TH[illegible]
INCIDENT

THE Z-5 INCIDENT

America's Ultimate POW/MIA Betrayal

Bob Miller

Library of Congress Control Number: 2014907146
ISBN: Hardcover 978-1-4990-0505-9
Softcover 978-1-4990-0507-3
eBook 978-1-4990-0504-2

This is a work of fiction. Names, characters, places, and incidents either are the product of the author's imagination or are used fictitiously, and any resemblance to actual persons, living or dead, businesses, companies, events, or locales is entirely coincidental. Dialogue, including those involving living and dead individuals are completely contrived and not to be construed as real.

This book was printed in the United States of America.

Rev. date: 05/02/2014

To order additional copies of this book, contact:
Xlibris LLC
1-888-795-4274
www.Xlibris.com
Orders@Xlibris.com
543593

CONTENTS

April

DEDICATION

This novel is dedicated to thousands of American veterans: patriots who answered the call to arms in WWII, Korea, Vietnam, and the Cold War, were captured, and declared dead, when in fact it was known they were still alive in captivity in the USSR.

"They shall not grow old
As we that are left behind to grow old.
Age shall not weary them
Nor the years condemn
At the going down of the sun.
And in the morning
We will remember them."

For the Forgotten
By Laurence Binyen

ALSO BY BOB MILLER:

NONFICTION BOOKS

America's Disposable Soldiers
America's Abandoned Sons

NONFICTION MONOGRAPHS

The Legal Dynamics of Women in Iran's Judicial System
The Ultimate Cyprus Solution: U.S. Unilateralism, 2001-2008
Iran's IRGC, Nuclear Weapons and Caspian Security
The Long Term Impact of WMDs on the Future of Iraq's Kurds
Quo Vadis: Kurdish Dreams and Unviable Alternatives
WMD's Impact on Iraq's People
Abu Ghraib: An American Scandal
Iraq's Urgent Need for an International Mandate
The Case for Iraq's WMD and Gulf War Syndrome
Collateral Damage: Depleted Uranium Munitions in Iraq
An Oil Trust Fund: The Key to a Democratic Iraq
Pakistan's 1982 Air Superiority Fighter Decision,
Turkey's F-16 Program Decision
Guns versus Missiles in Air to Air Combat in Crowded Skies

The Story

In the final three months of WWII in Europe, Soviet military forces overran Poland, Czechoslovakia, and Eastern Germany, along with hundreds of German prison camps holding captured allied soldiers. Tens of thousands of these soldiers were then secretly removed by Soviet forces to Gulag camps in Asiatic Russia, and never seen again. The Kremlin denied any knowledge of their whereabouts. Washington knew the truth, but with victory over Japan a long way off, Washington was unwilling to declare war on the USSR to get the prisoners back.

Throughout the war the German military had produced monthly name lists of all American prisoners in their camps in Eastern Europe and handed these lists to the International Red Cross in Switzerland, who in turn passed them to Washington.

The unresolved missing prisoner problem was initially kept Top Secret in Washington. But with the onset of the Cold War, Washington's only alternative was to ignore the reality, keep it secret, and declare these men missing in action and their remains not recovered. Until today the fate of these men in the USSR has never been admitted by the Washington.

This is the story of Paul Carter, one of the last WWII American Gulag survivors who escapes Russia recently, and returns home to hold accountable those who betrayed him a half-century ago.

What others have said about the Z-5 incident.

- "An extraordinary read. The story's adventurer-agent uncovers a background of numerous mysteries regarding thousands of US personnel lost behind Russian lines after World War II."
- "The plot is clever and imaginative. The story is thoroughly detailed and convincing in allusion to fact and historical relationships."
- "A fantastic romp through today's world of intrigue and espionage in the tradition of John Le Carre."
- "Exceptionally well researched and written with a plot intertwined with historic facts and secrets still unknown to the public."
- "Miller is obviously the next leader of the future spy/intelligence genre game."
- "The reader is mesmerized with clandestine trips into the Mideast, through Russia and the orient, up and down the East Coast of the U.S. from Florida Keys into the covert halls of the government's secret services, and finally into the desolate remains the Soviet Gulag."
- "This author is the next Tom Clancy. Fast paced and impossible to put down, the story's fantastic pace adds incredibly to the reader's inability to stop reading."
- "Fact and fiction are incredibly intertwined in an unprecedented tale of 20th Century betrayal and skullduggery."

PROLOGUE

January 12, 1943, Port of Spain, Trinidad

"MR. ROOSEVELT, IT'S five-thirty. You are expecting Mr. Carter at six?"

The president put his index finger to his lips, a sign the butler should not mention the name of Paul Carter or Carter's visit to the president to anyone outside this room. The president smiled in anticipation of Carter's unwitting secret heist which he hoped would lead to impoverishing the idiot in Berlin. "Let me know when Mr. Carter arrives."

"Mr. President, Admiral Leahey also mentioned that the secret service would be here at quarter till six with the Pan American captain."

"Very well, Arthur, tell me when they arrive."

Franklin loosened his collar and pulled his tie askew. Moving his wheelchair toward the railing, he studied the backdrop of quaint whitewashed buildings along the harbor below. The scene seemed surreal, the distant shoreline suspended between sea and sky, a washed-out green-black ribbon of forest peeping through heavy wisps of haze almost imperceptibly separating heaven from earth. The sights and sounds of the anchorage almost brought tears to his eyes as long forgotten memories crowded his consciousness.

Twenty years earlier, as the undersecretary of the navy and in full control of his body, before he'd been struck down with paralysis in his legs, he remembered raising hell in the joints downtown—quaffing Cuba Libras, dancing away the evenings in the arms of delectable wraiths with musk-scented bodies. For a young man in those days, Trinidad's Port of Spain was a licentious place in a forgotten backwater.

God how he loved the Caribbean and wished he'd taken more time to enjoy it when he was young. Searching around in his pockets, he found his cigarettes and fit another Chesterfield into its holder. It was good to be out and about again. He'd been cooped up too long in Washington. Fourteen months of war on two fronts was a test he'd never wanted. The only ray of light in recent months were the Allied landings in Morocco. He knew America's young men needed to believe in themselves and he'd demanded a soft landing for America's first confrontation with the Krauts. Morocco was one of those places where even the worst unforeseen disaster would still enable them to get ashore, establish a beach-head, and then move east along the North African coast toward Rommel. The landings had caught the Vichy-French government of Morocco unprepared, and already American troops were pressing east through Algeria. With the English in Egypt on Rommel's East, and the Americans on his west, Rommel almost certainly knew his days in North Africa were numbered.

The tide in Russia had also turned. Hitler's Army Group South almost reached the eastern Turkish border recently but was repulsed in the Chechen Mountains near Grozny. Two hundred miles to the north, Von Paulus's troops were encircled at Stalingrad. Franklin knew General Paulus would break out, but all these events gave him hope that the tide of war was finally changing.

He sucked in a lung full of smoke and watched a gecko scurry along the balustrade, pausing as its tongue extended three times its length to a cockroach. "Competent little bastard," Franklin muttered as the cockroach disappeared into its maw. Mr. Roach never knew what hit him, the president mused. The forthcoming conference in Casablanca would also decide where, when, and how fast Germany's armies would be forced back into Hitler's lair in Berlin.

A debate raged among Franklin's planners regarding where to hit Hitler next. Everywhere around the president were cabals advocating how the future of the war should be prosecuted. Some pushed for landings in Sicily next, others for Greece the following year, or an end-run across Syria and Turkey by mid-1944. Strongest were those in favor of landings in southern France later this year; this they argued would end the war by 1944. He needed to be careful however. America had no experienced combat generals and might easily blunder. Germany's field commanders, on the other hand, were seasoned veterans: bold, even reckless. Hitler's generals had accomplished much with guts, guile, and ingenuity. Without comparable leaders for his own army, Franklin would play around with a half-dozen German Divisions in North Africa while he tested several of his generals and see who could best improvise and lead. America newly reconstituted military forces couldn't afford to be severely bloodied like the Russians had on day one of Barbarossa.

He removed his handkerchief and paused to wipe perspiration from his brow. He replaced his Panama hat. God! Every time he saw the Russian casualty figures, he wondered if Joe Stalin could hold on. The thought of Russia's collapse made him sick. Could Stalin continue like this for a decade? Stalin too was a consummate double-crossing lying piece of shit. Already in the fourteen months since the war began: twenty-eight Americans had become unaccounted for in the Soviet Union. Three in particular were troubling for Franklin. They were technicians involved in America's Top Secret B-29 project while a fourth was knowledgeable of America's nuclear research program. Allen Dulles insisted he had the facts. Moscow assured everyone it was all a misunderstanding.

Historically he knew this war's roots lay in the last war. Wilson's fourteen points were responsible. Especially points five and fourteen. Five called for an open-minded impartial adjustment of colonial claims based on the desires of those ruled. Nothing happened! The Great Powers ignored colonial claims and fought among themselves over who would rule the rest of the world not already under imperialist rule. Ethiopia had tried and been butchered by Italy. Libya also tried and was wiped out by the Italians. Wilson's fourteenth point was also a debacle. It called for a world forum, affording political independence and territorial integrity to big and small states alike. The League of Nations had failed because America left it, and the colonialists were not about to guarantee anything. With a host of small new states constantly arguing, the imperialists ignored the Lilliputians among them. This time Franklin would complete the job. He'd make the postwar world safe for democracy. He was certain his approach was righteous. The postwar struggle democracy faced would not be totalitarianism—but imperialism. The totalitarian states controlled nothing, but the Imperialists controlled almost the entire world. The British had half; the French a fifth, Belgium a tenth. Americans from coast to coast wanted to defeat the Hun, but not so Britain and France could preserve their empires. It was the imperialists who'd set the stage for this war. And it was the imperialists who must now be shorn of foreign possessions in the aftermath. For Americans it made no sense to shed their national treasure and blood to protect the world's empires. But America would fight to defeat the idiot in Berlin and to prevent yet another world war twenty years hence.

His thoughts were interrupted by distant flashes, which caught his eye. To the south stood an ominous gray wall of clouds whose sunlit tops punched high into the stratosphere while lightning flashes illuminated its interior. Around him on the verandah the high-pitched drone of cicadas paused, almost as if in awe of the distant pyrotechnics.

Franklin would create a United Nations to replace Wilson's League of Nations: a new postwar alliance to stabilize a new order. This one would prevent the hordes of little states from standing on an equal footing with the major powers. The United States, Britain, France, Russia, and maybe one or two others would be provided permanent seats on a security council which would oversee the new world order in the postwar era. And to hasten that day, Franklin would make copious concessions to the Russians. He knew he could work with Joseph Stalin, who—at heart—was a nice guy with a gruff shell from the wrong side of the tracks and a town where people only understood brute force.

Franklin's wife disagreed, insisting that unlike Franklin, who was a Harvard patrician devoted to his national heritage, Stalin was a ruthless son of a bitch! She cautioned that Stalin was someone he should avoid. Avoid him? How could he? Without Stalin's cooperation, concluding the war against the Axis would take forever. America desperately needed Stalin if the horrendous American losses incurred in the First World War were to be avoided in this one. Eleanor didn't buy Franklin's arguments about the Russian being a nice man. Eleanor wanted Stalin to immediately account for some 1,820 American Dough Boys, who Soviet forces had captured around Archangel in World War One and secretly imprisoned in Siberia for life.

On the other hand, Eleanor also reminded him that Stalin had also been a monk earlier in life and included Article 124 in the Soviet constitution—guaranteeing freedom of religion to all Russians. Like most suffragists, Eleanor knew little about the real male world, only that men were devious and women wily! Franklin drew a distinction between totalitarian and imperialist. He could work with the former but not the latter!

This time there would be no separate peace until the latter were gone.

Many around Franklin also advocated acceptance of a German surrender, especially if they sued for peace as they had in the First World War. Franklin would not abide it. He knew that to do so would result in a temporary respite, after which the Europeans would be at each other's throats again. To hell with the appeasers he'd repeatedly told his wife during their private moments. While the conflict raged, he would honor his secret understanding with the Germans. But when dethroned, the ruffian in Berlin would go to the wall, his people would be deflowered, and his garden despoiled. It was the only way. In the final analysis, he supposed it would be appropriate to mention in his memoirs, pointing out it was the German who was responsible for most of Europe's wars in history. Others might point to France or England and even the Low Countries, but for Franklin, it didn't matter. His opinion was already formed.

Anything cast upon the water created a ripple. And it was the undisciplined Germanic tribes always agitating the pot, which caused those around them to perceive them as a threat. Franklin recalled the tenth-century barbarian invasion of Europe, whose real origin really lay centuries earlier in China. China forced millions along its borders westward into India and Mongolia, and it took two hundred years before the ripple eventually displaced the Vandals, whose Hun cavalry then ransacked Europe at the close of the millennium. And the result? Until today Europe remained a patchwork of warlike states. Now the patchwork would perish under a Pax-Americana: America with half of it and Russia the rest.

The rumble of distant thunder diverted his attention again, and he noticed the ash of his cigarette had dropped into his lap.

"Shit!" he exclaimed as he swiped at yet another small burn mark in the material. Good thing Eleanor wasn't around or she'd complain to him about his penchant to ruin trousers.

The thunderclouds were closer now, and he wondered if he would have to fly through them tomorrow. The big Boeing flying boat was pleasant enough in clear air but bounced around too much in clouds. He'd tried to conceal his discomfort on the flight this morning. Bumpy airplanes were like contentious women. One had to endure them. He heard his valet clear his throat behind him.

"Yes, Arthur?"

"Mr. President. The secret service is here with the Pan American Captain."

"Show them in, Arthur."

Franklin snugged his tie as he spotted Captain Cone emerging onto the terrace. He liked the man and hoped nothing was wrong.

"Excuse me, Mr. President," Cone stated respectfully, "I needed to discuss our departure for Belem in the morning."

"Any problem?"

"A minor one, sir. The schedule calls for a seven-o'clock departure, but the weather is warmer than I anticipated. Once the sun comes up, it will get hot. We shall have to further reduce our takeoff weight so the Clipper can get enough lift to get us out of the water. If we could depart an hour earlier, Mr. President, while the air is still cool. Would you object to a six-o'clock departure?"

"What about the weather?" Franklin asked. Pointing to the approaching squall line.

"It will be north of us by midnight, Mr. President. Tomorrow is forecast to be clear and hot."

"What is your opinion?" he asked the secret service man standing beside Cone.

"An earlier departure should pose no problem, Mr. President."

"Then whatever our pilot recommends is fine with me," Franklin replied jauntily.

"Thank you, sir," the Secret Service man replied. "I will inform the rest of the staff."

Franklin returned his gaze to the verdant hills beyond the anchorage. The most important objectives for him at Casablanca were twofold; unconditional German surrender and let the Russians bleed the Hun for the next two years. The most reliable estimates were that the defeat of the Hun could take until late 1945 or, maybe, even the summer of 1946. Any faster resolution of the war in Europe would require an earlier invasion from the West and involve tremendous American losses. The Asian war would take even longer, and he would not countenance American casualties in either theater like he'd witnessed in France during the last war. There would be no days in which a quarter-million Americans would be senselessly slaughtered in two hours. There would be no heroic battles in which seven hundred thousand would be killed and maimed in a couple of days. He would concentrate on the Japanese in the Pacific while Russia exhausted the

Kraut like a horde of leeches inexorably osculating the Wehrmacht across the vast reaches of central Russia. Better millions of Russian dead than Americans. Russia already had an incredible twelve million men in the field, and still Hitler's generals had repeatedly stopped them in their tracks, each time inflicting a grisly toll in dead and wounded Russians.

Franklin had recently diverted fifteen Air Groups of newly produced American bomber aircraft away from Europe and shipped them to the Pacific Theater. Planning for the invasion of France later this year would also be delayed per his arrangement in plan CASE JUDY. It detailed Franklin's top secret agreement with certain 'not to be named European parties: not to invade Europe before mid-1944. The date was mutually advantageous. Russia would slowly exhaust the Hun in the east and, and in return, obtain half of Europe as a buffer against future German bellicosity in the decades after the war. The intervening months until mid-1944 also provided Hitler with enough time to resolve his minority's problem. The former suited Franklin's commitment to the American voter not to shed American blood while the latter addressed Winston's postwar concern to secure their empire East of Suez. And finally it suited certain parties urge to smuggle stolen treasure from Europe . . . insurance should the war end with Berlin's victory.

Stubbing out his cigarette, he removed it from its holder and searched in his pockets for another. The scent of jasmine floated over the balcony as the wind shifted, and he paused to enjoy the aura of the moment. He also feared for the British. Could they survive the current test of their national resolve to stay the course? Twenty percent of London lay in ruins. Sixty percent of her merchant shipping was gone. A third of her industry smoldered and what remained of her Empire lay on the brink of anarchy. The First World War's debts had already weakened her financial stability, and this war now threatened what was left. He'd seen the secret British statistics. Forty percent of the English national budget went to the admiralty, a third to the army, three hundred billion so far. In round terms, it came to about one hundred thousand dollars for each man, woman, and child in the British Isles. It was a hemorrhage he doubted they could long endure. America's outlays too were staggering, already surpassing the sublime and headed for the ridiculous. America's war debts too would also have to be repaid. But when and how would fall to his successors.

British Prime Minister Churchill had explained his dilemma privately to Franklin months earlier at Argentia: only the perpetuation of Britain's Empire in the postwar era would make it possible for Britain to recover economically after the war. Franklin thought the argument spurious. But had withheld comment on Winston's concern. Britain's postwar linchpin according to Winston was Suez. Twice the Hun had threatened the canal, and twice Britain was almost cut off from her eastern Empire. So Winston had pushed for the Balfour initiative—a future Jewish State athwart the Arab heartland and astride Suez. It would be a future ally in a troubled area. But there were issues? How to make it work? Palestine was a godforsaken wasteland where only a handful of Jews had emigrated since the end of the last war. Winston's projection of an influx of ten million to the region after this war was clearly unworkable. Still, Winston waxed eloquently about the need to secure the Canal. Franklin had countered with Cyprus as an alternative location for Europe's postwar refugees. Winston dismissed it. Franklin proposed other alternatives, but Winston dismissed them too. Franklin suspected Winston had somehow learned of Hitler's secret initiative.

The mid-1941 German initiative, to the American president, sounded preposterous. Germany did not want problems with the United States. If the United States allowed central Europe's minorities to immigrate to America within the next five years, Germany would renounce aggression and withdraw behind negotiated boundaries. Franklin refused. The German ambassador knew he would. The German ambassador opined that Americans were nurtured in bucolic innocence and refused to acknowledge their own bestial banality. Germany's minorities did not include the Native American Indian or Blacks which were Washington's dilemma. The ambassador concluded that in light of America's refusal, that given some time, Europe's minority question would be resolved internally. Germany needed three years. Since that meeting, Franklin believed Winston's postwar Palestine plan might have serious merit.

Flicking his Zippo to the end of yet another Chesterfield, the president inhaled and then coughed repeatedly. The doctor had warned him about smoking too. But no one lived forever.

Smiling as he studied the harbor and reflections of the two Pan American flying boats lying in the placid dark blue-black waters below, he recalled one of the lithe local ladies he'd liaised with across this harbor many years ago when he was younger and foolish. Another knock at the door interrupted his thoughts. "Crap," he muttered. He wanted more time to enjoy the ambiance. "What is it?" he demanded without turning.

"Mr. President," His butler announced in a muted voice. "The other gentleman you were expecting is here. Shall I show him in?"

Franklin motioned his visitor forward with a wave of his hand. He smiled as the younger man approached. Franklin flipped his just-lit cigarette over the wall and unconsciously fidgeted with his tie.

"Mr. President," the younger man said.

"Good to see you, Paul! You enjoyed the flight down from Key West today?"

"Yes, Mr. President."

"Your first time in one of them?" he asked, pointing to the two aircraft below.

"No, sir. I came back from the Philippines on Pan American's Yankee Clipper."

"Of course! I forgot! I regret we were unable to speak on the flight here from Key West this morning. The less known about all this the better. You understand?"

His visitor nodded.

"And that includes the fact that I had the plane stop to pick you up at Key West."

"I understand," the younger man replied.

The president loved the minutia of special operations, especially when it involved intrigue. And this man's mission involved both. Franklin thought of Carter's mission as a feint within a feint, then within another feint. The allies would use German gold, probably stolen from the Russians who in turn had relieved Spain of it—and America would use it to secretly pay the Chinese so they would continue fighting the Japanese. Hitler would get the time he needed to complete his final solution, and the transaction would enable the State Department's intelligence code breakers to find out if the Japanese had broken America's secret communication code. The last was by no means the most important question because codes could always be changed. But if Hirohito's Jap fighter planes were out searching for an American flying boat next month between Ceylon and Australia, then Franklin would mercilessly search out the American traitor in his government and make that person or persons wish their mothers had never conceived them.

"Review the details with me, Paul?"

His visitor knew only about the first of the three feints, and spent the next quarter hour reviewing it. Months had gone into putting it together. The president leaned back after the younger finished and lit up yet another cigarette. Exhaling a thin column of smoke, Franklin studied the squall line which had now enveloped the two flying boats in the anchorage. "Tell me, Paul, who else knows about this?"

"Aside from you and I, Mr. President, only four men. My partner in Washington, Mr. Churchill, Mr. Inishkeen, and the English courier."

"Good! Keep it that way. Your arrangements are superb, and everything has gone without a hitch so far. Good job!"

"Thank you, Mr. President."

"The aircraft are prepositioned?" the president asked as a large raindrop splattered on the terrazzo floor beside his wheelchair.

"They will be shortly, sir," Paul replied. "Captain Gray left a week ago for Bahrain with a cargo of tires for the Flying Tigers. They'll be off-loaded in Bahrain, and the Royal Air Force will deliver them to Delhi. The second aircraft left LaGuardia three days ago with a load of .50 caliber ammunition for British forces in Egypt. It should be in Khartoum tomorrow. The one inbound for Khartoum is the one that I will proceed to Ceylon with."

"Good, good!" Franklin replied with a jaunty smile. "And the gold? It will be picked up on schedule?"

"Yes, Mr. President."

"And the cutouts, Paul?"

"Yes, sir. In four days! The .50 caliber ammunition will be offloaded at Damietta in the Nile Delta. A British crew will be waiting and they will take the Clipper to retrieve the gold off the coast of Cyprus and, on return to Damietta, return the aircraft to its Pan Am crew for the onward flight to Bahrain and points east."

"And the . . . Aahhhhhh . . ." Franklin glanced around the balcony to make certain they were alone. "The meeting point?" He was obviously reticent to mention the German submarine.

Paul understood. "It's arranged. It will wait southeast of the Cyprus coast for seven nights."

The president knew if the local seas were too rough, the sea plane would not land and the rendezvous would fail. "And if the weather is bad?"

"Prevailing winds are northwest this time of year. Inshore waters along the Cyprus coast there are calm enough for about six miles out. It should be more than adequate. The only risk would be an errant Royal Navy unit in the area. But these too have been diverted to U-boat patrols off the Syrian ports."

"Excellent! Excellent," Franklin observed with a broad grin. Franklin was impressed with this man and thought he would go far. The clandestine world of skullduggery needed such competent conspiratorial types.

Both men flinched involuntarily as a thunderclap rumbled overhead, and a couple more large raindrops spattered randomly on the terrace. "Your immediate plans, Paul?"

"I continue to Africa with you tomorrow, and then depart the next day across the Sahara to Khartoum. I should be back in Washington by mid-February."

"How do you get to Khartoum?" The president demanded as he began slowly moving his wheelchair off the balcony. The roar of rain already rattled through the trees below, and errant drops were now splattering more insistently around them as they moved toward the door.

"A ferry flight."

"Interesting. What kind?"

"A B-25, Mr. President. It's one of our "Lend Lease" twin-engine bombers en route to Basrah to be handed over to the Russians.

"Ah, yes. My good friend Stalin." Several hundred American fighter aircraft and twin-engine light bombers had already been delivered through the Belem/Basrah/Tehran axis. They followed the same route Franklin was now taking to Fish Lake on the African coast, and thence across the southern Sahara, thence to Basrah, and Tehran. Hopefully the meager supply would provide the courage to stiffen the Russian spine enough to prevent another unilateral Russian peace as the Bolsheviks had done in the last war. The president knew communism in Russia was almost dead and would in fact probably have died had the current war not began. It now allowed Stalin to once again divert his people's attention away from their own hardships to that of protecting mother-Russia from the barbarian fascists.

"Well, Paul, I guess you have everything under control. Anything I can help you with?"

"No, sir, Mr. President."

"Thanks for stopping by. See you aboard the flight in the morning."

DECEMBER

TODAY,

ONE

Fort McNair

A TAP ON HIS shoulder interrupted his concentration on the man speaking at the podium. The man behind him whispered in his ear, "Alex Balkan, you son of a bitch, I never thought I would ever see you at a place like this."

"Thought it might be good for my career," Alex whispered back acerbically.

"I thought you had retired." His friend observed, informing Alex he would see him later and moved away.

Alex had suspected beforehand that the evening would be a waste of time. Most in attendance were those who'd retired years ago, accompanied by their plump wives, the majority of who were primped with too much perfume, rich clothing, and painted nails. The younger men, he'd observed, sprinkled among the tables were also not the archetypal prime movers of his world but the cogs, hoping someone would notice them in the rapidly exploding population of new intelligence officers being recruited by the thousands on America's streets since 9-11.

The old order had been anesthetized for so long that it was functionally inoperative, spewing out fifteen thousand classified intelligence reports daily, most of which replicated the headlines of the hundreds of the world's newspapers being reported on by foreign embassies. Everyone knew that Washington knew everything, and yet its most useful intelligence report was the daily *Early Bird*, a cut-and-paste summary of the leading stories of America's newspapers and those of the English speaking world. Personnel cuts which had once threatened to slice huge chunks of flab from the federal intelligence carcass and had been de rigueur in Washington in the aftermath of Desert Storm had almost instantly stopped with the end of the Trade Towers. Many here tonight, who'd been confronted earlier with retirement, were now lucratively devoting the rest of their working lives to the new war on terrorism.

The events of September 11, 2001, had instantly brought into focus the overall incompetence of a fifty-year system created at the close of the Second World War. Designed for a pencil-and-paper world and functionally unchanged for a half century, its goals, objectives, leadership, and sacred shibboleths had virtually insured its sudden death. The FBI had been shadowing the Trade Tower villains for years but unable to see the big picture: had drowned in a sea of minutia and become blindsided by the collective wisdom of institutional bias and completely missed the obvious. Today in the era of Homeland Security, earlier institutional ailments were more prevalent than ever.

The intelligence reorganization which should have taken place after the collapse of the Soviet Union and the 1991 Liberation of Kuwait hadn't. The 9-11 Commission recommendations had been strenuously fought by the White House while Homeland Security gobbled up its competition, emerging as the largest federal budget line item for the first decade of the new millennium. But its brain stem had atrophied and metastasized into an incompetent but politically correct stupor while its clandestine field officers—the spear point of the huge new system—were still being assigned abroad for only one three-year tour in their career. The rest of the time they went on TDY's and stood out as typical Americana wherever they traveled: with penny loafers and neat haircuts. Even in the Central Intelligence Agency's feared Clandestine Service, only one in twenty of its case officers had ever recruited a spy for the United States. One in eighteen was fluent in a foreign language—60 percent of those only in French. Arabic speakers numbered sixteen, Farsi nine, Afghani seven, and Hebrew—418. It was a recipe for what was to come—whatever that was to be?

All of this infuriated Alex when he thought about the constellation of lights which had lit up one by one, warnings, threats, and disasters, which had warned America that its defenses had been breached . . . its security compromised, and its incompetence consistently downplayed by his peers and superiors. Everyone now was convinced the war on terror was endless. It had all started with managed intelligence by the executive branch, fed to and digested without complaint by the legislative branch, and the threats then dutifully followed up by the

Department of Defense. Threat after threat had been belittled and debunked until it was too late. Alex also knew that his bosses were no longer addressing the internal domestic threat since 9-11 and that within a decade civil liberties in America could be a thing of the past. The new "War on Terrorism" was allowing a government octopus to stifle free enterprise, the Constitution, the Bill of Rights, and most importantly the American's trust in those who led them.

The first round of systemic chaos had begun a decade back when communism suddenly evaporated like a Potomac mist on a damp summer morning. The Evil Empire had imploded, suffocating those within it in a vacuum inhabited by untold thousands of leeches who had made a career of feeding at the public trough. The hi-tech wonder referred to as the military-industrial complex of Russia and the United States stood exposed. Russia's heavy industrial capability had rusted while America's had moved abroad. Both countries vested interests sought to foster new international threats with which to perpetuate systems incapable of dying without a fight. The contrived mini-crises of Kuwait, Somalia, Iraq, Haiti, Bosnia, and Afghanistan had all failed to convince the public that an enemy lurked in the darkness beyond our shores while the Bushes' "Iraq One" and "Iraq Two" experiences illustrated America's ability to destroy all enemies but inability to secure the peace.

The trauma and gore of September 11 in New York City had exposed the reality. The intelligence system was dysfunctional for the new millennium, but the old guard's acolytes were entrenched, knew the levers of power, and now employed fear of the unknown to secure their continued patrimony. For Alex it was the same old guys who had bought the hi-tech wonders of espionage at the expense of human intelligence. It would take twenty years to develop a new cadre of deeply buried case officers in a wide variety of roles around the world where few, if any around them, might ever suspect who they really were. And in the meantime there was no defense against the rogue dissident with weapons of mass destruction. Alex suspected Washington would gradually emulate Russia's intelligence organizations: change the focus, change the faces, create new titles, burnish roles and missions, and repackage incompetence. What the American Congress and Senate really needed to do was to give the U.S. intelligence leadership a systemic enema.

Alex recognized the fat woman at the table across from him. She was a new Green Badger, one of the Agency's thousands of newly recruited contract staff whose ultimate security clearances were still pending. You could tell them all a mile away by their green badges. Would it be people like her and a host of others like her who would be the future of America's success against those wishing us ill? The fat woman laughed loudly, her voice more like the cackle of a hyena than a human. She smiled at Alex, her feline eye contact suggesting he might later find a place between her plump thighs if he pursued her look further. Beside her was a gorgeous waif in a black body sheath, with green eyes and auburn hair. She too was a Green Badger, and Alex wondered how many foreign men's lives she would destroy unwittingly.

He had his own woman. Heather Maldutis was his childhood girlfriend and had just spent four days in his bed here in Washington. Rubbing his crotch involuntarily Alex adjusted his equipment as thoughts of Heather momentarily stimulated areas best left dormant for the moment. He smiled, recalling Heather's comment that it was the first time she'd been stark naked for four solid days: only leaving his bed long enough to bathe and eat. He intended to join her in Salt Lake for the coming holidays.

Alex rubbed at his eyelid and the involuntary tick that pulled at it. The effects of years of neglect of his health and a perennial diet of junk food had dulled his senses. Too many years in the fast lane had taken their toll on him. But he had a way to go before he was ready to fade away. He was a little overweight from too much rich food, and maybe his skin seemed slightly pallid from too many months in northern Russia, but his eyes were clear and his temples marred only slightly by a few strands of gray. His eastern European bloodlines were strong, and his genealogy suggested that with luck, he could easily be drawing retirement checks when he was into his nineties. The tick in his left eye twitched again. It annoyed him as he couldn't control it as he had so many other minor irritants in his life. He'd been under too much stress these last few months in Russia and sorely needed a vacation. Soon, he thought. The day after tomorrow at the latest, he'd take off for two weeks skiing with Heather in Utah.

"So," the new CIA Director at the podium concluded, "When his Holiness arrived after an hour and a half delay, the visiting American delegation was immediately ushered into his Vatican chambers. But former Secretary of State Henry Kissinger, having just lit an expensive

Havana cigar in the outer foyer, could find no ashtrays. Rather than throw it on the floor, Henry flicked off its flame and put the cigar in his pocket. You can imagine the Pontiff's consternation a quarter hour later when he saw Mr. Kissinger, who now stood before the group and began slapping his suit pocket which was billowing smoke. And as Kissinger did so, his colleagues behind him thought Henry was applauding something the Pontiff had said, so they too began to applaud. What must his Holiness have thought? Here were the most senior policy advisors to the American president, applauding a former secretary of state as he attempted to immolate himself?"

Laughter erupted among the audience.

"Thank you for inviting me to tonight's banquet," the speaker concluded. "It was an honor."

The audience rose to their feet as the master of ceremonies returned to the podium and observed, "I'll bet our guest speaker never suspected he would be beset with the types of exposes he's endured recently. We wish him well."

Again the audience applauded and some laughed. "Ladies and gentlemen," the master of ceremonies continued, "this concludes this year's annual Intelligence awards banquet. Thank you for coming."

The tick in Alex's eye stopped as he rose to stretch. The man who'd stopped by earlier and whispered to him now stood beside him. "Mind if I get a ride home with you?" he said.

"Sure, Marvin! I'll be ready to leave in a few minutes. I want to say good night first to someone."

"I'll wait outside," his friend said.

Alex made his way between the tables toward the far wall to a tall man animatedly speaking to a knot of men, stopping alongside he gently squeezed the man's elbow. "Ted, I'm leaving. Will I have a chance to see you before I return to Europe after the holidays?"

"Alex!" his boss exclaimed. "Have you met Colonel and Mrs. Banaris? Banaris retired just before the Liberation of Kuwait in 1992 and was one of our best."

"A pleasure." Alex observed politely, wondering if Ted had deliberately used the opportunity to insert the word *retired.* On more than one occasion Ted had suggested that Alex should go play golf and get out of the business. But Alex enjoyed his work. It provided something to do until he found a better way to pass his time. "I really have to go, Ted. Will we have a chance for a cup of coffee? Maybe tomorrow afternoon?"

"Certainly, Alex," the taller man replied with a feigned smile. "I'll make time. Have you seen her?"

"Tomorrow morning," Alex replied.

"Good. Call me as soon as you're through."

Alex excused himself and made his way toward the side exit. He winced at the wall of icy air which hit him beyond the threshold. It was the eighteenth of December and already the weather was bitterly cold for the time of year.

"Jesus," he exclaimed, sucking in his breath as he joined Marvin Raoul on the steps and headed for his car.

He and Marvin went back decades. In Alex's business few men had real friends, and most were only professional associates. Still, he supposed Marvin knew him better than most, and the two shared a bond of mutual respect which provided Alex with a certain comfort gradient.

"I thought the cold didn't bother you." Marvin observed sarcastically.

Alex started the car but didn't reply as they skirted Fort McNair's parade ground and exited the main gate, turning right toward South Capitol Street.

"How's Ted LePage these days, Alex?"

"A pain in the ass! And his deputy, Chuck Bunn, is even worse. A real 'flamer' as the British say."

"Like the clown in the White House?" Marvin inquired.

"Yeah, they're all the same."

"What I cannot understand is why LePage hangs around. Christ, he's older than Methuselah. The son of a bitch must be in his mid-eighties," Marvin replied, "but is still as sharp as a tack. Looks like a man of sixty too."

"Too many of our intel types know so much they become Machiavellian," Alex countered.

"A big word," Marvin replied.

"Not a word," Alex corrected him. "A person. By the way, did you get a chance to meet the CIA Director before dinner?"

"No," Marvin replied. "But he's on the way out, and of no value to anyone anyway so why bother?"

Alex had been in the States almost two weeks and should have left for Provo already, but he'd been unable to arrange his final debriefing here in Washington until tomorrow morning. The person he was to see, an old defector from Russia, had suddenly blown town a week ago and was expected back tonight.

Marvin was slightly older than Alex and currently employed with the navy's historical department at the nearby Anacostia Navy yard. Over the years they'd served together at various places in Europe and experience and knowledge of the intelligence game had enabled both to remain in the business long beyond their normal retirement age. Marvin lived off lower Wisconsin in Georgetown, and Alex wondered why the son of a bitch had left his car at home tonight. But since Alex's apartment lay just across the river in Ballston he'd drop Marvin on the way. The man beside him was also an ex-CIA operative laid off during one of the most recent of scores of Agency reorganizations since 9-11 and—with decades of service—had been shuffled laterally into one of the agency's various holding positions until retirement became inevitable. Marvin had eight months to go before he reached yet another of his mandatory retirement gates, but he too had arranged to find a way to hang around now that the pay and benefits were increasing so sharply.

Alex turned up South Capitol Street toward downtown. "Shit," he muttered as he saw the blinking red and blue lights of yet another security road block at the 395 on-ramp. The police were abrupt and insisted on seeing a second picture identification for Marvin, informing him his current license reflected a man with a beard and he no longer had one. The officer made a digital photo of the license and instructed Marvin that he had two weeks to get a new photo ID. The officer opened the rear doors to the car and flashed his light around the interior. "Okay," the officer said, "Get out of here."

"Thank you, sir," Marvin replied as they drove away, "and fuck you! America ain't what it used to be. Sometimes I think I'm living in a goddamn police state."

"It's for your own protection," Alex replied. But he knew what Marvin was referring to. Keeping America safe was eroding everyone's freedom. The anthrax pranks at Congress and constant media references to dirty bombs and such had traumatized everyone. The Bush Administration had held onto the White House by constantly reminding Americans that the country was under attack.

The government had recently conducted yet another of many secret terrorist attack simulations to see if the country was more safe now than before 9-11. Called Dark Winter, the exercise supposedly determined what a biological problem could do in the United States. It concluded that a smallpox release in just three U.S. cities would cause a pandemic spreading to twenty-five states and fifteen foreign countries within two weeks. And probable casualties . . . eighteen million deaths . . . in six months.

"You making any progress, Alex?" Marvin asked as they hung a left on Independence Avenue. "In whatever it is you are up to here in Washington?"

"I have a meeting in the morning which should wrap things up. Then I'm gone."

"A meeting with whom?"

"Someone."

"Someone?" Marvin mimicked dumbly. "Male or female?"

"You don't know her."

"Her . . . then she must be the woman from Berdsk?" Marvin observed glibly. "The one with the grocery store. You know . . . the one with the tight ass and great thighs?"

Alex glanced at his friend as they crossed the darkened mall near the Aerospace Museum. Alex was miffed. Someone obviously had leaked the information that he would see Tatiana.

"And who might that be?" Alex inquired acerbically.

"Come on, Balkan! You know damned well who she is."

"Who told you?" Alex demanded angrily.

"No one! It was good elicitation, don't you think? You gave her away yourself." His passenger laughed. "How many years have we known each other?"

"Another 'A plus' for the CIA's art of elicitation." Alex laughed, his voice laced with sarcasm.

"But I doubt you'll get anything from her," Marvin replied seriously.

Alex's eye twitched again, and he rubbed it, willing it to stop. "How come you know so goddamn much?" he asked more to be polite than because he gave a crap. The reality was that he didn't really care.

Alex had attended tonight's dinner at the insistence of his boss who thought the evening out would do him good. Ted LePage liked to see his older contract case officers keep in touch with their younger compatriots, arguing that the social interaction and intercourse stimulated esprit de corps. Alex liked the intercourse aspects of it but not the rest. Society today was not like it once was. Today everyone was uptight, especially the young female case officers. He had stood back over at the headquarters the other day to allow a younger woman to enter the elevator first. The bitch had stood back and told him she did not appreciate older men hitting on her. He'd wanted to tell her to get a bigger dildo but knew better and said nothing.

Most of the attendees at the dinner were the staff types who'd left fieldwork years ago for politics inside the beltway. They were all whores only interested in perpetuating their careers, building empires, and when the opportunity availed itself, working the promotion game. Intelligence fieldwork had always been where the action was for Alex, not driving a desk in Washington or one of the thousands of intelligence-related organizations beyond the beltway. His peers in Washington were those who had to kiss ass and, in the process, too often compromised their beliefs. Alex could count those he respected on the fingers of one hand. He'd known Marvin since Christ was a corporal, and he trusted Marvin.

With the demise of Perestroika, the academic types had divined that capitalism would soon flourish throughout Russia. But the academics knew nothing about the real Russia. Americans naively believed the entire world would instantly adopt the concept of one-man one-vote. In the Middle East, Africa and the Steppes of Asia where the misguided liberals were now espousing these concepts along with women's rights, the locals really only understood food, work, and power. These were the cornerstones of reality in the third world. Alex understood Russia. He had frequently traveled the back roads, broke bread with the Kulaks, guzzled vodka with the peasants, schmoozed the bureaucrats—and cried with their high-ranking generals who'd lost their perks. These were the men who had already swept away the new bourgeois pseudo-communists experimenters. The Washington pukes didn't drink . . . didn't smoke . . . didn't swear . . . didn't screw around . . . and sprayed their mouths with breath freshener. They didn't understand shit about clandestine fieldwork as far as Alex was concerned.

"I don't know much," Marvin replied, "but you were into her, so I assumed you probably forgot to ask her something?" Marvin smiled.

He knew Alex had once had a thing going with this defector and suspected he still did.

In the beginning, Alex and this Bolshevik bitch had been physical. Alex knew it was against regulations, and those around him at the time who realized what was happening, did so too. But in those days, everyone looked the other way in such cases. Alex had been assigned to debrief Tatiana Slavchenko in Europe after she'd defected in India. Defector debriefings took a long time, and for those who cooperated, sanctuary and resettlement in the West awaited. She'd cooperated all right, even to the point of spreading her gorgeous thighs for his every whim.

Tatiana had first appeared at the front door of the American Embassy in New Delhi, India, when she'd requested to see a consular officer. Her defection was never announced by either the Russians or the United States, and the entire incident was soon forgotten. At first, her request for asylum was refused until the embassy realized who she really was. Then she was quickly ferreted to Frankfurt and then Rome where she turned out to be a gold mine. Not only did she know the intimates about the top Soviet Rocket Force leadership but also provided the first accurate ICBM target updates in many years, matching individual silos against individual U.S. targets.

The air force assistant chief of staff of intelligence at the time opined she was the most valuable defector since World War II. She knew the American cities and bases targeted, the warhead types dedicated to each, their yield, and their preset detonation altitudes. She also revealed the locations of seventy-six previously unknown SS-18 silos in central Asia which were dedicated to the obliteration of hardened American targets like Cheyenne Mountain, SAC headquarters, Boerfink, and leadership bunkers in northern Virginia. Buried among the hundreds of high-value intelligence reports produced was one of the almost insignificant value at the time, a report about some mysterious American prisoner reported to still be alive in central Asia.

Eventually, Tatiana's brain had been picked clean, and she was resettled and set up with a small grocery store in Washington. In the ensuing years, she'd refused to cooperate with other CIA case officers, insisting she'd only talk to Alex Balkan. No one seemed to object at the time. Everyone winked, knowing she probably hoped to get Alex to eventually make her his mistress or, better, his wife. She'd been squeezed dry anyway, had nothing left of value, and now wanted to be treated as something special. She was a concealed turncoat being provided sanctuary, and her petulant demands annoyed the agency. Defectors were not supposed to be prima donnas, but as long as she was good-looking and still willing, Alex didn't mind. He fitted in meeting her when he had time.

He hadn't seen her now for two-and-a-half years and wondered how much she'd changed. Flecks of gray were discernible last time they'd met, and she'd spread slightly through the hips but still turned heads on the street.

Slavchenko had been magnificent when he'd first met her, a cross between Marilyn Monroe and Cher. The evil empire in those days awed even the bravest of the Cold War warriors. It was the blue against the red, good versus evil, life and death, and Alex was debriefing one of the evil empire's hottest defectors and exposing the Soviet Union's darkest secrets, information critical to the survival of the Free World. In those days, everyone knew who Alex Balkan was but not Marvin who was assigned to maintenance of a safe-house in Rome.

To hell with it, Alex thought as he passed the National Gallery of Art on to Constitution Avenue. He'd take a chance and stop by her place tonight after he dropped Marvin off. He glanced at his watch. It was a quarter to eleven, and she'd probably still be up watching the eleven-o'clock news.

"It's getting late, Marvin. I've changed my mind about dropping you at your place. Hope you don't mind? There is a taxi stand two blocks from here. It should be less than five bucks to your place."

"Okay. Will I see you before you leave?"

"I doubt it."

Marvin turned briefly to Alex before closing the door. "Let's do it again. Call me sometime and let's do lunch or dinner. Have a Merry Christmas, Alex!"

"Kharasho!" Alex replied. He wheeled a U-turn at the corner and headed west along Constitution Avenue.

* * *

Six hours later, Alex shook his head and tried to drown out the alarm clock which played sounds of bugs and insects in the forest at a high volume. Tatiana hadn't answered her door last night, and Alex got the same response from her answering machine when he'd called from a pay phone down the street last night. He slammed his fist on the alarm and reached for the phone. But again got the familiar message saying she wasn't in. Well, he thought, she'd damned well better show up today or he'd really be pissed. He showered and after a light breakfast, headed downtown.

At eight-thirty, he parked around the corner from her store which stood among a strip of dingy ethnic stores supporting a growing neighborhood population of immigrants from the Indian subcontinent. A Vietnamese clerk stood behind a counter of outdated inventory observing Alex as he came in. Alex hadn't seen this man before.

"I'm looking for Yelena Yefimova?"

"Not in."

"What time do you expect her?"

"I don't," the Vietnamese replied. "May I be of assistance?"

"I thought she'd be in."

The elderly man shook his head.

"This afternoon?"

The Vietnamese hunkered his shoulders and shook his head again.

Alex hunched his shoulders too, waiting for an explanation.

"May I ask who you are?" the clerk inquired.

"I'm a friend. The name is Alex Balkan."

"I see," the Vietnamese replied, making a note on a pad by the register. "I don't know exactly when she'll be back."

"You're certain you don't know?"

"You ask many questions. You with the police or immigration?"

"No. I expected her to be here this morning. May I ask your name?"

"Tran Vung Tha."

Alex scribbled a note. "Please give this to her when she returns." He walked to the corner pay phone and called his boss at Scion Consultants. Since his meeting with Tatiana had once again fallen through, he was pissed and decided he needed to call the airlines and confirm his reservation to Salt Lake City, Utah, before the Christmas rush made that more difficult than it needed to be. Someone else would have to talk to the Tatiana about the American named Paul Carter who had disappeared decades back and been declared dead by

Washington but then reported as still alive many years later by Tatiana during her debriefings.

During her initial debriefings in Europe, she'd mentioned Carter's name, indicating she'd physically seen him at one of the KGB's Silent Camps near Novosibirsk in Central Asia. She said it was at a riverside camp along the Ob River near a town called Kolpashevo. Washington never figured out exactly who this Paul Carter was at the time because there were no records indicating a man by that name was missing. The only possible connection was another man by the same name who'd disappeared in West Africa back in early 1943. But thirty years separated the two names, and no one in the intelligence community believed it was the same person so the issue was forgotten. Outside on the pavement, Alex dropped a quarter into a pay phone and dialed Ted LePage's office.

"Glad you called, Alex. How did it go?"

"It didn't! She's not back yet. And the guy who works for her doesn't know when she'll be back. This will have to wait. I'm going to take two weeks' vacation and get out of town if you don't mind. I'll see her when I get back. Christmas will be here in a week and things should be quiet until the New Year."

"Where will you be?"

"Haven't decided yet." He lied. He'd always kept his personal life separate from work, and felt it was none of his employer's business what he did with his off time. Besides, he also didn't want them calling him.

"Okay, but call me before you leave town?"

"Thanks, Ted. I'll be in touch." He and Ted didn't always get along. He'd known Theodore LePage for many years, and Ted had helped Alex one time when Alex really needed it. The rest of the time Ted had let Alex know he was walking on thin ice and to be careful. Lately the warnings seemed more frequent, and Alex suspected it meant they were coming to a crossroads. But Alex couldn't change his past, and if it came to a parting, so be it.

The younger of two children of Martha and Jakob Balkan, Alex was a third generation immigrant from the city of Zagreb in Croatia, which at the time was part of the Austro Hungarian Empire. His sister Marsha was five years his senior and lived with her husband fifteen miles away from his parents' home in Pennsylvania. Unfortunately

Marsha had no children and neither did Alex, so without a miracle the family line would soon be extinguished.

His grandfather Havel was a Catholic who hadn't endured religious persecution well in Croatia and, at age thirty, fled to the German ghetto of Altoona in Central Pennsylvania, which in those days was good for Croatians needing work. People from Altoona had beer on their breath, greasy hands, wore subdued clothing, but had money in the bank. Altoona back then was a thriving town producing rolling stock for the nation's expanding rail system. But by the time Alex was ten, the railroads were being eclipsed by the automobile, and hard times had come to Altoona.

By the time Alex was eighteen his father was out of work and his mother was forced to labor as a waitress and there was little money in the Balkan house. The family's plans for his college education evaporated. So he'd joined the air force where his proclivity for languages took him to Skytop near Syracuse where he studied Russian. The next two years were among the best in his life. He had money in his pocket, a light class-schedule, and life was endless parties on fraternity row. Russian came easy to him, and most of his time was spent chasing women and hanging out at the Orange Bar on Marshall Street. Two years later, he graduated with honors at the top of his class.

Then came his first reality check when he got orders for Vietnam. His mother was distraught. His father was furious. What little taxes he paid for the government to teach his son Russian resulted in his son going to Vietnam? But Alex didn't care, he was young, he was immortal, and he was about to see the world. He arrived in Saigon in time for a couple of pieces of good pussy before the embassy was evacuated. Years later he realized the whole thing had been screwed up from the outset. Southerners were not really interested in fighting their northern brothers and let America do it for them. The 365,000 Americans were in country in 1966, 436,000 six months later, and then a half million the year before Alex arrived.

Assigned to a special communications unit at Tan Son Nhut Air Base near Saigon, Alex's job was to monitor Russian transmissions around Hanoi and Lach Cao. The work was mundane and only a few times did he overhear anything important enough to be forwarded up the chain of command. All around him the war raged as his friends "wasted slopes" while the Viet Cong "rat caged" captured round eyes, and both sides wasted the local villagers around Saigon.

Located at a remote site twenty miles out in the boonies from the air base, the thought of being suddenly overrun and captured frightened him. But he survived and came back to the world. On arrival in California, the air force offered him a commission and training with CIA. He liked the intelligence business, especially after what he'd seen in Vietnam. Following Officer Training School he got his first assignment to Moscow! Now he was really off to see the world. Six years later he got his college degree, and his career seemed assured. But like most things in the intelligence world, nothing was guaranteed, and he barely got through twenty years as a twice passed over major before the air force forced him to retire.

Alex's biggest problem as a commissioned officer was his inability to compromise. Things were always black or white to Alex, evil or good, unacceptable or okay. To his superiors though, almost every shade of gray was fine. This offended Alex's Catholic upbringing and American values drummed into him by his parents. He'd also seen too much dirty laundry done behind closed doors, too many instances where superiors looked the other way when someone should have been shit-canned for incompetence. So with twenty years under his belt, Alex ambled out the front gate of Andrews Air Force Base, bought himself a half-gallon of Dimple Scotch Whiskey, and tied one on for *auld lang syne* at a local motel. He had no idea what he was going to do next and didn't care. Still in a stupor three days later, he'd answered a knock at the door. Defense Intelligence Agency informed him he was to be hired as a case officer.

But Alex's proclivity for honesty plagued that relationship too, and six years ago, he'd left them also, this time for Scion Consultants, a clandestinely owned CIA Beltway corporation supposedly involved in obscure intelligence research.

Roslyn

It had been three days since he'd spoken with the Vietnamese man at Tatiana's store, and Alex was still waiting around. The day before yesterday when he'd called his boss at Scion to sign out on leave, he'd been instructed to cancel his vacation plans and await further orders. Something had come up, and Ted LePage wouldn't elaborate over the phone. Yesterday afternoon he called in again and was told to be in LePage's office this morning at nine o'clock.

The last few nights sleep had been constantly interrupted by dreams which had been so graphic he'd had involuntary emissions from sex with the greatest imaginable mate with perfect breasts, tight thighs, and a vagina to die for. Consciousness gradually broke into his thoughts as he realized it was only a dream. He turned on his bedside light and studied the large wet mark on his sheets as his bedside alarm went off, filling the room with the sounds of the morning's news. He arose, anticipating the pleasure of a long hot shower. Beyond his balcony, he noticed the gusts of snow flurries obscuring traffic along Wilson Boulevard. A couple of inches of new snow had fallen during the night. A crappy day, he thought.

The view from his fourteenth floor apartment always exhilarated him, and on a clear day, he could see aircraft landing at Washington Reagan airport. Now he could barely make out the cars on Wilson Boulevard below. The telescope in the living room stood forlorn. He suspected it would be a while before was able to use it again to watch people walking along the mall in front of the White House, or the couple two buildings away toward Clarendon, who endlessly copulated on their living room floor.

He flipped on the TV and coffee pot and headed for the shower. After a quick breakfast of black coffee and a bagel, he rode the elevator to the lobby, crossed the street to the Metro, and bought a newspaper. As he descended the escalator to the Metro platform, he noted the front page advisory that there were only two shopping days left before Christmas. Thank God he'd remembered his mother and sister in Pennsylvania and mailed their gifts already. His mother lived alone, and while his older sister lived in the next town with her husband, for the number of times his sister saw his mother in the last two decades, she might as well have been in California. His mother was a woman with a strong constitution, but he'd taken her for granted too long and only recently realized that beneath her tough shell was the little girl she'd once been long before her family came along. Now she needed family around her and had chastised Alex for not providing grandchildren for her to bounce on her knee. He'd promised to drive up and spend a few days with her after the holidays.

Emerging at ground level on Wilson Boulevard in Roslyn, he made his way along the slick sidewalks toward the familiar mirrored building along the river.

He purposefully looked at his watch as he emerged into the fifteenth floor lobby and approached LePage's secretary. "You are on time, Alex. He's not."

* * *

At twenty past nine, LePage pulled into the underground parking lot and flashed his badge to the guard as he emerged from the elevator on the fifteenth floor. The guard had the best view in the building: a solid glass wall behind him with an eagle's eye view of the Potomac, Key Bridge, and the panorama of Georgetown. But this morning the heavy snowfall obliterated the view.

"Coffee for both of us!" Ted ordered his secretary as he slapped his newspaper against the sole of Alex's shoe. "Come on in, Alex." Ted slammed the office door behind them.

His demeanor changed almost instantly. "What the hell happened, Balkan?" he demanded.

Alex stared at him blankly. "Excuse me?"

"You heard me. What the hell happened?"

Alex gave him a perplexed expression. Ted's anger was obviously rising as he waited. Alex too was now getting annoyed. Alex didn't have to take this crap from him, and he had no idea what Ted was pissed about. He decided to tell him to go to hell if he persisted. "Beats the shit out of me," Alex replied in a calm voice, "Why don't you tell me?"

"The Slavchenko woman?"

"What about her?"

"Are you kidding, are you an idiot, Balkan?"

"What's the problem?" Alex replied

"Jesus Christ!" LePage said, "You tell me."

"I did. She wasn't in."

"She was found murdered two days ago with a screw driver in her forehead and, attached to it, a photocopy of a recently declassified intelligence report which you sent in years ago!"

"Are you kidding?" Alex replied. "I didn't know. I didn't see anything in the newspapers."

"Of course you didn't! Asshole! The director put a blanket over it."

"So, LePage. And now you tell me about it two days later? Am I a fucking suspect?"

"No. But the agency wants to know how they found her and what your report was doing there. And they want to know what the fuck SM-72 means. I just returned from a meeting with the Washington Police. Since it happened within their jurisdiction, they also insist on investigating the murder. The agency advised them of the sensitivity, so the local fuzz haven't told the press yet and have agreed to let us stay in the loop. An agency liaison officer has been assigned to make sure they don't leak any of this to the press."

"Who is the liaison?" Alex asked.

"Bert Combi."

Alex knew him but only in passing.

"Did you kill her, Alex?"

"You serious?"

"Well?" LePage demanded petulantly.

"No."

"You got an alibi?"

"Screw you, Ted! If I am a suspect, then have the police see me. I told you, I have not seen her in two years, and I did not kill her."

"Who did?"

"No idea."

"Can I trust you, or do we need to put you on the box?"

"If it makes you happy. But I didn't do it. Christ almighty! Why should I?"

"Where were you the night before last?"

Alex smiled at him. "You getting senile, Ted? At Fort McNair?"

"I know. But afterward?"

"I went home and went to bed, Ted. What was this classified report you mentioned?"

It dealt with a missing American named Paul Carter. She told you she'd seen him before her defection. In one of the KGB's silent Gulag camps along the Ob River. She informed you that World War II American prisoners were also there, thousands of them, many of whom had been recently executed and buried in mass graves beside the river."

"The name of the place, LePage?"

"Your report stated it was near Kolpashevo."

"If you say so, Ted. It was a while ago."

"On the reverse of the document left at her apartment," LePage continued, "in bold letters someone scribbled SM-72 with a black magic marker. What does it mean?"

"No idea. Who found her?"

"A neighbor's dog kept barking outside her apartment last night until they got the custodian to open the door. She'd been dead at least three, maybe four days."

"So . . . Ted . . . who declassified my report?"

"It was an error. Shouldn't have happened."

"You think it led to her death?"

"Possible. But not conclusive."

"How did it get out?"

"The Kerry Committee."

"The what?"

LePage gave him an annoyed look. "Don't you ever read the newspapers? Senators Kerry and McCain appointed themselves back in the early 1990s to look into prisoner of war and missing in action reports from the Vietnam era. You have heard of the POW/MIA committee? Their committee ordered all pertinent Vietnam and World War II records be declassified."

"All declassified?" Alex replied in disbelief. "Yeah sure. And pigs can fly too."

"Not all obviously, but tens of thousands of POW/MIA families at the time believed him and that was all that counted."

Alex was feverishly thinking back over the details of Tatiana's case and the piss poor internal security system within which he'd worked at that time and was still working within today for that matter. Someone had obviously gone to the trouble of leaving the document at the murder scene. America's capability to protect those who defected from hostile states, never the best, had become abysmal since the end of the Cold War. The concept of personal security in the espionage business was based on anonymity, and anonymity stank around Washington. Americans thought anyone could obtain all the protection anyone needed through a lawyer. The lawyer in turn could threaten those who bothered his client with expensive litigation, and the payment of huge legal claims. Hostile security services laughed. They didn't need justification to make you disappear; all they needed to know was where you were. And once they did, even the best locks and security barriers were useless.

Alex had personally assured Tatiana, using the old Croatian expression, "swearing on his mother's milk," that she would never have to worry about the bad guys finding her. America would protect her. America would give her a new identity, new friends, and lots of backup in official records to support her new life's story. If her death had been at the hands of some political assassin, her last thoughts must have been that Alex Balkan's word wasn't worth crap and his mother's milk must have been bile!

"Assign her investigation to me, Ted!"

"We'll have to work the problem."

Alex shook his head in disgust. He hated that expression. Anytime anyone told him they had to work a problem, it meant the truth would never come out.

Theodore LePage was the ultimate intelligence system manager, only interested in promoting . . . number one, himself. Alex's passion was the establishment of intimate one-on-one trust with spies planning to betray their country. Ted arranged amorphous accommodations in a milieu which mocked all human relationships. It was just a job to Ted. Information to Ted was knowledge, knowledge was power, and what one knew equated to power and position over others. Ted was at the top of the power charts inside the Beltway. A real-life Potomac Potentate. Alex on the other hand was a lowly soldier, an expendable trooper on the front-line in the war of espionage. It explained the chasm between them. Alex was a lousy GS-12, grossing seventy-two thousand a year while Ted was an appointed public servant, bumping against the congressionally mandated maximum wage ceiling. At one hundred and eighty thousand a year, Ted had attended every conceivable management, leadership, and academic seminar in the world, but only to enhance his visibility. All you had to do was look at the wall behind his desk. An incredible eighty-three frames of paraphernalia documented Theodore J. LePage's rise to power.

Ted also yearned for everyone to like him. It was important to Ted that people like him. From a wealthy Virginia family, "Trust me!" was Ted's favorite moniker. It was important to him that his listeners believed him and that they consider him a patriot and a conscientious man: who helped the world's needy by dropping a couple of bucks into the collection plate each Sunday. Dilettante was a ten-dollar word which Alex thought best described his boss.

"Any other clues which indicate who the murderer was?"

"None except your declassified document."

"I'd like to see the murder scene."

"Sorry, Alex! It's not in the cards. Besides you aren't involved. I told you. This is a compartmented case."

Alex could feel his bile rising. The dead woman risked everything to defect. And now it had cost her her life. The eldest of three, Tatiana Slavchenko, represented the quintessential core of the Russian peasant class. Her ancestors were dirt farmers, indentured servants of the aristocracy. A good-looking child, she'd learned early what men wanted. At seventeen a commissar took a fancy to her and arranged for a position with the Party. A year later, she'd contracted a venereal problem, and the commissar shipped her off to a Russian air force intelligence job in Central Russia. Six years later, now aged twenty-four, she arrived in the city of Novosibirsk where her new boss was also a party hack and who also took a fancy to her. But by this time she had other things in mind.

Young, beautiful, and more knowledgeable in the ways of acquiring what she wanted, she became the commanding general's woman. Base housing for the enlisted was crap. With the general's attention came better quarters, plumbing, food, cars, and vacations at Sochi on the Black Sea. And as time passed, the general saw to it that her responsibilities were expanded. Five years later as a senior captain, she was placed in charge of ICBM target coordination for the Fourteenth Military District, which contained half of Russia's ICBM missile fleet and 80 percent of the heavy—launch vehicles—all targeted against the United States. The fourteenth military district was the largest: straddling the heart of Russia from the Arctic to Mongolia. With her new position came lots of travel, and within a year, she'd become familiar with the launch complexes throughout her district.

In the fall of 1991, her boss informed her of a special mission and ordered her to Moscow. The assignment turned out to be a special military intelligence school, which months later led to the interrogation of an American prisoner at a riverside camp along the Ob River north of Novosibirsk. The interrogation hadn't proceeded well, and superiors became disgruntled. They'd hoped Tatiana's beauty and congenial personality might change the prisoner's outlook and make him talk. It hadn't. And a few weeks later, she was reassigned to the military attaché office at the Russian Embassy in Delhi. India opened Tatiana's eyes to the fact there was another world out there which she decided to see. Weeks later, she walked into Delhi's United States Embassy and informed the marine guard who she was and wanted to see a CIA Officer about defecting. Two days later, she was in Western Europe.

She'd first mentioned the American she'd interrogated near Novisibirsk, to Alex, who'd been assigned as her debriefer in Germany. Alex had dutifully reported it among the four 418 intelligence reports which had been generated by her defection. But no one by that name was missing in American archives and eventually the report was forgotten.

"It's still not clear to me how my report was released," Alex complained, hoping Ted would clarify the point for him.

"The Kerry Commission was declassifying records and reports from Vietnam. John Kerry headed it up, along with others like Senators Smith and McCain.

"My report on Paul Carter dealt with the Second World War, Ted, and Kerry's focus was Vietnam—thirty years later. What's the connection?" Alex knew a lot more about the Vietnam question than LePage suspected. In the 1980s, a decade after the Vietnam War ended, Americans had become tired of the never-ending rumors from Southeast Asia about live American prisoners still being held in captivity in Southeast Asia, and after a yearlong investigation, the Kerry Committee had concluded: quote—"we found nothing to substantiate the rumors."

From what Alex now recalled about the hearings so long ago, he thought it might have been Kerry's objective at the outset, to find those who were still missing but then he had been convinced to forget about it by his powerful Senate friend, John McCain of Arizona. So the committee concluded its work with the observation that they sought nothing more than to create a healing document, one which would end the roller-coaster ride of family complaints about their missing loved ones which kept flowing into Washington.

"If you'll recall, Alex," Ted broke into his thoughts, "your report also mentioned there were Americans captured by the Soviets in Eastern Europe as World War II concluded, who ended up in Russia for exploitation and were then executed and buried in mass graves along the Ob River. That's how this happened."

Alex shot him a sarcastic expression. “What crap! You’re a manager, Ted. You’re supposed to make reports like that from her never see the light of day. Okay? How did it get out?”

“The report was not released by the committee at the time because of its sensitivity and was returned to the National Archives for long-term storage.”

“And?” Alex demanded.

“Someone made a mistake.”

“A mistake! Say it, Ted!”

“A researcher at the archives requested documents relating to another issue, and somehow your report got included among them. But the official in charge did redact the document before it was released.”

Alex said nothing and just stared at LePage with obvious hostility.

“Her true name was mentioned?” Alex muttered. He could feel his bile rising again.

“Yes. It was an oversight.”

“What in hell does that mean, Ted?”

LePage opened his briefcase and withdrew a paper. He handed it to Alex. “This was left at the murder scene.” Among all the excised spaces, Alex spotted the oversight immediately. Halfway down the page next to her six-digit B number was her true name. Her true name should not have appeared and it was his fault. He flipped it over and saw the letters SM-72 scrawled on the back. He rose and walked to the window and stared out over the river toward Georgetown, watching the ribbon of traffic making its way across the Key Bridge. He knew he’d have to cool down for a couple of minutes before he continued. Even he knew that there was a limit to what he could say to Ted in anger and get away with it. “We all took an oath, Ted!” He said finally, “To protect the anonymity of our sources. We betrayed her trust!”

“Yes. But you did not help by including her true name, so calm down, Balkan! Don’t go pulling a Jesus Christ act. It happened.”

“Who’s the cretin responsible?”

“Cretin is a strong word, Balkan.”

“The guilty bastard.”

“If you want to crucify someone, Alex, forget it.”

“I don’t believe you said that, Ted. We should execute the asshole who sanitized this report.”

"If you insist on demanding a pound of flesh. Then I'll have to ask for your resignation. It's your call . . . !" LePage leaned back in his expensive leather executive chair and explored his left ear with the end of a paper clip, his eyes riveted on Alex.

Alex supposed he'd known all along that the son of a bitch would take the collective approach. The system had obviously fouled up again, but the system was not about to offer up a scapegoat. Alex wanted to puke. This was the reason he'd never been able to get promoted during his air force career, because the system promoted the "get-along and go-alongs" while ignoring the conscientious types. The system had erred badly this time and someone had been killed because of it, but no one was going to be fired, probably not even disciplined? It would all be forgotten. "You think the Russians did it. Ted?"

It was a dumb question. The KGB hated defectors. And the higher a defector's rank, the harder the Russians searched for them. Treason was the ultimate transgression in Russia, and to defect from the KGB, that compounded the sin tenfold.

"We're checking. There might have been something else behind it."

"Meaning?"

"No one seems to know what the meaning of SM-72 scrawled on the back means."

Alex turned the document over and reexamined the large black letters. There was an empty space in his gut. He'd miss Tatiana. They'd been lovers in the vernacular. He preferred the portion of the dictionary definition, which referred to a strong physical attraction and desire. That's all it had ever been between them.

"Ted, I want you to let me look into who did this. It's the least you can do."

"Will you agree to keep this all to yourself?"

Alex gave him a pained look.

"You would have to report exclusively to me if I did agree."

"Then you have my word, Ted."

"I'll think about your request."

"When?"

"Soon. Trust me!"

Arlington

"How are things?"

The ensuing few minutes were spent in trivialities. Then the voice on the phone got down to the real purpose for the call.

"And this subordinate?"

"He'll do what he's told."

"We need to be careful, LePage. This guy must not find out. You and I must be absolutely clear on this."

"He's the same guy who originally debriefed the victim just after she defected. He's also experienced a troubled career and lacks polish."

"Is he any good?"

"Among the best."

"What is his name?"

"Alex Balkan."

"Sounds Yugoslav?"

"I believe his grandfather was from Zagreb."

"A Croatian? Christian or Moslem?"

"Come on, for Christ's sake!" Ted demanded with obvious annoyance. "What kind of a question is that?"

"Don't be abrupt with me, Ted! Damn it! What's his normal job?"

"A contract case officer. Still works what is left of our MBFR treaty with Moscow."

"Why? Mutual Balanced Force Reduction issues with Russia seems odd for a case officer?"

"Also gives him cover for action in a host of other areas we are interested from time to time."

"I see. He speaks their language?"

"Fluently. It's mandatory for the job," Ted replied. "He spends almost half each year wandering around Russia and other States of the former Soviet Union, to make sure they are still complying with the treaty."

"So he spots and assesses?"

"He meets a lot of interesting people."

"Thank you," the voice on the phone said. The caller needed to be sure all options were considered. Americans thrived on an insatiable urge to pry into everyone's personal life. This worried the caller, so he had to be sure that Ted LePage had considered everything. In life's successful voyages, it is always the first steps which were crucial: and most prone to establish the success or failure of a mission.

"Is it possible this man could betray you?"

"Shouldn't think so," Ted replied.

"What leads does he have?"

"Only two which relate to Carter," Ted said.

"Specifics?"

"His original report, and the letters SM-72 on the back."

"There was no report in the newspapers about the murder," the caller observed.

"Naturally. The local police understand it's a compartmented case. We will tell the press what they need to know and neither Balkan nor the media will ask for clarification."

"You are reassured?

"Trust me."

"Thanks for the update, Ted." The line went dead.

Ballston

Alex was noticeably relieved when he saw Ted the next morning. Ted suggested he take some time to follow-up the Slavchenko thing. Their conversation was terse and to the point. Ted LePage had already run a system-wide inquiry on the alphanumeric SM-72 on the back side of Alex's redacted intelligence report about the dead woman, but it had produced a dead end. A State Department review on the subject of the declassified report about Carter had also produced nothing. Even the original file was no longer available, misplaced, or lost years ago. State did have a copy of Alex's reports and State's subsequent inquiries to Moscow. But these too revealed nothing. Ted LePage had next poured through Slavchenko's phone records, and among them were three calls in the last year to a number in Key West. That seemed unusual and was about the only curiosity so far. The number was registered to an old woman. A system check through the FBI's personnel-link indicated the woman was born in Europe in 1919 and, at age two, had been adopted by a family in Wisconsin, where she'd been raised through high school. She'd worked for the government most of her adult life and only come under suspicion once in her entire career during the Second World War, regarding an issue about ships torpedoed near Key West. But an investigation at the time had cleared her. Beyond that, zero.

"Alex, I think you need to spend some time at Key West."

"You crazy?" Alex shot back. He knew immediately it was a dumb thing to say.

LePage balled up a piece of paper and threw it into a trash can." You said you want to be involved, Balkan. Maybe it's better if you just forget this entire issue. I should have known better."

Alex apologized.

"Before you leave for Key West, Alex, I also want you to see this guy. LePage handed him the name of an army analyst who was reputed to be an expert on wartime German submarine operations.

"What for?"

"An old woman in Key West was once suspected of involvement with ships torpedoed down there during the war. She's still alive and Slavchenko called her a couple of times last year. Find out why. She might know something. See this WW-II sub expert before you leave. It's not much to go on, but it's all we've got. When you get there, snoop around for a couple of days and see what you can find out before you see her."

"What are you driving at?"

"This is serious, Alex! You are not the only one, asshole. Higher-ups here are pissed also about her murder and they want answers, so don't fuck this up! Do it by the numbers."

"Why all the mystery?"

"Look, Alex!" LePage's face was now pained. He was losing his patience. "I'll be frank. It's common knowledge up the river that you were fucking the bitch here, right from the start! Been doing it for a long time from what I understand. It contravenes all regulations regarding case officer/agent operations. You knew it was wrong and should have withdrawn from the case long ago. You obviously didn't! Were all this known to me earlier, I would have shit-canned your ass for gross negligence. Now she's dead, and you come in here like some fucking prima donna, some grieving lover screaming you want revenge because someone killed your whore! Well . . . ? I'm sorry! You can't have it both ways. I'm giving you a chance. Don't mess up this one too."

Alex looked crestfallen.

"I apologize for having to be so direct, Alex, but you needed to be reminded." It really wasn't exactly the way LePage had just said it, but hopefully it would put Balkan on the defensive, and that might make him more cautious about what he did and said as things developed.

TWO

Key West

"MAY I HELP you Mr . . . . ?"

"Balkan. Its spelled like the place where Yugoslavia used to be."

"Yes, sir! A room for how long?"

"A week, maybe longer."

"You're lucky. A week will be no problem, but more might be. The holidays are upon us. Occupancy is heavy."

The effeminate young man studied the reservation book. His left ear sported not one but two rings and a line of diamond studs across the top outer rim of the auricle. Pimps in Italy, Alex thought, would describe this boffo character as *delicato* and the addition of the studs would also earn him the epithet of *corno.*

The flight south from Miami had been a relaxing experience, and Key West promised to be a respite from his hectic pace. It was Alex's first time to the Southernmost Point of the United States and already he liked it.

"Yes, I believe we can provide you with a very nice accommodation. Second floor! It has a nice view of the Atlantic, even a small balcony in the event you might want to work on an all body tan." He winked at Alex as he raised an index finger, which also bore a ring, and pointed to the area above and behind the reception desk. "It's up there."

He pushed the registration book around. "Kindly sign the log. I will also need a major credit card. Here on vacation?"

"Yes," Alex replied. The receptionist's expression left little doubt he was sizing Alex up. The tick in his eye twitched again, but it was gradually improving. "I'm doing some research. Is there a local library?"

"Certainly, it's six blocks away."

A half hour later, Alex pulled up before the Key West Public Library. He'd decided to present himself as a struggling author, gathering information for a story about Key West. It would provide him with a reason to ask lots of dumb questions. Before leaving for Florida, he'd spent a couple of hours with the analyst Ted had insisted he see at the army's historical records section at Fort Meyers. James Nolte was one of those obscure feckless types who miraculously survived a lifetime in government by amassing trivia about long forgotten histories. Knolte also knew about German submarine ciphers.

Nolte discussed German submarine operations along the east coast between 1940 to 1945 and expounded on wartime espionage, which was run by Branch-One of Germany's Abwehr. Abwehr, Nolte explained, was the legendary Admiral Canaris's stepchild, dedicated to ciphers. One of Canaris's wartime coups was his 'Postal Unit,' an obscure organization developed to secretly break the American wartime military ciphers. Run by a young man named Vetterlin. Vetterlin had broken the Top Secret American Telegraph and Telephone cipher known as A-3 long before the United States declared war on Germany. The American code used a random changing group of sub-bands with division points, and inversions plus intersubstitutions, all of which changed thirty-six times in twelve minutes. Alex didn't understand it and didn't care. The United States only learned about Vetterlin after the war, when bits and pieces of his records were recovered by the American Army in Europe. Unfortunately Russia captured most of Vetterlin's work, and Nolte suspected that the Russians were able to read American codes for many years after World War II ended. It was Nolte's conclusion that many wartime German secrets remained to be exposed some day.

Nolte's expression had become conspiratorial when he related a story about the night of February 13, 1942. The German U-Boat U-202 had dropped a team of five on Long Island, all of whom were captured because of a suspicious telephone tip, but the FBI never was able to trace the tip. The agent's mission was to blow up military factories in Philadelphia. Another sub dropped five more on the beach at Jacksonville, who were also all rounded up following yet another anonymous phone tip. Both groups were subsequently executed for espionage.

"But we now know there were other groups put ashore that we never knew about."

One, Nolte recalled, was Operation Rossbach, which U.S. Army researchers stumbled across in East Berlin records after the collapse of East Germany in 1989. Initially, investigators assumed Rossbach was the operation we already knew about and involved a Wolf Pack operation to intercept allied convoy ON-204 in the Greenland-Iceland channel in early October 1943. But the East Berlin Operation Rossbach that U.S. researchers uncovered was a completely different operation, and involved agent landings in the United States. Nolte's expression became conspiratorial.

"Following the landing of the five agents at Jacksonville, which we now know involved two German submarines, the U.S. Navy spotted two more U-Boats along the Florida Keys on February 21, 1942. Both submarines were forced to dive and were repeatedly depth charged but failed to produce any evidence that either had been sunk—such as oil or debris coming up. There are also only two ship logs during the entire Second World War, which end exactly the same way, and these were the ones involving the two surface combatants who depth charged these subs."

"So? What are you trying to tell me?" Alex asked.

"Until now . . . I thought it was a fluke." Nolte replied.

"So?" Alex had finally replied, realizing that Nolte was enjoying the recounting of his story and was waiting for Alex to show more interest?

"Well, it wasn't, and now I suspect there was something else afoot," Nolte continued.

"Where could I find this report?"

"Volume three of the Dictionary of American Fighting Ships for 1981. The logs state both American ships made an attack without success off Bahia Honda on the twenty-first of February 1942. Involved were the Coast Guard cutter Triton, whose hull identification was PC-445, and the Navy Destroyer Hamilton, DD-141."

Alex made a note. "What about German Navy records?"

"Zilch," Nolte replied.

"What do the German records report about their U-Boats that were in the area, Mr. Nolte?"

"On February 24, 1942, only two." Nolte smiled. Again his expression became even more conspiratorial. "We were reading their encoded traffic and knew two were in the area, the U-128 and U-504. The other two I referred to were further down the Florida Keys, and we didn't know anything about them."

"So what are you saying?"

"Don't know," Nolte replied. "It's so unusual for us not to have come across the final bits and pieces of their wartime U-Boat operations. The histories of all of the German's U-Boats ever produced have been documented in incredible detail, from the components that went into them, who produced them, the type, date its keel was laid down, date launched, put into operation, its captains and crews, wartime missions, and the date and place each was finally lost or captured. Just thought you'd be interested. According to Mr. LePage who called me, he said this was the type of information that might be useful to you. You are obviously looking into a gap in our intelligence records, and I wish you good luck."

* * *

Alex recalled Nolte's observations as he mounted the steps to the Key West Library. The librarian's office in a rear room was a mess, permeated by the odor of dank paper.

"Mr. Benson?"

A kindly face nodded.

"I'm Alex Balkan from New York. I'm a writer, doing research for a novel about the war years and need information about German U-Boat activity around here."

"My favorite topic," Benson replied with gusto. "I've got it all up here," he pointed to his bald main, "and what's not here, I can find. What's the question?"

"What was happening here in the early part of 1942?"

Benson stood up and moved to the window and crossed his arms, resembling a professor about to inculcate knowledge to a waiting freshman. "German Ministry of Defense records showed nineteen U-Boats along the East coast," his voice was officious, "of which three were in Florida between mid-February to mid-March. The three were involved in Operation 'Paukenschlag—Drumbeat!' Ever heard of it?"

"No," Alex replied.

"The three boats here were U-106, 128, and 156. In fact the Bremen built U-156 under the legendary Captain Werner Hatenstein, who at the time, as far as my research has shown, was actually in transit to Trinidad in late February. Around mid-March two more arrived."

"It's a long way from Germany. How were they able to get this far?"

"Drifted with the currents mostly. They were Atlantic class boats of about twelve hundred tons. 238 feet long and a 15 foot draft, fully loaded they could cruise 16,300 miles at ten knots with a 48 man crew—goddamn mean machines for those days! For their Caribbean cruises the German's augmented their on-board fuel supplies by storing fuel wherever possible—even their fresh water tanks as well as trim and compensating tanks. It's how they got the name Pig Boats. The crew smelled pretty bad after a month."

"How long did they hang around once they got here?"

"Less than six weeks usually."

"And the result, Mr. Benson?"

"Call me Lew! Key West is an informal place. The last time someone called me mister, was when I was asked to speak at a high school graduation. The U-Boats did a lot of damage. U-128 alone sank three ships in two days, almost twenty-four thousand tons—a lot of shipping back then."

"The skipper must have been good!" Alex replied, interested in developing rapport with this man who he hoped knew something about the real issues behind his visit, when he got around to it.

"Captain Ulrich Heyse. One of their best!" Benson continued, "But the poor bastard bought-it in mid 1943."

"What about others?"

"You mean what happened to them?"

"Did any of them survive the war?"

"All eventually went down with their ships."

"And the cost to the United States?" Alex said.

"Very high. We lost ninety-nine surface ships in eleven months. They lost two subs. There were many nights in 1942 and 1943 when three or four burning ships lit up the skies off Key West."

"And none of the crews survived the war?" Alex asked.

"Not that I know of. One might have," Benson replied.

"Which one?"

"Their most famous. Captain Werner Hartenstein of U-156. He was reported killed on his third patrol. He was one of their gutsiest, even took on the U.S. Navy Destroyer Blakely. Blew away most of her bow with a throat shot."

"What happened to Hartenstein?" Alex inquired.

"A navy flying boat caught Hartenstein's sub napping on the surface one day and dropped some depth charges which broke his sub in half. The PBY counted twenty survivors in rubber rafts after she went down, two of the men in the rafts had white Officers shirts. One of them could have been Hartenstein. When the PBY returned to the same area two days later, there was no trace of any of them, and a long search of the area turned up nothing. Either sharks got them or they were picked up by another U-Boat. But it's improbable they were rescued by another sub because there were none ever reported anywhere in the area."

"A surface ship, maybe?" Alex asked.

"Possible, but none of the crew showed up anywhere else later in the war in German records."

"What about an engagement up the coast at Bahia Honda, Lew?"

"Oh. You've heard about that already?"

"Yes."

"From whom?"

"A friend up north said it might make an interesting story."

"You'd have to make your book fiction. There's nothing to the story."

"For certain?" Alex asked.

"It was a false sighting! Take my word for it, Alex. Sonar was unbelievably bad in those days. It was a false sonar report."

"How can you be so certain?"

"I've been studying this stuff for years. I've examined all of the German Navy's histories, which we captured when the war ended. They're up at the National Archives. I also served in the navy for twenty years in sonar. Believe me, I know what I am talking about."

"What about German agents landing in the Keys?"

A huge smile erupted across Lew's face. "You've really been talking to too many people who drink their own bath water around here."

"I don't understand."

"Nothing to it either. Key Wester's thrive on tales of treasure, intrigue and get-rich—quick schemes. Jesus. I could tell you yarns for days if you got the time . . . all fiction."

"Anyone else I could see who might know something about life in the Keys during the war years?"

"Sure." He scribbled several names and phone numbers. "You might try these."

"Mind if I call on you again?"

"I'm here six days a week. Anytime! Try the old man at the top of the list first. He hangs out at the Armory over on White Street. He's usually there after lunch. If he's not, his place is two blocks away."

"Much obliged."

* * *

At the end of Fleming, Alex turned right onto White Street and parked across from the traffic light. The armory was another of the perennial wooden clapboard structures that abounded everywhere on Key West. Inside, an assortment of shriveled elderly snowbirds sat around silently playing bridge. Edgar Nutt was not among them and an elderly woman scribbled directions on a score pad. "Its three blocks toward Duval," she pointed.

He rang the doorbell on the quiet palm studded street. Nutt's house had seen better days, and dense bouquets of red Bougainvillea lent a grace to the dilapidation. The man who opened the screen door was ancient.

"Mr. Nutt?"

Nutt invited Alex in once he'd explained his purpose. Nutt continuously squinted as if he'd just stepped into direct sunlight. His head also twitched to the left, and between the squints and twitches, it was difficult for Alex to watch the gaunt face. Over Nutt's thin lips hung a gray mustache and two hollowed-out eye sockets. His resemblance to the famous movie star Jack Palance was uncanny.

"What can I do for you, Mr. Balkan?"

From the loud voice, Alex also suspected another of Nutt's ailments was deafness. "I'm doing research for a book about the war period here. I understand from Lew Benson at the Library that you were here then?"

"Sure as hell was! What you want to know about the Cubans?"

"Cubans?" Alex inquired.

"The Cuban Missile Crisis, right!"

"No, Mr. Nutt. World War II."

"Sorry! Wrong war."

"Where you here in 1942?"

"Sure as hell was! Was here for that one too! What do you want to know?"

"What was it like?"

"Exciting. After the Jap's attacked Pearl Harbor, my Reserve Unit was activated, and I went off to the west coast for basic training and then the war in the Pacific."

"But," Alex interrupted, "I thought you were here in the Keys?"

"Hold your horses, son! Let me finish! I was. But only for a while. Once we finished basic training, we spent a few months in California and then got reassigned back here. I thought I was going to be able to sit out the war here and enjoy myself. But it didn't last long. The army thought we'd do better here as road guards on the bridges from the mainland 'cause we were all from Key West. It was a small place, and we knew everyone. The army's biggest security problem then was the bridges to the mainland. Always afraid someone come down and blow them up."

Nutt fidgeted for a few moments and seemed as if he'd lost his train of thought. "You were going to tell me why you came back," Alex repeated.

"Yeah! First the army assigned a bunch of northerners to guard the bridges. But they were no damned good. There was a drinking place on Pigeon Key, you know, a shack with a refrigerator and cold beer and some whiskey. These clowns would stop for a brew, or two, then go and pass out somewhere along the roadway." A laugh gurgled up from Nutt's chest as he smiled. In three months, the army lost nine men."

"Murdered?"

"Hell no! Them bastards was run over where they lay."

"I don't understand, and where is Pigeon Key?"

"It's just south of the beginning of the seven mile bridge. During the 1940s it was one of the few places of inhabitation because of its deep water channel which supply ships could come in through at the time. You see, in those days the bridge was just wide enough for a single car. Them what fell asleep along the roadway at night was run over by the occasional cars coming through. Plus them what weren't known to the guards ended up always being held needlessly, so the brass down at Key West figured we local guys could do better! Plus, we knew everyone and didn't get bored and drink like the Northerners."

"When did you start?"

"February 5, 1942."

"You seem so certain!"

"Damn right! I ought too! I got married here on the first of February. Four days later I got orders to go up to Pigeon Key." He smiled, knowing Alex understood the implication. "I spent three months up there and never got a pass. Didn't see my bride for ninety days." Noting Alex's incredulous expression, Nutt relented a little. "Well, we did get it on a couple of times, and in between she'd stop by and I got some quickies."

Alex was wondering where the conversation was leading. The old man was here only a few weeks after the submarine incident, so maybe he didn't know anything. "Ever see any Germans?"

"I didn't! But others did. I heard about them on the QT you understand. At the time one didn't ask questions. Everything was top secret."

"Anything specific?"

"I know they caught one guy. An older German who was sending messages to submarines offshore."

"And?" Alex asked.

"He was a clever bastard and used the portable generator on his ice cream truck to power his transmitter. Like a Good Humor Man. The army kept picking up his transmissions from different parts of Key West. But by the time they triangulated it and went there, no one was there. One day he made a mistake and they caught him."

"Anything else?" Alex asked.

"I remember we also found five German uniforms on Big Pine, buried in a shallow hole."

"When?"

"Late March I guess it was."

"Ever hear about any dead Germans?"

Nutt seemed concerned for a moment. "Once, but I don't know if I should talk about it." The old man glanced around as if trying to determine if anyone was listening. "It's been sixty years," he said, "and I suppose it's probably not top secret anymore. You ain't with the police or FBI, are you?"

"Hardly," Alex replied. "Just a writer looking for a story."

"This may still be top secret," Nutt continued, "so you didn't hear it from me. There were three I heard about around mid-February

1942. Three dead Germans up on Boot Key. But it was all hush-hush you understand."

"Only three."

"Right!"

"You sure?"

"Just telling you what I heard."

"Mr. Nutt, how come none of this was ever published in any of the postwar histories?"

For a moment, the old man seemed confused. Then became angry.

"I just told you, young feller, that it was hush-hush. Secret . . . get it? Probably still is for all I know."

Alex decided he'd better change the subject.

"So what happened after you came back from Pigeon Key?"

"We were isolated in a barracks. The security people warned us not to talk about anything we'd seen or heard under pain of death. That included the dead Germans too. I was given a week's leave with my wife, then got shipped to the Pacific. Didn't get back till I was mustered out in early 1946."

"You were going to tell me something about what happened while you were at Pigeon Key?"

"Wasn't really on that Key. It was on one further south."

Alex waited as the seconds ticked by, and the old man stared out the window into his garden, saying nothing for a while. "And?" Alex asked again.

"Changed my mind, young man. Something real serious did happen there, but it's better if I say nothing."

"You sure?"

"I'm sure."

"Well, you have been very kind. I've got to be going. Mind if I call you if I have more questions, Mr. Nutt?"

"Welcome anytime. I'll ask around if you like."

"Not necessary. Thanks for the information."

* * *

At three o'clock Alex stood before a picket fence two streets from Duval. The house was attractive but also needed repairs. Inside the front door he could see a young man sitting at a desk.

"May I help you?" he inquired.

"Is Eugene Sharrold in?"

"No. Who's looking for him?"

"I'm doing some research and was told to see him."

"He's up on the mainland."

"Does he have a wife I could talk to?"

The young man got up and walked out to the gate. As he did, Alex noticed he too sported a diamond stud in his left ear.

"What did you say your name was?"` he asked Alex with a strange expression.

"I didn't!" Alex replied. Alex was visibly annoyed at the earring and supposed his face showed it.

"I live here," the younger man replied. "I know Eugene. But I don't know you! You ask a bunch of questions, and I ain't never seen you round here before."

"Name's Alex. I'm from New York."

The younger man returned to the porch. "I think you've got the wrong Eugene." He observed in a haughty tone.

"Oh! Why's that?"

"No women live here."

"None?"

"None."

"How unusual."

"Not at all."

"Why?"

"This is a gay hotel, whatever your name is, and I can assure you, Mr. Eugene does not have a wife. Not like you think anyway."

"I see. I still need to talk to him. When will Eugene return?"

"A day or two."

"I'll check back."

"A bientot," the queer replied, turning his back as he swished back into the lobby.

"*A toute a l'heur.*" Alex observed sarcastically after him as he turned and headed toward Duval Street. Stopping a couple of blocks away at a bar with the sobriquet, Bull and Whistle, he watched the tourists parading past him toward the sunset spectacle at Mallory Dock.

* * *

The next morning he drove up the Keys to see the third name on the librarian's list. Catherine Rhiener's place lay to the right of mile-marker thirty-two. Her residence sat among a hodgepodge of old buildings long past their prime. As he got out of his car, a woman emerged from the channel behind the house, wrapped a printed cloth around her waist, and plopped a straw hat on her head as she crossed the sand toward him. He guessed she was in her late sixties and obviously in fantastic shape. She'd probably sported carrot red hair in her youth, which today was faded with flecks of gray. From her gun-barrel frame and long legs, Alex guessed she'd once resembled a Playboy centerfold.

"You Kate Rheiner?" Alex asked.

"And who might you be?" she replied.

"Alex Balkan, an aspiring writer, Lew Benson at the Key West library listened to my spiel yesterday and mentioned you as someone I should try to see."

"About what?" she asked, pointing that they should move into the shade of a nearby Ficus tree.

"Intrigue. Second World War and that era here in the Keys."

"Lots of sex and loose women?" she asked inquiringly.

"Haven't got that far yet."

"What?" she exploded. "Half the male animal's life is dedicated to the pursuit of sex in all its glorious forms! You did know that?"

"Not offhand."

"Kinsey Report! Being a writer I thought you'd be up on this kind of thing!"

"I'll make a note of it."

"How many books you published already?"

"None."

"How many you written?"

"None."

"None?"

"This is my first."

"I see! What's the subject?"

"U-Boats and secret agents around here years ago."

"Ahaaa!" She winked at him. "Now I know what type of a guy you are. Want me to tell you?"

He stared at her in anticipation.

"The minute I laid eyes on you, I say to myself, Kate! This guy is honest! He's reliable and you can trust him. And he's probably dedicated his life to working behind the scenes for his country. And he's a spy. Am I right?"

"I'm flattered!"

"Flattered . . . or exposed?"

"The former."

"If you say so. Since you are a spy, got any creds?"

"Sure." Alex fished into his wallet and showed her his Virginia driver's license and his Department of Defense identification card, both of which were in his true name.

"I knew it." She laughed. "You even showed me your government ID card. I know how that works. It's a big government. But being a gentleman I suppose I must believe you. Come on, let's go inside. What would you like to know?" she asked him as they threaded their way along a narrow path through the dense vegetation of what had once been a garden.

"Lew Bensen told me about a navy engagement which took place around here in early 1942, involving a submarine. You know about it?"

"What possessed you to get interested in such a subject?"

"It's an interesting angle."

The inside of the house reflected the tastes of someone who'd done some traveling. What set off the assorted knick knacks of world travel was the white marble floor which extended throughout the house, and had obviously cost a bundle to install. Pointing him to a white wicker chair, she left and returned moments later with two glasses of Seltzer water. In the next twenty minutes, she regaled him with several stories which confirmed his belief that lots of mysterious things had happened throughout the Keys in the last two hundred years and that most of it had long since been forgotten.

Alex finally got around to asking her about rumors of Germans landing nearby just to the north of Big Pine during the war, her response was almost instantaneous.

"The reason I know the incident is true," she continued, is I heard it firsthand from Corky. He was a retired British battleship captain from the First World War. Corky knew what he was talking about when it came to Naval matters. He retired here in 1926 and stayed here until he died thirty-six years later. On numerous occasions in the late forties, he related a story to me and others around here about old man Tollway. Ever heard the story about Tollway?"

"Not yet."

"He was a hermit who hung out on a small Key north of here. He did his shopping at the general store on Marathon, and in the early 1940s the old codger suddenly began buying the damnedest things at the Marathon General Store: and all with cash. An electric refrigerator, an electric fan, and an electric washing machine for instance, then a generator and lots of cans of diesel fuel which he hauled away to his hootch! Where would the old bastard get the money which was all in twenties and fifties? Then during the summer of 1943, no one saw Tollway for a while, so in August Corky went to see if he was all right. The old geezer had been dead quite awhile, and his body was badly decomposed but still recognizable. When Corky nosed around, he also found three shallow graves near Tollway's hootch. According to Corky, the bodies were partially exposed and had been pretty well cleaned up by the crabs. But from their clothing it was obvious they were men. Corky reported all this to the coast guard at Marathon who immediately swore him to secrecy, but then he never heard anything more about it. He said it was strange when he heard later the authorities decided the three skeletons were unknown animals and not human! Corky knew what human skeletons and skulls looked like. The authorities were lying and covering up something, and Corky wondered about it and where old man Tollway got all the money from."

"You think he killed them and stole their money, Kate?"

"I think he got it off some dead Germans who washed ashore. That's what I think!"

"Corky said that?" Alex asked.

"Sure as hell did! To my face. Corky read a book after the war which talked about Germans agents put ashore by submarine in Maine, New York, and Jacksonville. Each of the three German teams that came ashore had over forty thousand dollars in cash on them when they were caught." She winked at Alex.

"How much could this old man have spent at the General Store Kate?"

"Maybe a couple of hundred."

"And the rest?" Alex asked.

She laughed. "The place he used to live is not too far from here. If you want, you can nose around and look for some buried chest with cash in it. But in this climate and the high water and moisture, it's doubtful paper money would last more than a couple of years."

"You know about the Triton and Hamilton?" Alex asked.

"Sure," she replied giving him a knowing look now. "Corky used to talk about them too. No one said a word about it during the war, and when Corky brought it up with a navy officer who came to see him during the war, he suggested Corky never talk about it again or he would end up in an isolation cell in a military prison."

"Kate, the librarian alleges all this was a wild-goose chase."

"Maybe. Maybe not! Corky was no fool."

"Lew's adamant!"

"Sure, I know Benson. He didn't get here until the nineteen sixties. He's one of them types that if he didn't think it up or discover it first, then it probably ain't so. He also tells people stuff from time to time that completely throws them off the scent."

"Like what he told me?"

"Maybe. In this instance I think you can be certain he's wrong. I'm not going to dispute Lew Benson's word," Kate said, "I'll just tell you what I think, and don't you mention anything I've said to him, okay?"

"Not for attribution?" Alex asked.

"You got that right, young man."

The old woman had class. Alex thought. She'd obviously spent her life among the mangroves with Conch's and rednecks, but still had the polished demeanor of good breeding which shone through. "You have my word, Kate."

"Good! The Triton and Hamilton thing happened right out there in Hawk channel." She turned and pointed out the window. The two submarines were out there too. "Don't let any of those pretty boys in white uniforms at the Trumbo O'Club tell you otherwise! Know why I'm so certain? Because I talked to an eyewitness!"

"Why didn't you say so earlier?"

"Got my reasons."

Alex waited.

"Maybe ten to fifteen years ago I think it was. Around 1992 maybe? I met a guy passing through. Just like you. He'd served at a gun battery on Bahia Honda in 1942. Name was Allen Svoboda. Good-looking guy! I was in between husbands at the time and liked him, but he only stayed a few days then I had to throw him out before he wore me out." She smiled. "He was over seventy at the time, and at my age, he was too much for me to handle in bed." Again she smiled.

"Okay." Alex laughed. "How old are you?"

"Be ninety-five in a few days."

Alex was amazed and thought she looked somewhere in her midsixties.

"This guy Svoboda's dad," she continued, "had also been a general over in Europe in World War I. Anyway he told me he'd been an army second lieutenant in charge of a French 88 cannon on Bahia Honda in February 1942, and that he and his crew fired on a submarine in Hawk Channel. He alleged he hit it."

"Anyway I could verify this, Kate?"

She shrugged. "You could ask the navy."

"I have."

"They denied it, didn't they?"

"Assured me it never happened."

Her eyes twinkled. "I knew I was right about you. Silent waters run deep. Maybe you do have a good story to write after all, Mr. Balkan. Have you checked in Washington?"

"Sure have," Alex replied. "Navy historical society, Department of the navy headquarters, and the Bureau of Records, and the National Archives. Zero at all four." He didn't tell her what Jim Nolte in Key West had just told him. That he would keep this for later.

The old woman continued, "This guy Svoboda told me he saw all this firsthand."

"Where could I find him?"

"Somewhere on the north side of Baltimore as I recall. A place called Lutherville or some such place."

"Anyone around here who might know more about this?"

"The navy at Key West. But they're officious assholes! Doubt they'd give you the time of day, besides all their WW-II records were transferred up to Georgia decades back, and I doubt anything from that time is in their records here." Kate searched through the wreckage of an address book she'd retrieved from an end table, then dialed a number.

"Euell? Kate here! You remember anything around here about a German submarine being fired on back in 1942? Yeah . . . !" She winked at Alex. "Okay, I've got a young fella here with me. Seems like a good guy and I like him, he needs some help on a story he's looking into, mind if I send him around this afternoon? His name is Alex Balkan. Yeah, he's a friend of mine. You can talk to him. Tell him what you know!" She winked at Alex again as she hung up.

"Stallings is a damned fine guy and will help you as much as anyone. And he's discreet. Worked for the Park Department and American Legion here for years. But don't let this confuse you. Before that he spent forty years in the Diplomatic Service in the Mideast and Asia. He's sharper than a god damned tack and has an interesting outlook on life. If anyone knows about this, it's him."

"You mentioned Hawk Channel, Kate. Is it deep enough for submarines?"

"Absolutely! I've done a lot of diving out there. It parallels the reef all the way to Key West, and around here, it's at its widest and deepest, with sixty feet of water in most places at low tide. There are also several openings in the reef which are deep enough for a submarine to get through."

"How long you been in the Keys?"

"Sixty years and three husbands worth."

"You married now?"

"Yep. He's upstairs!" She pointed toward the corner of the front room. "First ones ashes are over there in that Ashanti gold pot. Second ones opposite him in that Greek urn. They didn't care much for each other in life; second one was real jealous of my first paramour, so now they watch each other. My first husband also built this place, and it's the only house in the keys with imported Greek marble floors. He said the marble made him feel special! He'd spent a few years in Greece before I met him and knew some Greek shipper who owed him a favor and delivered the marble here as a favor to him."

Alex glanced around at the faded decor and stains marring what was once a pristine white.

"What happened to him, Kate?"

"The poor man drowned."

A half hour later, Alex excused himself and headed south toward Key West to see Euell Stallings.

* * *

Stallings was a real oddball just like Kate Rheiner had promised. His voice drifted into staccato crackles when he laughed. His bushy mustache and egg-shaped head encircled by a band of white hair reminded Alex of old sepia photographs of Germany's Kaiser Willhelm.

"Come in! Want a drink, Balkan?"

"No thanks."

"What did Kate tell you about submarines off Bahia Honda?"

As Alex recounted the highlights and the reason for his visit, Stalling's plump pink hand wandered around the table between them and into and out of his pockets like little guinea pigs looking for their mother's teat. Alex decided his host was a pertinacious creature whose studied exterior concealed a deep seated fear of criticism.

"What Kate has told you is accurate as far as that goes, the navy recorded a contact that day in the area near Bahia Honda! But the official record concluded "no blood was drawn! But having said this, it's also technically not true because the official navy contact reports available today states the contact was actually outside the reef . . . not inside the reef! It's a fine point but important in the historical perspective."

Alex paused for a moment, trying to comprehend the statement. "Can you be more specific?"

"There were actually, in fact, two separate engagements that day! One inside the reef in Hawk Channel and another outside the reef! The navy accurately recorded only the second encounter, which never happened but not the first engagement which did!"

"Could you say that again!" Alex asked.

"It's simple, Alex!" the navy lied.

The old bastard had put his finger on the issue. Why hadn't Kate or Nutt figured it out? Lawrence Benson had also missed it completely! If Stallings was correct, then the navy had deliberately falsified the location of the encounter and placed it outside the reef instead of inside?

Stallings continued. "Sure! Kate and I know of a man up north, near Washington, who knew about the engagement with the submarine in the channel first hand. He also knew the sub was hit. He saw the hits on the surfaced sub. But he doesn't know if the hits resulted in it sinking or not. When he inquired about it two days later in Key West, he was ordered never to speak of it again."

"I don't follow you."

"His superiors told him nothing happened and to forget about it!

"They denied it?"

"The poor bastard was ordered to forget what he'd seen, what he'd officially reported in his written report. They told him to tear up his report."

"Did he?"

"Of course he did! He had no choice! The encounter had been classified top secret by his superiors, and people didn't ask questions in those days about National Security and such."

"Kate mentioned a man named Svoboda. Is he the one you are talking about?"

"One thing at a time," Stalling insisted. "The officer of the gun crew at Bahia Honda was transferred to the West coast the next day! His gun crew on Bahia Honda were also transferred to various assignments in the Pacific two days later. So within forty-eight hours of the encounter, there were no witnesses left anywhere in the Florida Keys. And no witnesses, no engagement, and no German submarine! Poooooof, just like that, the whole issue vanished into thin air."

"Why?"

"Obviously because the navy didn't want anyone to know about it."

Alex waited.

"Ever do any diving?" Stallings inquired.

"From a diving board?"

"Underwater?" Stallings asked

"Not with scuba equipment."

"What about snorkeling?"

"Sure."

"That's all you'll need anyway."

"Where?"

Stallings got up. "Hang on just a second, I've got something I want to show you." Stallings went into a bedroom and emerged moments later with a rolled up map of the lower Florida Keys. He spread it out on the dining room table.

"We're here, and where you want to go is here. Its Boca Chica. Just a few miles from Key West. See this series of indentations in the coast here? There are seven of them. Each are deep water channels connected to deep water through this channel to the right. There's an access road off the main road which will take you past them. You will want to turn left at this one here, it's the next from the last. You got it?"

"I think so."

"Good. Each of the channels is sixty feet wide, forty feet deep, and precisely one thousand three hundred and twenty feet long."

"Precisely?" Alex countered with amusement.

"Correct!"

"Why precisely?"

"A hair short of a quarter mile."

"You are suggesting I swim in them?"

"You bet your ass I am! You want a story . . . this is a story worth checking out, but like I say, you better be careful because its posted as navy property and no one goes there, and they do have random security patrols, so be careful." With a pencil Stallings drew a line along the right side of the canal. "It's not deep, and you appear to be in reasonably good health. I believe you should be able to dive down twenty feet with no problem."

"What will I be looking for?"

Stallings smiled. "Don't know exactly."

"Is the U-Boat there? The one hit out in Hawk Channel in 1943?" Alex asked.

"Don't know young fella. Go have a look and see what you can find. I can tell you that there was one there many, many years ago, and then it disappeared. Maybe you'll find something?"

"Would you come with me?" Alex asked

"No goddamn way!"

"Why?"

"Too old! Besides, it's your story. You do the research! You are the first person I have ever mentioned this to so forget we ever talked."

* * *

Alex found a policeman waiting when he returned to his hotel on Key West. The receptionist regarded Alex with disdain, obviously concerned that his clientele might worry that the hotel might harbor dangerous people. The deputy asked Alex to accompany him as the sheriff had some questions.

On the way Alex inquired what it was all about, but the deputy didn't say much. He did learn though that sheriffs in Key West didn't change very often as the locals were an odd assortment of homosexuals who owned over 50 percent of the local establishments and wanted three things: tourist's dollars, no violence, and no interference in their unique personal lifestyles. So when the locals got a sympathetic sheriff, he was a keeper. They locals weren't bad people the deputy observed and even funded a hospice for Aids victims, so they'd have a place where they could die with dignity. The deputy smirked, but I gotta admit, they do cover each other's back sides!" He glanced at Alex to see if he'd understood the innuendo.

Alex ignored it. "They give you more trouble than the straights?"

"Less. But they sure are funny. Had a call a couple days back, a domestic dispute. A dike stole her roommate's dildo and tried to check out of the room they were sharing. The Lezzie accused the dike of grand larceny. The dildo was one of those squirting types worth maybe fifty bucks! It was four-thirty in the morning when I got there, and it only took a minute to resolve it."

"How'd you settle it?" Alex inquired with feigned interest.

"The one with it in her suitcase obviously owned it. Possession is nine-tenths of the law. Right?"

Both men laughed.

"What's the sheriff want to see me about?"

"Didn't say. Probably just wants to welcome you to Key West. You some kind of dignitary?"

"Hardly. Wish I was!"

Monroe Country Courthouse was among the more substantial buildings on Key West. It reminded Alex of a hybrid Georgian Mansion. Monroe county was named after President Monroe at a time when Key Westers hoped the federal government would set up a ship wreck court at Key West, to handle the many salvage cases for shipwrecks in the Keys. The gambit paid off and by the late 1880s Key West's per capita income was the highest in the United States.

At the top of the stairs a secretary showed Alex into an ostentatious office overlooking the street and announced him to an elder man in casual clothes.

"Name is Sheriff Roth. Have a seat, Balkan. What brings you down here?"

Alex decided he'd play stupid until the sheriff showed his hand.

"I'm a tourist."

"Like some coffee, Mr. Balkan?"

"No thanks."

"Where you from, Balkan?"

"Up north."

"Whereabouts?"

"Virginia! Have I done something wrong, Sheriff?"

"No, but you been asking a lot of questions around town."

"Anything wrong with that?"

"Mind if I ask why?"

"I'm doing research for a book."

"You published anything I've heard about?"

"This will be my first."

"Fiction?"

"Correct."

"About Key West?"

"Maybe."

"Meaning what, Mr. Balkan?"

"I'm still gathering information. Key West may play a part—maybe the beginning and the end."

"When will your book begin?"

"When I start writing it." The response was a mistake. Roth was following up on a stranger who was asking questions around town and someone had obviously complained. Alex probably would have done the same thing in the sheriff's place.

"Don't pay to be a smart-ass sometimes. Even if you're right, Balkan!"

"My apology. I don't have the outline completed yet. But it will probably begin here during the war years, and then move elsewhere and end here in the present."

"That why you been asking question about people around here during the Second World War?"

"Yes, sir."

"Anything I can help you with?"

"Who complained about me?"

The sheriff smiled and asked if anyone had suggested that someone complained.

"Okay," Alex continued. "Do you know Kate Rheiner up on Ramrod Key?"

"Sure! Kate's been here forever."

"She told me there was a report of three graves found near Big Pine around 1945. Do county records provide any information about it? Coroners reports maybe?"

"Let me check." He picked up a phone and called records. "Sorry," he replied, "all records before 1947 were transferred to Miami years ago. It's almost sixty years you know!"

"Anyone come to mind who was in Key West during the War who could tell me about local color and such?"

"Sorry!" the sherriff replied. "Can't think of anyone."

"Well, if there's nothing else, Sheriff, I'll be on my way."

"Balkan . . . !" The sheriff's omission of mister got Alex's attention as he turned.

"Be discreet when you ask questions. This is a small place."

"I'll keep it in mind. Sherriff."

"Please do!"

"Am I free to go?"

"Sure!"

There were two places left, Eve Albion's and the canal. He'd visit the old woman's place before dinner and do the Boca Chica canal in the morning.

* * *

Eve Albion's residence fronted Key West's central cemetery across Catherine Street. The eaves of the two floor clapboard, 'Belle Epoch' residence were completely enveloped by a thick stand of Acacia while the street-front balcony was impassable by a thick tangle of vines. It was obvious the house had once been a classy place but ignored to the point that the realty market classified it as a TD, a tear down. Only Key West's historical society would mandate that no one tear it down but restore it instead. The woman who peered out through the dirty stained glass window as also a faded flower of a bygone era. Ms. Albion?" Alex asked.

Opening the door, he explained Lew Benson's recommendation to see her. She resembled many of the faded flowers Alex had seen everywhere along Duval street—ancient divas with leather skin and faded sun-damaged hair who refused to accept the vagaries of age and time. A large photograph in the front hallway showed an attractive young woman in a bathing suit with a well-proportioned body and mop of blond hair."

"Come in!" she replied. "If Lew Benson at the library recommended me, then I'm the person you should talk to. What's the subject?"

"The Second World War years here," Alex said as he followed her toward the kitchen at the rear of the house."

"You wouldn't recognize this town in those days." She laughed as she stepped on a cockroach skittering along the base board before them. "Even these roaches were here back then, one would have thought science would have come up with a final solution for the cockroach? Oh well?" She pointed to a chair after she pushed papers off of it onto the floor.

"What was it like back then?" Alex asked.

"Better . . . worse . . . more fun," she observed. "When the war started, the navy owned only fifty acres on Key West, and when the war ended, they owned three thousand, all dredged up out of the reef to create space for everything they needed here. Trumbo Annex, Sigsbee Island, and most of Truman Annex were all underwater reef back then."

"How old were you when the war started?" Alex asked. Her face wrinkled as a grin formed. "I'm only asking so I'll have some idea of what questions to ask." Alex smiled diplomatically.

"I was twenty-four when the war against the Japs started."

"How old are you now?"

"Do the math," she replied.

"What did you do back then?"

"I worked as a secretary with the navy here. Captain Walt Jacobs was my first boss. He was the commander here from February 1940 through May 1941. I also worked for the men who replaced him through the end of the war."

"You must have seen a lot."

"Yes, sir, sure as heck did!"

"Who did your boss report to?"

"The commander of the Seventh Naval Division at Charleston."

"Must have been a great time for women with all the sailors around?"

"There were nineteen thousand of them. Their morale was terrible, and the navy had to keep a third of them on leave all the time just to stop them from going AWOL. There was also a curfew to keep them out of the bars and off the streets at night."

"Where did they go for fun?"

"Chased girls mostly!" She laughed. "It was all they thought about! The red light district here in those days was huge! Probably half of the entire navy payroll went into pussy." She smiled at him. "I'm not offending you I hope?" She laughed. I could have become a millionaire if I'd sold what I'm sitting on, but I had a responsible job working as a secretary, and such things were frowned on if you were employed by the navy! Yes, sir, I was a good-looker back then and all sorts were buzzin' around. But I knew what they really wanted! The few who got it, well . . . they were nice boys."

"What were the famous girlie places to go to back then?" Alex asked.

"The most famous was Mum's Tea Room on Stock Island. It was the biggest whorehouse along the entire East Coast. Next to it was another dive called the Horse and Cow Saloon which was another pleasure emporium. Here on Key West there was the Bucket of Blood and Captain Tom's Bar which were the most notorious. By 1942 there were more than three hundred girls catering to the boys' needs."

"Yes, sir," she exclaimed, "Key West was a great place in those days. You could watch cock fights at the Cuban Club on Virginia Alley, place bets in the back room of Dewey Riggs Cafe on Duval, and get a great meal at Peppis Cafe. Sometimes in the evenings, I'd sit on the balcony of the Customs House and watch the Shore Patrol haul the sailors to the Brig which used to be across from where Mel Fishers Museum is now. The Brigs gone of course, replaced by a parking lot."

"Who's the most important person you ever met down here during the war?"

"President Roosevelt!"

"I didn't know he'd been through."

"Yep! It was all hush-hush back then, probably still is, but who cares about such things anymore. Over fifty years have passed. It was early 1943. He was en route to the Casablanca Conference in Morocco. Only my boss and I knew because we needed to arrange some details for the stop. They were flying boats which came through. One of them landed here while the other circled around nearby for an hour until the president left."

"Why did he stop?"

"To pick up someone."

"Who?"

"A real good-looking young man. 'Course you understand you cannot speak about what I just said because it never happened."

"Did you meet him?"

"Only briefly."

"Do you recall his name?"

"Paul something or other. Why do you ask?" she demanded, suddenly suspicious.

"Just curious."

"I think his family name was Carter," she added.

He detected more annoyance in her voice now.

"Where did you meet this young man?"

"At my office when he met with the captain." Now her annoyance was palpable.

"You certain about his name?" he persisted.

"You are a nosey bastard. Why?"

Alex changed the subject. "One of the other things I'm interested in, Eve, is anything you might know about German submarine activity here in 1942. Anything come to mind?"

Again her face hardened and her body tensed perceptibly.

"You all right?" Alex inquired.

"Aaahhhh . . . !" But she didn't complete the sentence. She seemed distracted, blinked repeatedly, and for a moment appeared not to have not understood his question."

"Is there something wrong, Ms. Albion?"

"No, just indigestion I guess. What was the question?"

Alex suspected he'd just hit on something, and it had nothing to do with her indigestion. "I was curious about submarine activities here."

"Well, there was the Santiago de Cuba, but I'm not sure that you would be interested in it."

"Sure, I would," Alex replied.

"Oh, . . . and why is that?"

"As I told you, I'm gathering tidbits and background about the war years here, and local color and weird stories help flesh out a good story." Alex could tell she was mentally struggling with something.

"Okay," she replied casually, "it involved a ship torpedoed outside the reef. My boss suspected it was the work of spies. The United States in early 1941 was not yet in the war against Germany but had already sent hundreds of millions of dollars in assistance to Britain through Africa, and much of it transited through Key West. On any particular day, there'd be eight to ten brand spanking new fighter planes from the factory flying into the local airfield here on Key West, while several transport ships a week refueled in the harbor. They were all loaded down with military supplies for Europe. The German government knew what was going on, but we were not formally at war with each other yet, and at any particular time there were several of their U-Boats hunting our ships along the east coast. And German submarines were having a field day around here."

"It seems that the particular ship I'm referring to that was torpedoed and had to do with a meeting between Roosevelt and Churchill in Newfoundland in August of 1941. At that meeting Churchill demanded British radio detection finders to help triangulate the locations of U-boats communicating with Berlin from the Caribbean, and Roosevelt agreed." The radio detection finders arrived in Key West in late 1942, and . . ."

Again there was that hesitancy in her voice and Alex surmised it might be due to her age and the fact she'd once been under suspicion herself.

"Do you recall the approximate date, Ms. Albion?"

"August."

"Thanks! What happened next?"

"Well, there were five ships in the convoy, three big ones and two tramp freighters. When they arrived in Key West my boss ordered all the RDF's removed from the largest ship and placed aboard the two smallest ones. He believed the Germans might try to torpedo the larger ones when they sailed further south to deliver them to Cuba, Jamaica, Trinidad and Caracas. So the transfer was made at night under the strictest security. The convoy sailed for Cuba before sun-up, and when they were beyond the reef, torpedoes slammed into the two smaller freighters which sank within minutes. The incident was investigated by the navy for years but no one ever figured out how the German's knew which ships to hit?"

"Was anyone ever able to find out which German submarine did it?"

"After the war we learned it was the U-508 whose commander was named Staats. He filed a report with Berlin indicating he'd sunk both ships at 1355 that day."

Alex thought a minute. "But that would make it in the afternoon, not the morning."

"U-Boat sinking's were filed in Berlin time, so 1355 hours in Berlin was 0755 in Key West."

"Did Staats survive the war?"

"No."

"And the navy never found the leak?"

"No!"

"Anyone ever locate the two ships?"

"Locals have looked but never found them."

The old woman possessed a good memory. He wanted to get around to the subject of the telephone calls to Albion by Tatiana Slavchenko, but decided to wait a few more minutes. "How come?"

"Water depths beyond the reef drop rapidly to six thousand feet and the Gulf current moves along at one to two knots beyond the reef, so the ships could have drifted several miles northward before hitting bottom."

"Mind if I change the subject?"

"If you want."

"How long have you lived in this house?"

"Almost ten years."

"Your phone number's always been the same?"

"Sure, why . . . ?" A trace of suspicion had again crept into her voice and her demeanor changed slightly.

"A dumb question, Ms. Albion, excuse me. Was it difficult for people to get around on the Keys during the war years?"

"Not at all," she replied, "the curfew applied only to the military. Even bridge traffic was not controlled. It should have been . . . but the services couldn't agree who should be in charge. Army intelligence wanted a check point at Card Bridge north of Key West, but the navy forced them to locate it up on the mainland."

"So anyone could travel all the way up the Keys without ever being stopped or checked?"

"Correct!"

"What was over on Boca Chica in those days?"

"Nothing."

"Nothing at all?"

"No! The Naval Air Station wasn't opened until long after the war, and the only airfield was Meachum Field which today is Key West International. There was also the Trumbo sea plane Base."

"But nothing at all on Boca Chica?"

"There was a small navy operation there, but no airplanes and no one paid much attention to it."

"Ever hear of submarines being stored there?"

"Sure. Until this day the locals still refer to that area on Boca Chica as the sub pens."

"Whose subs?"

"American submarines, who else's?"

"Could you see the sub pens from the main road on Boca Chica?"

"No," she laughed. "You been out there? Times have changed since then. During the war the main road was along the south side of Boca Chica. The new road which was put in the sixties, runs along the north side, which is the one you're talking about! Tell me something? You really writing a book or investigating something?"

"Do I seem suspicious?"

"Like a hound dog after a coon!"

"I'm trying to tie loose ends together for a novel which I hope will fool everyone."

"You for real?"

"Sure. Why?"

"If you are, then you should talk to Euell Stallings on Big Coppitt Key."

"I already have."

"You get around! What did Euell tell you?"

"He suggested I go for a swim in the channels on Boca Chica."

"I see . . . and have you?"

"Not yet, but I will. Any idea what I might find?"

"Damned if I know! Let me know when you do."

"One last question. What do you know of a woman from Washington called Tatiana Slavchenko?" The old woman's eyes gave her away instantly. The name had obviously clicked, and her eyes had narrowed to slits as an expression of anger swept her face.

"Don't know her!"

"But you have heard of her?"

"No!"

"She's called you repeatedly during the past year. I've seen the phone billings."

"Look! Whoever you are, I don't like your tone, you barge in here asking me questions! I'm an old woman, leave me alone! Get out!"

"Ms. Albion. Are you denying you know her?"

"Leave!" she shouted.

"What is your relationship with Slavchenko?"

"I think you should leave, Balkan, or whatever your real name is! Get out!"

"Tatiana was my friend, Ms. Albion," Alex tried to explain. "I've known her for many years and want to know why she was calling you."

"Get out!" Eve screamed.

"Did you know she was murdered last week?"

The old woman opened the kitchen drawer and pulled out a carving knife and pointed it at him menacingly. She followed him as he backed up through the house, repeatedly screaming at him to get out. As he withdrew onto the porch, her obscenities would have made neighbors' blush. As he reached the gate, she picked up a flower pot and threw it at him.

Duval Street

Albion obviously knew much more than she had let on. He'd have someone serve her a warrant or subpoena when he got back to Washington. He glanced at his watch as he hit Duval Street. It was just after three o'clock, and he decided to make one last stop before calling it a day.

Unfortunately the Key West Historic Society had only involved itself with maintenance and upkeep of historical buildings, and the flaky young curator knew nothing about events during the war. The curator provided a business card with the name of a retiree who lived nearby. "It's just a couple of blocks from here," he told Alex. "If anyone knows about this, it will be him."

Bahama Village was a twelve-block area of Key West, whose Caribbean inhabitants had migrated over the years into Key West in search of a better life. It was also a ghetto of run down homes, graffiti sprayed walls and barred store fronts. As Alex approached the address, an elderly man and woman on the sagging porch observed him. The old man drove away a couple of kids playing before the house as Alex stopped. "You the man the curator called me about a few minutes ago," he asked.

Alex nodded. "And you are Mr. Solomon?"

"Come on in."

"Thanks."

"You CIA?"

Alex laughed. "Yeah! I'm the director!"

"Don't want no problems, that's all," Solomon replied, "Doi ce pap, bayonet ce fer! Comprende?"

"Huh?" Alex asked politely

"It means the law is paper, but the bayonet is steel!" Solomon laughed, "It's a Creole proverb."

"I'm a writer looking for a million dollar story! Got any about the war years?"

"What sort?"

"Spies, intrigue. That sort of stuff."

"Maybe! Ever heard of Santeria?"

"Who?"

"Santeria . . . ! The way of the saints."

Alex gave him an expression which showed he hadn't.

"It's okay, Mr. Balkan. Most Anglo northerners haven't."

Alex cocked his head.

"It might make a good story. They're a homegrown Cubano movement! There's a lot of them right here. They're a cross between Catholic and the Yoruba of Africa, with a dash of communism thrown in and a pinch of black magic. Right now they're just a small outfit, but they'll destroy this great Republic some day!"

Before Alex could clarify his real interests, the old man was off into a long-winded monologue that Alex suspected he repeated to everyone who came by.

"First, there's Olodumare, whose is the owner of destinies, then Ashe—the blood of cosmic life, and Ara Orun—the ancestors of people already in heaven. Finally, a guy named Cimarrones, whose a Cuban dude who fled Cuba in 1963 and hunkered down in New York where he started this religion. You following me, Mister? This guy called Cimarrones, he alleges a man called Ifa Marote who also came to New York in 1946, is the Padrino or godfather of the movement."

It had been a long day and Alex was tired and the sun was getting low in the sky. He wanted to have an early supper on Duval Street and then catch up on his sleep before he swam in the canal in the morning. "It's all very interesting, Mr. Solomon. But what can you tell me about the war years?"

"You ain't listening!" Solomon's voice was terse. "I told you, the movement had a tinge of communism. It's what led up to the Cuban Missile Crisis?"

Alex laughed briefly. "Wrong war! I'm after background on Key West during the Second World War, not the Cuban Missile crisis."

"Ooooops. Sorry! I misunderstood the curator. What specifically you looking for?"

"How about missing people and secret agents?"

"You familiar with the Grossjean case in 1945?"

"No."

"A body was found up on Big Pine. It was dead for quite a while and there was disagreement at the time as to who it was, but the police finally decided it was Grossjean."

"Anything to do with the war?"

"Maybe! Maybe not!"

"Anything else?"

"The ice cream man comes to mind."

"I've already heard about him."

"Okay, what about Essar?"

"Who?"

Solomon rubbed his hands in anticipation. Alex could tell he was really enjoying himself and had probably done this a thousand times. Even Solomon's indolent wife who'd also been following the conversation had begun to chuckle.

"Essar was a German American who came down here in nineteen forty-one for a vacation, and then disappeared! He stayed at a motel on Boca Chica for several weeks until a couple checked in. The couple were older, and had just got married, and were on their honeymoon. A few days later Essar and the new groom went fishing and neither were ever seen again. The strange thing about Essar was that he was always carrying a small briefcase which he never let out of his sight, and he took it with him the day both of them disappeared. A couple weeks later the widow accused Essar of being a German spy. This the kind of stuff you're interested in?"

"Possibly. How did it end?"

"The FBI got involved. Seems Essar was a German immigrant who had a distinguished military service record with the German Army during the First World War. He'd returned several times to Germany between 1918 and 1938. Eventually everyone forgot about it. Now comes the best part! Three years after Essar disappears, in nineteen forty-four, the FBI picks up secret radio transmissions around West Palm Beach. They raided a house in West Palm. Guess who they found? It was Essar."

Alex was beginning to wonder if the old man had something of interest, and he decided he'd look into the newspaper reports at the time and see what they said.

"Sure enough," Soloman exclaimed. "And when they caught him, Essar was actually transmitting. The FBI ordered him to stop at gunpoint. But he ignored them. So they shot and killed him."

"You certain about all this?"

"Absolutely! The FBI stated he was someone else. But I know it was Essar!"

"Someone else?" Alex asked.

"The physical description and characteristics given by the proprietor at Boca Chica Motel where Essar stayed. It matched the man they killed in West Palm to a tee. It was Essar all right."

"So what's all this leading too Mr. Solomon?"

A conspiratorial look clouded the old man's face as his wife excused herself and went into the house. "In 1941 we were still not at war with Germany. Essar needed to get out to Hawk Channel, so he could be picked up by a U-Boat which was waiting to take him back to Germany. The briefcase he had was the same type the FBI captured in West Palm Beach three years later. The briefcase was actually one of those ULTRA typewriters! Essar's suitcase in 1941 contained one of them."

"You seem awful certain?"

"You bet!"

"And the conclusion?" Alex asked.

The old man laughed. "We'd been reading German code between 1938 and 1941, and the Germans suspected it. So they added a fifth wheel to their Ultra typewriters. It's in the history books, you can find it at the local library. The Krauts added a fifth wheel in early 1942, after which we couldn't decipher their communications for almost a year.

Don't you see! Essar had to get his typewriter modified in Germany, and needed someone to help him row a boat out into Hawk Channel. So he enlisted the help of the newlywed groom to help him go fishing out in the channel, and then killed him when the submarine arrived."

"An interesting story. What about submarines at Bahia Honda in 1942?"

"There was at least one there, maybe two. In mid-February of forty-two."

"You seem certain?"

"Damn right!"

"Any proof?"

"A signed affidavit!"

"A what?" Now Alex was really surprised. "Which says?"

"A German submarine was inside the reef and engaged by a shore battery, and some Germans were taken prisoner."

"You serious!"

"Serious as a heart attack!"

"Could I see it?"

Alex recalled Kate Rhiener's story about the man who'd spoken to her after the war. Maybe it was the same man. Kate had said nothing about a statement. Alex also recalled Kate saying that Allen Svoboda lived on the north side of Baltimore. Maybe he would be worth a visit when Alex got back to Washington.

"What's his name?"

Solomon's face became distant. "For the moment, I think that will remain my secret."

Alex already knew the name. "Might I at least have a look at it?"

"I suppose. But I don't want to give you his name and address."

Solomon returned with an envelope from which he extracted a dog eared sheet of paper. He folded down the top and bottom then held it out for him to read. It was obviously a photocopy which stated that one submarine was sunk and a second ran aground, and some Germans taken prisoner.

"So tell me Mr. Solomon, what do you make of all this?"

"Simple. They were inside the reef and we nailed them."

"But the official logs of the two navy ships in the area."

"I know, I know!" Solomon interrupted him.

"So?" Alex asked

"So," Solomon replied. "They lied!"

"The navy?"

"You got it!"

"Just like that? For what purpose?"

"The government does it all the time!" Soloman laughed. "It comes naturally to bureaucrats. But better be careful. If you accuse the navy of a cover-up in 1942, what are you going to say? That two U.S. Navy ship captains lied? Falsified official records? Such things were courts martial offenses in those days and still are today. No one is going to change their story now. Besides, all of them are probably dead anyway."

Alex changed the subject. "Any idea how many submarines they had?"

"Sure." Solomon pulled a book from a shelf and found what he was searching for. "They started with fifty-seven when the war began, built 908 of Types II through XVII. Plus another 181 of Types XXI through XXIII. They also built seven experimental boats; for a grand total of one thousand one hundred and fifty-six"

"Does your book say how they were lost?"

He flipped to the rear. "six hundred and thirty-six were sunk by gunfire torpedoes and depth charges. Sixty-three were lost to air attack, and seventy-five to collision and internal explosion. Two hundred and fifteen were captured when the Krauts surrendered. One hundred and fifty-four were turned over to us. And only ten were never accounted for. All the rest were scuttled, mostly in Europe."

"You are very well informed, Mr. Solomon. Maybe the two at Bahia Honda were among the ten?"

"Could be!" Solomon agreed.

"Something has been bothering me Mr. Solomon. Why would two German submarines have come inside the reef?"

"Probably putting people ashore. You familiar with the two ships torpedoed a year later just outside Key West?"

"The ones with the radars aboard?"

"You've heard about them?"

"Yes."

"Mysterious don't you think?"

"I suppose."

Long shadows crept across the balcony as the sun sunk behind some palms. Alex looked at his watch. "You've been very kind, I've got to be going. Maybe I'll see you again before I leave."

"I'm always here, Mr. Balkan. Any time."

Boca Chica

Alex rose before dawn. Unable to sleep he suddenly was feeling all alone and sorry for himself. Tomorrow was Christmas eve and he had no friends with whom he could hang out. He decided he'd visit the local Catholic Church later in the day and listen to its coral group who he'd seen advertised in the newspaper. The paper said they were supposed to be among Florida's finest. After lunch he called his mother in Pennsylvania and at her insistence also called his sister who lived down the road from his mother. Just after seven he watched the sunrise from his balcony, then went down to the dining room for black coffee and a newspaper. Later he retrieved the rental car and wandered the side streets for half an hour, checking for surveillance. Reassured that no one from the local cops was keeping tabs on him, he pulled into the K-Mart on Roosevelt Drive, bought some flippers, a face mask and snorkel. Just after nine he headed to the canals Euell Stallings told him about on the Gulf of Mexico side of Boca Chica.

Ten minutes later he parked in a Pine thicket and shut off the engine. Stallings instructions were perfect. As he drove the heavily overgrown access road he'd turned left after the fifth turnoff to the left. Through the thick undergrowth he could see nothing, but knew he was on a peninsula with canals of both sides. He put on his bathing suit and headed into the almost impenetrable underbrush.

The clear warm water of the canal teemed with fish. Swimming parallel to the bank he could discern little of interest on the bottom as he moved along. As he returned he dove on two shapes he'd noted. The first was a large, heavily encrusted brass propeller. After repeated dives he was able to make out the inscription "Kiel 1938" and Eisener Gesseleschaft, Fabriken 22/X/1942/No: 399736 on one of the blades. Further along lay a pole-like shaped object laying in the sea grass which turned out to be the remains of a periscope, its glass still fitted. It bore no markings. He could find nothing else.

The propeller was definitely of German origin and he suspected its date of manufacture was October 22, 1942, while the other numbers were probably production serial numbers. He walked the length of the shore line but discerned nothing in the undergrowth either. The area was heavily treed and looked as if it had never been inhabited, but he knew it had been because here and there he could see the concrete pads and base walls of what had obviously been canal-side workshops or warehouses at one time.

He found what he'd come for and after toweling off, made a note of the serial number and got dressed. Driving back toward the main road, he rounded a corner and braked to avoid a collision with an oncoming van. He was about to back up when a navy policeman emerged from the driver's door and directed him to get out of his car.

"A problem?" Alex asked through the window.

"This is a restricted area, sir! It's posted!"

"I didn't know that," Alex replied.

"You must have seen the sign as you came in?"

"I didn't," he lied. "But don't worry, I'm leaving."

"Please get out of your car," the policeman ordered.

"What's the problem?" Alex inquired

"Please get out of the car, and keep your hands where I can see them."

"What's the problem?" Alex demanded again.

The Shore patrolman opened Alex's door. "Get out!"

"Look," Alex told him, "I'm sure this is a mistake, I'm a tourist. I'll be on my way, let's just forget about this!"

The passenger door of the van opened and a second man emerged with a carbine with a clip inserted.

"Just get out of the car, slowly . . . ," the man beside him ordered. They spread his legs as he leaned over the hood. They handcuffed him."

Two minutes later they passed through the chain link gate and onto the paved road to Key West. The driver pointed out the Restricted Area sign.

"It's covered with scrub!" Alex observed sarcastically. "Who the hell would see that?"

The policemen ignored him.

Truman Annex

"Who the hell is this clown?" Admiral Lange demanded.

"An air force contract type. But I'm not certain beyond that."

Key West's Two-Star was not used to being told that his staff couldn't get to the bottom of simple matters in a hurry. Key West was one of those dead places where nothing exciting ever happened of military significance and Lange was up for promotion and wanted his third Star next year. He knew admirals only made three-star rank by being astute players of the big power game in Washington. Politics was like chess and one always had to be a couple moves ahead of the competition and never exposed their strategy to peers or subordinates! Lange also had every intention of letting his subordinates know that he was annoyed over the Shore Patrols screw-up at Boca Chica.

For a decade NAVCARIBCOM had also been a stepping stone to three star rank. But the end of the Cold War had changed all that: and without the Soviet threat from neighboring Cuba, the nature of American Naval Forces in the Caribbean were gradually changing into a caretaker status—for a host of inconsequential bases, in an archipelago, of tourist resorts, and benevolent backwater banana republics. September 11, 2001, had temporarily brought some notoriety to the dog cages at Guantanamo which were used to house Al-Quaeda terrorists sent to Gitmo from Afghanistan.

The admiral's only operational mission these days was catching drug runners from South America. This portfolio provided the high level visibility Lange needed in Washington to get promoted. But yesterday, some stupid son of a bitch at Boca Chica had caused an uproar in Washington, and Lange couldn't figure out what the fuss was about?

Boca Chica's Shore Patrol caught a tourist in a restricted area three days ago. But the enlisted man who'd made the arrest compounded his mistake by calling the Key West Police to find out if there were other problems with the suspect. When he learned that other complaints had been received for suspicious activities on Key West, he told them he'd hold Balkan until they came and picked up his suspect. There was a complaint but no charge. The Key West Police had no authority to pick up or detain this guy called Balkan because he'd been detained by the shore patrol for trespassing on government property. So they'd never arrived. And the result was that the navy illegally detained the suspect incommunicado for forty-eight hours in the brig. This morning Lange had a message from the judge advocate general's office in Washington, asking what kind of illegal operation he was running at Key West? Lange had twenty four hours to explain.

"What the hell was he doing snooping around the old Hawk Missile Site in the first place?" the admiral demanded.

"We don't know, sir," his aide replied. "The subject alleges he was sightseeing and didn't see the Restricted Area sign."

"Is that possible?"

"Yes, sir. The sign is overgrown with weeds, and portions of the perimeter fence have been down for a long time. Kids have been using it as a lover's lane for years."

"So why did he arrest him?"

"He was within his authority, Admiral. He just didn't use good judgment. That's all."

"And the Key West police? What the hell is their excuse?"

"It was Christmas, sir, they just forgot to explain to the Shore Patrol there was no reason to hold him."

"And the suspect?"

"He's really pissed."

"Anything else?"

"Seems he's been telling everyone locally, he's an author, gathering information for a novel about submarines in the Keys during the Second World War, but that's crap."

"So who is he really?"

"Appears to be a contract officer with a Washington outfit called Scion Consultants! Seems like he spends most of his time in Russia."

"Doing?" the admiral demanded.

"Nuclear force reduction verification."

"They tell you what his specialty is?"

"Eight hundred series, an air force intelligence case officer."

"Great! What's he up to down here?"

"Don't know, Admiral. Only that he's willing to forget this ever happened."

"You believe him?"

"You want me to check with the air force or Scion Consultants?"

"No. That's all!" Lange studied the hand written note they'd found on the suspect the morning they'd arrested him, and wondered what it meant. 'Periscope with glass still fitted, and four bladed propeller with inscription, Eisener Gesselleschaft Fabriken 22/X/1942/No:399736.' Had Balkan obtained it at the old Hawk Site?

The admiral picked up the phone and called the one man on his Staff he hoped might get to the bottom of the issue fast. He'd ask Commander Lynn Davis to look into it and prepare the response for the Judge Advocate's Office. He heard the crisp authoritative voice of the man he considered among the most competent in the entire Command. "Lynn, I need you to do something for me. Get in touch with Navy Historical Records in Anacostia. Ask them if our navy captured any German U-Boats around here during World War II? Secondly ask them if there were any German subs stored around here during or after the war?"

He picked up the phone again and waited for his secretary to answer. "Be a dear, and call the Hampton House in Key West, and ask for a Mr. Alex Balkan. If he's in, tell him I'd like a word with him."

Balkan was not in, and his secretary left a message. A half hour later Commander Lynn Davis called back with the information the admiral had asked for from Anacostia and asked him to bring it over immediately.

Lynn was one of his "fast burners" and if Lange made his third star, he'd see to it that Lynn's career advanced too. He'd arrange a heavy cruiser command for Davis. Lynn was sharp as they came, and a Cruiser Command was a surefire ticket to promotion to Flag rank.

"Morning, Admiral."

"What did you find out, Lynn?"

"To your first question. There were only two ever captured at sea during the war, the U-570 by the British off Iceland, and U-505 which was taken by us in the south Atlantic. U-507 was later recommissioned in the Royal Navy as HMS Graph. The U-505 was exploited by us during the war and later placed on permanent display at the Museum of Science and Industry in Chicago."

"And my second question. Lynn?"

"Again there were two. The U-2513 and the U-3008. Information about both is still classified Top Secret and not subject to automatic downgrading, so it will remain Top Secret forever I guess."

"Why classified for so long, Lynn?"

"Probably because the Russians didn't know we had them?"

"Your opinion?"

"U-2513 was brought down here for test and evaluation. But no one saw here as she was stored secretly around here somewhere between sea trials. From what I understand 2513 was sunk off the Tortugas in 1951. But her presence here in the States and location of her disposition is still Top Secret. So What I just told you is close hold and be careful with it. The U-3008 on the other hand was broken up for scrap around 1956, but there is nothing suggesting she was around Key West."

"How did we acquire them?"

"Spoils of war after Germany surrendered. We and the Brits decided before the war ended what would happen to all the captured German sub inventory, especially these two which we got secretly for exploitation."

"Why?"

"They were so shit-hot operationally that they were a quantum jump in technology. We used it for the design of our nuclear boats in the 1950s."

"Mind if I ask you another favor. Lynn? Same caveat as before."

"No problem, Admiral."

"Look into the second question further. Let me know if there is anything that doesn't seem straight-up! Secondly, see what you can find out about the canals at the Hawk Missile site on Boca. Who built them, when, why, that kind of stuff." He handed Lynn a folder with the Judge Advocate General's message in it. "You'd better read this too, and talk to those concerned. I'll need a reply by 0600 tomorrow morning."

* * *

It didn't take Lynn long to get the information. Following the 10:00 stand-up, the admiral found Davis waiting for him outside his office.

"Come in and close the door!"

"Admiral, the U-2513 was a Type XXI built in late 1944 by—," he glanced to his notes, "a company called Weser, in Bremen. She never saw combat and secretly surrendered to us in Germany in April 1945."

"The war had still not ended."

"That's right, sir. And a month later we sailed her to New London. In July 1945 we began testing her along the East Coast during the next two years. She also visited Key West twice before being taken out of service. Her disposition seems fishy."

"How?"

"It's a gut feeling. You asked, and I assumed you have your reasons. Excuse me if I'm out of line on this."

"I'm listening, Lynn."

"This happened a long time ago, so records are a little scarce. I could request her service records from the archives if you desire. But they will ask why we want them and that might be problematic for you, sir"

"What have you got?"

"As I said, both were Type XXI's, but the second Boat's record is strange. U-2513, was built by Blohm and Voss in late 1944. But she sailed to the United States and her record, becomes, well . . . a little too stilted to my way of thinking?"

"Stilted. Meaning?" Lange demanded.

"The record's too pat?"

"Go on?"

"I don't want to get sideways with anyone on this, Admiral, especially with the navy brass in Washington. I mean . . . you did ask me to look into it, and her U.S. Navy record is strange. It's just that I've got a bad gut feeling about it and I don't know why."

"Tell me what you've got Lynn and let me decide." Maybe this Alex Balkan character was on to something after all the admiral thought. If Lynn was suspicious, it probably was significant.

"Admiral, I spent an hour reading ship histories in the *History of American Naval Fighting Ships*. They are all well documented, factual, incredibly detailed. Each entry was prepared after laborious research and contain excruciating detail. First of all there is no record of either sub's whereabouts between the end of the war and June 1948, when U-3008 suddenly appears in our records. That's almost thirty months! And the gap is covered . . . just a second . . . ," Lynn referred to his notes. "It says here, she might . . . and I quote, might have lay at dockside in some port in occupied Germany or perhaps in an Allied harbor! Unquote."

"Not conclusive?" the admiral observed. "What else Lynn?"

"There's more, Admiral. The record also states the first indication of her appearance was in August 1948 when, and I am quoting from the navy record here, 'she presumably arrived from Europe.' The wording 'presumably' is so unusual, admiral, no one uses presumably in an official navy log! It is suspicious! As a matter of fact, in my opinion, it stinks!"

"So what happened after she arrived, Lynn?"

"She was damaged and laid up at Portsmouth, New London and then scrapped."

"What's the problem?"

"The problem, sir, is, I just spoke with my dad who was stationed at Portsmouth between 1949 to 1952. He said everyone at New London had to sign secrecy statements never to talk about her presence or disposition. But he insists she was scrapped in the midfifties!"

"Not earlier?"

"Correct, Admiral."

"So your father's an old man, maybe he is confused."

"No, sir, he has some notes he found on it. He is certain of the year."

"Okay, Lynn. I'm with you so far. What does it say happened to 2513?"

"Her file stinks even worse! There's no record at all of her whereabouts from the end of the war until 1951. That's six years, Admiral."

"Nothing at all, Lynn?"

"No, sir! I'd better read this to you. It's from the official navy record. It says, quote, 'she was moved to Key West on 2 September 1951, when the chief of naval operations ordered U-2513 to be sunk by gunfire. Presumably, that decision was carried out soon thereafter although the exact date and location of the action is not recorded.' Unquote!"

"I see," Lange observed. "So you are telling me that this was the official U.S. Navy record for the final disposition of an operational German U-Boat?"

"Yes, sir."

"Is that it, Lynn?"

"No, sir," he replied. "You know that guy who's in charge over the at the Truman White House here at Key West."

"You mean Bob Wolz?"

"You are not going to believe this. I guess the U-2513 was such a hi-tech curiosity at the time that, Wolz commented to me that he has some of Truman's personal records that indicate President Truman personally went for a top secret sea trial on U-2513, on November 21, 1947. The sub went to sea, if you can believe it, with the president and twenty-three senior government leaders then visiting Truman in Key West. Once beyond the reef, the submarine submerged and dived to 450 feet. While at depth, the sub mysteriously developed several serious problems. She began to leak, she took on water, one of her engines flooded, and a fire broke out in the engine room. Twenty-five of America's most senior leaders were onboard. If she hadn't surfaced that day, it was unclear who the next president would have been."

"Did Wolz have any comments in particular?"

"Interesting," Lynn continued. "The possibility of an attempt on the life of the president had a lot more credence than most realized at the time. When Roosevelt died, Truman became vice president after only eighty-three days in office, and for the rest of Truman's four-year term, there was no serving vice president. If Truman had then died before completing his term, Sam Rayburn or Joe Martin would have replaced him as Speaker of the House. But there was an argument raging behind the scenes as to whether the Constitution should be changed to alter this process. And Wolz reminded me that there were a hell lot of problems in the country right after the war: widespread inflation, unemployment, labor problems, while Truman's public support plummeted from 87 percent in the beginning to 32 percent a year later."

"So?" the admiral interrupted.

"I guess Truman's Secret Service concluded that an attempt had just been made to assassinate the president. The subs sudden problems while under water all seemed too suspicious, so the entire incident became classified."

"And that is the explanation?" Lange asked.

"There is more, Admiral. There were rumors that Truman had secretly signed off on the fates of thousands of our captured servicemen in Germany who were kidnapped into Russia as World War II ended. These men were then declared killed in action and their bodies not recovered, while our highest officials in Washington knew these men were still alive in Russian captivity. I guess someone may have wanted Truman out of the way because of it."

"Any truth to any of this?"

"Who knows, Admiral. If it was true, it's undoubtedly still buried behind a Top Secret stamp."

"Interesting." Lange observed.

"Admiral, I also have an answer regarding this guy Balkan. You want the long story or an abbreviated one?"

"I've got time."

"Good, 'cause this also smells. Before the war Roosevelt started a WPA airfield construction program on Boca Chica. I guess he knew there was going to be a war, and we'd need plenty of airfields. Once the war started the Army finished the airfield on Boca Chica, and it remained an army air field until after the war when the navy took it over and renamed it Boca Chica Naval Air Station. While WPA was building the airfield, they also dug the channels near the Hawk missile site as well as the turning basin and connected the canals with an access channel through the reef to deep water, sufficient to accommodate large warships. The channels too were deep enough so large ships could get in. After the war, a local outfit was hired to build residential housing around the channels, but before they started, they were advised their permits had been canceled on environmental grounds. Its remained like this down to the present time."

"Environmental grounds, in 1945?" the admiral mused.

"Correct, sir."

"What do you think, Lynn?"

"Like I said. Fishy."

"So what's your conclusion?"

"A cover-up!"

"Meaning?"

"Meaning we might have built those canals and the turning basin to store someone's submarines during the war and then, for unknown reasons, got rid of them afterward."

"Who owns the land now?"

"That's another thing that's strange. It's not government property at all. It never was! We've illegally posted it as government property when it is not. Some Bank on the mainland holds the title."

"A bank? I don't believe it."

"That's what the record says, Admiral."

"You absolutely positive?"

"Yes, sir. We've assumed it was government property for sixty years and it's really private property, but no one knows it."

"This takes the cake!" Lange exclaimed. Christ! We didn't even have jurisdiction for an area posted as U.S. government property . . . and it isn't?"

"You want me to look into this further, sir?"

"Forget it for the moment, Lynn. Get me a reply for Washington, and leave out all this stuff you just told me. Just explain that such things will never happen here again."

"Aye, aye, sir."

As Davis left, the admiral asked his secretary to try to reach Balkan again, and also to remind him in a week or so that the navy needed to look into the property ownership question on Boca Chica.

Trumbo Officers Club

The admiral knew naval hagiographers were not noted for the religious pursuit of changes to historic documents.

The official history of the German navy mentioned that records for U-Boat 2513 were unavailable. And based on this, Lange surmised the allies involved with her capture and disposition had obviously ignored this portion of her pedigree. Was this unusual? He supposed not. But was it suspicious? Absolutely! And despite all this, the gap in German records as well as those of the American navy who'd disposed of her had slipped unnoticed into history, and no one had ever looked into it since? He swung his chair around and scanned a row of books on the shelf behind his desk. He recalled the name Lockwood and withdrew a book about submarine warfare during the Second World War. Lockwood was among the famous American submarine commanders in the Pacific, whose career ended when he'd tried to get the navy to create a new position, Deputy of Naval Operations for Submarines. Lockwood's argument in the 1950s was that the navy needed to exploit captured submarine technology if the United States were to retain its military superiority in the Cold War. But Lockwood's concerns fell on deaf ears. Any such effort at the time would only be done at the expense of the navy's surface carriers and battleships, and none of the surface ship lovers were about to listen to anyone who suggested that submarines might be a significant future threat either to surface navies, or the United States.

Everyone knew wartime German technology was superior across the board to America's. Hitler's U-Boats dove deeper, moved faster, were quieter, had better engines, better batteries to say nothing of optics, sonar, and hull design, and without a doubt, the best torpedoes. Lockwood also raised the contentious issue of ships and tonnage lost, which, in any war, is the *sine-qua-non* of success. American statistics were abysmal. American submarines were dismal affairs by comparison. Primitive German models from World War I had butchered five thousand allied merchant ships totaling eleven million tons. Two decades later, the Germans went on to sink fifteen million tons and by comparison, American subs sunk an insignificant three million, and half of this total was questionable.

Lockwood knew the German Type XXIII were the best ever built. And yet, for some inexplicable reason, none were ever exploited by the United States after the war. Its innovative fish-shape configuration—critical for high-speed underwater travel—was instantly recognized by the Russians however and incorporated into their Whiskey Class nuclear boats, which appeared for the first time off U.S. coasts during the Cuban Missile Crisis. They were so fast underwater that they could walk away submerged from most American Destroyers at the time. And then the Cold War ended and once again everything changed yet again. With the advent of space based satellites which most countries around the world now had, today almost everyone knew exactly where each American aircraft carrier in the world was, the direction it was going, and the size and number of its escorts. They even knew where all of America's international stealth bombers were when they were flying around the world to attack foreign enemies like in Afghanistan, the Balkans, and Iraq.

Lange picked up the phone and waited for his secretary to answer. "What time is my appointment with Millican?"

"At half past eleven," she told him.

"Good!"

Retired Captain Millican had left the navy two decades earlier, and moved to the Florida Keys when his wife died. Millican was a walking encyclopedia about submarines and Lange hoped Millican might resolve the question of German submarines brought to the Keys during or after the war. "What about Alex Balkan? You reached him yet?"

"No, sir. He's still out."

"Keep trying."

Balkan had slipped out of Key West when the police released him, but was still paying for his hotel room. His departure further whetted the admiral's curiosity, especially when he'd learned the Key West police were again looking for him; this time in reference to the death of an elderly woman who Balkan had seen the day before she died.

His buzzer rattled. "Yes."

"Millican is here, Admiral."

"Show him in."

"Captain Millican, a pleasure! Please, have a seat." He noted that his visitor had aged significantly since he'd seen him a year or so back at a Fourth of July ceremony at Homestead. He needed a cane to steady his walk.

"Thanks, Admiral."

"Coffee?"

"Yes, sir, thanks. Just black please."

Lange asked his secretary to get two cups, one for each of them. "My Staff inform me you know something about German submarine history?"

"It's a hobby," Millican replied.

"Any time in subs?"

"Four cruises during the war. Got off the Legarto at Pearl Harbor before her last cruise. She went down in May 1945."

"Lady Luck was smiling on you."

"Seems so."

"And after that?"

"I spent another twenty-five years in oilers and supply ships. Then retired in 1980."

"Never went back to subs?"

"No, sir."

"Ever have a command?"

"No."

Already Lange knew he'd never establish a close bond with Millican. Lange liked men with command time under their belts. Commanding a warship at sea was the litmus test of manhood! Without it, leaders were incomplete. "You might be able to help me."

"I'll try."

"I understand you've done research on U-Boats?"

"Some."

"You know what happened to those we captured?"

"Which war?"

"WWII."

"Most."

"What happened to those we got from the Germans?"

"How much time do I have?"

"All you need."

"One hundred and seventy-one were captured and later disposed of. A hundred and thirty-eight were also scuttled by their crews before we could take possession."

"What happened to those scuttled by the Germans?" Lange interrupted.

"Most were refloated to clear harbors and ship channels along the Baltic coast. Those refloated were sent off to the scrap yards or rescuttled in deeper water."

"Where?"

"In most cases, outside the Baltic ports during the first two weeks of May 1945."

"By whom?"

"Allied crews. They were towed out and sunk in deep water by gunfire."

"Any details?"

"About fifteen were sunk off Wilhelmshaven, maybe ten near Hamburg, thirty or so off Travemunde, and maybe twenty-six north of Kiel. The rest of them, maybe about fifty-six I think, went down outside the port of Flensburg."

"I'm impressed!" Lange replied seriously. "You want a position on my staff?"

"I enjoy my free time and golf."

"Do you happen to know how many of those scuttled were Type XXIII's?"

"Maybe twenty. But most were still under construction!"

"Do you know if any surrendered here in the States."

"None, far as I know."

"I hope you don't mind all the questions, Captain?"

"No problem, Admiral."

"How many of all types were operational?"

"Almost 1,200."

"How many Type XXI and XXIII's?"

"Sixty of the former and four of the latter."

"Was any exploitation of the XXIII done by the United States after the war in Germany?"

"Sure."

"Where?"

"Mostly at the port of Flensburg. It was the last seat of the Reich before the armistice, and after the surrender we, and the British, took possession of their surviving assets. The 17,000 ton Hamburg-America liner called Patria, was sailed to Flensburg and served as the headquarters for Major General Rooks and his staff. Rooks as you may know, accepted the surrender of the German Navy. Hundreds of German warships of all types were involved, and because the war with Japan was still on, our technical people were all over the U-Boats like locusts to find out how we could improve our own designs. Once we'd divined their secrets, their surface ships were disposed of."

"How?" Lang inquired.

"The British handled it under Operation Deadlight. In late forty-five the Brits took all the remaining surface ships and their U-Boats too, out of German harbors and towed them to Belfast in Northern Ireland. From Belfast they pulled one or two a day out into the Atlantic and sunk them by gunfire. You sure are asking a bunch of questions, Admiral, what's this all about?"

"Just curious how the U-Boat issue was finally wrapped up after the war, that's all!" Lange wondered if Millican had bought the explanation. Up until now it was obvious Millican knew his stuff. "How many were evaluated here in the States?"

"By treaty, Admiral, each of the powers were allowed to exploit ten ships, and the rest had to be sunk. We had four of their U-Boats here in the States, the U-505, 858, 873, 1288. They were Type XXI's."

"No Type XXIII's?"

"No."

"Isn't that strange?"

"How do you mean?"

"It was one of their best and we didn't evaluate any?"

"I would assume we got what we needed from those we looked at in Europe."

"I see. Have any of their Boats survived here?"

"Only 505, which is on display at the Chicago Museum."

"And the others?"

"Sunk or scrapped."

"I can't understand why none of their Type XXIII's were exploited."

"What's your interest in this Type, Admiral?"

"It was their best?"

"Yes. They were huge 1,750 ton ocean going types, with two, six-thousand horsepower turbines. That honey could move along at seventeen knots on the surface and an incredible twenty-five submerged! It's still among the fastest, even today. German records show they never deployed any of them operationally."

"Why?"

"You might not like it!"

Lange realized he didn't really care for Millican even though he seemed nice enough. "Please continue."

"I would presume the evidence points to what we already knew."

"You've lost me, Captain."

"Our intelligence types were involved! They 'doctored' the records!"

"You can't be serious?" Lange's voice betrayed his surprise. "Why would we want to do such a thing for?"

"Why not, Admiral? The testimony of our Naval leaders at the Pearl Harbor hearings in 1946, indicated the code breakers knew more than was said publicly. We all suspected Roosevelt knew of the Jap attack on Pearl before it happened. The intelligence types denied it of course. But they knew! We were reading Jap and German traffic within hours of dispatch. Hell, Admiral! I'll bet you don't know one percent of what NSA and CIA are picking up right now!"

"What's your point?"

"Admiral. I learned a lot about the code breakers after the war, and most of it I didn't like! Some of it made me sick! They knew more than you or I will ever know, and they still do today!"

"For example?"

"The capture of the U-505 at sea was a big coup for the navy because heroic Navy seamen risked their lives to board her after she'd been scuttled and abandoned by her German crew. But she was captured against orders! The navy had standing instructions to all its ship captains never to capture a U-Boat at sea. So when Admiral Gallery's Task Force captured the 505 in June 1944 in mid-Atlantic, the admiral thought he was going to get a medal, but instead he was almost court-martialed. The code breakers were furious! Gallery had endangered their entire program. Gallery only saved his ass because the war department knew it would have a hard time keeping the secret if something more radical was not done. So the navy ordered all three thousand men under Gallery's command to sign a top secret statement, not to ever discuss the incident . . . even after the war ended. So the Germans never knew we'd captured their codes intact. The information is still classified Top Secret today, did you know that?"

"Any idea where the U-2315 is today?"

"Near the Dry Tortugas." Millican could see the surprise on Lange's face. "That's right Admiral, somewhere near the Tortugas."

"Where exactly?" Lang inquired.

Millican's face broke into a smile. "I don't know. But the navy should."

"I'm sure it does!" Lange smiled.

"But not her exact location?" Millican said caustically.

"Meaning?" Lange shot back.

"They do not know where she is either."

"Then why tell me to ask them?"

"Because you are in the Navy's chain of command."

Lange smiled. "It would take time and it would be quicker if I could find out from somebody here in Key West."

"What's this all about, Admiral? If all this is not 'Official,' then I'd like your word I'll be included in whatever it is you are looking into when the time is right!"

Millican could smell money and his request was not out of order. Lange had no objection but hoped when he himself retired, he wouldn't become an ambulance chaser like this old son of a bitch . . . it made Lange sad to see a fellow officer negotiating with him to make a few bucks. What Key West did to retired military saddened him. Lange would rather starve than stoop to such depravity. "It's reasonable. But you'd have to take my word."

"That's good enough. There may be some professional divers who know where she is. But they're a secretive bunch who don't discuss wrecks with outsiders—for obvious reasons! I'd have to ask around."

"Anyone come to mind?"

"Mike Grigoriou. He runs Dives Unlimited, on Stock Island. You heard of him?"

"No."

"I think he knows."

"What's the best way to approach him?"

"Not sure! But as soon as he knows, it's you whose making the inquiry, he'll clam up like a crab's asshole!"

"This isn't official!"

"Come on, Admiral . . . ! Jesus . . . ! You call it whatever you want! But don't try to tell me or Grigoriou that!"

Up your ass Lange thought! He had a job to do and this son of a bitch was not only an ambulance chaser but insubordinate. "Think about it, Captain Millican! See if there's some reason you could ask Gregoriou about her location?"

"I'll nose around, Admiral. Thanks for the offer for coffee. It never arrived."

Monroe County Sherriff's Office

Alex was on his way back to Key West this morning from Miami. He intended to confront Albion again and try to get her to reveal the nature of her association with Slavchenko. His visit to the navy records library in Miami had surfaced even more concerns about her. The Miami historical navy library custodian produced a set of eighteen microfiche rolls for Alex to review. Entitled "The WW-II Naval History for the Southeast United States and Caribbean Basin. 1940-1945," two facts surprised him. The first was in the Personnel Annex. All references to Eve Albion in the alphabetical lists appeared to have deliberately been blacked out before being placed on microfiches. The name following Albiate on the alphabetical list of all civilians employed by the navy throughout the war in Key West was blanked out. And the name following the blanked out Albion was Albionate. The second curiosity was in the operational annex. There was no mention of old man Edgar Nutt's allegation that he and his gun crew on Pigeon Key had ever engaged a submarine inside the reef near Key West with their cannon in February 1942.

As Alex got out of his rental car, he found a deputy waiting for him in the hotel lobby. He informed Alex that Eve Albion was dead. Her body found yesterday morning by a neighbor. The neighbor described a man fitting Alex's description and said Alex had visited Albion the afternoon before she died. The neighbor also reported that Albion had obviously been upset when Alex left because Albion had shouted at him repeatedly to get out of her house, and even thrown a flower pot at him.

"So what did you do that made her so angry?" the deputy asked.

"Nothing," Alex replied. "She didn't like my demeanor."

"Is she the reason you came down here?"

"No," Alex lied. It was none of the deputy's business, and the old woman, according to the coroner, died of natural causes.

"Related to your work?"

"Maybe."

"What about all the others you've seen? And your cock-and-bull cover story?"

"Just following some leads."

"You threaten her?"

"Of course not! She was alive and kicking when I left. You have a witness."

"Like I said Balkan, be careful, or the sheriff might hold you on suspicion of murder!"

Alex couldn't hide his surprise at the mention of suspicion of murder. "Was she murdered?"

"Could be. The sheriff is waiting for some information."

* * *

"Just between us?" the sheriff replied. Balkan, you're bad news! I think you're an arrogant son of a bitch! You are no more a writer than I am a nuclear scientist. But your biggest problem is with me as you seem to think because you're some kind of spook, you can come down here and crap on local law enforcement! Wrong! I know about people like you! I see your type here every day, ex-military and retired government types, who think they're special. Well . . ."

"Sheriff I . . ."

"Let me finish, Balkan! They're not special and neither are you! Look around. Places like the Bull and Whistle, Sloppy Joes, they're packed with the has-beens who thought they were special! And every morning, the county jail is full of these types who all think they're a cut above the rest of us!"

"It wasn't my intent, Sheriff."

"Be careful!"

The threat was obvious, and Alex knew his nose was out of joint. He decided he'd better tuck in his horns and let the storm blow over.

"I'd strongly suggest you get the hell out of Key West, pronto!"

"I will. I just need a day or two."

"You trying to give me a bad time, Balkan?"

"No, sir."

"You looking for trouble?"

"No, sir."

"Then you'd better listen!"

Alex bit his tongue. He'd driven up to Miami yesterday to get answers which the local library and courthouse were unable to provide. What he'd learned in Miami, convinced him the Slavchenko's phone calls to Albion had been more than coincidence. The old woman had once been a prime suspect during WWII, when the two radar ships were sunk by U-508 near Key West. He recalled the dead woman telling him about the incident, but she'd said nothing about her becoming the prime suspect in the investigation that followed.

From Naval intelligence and the FBI, he learned both organizations shadowed her in a vain effort to find a connection but were never able to prove anything and eventually dropped the probe before the war ended. Eve's original name before she'd been adopted and brought to the United States was Ramkoettle. Her German parents were from East Prussia and had died in a fire, leaving no relatives to care for her. An American family visiting Germany at the time, saw her in an institution and adopted her, taking her back to Versailles, Ohio. Nineteen years later, the daughter gets a very sensitive job with the navy at Key West and a year later comes under suspicion for espionage. But nothing comes of it. Then, fifty years later she's again in contact with a Russian defector! And she'd mentioned that she'd met some man called Paul Carter when Roosevelt stopped at Key West during the war. But no records report Roosevelt ever stopping in Key West. Too much coincidence, Alex thought.

In Eve's personnel file which he'd had faxed down from FBI archives, he'd learned she'd moved to Washington after the war and held a series of increasingly responsible positions over the next thirty years, and ended up a senior advisor for Russian military capabilities at the Joint Staff in the Pentagon. And while at the Pentagon, she's also been involved in some stillborn mid-1990s secret U.S./Soviet negotiations for the return of American prisoners of war from the USSR. Then she retired ten years ago, just after the end of the Gulf War, and dropped out of sight, but is contacted repeatedly by Yevchenko from Washington. Again, happenstance or design?

"Take my advice, Balkan," the sheriff cautioned. "Leave Key West today."

* * *

At the corner of Duval and Truman, Alex pulled over. He dropped a quarter into the phone and dialed. He hoped the local cemetery might know Albion's funeral plans.

"Hello, would you happen to know the funeral arrangements for Ms. Albion?"

"Who's this?"

"A friend."

"It's tomorrow, at two-thirty, at the city cemetery. If you would like to pay respects, there will be an open casket viewing at the Pritchard Funeral Home on White Street. Viewing hours are from four to six this evening."

"Did she have a lot of friends here?"

"No."

"One more question? You been here many years?" Alex asked.

"Since the forties."

"You recall the internment of three unknown males here sometime in late 1945?"

"Do you have their names?"

His investigation in Miami had also failed to substantiate the rumor about three dead Germans on Big Pine. He'd asked the sheriff who'd told him records were no longer available at Key West before 1948. But he'd found nothing in Miami either.

"No. I don't think anyone ever positively identified them, so they may have been buried in unmarked graves."

"What did you say your name was?"

"I didn't! Can you help me?"

"Were they locals?"

"I don't think so."

"I see. How about yourself, you a local?"

"No."

"To be honest, I don't recall anything that fits your question! But it's possible. Hell the navy alone had almost thirty thousand here back then."

Alex hung up and dropped another quarter into the slot and dialed Euell Stallings residence.

"Good morning, Mr. Stallings? Alex Balkan here. We talked three days ago?"

"Sure, what did you find?"

"A propeller and what appeared to be a piece of a periscope."

"That's it?"

"Yep!"

"Sure you got the right canal?"

"Yep!"

There was a momentary pause. "They must have cleaned it out then. It's been a long time."

"Cleaned what out?"

"I thought you would have figured it out by now. A German sub was tied up there in late 1946. Early in 1947, the navy cut her up pretty bad and dropped pieces of her into the canal. I know because I saw it. The stuff was all over the place. They must have cleaned the bottom."

"Who?"

"The navy, I should think! Around December 1946, they relocated the boat to the northwest shore of Fleming Key and submerged her on the bottom there for a while. She disappeared the next year!"

"They parked her on the bottom on the northwest shore of Flemming Key?"

"Yep! But you couldn't see anything from the shore!"

"Why did they do that?"

"No idea. My guess is they wanted to conceal her! Isn't that what this is all about?"

"What do you think they did with her?"

"No idea! There were rumors, but I never believed any of them."

"Such as?" Alex asked.

"One was that she was moved to Bikini for the Baker nuclear tests. Another was that she'd been disassembled because the navy was looking for something."

"Where's Fleming Key, Mr. Stallings?"

"Go through the Trumbo Annex gate, you'll find it."

"Where exactly?"

"You going out there?"

"Why not."

"You'd need a government ID to get through the gate."

"Let me worry about that!"

"Turn left at the first intersection inside the main gate. You'll see an aircraft hangar, turn right after it and you'll cross a small bridge onto Fleming. Follow the road about two miles until you come to the Department of Agriculture building. To the left is an unpaved road which follows a fence to a small bay. You shouldn't have any trouble. But make sure you avoid the Special Forces camp at the north end; they don't take kindly to folks snooping around."

"Who told you about the submarine?"

Stallings laughed.

"Who in the navy knew about it?" Alex pressed.

"Who knows? I heard it from a guy who lived down the street from me years ago. He'd had a few too many at my place one night and mumbled on about it for almost an hour. Next day he swore me to secrecy; said he'd go to Leavenworth if I said anything. He's dead now, so my guess is that it probably don't matter anymore . . . but then maybe it does. So be careful . . . just in case."

"Thanks for the info. I'll be in touch."

* * *

Five minutes later, Alex passed the yacht Basin at Garrison Bight, flashed his identification to the military policeman at the Trumbo Annex gate. The small bay was right where Stallings described it. Parallel to the shore was a blue swath of deep water which led to an opening through the reef. Thick mangroves concealed the view seaward and made it difficult to view the offshore area. He stripped and donned his flippers and mask. He shivered for a moment as he entered the water which was much colder than his earlier swim in the canal. He could feel his nipples shrink.

He estimated its low tide depth at forty feet; more than enough to conceal a submerged U-Boat as he scanned the entire area. One traverse of the shore line was enough! If it had ever been here it had left no record of its presence. He dressed, crossed Key West, stopping at a greasy spoon hamburger place for a cup of coffee before proceeding on to Stock Island, where he parked along the wharf at Dives Unlimited. To his right a line of small to medium sized pleasure craft tied up along the wharf highlighted the turquoise water, and as Alex approached the shop he could tell the place was obviously a thriving business because hundreds of compressed air bottles lay everywhere along the back wall.

Inside he noticed a large nautical map hanging on the wall behind the register with the locations of local wrecks.

"Can I help you?" a bronzed man inquired.

"Is Mike here?"

"He'll be here shortly. Interested in diving lessons?"

"Just wanted to ask him a question."

"Maybe I can help?"

"I'm curious about old wrecks like those on the chart over there. Are they the ones you take people to?"

"Correct!"

"What about others?"

"You'd have to ask Mike."

"Mind if I wait?"

"There are chairs outside, help yourself."

An hour later a boat tied up and a slender man approached Alex. "You waiting for me?"

"You Mike Gregoriou?"

"Yeah!"

Grigoriou's frame looked like chiseled walnut. One of the shop's employees had told Alex that Grigoriou was a triathlon freak who ran ten miles a day, swam, and rode a bike. Alex subconsciously sucked in his gut.

"I'm looking for information about a wreck."

"Then you've come to the right place!"

"A submarine."

Curiosity erased his smile lines. What type?"

"A U-Boat."

Grigoriou's expression was now dead-pan. "Anything specific?"

"According to navy records it's near Dry Tortuga."

Grigoriou's face broke into a smile. "Must be open season for research!"

"Sorry?" Alex inquired.

"You're the second person whose asked recently."

"Oh?" Alex replied, trying not to show his surprise.

"That's right. Something you want to tell me? I don't think I caught your name. Mr . . . ."

"Alexander Balkan. Do you recall who the other person was?"

"Some retired navy guy who came by yesterday. He asked about the U-2513. That the one you are interested in too?"

"Yes," Alex replied a little sheepishly. Who was the other man?"

"Sorry. I don't discuss client business. What do you want to know about her?"

"Do you know where she is?"

"I'll tell you the same thing I told the other guy. I've been diving here for twenty years, I've dived every wreck from Tortuga to Key Largo. Diving is my business! There's very little available about the U-2513, mostly rumors!"

"So you don't know where she is?"

"Did I say that?"

"She is a phantom submarine. She exists in German records but not American records because she was some kind of Top Secret experiment that the American Navy got involved with after the war. And near as I can tell, everything about her is still top secret."

"So I'm wasting my time?"

"I did not say that. Only that her existence is still a closely held government secret that no one is supposed to know about. What did you say your name was again?" Gregoriou demanded.

"Alex Balkan."

"You want to dive on her? Assuming anyone knows where she is?"

"Not my bag, just looking for information."

Grigoriou's face broke into a smile. "Mr. Balkan! Wrecks are treasure. So no one will tell you squat until they're absolutely certain they're worthless. Mel Fisher did secret research down here for years until he found a Spanish Galleon called Atocha! It put him into the history books and a hundred million into his bank account."

"I work for the government, Mike, and the U-Boat came up during an investigation I'm involved in. I don't think it has anything to do with my investigation. But I need to be sure."

"Any ID?"

Alex flashed his credentials.

"This official or unofficial, Mr. Balkan?"

"Unofficial."

"And the other guy who was here yesterday?" Grigoriou asked.

"Unofficial too as far as I know, unless he said otherwise." Alex made a note to call the navy in Washington and find out who this other guy was.

"So what is your 'unofficial' interest in this submarine then?" Gregoriou asked.

"I'm going to try to find some of her crew in Europe and thought I'd see if anyone knew where her last remains were before I go over." It was a lie, but Alex suspected that before it was all over there might be a reason to try and find more information on the genesis of the U-Boat,

He hoped Gregoriou would accept his explanation without going into a long litany of questions.

"You got a few minutes, Mr. Balkan?"

"Sure, why?"

Grigoriou shouted to his assistant to take care of the shop. At the rear was a metal shed with an air-conditioned office. Grigoriou searched through some cassettes. He found one and pushed it into the VCR, watching as it whirred in fast-forward. When it stopped, the screen displayed what appeared to be the bow of a submarine.

"Is it her?"

"No. It's a First World War American type up north, she went down in the nineteen thirties. Her skeleton is so rotten, her hull will collapse any day. There!" Mike leaned forward and pointed to a large dent in her side, "See the sag? Her internal bulkheads have rusted away and her skin is collapsing inward. I've done a lot of diving on her years ago, but not anymore. Better quality steel in the later boats makes them last longer these days thank God, otherwise I'd lose about a third of my business here."

"A third?" Alex asked, indicating he didn't understand the significance.

"That many come down here to dive on wrecks, and they need people to get them out there and back, provide provisions, and recharge tanks."

"I see, and how much longer do the newer hulls last than those of the First World War?" Alex asked, wanting to appear interested.

"The older ones were unsafe after twenty years. The World War II types will last as much as seventy or more years."

The screen flickered for a moment and a ship's anchor came into view. "This is probably what you are looking for." Both men watched as the camera panned along an anchor chain across the sandy bottom toward the knife-like bow of a submarine. The view moved along the left side of the hull, rounded the stern and followed the hull forward, then doubled back along the foredeck and up the sail. Inside the weather deck the screen brightened as an underwater flood light came on. Grigoriou leaned forward and stopped the tape.

"Is that her?" Alex asked

"TBD," Grigoriou replied, "But it could be."

"Did you show this to the other gentleman who asked about it yesterday?"

Grigoriou looked at him for a moment, obviously considering his reply. "No, I did not. As a matter of fact not many have seen this footage because it's one of . . . shall we say, my findings which I came across recently, but do not really know what to do with. I am going to have to look into it more closely. I'm still not certain of her status and some low-level inquiries of an innocuous nature have turned up nothing. So I am still trying to decide how to proceed. Does that answer your question?"

"I didn't see any significant damage," Alex commented.

"Were you expecting some?"

"I'd heard she was sunk by gun fire," Alex observed. Immediately wishing he had not said it.

"In fact by navy hedgehog ordinance I am told," Gregoriou replied. "But you are correct the damaged noted is not enough to have sunk her." Grigoriou shrugged, obviously trying to conceal his interest in what Balkan had observed.

"The hatch on the bridge was closed and looked like it hadn't been disturbed!" Alex threw in.

"Yeah, so what?" Gregoriou asked, more interest now evident in his voice.

"How did you get inside?"

"Did I say I had?"

"What's the water depth?"

"That information I'm keeping to myself. Let's say below three hundred feet."

"Difficult to reach?"

"Very! Scuba is good to about two-hundred. To get below three hundred requires gas, and long decompression stages. A three hour dive might not get you ten minutes on the bottom. You have to know what you're doing!"

"I didn't see any hull markings?"

"Paint don't last long in salt water!"

"When did you make the dive?"

"Awhile back."

"Recently?"

"Awhile back."

"And how did you find her?"

"By accident," Gregoriou replied.

"And you haven't been inside?"

Again his broad smile created smile lines everywhere. "What exactly do you want to know, Mr. Balkan?"

Alex didn't answer.

"Well then. Maybe you would be interested in financing a dive on her?"

"What would it cost?"

"Mmmm. Minimum, ten grand to get started! Twenty would be acceptable, and cover a couple of days. Beyond that it depends on what we find and what it might be worth? In return I might offer a two percent interest in whatever's inside . . . maybe more."

"I'd have to think about it!" Alex replied.

"You do that. There's plenty of time, Mr. Balkan. I'm up to my tail feathers through this April. After that it would take about a week. Let me know."

As they traversed the parking lot, Grigoriou assured him something might be worked out financially. Alex didn't inquire further about details and promised to get back to him within a couple weeks with a more definitive expression of interest.

* * *

Alex couldn't miss the tanned navy officer in the immaculate white uniform, as he entered the lobby of his hotel.

"Mr. Balkan, I'm Admiral Henry Lange! I tried to reach you earlier."

"I got your message."

"You didn't call back."

"Busy."

"You have a few minutes?"

"Maybe."

"How about lunch?"

Alex looked at his watch. "I've got to make a phone call first."

"No problem, I'll wait."

"Be right back." He punched in the number for Scion Consultants in Washington and waited until Ted LePage's voice came on the line. "Alex here!"

"What have you found out?"

"Albion told me nothing! But she obviously recognized the dead Russian woman's name when I mentioned it. She got so pissed-off the second time I mentioned it, that she threw me out. Then I found some anomalies, and I tried to see her again, but unfortunately she's died."

"What?" Ted exclaimed, annoyance obvious in his voice.

"Croaked of natural causes near as I can tell, but the local fuzz are suspicious, and looking into it further. They've also been to see me because I may have been the last person to see her alive."

"Suspicious, why?"

"Don't know yet."

"Damn it Alex, this was supposed to be low key, remember, how the hell did the Police get a line on you?"

"Explanations later, there are more important issues I need to tell you about."

"What about the phone calls from Slavchenko? Did you ask her about them?"

"That's why she threw me out."

"So they knew each other!'

"Absolutely! No doubt about it."

"What about the war years down there?"

"There may be something to that too. But the exact details are still a little fuzzy. Albion might have been involved, even way back then!"

"Meaning?"

"I'll find out and let you know."

"I really think it's time you get back here. There are other places we need to look."

"You mean in Washington?"

"No. In Russia!"

"You want me to head back then?"

"Right away."

"And down here?" Alex asked, wanting to be certain that LePage had thought through his next move.

"Forget about Key West. I'll see you tomorrow."

* * *

Alex replaced the phone and went downstairs.

Lange's choice in restaurants was expensive. Nothing on the menu was below fifteen bucks. The admiral ordered a double dry Martini and Alex stuck with ice tea. Stilted small talk occupied them until lunch arrived. Then Lange got around to the purpose of his invitation.

"I owe you an apology, Mr. Balkan. My people at Boca Chica acted precipitously when they detained you, and I hope you will accept my personal apology?"

"You got some cowboys working for you, Admiral. Some may need a whipping."

Lange leaned back and templed his hands. Alex wondered what he really wanted. He didn't have to wait long.

"What's all this about, Mr. Balkan?"

"Admiral?" Alex replied naively.

"I know who you really are! I know what you've been telling everyone about being a writer and all that crap! But we both know it isn't the case, don't we? You're really a contract hire who specializes in Russia, you even speak Russian! You were recalled to Washington in mid-December for consultations, and then flew down here to snoop around asking lots of questions. Then you see an old woman. She dies. Where's all this leading?"

"I resent the implications of your remark, Admiral. Are you asking because you had something to do with her death, or just trying to be obnoxious?" Alex smiled, waiting for the comment to sink in and watched with satisfaction while the admiral again apologized.

"Like I said, I'm writing a book, Admiral." From Lange's pained reaction, he could tell the admiral was obviously annoyed and trying hard not to show it. Admirals weren't used to people avoiding their questions, or being disrespectful. But he owed Lange nothing, and Lange obviously had people working for him who needed to be shit-canned for stupidity.

"It's not the case and you know it." Lange's eyes narrowed as he dabbed at his mouth with his napkin. His eyes riveting Alex.

"I thought you invited me to lunch, Admiral? Not to a hostile interrogation!" Alex speared some lettuce and deliberately took his time masticating it as he studied the view along the shore. Lange withdrew a photocopied page from his pocket and placed it on the table.

"What's Eisener Gesseleschaft Fabriken 22/X/1942/No: 399736 mean?"

Alex's boyish face grinned stupidly as he continued to masticate his salad. "No idea."

"It was found among your possessions, Alex."

"Found? You mean illegal search and seizure by your Gestapo and the local Key West Police don't you, Admiral? Thanks for returning it." He'd wondered if he'd ever get the note back after they'd taken it from him a few days ago. He folded it and set it beside his plate. "Sure is a beautiful view of the reef from here, Admiral. My compliments on your choice! Lovely restaurant. Good food too." Alex wasn't about to tell him anything, but he wouldn't be rude. Protocol required that much!

JANUARY

ONE

Ballston, Virginia

ALEX WAS IN a foul mood and the lousy January weather of Washington wasn't helping. He'd slept fitfully, was tired, he needed some time off. He'd returned from Key West three days ago, spent Christmas alone, and yet already missed the balmy weather of south Florida because it didn't remind him so much of the festive season that had just passed. Since he'd been back, Ted LePage had been making him run around Washington like a god-damned junior research assistant, trying to uncover more information about Roosevelt's trip to Casablanca, and Alex wasn't getting anywhere.

This morning he'd tell Ted to either let him pursue the Russian angle of the case, or take him off of it all together. Since the document left at the Slavchenko murder scene indicated that an American was last seen at Novosibirsk in the early 1980s, this was probably the next logical place for anyone to look.

Emerging from the Metro escalator at Roslyn Station, he made his way to the side entrance of the building housing Scion Consultants. He flashed his credentials at the familiar faces beneath the large logo on the fifteenth floor. Halfway down the hall Ted spotted him, motioning him into his office.

"What did you find out from Fort Leavenworth?" LePage demanded.

"Nothing. I spoke with two of their research people yesterday. There is no reference anywhere to any stop at Key West by Roosevelt in 1943. They assured me it never happened. The old woman at Key West must have been full of crap."

"Why did Roosevelt choose Morocco?" LePage asked.

"Because Churchill and DeGaulle were close by, and half million American troops were already ashore. Stalin refused to come because he was busy with the Germans at Stalingrad, and didn't want to take the risk of being out of Russia if Von Paulus's army broke out of the Stalingrad pocket."

"What about other sources you checked?"

"Same dead end. Everyone looked at me like I was crazy, and assured me that President Roosevelt never stopped at Key West en route to the Conference."

"Libraries?"

"I checked with the National Archives . . . ditto!"

Alex had searched everywhere in Washington for references to the two Pan American seaplanes which Eve Albion alleged stopped at Key West while en route to Casablanca. Alex had also spent half a day at the local Library, poring through books about the Conference. Only three alluded to how FDR got there while only one bothered to mention the type of plane and routing used. There was no reference to Key West anywhere.

LePage changed the subject. "What about the stuff you saw in the canal?"

"The propeller and periscope?"

"Yeah."

"I checked with navy archives, none indicate any submarines were ever kept there."

"Shit," Ted muttered, he'd hoped to solve the puzzle by now and they still had too many unanswered questions and the clock was running. "Have you checked with Roosevelt's Library in New York?"

"Affirmative, nothing there either."

"What about the personal papers of his Chief of Staff, Admiral Leahy? He must have kept an itinerary for the trip.

"Neither he nor Harry Hopkins made any mention of it." Admiral Leahy's hour by hour description of the trip is the most comprehensive history of the trip and it too says nothing."

"What exactly does his diary say?"

Alex withdrew a note pad from his brief case, and searched for the reference. "It says, they left Washington by train on the evening of 9 January 1943, and arrived in Miami before sunup on the eleventh. They left Dinner Key at 0605 with two flying boats and landed in Port of Spain ten hours and forty minutes later—1645 hours Trinidad time to be exact."

"Who went with him?"

"Hopkins listed fourteen passengers. Himself, the president, Admiral MacIntire and Captain McCrea—who was FDR's aide, plus six secret service men, and a man called Arthur who was his butler. There were also three unnamed army officers aboard."

"No names?"

"No."

"No mention of their names on the manifests?"

Alex hunched his shoulders.

"What about other aircraft which might have accompanied them?"

"Aside from the second flying boat, none."

"How about the return flight?"

"Again zero. Hopkins didn't cover the return, because he never made it to Morocco. He developed a fever in Trinidad and was left behind, so he never made it to the conference."

"Pan Am?"

"They're out of business, and a new company by the same name operated out of Sanford on the north side of Orlando in Florida for a while. But that was a long time ago too. One of their folks told me they bought the old company's name but none of its liabilities or assets—including historical records."

"Find out where the old company's records are. They are probably in New York somewhere. The old Pan Am went tits-up in 1991 after the Lockerbie disaster. There's got to be tons of records in storage somewhere. When can you get back to me?"

Alex shrugged. "I should have something by lunchtime I suppose."

"Okay, I've got to go over to the Pentagon. I'll return around twelve. Meet me at the deli across the street for lunch at noon."

Alex was tired of all the bullshit and wondered why someone else couldn't look into all this crap? He and LePage had also heard nothing about the local police investigation and assumed it too was dead in the water.

* * *

Three hours later, Alex spotted Ted in a booth near the window. The waitress had a cute ass which wiggled suggestively like two semi-inflated volleyballs as he followed her to the table. Alex wished he were having lunch with her instead. She took their order and left.

"You seem to be in a better mood, what's the big smile for, Balkan?"

"Good news for a change."

"It's about time."

"I checked with Pan Am. Their New York archives are hopeless. Most of their records it seems were lost. Some of what remained was bought by the Trippe brothers, whose old man Juan Trippe, was the guy who started the company and was involved in it almost to the end. There's nothing from the war years so it's a dead end. However, I also checked with some folks in Miami who opened a Pan Am museum down there. They got lots of paraphernalia which used to belong to the defunct company, like old models, uniforms, old engines . . . but no historical records. I even called some guy in Ireland where the old film actress, Maureen O'Hara, set up a small Pan American museum at Foynes. Again zero. Then I got a lucky break. I located the widow of one of their retired executives in Staten Island, whose husband spent thirty-five years with Pan Am. She had a phone book that had addresses of two of her deceased husband's old buddies. She provided them, one in Daytona and the other near Tampa. I was unable to get the guy in Daytona on the phone, but his answering machine works so he's obviously there. The guy in Tampa has agreed to talk to me if I stopped by."

"Another vacation in Florida Balkan?" Ted LePage asked, his innuendo dripping with sarcasm.

"There's more." Alex smiled.

"It better be good." LePage observed.

"It is. The guy in Tampa used to ferry American 'Lend-Lease' fighters from Robert's Field in Liberia, across Africa into the Middle East during the war, and he remembers seeing one of Pan Am's flying boats in the Nile River near Khartoum. Said he recalled meeting one of its crew in Khartoum who told him the flying boats name was the Anzac Clipper."

"Any significance?"

"Anzac was one of the four sequestered by Roosevelt for the Conference."

"Did he recall the exact date?" LePage asked.

"He checked his flight logs while I waited, said it was January 20, 1943."

"FDR was at Casablanca from the fourteenth through the twenty-forth, wasn't he Alex?"

"Correct."

"So what's the significance?"

"He said this guy told him the Anzac was on a special mission. Seventy-one. Get it? SM-71? It's a break."

"Christ," LePage muttered. It was a lead. SM-71 was the symbol scrawled on the back of the document at the Russian's murder scene. "Congratulations, Alex. Can we assume that if there were four flying boats involved, that the special mission numbers of the others were in sequential order?"

"Correct," Alex replied. "Seventy-two and seventy-three were the two Roosevelt used while seventy and seventy-one were apparently other Pan American aircraft off to the east."

"Okay, Alex. This is what I want you to do. Instead of leaving for Russia next week, catch a flight to Florida tomorrow. See these two clowns down there. Then leave for Novisibirsk from Miami and see what you can find out about this guy named Paul Carter. The last we heard anything about him, according to the Slavchenko woman, he was in the Novisibirsk area. Maybe you can pick up his trail there again. Call me before you leave Florida. I don't care what time it is."

Arlington

Opening his desk drawer Rinehard Staples removed another Excedrin, downing it with some coffee. At eighty-four he knew he was out of his depth and should have retired from his third government job a couple of years ago and headed south to play all the golf courses in Georgia. On days like this he swore at himself for not having done so.

Having spent a career in the Army and becoming associated with intelligence tangentially late in his career, Rinehard now had an egalitarian outlook on his world and its endeavors. Most of his Army career had been spent in an eclectic assortment of dead-end assignments designed to enhance morale, and ignore the realities needed for promotion. Before he retired he'd studied Russian and become somewhat proficient in its use—which had opened doors to his present dilemma. He'd jumped into a crucible which had elevated his endeavors into one of verisimilitude: ensnaring his efforts to find thousands of lost Americans in Russia. Special Group Moscow, or SGM as it was affectionately known inside the beltway, was Washington's executive agent in Russia: empowered to find missing Americans from any of America's twentieth century wars. SGM had the appearance of sincerity, but was in reality a carefully orchestrated sham to conceal and forget ugly old secrets which both Washington and Moscow agreed from the outset were to be buried and forgotten.

Rinehard remembered some of the old WWII veterans he'd met when first appointed to his SGM assignment. They'd described the thousands shipped into Russia in 1945 as our missing sons and our soldiers of misfortune. They assured Rinehard that he was among the few in America who now knew what had really happened to these misfortunate abandoned bastards, and prayed Rinehard would find a way to bring them home dead or alive. But at his place of work Rinehard was cautioned that the entire issue of what had really happened was Top Secret and Code Word to boot. If he broke security he would end up in a padded cell at Fort Leavenworth, Kansas.

Rinehard had adopted the easy way out, he listened attentively to the POW/MIA families entreaties: confirmed nothing, expressed his condolences, and assured them Washington was doing everything humanly possible. His betrayal had plagued him endlessly. Then his nightmare got worse when his limited Russian language ability brought him to the attention of those looking for someone to send to Russia to find these tens of thousands of missing American servicemen who'd perished there secretly throughout Stalin's Gulag in the years after WW-II. Rinehard's lack of intelligence background was also a problem so a decision was made to rush him through a basic Army clandestine intelligence school in California. But he'd flunked the course, and somehow the Russians later learned of it and tormented him in thousand little ways with minute professional razor cuts to his ego.

They were mocking him and his make-work efforts that produced naught. Rinehard's superiors did not want to embarrass the United States Government nor did they wish to have anyone view their mission as one of redeeming the sins of former American administrations. The program was all make believe. He'd seen it in the faces of his Russian counterparts and KGB archivists who he knew had seen Americans by the thousands in the USSR, and in many cases murdered them. He'd also seen it in the eyes of old Russians who started to say something to him about what they knew until interrupted and reminded by "minders" present, that to speak about what they knew was treason. In the few instances where Rinehart thought he'd hit the jackpot, and his sources would refuse to back down, they too had always mysteriously changed their minds, died or disappeared.

What the hell was he going to do next? For a few moments, he studied the emblem on his cup: Rinehard Staples, Headquarters United States Air Force, Office for Prisoner of War and Missing in Action Affairs—WWII and Korean Conflict Division. A second cup on the window sill bore his name and Special Group-Moscow. He rubbed at his temples a few moments, willing the Excedrin to kick in and lessen the pain. For a while he'd thought he'd finally brought his nightmare under control and could forget about it. But yesterday it had suddenly resurfaced when he'd met downstairs in a Mall coffee shop with a retired Marine Corps Officer from DesMoines, Ohio. This retired guy had somehow learned of the Russian offer made to Rinehard a few months earlier through a Swiss professor in Luzern. The retired Marine officer had offered a lame explanation concerning his role in the affair, insisting he did not know the Swiss man and was only an intermediary in the affair. But he clearly now knew details of something which he was not supposed to know about! In fact the Russian's had made an official government-to-government offer to provide Washington with what Moscow had done with some twenty-plus thousand WWII American soldiers kidnapped by Stalin into the USSR as WWII was ending. The offer would start with an initial 5,000 files, all of which were systematically murdered in Siberia in the decades after World War II.

The Swiss man was a professor with the Institute for the Prevention of War and Conflict in Luzern, Switzerland and for many years had been involved in research for missing European POW/MIAs captured in the Soviet Union and Europe by the Red Army during the Second World War. The professor had already accounted for hundreds of thousands of missing Europeans who'd also died long after the war in Russian prison camps across Asia and Siberia. The Swiss professor had also been retained as a consultant by several other European countries to locate their unaccounted wartime missing, and again here too he had produced noteworthy results. And now the professor indicated that there were Americans who the Russians had agreed they could account for?

The professor, whose name was Schenke, had recently called Reinhard at the request of a Russian archivist in Moscow. The Russian archivist had told Schenke that he had tens of thousands of American dossiers in his archive. The professor had in fact already seen some of them so he told Schenke he personally knew they existed. The secret Russian dossiers for these Americans documented each of their final dispositions in the years after World War II. The Russian had asked Schenke to pass this information to one of Schenke's trusted American archivists in Washington, and for someone to get back to the Russian archivist with a response. The Russian archivist had also suggested some neutral American organization undertake the work in Moscow: maybe some nonmilitary charitable foundation involved in world peace, conflict avoidance and/or human rights. The Russian suggested the National Alliance of Uniformed Services, or alternatively the Soros Foundation in New York.

Rinehard had immediately coordinated the offer with his superiors in Washington, only to be ordered to forget about it. America was at war with terrorism they told him. Al-Quaeda were strong in some of the USSR's former Soviet Republics and the American people were not strong supporters of being nice to Moscow. But most important, he was warned . . . the appearance of such incriminating information now would inflame American public opinion not only against Russia, but America's bureaucracy who had obviously betrayed the American people's trust. Therefore it was not in the national interest to surface a half-century-old scandal now, or ever. Through a back-door Rinehard notified Moscow's highest authorities to 'back off,' and if need be, to get rid of those involved with the "initiative" in Russia. Rinehard's superiors reasoned the retired American Marine's inquiry was a "one-off" and would forget about the issue. The Swiss professor, on the other hand, was more problematic, and Rinehard suspected more complex ways might be needed to discredit and/or sever that man's association with Moscow. Washington's Moscow embassy would attend to that.

Thousands of American military prisoners had been held in German POW camps overrun in Eastern Europe by the Russian army in the final months of WWII. General Eisenhower at the time reported twenty-five thousand then under Russian control and demanded the

Ruskies identifying who they were, where they were, and get them repatriated to U.S., control pronto. Regrettably only a few were, and the rest were secretly written off and forgotten as the Cold War started. Rinehard was assured his instructions to say nothing were made at the highest levels of the American government.

The Russian archivist in Moscow was a man named Yakov Ghranov. Rinehard recalled meeting Ghranov on several occasions in and around Moscow. Cosmopolitan, outgoing and with a sense of humor, Ghranov was well educated, suave, and had risen through the KGB's ranks as a trusted party member of impeccable background. Ghranov, had informed him that Moscow had now decided to close this secret scandal and provide the United States with the information in its files, and on the same basis that Moscow had already been doing for almost a decade for hundreds of thousands of captured European's who had also been disposed of in the Soviet Gulag. Deep down Rinehard knew the Russian offer was the Holy Grail for twenty or more thousand American families of the missing who knew something had happened and wanted the truth. But he had his orders.

"Shit!" he exclaimed as he continued to rub his temples. His headache was not lessening, and he suspected it was his nerves. He had his orders but had difficulty looking at himself in the mirror. Some of these poor bastards still alive out there across the former USSR called out to him in his dreams to bring them home from a living hell.

Many outside government in the United States had been looking for these American's records since the Cold War ended. Russia's Gulag and GUPVEE prison system's kept impeccable records and—if they could be made available—would close a sad saga. But until now the records were undoubtedly laying in unmarked boxes at the back of some closet in some forgotten dark Kremlin room.

Rinehard knew they existed. He'd seen some of them. In particular 618 of them for American Army and Army Air Corps prisoners captured in Poland who'd died between 1945 and 1947 at Rybak about a hundred miles south of the Severnaya Zemyla Island which lay north of the Arctic circle. A land of intense cold and endless snow, the Americans there had died along with thousands of others sent there around the same time. Hundreds more had died at Kirovskij and Peveka, northeast of Krasnoyarsk and 318 at Bodaybo on the Vitim river, two hundred miles north east of the Lake Baikal. And these were but a few.

The massive Russian labor camp system known by the acronym GUPVEE, had extended for six thousand miles across northern Russia from Archangel to the Pacific coast. By Rinehard's estimate, some eighty million people had been consumed in GUPVEE during the three quarters of a century between 1925 and 1990. Some twenty thousand American servicemen from Hitler's Stalag's were a small portion of the total, and their physical remains would never be located.

The GUPVEE registries, if ever found, would document the disposition of every last one of the untold millions of poor bastards who'd passed through that system into oblivion. Rinehard had also seen some of GUPVEE's files for a few of those lucky enough to have survived because of their notoriety beyond Soviet borders; men like Sakharov, and Solzchynitzen. But in recent years, senior Russian officials had blandly assured everyone that all had been lost long ago.

Rinehard recalled his meeting with the Marine, suspecting the Marine had seen through his argument. Especially when he'd asked Rinehard if he were deliberately lying to him within the provisions of the "Missing Servicemen Personnel Act." The Act, sponsored by Senator John McCain toward the end of the Cold War, allowed U.S. Government officials to knowingly and willfully withhold and deny any information they might have concerning the disappearance, whereabouts, or status of missing servicemen. The Act had been passed to provide government officials being confronted by those with loved ones missing, with a means to legally avoid telling them things that would cause endless pain, help no one and also complicate the government's ongoing efforts to negotiate the release of missing servicemen still under the control of foreign governments. McCain, having himself been a POW for many years, was the only one who could have authored such legislation, which in reality was designed for an honorable purpose. But like most such legislation, could be skirted and misinterpreted. Rhinehard was now in fact using the legislation to deny the existence of the Russian archivist's offer.

And to throw off the retired Marine officer's inquiry even more, Rinehard's response had been to insist that the McCain legislation was treasonous; and had actually been introduced only to conceal Washington's illegal cooperation with the North Vietnamese during the Vietnam War, and at a time when McCain himself was a prisoner in Hanoi. The Marine hadn't bought Rinehard's observation and suggested that Rinehard might be a Benedict Arnold. The conversation became testy after that, and the Marine concluded that he didn't believe Rinehard, and hoped none of the 5,000 files being offered were still alive, because if any were, and somehow learned of the Swiss professor's offer and how it had been side-tracked by Rinehard and the POW/MIA Agency, then no one could blame any of them for 'wasting' everyone in the POW/MIA Agency if they ever escaped and learned about it.

Lisbon

As the captain's voice floated through the cabin's public address system, advising his sleeping passengers they could now see the Portuguese coast from the left side of the aircraft, Alex stood into the isle and headed for the latrines, reflecting as he did about his latest visit to Florida. Both people he'd seen there were important.

First he'd met with the retired Pan American flying boat captain in Daytona, and yesterday he'd seen the elderly ferry pilot in Tampa. Unfortunately the former had not been aboard the president's flight to Casablanca, but had flown flying boats during the war, and knew a lot about Pan Am's operations in those days. The Daytona man also recalled the name of a retired oil company executive in Lisbon, a Mr. Higgs; who he said had commanded Roosevelt's flight, and provided the man's phone number and address.

In response to Alex's question about other Pan American aircraft in Ceylon at the time of the conference, the Daytona man thought it unlikely, as the Company operated only land based planes in the India-Burma theater in those days. He doubted large seaplanes would have ventured that far because of the proximity of Jap fighters in nearby Chittagong. The day before yesterday Alex had driven to a motel in Clearwater, and yesterday morning, visited the retired ferry pilot whose name was Harold Rice.

Rice's place on Scimitar Drive looked like most of the area's retirement homes. But the inside of the house surprised Alex. Rice had hollowed out its interior to accommodate a huge aviary, and the center of the house was a mess of birdseed and guano droppings. Rice no longer had such a good memory, but had an incredible collection of reference material, which he stored in old cardboard boxes which almost completely filled the garage. It was from these that Rice extracted the information Alex needed.

In the three years between 1941 and 1943, Rice made seventeen fights to the Mideast, ferrying combat aircraft to Iraq and Iran for delivery to the Russians. He remembered seeing a Pan American World Airways flying boat in the Nile River near Khartoum during one of his trips, and from a mildewed log-book showed Alex an entry for the twentieth of January 1943. At the bottom of the page he'd scribbled: "Anzac in the Nile! Special Mission-71? Bahrain? Probable destination . . . somewhere east?"

Rice recalled obtaining the aircraft's destination information from one of Anzac's crew at a refueling barge in the Nile river, and recalled the man becoming agitated when Rice offered to accompany the Anzac as far as Basrah. Rice pointed out to the Pan American pilot that his twin engine B-24 light bomber carried six .50 caliber guns and could provide protection for the lumbering flying boat if they encountered any Krauts along the route. The pilot insisted that Rice forget what he'd said and abruptly left. Two days later Rice spotted another flying boat. This time parked on Lake Habbaniya in central Iraq. But he was certain this one was a Royal Air Force Sutherland, and not a Pan American Boeing B-314. The two were similar but the British model had a stockier fuselage, and a nose turret!

In retrospect Alex was uncertain what to make of most of the information. He would try to make sense of it from the next man he would see in Lisbon.

The view from Higg's balcony above Lisbon's harbor where Alex now sat in the early afternoon sun, was a scene most people dreamed about from old travel posters. Alex felt fatigued after his flight over from Florida, but the day was splendid and his jet lag had now dissipated. Spread out beneath him was a panoramic view of the entire expanse of Lisbon's harbor. From the decor of the old Spanish red tiled villa and expansive well-manicured balconies, Alex imagined that the ex-Pan American pilot must have owned the princely estate since the days when such things were affordable to those who were not born to incredible wealth. An immaculately attired servant whose dark skin and white turban probably signified Moorish or maybe Sudanese origins, proffered a tray with Alex's double gin and tonic.

Mr. Constantine Emliovitch Higgs, the former Pan American pilot who'd flown Roosevelt to Casablanca in 1943, was attired in dapper late British Empire style, with a white straw hat and a blue ascot around his neck, a pale blue shirt and white flannel slacks.

"There, there," he said with affection, signaling to the houseboy to bring a wash towel with which Higg's wiped away the African gray parrots droppings from his sleeve. "There's a good boy," Higg's said, passing the parrot to the houseboy. "The bird is anxious because you are here. Grays enjoy social contact with humans and can sense our moods and anxiety. He normally avoids defecating on me and must be in one of his rebellious moods."

"How old is he?" Alex asked, not really giving a damn but reticent to let Higgs think he was not interested in such things.

"Six years. They normally begin forming words around a year and a half to two years, and by age six acquire a pretty good vocabulary if properly trained."

Higgs had flown with Pan American for ten years at the beginning of his career. Higgs corrected Alex's observation about the Daytona man's statement. Higgs was not the pilot on Roosevelt's flight to Casablanca, but copilot. After the war Pan American had sold-off all of its Boeing-314 flying boats and Higgs had decided to pursue his fortunes elsewhere. He'd gone to work in Saudi Arabia for ARAMCO, the American Arabian Oil Company.

"In those days," Higgs concluded, "I made four times more than my earlier Pan American salary; hung around with incredibly rich people, and became involved in lucrative opportunities that only come to well-placed people when boom times suddenly come to backward areas of the world."

Alex asked him what he did for ARAMCO?

"Flew ARAMCO's DC-6 back and forth to the States and Europe, and in between flew throughout the Mideast on company business. Later one of the young Princes took a fancy to me and I signed on with the Prince. Those were really good years for me. Everything was super first-class and the money was fantastic."

"What do you recall of the presidential flight to Morocco, and especially if they stopped at Key West?

Higgs eyed Alex with surprise and sat back for a moment as he stared off into the distance, his fingers drumming on the table as an expression of resignation came over his face. "What the hell." Higgs sighed. "I always suspected someone might eventually ask me about it. I guess I'm surprised that it took so long."

"Mr. Higgs?" Alex asked, obviously surprised at the way his host had phrased the response.

"Sure, I remember that trip. It started on 11 January 1943. Even to this day there aren't many who can say they flew an American president overseas in wartime. Of course . . . all this stuff about America's War on Terrorism is a lot of crap. If the assholes in Washington would give the goddamn Palestinians a homeland the Arab world would calm down and leave America alone. Unfortunately for America, almost all of its recent presidents have been bought and paid for by the Israeli lobby, so if any of them crosses the Israelis they'll nail his ass to the wall and throw the son of a bitch out of office."

"Mr. Higgs, I appreciate your views on America's problems, but could you go over the entire sequence of events as you recall them in January 1943?"

"Sure! We'd been told to have two flying boats ready at Dinner Key near Key Biscayne two days before the president actually showed up. Even the captain didn't know our final destination, only that twelve government employees would show up and that they would provide destination information. It was still dark when they arrived and we were running our departure check lists which we'd already done for three mornings in a row. The air instantly became electric when word spread that the president was being carried aboard!"

"We were airborne twenty minutes later and flew south on a heading of one hundred thirty five degrees at a thousand feet toward Trinidad. About ten minutes after takeoff the Captain received a note that the president wanted a word with him. Roosevelt told him to change course and proceed to Key West, and land at the seaplane base near Trumbo Annex.

"So we landed at Key West, picked up a passenger, and continued on to Trinidad where we arrived that afternoon. Between Key West and Trinidad one of the president's secret service men came to the flight deck and instructed everyone in our crew to sign a handwritten statement. Under penalty of death we could never discuss the Key West stop with anyone . . . ever . . . period. So if you tell anyone what I just said, I suppose some spook could be dispatched from Washington to assassinate me." Higgs laughed.

"What happened?" Alex asked.

"How do you mean?"

"While you were on the ground at Key West?"

"I hope you realize, Mr. Balkan, that you are the first person I've ever mentioned this to, and I am only doing so because you obviously already know about it and appear to have some interest in the issue which transcends making a public expose about it."

"You are correct. You will never see our conversation or your name mentioned in the media or a book."

Higgs continued. "We landed just before sunup. The second seaplane with Captain Vinal at the controls didn't land and proceeded about halfway to Cuba and then circled out of sight of Key West until we took off again and rejoined him. There used to be a huge seaplane hangar at Trumbo, it may still be there"

"It is," Alex confirmed.

"Well, we taxied up to a jetty on the left side of that hanger, and tied up while the president went ashore. He sat beneath some palms and smoked a few cigarettes in the dawn light. A man arrived and sat alone with the president for maybe five minutes, and then the two men reboarded and we left."

"Who was he?"

"No idea. The captain might have known, but none of us asked any questions at the time and soon forgot about it."

"Where's Captain Cone now?"

"He died years ago."

"Wasn't it unusual for you to make such a deviation?"

"Not when the president tells you to."

Alex was still trying to comprehend the significance of what he'd heard. No where did the official log for the trip match what Higgs had just told him. Admiral Leahy, the president's chief of staff at the time had produced a comprehensive fifty-one page log documenting the entire trip. It detailed everything in the minutest detail. But nowhere did it mention the stop at Key West or who this person was that came aboard with the president. Why?

"What did this passenger look like?"

The old man gave him a look of disbelief, then leaned back and thought a moment. "Nice-looking guy, mid to late twenties, tall—just over six foot, maybe 170 pounds. Auburn hair and well dressed."

"How far did he go?"

"To Bathhurst on the Africa coast."

"Not Casablanca?"

"No."

"You certain?"

"Yes."

"Do you know where he went after Bathhurst?"

"No idea."

"But you're sure he didn't go to Morocco with the president?"

"I heard he'd traveled elsewhere!"

"And the flight over to Bathhurst?"

"From Key West we flew to Trinidad. Next morning we left Trinidad for Belem in Brazil, and at sunset the following day flew across the Atlantic to Bathhurst, which is at the mouth of the Gambia River. The American Cruiser Memphis was already there, anchored in the river when we arrived, and we parked alongside her while the president and his party deplaned."

"And the second flying boat?"

"Her passengers also transferred to the Memphis. Then we lay around and twiddled our thumbs for almost two weeks until Roosevelt returned from Casablanca and we flew him back to Miami."

"How did the president get up to Casablanca?"

"A four-engine C-54 cargo plane."

"Do you recall the date you returned?"

"Twenty-seventh of January."

"Were you aware of any other flying boats further east while you were waiting for the president to return from the Casablanca Conference?"

"No. I wasn't!"

"Think back? Are you certain?"

"Hell yes! Of course I'm certain. What's this all about anyway?"

"There's no record anywhere of a stop at Key West!"

"I know that, Mr. Balkan. So what? I told you we had to sign a statement never to talk about it."

"Why do you suppose that is?" Mr. Higgs.

The old man's eyes slitted, and his fingers once again began drumming on the table cloth in front of him. "You accusing me of lying?"

"My god, no! Of course not! It's not an issue here."

"It was unscheduled! Maybe they forgot. The president obviously didn't want any of us to ever discuss it, so I assume the answer lies somewhere in the president's archives. Maybe that's where you need to check?"

"All of the official records," Alex replied, "which I've seen, document everything about that trip right down to the minutest detail, even the meals served, the types of liquors consumed, etc., but not Key West"

"So what's your point?"

"Even so many decades later, it's been deliberately left out of history books."

"Any why is that, Mr. Balkan?"

"It must have had to do with the man you picked up."

"Well, Higgs continued, "I don't know about such things. But I can tell you that for damned certain we landed at Key West, and what I saw is what I've already told you."

"I believe you. What can you tell me about flights across the Sahara back then?"

"If you're talking about B-314 flying boats, I doubt you'll find much. They seldom ventured across the desert because the Krauts were everywhere in North Africa. There was also the problem of no place to land if you had engine trouble."

"Mr. Higgs, I spoke two days ago with a man in Tampa who ferried replacement fighters across the Sahara around the time of the Conference. He swears he saw a Pan Am flying boat in the Nile River near Khartoum on the twentieth of January 1943. He also saw a British flying boat on Lake Habbaniya in Iraq two days later."

"If he saw them," Higgs replied, "then they were there."

"Any idea what they might have been up too?"

"None."

"Take a guess?"

"Probably Ferrying supplies or mail," the old man replied.

"Ever heard of Special Mission Seventy-Two?" Alex asked him.

"No!"

Alex studied him for a few moments, wondering if Higgs might also be involved somehow and playing dumb? "It was the special mission number assigned to your trip with the president."

"If it was, I didn't know about it!"

"There were four flying boats involved in the trip, the two you know about and two more which were already further east."

"Where you getting all this from? What's the point?"

"To be honest Mr. Higgs I wish I knew."

"If I were to guess," Higgs speculated, "I suspect the others were involved with Winston Churchill's attendance at the conference. He also flew down from England as you probably know."

"Not possible," Alex replied

"Why not?" Higgs observed. "Churchill went to Egypt after the conference and then on to Palestine and Turkey."

It was a point Alex hadn't considered, but it still didn't fit.

"Maybe you're counting apples and oranges?" Higgs pressed him. "Pan American had twelve 314's before the war started, all of them were seconded into government service and three of them were then transferred to the British when we got involved in the war in Europe."

"And the Anzac Clipper spotted near Khartoum?"

"Maybe the retired Pan Am guy in Florida was wrong! Have you checked historical records in Washington?"

"They are all lost."

A smile spread across Higg's face. "Typical!" He said sarcastically. "The government never could hold on to anything. And what it does it never seems able to find when you really need it."

"Anyone you can think of who might could help with this?"

"Sorry. Almost everyone I knew from those days are dead and the few left don't keep in touch with me. I'm curious about one thing though, what is this all about?"

"I'm still not certain myself."

"Oh, come on, Mr. Balkan?" Higgs hadn't believed a word Alex had told him.

Novosibirsk

Gathering his overcoat around him and vigorously rubbing his hands together beneath the table, trying to warm them in the cold damp air, Alex eyed the old Russian across the table from him . . . waiting for him to start talking. Pyotr Kaminski had come to see him voluntarily. But like all Russians, Kaminski needed a couple more vodka's to thaw out the wall of suspicion which perennially gripped all Russians, especially during the endless winters of Central Asia.

"So how did you know I was here, Pyotr?" Alex inquired.

"To survive here today one must be able to see the crumbs before the bread. You arrived a couple of days ago. Where have you been?"

"You ask officially."

"You must be joking. I am retired, the old days are gone. I come as a friend. Why not? Are our countries not friends now?"

Alex had already assessed the old man's motives for coming, and believed him. Kaminski was looking for a free handout. They'd first met a decade earlier when Alex had wandered around the area as a member of a nuclear reduction program under SALT II. Kaminski, a former intelligence officer was now obviously retired, and from his appearance was having hard times making ends meet in modern Russia. If time permitted Alex would pitch him as a potential future spy before he left Novibirsk. Recruiting clandestine sources was one of Alex's favorite past times, and he was good at it. And why shouldn't he be? In his career he'd brought aboard 218 assets for United States Intelligence so far—sixteen under a false flag, thirty-one with promises of resettlement, fifty-four for patriotism, twenty for blackmail, and 101 for the most popular of all incentives that drove people to betray their country—money.

Reflecting back on the Lisbon stopover, Alex was happy he'd caught the plane for Russia when he had. For just a moment at Lisbon airport he'd become indecisive, and seriously contemplated taking a couple of days off to enjoy himself in the balmy winter weather at one of his favorite hangouts in nearby Estoril.

Novosibirsk on the other hand, now blanketed with a new dusting of snow, was still a barren drab cookie-cutter creation of communism's worst architectural nightmares. Alex glanced around furtively at the impoverished clientele of the restaurant-cum bar as the Russian across the table from him droned on about his marital problems with his fourth wife, who was now a fat unloving pig who threatened to throw Kaminski out of his own government provided apartment

No one seemed to be paying any attention to them as Alex leaned as far forward as he could, and in a low tone demanded, "Tell me about the American's held in your camps? Tell me what you know about one in particular, who was held near here—a man called Paul Carter."

"You interrupted my story!" The Russian observed with feigned offense.

"Because what you say does not interest me!" Alex shot back. It was the third time Alex had posed the question and the third time the Russian had rebuffed him. Now with a bottle of expensive local vodka between them, the son of a bitch across the table was more interested in finishing the bottle than he was in their conversation. This man knew about the camps and could probably find the man Alex was looking for.

Times were hard in Russia these days, and Kaminski had retired a few years ago and obviously had not received most of his government retirement checks. The Russian government was bankrupt, and all the old Party hacks had been told to forget about their government subsidies. And now inflation had eaten away ninety-five percent of what little Kaminski did receive. A year ago the old Russian's pension barely kept fat on his wife thighs. This year's inflation along with Kaminski's un-indexed monthly checks would hardly keep fat on a mouse. By Alex's calculations it might exceed about $4.60 a month in new Rubles.

Pyotr Kaminski was a proud man. He'd served the motherland with honor. And now they were shunting him aside, along with millions of others—into a vacuum where they were supposed to go away and die quietly without complaining. Alex knew a couple of hundred dollars would take care of this Russian for the rest of his life.

* * *

Somehow Pyotor Kaminski had got wind of his presence in Novisibirsk. Alex assumed it must have been the hotel's desk clerk who might have recalled him from earlier visits a decade ago, or maybe one of the Russian staff at the local American consulate.

He'd first met Kaminski almost a decade ago, when Alex had first shown up to tour Russian SS-20 sites where the American and Russian government's had agreed the Russians would destroy their intermediate range theater missiles. The thirty-five foot rockets moved around the country side on large mobile tractor-trailers which when launching, raised the missiles upright. With a range of several thousand miles they could reach most places in Europe where their twenty kiloton warheads would take out most tactical military targets. The rockets were brought from their remote dispersal sites in western Russia to a place where Balkan and several other Americans first verified their operational status, inventory numbers, production markings, and then stood by and watched while the rockets were first cut open and their solid fuel removed, then cut into pieces before being driven over with bulldozers. Pyotr's part in all this was to escort the Americans and make certain they didn't wander off from their preagreed MBFR missions to go spying. He and the American had formed a professional bond over several years, but had never become friends insofar as being invited to Proty's home or meeting any of his family and friends.

Two hours ago Kaminski had found Alex and seated himself here, across the table from him in the hotel's bar, and tried to make the meeting appear casual. He knew Alex needed information and Kaminski no longer gave a damn about narodny, izvestia, pravda or patriotism. Pyotor needed hard currency, dollars or Euro's. Russia's money was worthless and Kaminski would even sell his mother for dollars if he could. The Russian's life had turned to shit in the last few years, and what little pride he still had, he would trade for dollars or even a bottle of vodka.

* * *

"So you see," Pyotr continued with the point he'd been trying to make, that it was okay to sell out one's country for money when times were rough. "I definitely see a difference between truth in the news, and news in the truth!"

Alex leaned back and ignored him. All he wanted to hear was Kaminsky's price.

"American's only distinguish," the Russian continued, "between things which don't matter! Why is it my friend?" Alex noticed the sudden use of the word 'my friend.' It was a good sign! Kaminsky was obviously coming around.

Four days earlier Alex had flown into Novosibirsk to see if he could pick up the trail of Paul Carter or other WWII American survivors that might be in the area. Situated in the Ob River valley, hundreds of miles north of Novosibirsk, it had once housed thousands of Gulag camps, most of them known as "silent camps," some holding Americans from WWII and Korea . . . those to be systematically liquidated by the KGB and NKVD. Novosibirsk was a dreary place, enshrouded beneath a pall of pollution within which the population groped its way around like zombies. Because the local American Consulate was unable to assist visitors with such mundane things as reconfirming return air reservations, Alex had spent a day at the local airline office. Seats to Moscow were hard to get.

Easternmost of four "Russianized" cities sprawled in a three thousand mile arc from Europe to Asia, Novosibirsk intersected the historic trade routes to Asia, Alex's father would have loved its huge railroad switching yards, which contained miles of rolling stock like those once so prevalent in his home town in Pennsylvania.

Alex suspected Kaminski was still somehow associated with the secret police. In the days before the collapse of Communism, Kaminsky's employer had been the Second Chief Directorate of the KGB, and before that he's spent decades in the now defunct NKVD. When the KGB failed to seize power in the August 1991 coup against Gorbachev, revanchists, fearing the KGB might again try to seize power tried to castrate it, but had only succeeded in renaming it Federalnaya Sluzbah Beznopasti, Russia's new internal security service. Security organs in Russia never went away, and renaming things every couple of years was an old Russian pastime. The director of the new "reformed' MBFR had confided to his CIA counterpart a year ago that "our organizations are too powerful to be eliminated. There is no one in Moscow or Washington with balls big enough to neuter us!" Alex knew it was true.

"I'll tell you why this is so," Kaminsky droned on. "We Russians make a subtle distinction between truth and news. One must," he smiled indolently at Alex, "if one is to reach old age."

"We in America value the worth of the individual more," Alex replied.

The Russian shrugged with a look of disgust on his face. "Bravo!" he laughed. "We don't! A little bread, some cheese and vodka, it's enough for a Russian."

"And the soul?" Alex asked.

"Food for the soul turns to shit!" Kaminski replied sarcastically, "And too much shit causes constipation. And constipation makes one unhappy. Especially little fish in a big pond." A smile spread across his gaunt face and his lips parted, revealing his uneven brown teeth.

Alex leaned back and sipped his vodka as he surveyed the motley assortment of men in the room who'd drifted in off the street for tea and vodka. Alex hated the Svetlana hotel from the moment he'd first seen it a decade back, and the advent of capitalism in Russia had not reached Novisibirsk yet. Even the hotel's proprietor had obsequiously apologized when Alex checked in. Hotels in Novosibirsk were still only priority 37 on Moscow's list, so the Svetlana hadn't been renovated in four decades. Alex suspected that Ghengis Khan would probably recognize it from his last visit in the twelfth century! The tiled bathroom in Alex's room contained only a floor bomb-sight beneath a wall pipe which emitted spurts of hot water when-ever one flushed. The hot water pipe also served as the shower. Named after Stalin's daughter, who'd fled to the United States in the sixties, the Svetlana was worse than the worst Brooklyn tenement. Alex gathered his coat around him again as yet another blast of cold air accompanied the latest group of Kulaks, who'd just come in and forgot to close the street door behind them.

Kaminsky raised his glass, "Nastrovia Kamaradsky!" He downed his fifth vodka. Alex leaned forward again. "What about the camps?" Alex suspected Kaminsky knew all there was to know about the camps, and probably knew people who could tell Alex about Tatiana Slavchenko, and Paul Carter! Alex had seen Kaminski blink earlier when he'd mentioned the two names.

"You know what your problem is?" Kaminski observed, wiping phlegm from his mustache with the back of his hand before pouring himself another half glass. "Americans have too much freedom. We need some changes in Russia, but we still know what responsibility is. We know how to work and respect other's property. You don't in America."

Alex leaned forward and in a low tone whispered, "I don't care! Tell me about Carter."

Kaminsky belched. "How much money is there in the world?" He laughed.

"Sutkin Yar!" Alex formed the words quietly with his lips as he rubbed his index finger and thumb together in the age old signal for money.

Kaminski chuckled. "You tell me to fuck off! What do you know of fucking off? People like to fuck off in America, isn't it? Sex rules your country! Your wives get raped and no one cares! Your daughters get fucked before they're ten years old, and you give them rubbers and abortions. Your president gets blow jobs in the Oval Office, and no one cares when he lies about it under oath before your highest courts." Kaminski laughed. "Half of you are bastards, born out of wedlock. Even your poor are too stupid to work! What does it all mean my friend? Tell me about freedom as the truth? And tell me how many dollars you have with you?"

"You came to find me old man. Not the other way," Alex replied. "I'm not going to tell you shit. You want some kopeks in your trousers. Talk to me! Talk to me about what I want to hear, or find someone else to buy your god-damned vodka!"

"Talk to me!" Kaminski mimicked.

Alex hoped the liquor had not gone to the man's head already. He didn't need Kaminsky to make a public spectacle of himself just now. Not before Alex got what he wanted. He knew the nearby prison camps existed. He'd seen the CIA satellite photography of the camp complexes, which still bore the vague outlines of the buildings and perimeter areas which now had new stands of timber growing over them, and yesterday he'd driven out to see the area where Carter's camp was last reported to have existed in 1982 by Tatiana Slavchenko in Washington. Alex leaned forward. "Talk to me Kaminsky, or I'm leaving!"

* * *

Alex had taken a night flight from Lisbon and arrived the next morning in Novisibirsk. Downtown he caught an afternoon bus to the city of Tomsk and found lodging at a kulak pseudo-parasha dump near the bus station. The following morning he took another bus, this time two hundred miles north to Kolpashevo on the east bank of the Ob River. Kolpashevo was another dreary nondescript Siberian town with several prominent pedestals here and there at traffic intersections upon which had once stood massive metal and stone statues of Stalin, Lenin, and various other heroes of the now defunct communist revolution. At the northern edge of town he spent the day wandering downriver through the birch and poplar forests along the river's banks. The day was pristine, cold, with a bright blue sky overhead. From intelligence reports he'd seen years ago in Washington, Alex knew about Kolpashevo's dirty secret. Today he hoped to find some scent or actual evidence of what had happened here decades ago. The entire area had once contained silent gulag camps in which hundreds of thousands of victims had been systematically exterminated, and their remains dumped into shallow pits in the permafrost. Estimates were that somewhere upward of a half million had met their fate in the area between 1940 and 1968, some of whom were American servicemen. Alex had seen the reports concerning these American servicemen captured by the Red Army just as WWII ended and dispatched to the Kolpashevo area.

In 1978 Kolpashevo residents noticed scores of dead bodies floating along with the river current everywhere in the area. All were perfectly preserved and seemed to have died recently. Their faces were still recognizable and their clothing intact. All had one or more bullet holes in the backs of their heads? Local residents were appalled. Then Moscow's security services arrived—warning residents to say nothing, forget what they had seen, but to report locations from which the bodies came so they could be disposed of. In the spring of 1979 the problem became more serious. Moscow got involved. Upstream and downstream of Kolpashevo the river's flow had eroded lengths of permafrost cliffs along its banks. The process had undermined mass grave sites, dumping still frozen bodies into the river. Hundreds a day floated through Kolpashevo and nearby towns: men, women, children, babies—even pregnant mothers.

Reports of these events reached Washington, the reports and photographs kept secret to protect sources identities. American satellite photography of the area also revealed the thousands of corpses floating along for miles in the river. This information too was top secret to protect American satellite imagery capabilities. Then the Cold War ended and Washington and Moscow signed new government-to-government agreements—that such information would remain secret to protect both governments from criticism: and in the case of Americans murdered around Kolpashevo—protect the privacy of Americans disposed of there.

To eliminate the evidence at Kolpashevo at the time, Moscow brought in large tugboats, put heavy fishing nets across the river downstream, then ran the tugboat's engines at high speed, the backwash from their propellers wearing down the permafrost cliffs, and in the process—grinding up all solid matter that fell into the river. Four months later the evidence was gone. The crisis had passed. But everyone around Kolpashevo suspected it might happen again. The only question was when?

Along the river bank north of town Alex encountered an old woman sitting before a small samovar of tea. She invited him to sit with her. She was grieving for her husband she told him. In 1980 her husband had been recruited to help get rid of the evidence here, but then he too had disappeared afterward. Today was the anniversary of his disappearance. Local authorities had told her not to ask about what had become of him. They suggested he got 25 years at hard labor for bourgeois anti-state activity. Alex asked her what she thought? Her response surprised him. Her husband had mentioned seeing Americans among the dead.

"What did he say?" Alex asked.

"I will tell you," she replied. "But why do you ask?" she demanded, her voice now accusatory. "Are you with state security?"

"No. Do not be afraid my mother."

"Well, if you are . . . and you are going to arrest me, at least wait until we finish our tea. I no longer care to live in this horrible place, and I pray for the day I can join my husband in heaven."

"Have no fear old woman, I am a private person like you."

Tears came to her eyes and she sobbed. "Of course we are all guilty," she blurted out. "No one said anything in those days. I too . . . God, forgive me. Now their names must be made known. These were all innocent people." Her words now came forth, tumbling from her mouth in a torrent. "Babies . . ." she exclaimed through sobs. "Pregnant women in advanced pregnancy," she exclaimed. "All had bullet holes in their heads. Many their eyes still staring at me in death." She reached out and held Alex's hand. "What kind of animals do such things? My husband told me one pregnant woman he saw, the head of her baby had partially emerged between her legs." The old woman regained her composure after a few moments while Alex waited. "And then they killed my beloved Dimitri . . . my husband of thirty years . . . and for what? For speaking about such things? what kind of Russians are these?"

"Bad leaders," Alex said quietly.

"Scum of the earth," she spat. "Worst was that fatherless shit . . . comrade Stalin." She smiled mirthlessly. "And now it's Putin and his SRV fatherless shits. He is another Stalin. He and his yes-men in Moscow do not allow our history to be revealed. They are all the same, and it is our flesh they live off in their capitalist dacha's and palaces around our country."

Tears came to her eyes. Alex waited an appropriate time, squeezing her hand reassuringly in his.

And the Americans," Alex finally asked. "What did your Dimitri say?"

"My husband said he was sure they were Americans from their clothing. Some wore tattered American military uniforms and boots of good quality. Others," she said, "had tattoos, one was an American flag, and another a place in America—Brooklyn, New York, as I recall. One, Dimitri said, had God Bless America across his chest. Another he said, a tattoo of a statue of a woman holding a torch in her right hand. All of these men too had been killed in a mass grave and had bullet holes in their heads."

"Strange," Alex observed compassionately. "How many Americans did Dimitri think were here?" he asked.

"Hundreds," she replied. "Maybe thousands. My husband told me the tug boat the men from Moscow were using at one place here . . . was excavating a river side mass grave at which all were Americans."

"Do you remember where that was?" Alex asked quietly.

"Just up the river there." She pointed northward. "There in the river bend, maybe a half kilometer."

Alex squeezed her hand. "Maybe things will get better in Russia now. The people seem to have faith. Maybe Putin will make things better?"

A cackling sound came up from her chest as she wiped away her tears. "Do not be stupid." She sneered at him. "No one will be held accountable, so why bother. We have too many Ligachevs and Putins in Russia today."

A half hour later at a dense stand of pine trees along the river bank where the old woman had pointed, Alex could discern no unusual disruption in the terrain that might indicate other undisturbed mass graves in the area.

* * *

Returning to Novisibirsk last night, Alex checked into the hotel Svetlana, and this morning rented a taxi for the day near the local railroad station. This time for a tour of the countryside to the south-east toward Berdsk and Iskitim. Other camps were in this area, one of which in particular Alex was interested in. At the village of Yevsino he'd ordered the driver to take a left, and a half hour later turned onto a remote track through the forests. They followed it for thirty miles to a crossroads which today stood in the middle of nowhere. But Alex knew the intersection had once been the center of the vast prison complex known as the Krasnoyarsk Administration. Two miles north from the crossroads had once stood a NKVD Controlled Gulag subcamp called Buytenlag-23V. His driver, a Kulak, was noticeably nervous but Alex suggested his KGB intelligence work was critical, and it would go badly for the driver if he refused.

The entire area was now veiled in thick forests and all that remained of Buytenlag-23V was a dilapidated assembly of collapsed wooden buildings. Perimeter fences were still discernable but in shambles, and the once cleared fields beyond the strands of rusting concertina wire were now overgrown with thick stands of Siberian spruce and birch. Through the trees he could see thousands of wooden stakes poking through the snow everywhere. Alex struggled toward them, realizing the entire area was obviously a vast cemetery. Returning to the buildings he checked those whose roofs were still intact and found nothing of interest.

The countryside around Novosibirsk was dotted with hundreds of such abandoned camp complexes where so many had disappeared in the last eighty years . . . and without anyone to mourn their passage. Sniffing the air, Alex wondered about the millions who lay out there toward the horizon? If only they could now tell their story.

On the way out he'd checked for surveillance but detected none. He wondered if they might be tracking him discreetly, but suspected that in Russia's deteriorating security system, they had probably completely missed him. Alex knew too that just over the northern horizon, maybe thirty miles away, lay all that remained of the cream of Russia's ICBM fleet: eight hundred Intercontinental Ballistic Missiles buried in hardened silos, each loaded with MIRVED J-23 series warheads: five, ten and twenty megaton behemoths designed to excavate huge craters all over the north American landscape: if and when Russia ever had to mount a nuclear exchange with the United States. All together the silos contained enough atomic pollution to turn North America into a radioactive wasteland. Alex wanted to call out in the silence, suspecting that somewhere out there, beyond the wire, might be the remains of the man he sought.

The cold was starting to penetrate his clothing, so he'd signaled the driver they would head back. A half hour later they approached a group of buildings they'd passed earlier. From the maps in Washington he knew this was once the main gate for the complex.

"A stantya-v-avtomobiley!" Alex ordered.

The driver looked over his shoulder. It was almost four o'clock and the night shadows already were creeping across the landscape. The temperature too was dropping rapidly, and the driver didn't want to stop until they reached Novosibirsk.

"Ya predo chairez prots minutez!" Alex warned him as he got out of the car.

"Where are you going?" the driver demanded.

"Ya predo!" Alex shot back.

"Okay, but I'll leave the engine running while you look around."

"Suit yourself." Alex walked away from the car and banged on the door of the roadside cabin which had smoke coming from its chimney.

A decrepit man opened it a crack, pushing aside a goat and its bleating kid. "Da!"

"Shtoe schluchilus Buytenlag?" Alex asked.

"Ktoe vwe?" the old man demanded.

"Diplomat ez-Moskva!" Alex lied. He knew if the man also thought he was a diplomat employed by the KGB in Moscow, it would frighten him enough to confide whatever he knew.

"Gavno once ne vazhna!"

The old bastard's response surprised Alex. The old man didn't give a shit about dignitaries from Moscow anymore, even if they were KGB or SRV to boot.

"Tea hochsh yitsea butlika vodka?"

The promise of a bottle of vodka worked. Vodka opened doors everywhere in Russia. Alex took out his handkerchief and covered his nose against the stench as he crossed the threshold and stood near a cast iron wood burning stove.

The old man said his name was Gavodny. He'd manned the main gate to Buytenlag-23V for thirty years, and his roadside cabin was as far as anyone went when the camps were in operation unless the visitor was not coming back. To Alex's question about how many had left the camps the old man laughed. "None!"

Alex didn't reply and watched him skeptically.

"There were a few," the old man muttered "maybe one in a thousand, maybe one in ten thousand, I was never informed how many poor bastards were in the trucks that passed by constantly!" The old man also confirmed that the camp known as Buytenlag-23V, was finally closed in 1991, and the last of its inhabitants moved east. Furthermore that the entire area had remained off-limits and the gate stayed up until two years ago. Now no one came and no one cared the old man observed.

"And when the camps closed," Alex pressed him, "who left?"

"Only four or five truck-loads as I recall. Maybe three or four hundred men." He shrugged, looking at the bulge concealing the vodka in Alex's overcoat. He pointed at it inquiringly. "I was warned to say nothing."

"You are a wise man," Alex assured him, reaching into his overcoat and withdrew a pint of the local Krasny Vodka and placed it on the table. The old man's attention immediately was riveted to it and his eyes began to glaze over. Alex thought the old man's eyes even puddled a little. Vodka was difficult to find. The old gatekeeper recalled that it was precisely mid-September 1990 and the weather was warm.

"That was all that were taken away?" Alex inquired.

"You are surprised?"

"Do you recall any Americans among them?"

"No one spoke of such things. I didn't know who any of them were, I didn't care, and I minded my own business."

"Who was in charge?" Alex asked

"Of what?" The gatekeeper smiled stupidly.

"What was the name of the man in charge of the entire complex?"

"Comrade Igor," Gavodny replied. "And before him, Comrade Topolin." A hint of suspicion now evident in his voice.

"Igor and Topolin. Their first names?"

"There was only one Comrade Igor! I am surprised you did not know that?"

"Just answer my question? He had no family name?"

"Who did?" The old man asked, again flashing a stupid smile.

"Thanks, the vodka is for you. I'll be on my way."

The gate man obviously knew nothing and Alex suspected the answer to his question lay in Moscow.

"Pacho moo eta billa tak dolga?" the driver asked as Alex got into the car.

"Et fe foreda," he replied. It was time to start back.

*   *   *

Alex smiled as Kaminski continued to drone on about some arcane problem regarding the local water supply from the river being polluted from time to time with decomposing human bodies. "I am boring you?" Kaminski asked. Alex remained silent and wanted to laugh thinking about how fucked-up Russia really was, and yet how much it was still the same. The driver of the car he'd rented yesterday had run out of gas on the way back from the boonies, about twelve miles from Novisibirsk. Thank God it had happened on a main road. Alex had paid the driver off and hitched a ride with a passing heavy truck. Had the stupid car driver run out of gas a few miles earlier, both of them would probably have frozen to death before they reached the main road, and for all he knew the old man driving the car may have.

"Supposing I had what you want?" Kaminsky replied. "And supposing it cost you some dollars?" The comment immediately had brought Alex out of his thoughts about his visit to the camp yesterday. "How much money will you pay?" Kaminski demanded, leaning forward conspiratorially so their conversation would not be over heard.

"It depends on what you tell me."

"Not good enough!" Now Kaminski rubbed his index finger and thumb together.

"It can be arranged!" Alex replied, holding his thumb and index finger about an inch apart to signify the number of dollars it might take to close the gap.

The Russian's nose was bulbous and looked like a raspberry from the cold and too much vodka. More mucous dripped onto his mustache which Kaminski wiped away with the back of his sleeve. "How many dollars? Ones or hundreds?"

Alex laughed. "Many!"

The Russian's eyes riveted Alex's, his greed radiating in anticipation.

"And dollars go a long way these days in Russia my friend." Alex observed.

"All with the silver strip in them?"

"Of course," Alex replied with a feigned hurt expression. "Do you think I would bring counterfeits?" I will give you enough to live comfortably and feed you and your babushka for the rest of your lives."

Kaminski's eyes revealed his pleasure. Bogus American currency had become a serious problem in Russia in the 1990s when the Russian Ruble was worthless. The Russian Mafia counterfeited billions of bogus twenty, fifty and hundred dollar bills using high quality Cannon color photocopiers. Some sixty billion had gotten into circulation before most Russians realized that the real McCoy's had the small silver metal strips down their left side, and began rejecting the those without them. The whole affair had severely strained American/ Russian relations, and in the mid-1990s President Clinton demanded that the Federal Reserve issue new American currency with larger pictures and traps which would make the dollar more difficult to copy.

Over the last thirty years Kaminski, like his Russian brothers, had always had enough to eat in the winter, but stores these days didn't even supply the basics of potatoes, cabbage and beets. The last two winters had seen starvation stalk the remote areas of central and eastern Russia. To Kaminski Alex's dollars represented salvation.

Alex egged him on, realizing that greed was about to curtail their protracted negotiations. When Perestroika swept Russia in 1990 one dollar had bought one ruble. Two years ago the exchange rate was five hundred rubles per dollar, and now it was over six thousand. Two thousand dollars would make Kaminski comfortable for life. Five thousand would buy him a dacha in the country, and another thousand would get him a young wife to warm his bed and take care of him until the day he died.

"How many dollars do you have with you American?" Kaminski probed

Alex wondered what would it take to overwhelm the old Russian? Two thousand would be a princely sum. Alex recalled the Russian description of heaven: a place where the police were Russian, the cooks Polish, mechanics Ukrainians, the women Armenians, and those who organized things—with dollars from Moscow! In hell on the other hand, the chefs were Mongols, the mechanics Tajiks, and the organizers with kopeks from Uganda! Alex leaned forward until their faces were close. "You want to be rich?"

"Da!" Kaminski replied."

"What about your own dacha?"

"Daaaa." Kaminski smiled, his voice obviously elevated at the thought.

"Tell me what happened to Carter?"

"I will."

"Now?"

"Nyet!"

"When?"

"In a few weeks!"

"Why not now?"

"Because I must get the information first!"

"There are others who could tell me about him, and I need not wait," Alex threatened.

"There is no one!" the Russian shot back.

"You are not the only one who knows?" Alex asserted with obvious scorn.

"Then, Alex . . . why do you waste your time here with me? Go upstairs to your room and play with your penis, it will be more useful."

"One thousand dollars," Alex whispered.

"Five thousand," Kaminski countered in a whisper, his face now six inches from Alex's.

"No," Alex whispered back.

Kaminski leaned back into the chair, downed yet another shot of Vodka, and became nonchalant, feigning disinterest, tweaking his mustache, flicking flecks of dried mucous onto the floor. "It is not enough!" He replied and began to button his overcoat as he stood up. "I will leave you. You are not serious."

"I will split the difference with you, but no more," Alex said in a low serious voice. "But for so much I also must know what became of him and if he is still alive, and if so, where?"

Kaminski leaned forward again. "I agree. Five hundred now, five hundred tonight, and another two thousand when I get you the information about Carter. Take it or leave it!"

"I told you I would split it with you. Twenty-five hundred."

"Then forget it and go fuck yourself," Kaminski shot back as he started to walk away.

"I agree," Alex replied.

Kaminski sat down again and poured himself another shot of vodka. "To good times," he whispered as he downed it. "Deliver the final two thousand to the name on this paper," he said putting the paper into the glass and pushing it across to Alex. "He's my brother-in-law in Moscow."

"I will do it, but one more question, some free information."

"What is it?"

"An old woman came to see me last night. I need to verify what she told me?"

"Her name?" Kaminski asked.

"Not important. She's in her mideighties and told me a strange story. She alleges that in the late 1940s she worked for twenty years near Krasnoyarsk at one of the "silent camps" nearby. She alleges there were thousands of Americans near Teya on the Velmo River. She felt sorry for them and one day she approached a group of them and asked thirteen of them to write their names and home addresses in America on a piece of paper. She smuggled the paper out of the camp and hid it beneath a floorboard of her house and forgot about it. A few years ago she recovered it and gave it to a local policeman named Vassily Bestamak. She told me she saw notices in the newspapers that the American and the Russian government were interested in hearing from anyone with evidence about missing Americans in the Gulag. Instead of getting a reward which she thought she would, she received threats against her life. A week later the local KGB office in Krasnoyarsk moved her to Novisibirsk where she now lives with her grandson. Do you know this man?"

Alex recalled from one of the TFM people in Moscow a year or so ago, that a similar incident had happened at the town of Ukhta in north central Russia near the Arctic Circle. In that case an elder Russian had also turned over the names of twenty-two Americans from the Korean War who'd written their names and addresses on some newspaper which the Russian had hidden for fifty years and then turned it over the a local Russian law enforcement official. In that case too when the American Embassy team arrived from Moscow and saw the official, he was terrified and reported it was all a mistake and he had fabricated the list. But on checking back in Washington it turned out that all of the names the old Russian had provided were in fact still 'missing in action' cases from the Korean War.

"I know of this man Bestamak of whom you speak," Kaminski replied.

"Could you find out where he is for me? I would like to talk to this Vassily Bestamak."

"When did the old woman say she gave this document to Bestamak?"

"Years ago, maybe ten or more."

Kaminski shook his head and as a troubled expression came across his face."

"What?" Alex asked.

"I believe Vassily Bestamak was reported killed in a shooting accident about that time. At least that is what I recall."

"Where?"

"In Krasnoyarsk and a reward was offered for anyone who could lead to his murderers."

"And what did this Bastamak do?"

"He was a liaison man with people you should know well. They are with your embassy in Moscow."

"Special Group-Moscow?" Alex asked with increased interest.

Kaminski shrugged, an expression of understanding on his face. There are risks. Maybe Bastamak died because of what the old woman gave him? Maybe that is why she is afraid and moved here? Do you know her name?"

"Yes," Alex replied. "But it is not important."

"If I were you I would mention it to no one. She is obviously a witness and if so, there will be those looking to silence her."

"Will you see what you can find out about him and how he died?"

"For no charge?" the Russian replied.

Alex slipped him five bills under the table.

Kaminski smiled. "I shall return for you at seven this evening," he said in an almost inaudible voice. "We will go and see a friend of mine. A word of advice to you," he said.

"No charge?" Alex inquired.

"No. Get some rest, Alex. You look like death warmed over."

* * *

That night as Alex crept beneath the covers, he was pleased with himself. Kaminski had appeared at the appointed time and taken him via a circuitous route to see an elder man by the name Tukhachevsky in the city's northern suburbs.

Tukhachevsky assured Alex he would get the information about Carter in a few weeks and would relay it to him through Kaminsky.

What had made the meeting worthwhile for Alex were three things. First the old man provided a grave report from the local area for a man named Paoulo Cater who'd once been held in the Buytenlag system. The name was similar and the old man doubted it was the same man Alex sought, but it could be, and the old man would check further. Secondly, Tukhachevsky believed the last survivors from the camp were shipped in the late 1980s to a place called Marba, nine hundred miles to the north-east on the Lena River in Siberia. At this point Kaminsky excused himself to go down the hall to urinate. Once out of the room the old man removed an envelope from his pocket and handed it to Alex and asked him not mention it to Kaminski.

"You will understand when you read it later," he said. "It is not something we Russians are proud of. There were probably five to six thousand of your American countrymen up north of here in the late 1940s. They died like flies within a few years and by the mid-1950s I doubt there were a thousand left. Many of them were executed in large numbers in mass graves, and each spring the thousands and thousands of others who'd died each winter and been stored like frozen beef in the open, were either dumped in mass graves or burned on huge funeral pyres. I recall that some of the stacks burned for days and you could smell the stench miles away." The old man speculated that from rumors he remembered in the early 1950s most of the Americans who perished north of Novisibirsk were captured from the Germans somewhere in Poland and eastern Germany. Two camp names he recalled were Stablack near Jesau and Hohenstein near Allenstein.

Alex thanked him for his candor, now understanding that Tukhachevski had personally been involved with the camps, had blood on his hands, and the nightmares old men experienced from such horrors. Tukachevski had probably witnessed spectacles which would have even sickened men like Cecil Carlo Ponti and David Lean when the conjured up scenes for the movie Doctor Zhivago. The endless columns of humanity trudging through the deep mid-winter snows toward destinations they would never reach: human rivers perishing in agony from exposure to the elements: from pneumonia, typhus, pleurisy, syphilis, starvation, cannibalism, and for those who survived, eating their own excrement. The Asiatic Steppes still howled with the demented whines of these phantoms of misery and misfortune, and Alex knew that even here in Novosibirsk, many had born witness but all were still terrified to speak about it.

* * *

Looking out over the snow covered airstrip as it flitted by the next morning, Alex smiled as the Antonov-12 turboprop climbed quickly through the pollution and emerged into bright sunlight. If he never solved the Carter and Slavchenko cases, he knew now that it might not matter. The envelope the old man gave him last night would create an incredible splash if made public in the United States.

For decades after the Second World War Washington had clearly known that thousands of its captured American servicemen were being detained in Russian camps, and that they had never been accounted for. But without proof at the time, the issue was considered a secret internal Russian/American affair which both denied. So the problem disappeared and was forgotten by the end of the 1940s.

The contents of Tukhachevski's envelope was a smoking gun.

The first document dated 1948, showed forty-seven million prisoners of all types being detained in Russia's camps when the war ended. Forty-seven million was an incredible number, which Alex knew analyst's at Defense Intelligence Agency and Central intelligence Agency might find hard to believe. Even more unbelievable would be the next to last entry on the first document. Beria's signature on it indicated 26,854 American servicemen were being secretly detained in Russia just after the war, of whom 13,022 were still alive in the Gulag in mid-1948—three years after the war had ended.

A second document dated 1960, showed a total of nine million prisoners still alive in the camps twelve years later. But there was no mention of any Americans in the second document. What had become of the thirty-eight million? What had become of the Americans? Alex assumed they'd all been worked to death? He committed the two documents to memory before concealing them in the lower hem of his overcoat. The numbers of American prisoners paled next to those of the other countries, but still, almost twenty-seven thousand Americans had been kidnapped by the Russians own admission. Might some of them still be alive today? In Alex's mind, he once again recalled the particulars of the document Tukachevsky gave him:

TOP SECRET/NKVD
(Case Alyati)
Official report forwarded to Comrade Beria

Occupants of the Gulag Camps
(At 31 August 1948)

RUSSIANS (From Western Europe)	1,853,583
RUSSIANS (From Central Europe)	3,397,663
WHITE RUSSIANS (From Southern Europe)	18,311

POLES	971,929
CZECKS	1,130,229
SLOVAKS	389,190
UKRAINIANS	3,211,139
EUROPEANS	867,610
AMERICANS	13,022 (1)
OTHERS	34,716,865 (2)
TOTAL Prisoners(3)	46,569,457 (3)

(1) NKVD records indicate the original number of American POWs liberated from Nazi prison cages and shipped via Odessa to the Gulag as of 31 July 1945, as 26,854.
(2) Suspects of anti-state activities. No documentation for imprisonment or execution required under Soviet regulations.
(3) Based on one guard per two hundred prisoners, and 239 Rubles per guard, a 1949 appropriation of 140 million rubles is requested. Comrade Beria reminds the Committee that coal, diamond and gold production for 1947 was 498 million rubles; three times the cost of operating the Gulag system. 1948 production will rise 22 percent and 1949 another 20 percent. These increases assume no budget cuts.

Two Copies: 1. to NKVD Comrade Beria
2. to Alyati File

When Alex thought about the third footnote on the second document, he wanted to laugh. Beria, as big of a son of a bitch as he was, still obviously needed to remind his boss that "their camp system business was very profitable!" The latter document from 1960 didn't specify how many Americans might still be alive, but it contained thirty four specific locations which still held nine million people. The Krasnoyarsk Administration camps of Siberia, which was where Kaminski's friend thought the survivors of Buytenlag-23V had gone when that camp closed in 1990, reflected 189,000 prison inmates in 1948; but only 12,599 in 1960.

Alex studied the desolate landscape as it drifted by. When Kaminsky had returned from his visit to the parasha last night, Tukhachevky's research suggested Paoulo Cater was Italian while his grave location, although in the record, was probably lost due to the dense forests which had reclaimed the open fields. He also repeated his belief that in any given year most of the prisoners not shot, had died during the winter months from exposure. Unable to dispose of the bodies in the permafrost they were stacked like cord wood and burned each spring. Tukachevsky had also reminded Alex that all the camps where Americans and Europeans were held, were under the exclusive control of the former MVD and not KGB. Both kept extensive records of all dispositions. At some point Alex might turn over the information to the American 'Graves Commission,' or the POW/ MIA identification group known as the Unified Missing Prisoner Command in Hawaii, and let them try to determine were the grave was and who was in it? But for the moment he was still troubled by the two documents and in a quandary as to how to proceed and who to involve?

TWO

Rosslyn

"IS THIS MR. Theodore LePage?"

"Yes. Speaking."

"We haven't met. My name's Harold Rice. I'm calling from Tampa. I'm retired here. A Mr. Alex Balkan stopped by to see me two weeks ago and asked me to call you if I heard anything."

"Sure, Mr. Rice. Alex works for me. He's out of town right now. I'll pass the information along to Alex next time he calls in. What is it?"

The retired ferry pilot explained that after Alex's visit, Rice had contacted several of his old buddies and asked them about Paul Carter. Rice explained to Ted that Carter was the name of the man who'd been aboard the Pan Am flight between Khartoum and Sri Lanka in early 1943. Ted LePage listened with mounting interest. One of Rice's buddies recalled two other civilians aboard that flight. One was an English courier whose name none of them could recall. The other man was an Irishman from a place called Shanagolden in western Ireland. The Irishman's name was Sean Inishkeen. "It's not much," Rice concluded, "but if Inishkeen is still alive, Alex should be able to find him."

"Thanks for the help, Mr. Rice."

It was the break LePage had been waiting for.

When Alex called in that afternoon, Ted told him about the call from Rice, and suggested Alex head for Ireland immediately and find out whatever he could about this guy called Inishkeen. Alex insisted he first had to see a German in Berlin.

Berlin

The red glow of the table top alarm clock LED focused his sleepy brain as Alex ran his hand across the top of the radio trying to find the off button. His brain raced into overdrive trying to determine if he'd also slept through the night and forgotten to get up for dinner the previous evening?

After a week in Novosibirsk, and then a few days in Moscow, yesterday's departure for Berlin had been a nightmare. Airline officials at Moscow's Sheremetyevo Airport had assured Alex that his ticket was good, only then to acknowledge that their computer had obviously made a mistake. His name was not on the manifest. Unable to board he'd been detained in the transit lounge until midnight when another flight had an available seat. He'd landed at Berlin's Taegel at five this morning.

He'd decided when he checked into his Berlin hotel that he would sleep through the day, have a good dinner and then turn in for the night and catch up on his sleep. He was exhausted and his body was letting him know it. Eight hours in deep sleep had left him so sluggish he had trouble struggling into the pristine German bathroom for his first hot bath since he'd left Lisbon. Feeling rejuvenated a quarter hour later, he emerged naked into the bedroom and laughed . . . realizing he had no clean clothes to wear. He doused himself with bathroom cologne and threw his most soiled clothes into a hotel laundry bag.

During his three days in Moscow he'd repeatedly visited the Ministry of Public Order, which maintained records for all citizens sentenced to prison by the Russian courts. Their records showed only twenty-eight thousand behind bars, all Russians, none of whom were located in the Novosibirsk area. Records going back more than four years the officials lamely explained, were forwarded for safekeeping to the Zelenograd archives ten miles northwest of the beltway.

At Zelenograd, Alex was assured that the idiots in Moscow didn't know what they were talking about. Nothing had been sent to them. They also pointed out that the destruction of state records was a death penalty offense. He'd known from the start it would be an unproductive effort, but he'd tried anyway.

Everywhere his reference to American prisoners had raised hackles. One department head personally escorted Alex to the front door of his Ministry and then locked the front door. Some nondescript man with the name Uripov had left a note under the door of Alex's Moscow hotel room, suggesting he call a Professor William Schenke at the Vilvoorde Institute near Brussels. Then, yesterday morning his Russian visit had ended abruptly when he'd tried to sweet talk a Russian State archivist at Podolsk into letting him look at the records for which Alex proffered a fifty dollar bill. This time armed guards escorted him the seventy miles to his Moscow hotel, informed the Hotel's reception that Mr. Balkan was leaving for the airport immediately. They'd dropped him at Sheremetyevo, warning him not to return.

Everywhere in Russia it was the same; deceit shrouded in mystery. Secrecy entombed in misinformation. Russia's history was a conundrum of shameless disregard of human rights and decency. Everyone knew about the Gulag, but no one ever asked about it. Somewhere were records that dealt with the grisly disposition of fifty million human beings. And amongst those records, if Alex ever found them, he suspected, were those dealing with the thirteen thousand Americans. Russia had signed protocols with the United Sates during the War to account for all American prisoners in their control, and to quickly arrange for their repatriation. Russia had pissed on the protocols and ignored them. She'd also signed the Hague Convention in 1954 and taken a crap on that too.

The worst mistake Alex had made before he left Moscow was to call Ted LePage. Ted had ordered him to fly immediately to Ireland. The tick in Alex's eye was his bell-weather; and it continued to remind him about the stress of travel and long days that were taking their toll. As soon as he got back to Washington he would make his report, and then take a month vacation. But first he had to see a German submarine expert here in Berlin named Erwin Bertmeir. Tomorrow morning he would see Bertmeir. After that Alex would go to Ireland.

Feeling better after the long hot shower, he went down for a German dinner of Jaegerschnitzel followed by a side order of Handkaese mit musik. Several Pils beers almost put him to sleep over dinner, and he ordered a large glass of schnapps before retiring. A quarter hour later he was asleep.

Parting the curtains the next morning Alex could barely make out the other side of the street through the heavy snow flurries whipping the street. After breakfast he took the U-Bahn to the Pankow district in the former Russian sector of East Berlin.

When he emerged above ground, unpainted buildings and peoples appearance convinced him that capitalism had still obviously not fully permeated Pankow area of the city. After a decade of capitalism, the former West Germans were furious over the huge and seemingly never-ending costs involved in reconstruction of Germany's eastern areas. The former western areas of Germany were filthy rich, and unification had solved the simple issues. Providing for their East German brothers was bad enough, but it was the minorities that were straining Germany's patience. The "untermenschen" and former "gastarbeiters" accounted for almost a fifth of Germany's people, and every small town had its immigrant ghetto's who refused to join the German mainstream.

Getting his bearings Alex headed east along the main Boulevard toward his appointment. Several ethnically attired women approached as he moved along the sidewalk but they refused to move aside. The shrouded Moslem women laughed as Alex was forced to step into the street to let them pass.

He'd read in this morning's paper, that Germany wanted to rescind citizenship for the millions who'd emigrated to Germany during the cold war. Another article reported that four hundred and eighty-three billion German marks had moved East in four years, and, another one point eight trillion would follow within a few years. A third article reported the murder of several people in a skinhead confrontation with ethnic minorities in a small town near Berlin. The article concluded that German government outlays in recent years were enough to build a new home for every man woman and child in the East.

Bertemeir's apartment building on Mertzstrasse was a six-floor walk-up, and Alex paused on the poorly lit landing to catch his breath. He traced his fingers over the outline of 2D before knocking.

"Ja. Bitte," a voice replied.

In his best German, Alex replied, "Herren Erwin Bertemeir, dist is Herr Balkan."

The door opened, and an elder man motioned him forward pointing to a room at the end of the hallway. The apartment was damp with heavy condensation on the windows while the air was permeated with the stench of stale Rothhandle cigarettes and schnapps.

"I called earlier."

"Ja, I know who you are." Bertemeir's voice was mechanical, almost robotic. "You are interested in discussing the question of submarine history? Have a seat, I'll be right with you."

Alex suspected Bertemeir was no simpleton. For years Bertemier had obviously stood in the shadows and was now about to be shunted into retirement. He'd worked in section B-3 of Germany's Maritime Ministry, which after reunification, was incorporated within the new Ministry of Interior. Prior to unification, B-3 kept all of East Germany's still secret wartime records. In fact Bertemier's section had actually been a part of the Fifth Bureau of East Germany's Ministry for State Security.

Alex would not come right out and ask the old man to commit espionage, but would lead him around to the subject. Then it would be up to the old man to take the bait and make the first move. "Herr Bertmeir, you were once considered to be, how should I say, an expert on certain aspects of the Third Reich's U-Boat war?"

"Ja, thank you for the compliment. It has been many years now."

"I am interested in certain U-Boats from the war years."

"I see. There are excellent documentaries available in the West," the German replied. "You are familiar with them?"

"Yes, I am."

"And it was not there?"

"No."

"How can I help you then?"

"Certain missing documents. I believe some of the histories are incomplete."

"Incomplete?"

"Correct."

"I see. Incomplete because they are . . . , ahh . . . missing or . . . possibly unavailable?"

"Both!" Alex replied. "Probably because the Russians may have captured them." Alex would blame it on the Russians and see if Bertemier disputed it. "I thought you, as former chief of section B-3, and still associated with them through volunteer work, might be able to . . . aaahh, shed some light on the problem? In other words, might the documents still be available?"

"You could make an official request through the Ministry of Interior." Bertemier observed, "This would be the correct way."

"Of course. This is true," Alex replied. "But I believe it would needlessly consume valuable time."

"An official request would only require a few weeks."

"It's not the point."

"Why is that?" the German asked.

"Because they would not reply favorably." Alex watched him for a moment, hoping his meaning would be obvious.

"I see," the German replied after a pause. Bertmeir obviously appeared to have understood his meaning.

"Of course," Alex continued, "I would be willing to make it worth your while. I mean for whatever time you might devote to it." Phase one of ten, Alex thought. Now he'd find out if the old man would to do it for money?

"You are referring to things which might be, ahhhhh, difficult?"

"Correct." Alex observed with his most congenial expression.

"And you assume I might be able to obtain it?"

Alex's palms opened. "Of course. You have followed developments in the submarine business?"

"Ja," the German replied, "Of course! We were good and we're still the best!"

Alex waited. He wasn't certain how far the old man would go, so he waited while he rambled about various immaterial aspects of the submarine business, probably in an attempt to fill the vacuum while he tried to figure out how deeply he wanted to get involved with this American. "Only nuclear boats can stay down longer than ours," Bertmeir concluded with obvious pride, "but they are noisier and easier to find, and of course ours are only a tenth the cost. The German Type 209 today is superior to anything out there. At eighteen hundred tons, it carries 14 torpedoes, and with a single propeller, runs submerged for four hundred nautical miles at 23 knots. It can also stay down for five days which is a significant improvement in the 'indiscretion ratio.'"

"Excuse me?" Alex asked. "What is that?"

"They're vulnerable when at or just below the surface, which is indiscreet to do while on patrol, because satellites can detect them, but only when they are within a hundred feet of the surface and moving at four knots."

Alex didn't really care about the technicalities but the old man was obviously warming to the discussion "How?" Alex asked with sincere interest.

The old man went into another monologue about the concept of inverse footprints and pressure waves and surface cones, such as trailed behind aircraft in flight or submarines on the move. In the case of a submarine, minute bulges in the surface above, were imperceptible to the naked eye, but satellites could detect such minute changes, exposing course and speed. Bertemeir stopped. "But I ramble about incidentals. You had specific questions?"

"I'm interested in U-Boats around Florida early in the last war?"

"I see." Bertemier paused for a few moments. "How did you get my name?"

"Does it make any difference?"

"You're American?"

"Of course."

"May I see some documents?"

Alex dropped his Diplomatic Passport on the table and waited as the old man thumbed through it.

"This matter is intelligence related?"

"Does that matter either?" Alex inquired evasively, waiting while the German decided how to proceed.

"You are with the CIA?"

"Yes," Alex lied.

"What specifically do you want?"

"U-Boat records not available in the West because the Russians got to them first after the war."

"Such as?" the German inquired.

"U-Boats unaccounted for after the war."

The old man said nothing, obviously waiting for Alex to continue. Alex knew that the Russians had shared what they'd found with the East Germans after the war. He also knew that about two weeks after Germany's surrender, a meeting had taken place in Moscow, between the American Secretary of State, Henry Hopkins, and Joseph Stalin. At that meeting Stalin's notorious security chief, Laventri Beria, had admitted that Russia knew about several U-Boats which were then still at sea, and had no intention of surrendering because they carried cargoes of stolen gold and precious stones to provide for certain Germans after the war. Stalin later denied discussing any of this with Hopkins. The United States knew that the Russians had learned about the still missing U-Boats through document exploitation.

"I'm not certain," Alex lied, waiting for the German to pick up the obvious trail he'd already alluded too.

"Not certain about what Mr. Balkan . . . if they were missing or if they were unaccounted for?"

It seemed as if Bertemier would need more coaxing, or maybe would respond to an offer of money. But Alex didn't want to raise the issue of a bribe until the German raised it first. He decided he'd change the approach slightly. "Both," Alex said. "What can you tell me about U-Boat operations in Florida?"

"What period?"

"February 1942," Alex replied.

The old man smiled. Alex realized the date obviously meant something as Bertemier nodded his head, "I think I understand." He chuckled to himself and said something in German.

"Is there something I said which is humorous?" Alex inquired.

"Maybe. As I recall there were about nineteen U-Boats along the East coast at the time you mentioned."

"And those south of Miami?"

"Mmmm, maybe four, certainly not more than five."

"You recall their hull-numbers?"

"I recall three. The U-156 was in transit to the Caribbean and the other two were on patrol in the Florida Straits . . . U-128 and U-584."

"What about the last two?"

Bertemiers reaction was slow at first and then a quizzical expression developed and he smiled. "Now I think I know what it is you are looking for."

"Good. I don't know myself, so tell me."

"Why not."

Alex waited but Bertmeir didn't continue and just stared back.

"I'm sorry?" Alex finally inquired.

"There's a question of remuneration, Mr. Balkan." Bertemier observed caustically.

Now that it was out in the open, Alex felt better and suspected the visit would be productive. "You had a number in mind?"

"Ja! What about one-thousand Euro's?"

"Agreed, if you give me everything I need?"

"The first U-Boat was on patrol while the second . . . , the U-584 was dropping agents."

"Off Jacksonville. This much we already know," Alex replied. "Please continue."

"Jacksonville was a diversion," the German shot back. "She made two drops, a four man team near Jacksonville on the night of 19 February 1942 which you obviously know about. But then she continued south and dropped four more inside the reef near Key West."

Now Alex was surprised. But he wasn't about to confirm what he'd already learned in Key West. "And their purpose?"

"Sleepers."

"I see." Alex recalled Kate Rheiner telling him about the retired English ship captain, and the old hermit with all the money, and the three skeletons near Big Pine Key. "Tell me Herr Bertmeier, did the group put ashore near Key West have American dollars with them?"

"That's a strange question?"

"Did they?" Alex repeated.

"Yes, of course. How would they get around if they didn't?"

"Do you recall how much?"

"Why do you ask? What's its import?" the German asked.

"I'm just curious?"

"Is this about counterfeit money?" Bertemier asked with a smile now beginning to cover his face.

"No," Alex replied. "Some of it was found, but it is not the reason for my question.

"They carried about forty thousand," Bertemier replied. "As best I can remember it was in tens, twenties and about half in one hundred dollar notes."

"Thanks," Alex replied. "Do you recall what happened to the second group?"

"There were problems. As far as we know they drowned"

"Why?"

"The U-Boat came under fire from a shore battery and was forced to submerge, leaving not only the four agents, but five of her crew in the water. I looked into it further after the war, but was never able to find out anything about the incident."

"Then how do you know they died?" Alex asked.

A conspiratorial expression crossed the old man's face and he shrugged.

"Herr Bertemeir, you mean to tell me you never found out?"

"Of course, but not until long after the war. You see, the U-Boat waited outside the reef for two days, hoping to recover any of her crew who might still be in the water, but some U.S. Navy ships appeared and dropped depth charges, so a week later her captain decided to return to Germany. Almost three decades passed before I was asked about it again," Bertemier continued, now with a noticeable change in his voice. "It was just after the Berlin Wall came down. Washington informed Berlin they were deporting three Germans. All of them had been held incommunicado since their capture in 1942. They were our agents dropped near Key West who we thought were dead. In 1952 my boss asked me to see if I could find out what happened to them, and a few months later I learned that three bodies had been found near Bahia Honda during the war and I assumed they were our men. They obviously were not, but we closed their files. It was from these three that we learned what had really happened."

"Why did we hold them incommunicado for so long?"

"Don't know. No one ever told them, or us."

Alex recalled the three skeletons at the old hermits place. "So who were the three bodies found in the Keys?"

"No idea," the German replied.

"And the fourth person?" Alex inquired. "Is he still alive?"

"Maybe . . . maybe not."

"Who would know?"

"My old superior, but he may not want to help you."

"Where is he?"

"What about another thousand Euro?" the German suggested.

"Fifteen hundred is my limit," Alex replied.

"Okay! He's north of here. On the Baltic coast. His name is Untermann. I have his address and phone number somewhere. I will find it and give it to you in a moment."

"What did Untermann do?"

"He worked in Branch 1 of Abwehr, special agent operations."

"So he knew about all the teams."

"Undoubtedly."

"Have you ever heard the name Paul Carter?"

"No. In what respect?"

"Forget it. One last request? Could you ask around and see if you could find production records for parts placed aboard certain U-Boats."

"Some might still exist. Which parts?"

"A propeller produced by Eisener Gessellschaft." Alex wrote down the production date and serial number of the propeller he'd seen in the canal at Boca Chica and handed it to Bertemier.

Ireland

Shanagolden lay twenty miles from Limerick on Ireland's southwest coast. At eight hundred feet above the bay, it afforded residents a spectacular view of the Shannon estuary and the Airport to the northeast. The area had a quaint impoverished look about it. Lots of weathered stone and badly worn thatched roofs dotted the landscape while the town itself was a compact assembly of field stone buildings, most of which bore newly thatched roofs. A quarter mile up a narrow road stood a lone building whose postbox bore the inscription Sean Angles Inishkeen, Esquire.

A decrepit-looking man with opaque skin, sunken cheeks and several teeth missing, answered the door, sneezing repeatedly into a filthy handkerchief as Alex waited to introduce himself. The old man had no phone, so Alex's visit was unexpected. The old man lived alone and appeared pleased to have a visitor.

As it turned out, old man Inishkeen was once an operative in Her Majesty's intelligence service and had retired in 1972 after a long and interesting career. Since then he didn't appear to have done much. From a pub in town, Alex learned the old man was gone most of the time and always returned with a good suntan—Spanish sun the bar—keeper confided.

Inishkeen's Shanagolden residence was not ostentatious, but its cobweb-covered appointments bespoke a long career outside the UK; fine Nain carpets from Iran, silver Khanjars from the Hadramaut and a faded silk screen of elephants and bearers from India or northern Pakistan, and sprinkled amongst these, a melange of silver and gold artifacts, most blackened from tarnish. The house was in need of good cleaning.

Following his graduation from Eton, Inishkeen had offered his services to Her Majesty's Government. The son of a Dublin barrister who'd himself spent his youth in Asia; Sean Inishkeen possessed a keen interest in the Orient, and because of his international experience and language capabilities, on joining the government, was immediately offered work in intelligence. His first assignment was a place outside London—Bletchley Park. Britain was about to make war on the Hun in 1939, and young Sean's bent for analysis, languages, and puzzles, was quickly put to good use at Bletchly Park, where he tinkered with German and Japanese cyphers until the summer of 1942. Then he was ordered to New York, and a few months later, to Canada, for special "secret agent" training with the Yanks.

"Mind if I ask what kind?" Alex interjected.

"Not at all. The forerunner of your CIA . . ."

Alex had just learned another piece of the puzzle, and made a note to find out if Carter had also worked for the OSS?

"May I ask what the exact nature of your interests are Mr. Balkan?"

"A Pan Am flight to Ceylon in early 1943. It's my understanding, you were aboard that flight."

"Correct."

"So you knew an American aboard the flight named Paul Carter?"

The old man's demeanor changed but only for an instant. "Yes, I knew Paul Carter. The bloke attended the same OSS class with me in Canada. Mind you, I didn't think he was so good. Why do you ask about him?"

Alex assured him it was in reference to a sighting of Carter almost two decades ago in Russia. It was a loose end Alex which was trying to tie up, and it appeared the American had died somewhere in the Russian prison system long after the war.

"I didn't care for Carter," the Irishman observed. "Maybe if he had not been a U.S. Marine it would have been different."

"Carter was a marine?"

"Yes," Inishkeen continued. "When I met him he'd recently been discharged. At least that is what I was led to believe. For all I know he might still have been on active service and merely documented as a civilian. You know, . . . as a spy."

"And you didn't care for him?"

"He was an arrogant young puppy who granted, appeared to have done some fascinating things, but he liked to tell you about it."

Alex waited, hoping the old man would continue the data dump because he was filling in huge gaps in the story. "Carter had spent four years in China and the Philippines before I met him. He spoke excellent Chinese. That much I know for certain, because I too had gone to a Chinese school when I lived in Shanghai as a school boy, and Carter's command of the language was superior to mine. He supposedly also knew your president quite well. Carter thought highly of himself too because of it. I suspect it was the president who got him into the OSS. I can see from your expression Mr. Balkan that you didn't know most of this?"

Again Alex shook his head as Inishkeen went on to explain how he'd waited around in Ceylon for almost two weeks for Carter to return from his mission to northern Burma. And when he didn't, it became apparent that something had gone amiss and London ordered Inishkeen to go and find Carter. But he never had.

"So when was the last time you saw Carter?"

"End of January 1943," Inishkeen observed.

"Who else was aboard the flight to Ceylon?"

"Aside from the air crew, only three, myself, an English bloke named Jack Horner who was a courier, and Carter."

Alex made a note of Horner's name. "How did you get to the rendezvous in the Sudan?"

Inishkeen stood up and motioned for Alex to follow him to a window. "Right down there."

"I'm sorry, I don't follow," Alex observed, studying the large estuary below.

"I was picked up down there up by a Royal Air Force Sutherland flying boat and flown to Liberia. From Liberia I caught a hop with a Yank transport plane across the Sahara to Basrah in southern Iraq. The transport landed near Khartoum where Carter's flying boat was waiting for me in the Nile River." Inishkeen laughed. "Jesus, think of it. So much time has passed and you tracked me here. You must be with the CIA?"

"No."

"No? With whom then? And what do you really want, Mr. Balkan?"

"Pardon me?"

"What's this really about? "How could this man have been reported alive in a Russian prison camp almost forty years later?"

"That is what I am trying to learn, Mr. Inishkeen?"

"I doubt it," Inishkeen replied.

As Alex studied the old man, Inishkeen's mind seemed to be drifting. The pace of the conversation had probably exhausted the old man. Alex suspected the old man might be gathering his thoughts. "I spoke with someone a few years ago," Alex replied, "who swears they saw Carter alive."

"I see," the old man replied as if in a trance, and he seemed to drift into sleep for a moment. His head nodded off to the side.

"Mr. Inishkeen." The old man had obviously dozed off.

* * *

The war years were a time Sean Inishkeen frequently wished he could relive. He'd flown across the Atlantic repeatedly and also into Africa and South America, and this time into Ceylon off the southern tip of India. Once again Sean recalled of the morning he stood on the spacious flight deck of the flying boat as it floated in the huge anchorage of Tricomallee in 1943. He'd always loved airplanes.

"Mr. Inishkeen," the flying boat captain said, "if you would kindly stand there against the bulkhead while we complete the preflight checklist."

"Certainly!" He loved watching the drama.

"Right and left outboard wing tanks?" The captain called to the first officer.

"Four hundred fifty gallons indicated, sir. I also verified it with the fuel probe."

"Very well, and the main wing tanks?"

"Gauge indicates full also."

"What about the main fuselage tank?"

"One thousand nine hundred gallons indicated."

"Make a note, engineer, if temperature exceeds ninety degrees before takeoff tomorrow, we download one hundred gallons."

"Yes, sir."

"What's the reading for the main oil reserve tank?"

"Three hundred fifty gallons."

Four minutes later, they were done. "Very well," the captain said. "That completes the checklist." He arose and turned. "Gentlemen, with the exception of the radio operator and Mr. Inishkeen, would everyone please go below." Once they were alone, the captain moved to the radio operators desk at the rear of the flight deck. "Is this the latest transmission you received from Australia?" he asked.

"Yes," the radio operator replied, "if you'll verify the decode which I and Mr. Inishkeen made earlier, I think you'll find its accurate."

The radio operator placed the pad before the captain. It bore the inscription: Top Secret. Property of U.S. Navy. Wireless Codes for 10 Jan 1943 to 20 February 1943. Special Mission—69. He checked it against the decrypted message.

> TOP SECRET
> From SPA/A/-Zenith.
> Msg No 22/A-17C
>
> Upon receipt of this transmission, wait twenty four hours due to bad weather en route. Depart on 29 January 1943 with Wedemeyer and staff for Perth, Australia. Refuel at Cocos Islands. Repeat, refuel at Cocos. No fuel available at Exmouth Gulf.
>
> Zenith sends.

He handed it to the radio operator. "Destroy it," the captain ordered. "Well, Inishkeen, it seems you will be leaving finally."

"Not I, Captain, I must remain here."

"Your superiors in London are aware of this?"

"Yes, Captain."

"I see." The captain toggled two rows of switches to the off position, noting each of the fuel and battery gauges as they dropped to zero. Picking up the log book he checked the calendar, then signed and dated the log. "Okay, let's head for shore."

Since they'd arrived two weeks ago, the captain suspected a high level meeting must be in the offing somewhere in Asia. What other reason was there for the huge British fleet anchored here at Tricomallee; the presence of General Wedemeyer and his staff, and the Pan American flying boat sitting around doing nothing? Captain Baslund's chief worry, aside from the Japanese nearby, was the humidity. It was Monsoon time in south India, and between the never-ending rain squalls and intense heat, everything aboard his aircraft was damp and corroding.

His mission to Ceylon had begun fifty-five days ago on 4 December 1942. Baslund had been visited at La Guardia Field on Long Island, by a young Army Colonel from Washington. The Colonel asked him and his boss to close the door to their office and to sign secrecy statements. Then he'd opened his leather case and withdrew a Top Secret document.

Four of Pan American World Airways Boeing B-314A's were to be made available for a mission. Two aircraft would be at Miami on January 11, a third at Bahrain in the Persian Gulf, on January 12, and a fourth in Ceylon, on January 14. Baslund was to personally see to the details and the aircrews involved were to be told nothing. Nothing was to be written down about any of this. None of the aircraft were to break radio silence outside the United States, and all aircraft were to rely only on their own on-board navigation equipment. The purpose of the mission was also unstated.

After Bahrain, Baslund suspected that the delivery of the mysterious boxes aboard his aircraft was the purpose of his portion of the mission. Now he wondered if the whole mission might have been a feint for events elsewhere? Maybe President Roosevelt was already in Australia and General Wedemeyer was to join him? He turned to the radio operator as they neared shore. "Double check for incoming messages every two hours. Get provisions too from the commissary." He looked at Inishkeen, "You ready to meet General Wedemeyer?"

"Yes. I am."

Ashore, a Royal Navy launch waited to take them back into the anchorage where the huge silhouette of the flagship, HMS Rodney ominously darkened the horizon. Once aboard Baslund would raise the question of his 'no-show' passengers with the General, and their departure tomorrow. On the inbound flight to Ceylon, the other B-314 captain in Bahrain had confided to Baslund that Inishkeen had literally hijacked his plane at Damietta, in the Nile River delta. Another British flying boat there had been damaged and couldn't take off until repairs were made. So His Majesty's government urgently needed to borrow the American flying boat. Inishkeen presented orders from Cairo, authorizing the British aircrew to commandeer the Pan American Clipper, and an hour later it left with an all British crew.

At three the next morning the flying boat returned to Damietta. Baslund heard its engines overhead and became apprehensive when he realized the British intended to land it in the dark. Flares were placed in the river and Baslund's airplane miraculously landed in one piece. The British crew seemed ebullient as the aircraft was refueled. Baslund had to admit the Limeys had guts. Then they ordered Baslund to leave immediately for Bahrain. A brief argument ensued regarding the weight of the cargo the British had placed on-board. With a full load of fuel Baslund was concerned he might not be able to get the Clipper out of the water. The British told him either he flew it out, or, they would do it for him. The rest of Baslund's trip to Ceylon was uneventful.

Approaching Rodney, Baslund could tell she'd seen hard service. Battle damage was evident, and rust streaked her gray paint everywhere. The first thing he saw as they reached the top of the boarding stairs was her polished brass commissioning plaque.

H.M.S. Rodney

Displacement: 38,000 tons
Keel Laid down 1923, commissioned 17 December 1925
Length 702 feet OA, Beam 106 feet, Draught 30 feet
Complement 1361

> Second of two battleships designed by Sir E. Tennyson D'Eyncourt while D.N.C. Main armament forward, and arrangement of three triple turrets and nine 18 inch guns, complies with 1918 treaty limits not to exceed 38,000 gross tons.

At thirty-eight thousand tons, she was among Britain's largest and most unusual in layout. Three massive gun turrets forward, the middle towering on a pedestal above the other two—allowed all three to focus simultaneously on a single target; against which, nine eighteen-inch barrels could hurl eighteen tons of armor piercing explosives to a distance of twenty miles. Baslund wondered what would happen if she were surprised from behind by one of the new Jap dreadnoughts? With no large-caliber guns at her rear, she'd have no option but to turn and fight.

He mentioned this to the captain who bragged of Rodney's contribution to the recent demise of Bismark. Rodney had pursued the Kraut battleship for four days only to lose Bismark when HMS Hood exploded. But Rodney caught up with Bismark again a day later; and exchanged volleys for two hours until the German's forward section glowed red from internal fires, and each time Bismark's bow went into the waves, she was enveloped in clouds of steam.

"We taught the Hun a lesson that day by God!" The British captain observed haughtily, "We lost 1,500 aboard Hood and the Hun lost 2,100 when Bismark joined her in Davey Jones's locker."

It wasn't until Rodney's captain described the physics of projectiles in flight to the Pan American captain that Inishkeen appreciated the futility of all war. At 3,700 feet per second, with two thousand pounds of hi-explosive, each two ton projectile penetrated seven feet of reinforced steel plate before detonation. Rodney's thickest armor was only three feet while Japan's latest models had four.

"So, Baslund," the captain continued, "if you and Mr. Inishkeen will follow me, we'll proceed to the mess for a spot of port with the admiral and General Wedemeyer. And then some lunch. Eh . . . what?"

After toasts to His Majesty and Roosevelt, Wedemeyer asked Baslund if he'd received a message.

"Yes, sir, we leave at 0600 in the morning."

* * *

"Mr. Inishkeen?" Alex repeated insistently, gently shaking the old man's shoulder. "Mr. Inishkeen . . . are you all right? What became of Paul Carter, or . . . the courier?"

"You already asked me that!" Inishkeen replied, now completely lucid and wondering why the American had been shaking him. "What is it that you really want to know? You realize that under the British Secrecy Act; there are many things I cannot divulge?"

"But it was fifty years ago, sir. Will anyone really care?"

Inishkeen guffawed. "My dear boy!" He exclaimed in a loud patronizing voice. "I am always amazed by you Yanks! You hold nothing sacred, do you?"

"Can't you bend the rule a little?"

"Absolutely not! But if you want to tell me what you know, Mr. Balkan, maybe I can fill in some of the gaps for you."

"Whatever you can, would be most helpful," Alex replied in an expectant voice. "Two Pan American flying boats were assigned to transport Roosevelt to Casablanca; they were mission numbers seventy one and seventy two. Was your flight to Ceylon ever referred to as Mission sixty-nine or seventy?"

Inishkeen smiled and shrugged. "It sounds logical enough, doesn't it?"

"But am I correct?"

"Maybe." He nodded his head in affirmation.

"Okay. What happened after Khartoum?"

"We proceeded north to Damietta, it's a small truly dismal place in the Nile Delta where the water is filthy, the food abominable, the bugs horrible, and the locals stink like rotten Stilton cheese. We refueled at Damietta, then proceeded across Arabia to Bahrain. In those days Bahrain should have been called mozzyville. The bloody mosquitoes were as bloody thick as flies on a wogs ass. We changed aircraft there and proceeded the next day on to Ceylon."

"In another flying boat?" Alex inquired. "That could have been the fourth airplane?"

"I suppose. It was a B-314."

"What was the cargo loaded aboard at Damietta?"

Inishkeen looked surprised. "Did I say we took on cargo?"

"I thought you did. Didn't you?"

The old man looked perplexed for a moment. "I'm certain I did not say that."

Alex decided to press his luck. "Are you certain? I thought you did."

"I'd rather not say," Inishkeen replied, his eyes now boring into Alex's in a suspicious manner which left little doubt in Alex's mind that the old codger had almost been tripped up and was now suspicious and probably annoyed.

"Okay." Alex continued, "Why did Wedemeyer hang around in Ceylon for so long?"

"I don't really know. There was a rumor he was to fly to Cairo to meet with FDR, but of course he never did." He stood up and stretched, arranging his shirt cuffs as he moved into the kitchen. "What about a spot of tea?" he asked as he turned on the gas stove.

Alex sat and thought while the old man made tea noises in the kitchen. Maybe now was the time? Alex would trade secret for secret. It was worth a try. "I wasn't going to tell you this, Mr. Inishkeen, and it must be kept strictly between us."

The Irishman's head poked around the kitchen door. "You have my word," he whispered with a devilish smile. "I knew there was more to you than you'd told me at the outset."

Alex joined him in the kitchen and gave him an abbreviated version of what Alex had learned so far about the Slavchenko woman's murder in Washington and her meeting with the man named Paul Carter near Novosibirsk in the early 1980s.

"An astonishing story," the Irishman replied as he poured tea. "I would not have wished such a fate on anyone."

As Alex drove back toward the airport, he knew that seeing Inishkeen had been a complete waste of time. The old man obviously knew more than he'd let on, but had not reciprocated as Alex had hoped. The only new piece of evidence Inishkeen had surrendered was that the Ceylon cargo consisted of ninety-two wooden crates, each weighing fifty kilos. Their contents—unknown.

Bansin, Germany

Portugal, Novisibirsk, Berlin, Ireland, and now the tiny town of Bansin along the Baltic coast of Germany. The travel was starting to take its toll. Before he'd left Moscow the tick in his eye had reappeared; brought on he knew by the cumulative effects of poor sleep, exhaustion, and stress. He'd slept well last night and already felt better. An immaculately coifed waiter in black trousers with a white apron inquired if Alex wanted more coffee. He signaled a refill.

The temperature outside hovered just below freezing and the wind reduced the chill factor to around five above zero. Snow whipped in through the dark gray background concealing the Baltic, whose crashing waves along the nearby breakwater created a constant roar. The streets of Bansin were deserted, the town looked as though it were lifeless. A black and white snapshot of a cold midwinter night in the Arctic.

He'd planned to see Bertemier's ex-boss before he'd flown off to Ireland. Now he would close the loop and find out what Uli Untermann knew about the German team which had landed sixty years ago in the Florida Keys.

Usedom, the spit of land on which Bansin stood: according to the slick Teutonic travel brochures on the table before Alex, was a prodigy of the so-called Vistular Glacial Period. The most recent ice age which bulldozed up the three gravel bars, which today bore the names of three islands just off Germany's north coast, Rugen, Usedom, and Wholin. The brochure contained the usual German detail about the mundane. "Usedom,' it proclaimed, "is a quaint out of the way place, which obtained recognition even in Roman times for its Amber. Phyleas of Massilia in AD 350 referred to Usedomians as the Goths of the Sinus Venedicus because they'd refused Christianity until the fourteenth century. After that the Islands remained an obscure place until the twentieth century when Berlin's "haute vole" made Usedom their summer vacation place!"

Jesus! Alex thought. Who gave a goddamn? The place had probably always been a barren icebox! As he watched the low scudding clouds over the gray landscape, and spindrift sailing through the air above the nearby breakwater, he supposed it was the weather which made everything appear so depressing. The place was cold, damp, white and lifeless.

Two hours later he stood in the screaming winds roaring off the slate gray seascape, waiting for someone to answer the door of the sea-front cottage. The German he'd come to see lived twenty yards from the break-water in Bansin, and when the door finally opened a crack, a nondescript man stared back at him; just over five feet, corpulent, with thick black hair stinking of shoe polish. The German pulled his black leather coat off a peg in the hallway, and insisted they walk around the corner to a bar where they could talk over lunch—and that Alex was to pay for it.

The German said that Bertemeir had called already. So Alex wasted no time inquiring about the four agents at Key West. But Uli Untermann preferred small talk, avoiding Alex's demands for instant information. Alex suspected the old bastard was starved for companionship and had few visitors. Bansin was the type of place where anyone used to big city life would quickly go crazy. As lunch came and went, Untermann loosened up with repeated refills of beer. Around two o'clock Alex began glancing at his watch. "Time is passing," Alex observed. "Carter . . . ?"

"Yes," the German replied, "my associate said you asked about him? I haven't heard that name for a long time?"

"You knew him?"

"I knew of him. But he died during the war."

"Maybe not," Alex replied. "He was seen in a Russian camp in the early eighties."

"So I was told by Bertemier. Amazing! Who told you this?"

"An eye witness!"

"Truly amazing

"What do you mean by that, Herr Untermann?"

"Mr. Balkan, you are familiar with the 'Gauk-Behorde' legislation?"

"No!"

"You should be!"

"What is it?"

"My American friend . . . people should not be asked to place themselves in danger. Especially little fish being hunted by sharks! Americans think they have a right to know everything about each other, their neighbors, friends, and those they do not like."

"Are you a little fish being hunted by sharks? Alex asked sarcastically."

"Maybe," the German replied.

"And who are these sharks you refer too?"

"Those for whom we once maintained files. The Gauk Behorde legislation is named after Jaochim Gauk, who used to be a Lutheran pastor from Rostock! His legislation protects all of us from our past! Perhaps you were aware that hundreds of thousands of dossiers were maintained by the former East German Ministry for State Security or MfS and Stassi as you Americans used to call it!"

"Yes, I did." Alex knew that the MfS was one of the most aggressive security services in the cold war era, even surpassing the Russians and Chinese in the depth and scope of secret files they kept on almost seven and a half million people.

"Well you see, my friend," Untermann continued, "now everyone in Germany wants to know if there was a secret file on them. And if so, what does it say? So what you ask puts me at risk!"

"Herr Untermann, are you telling me a file exists for Carter?"

"I cannot say!"

"Cannot, or will not?"

"Cannot."

"What do you want?" Suspecting it might boil down to money, Alex wanted to find out how much? If the German wanted to be paid for what he knew, which Alex was almost certain of, he could arrange it. One of the briefings Alex had received in Washington before leaving for Europe, had covered developments within the German intelligence structure since unification. It had also addressed the new German Erkennungsdienst, Leidstelle and Mordkommission, organizations which were now tasked to provide personnel to the Kriminalamt and Abteilung—for the purification of the former East German intelligence services. Few of the former 2.2 million East Germans who'd committed criminal acts under West German law, had yet been called to account, and hundreds of thousands of Germans were still hiding anonymously in the former East German files, behind cryptonyms such as Maximillian, Czerny, and Tilly.

Some of them had been unmasked, but the work would take forever. Alex knew for example that Maximillian was Ibrahim Boehm—the founding father of the former West German Socialist SPD Party, and its first chairman after the collapse of East Germany. Czerny on the other hand was Helmut Kohl's deputy, and Chairman of the Christian Democratic Union. No one yet knew who Tilly was, but from his dossier, his position was obviously so prominent in the German government that it was only a question of time before he too would be exposed. Alex wondered what Untermann's pseudonym was, and what sins his file harbored? He studied the old man, trying to decide how much would be required to bribe him.

"I want two things," the German replied, "your silence and ten thousand euros."

"Silence is no problem. But you ask a considerable amount. More than I can give."

"The information is worth even more!"

"Why?"

"You will see."

"Not good enough . . . not for that much!"

"I am a reasonable man. You can agree to my demand after I've told you what I know. Would that make you more comfortable?"

"No commitment?"

"I'll trust you."

"Okay, I accept."

"There are several things," Untermann observed, "I think you would be interested in. One obviously is the Key West survivor. Then there's the Caballero bullion." He held up his hand to the bartender. "Zwei mal Bier, Bitte!" Then he turned back to Alex. "Of the four who came ashore that night near Key West, only one survived."

"But your associate in Berlin," Alex interrupted, "informed me the United States held four at the end of the war."

Untermann laughed at the comment. "It is why you are paying me so well my dear friend." He repeatedly patted Alex's arm reassuringly. "They were crewmen. The United States offered them citizenship . . .

and certain other rewards, in return for their silence about the attempted Key West landing."

Alex's face remained deadpan.

"I'll come back to this in a moment," Unterman continued. "First let me tell you about Carter. I recall him in reference to an operation we conducted during the war. He was with your State Department, and known to your president, who picked him up at Key West and traveled with him as far as the African coast. From there he went to China where he unfortunately met with an untimely end."

"Why?" Already Alex was amazed at how much the German knew and suspected he was going to amaze Alex even more.

"The entire operation was a set-up."

"He was deliberately betrayed?" Alex inquired.

"Yes," the old man replied casually, thanking the waiter for the new beer delivery with which he offered yet another *prosit* to Alex before draining away a quarter of the mug. "How much was involved?" Alex asked.

"The equivalent of thirty-eight million Reichmark."

"Clear up a point for me, Herr Untermann? Why were Germany and the United States cooperating, when our two countries were at war?"

"That I do not know. But who cares? It is what you will eventually find out I assume! And in the interim, I will tell you who I knew to have been involved. Himmler, he was involved, and one did not ask Himmler why. Goering too was involved, and no one asked him about it either. I also know that one of our U-Boats made a rendezvous with an American flying boat off Cyprus, and this is where some of the gold was transferred. We also knew the gold's ultimate destination, and betrayed the secret, so that the cargo was diverted."

"To whom?" Alex inquired.

"Back to those who gave it to them."

"So you got the gold back?"

"Not me." Untermann raised his glass again and rolled his eyes as he drank deeply from the mug. *Prosit.* "Himmler and Goering did I suppose. But who knows for certain? Were you able to follow this so far?"

"I think so."

"Interesting, *nicht wahr*?"

Alex nodded.

"Excellent!" The German rubbed his palms in anticipation. "You see, there was some kind of an agreement between Hitler and the British, I never got the details and can only guess. I know America was involved also because the plane which arrived off Cyprus was a Pan American seaplane, which had a British crew aboard. Also aboard the airplane were Carter and two Englishmen."

"Do you know their names?" Now he understood why Inishkeen had been reluctant about details. Inishkeen obviously knew all about the conspiracy. Hell, Inishkeen had also been aboard the aircraft.

"No," Uli replied.

"Herr Unterman, do you know where the gold is today?"

Uli laughed. "If I knew that, . . . do you think I would be here talking to you."

"What about the man who delivered it?"

Uli shrugged.

"Why should I believe any of this?"

"Because my dear American friend, you are paying me handsomely for it."

"But can you prove any of this?"

"Over sixty years later? Who even cares? It was a long time ago."

"I must have proof. Are there others who can corroborate anything you have told me?"

"Unfortunately they are all dead. But unlike people who have a short life span, documents survive longer. You ever heard of Case Judy?"

"No."

"Check it out!"

"Where?"

"After all this time, how should I know? Washington I suppose. But if I were you, I would be very, very careful when you do it."

"What does it have to do with?"

"A dark secret which should not be disturbed, even by you."

"Who's involved?" Alex insisted.

"It deals with what I have been telling you. The Third Reich, America, Britain, the Russians, and God knows who else."

"Case Judy?"

The old German nodded his head slowly. "It is a dirty dark secret of the worst kind."

"Okay. What about the person who survived at Key West?"

"First let me finish with the question of the bullion. There were a total of four shipments. The first, which I have already mentioned. A second was made five months before the war ended but was sunk by a British submarine off the Norwegian coast. One of these days her case will become better known once someone gets around to looking into her cargo."

"Meaning?" Alex inquired.

"In addition to the bullion aboard," Untermann continued, "was seventy tons of mercury. It is a very toxic substance and the wreckage of the submarine now lies in about five hundred feet of water off Norway's second largest city. It will become an environmental disaster when its containers eventually begin to leak into the water at the wreck site."

"And the third?"

"It was the U-864 which was destined for Japan with technology for jet engines and missile technology and guidance system data. The British Code Breakers figured out her route and had her intercepted. She was sunk in February 1945."

"And what is unusual about her cargo?" Alex tried to sound interested.

"It was one of Hitler's ideas and known as ERR, which stood for *Einsatzstab Reichleiter Rosenberg.*"

Alex made a mental note of the acronym. "It's significance?" he asked.

"Hitler, Goering and Himmler's little war-time ring of stolen art and treasures from across Europe, all taken back to Germany, sorted, documented, and stored away. Some of it was laid aside for certain Nazi's postwar personal convenience. As the war ended some 350 Americans were assigned to Washington's Monument Commission and spent years trying to find everything the Nazis stole in Western Europe. Probably eighty percent of it was found and eventually returned to its rightful owners. The Russians too had their search teams . . . their Trophy Commission hauled off everything they found to the USSR, and most of that stuff has still to be returned. The rumor is that it is in the cellars of the Heritage in Saint Petersburg. So you—"

"What is the relevance of this?" Alex interrupted him.

Uli smiled. "It's all interrelated, connected, glued together . . ." He smiled insidiously, holding up his hands for Alex not to interrupt again as he continued. "These men had a grand secret which they have taken with them to their graves and you are probing around its edges and . . ." He raised his beer and drained away a quarter of its contents, "this is all about money, greed, and King Priam's gold. Enough to make great men willingly sell their mothers in the local whorehouse. Enough to make great men betray their friends, their own families into slavery. That is what this is all about. My dear American friend, you expect me to believe you are doing all this for the love of your country? You are just like me, only a little younger and maybe a little more idealistic? So you see ERR is about the theft of incredible wealth which is still unaccounted for, and this man Carter you look for was somehow involved in it."

"And the last submarine?" Alex countered, trying to get back to the real issue.

"July 1945." He watched the American for a moment until the date sunk in.

"Three months after the war?" Alex replied, his voice now slightly incredulous.

"Ja," the German replied

"For whose account?" Alex said.

"Himmler I assume," the German replied.

"Where exactly did it take place?"

"The last delivery was to Uruguay."

"How was it made?"

The German seemed puzzled by the question and hesitated a moment. "By submarine of course. And the same submarine each time . . . U-864."

"Do you know who commanded each of them?"

"Of course I do. His name was Heinrich Kaufmann. The first delivery off Cyprus involved five thousand-two hundred kilos of bullion. The second delivery was much more. The third, I believe had almost sixty tons aboard. The last was so large that Kaufmann's U-Boat had to be specially modified so it could carry the extra weight."

"Whose gold was it?" Alex said.

"Spain's. And well, let us just say, others in Europe who no longer needed it."

Alex laughed out loud. He'd heard some preposterous stories, but this was the best. "I don't know if I believe you!"

The Germans slammed his beer mug on the table and began to get up. "Du bist ein arschloch!" he exclaimed. "I obviously have nothing further to say. You think I am lying? You think I am some buffoon? A lightweight? Fuck you dumbkopf Amerikanerisher!"

Alex had underestimated the old man. "Please excuse me," he said deferentially. "I apologize. Enschuligen." He repeated several times in German, "Please excuse me."

Uli Untermann gradually regained his composure and resumed his story. "Okay! We captured it from Russia!" Now he relayed a story that was so incredible, Alex promised himself he'd look into it in more detail when he had a chance. Its main components went something as follows:

Russia supported the communists during Spain's civil war. In September 1937 General Francisco Franco's anti-communist forces were about to capture Madrid. There was a half billion dollars of gold bullion in Madrid's central bank vaults. It backed Spain's currency. Largo Caballero, a communist sympathizer, and the man in charge of Spain's finances, fearing general Franco's forces were about to capture Madrid, ordered the 520 tons of gold moved by train to caves in the hills near Valencia on the Mediterranean coast. Moscow at the time was also demanding payment for armaments provided, so Caballero agreed to transfer the bullion to the USSR for safe-keeping, and help pay Spain's debts to Moscow. On 25 October some 7,800 crates of bullion, then worth about half a billion dollars, left Spain in Soviet ships destined for Odessa. The gold arrived in Moscow in early November 1937. Then three years later, in late 1940, as German armies closed in on Moscow, Stalin feared the city would fall and ordered the Spanish gold evacuated. During that evacuation the railroad shipment with the gold was captured by Hitler's Wehrmacht and never seen again by either the USSR or Spain.

"Where did the German army capture it?" Alex inquired.

"I'm getting to that." Again Uli rubbed his hands, enjoying a tale which he probably hadn't confided anyone since the war.

"German Generals Leeb, Bock, and von Rundstedt's armies swarmed into Russia so fast in August 1940, that they captured Minsk within two weeks. Northeast of Minsk, German ground forces pushing toward Moscow, overran a freight train trying to escape to the north-east. It was sitting on a rail siding as Russian troops frantically tried to remove the wreckage of another train blocking the line ahead of them. Inside the train on the siding were hundreds of wooden crates containing the Spanish gold. The entire shipment was secretly transferred to Berlin, and as I have already explained a portion of it was subsequently delivered to China by Carter while the second and third deliveries later in the war were made to China and South America."

"Case Judy?" Alex asked.

"Ja! Correct!" the German replied. "Case Judy!"

"I'll look into it when I get back to the States," Alex said.

"You do that. But be careful!"

"What about the agent you mentioned in the United States?" Alex asked.

"Ah yes! Her name was Marta Schaeffer."

"She knew Carter?"

"Yes." Uli grinned, repeatedly poking his index finger of his right hand into his clenched left fist, signifying a sexual liaison.

"They were lovers?" Alex asked.

"I think so." Uli smiled. "And Schaeffer was not her real name in America."

Alex had a nagging sensation that he knew what he was about to hear next. "Is she still alive?"

"Maybe."

"Where?" Alex asked.

"Virginia, last I knew."

"Under what name?"

"Eve Albion."

* * *

As the twin-engine Air Germania Turboprop droned through the turbulence toward Berlin, Alex knew Case Judy had to be the key. It was time to get back to Washington. He suspected he now knew who'd killed not only Slavchenko but Eve Albion as well. If Albion too had betrayed Carter, it would explain why he'd killed her as well.

The Case Judy plot was now thickening so fast that Alex knew he would have to be very careful if he too was to avoid becoming a casualty of his investigation.

THREE

Cameron Station

THERE WERE SEVERAL reasons for Ted LePage's decision to seek out the man he was about to meet at Cameron Station on the north side of the Washington Beltway just west of the Potomac bridge near Alexandria. The most important reason was that Alex Balkan's investigation was obviously spinning out of control and Ted desperately needed some answers.

Alex's latest calls from Moscow and Berlin had also clearly proved that his investigation had entered areas no one ever imagined. He had to be stopped. Then too there were the official inquiries from the American Ambassador in Moscow which had been sent to State and the CIA, demanding to know what was going on, and by whose authority? And now Alex was excited about long forgotten American prisoners somewhere in Russia. Ted would have DIA down on his ass too if he didn't stop Balkan's investigation. But first he needed to find out if there was any truth to Alex's allegation regarding a cover-up about American troops who'd disappeared into Soviet prison camp system after World War II.

This morning Ted had received yet another back-channel message from the American Ambassador in Moscow, this time demanding to know what the hell Balkan was really doing. Alex had accused a Russian government minister of illegally holding American soldiers in Russia. Alex had also tried to bribe another minister in Moscow for information. None of this had been coordinated with either the Embassy or State Department. The Russian Foreign Ministry was about to file a formal complaint. State wanted Balkan shit-canned, and to make matters worse Alex had refused to leave Europe, and had told Ted he would remain for several more days. Ted had ordered him home immediately and Alex had refused. It was time to get rid of him. Alex Balkan's future with international weapons verification programs in Russia was also over. Ted would pass the bad news to Alex the next time they spoke.

But first Ted had to see Stanley Citwits at Cameron Station. The man he would see would update Ted about the United States government's role in rumors concerning the abandonment of American POW's in Russia during 1945 and the years after. From what Ted already knew there appeared to have been a massive cover-up. Some had obviously taken a vow of silence while others seemed to know bits and pieces but were unable to piece it all together.

For fifty years the two superpowers had glared at one another across an ideological gulf, each threatening the other with atomic holocaust at the drop of a hat. To add to the fear of war, ruthless men with names like Stalin, Kruschev, and Brezhnev had relentlessly sought military superiority over capitalism at any cost while the superpowers had relentlessly confronted each other in Asia, the Middle East, Europe and the Carribbean.

Ted stopped at the rent-a-cop booth at the gate to Cameron Station. The guard asked him to pull over while a temporary pass was prepared because Ted's U.S. government vehicle pass had expired. When Ted arrived for his appointment, the man he was to see had stepped out. An overweight, effeminate-looking man finally appeared a quarter hour later. Ted at first thought he was some flunkie delivering interoffice distribution. "Hi, I'm Stan Citwits." The flunkie announced as he approached Ted handing him his card.

Ted noted his garish shirt, starched dirty collar and paisley Mickey Mouse tie with disdain. The analyst obviously considered himself an Hombre. Probably the type, Ted thought, who fondled little girls asses in the Metro. Ted decided he'd think of this analyst in future as Stud-Muffin, as it definitely fit his character.

"No one can get my last name right," Citwits laughed, "phonetically the family name its pronounced Citwits, so don't let the spelling on the card confuse you." Ted looked at the card. Jesus, he thought to himself, one vowel and eight consonants. No wonder the Polish people were made fun of.

"If you will follow me, Ted," he said, "we'll talk in the conference room."

Stud-muffin's chest made a hollow sound as if he smoked too much. He also rolled his eyes and Ted wondered if he might place his hand on Ted's knee. "Sorry I had to step out, Ted, but you were late and it has been a hectic morning!"

Screw you Ted thought. Who cared? "How much time you got"

"As much as you need!" Stud Muffin replied.

"Half an hour should do it," Ted replied. Ted was a Senior Executive Service appointee and unused to being stood-up even when he was late for appointments with underlings. Ted assumed Stud Muffin knew he was the equivalent of a Three Star General.

"Have a seat, Ted."

"It's Mr. LePage," Ted replied acerbically.

Stud Muffin seemed to have been taken aback for a moment. "Very well, Mr. LePage." Stud Muffin repeated with respect. "If you will have a seat, we'll get started. I think I have what you're looking for. Are you doing a work-up for some senator looking into the perennial problems under investigation over at DMPO here in Washington or UMPC in Hawaii?"

"No!"

"Prisoner of war and missing stuff is getting a lot of coverage in the media these days and the organization is being hoisted on its petard: and probably with a lot of justification." Stud-muffin rolled his eyes again and explained how he'd been researching the issue for years and considered himself among the experts in Washington. "Is Vietnam era missing in action what you are looking for?"

Ted wanted to laugh. The Beltway was crawling with tens of thousands of useless bureaucrats like this guy who all drank each other's bath water. No wonder folks in Oscaloosa, Ohio, and Podunk, Mississippi were fed-up with a bureaucracy that served no one. Washington today resembled London after Nelson's 1805 victory at Trafalgar: a time when Britain no longer needed a huge fleet and Army. Parliament's requests for manpower reductions at the time were continuously ignored by Britain's military leaders, so in 1817, Parliament ordered the entire British fleet beached. After September 11, 2001, and hundreds of billions wasted on 'Homeland Security,' Ted wondered when the American voter might try to repeat Britain's 1817 experience in Washington.

"As you know DMPO stands for Defense Missing Personnel Office, and UPAC is its Unified Personnel Accounting Command. The former here in Washington does research to find out where the POW/MIAs are while UPAC in Hawaii goes and recovers them."

"I know that." LePage's voice now more annoyed.

"At the outset Mr. LePage, do you really mind if I call you Ted?"

"If you must," Ted replied. "I do." Knowing it was probably futile to expect any sign of respect anyway.

"First some background, Ted," Citwits began, ignoring his objection, "As you probably know, prisoner repatriation in history was the exception and not the rule. Historically male prisoners were almost always put to the sword because it took care of feeding and housing them, and the victor also didn't need to worry about a Fifth Column. Women on the other hand were raped then killed. The Greeks, Romans, and Chinese interestingly enough viewed healthy prisoners a source of wealth—slaves to build roads, till the land and erect buildings. The Romans used many of the young men too as professional gladiators to entertain the Roman mobs. The only prisoner exchange ever recorded before the birth of Christ, was Moses' Exodus from Egypt, and the Jewish return from Babylon."

Ted's expression left little doubt he was bored.

"It's only in the last two hundred years, Mr. LePage, that anyone thought about prisoners' rights. And it was the Americans and Europeans who thought about it. These concerns were subsequently codified by the Geneva Convention of 1864. More conventions followed after the First World War. But to most of the world even today, the traditional approach still persists. The next four slides will cover the United States' experience in the last century. From these you'll quickly note that we've learned almost nothing about how to deal with the prisoner of war problem, especially our own who are captured."

Stud Muffin's first slide which was marked Top Secret at the top and bottom of the slide, indicated that 800 American prisoners were never repatriated from the port of Archangel in northern Russia after the First World War. Another twenty-one thousand never returned from German POW cages overrun by the Russians during the closing days of the Second World War. And in Korea, we saw another twenty five hundred transferred alive into China and Siberia. And in Vietnam, several thousands more were abandoned. About two hundred of them ended up in the USSR for exploitation. The rest never came home and rotted away in North Vietnam and Cambodia when Washington told Hanoi there would be no reconstruction funds forthcoming."

"Why the asterisk after the twenty-two thousand figure you show for those taken to Russia?" Ted asked.

"It's an estimate," Citwits replied. The estimate is probably too high. A more accurate number would probably be in the range of nine to twelve thousand. Others at the national archives dispute both figures and admit a number of about three to five thousand is probably accurate. But no one wants to talk about a larger total for obvious reasons because of political and emotional issues."

"What's the bottom line," Ted interrupted.

"The bottom line is sad because we're probably the only nation in the modern era, who periodically mobilize huge civilian armies for war, we win them, and then quickly disband our army. And once we disband, those we fought, on most occasions, were still our enemies, such as in Russia after the First World War, Russia in the second, Korea and Vietnam, so we forget about it and move on.

"A little simplistic, don't you think?" Ted observed, his voice making it obvious he was not at all impressed with Stud Muffin's conclusion.

"You asked for my views Mr. LePage."

"Okay." Ted decided he'd ask about the Russian experience. "What about those you mentioned who we left in Russia after 1945?"

"Today? God knows! Probably none. Maybe a handful. When the war ended in Europe we knew there were one hundred and two thousand of our prisoners in Axis camps, of which almost thirteen thousand were never accounted for. Then there were maybe twenty thousand more who we thought had been killed in action and their bodies not recovered, when in fact they had survived and were in German captivity as the war ended. Until this day, we are still uncertain about the final disposition of many of them."

"The Germans had them?"

"Yes, they were all documented as being alive in German POW camps until the Russian's overran those camps in eastern Europe during the final months of the war. We knew they were there. We had the Red Cross reports attesting to it. And when it was all over, the Russians couldn't account for almost thirteen thousand of them."

"Meaning?" Ted demanded.

"The Russians secretly moved them east into Russia and kept them after the war and never returned them to our control. I feel sorry for the families. It's a bummer! Just over eight thousand of our men were also missing in Korea. Don't you think it's incredible that we assumed only one hundred and one out of eight thousand missing in Korea were captured?"

"Today," he continued, "I can't blame the Russians for saying nothing. Not only is it an embarrassment to them, but now there's the legal aspect for both them and us. The Japs are about to get financially reamed because of their behavior in World War II. And in Korea the Russians were not a participant but secretly they were helping the North Koreans. I think we were making a lot of progress with the Russians in the mid-1990s, but the Robert Hansen FBI spying case really threw a wrench into our association with the Russians and gave them a perfect excuse to get rid of a lot of problems. You may recall that in March of 2001 we threw out a bunch of their diplomats in Washington because of the Hansen case. The Russians reciprocated by throwing out forty-five of our people in Moscow, but among them they targeted five of our best people assigned to find our missing POWs somewhere in the former USSR. It's doubtful now that we'll ever get back on to the trail of any of our people they've had from World War II. That son of a bitch Hansen cost this country a lot. We still have working groups in Moscow for World War II, Korea, Indochina and the Cold War, but they haven't done anything since the Hansen issue."

"It's a damned shame," Stud Muffin said, "because in a decade we've only identified 146 remains from the Second World War, 256 from Korea, 591 from Indochina and 18 from the Cold War, and in future it will be much less."

"Sounds to me," Ted opined argumentatively, "like a fine record of accomplishment which our POW/MIA Agency ought to be damned proud."

"If you say so Mr. LePage. As of this moment eighty-three thousand American soldiers who fought for us in Europe and the Pacific since 1941 are still to be found and identified. So the last decade's accomplishment represents less than one percent of those still missing." He could tell from LePage's face that his visitor was now really annoyed. Citwits continued, "1,842 from Vietnam, 8,100 from Korea, 125 from the Cold War, and 78,000 from World War II. As regards Russia, you are familiar with the U.S. Russia Agency formed in 1992?"

"Don't patronize me." Ted ordered him. "Just get on with it!" But Ted had never realized that the number still unaccounted for was so high, especially from the Second World War in Europe, and wondered how many in America knew this. "What's the 'Century Light' codeword stand for?" Ted demanded, pointing to the highlighted red letters at the top and bottom of the briefing chart.

"It's a top secret program monitoring the whereabouts of all our known and suspected American POW's worldwide."

"Whose program is it?"

"Defense Intelligence Agency."

"Why the top secret classification fifty years later?" It was a stupid question, but Ted thought he'd inquire anyway because a lot of time had passed and it was a question that the general public would certainly ask him in a heart-beat if they ever became aware of what Citwits had just told him.

"Some are still believed to be in captivity. So releasing this might endanger their status."

"Any hard data to prove any of this?"

"Yes. But most of its been discounted by DIA. In the late fifties for example we had eye witness reports of entire train loads of our captured air force and army prisoners being transported across the North Korean border into northeast China."

"Where?"

"A place called Manchouli."

"Reports from whom?"

"All kinds of people, some local recruited sources, some were Europeans along the route, and others, Russians who later confirmed the sighting. They all indicated that trainloads of American prisoners which contained upward of a thousand to twelve hundred each were seen moving across the border into China. There were others too. And in each instance, when we learned about it, we filed secret demarches with the Chinese and Russian governments. And each time they denied it, despite the fact we had carriage numbers, engine numbers, even several of the officers names who were aboard the trains."

"So they told us to screw-off?" Ted observed.

"Correct. In essence they told us it was none of our business and they knew nothing about them."

Ted had grudgingly begun to respect Citwits. "None of them ever escaped?"

"A few did," Citwits replied. "Twelve to be exact!"

"How and when?"

Citwits laughed. "Two actually escaped from Siberia. It's not the type of place that anyone escapes from. Virtually all who tried were caught and executed. The twelve I'm referring to were actually released during the Vietnam War. For example, one you might remember was an American air force pilot shot down in China who was held in solitary there for eight years. From time to time his Chinese captors repeatedly exposed him to older American prisoners captured during the Korean War, these older men warned him that he'd be held forever too, unless he cooperated. He never did but when the Vietnam War ended the Chinese for some obscure reason decided to release this pilot along with two of the Korean War prisoners. It was the first time we were forced to acknowledge that some of our Korean War dead were not dead at all, and had spent twenty years in captivity."

"What was the colonel's name?"

"Can't recall offhand. Do you want me to get it?"

"Move on," Ted ordered.

Citwits flipped on the room lights. Questions?"

"What's the total of our unaccounted American prisoners for in the last century?"

"You mean men we knew were illegally being held and not released?"

Ted nodded.

"Conservatively, right at 30,000!"

"Abandoned and forgotten in foreign prison camps."

"Yep!"

"Jesus, are you relatively confident about your data base?"

"Absolutely! I guess, Mr. LePage, that you are starting to grasp the magnitude of the problem?"

"How many disappeared in the Burma/Southeast Asia area during World War II?"

Citwits thought for a moment. "If you're referring to this man Carter who you have also asked about, there were two hundred and nine of them."

The number didn't seem that high to Ted, but then he was not an expert of that war. "How many of them were civilians?"

"Seventy three."

"And civilians captured during the year 1943 in that Theater?"

"Near as I can tell, seven."

"What happened to them?"

Citwits hunched his shoulders." They disappeared without a trace! The Japs didn't keep records and were notorious for brutalizing prisoners they didn't kill outright, so most of their prisoners did not survive more than a few weeks."

"And Carter?"

"There is no record of him anywhere."

"Nothing at all?"

"Zero. I've prepared a summary for you, Mr. LePage. Unfortunately it's drawn from highly classified multiple source data, so you will not be able to release it." Citwits flicked the view graph back on and placed another slide on the glass and waited for Ted to read it.

TOP SECRET/CJ

SUBJ: Paul Carter, (Case WP/378/PC-1943). (TS/CJ)

WARNING NOTICE: (U) The following information is Top Secret in its entirety, and subject to caveats for sources and methods. In addition, Under the Freedom of Information Act, it is automatically excluded and not releasable per Title XIV, sec 12, para 32,

DISCUSSION :

1. (TS/CJ) The last wartime sighting of Paul A. Carter was 24 January 1943 at Fish Lake in Liberia. He was placed on the 'missing list' by the Department of State on 5 February 1943, and declared dead 24 May 1944.

2. (TS/CJ) A live sighting per USAF Case File DR/R-095746, dated 22 March 1984, alleged that an American by the same name was seen at Camp Buytenlag-23V //Beno 3460W:1970E// near Novosibirsk in Soviet Central Asia. The sighting did not conclusively identify the subject as Paul Carter, nor did it conclusively establish he was American. The source, although considered reliable, could offer no forensic evidence regarding

subject, and the entire report was therefore considered unreliable by DIA's POW/MIA office. Three subsequent official State Department inquiries to Moscow in 1984, 1985, and 1986, were all negative and the case was again closed on 15 January 1986.

BACKGROUND: (TS/CJ) Born Paul Agnostio Carter in Brooklyn, New York on 5 June 1917, of Henry and Angelica (Adelos) Carter, he attended Bayshore Elementary and Bishop Grimes High School. After a year at Long Island University he was Commissioned a second lieutenant in the Marine Corps 12 August 1937. He served one year at USMC Headquarters, Washington, D.C., before being transferred to China in September 1938. In October 1940 joined General MacAuther's Staff in Manila. In November 1941 he returned to Washington, was promoted Major. Through the date of his disappearance he was assigned to the employ of an unnamed company in New York City, from whom he requested 30 days leave at Christmas 1942, and for reasons unknown, soon thereafter departed for Africa and disappeared.

DISPOSITION: (U) Case closed.

"Where the hell did you get this?" Ted demanded.

"I have my sources."

"Seriously."

"Old records in offsite storage."

"Does the State Department know you have this?"

"Probably not. Would they care?"

Ted suspected they might. "You know, Stan," Ted noted the sudden smile on Stud Muffin's face at the sudden use of his first name. "Until now I'd thought this guy Paul Carter was a dumb civilian who got lost in Africa. He obviously wasn't. Can this be declassified?"

"Impossible. Not in a month of Sundays. There's tons of stuff like this in the archives, all exempt from the Freedom of Information Act forever."

"What do the initials CJ mean?"

"No idea! Codeword obviously?"

"Can I get a copy of this?"

"No way," Stud muffin replied.

"You know I have the clearance!" Ted commented officiously.

"TS, probably," Stud Muffin replied. "But not CJ to my knowledge."

"Who can I see about its access?"

"Beats the crap of me. Someone over at State Department probably."

"What about Americans still in Russian camps?" Ted asked.

"No interest here in DC."

"You are kidding?" Ted demanded.

"Not for WWII and Korea."

"What's the problem?" Ted asked.

"Here the problem does not exist. And in Moscow it is probably about money. The central government in Russia is broke. No one is being paid regularly, and in most cases not at all. Then there's the facility and equipment maintenance problems. The lack of budget allocations in these areas has resulted in the permanent closure of everything not directly supporting high priority defense areas. Most of their archives have been closed for years and all those who once knew where everything was have either died or moved away. Their internal situation is increasingly hopeless."

Ted knew what he was referring to. Everyone in Washington knew about the deplorable state of Russia's front—line rocket forces and nuclear programs. Chernobyl's release of radioactive isotopes into the atmosphere were the equivalent of 400 Hiroshima bombs. That was bad enough, but now Russia's highly trained atomic bomb scientists had mostly been put out to pasture. Most had not paid in years while some were out moonlighting to put food on the table. Inspections were revealing worrisome gaps in bomb inventories, and even the Russian leadership were afraid that missing nuclear weapons had already fallen into the hands of international terrorists like Al Quaeda and Iran's Al-Qods. Ted had seen the top secret reports that a tactical nuclear weapon had allegedly been transferred to Iran's mullahs along with nine of Russia's top nuclear scientists who were now well paid for their work by their Iranian masters at Parchin. Those involved had been warned—get it back or suffer a Mafia type erasure of their extended family. "A few minutes ago, Stan, you said you'd give me your views off the record."

"Sure." Stud-Muffin closed the door to the room. "I'm sure that you realize Mr. LePage, that the published data on our missing prisoners of war is compiled by Inter-Agency groups, and seldom resembles the real truth because it deals with an incredible assortment of accommodations, trade-offs, and concessions made throughout the intelligence analysis process. Everyone has vested interests to protect, so what emerges oftentimes has little to do with actual realities. The most important question we all have to deal with is—will the outcome endanger present or future funding for our respective organizations?"

"A little cynical?" Ted observed, but he knew Stud Muffin was right. They were discussing the dark-side of an issue no one in Washington wanted to be reminded of. And Ted knew that if Stud-muffin ever made this information public, that this Pillsbury dough-boy would be pilloried into oblivion behind closed doors, his career and employment ruined, and probably a few decades behind bars in solitary confinement at Leavenworth. And that if Ted said anything, he too could kiss his career good-bye. The Patriot Act legislation rushed into law by the forty-third president after September 11, 2001, had successfully muzzled a wide range of American citizens rights to protest their government's activities, its past or future plans.

Ted didn't care much for libertarians and thought most of them were ex-cold war communists seeking a new mission in life. But the post 9-11 executive branch leadership's penchant for secrecy and un-American activities scared Ted even more because the Patriot Act provided the U.S. intelligence organizations with unsupervised police powers easily abused. Ted had even told his son to watch what he said these days on the telephone because the FBI had set up nation-wide monitoring of the airwaves to pick up all references to narcotics, certain names, statements, and places. When monitored these were closely examined and in some instances ended up in search warrants and telephone taps on those who'd used them. The American Moslem community had been pilloried like the American Japs under Roosevelt, and the Jews in Nazi Germany. But the white majority throughout the country were also becoming radicalized by invasive spying on the American people by their government.

For Scion Consultants the war on terrorism was a gold mine: an amorphous octopus without an end game, its success impossible to define, and therein lay its Trojan Horse. In each subsequent crisis government accumulated more power to the legislative and executive branch.

"Cynical maybe," Stud Muffin cut into Ted's thoughts. "But you know, just like I do, that its money that greases the skids in Washington and make it function, not morals or ethics. It's the money and special interest groups. It's that simple."

Ted looked at his watch. "Thanks for the information Ted."

As LePage left the parking lot he recalled his conversation the other day with Alex Balkan on the secure line from Moscow. Balkan alleged that he had a Russian document which proved there were twelve thousand seven hundred American soldiers who were still being held somewhere in the former Soviet Union three years after the Second World War in Europe ended. For all Balkan or Ted knew there could still be some of them still alive in Russia today. If Alex's documents were authentic, no American's would ever believe anyone could do such an uncivilized thing, and anyone still alive out there would have to be found . . . or else?

Rosslyn

"Scion Consultants. Julie speaking."

"This is Detective Arden Welsh with the Key West Police, I'd like to speak with Alex Balkan?"

"He's not in! May I take a message?"

"When will he be back?"

"A week, maybe two."

"Is there some way I can reach him?"

"What's the subject?"

"Murder."

"Hold on." She moved briskly through the maze of partitions to Ted LePage's suite along the exterior wall of the building overlooking the Potomac River and the Key Bridge. "Sir, there's a detective calling from Key West looking for Alex Balkan, I thought you should know."

"Tell him Alex's out of town and get his number."

"I did. He said it was important, something about a murder."

"I'll take it! Thanks Julie. Close the door behind you!" He punched in the flashing light on the console and picked up the phone. "Ted LePage here! Can you hold moment?" He found the folder and quickly scanned the photocopy of the eight calls made to Eve Albion's residence in Key West. "Sorry to keep you waiting, Detective."

"Who am I talking to?" the voice on the phone asked.

"Ted LePage."

"Name is Arden Welsh! I need to speak with Alex Balkan."

"I'm sorry, Detective, but he is unavailable and out of the country on the road somewhere. He works for me. Can I help you?"

"I'm a detective with the Monroe County Sheriff's Office. Can you tell me where I might be able to find Balkan?"

"As I said, he's not available and difficult to reach right now. Is there something I can help you with?"

"I'll call back."

"Might be awhile."

"How long?"

"Maybe several weeks."

"You familiar with his trip down here?"

"Of course! I'm his boss."

"He was asking about a woman called Eve Albion."

"He mentioned it to me."

"What do you know about her?"

"Nothing."

"He tell you the coroner listed her death as heart failure?"

"No, he didn't."

"He tell you we also suspect there was foul play involved in her death?"

"No."

"Who is he actually employed by?"

"Why?"

"Just trying to get some facts."

"What's this all about?" Ted asked, now becoming concerned that the detective might be getting into issues which could spill over into areas of national security. "Is Alex a suspect?"

"Could be! Who exactly are you?"

"I am the chief executive officer for Scion Consultants."

"Yeah, yeah, I know that. But what does Scion Consultants do?"

"Security consulting for government projects."

"Yeah, yeah, as I said already, I still don't have the slightest idea what the hell it is that you do for a living, or Balkan for that matter.

"Is Alex a suspect? Are you going to issue a subpoena or a warrant?"

"Maybe. There's been suspicious things going on down here, and he appears to have been involved."

"What kind of things?"

"He saw this woman the same day she died. They had an argument, she threw him out. We have a witness. You want to tell me about it?"

"If I could, Detective, I would! But I don't think Alex had anything to do with the old woman's death." There was a silence on the phone, and Ted thought the detective might have hung up. "You still there?"

"Yeah! If you don't want to say anything, that's okay, I'll wait. But tell him it would be in his best interest to call me ASAP."

"Meaning?" Now LePage's voice was testy.

"Nothing. We had the old woman's house swept for prints. Course we found Balkan's, but also some others we've had trouble with. An FBI inquiry came back negative. So I decided to follow up on it. Last week one of my temporary hires requested an archive search by FBI. This time we got a hit, but it's a dead end. They belonged to a dead man."

"So you called to tell Balkan that?"

"There's more. Four days ago two other people down here asked about the dead woman. This time it was a Peruvian and an Indonesian woman who'd flown in from the Bahamas. When they learned she was dead, they spoke with the Realtor handling the sale of her house. Luckily the Realtor called me first, so I was able to interview them before they got away."

"What were their names?"

"Eduardo Hernandez and Mary Malagang. You know them?"

"No."

"I don't have their passport data yet, but have requested it from Miami."

"What have they done wrong, Detective?" Ted hated local law enforcement, especially the types who had a little power and went off the deep end with it.

"We know they started from Saint Martin in the Leeward Islands and flew to the Bahamas on Blue Point Air! You familiar with Blue Point?"

"Never heard of it."

"It's a sleaze outfit. Belongs to a prominent family there. The air charter is part of a Carribbean based drug smuggling operation owned by the Castries brothers. They got their start in the eighties in the local construction business in Jamaica and then moved throughout the Carribbean. In the nineties they shifted into banking and money laundering. Then, a few years ago, into drugs. For several years now DEA has been watching them because they know they're heavy in the cocaine transportation business across our southern border in California, Arizona, New Mexico, and Texas."

Ted didn't care for the detective's manner. Neither was he interested in two-bit pushers. "So what does all this have to do with anything?"

"There's something going down. An associate in Saint Thomas confirmed this Hernandez creep also met with the local Chief of Police there, who just also happens to be one of the Castries brothers."

Jesus Ted thought. Welsh was a typical cop, who thought the entire world revolved around his case. "Get to the point!"

"Ever heard of the name Paul Carter?"

Ted's face blanched as he fought to control his breathing. Alex swore he'd mentioned Carter's name to no one at Key West, so how had this fucking flat-foot obtained it?"

"It's a common enough name. Why do you ask?"

"You didn't answer the question, Mr. LePage."

"Excuse me."

"You ever heard that name before?"

"No," Ted lied.

"You recall the prints I mentioned at the dead woman's house?"

"What about them?"

"They belonged to this Carter guy. But the FBI informs me there must have been a mistake because the subject died in 1943!"

"1943?" Ted replied dumbly.

"You got an echo in you?" Welsh demanded. "I thought maybe Balkan knew something about it because Carter's prints were as fresh as Balkans, so both men were definitely at her place just before she died."

"I see." But Ted didn't. He didn't know what to say, only that he'd have to ask Alex about it when they next spoke.

"You didn't put Balkan up to dropping a dead man's prints around her place, did you?"

"You are out of order, Detective, so I'm going to hang up, Mr. Welsh."

"My apologies, Mr. LePage, I was just thinking out loud."

"Well, think something else then."

"Tell your man I called. Ask him to give me a ring ASAP." The line went dead.

Ted stared out the window for several minutes while his blood pressure subsided. Fucking Balkan had somehow made contact with Carter and hadn't told Ted about it! Now he'd have Alex's ass! And Balkan was involved somehow with some drug pushers? He'd always distrusted Alex and knew his unconventional ways and free-spirited approach to collegial intelligence was unacceptable and would one day get both him and Ted in trouble. Balkan was clearly now beyond the pale. Ted picked up the phone and called his secretary. "Julie, what's on my schedule this afternoon?"

"The promotion board at Defense Intelligence Agency starts at one o'clock and will run all afternoon."

Damn, he thought. There was no way he could skip it. "And tomorrow?"

"The National Security Council at nine for an update on long range intelligence objectives for the five year plan. Then the round table with the two Senators from Iowa. After lunch you have the interagency group meeting at the Dirksen Building."

"Remind me. What's the afternoon meeting about this time?"

"Should CIA and NSA recruited sources be subordinate to the Director of Homeland Defense?"

"See if you can reach Balkan before noon." Ted scanned his Rolodex and found Langford Seeley's private phone number. No one answered. Damn! He needed to ask Seeley about what he'd just been told. Ted called his liaison man with the FBI and straightened out some problems. He received two more calls from State before lunch; the Russians were still hopping mad about Balkan, and State wanted to know what Ted intended to do about Balkan? Ted would put Alex out to pasture as soon as he returned, and meanwhile the Key West detective would have to spin his wheels for a while.

Foggy Bottom

Ted pulled into Twenty-first street's side entrance and parked in the General Officer parking area beneath the State Department building, paying attention not to get any slush on his trousers as he stepped out onto the concrete. The weather had deteriorated during the night and another six inches of snow blanketed Washington. Presenting his pass to the security officer at the ground floor entrance, he proceeded to a bank of phones on the main landing and called his secretary to see if Alex had called in yet? He hadn't. Where the hell was Balkan? It was several days since he'd ordered him to catch the first flight back to the States.

Proceeding to the second floor conference room he threw his overcoat over a chair. He was early and wanted to watch the others as they arrived for the inter-agency meeting. It had been called to discuss Alex's recent information concerning a grave at Buytenlag-23 for a man named Paoulo Cater. This morning's enclave would review all available data to see if Alex's lead might in fact be Paul Carter. Ted now knew it wouldn't be. All the way over he'd been debating whether or not to say something about the Key West detective's comment about Paul Carter's fingerprints at the Eve Alba residence. Without more definitive proof he'd decided to say nothing. Ted wished he'd never passed Alex's information to State. Ted's reputation was already seriously damaged by Alex's shenanigans in Moscow.

The conference room was luxuriously appointed even by Washington standards. A huge walnut table spanned the length of the room, surrounded by twelve matching ornate chairs. Along the far wall were another twelve matching chairs but without arms. A solid mahogany podium stood before a painting of president Millard Fillmore in a gaudy gold frame. How appropriate Ted thought. Fillmore had inherited the presidency when debate raged on the subject of American captives—only in Fillmore's case they were American negro slaves and not prisoners of war.

Ted's conscience had nagged him all night. The call from Key West, on top of Alex's report from Moscow about Carter's grave all seemed too coincidental. Last evening he'd discussed the question of the new information about Paul Carter's fingerprints with his legal advisor. Langford Seeley was annoyed about the information, and suggested Ted forget about it until Balkan showed up. Seeley also pointed out, that Balkan had obviously outlived his usefulness and needed to be put out to pasture because Moscow would never allow him to visit Russia again. Ted knew he was right. This morning he'd checked with Langley and arranged for Alex's termination with the personnel department. Balkan would get the word as soon as his trip reports were filed; then all his clearances would be revoked and he'd be on the street before the end of the month.

The room gradually filled and Ted was surprised when Stanley Citwits, the Analyst from Cameron Station, appeared and took a chair across from Ted.

"Small world." Stud Muffin observed to Ted as the hulk of Tucker Attarian closed the conference room door and took the chair at the head of the table.

"Ladies and gentlemen," Attarian announced, "let's get started!"

Attarian was a state's staffer, assigned to the chairman of the POW/ MIA working group, and handled meetings in the absence of his boss, who was out west skiing somewhere.

"As you know," Attarian began, "there was a report last week of a grave site near Novosibirsk belonging to, one Paolo Cater. The question is, might this be that of an American with a similar name reported in the Novosibirsk area in the early eighties?" He glanced at Ted, "So the question is, does this new information warrant reopening Carter's case?" He turned to LePage, "Ted, any new developments from your secret agent, James Bond in Russia, or where ever he is before we start?"

"No." Ted didn't appreciate the dig as several around the table smirked. "I've recalled him and believe this issue is a dead end." He noticed several more smirks and suspected Moscow's latest complaints about Balkan were already public knowledge to most around Foggy Bottom.

"Fine," Attarian said. "I want to keep this as short as possible, I know we are all busy, and such things need not take up our time, and . . ." He glanced to his left as a dour-looking woman across from him interrupted.

"The names aren't even the same for Christ's sake!" she whined. "Why are we even here discussing this?"

Ted noticed Stud Muffin roll his eyes.

"If you will kindly let me finish, Ms. Compton!" Attarian replied.

Ted didn't care for Compton either, and if she'd been a man, he would have suggested she shut the fuck up and go play with herself! But civil liberties and women's rights demanded that Attarian be civil even to the most obnoxious of that sex.

Attarian's voice was now more assertive. "Bear with me, Ms. Compton. We have a public duty to discharge, now let's move on. I'd like each of you to review the holdings." He looked at Henry Roderic from the National Security Agency next to him. "You want to start Henry?"

The NSA representative obviously wasn't going to tell them much! All he'd brought was a blank note pad which lay prominently before him. NSA was constantly beseeched by the powerful and prominent in government, especially since September 11, to provide more and more monitoring information. Added to NSA's hit list for monitoring were another six hundred and eighteen thousand American immigrants in the United States who although citizens, had all become suspect as possible terrorists, and were being periodically monitored on a regular basis just to make sure. But recent reorganizations and reallocations within Homeland Defense had resulted in various budget cuts and manpower reductions which had taken their toll. "Nothing to report, sir. During the last two weeks that Scion Consultants has had their man in Russia, we've monitored Moscow, Novosibirsk, and Marba traffic, to see if Carter's name cropped up. It hasn't. If the Russians know anything, they aren't talking. We'll watch for another two weeks but I doubt anything will show up"

"Thanks," Attarian replied and turned next to Compton, who was fidgeting with a pencil. "Ann, what you got?"

From the State Department's Bureau of Research, Compton had held her job so long, she considered peers and superiors alike as nincompoops. "Nothing!" She growled without raising her head. "We weren't even able to find a dossier on him."

Citwits shot another glance at Ted, as if to say, the bitch lies!

"About the only thing I can tell you," she continued, "is that this clown flew to Africa in early 1943 and then disappeared. In April of that year we placed him on the missing list, and two months later declared him dead. When his wife died in 1973, the case was permanently closed . . . and since then we have been unable to find his file."

"Unable to find it or lost it?" Ted demanded.

Stud Muffin glanced again at Ted, this time with an expression of "show me." Obviously fearing Ted would say something about the Carter file information Stud Muffin had shared with him.

"No change in status then?" Ted demanded.

"Isn't that what I just said!" She shot back.

Bitch! Ted thought. He wanted to embarrass her with the report Citwits had showed him the other day, and accuse her of participating in a conspiracy. State knew more than they were letting on. Why? And how much did they really know? Ted realized that now wasn't the time to push the matter, he had bigger fish to fry. He'd get Alex's report first and then decide how to proceed.

Attarian turned to the man to Compton's left. "Julius, what's OSR got?"

"The Office of Strategic Reconnaissance, as usual comes through with the 'show and tell' stuff," he replied. Several people smiled as Julius raised the screen of his lap top and pushed it forward so everyone could see it. "I've arranged these in date order," he said as he transferred the view to a screed which unrolled automatically before the picture of President Fillmore on the far wall. Julius punched a key and the screen changed from a picture of Julius at his desk. "I've got three slides which came in yesterday. The first is a quarter mile grid-shot of the Buytenlag-23V camp location, in which you can see the remains of individual buildings. Notice structural decomposition, snow depth, and the virtual lack of road traffic. The place has been deserted a long time." He punched a key again. "The second shot is a complex two miles, away which is also deserted." Again his finger stabbed the keyboard. "The last is a two hundred mile grid of the Krasnoyarsk Camp system. I've circled the sixty-two known Gulag and other local camp sites in the area, all of which are closed. In the southwest corner of the screen, you can see lake Obskoye Dkhr and suburbs of Novosibirsk."

Someone across the table inquired what the distinction was between Gulag and local camps?

"The former were their equivalent of our federal penitentiaries—but much worse!" The latter were equivalent to our State Penitentiaries and also much worse." If anyone is interested in what has been going on there for the last twenty-plus years . . . watch." His finger continued stabbing the key each few seconds as he summarized what the camp system had looked like in high resolution satellite shots taken in 1980 and 1986. "From these you can clearly see that the area was once heavily inhabited . . . but not anymore. The only other thing I've got are some recent shots of the Marba complex in Siberia. "There's little doubt the Marba complex is also closing down. Only two of thirteen known camps there showed some sign of use, and I've marked them with red circles."

"That's the second time someone has mentioned the Marba name. Henry mentioned it a couple of minutes ago. What's the significance?"

"Ted?" Attarian said.

"The information I got from Balkan a couple of days ago was that some source he'd spoken within Novisibirsk had mentioned that when the Buytenlag system closed down, its remaining survivors were shipped off to Marba."

"And for the rest of us," Ann Compton continued, "maybe you would have the common courtesy to inform us of where it is. Russia's a big place you know."

Screw you, Ted thought. He wished he had the coordinates, then he'd just rattle them off and let her go and find them for herself when she got back to her office. "It's about fifteen hundred miles northeast of Novisibirsk on the Lena River in Siberia," Ted said. "It doesn't show up on the maps so you'll have to find it in the database."

"When did the camps around Novosibirsk close?" Compton demanded.

"Near as we can tell," Hank Roderic cut in, "was between 1985 to 1991."

"We also have a cemetery plot, anything on that?" Compton asked again in an accusatory tone.

"Unfortunately OSR does not monitor such information. From the earlier photography you can see large areas of open fields which more recently are reforested. It impossible to get anything meaningful through the tree canopy."

"Thanks, Hank!" Attarian replied, turning next to an unfamiliar man seated next to Stud Muffin. "I believe you represent the deputy director for the Joint Agency Operations Office for POW/MIA?"

"Yes. Normally my boss, Mr. Kissling, would attend such meetings, but he unfortunately suffered a heart attack yesterday and died."

"Our regrets," Attarian observed dispassionately. "Hell, I thought he was out west skiing. Obviously my information is dated. "You have anything to add?"

"Nothing."

Attarian turned next to Stud Muffin. "For those of you who have not met Stan Citwits, he's the Army's expert for POW/MIA stuff. I asked him to attend in case we need the Army's help."

"I have nothing concrete to report." Citwits observed. "But if there is even the slightest truth to this report, we should push it to the hilt in Moscow! To do less, we'd just be playing with ourselves!" His remark drew a look of reproach from Ann Compton, who glared at him. He rolled his eyes then glanced at Attarian again before continuing. "Unfortunately I can't help much with these deliberations, as I'm concerned primarily with documentation. But I can confirm that Russia consistently lies, resorts to deceit, and in fact had many American prisoners which they denied were in their possession."

Ted could see Compton was becoming agitated.

"Why are you so down on the Russians?" She demanded. "For a decade now the State Department has been doing everything in its power to reach an accommodation with the Russian Government."

"You certainly chose the right word," Stud Muffin shot back,"

"Excuse me!" Compton asked accusingly.

"The operative word is 'accommodation!'" Stud Muffin shot back.

"I resent the inference!" Compton exploded.

"Resent what you like!" Citwits replied. "Everyone knows that for fifty years now the State Department has had unclean hands in this POW/MIA matter."

"How dare you!" She demanded.

"Ladies, Gentlemen . . . !" Attarian implored. "Let us maintain decorum. Please!"

Ted wanted to laugh as the little bitch had obviously misjudged stud-muffin, just as Ted had when they first met, and now she obviously knew she couldn't brow-beat him.

"State has worked this question diligently with the utmost zeal. Of that I can assure you!" Her voice was now more even.

"You might be," Citwitz replied, "but I'm not. Russia owes us an accounting! They've been screwing around with us since the First World War, and while you might be trying to get in bed with them, I want them to fess-up about our prisoners they are holding first! Let them come clean! Then I'll sit here quietly while they shove other falsehoods up your skirt."

Several around the table began to smirk. It wasn't often that anyone in Washington, especially inside the beltway seemed to really care about something passionately enough to ruffle feathers like this. Most around Washington didn't care for Compton anyway. Most in the bureaucracy just took their salary and avoided confrontation at all costs, because not to, indicated you were unsuitable for employment with the federal government.

Compton's face turned beet red.

"And if this guy called Carter is alive," Stud Muffin continued, "and they suspect we know it, they'll cover their tracks. So if we don't lower the boom on those bastards in Moscow, you can bet your ass they'll erase all traces of Carter's existence before we can get to him."

"How dare you!" Compton's face was now livid.

But Citwitz would not be cowed and spoke through her objection. "And if the American people ever learn the truth about the other thousands of our servicemen we abandoned in Russia after World War II, and you knew the details, Mrs. Compton, and chose instead to say nothing about it . . . well, the American people will probably take Washington apart, hang most of us, and tell Russia to go to hell."

Compton's ire was now at high heat. This Pillsbury dough boy had insulted her with his offensive language, and was obviously a male chauvinist pig who'd grievously violated government policies on sexual harassment. He'd just used the 'screw' word in her presence, he'd used ass, and other profanity. She'd find out who his boss was and have him face disciplinary board action. "A little presumptuous don't you think?" she needled with sarcasm. "And I find your language and sexual insults obnoxious."

"Madam." He shot back. "We must tell the Russians we know where he is, before they liquidate him."

Everyone was enjoying the confrontation. Even Attarian smiled and had sat back for a moment.

"For your information. They no longer liquidate people," Compton shot back.

"Then you are either naïve, stupid, or an ignoramus." She glared at him as he continued. "I happen to know that several hundred American Air Force personnel during the Korean War ended up at camps at Kul'dino on the Kolyma River. The project was run by General Georgii A. Lobov of the Sixty-fourth Fighter Aviation Corps at Andung. Seven Top Secret reports were filed with your office Compton!" Citwits said with a sneer. "Between 1980 and 1987 as a matter of fact. All of them dealt with American POW's from the Korean era who we knew were still in the Russian camp system. And what did you do with them? You suppressed the reports. State department ignored the fact that they were still there. Why damn it?"

"Because they were unreliable reports. Mister!" She shot back.

"Unreliable . . . That's crap, lady . . . !"

"If not unreliable, then certainly without forensic proof," she interrupted him.

"You don't know shit!" Stud Muffin needled her. "If it had been you they'd captured and you they'd gang raped into eternity, you'd call the reports reliable all right!"

Compton's face turned beet red as she started to stutter.

"And Ms. Compton . . . ," Stud Muffin continued, "if it were up to me, you and your boss would be tarred and feathered and run out of Washington on a rail for your part in all this!"

"Stan . . . Stan . . . !" Attarian cut in, looking imploringly from Compton to others around the table. Citwits had obviously gone too far. "Some decorum please. Ladies and gentlemen . . . let's not turn this into a dog fight. Please desist. Less needless vulgarity. After all we're all adults here."

"Thank you for inviting me," Stud Muffin replied to Attarian as he gathered his papers and arose. "I believe I have made my case, and placed it before you. Act on it as you see fit. Now if you will excuse me. I have another urgent meeting I must attend to." He left, closing the conference room door gently behind him.

Attarian turned to Rinehard Staple next, who worked for the department of the air force as a civilian, heading up DOD's office responsible for missing American servicemen from the Vietnam conflict. He was assigned to the Undersecretary of Defense's Agency on POW/MIA Affairs, and hid out most of the time in his Crystal City headquarters. As a retired air force colonel of intelligence, he also thought he was shit hot because he knew deep and dark secrets. Staples too didn't care for the roly-poly man whom he considered effeminate and a bore, and was pleased that Citwits had left in a huff. Ted on the other hand also couldn't stand Staples either; believing him completely incompetent. Staples also knew that Ted LePage distrusted the POW/MIA Agency, believing most of them ought to be shit-canned for their part in the conspiracy of silence about all those still unaccounted for from Korea and the Second World War.

"Jesus," Rhinehard Staples observed as he began his comments, "let's hope the rest of this meeting is a little less tense."

There was terse laughter as the atmosphere eased.

"My learned historian associate who just departed, knows that without a specific location or eye-witnesses as I'm certain everyone here realizes, it is difficult to challenge Moscow every time we have inconclusive information! We must have details! Only with details can we take action!"

Well spoken by a typical Beltway liberal, Ted thought. But he could tell from the expressions of others around him that no one had bought Staple's view. Ted frequently wondered what it took to make the Compton, Staple, and Roderic-type people of the world mad? Everything these people did was handled with such detached objectivity, it was enough to make one sick.

"So I am afraid," Staple concluded, "until more concrete information is available, we should leave this issue."

Attarian pointed across the table from Staples. "And the FBI? What have you got?"

"A records search indicates only two men with the name Paul A. Carter have ever been documented. A search of immigration and passport records produced a third who died in 1952. So whoever this person in Russia is, or was, it's clear he's not one of ours, and certainly not the one we're looking into here today."

Five minutes later the last three at the table had completed their comments, and Attarian thanked everyone for coming. He turned to Ted as they were leaving. "I didn't expect the confrontation."

"Me either," Ted replied. "Got a minute? There's something I wanted to mention to you in private." As he said this he noticed Ann Compton, stalking around the conference table toward them, probably to demand Attarian do something about Stud Muffin.

"Got time for a get together . . . maybe tomorrow"

Rinehart studied his electronic calendar for a moment. "Tomorrow morning?"

"Ten?" Ted asked.

"My office or yours?"

"Yours," Ted replied."

"You know the way. I'll see you then."

Ted turned away as Compton stood before Attarian. For a moment Ted had considered confiding to him what he'd just heard about Paul Carter's fingerprints from the Detective in Florida.

Rosslyn

"Alex Balkan please!"

"Who's calling?"

"Is he in?"

"No. He's away."

"Still . . . ?"

"Who is this?"

"Detective Welsh. Let me talk to Ted LePage."

"Just a minute." She cupped the phone, "Julie, some detective wants to speak with the boss."

"This is Julie speaking, may I help you?"

"Yeah. My names Welsh. I need to speak with Mr. LePage again! Is he there?"

"A moment, let me see if he's available?" She proceeded through the maze of gray partitions to his office and knocked. "Sir, that detective from Key West is on the phone again."

"Transfer it!"

Damn, Ted thought! After Welsh's last call, he hoped it would be a long time before Welsh called back. Ted had stopped by the FBI headquarters in Washington to see Eddie Kantez, an old friend. He'd asked Kantez to inquire on the "QT," about fingerprint records going back to the early 1940s and see if he could find anything available on Paul Carter. Kantez confirmed that the Bureau did have files, but from that era the majority of them were unreliable because the FBI never filmed them, and most of the cards were now badly deteriorated. Eddie had also confirmed that a request had been made recently by Monroe County regarding a Paul Carter.

"Hello."

"LePage?"

"Speaking."

"This is Detective Welsh in Key West! I got more information. When will Balkan be back?"

"Could be another week. I'm listening."

"Bad news about this Peruvian character I mentioned earlier. Seems the Blue Point plane that carried this Hernandez creep to the Bahamas, was involved in a drug drop."

"So?" Ted inquired.

"DEA informs me Blue Point Air filed a flight plan for the Bahamas with a cruise altitude of 9,000 feet. But en route they suddenly descended to sea level for a few minutes. The pilot later reported he'd experienced cabin pressurization problems. But an AWACS in the area noticed the aircraft suddenly lose altitude and then monitored what they believed was a narcotics drop. When the Piper arrived at Nassau, Bahamian customs took a look at the plane and decided that AWACS had made a mistake. I just found out the son of a bitch used one of the oldest tricks in the book."

"Look, Detective, I'm busy, none of this is of any concern to me."

"Mr. LePage, we now know it was carrying a form-fitted centerline luggage compartment underneath when it departed St. Thomas. The compartment stores 490 pounds of luggage, that's the equivalent of 230 kilos of cocaine! Eighteen million smackers wholesale! You running some kind of an Iran-contra deal down here LePage?"

"You're crazy, Welsh, anyone told you that lately?" But Ted was concerned, this son of a bitch was grasping for straws, and Ted didn't need some law enforcement outfit accusing Scion Consultants of being involved in narcotics operations. Not right now anyway!

"Maybe you got some dirty people working for you LePage?"

Christ, Ted thought. What the hell was happening? "I don't know what you're trying to prove, but neither Balkan nor Scion Consultants is involved. You're on the wrong track! I think you'd better back off!"

"Back off ?"

"Yeah!" Ted said in a soothing tone.

"Tell me why, Mr. LePage? Is this some kind of a secret Washington 'Sting' you guys got going down here with the Cartels? You want to know what I think, LePage? I think you got yourself a loose cannon, and you are into some kind of Iran Contra deal. The same people involved with the drug runners and the ones seeing your friend Mr. Alex Balkan. Level with me."

"You're crazy."

"Maybe so. But there's too much coincidence involved here. Your man Balkan sees her. She dies. He leaves fingerprints of someone dead forty years? A Colombian makes a drug delivery. He comes to see her, and also asks around. We ask him why, and he also blows town."

"So?" LePage replied.

"So . . . . Thanks for listening Mr. LePage."

The detective hung up before Ted could reply.

Ted redialed Eddie Kantez's number at FBI, and waited for the liaison number to pick up. Ted had to get a copy of Eve's Albion's FBI file, and see what they knew about her or the Castries Blue Point Air outfit. Also this Peruvian called Eduardo Hernandez. "Hello, Eddie! Ted LePage here! We need to have lunch tomorrow! Your busy? Is that the soonest you can get away? I see. How about the day after tomorrow? Fine. I'll see you then." Damn it, Ted thought as he put the phone down. Things were definitely moving too quickly.

Arlington

Ted emerged onto the Metro platform at Arlington and at the top of the escalator moved through the tunnel into the weather. Tightening his overcoat he briskly covered the distance to the gray-black five floor building housing the POW/MIA Agency. Its polished marble and opaque glass reflected the almost dark gray sky. Passing through the lobby security screen he took the elevator to the fourth floor.

"It is Mr. Theodore LePage to see Mr. Staples," he said into the wall phone and knocked the snow from his Fedora as he waited.

A pretty young woman opened the door and invited him in. Ted showed his pass and driver's license to the security person at the desk and then followed the young woman to the east side of the building.

"Nice view," Ted observed as he shook Rinehard's hand. "But I prefer mine, it is less noisy."

Both men stood silently for a moment and watched an ethereal shape of a Boeing moving up the taxiway at Reagan Airport. "The view," Rinehard observed, "is spectacular on a clear day. And for leased space I am not complaining. What's on your mind?"

"Could you update me on how your POW/MIA office in Moscow got started?"

"Sure! It was an ancillary outcome of the Kerry Commission decision on the Vietnam problem. But the overriding concern was to create something that would convince the American people that their government was being all inclusive and accountable before the fiftieth anniversary of the end of World War II." Rinehard smiled. Ted could tell they'd just reached a meeting of the minds. "It's how government works sometimes," Rinehard concluded.

"We obviously had a much greater interest in seeing it started than did the Russians. I think the last few years' experience clearly indicates that. Anyway, a working group was created in early 1993 and finalized later that year. We had four objectives and the Russians one. Hold on a moment. I thought you might be interested so I dug out some ancient history for you." He pushed a data disk into the projector on his desk and pointed at the screen. "There are the official objectives . . . for what they were worth. But unofficially, we never really did because no one wanted to open Pandora's box."

SPECIAL GROUP-MOSCOW
(TOP SECRET/AMBIENT)

The World War II U.S. Working Group
Objectives

- Determine why and how many U.S. prisoners of war came into Soviet military custody at the end of World War II.
- Describe what happened to these illegally hijacked POW's while in the hands of the Soviets.
- Describe the process by which all of these POW's were returned to U.S. military control.
- Determine whether thousands (as alleged in some accounts) of live American prisoners of war were ever abandoned in the USSR.
- Reach a final Soviet casualty accounting for World War II Russian prisoners who did not return to the Soviet Union.

"How much do you know about our missing servicemen in the USSR and elsewhere, Ted?"

"On a top secret basis, enough not to argue that many were there and some still may be."

"Not straddling the fence anymore, Rinehard? You've been doing this now for at least seven, maybe eight years?"

"You could say that," Rinehard replied. "It's a thankless exercise in futility, for the most noble of sacrifices, but enshrouded in mystery, protected by malevolent sentinels, and downplayed by political wags here . . . and disavowed absolutely by those ruling in Washington and the Kremlin."

"You have not had much luck."

"We were not supposed to right from the start."

"So why do you continue at it then?"

"It's a job, the view is good, the pay fantastic, the work a no-brainer, and when I retire the extra income will put me on easy street."

"And our government?" Ted asked.

"It makes the Congress feel good, fills the square, stops veterans complaints that its government is not doing something."

"And today?"

"There is still smoke from time to time. Sixty years ago, right after the war there were thousands of American's coming out of Eastern Europe, along with millions of other displaced persons fleeing the chaos of war. There were over a hundred thousand of our soldiers in German POW camps liberated by the Russians. Did the Russians let all of our people go? Did they keep some of them? Did they ship some of them into Siberia? You bet your ass they did. Behind the secret stamps we know that hundreds of thousands of allied prisoners also went the same way . . . Americans, English, French, Austrians, Belgians, Dutch, and Italians for starters. Some came back, but most didn't. Is it possible that in this huge river of humanity flowing east in the months after the war, that a couple, a hundred, a thousand, or twenty to twenty-five thousand Americans got caught in the flow—absolutely!"

"Our military set up a debriefing program worldwide right after the war, particularly in Europe, where the WRINGER prisoner interrogation project had interrogation teams all over Europe. They debriefed refugees and defectors flowing into the NATO area. Among the refugees were large numbers of former European military prisoners escaping from Russian detention camps. They reported seeing large numbers of Americans everywhere, so we knew our prisoners were there at that time. Talk to any of the ex-WRINGER personnel still around today and they'll convince you that this is an issue worthy of pursuit. This answer your question?" Rinehard asked.

"Got any of their names?"

"Colonel Bob Work was the commander. Others were Heinz Neblic, Gurth, and Riesbacki. I can get you more details."

"How many of our prisoners ended up in the USSR and what happened to them?" Ted asked.

"Where to start?" Rinehard muttered, "Without spending all day? By the time the war ended we had almost ten million people under arms. But you are only asking about those in Europe and the Mediterranean theaters. Hold on just a moment." He fiddled with the projector activation remote. The screen information changed.

Special Group-Moscow (unclassified)

Wartime Casualties in the European/Mediterranean Theater (U)
(Killed, Captured and Missing in Action)

1942	4,028
1943	60,217
1944	478,489
1945	222,548
Total	765,182

Source: Final Army Report on WW II.
Battlefield Casualties by Year in Europe.

"This is an overview of the size of the problem just in Europe. Keeping track of so many was a full time job. When the War ended in April 1945, SHAFE, which stands for Supreme Headquarters Allied Forces in Europe—had no idea where most of our captured personnel were physically. The Germans had been providing lists through Switzerland, but there were always weeks or months out of date by the time they reached Washington, and as the Russians overran Eastern Europe in late 1944, total chaos ensued. We'd agreed with the Russians at Yalta that both sides would immediately arrange to repatriate each other's captured servicemen from the Germans, but Moscow never adhered to its part of the agreement. So by the time the war ended they'd given us nothing about the status of any of our prisoners under their control for the six months between November 1944 to April 1945. And after Germany's surrender, some of our people began appearing along our lines. They were the lucky few who had somehow been able to walk out of the Red Army-occupied eastern areas. Some walked for hundreds of miles through the chaos of the collapsing Reich."

"How many of the total were captured," Ted inquired.

"An army adjutant general report published on 31 December 1946, a year and nine months after the war ended, put the number for the entire war in Europe at 93,941 captured and 23,014 missing in action. That covers 7 December 1941 through 31 December 1946."

"But what about those the Russians had in mid-1945, who we never recovered, and ended up somewhere else?" Ted asked.

"Back then the answer was more clearly defined. Today its more complex. There are many issues involved."

"I'm certain there are," Ted said with a note of annoyance in his voice. "He'd heard the same thing from Stud Muffin. What's your opinion?"

Rinehart changed the chart with another one. "Study this for a moment, Ted. It's kind of busy, but there are a couple of points that stand out."

Special Group-Moscow
(Top Secret/Ambient) (1)

Americans Captured and Missing in
European/Mediterranean WWII Theaters
June 30, 1946

	30 June 1945	**31 Dec 1945**	**30 June 1946**
Killed in Action	130,038	140,594	142,411
Returned to Military control	87,737	92,564	96,691
Prisoners of War	9,343	5,489	-0-
Declared Dead	5,798	12,261	14,331
Currently Missing in Action	20,391	3,023	433
Grand Total	253,690	254,792	255,206

(1) Source: Battle Casualties of the Army, War Department General Staff, Adjutant General, Washington. June 1946. This briefing is classified TOP SECRET because of serious irreconcilable casualty data (especially KIA, POW, and Declared Dead) between Department of Army, State Department, Pentagon, and Individual Military Services.

Ted took a moment to digest the totals. "What's the bottom line, Rinehard?"

"If you have never seen the referenced Battle Casualties of the Army Report from which this data was taken, you should. It's an incredibly comprehensive report of some forty large pages and includes all services. At the time it was considered the definitive study of our wartime losses in all theaters, and was updated in six month periods! That's June 1945, December 1945, and June 1946, and so forth. This was during a time when the Army was exhaustively trying to ascertain the final status of all U.S. personnel still unaccounted for in Europe. You'll notice that the totals for June 30, 1945, December 31, 1945, and 30 June 1946, are almost exactly the same. The Army had obviously agreed on the total in that regard."

"You'll also notice that the first, second and fourth of June 30, 1946, totals significantly changed over the proceeding periods, Killed in Action, up 12,373. RMC, or Returned to Military Control, up 8,954. And Declared Dead, up 8,533. That's a cumulative total of 29,860 personnel."

"You'll also notice that the third and fifth of the 1946 totals also fell significantly over the same period. POW's declined by 9,343 personnel down to 0 while current MIA's also declined from 20,391 down to only 433. The 433 were obviously those still considered missing in mid-1946, a year after the war ended. The respective increases and decreases cancel each other out almost completely." Rinehard paused, looking at Ted with an inquiring expression.

"So . . ." Ted enquired finally, "the POWs and MIAs somehow suddenly became killed in action?" Ted speculated.

Rinehard shrugged. "And the killed-in-action were also conveniently declared BNR for Body Not Recovered."

"A cover up for the Russian's perfidy?" Ted thought aloud.

"I didn't say that," Rinehard replied. "But, I cannot think of another explanation. Those involved in the wrap-up effort were loyal and patriotic Americans. They had a difficult job. And their endeavors were frustrated by three overwhelming considerations. First the American public was losing interest in the war-era as everyone focused on rebuilding their lives. The military was downsizing rapidly and manpower cuts were extensive. And most problematical was our public law." Rhinehard changed the screen again. "Ever seen this before?"

SPECIAL GROUP-MOSCOW (unclassified)

Public Law for Soldiers missing in Wartime

> Those reported as missing or missing in action will continue to be so recorded until twelve months from the initial date of the individual's report in accordance with Federal Statute. They will then be declared dead unless mitigating information dictates otherwise.

Ted looked at him. "So we declared them dead when it was suspected that at least some of them might still be alive in Russia?"

Rinehard nodded. "Correct. Near as I can tell those still alive and in Russian hands at 30 October 1946 were somewhere around 11,200. Behind closed doors here in Washington, among the cognoscenti, the consenus back then was that the real number was much higher."

"And today?" Ted asked.

"The folks over at State and Crystal City, behind closed doors, still agree."

"Reality or cover up?" Ted pressed him.

"Reality is a better term." Rinehard insisted. "The bureaucracy's concern is that if the Privacy Act legislation is changed, or classification restrictions lifted, the information which would come out, for the families involved, would be like manna from heaven. But for the government the result would be legal chaos."

"An interesting term. Why chaos?"

"Because the rest of them had probably already died at hard labor. Five months earlier—in May 1946, the army sent out 26,736 notices to next of kin throughout the United States, informing families that their sons, husbands, fathers, and loved ones' status had suddenly been officially changed, from missing to presumed dead, but no one was informed exactly where the missing were presumed to have died?"

"What about finding any of the Russian records about the survivors today?"

"I've spent a lot of time on this in Russia, Ted. If anyone in Moscow would know, it would be the former KGB's archive in Moscow."

"Where is that?"

"Either at their headquarters in downtown Moscow at Dzerzhinski Square, or #3 Vyborgskaya, which is in the city's northern suburbs. Some of their senior intelligence people know exactly where the records are. But would they tell us? In the mid-1990s I think some of them were ready to share them with us. But in the era of Putin, things have become very testy. You need approval now from hundreds of people who all want to know why, where, what, who and when?"

"I've got about 1,700 leads so far but all have led nowhere. We got a lead from a walk-in in Moscow a while back who told us about a place in the Kurile Islands. We found remains of a B-29 electronic reconnaissance aircraft crash and repatriated the remains of a crewmember found there."

"Why do the Russians try to hide it, even today, after so many years?"

"Think about it, Ted. An attorney told me a few years ago to call him if we learned about survivors still alive out there today. Rinehard had already worked the numbers. Based on a declining number yearly from the initial group in 1945, with only a few hundred alive today, he estimated that a Class Action Law Suit with the survivors as the plaintiffs and the families of the deceased as participants: that the financial claim for back-pay alone could exceed two and a half billion dollars today. And with punitive damages et cetera, maybe ten billion?"

"Yeah. But who would pay it?" Ted asked with incredulity in his voice.

"According to the attorney, no problem. Most of the people in the Gulag were employed by Russian government companies: oil, coal and gas, and other raw materials. Organizations like Gazprom today have assets worth trillions. Gazprom's annual delivery contracts with Europe today for oil and gas are in scores of billions. A class action award would tie up Russia exports, and in the end Moscow would have to settle out of court—for maybe half or a third of the amount. But it's still a enough to draw in thousands of attorneys who could lay back on easy street for the rest of their lives."

"Would money help loosen up tongues in Russia?" Ted asked. "You know, to get the ball rolling?"

"You'd think it would. But I don't think so. Too much bureaucratic red tape. And then there is what is in their archives that others are looking for? It's a real problem. And whose going to give them money? You?"

"What were you referring to when you mentioned what others are looking for?"

"The Hermitage in Saint Petersburg for instance. Europe suspects that a lot of its missing art treasures from World War II are in its basement. And they probably are."

"What do you think of Stanley Citwits?" Ted asked.

"For a historian he's a good man. Knows his stuff."

"Thanks for the time."

FOUR

Dulles Airport

A STACCATO WOMAN'S VOICE came over the aircraft intercom and pulled Alex Balkan out of a deep sleep. He glanced at his watch . . . it was nine o'clock in the evening in Germany, he'd slept three hours. "Ladies and gentlemen," the announcement droned, "please fasten your seat belts, put up your tray tables and seats back. We are approaching Dulles International, and the captain is pleased to inform everyone that we will be arriving fifteen minutes early. The local time in Washington is a quarter to three in the afternoon."

He'd deliberately not called ahead from Frankfurt to tell Ted LePage he was returning. Four days ago Ted demanded he return immediately. It almost seemed as if LePage was deliberately trying to annoy him, and there had to be an explanation. But what? Alex had ignored LePage's order because there were loose ends that he needed to look into. In the final analysis he thought he'd done a great job. He'd almost solved the Slavchenko case, and also picked up some incredibly interesting information along the way. But what good was information about POW/MIAs? It wasn't the type stuff LePage or others inside the Beltway wanted to hear about.

He had seen Untermann in Bansin on the northern German coast. Untermann had filled in a lot of the missing pieces and provided the name of a retired engineer in Bremen, who'd spent his life with the Krupp steel combine. One of Krupp's companies during the war was Eisener Gesselschaft Farbriken—the name stamped on the propeller found in the Boca Chica canal. He'd also gone to see the man with the Krupp Steel Combine in Bremen. But unfortunately, the man was unable to shed new light on Alex's problem. All records pertaining to individual propellers fitted to different Nazi warships were destroyed during an American Army Air Force bombing strike on Bremen toward the end of the war. There was no way to tell anymore. After Bremen, Alex spent two days slowly driving south through the Thuringian countryside toward Frankfurt.

Then there was the question of the three gold shipments. The Germans had obviously conspired with the United States and the British; but for what purpose? The gold aboard the three U-Boats? What had become of it and who had benefited from it in the last six decades? Alex pushed the call button for the flight attendant.

"Miss, could you bring me today's newspaper!"

She brought him the London Times. Toward the back he found the metals section, and yesterday's closing price for gold. After some quick calculations he whistled quietly to himself as he studied the snow-covered landscape as the Jumbo drifted south across the Virginia countryside.

Outside customs he headed for a bank of telephones and punched in the numbers for Marvin Raoul's apartment in Georgetown. It had been a while since they'd attended the Intelligence Banquet at Fort McNair, and he hoped Marvin had forgiven him for not taking him home that night. On the fourth ring Marvin answered.

"It's Alex. I just got back and need to see you. Could we meet tomorrow for dinner?"

Alex pressed the phone tighter to his ear to blot out an airport public announcement. "So what if tomorrow's Friday night Marv? Alex insisted they meet until Raoul relented. "Good, I'll see you at the place which used to be Pied du la Couchon in Georgetown, you remember where it is, it's a couple blocks up from M Street."

Marvin told him he knew why Alex wanted to see him, and hoped the rumors were not true. Alex's face drew taught as Marv told him of the rumor circulating, that Scion had decided to terminate Alex.

"When?" Alex demanded.

"End of the month."

"Thanks for the heads-up. See you tomorrow night at six." He hung up and dropped more change, and dialed the number given him by Professor Schenke in Brussels for Kissling at the Crystal City POW/MIA Agency. A secretary answered and asked him to hold for a moment. Kissling came on the line.

“I’m curious about a call you got six months ago with an offer for five thousand files on captured American soldiers in World War II who were never repatriated and sent to their deaths in Russia.”

“Who is this?”

“Names Balkan, Alex Balkan.”

“Who told you this?”

“A professor Schenke in Brussels.”

“Never heard of him.”

Alex held the receiver back, staring at it in disbelief. “You know nothing of the man or the offer for five thousand files?”

“Neither. You must have made a mistake. I have a meeting going on, so if you will excuse me.” The line went dead.

His next call was to Ted LePage’s office. Ted answered. “Where the hell are you?” Ted demanded.

“At Dulles.”

“Just arrived?”

“A quarter hour ago.”

“You were supposed to be here days ago! Isn’t that what we agreed on Monday? You don’t follow instructions very well, do you? What the hell does someone have to do to get your attention, Alex?”

“I’ll be in your office before five.”

“Not so fast! I’m tied up this afternoon and busy tonight. Be in at eight in the morning.”

“Ted!”

“Yeah.”

“What’s the matter?”

“What do you mean?”

“You’re uptight!”

“Mind your own business!”

Alex decided not to pursue the rumor about his being fired. “You still there, Ted?”

Again, that annoyed and abrupt intonation in Ted’s voice. “Yeah I’m here.”

“What do the next few days look like?”

“Why?”

“I was thinking about some time off.”

“No problem, Alex, you got plenty of leave time.”

“Meaning?”

“I’m busy Alex. See you in the morning!”

Alex hung up. Something was wrong! Maybe Marvin was correct! He contacted the Operator and asked for a collect call to Salt Lake, Utah. Five minutes later he'd made plans to leave Saturday morning from Washington National, and stay with a girlfriend in Chicago. He gave the operator his true name. With his last quarter he dialed American Airlines again, this time making a reservation to Salt Lake City in the name of Jonathan. Zilken. With all the shit which he suspected was about to happen, he didn't want to leave an easy trail if they decided to come looking for him. On the other hand, if the rumors were untrue, then he had less than three weeks before he'd leave for another season of missile and nuclear weapons verification work in the Russian missile fields.

He took a cab to his apartment in Balston and by eight was in bed.

* * *

"What did you find out?" Ted LePage demanded the next morning.

Alex started at the beginning and recounted the highlights of his trip from Florida to his stops in Lisbon, Novosibirsk, Marba, Moscow, and Europe. He mentioned the Case Judy question, and how the old German repeatedly cautioned him to be careful about whom he mentioned it to. But Alex deliberately omitted the part about the two Novosibirsk documents, and was waiting for Ted to mention them.

"What the hell did you do in Moscow that pissed them off so bad?"

"Told them I knew they were holding our soldiers from World War II, and asked for an updated list of their living survivors and where they were being held."

"Jesus. What were your accusations based on?"

"The two documents I mentioned."

"May I see them?"

"They're in my stuff, I'll bring them in later. What about here in Washington Ted?"

"Meaning?"

"What's happening?"

"Things have been quiet."

"Nothing new about Slavchenko?"

"That's right."

"And the police?"

"Zero," Ted explained. "And her case is almost dead in the water. No leads. They've decided to put it on the back burner."

"The other day when we talked, Ted, you said you thought you had something!"

"It was also a dead end."

Now Alex knew something was definitely wrong. LePage must be holding out on him. And if he was, then Alex too would hedge his bets. He had the information Ted needed, and Ted had no idea how incriminating it was. During the next five minutes they made polite conversation until Alex realized the rumor about him must be true. "What about my future Ted?"

Ted's demeanor changed slightly.

"What about it?"

"I've heard rumors."

"About what?"

"My employment being terminated."

"Who told you that?" LePage demanded, his voice instantly agitated. But his reaction transparent.

"Then it's true?" Alex's tone accusatory.

"I won't mince words, Alex. It's nothing personal you understand, and it has nothing to do with your performance. Anyone who asks, will be assured you were among our best. But unfortunately reductions are taking place. Such things happen. You understand. I hope you realize this was not my decision, the personnel folks called it," Ted concluded.

"Bullshit!"

"I'm leveling with you, Alex."

"Don't give me that crap."

"Calm down, Alex! It doesn't become effective until the end of the month, maybe we can work something out!"

"I don't think so," Alex replied. "Under my contract I'm entitled to double time for accumulated weekends and holidays."

"Correct! And you will be paid."

"I'm also carrying seventy-two days of overtime through December, and a shit-pot more since then."

"You'll get that too."

The meeting wasn't going the way Ted hoped. He wanted a complete debrief, and written report from Balkan, and after that he'd planned to break the bad news to Balkan. "Look, Alex, I don't have all morning to waste on this. I need the documents and your report."

"Excuse me!" Alex replied sarcastically as he got up. "You are obviously busy, and what I have to say will keep, so I'll put it in my report and send it when I get time." He got up and headed for the door.

"Where you going?"

"I'm going on leave. A long one!"

"I need your report, Alex."

"I'll mail it!"

"Alex!" LePage's voice was now insistent. "Balkan! Come back here and sit down!"

Alex left the door ajar behind him.

*   *   *

"From what you've told me," Marvin concluded over drinks that evening in Georgetown, "it's obvious you are on to something incredible. These are the documents?" Marvin peered into the manila envelope at the papers. "And you haven't mentioned the details of these to LePage?"

"Only about the Americans."

"You realize that unless you go public with this, it isn't worth much?" Marvin was concerned his friend might have missed the obvious. No one in intelligence would discuss any of this in public, and once classified, the information would disappear into the system forever and be forgotten. If any of the Americans in the document were still alive they'd now be over seventy; men who even if repatriated, would have few close relatives, and most would be transferred into institutions for the aged.

"I'll tell you this Alex! The Press would love to get their hands on this. What do you intend to do with it?"

Alex shrugged.

"You're undecided?"

"It will cause a lot of grief. So much time has gone by. But we abandoned these poor bastards and they deserved better. They are . . . were . . . Americans just like you and I, and we abandoned them."

"Yeah."

"So why delay making it public?"

"Because of what happened this morning. I think LePage is involved." Alex knew it was a serious accusation; he was talking about Murder-One. He was also talking about treason and interference with the justice system! Concealing evidence. Even conspiracy!

"If it were me, Alex, I'd give it to the newspapers?"

"Can't! Not yet anyway! CIA would find a way to quash it for national security reasons. They'd also call it a forgery and say I'd run amok; was unhappy and wanted to embarrass the country: and the Agency too because I'd just been fired. Then they'd roll up my charges under the Patriot Act and put me away forever."

"Sounds to me, Alex, like you've already thought this through. Who's behind this?"

"Wish I knew!" Alex suspected it was much bigger than good old Ted LePage.

"The agency?"

"Could be."

"The good old boys at Exeter?"

"Them too," Alex said. "It's possible." Exeter was an obscure association of Washington's power brokers who met periodically over lunch and established policy arguments directing the nation's political leaders. "Sounds like them. They're above the law most of the time."

"DIA?" Marvin asked.

"Maybe?" Alex realized Defense Intelligence Agency had the most to lose if the information became public. They'd been involved in all prisoner reporting over the years and their record was abysmal. On the flight in from Frankfurt he'd seen an article in the American Spectator magazine. Entitled MIA Cover-Up, it painted a dim picture of government's role in the POW/MIA problem. It pointed out that in the last four decades Washington had received fifteen thousand live sighting reports about Americans being held in Southeast Asia and elsewhere and discredited all of them as unreliable. The author observed such an abysmal record defied the laws of probability and constituted culpable negligence. The author concluded it was apparent Washington was involved in a huge conspiracy, and accused the Pentagon, CIA, and the Senate of also being involved.

Alex had thought about mentioning Case Judy to Marvin, but decided against it, recalling the German's warning to be careful whom he mentioned it to. Alex didn't want to endanger Marvin, not yet anyway.

"So what are you going to do, Alex?"

"Lay low. I've contacted a friend and will get out of town for a while."

"Need money?"

"Thanks, but I just cashed in my savings. It should last awhile. I need a couple of favors though."

"Name it!"

"I want all this kept between us?"

"You got it!"

"Can I stay at your place tonight?"

"Sure."

"Could you drop me at BWI tomorrow?" He planned to leave his rental car at Washington National after lunch, and leave from Baltimore a few hours later. If anyone were looking for him, they'd be watching National and Dulles. No one would be looking for J. Zilken at BWI.

"No problem. Will you stay in touch?"

"I'll leave a number."

Rosslyn

"Yeah, I know.

A long silence.

"That's a little strong don't you think?"

More silence.

"Okay. I'll try to find out if its Paul Carter."

Another long pause.

"Jesus. You say he's documented as Pavlo Krasnov, a Bulgarian! I'll see what we can do."

The old man listening in to the conversation smiled as he tweaked the receivers dial trying to fine-tune the acoustic signal, afraid he'd lose part of the one-sided conversation. Then it returned loud and clear.

"Alex Balkan . . . what about him?"

Silence

"No problem. He's off the Slavchenko case already."

Another pause.

"I think he knows a lot more than he's told me. Unfortunately he stormed out a while ago and didn't leave the Russian documents."

A pause.

"No. I don't know when he will file his report. He's been fired, effective the end of this month, and he knows it. So for all I know he may never file the report, and we may never see the documents."

More silence.

"I have no idea what the documents say. He suggested they were important. He picked them up in Novisibirsk."

More silence.

"No. Nothing to do with Slavchenko as far as I know. Carter, it could be about him."

More silence.

"Goddamn it! I know the timing is unfortunate, but we had to get rid of Alex Balkan, and somehow he learned he was going to be fired. There was no other way. Anything else?"

Another silence.

"Christ, I can't do this! It's murder!"

Silence.

"You will take care of it?" LePage's voice now sounded incredulous.

A momentary silence.

"Of course I won't say anything about it to anyone. I'm not that dumb, goddamit! I'll get his documents as soon as possible."

Paul Carter heard the sound of the receiver being replaced on the phone's cradle. He knew Ted LePage had just hung up the phone in his office an eighth of a mile away. LePage called his wife at home next, and told her to be ready to leave the house at seven thirty, as they had a dinner engagement this evening.

That's it, Paul Carter thought. Somehow they'd learned he was still alive, and figured out who he was. But they apparently still did not know he'd made his way to the United States. Paul smiled as he looked at the recorder on the table.

A block away on Kent Street in Rosslyn, overlooking the Potomac River and Georgetown, stood the mirrored glass building housing Scion Consultants. From Paul's warehouse window which earlier tenants had thoughtfully plastered over with newspaper, he had an unobstructed view of the corner office on the fifteenth floor which Ted LePage's Scion Consultants occupied. Paul couldn't see through the mirrored exterior glass, but the laser gun relayed all he needed off the exterior glass of Ted LePage's office.

He now had what he needed. It was time to pull the plug and drop out of sight for a while: he knew who they were, where they were, where they lived, what they were afraid of. And best of all, that they desperately wanted him out of the way. He also knew they wouldn't go to the police. But then his own agenda didn't involve him going to the police either. What concerned Paul most was how they knew his alias? For that he suspected there could be only one explanation? The Russians!

From people transiting the building's foyer, he'd also determined that Scion Consultants were involved with the Central Intelligence Agency. Two days earlier he'd spotted Theodore LePage in the lobby and followed his former associate. First Ted's car had disappeared into the grounds of the Central Intelligence Agency just up the road. When LePage emerged hours later he'd followed him home, and yesterday Paul had followed LePage from his residence back to work.

First he'd take out LePage and then sit back for a while and stalk Seeley and make the old bastard sweat his fate.

Northern Virginia

LePage's Camray stopped at the four-way stop sign in Lee Heights. Carter scanned the approaches which were clear, then leaned out the window toward the Camray alongside. Several inches of new snow and a light fog highlighted by a quartz halogen street lamp, cast eerie hues into the woods beside the residential intersection. Through the open window Paul hailed LePage, honking the horn. LePage noticed he was trying to get his attention and hit the passenger side electric window. "Can I help you?"

"Where's Wakefield Drive?"

As Ted explained, Paul's hand rose above the window sill. LePage saw the gun barrel six feet from his face and seemed perplexed as Paul extended his arm out straight. "Son of a bitch," LePage exclaimed. "Is it you Paul? Don't do it, I am sorry, forgive me!" But it was too late! His head jerked sideways against the driver's side window marking it with a red smear of blood. LePage's body bucked twice more before slumping forward against the seat restraints. The car and its lifeless occupant rolled through the intersection, side swiping a row of parked cars before hitting a tree. Paul turned right and minutes later was amidst the evening traffic heading west along Route 66 for the Washington Beltway.

Two down and one to go he thought. He'd leave in the morning with his girlfriend, for a few weeks at her cabin in upstate New York. Without Cimeon's car, he'd never have got this far. He had no driver's license and couldn't apply for one. She didn't know that, and since she rode the Metro to work daily, she left him the keys. When he'd first arrived from Canada, he spent several frustrating months trying to determine if Seeley was still alive. It was only with the help of a lady at the local library who'd helped him understand the Library's computer web-site equipment that he'd finally located Seeley, and as luck would have it, the son of a bitch was still right here in Washington after all these years. The librarian had opened his eyes to the simplicity of the Internet and its incredible use as a research tool.

With Cimeon's car, everything quickly changed for Paul, he had mobility and obscurity. The revolver too was no problem. Cimeon said it belonged to her deceased father and had been in the family for fifty or more years. Paul's biggest problem was making certain the police didn't stop him for some minor traffic infraction. But even in that eventuality he'd decided he would shoot the officer. Soviet police, American police, they were all the same to him now after sixty years in the Siberian Gulag.

Now only Seeley and Staples remained. But Paul would let him sweat for a while. He wanted Seeley to know what it felt like. To know he was going to be killed, but not the exact time and place, nor how his death would be administered.

Paul had first got to know Seeley at an OSS training camp on the north shore of Lake Erie in the summer of 1942. Even then Paul hadn't liked the ostentatious bastard. The only child of a wealthy New England family, Langford Seeley thought he knew it all. Daddy had already arranged everything for Langford: the best schools, the biggest parties with the crème de la crème and summer vacations in Europe with the scum of La Belle Epoch. Daddy had even arranged for young Langford to attend the 1936 Olympic games in Berlin.

Paul on the other hand, was the son of dirt poor immigrants. Brooklyn was the wrong side of the tracks. People of wealth smirked knowingly at those from Brooklyn. Public schooling had been his lot. But he'd always known where he'd come from and was never fooled by money, position and power. His big break was the Marine Corps, which had opened another world for him, one he'd never have seen had he remained in Brooklyn working one of the corner stores which dotted the area where he was brought up. A couple of years with the Marine Corps and service in Asia had exposed him to the seamier side of life, where he'd seen death up close, the frailty of human endeavor, and had drunk deeply from the cup of the seven deadly sins.

Langford on the other hand was unfamiliar with the close-up realities of human misery. Langford thought everyone had servants, could have their way with their female domestics, and buy off those he'd abused with money. Langford looked down on those of lesser fortune. Friendship and trust to Langford were trivial matters of little import while, to Paul, they were treasures to be nurtured and esteemed.

He and Langford wcrc thrown together as roommates at the Ontario OSS camp, and forced to work together for eighteen hours a day for three long months. By the time it was over, Paul truly disliked his roommate. He knew Langford's weaknesses, and idiosyncrasies and found them repulsive. Paul had also been forced to help carry Langford through the grueling syllabus. Without Paul, Langford would never have made it. Paul thought Langford totally unsuited to the clandestine world. To work with others confronting death, one had to understand what motivated men, made them trust you, love you, and to keep faith with you, even when their lives were being ripped from their chests. Not to care about those in one's care trivialized those whose lives too often ended in dark rooms—hideously tortured and broken in the process of extracting their last thoughts. In the end it was only daddy's money that finally got Langford admitted to the OSS, and Paul who got him through the program and accepted.

Five months later came Paul's betrayal in China, and were it not for Slavchenko's visit to Paul's Gulag camp near Novisibirsk so many years later, Paul would never have known of Langford Seeley's duplicity. The woman who'd come to interrogate him at Novosibirsk, had unwittingly supplied Paul with the who, the what, the where, and the why of his betrayal by Seeley. And even now he still didn't understand what the whole thing was all about, but didn't care. Now in his ninetieth year, settling old scores was all that remained to him in what little time he had left. The Russians were obviously still looking for the wartime gold stolen from them by the Germans, and subsequently lost in China. And while the part Seeley and others had played in his betrayal still intrigued Paul, it was of little consequence now. All that would quench

Paul's hatred was the thought that Seeley knew his own days were numbered, and that it was Paul who would end them.

Paul turned north onto the beltway and headed for Cimeon's apartment in Maryland. His urge for a sexual liaison with Cimeon was on his mind. It would not give her the satisfaction of a younger man, but the act with her, for him, was incredibly satisfying. First thing in the morning, they'd drive north to Cimeon's camp in the Adirondaks.

Salt Lake City

The United Airlines Boeing made its final approach over the white expanse of Utah's Salt Lake through a late February cold front which had already punched south through the Rocky Mountains from the Canadian Artic. Temperatures from North Platte to Kansas City had plunged within hours. The front was now stalled over southern Colorado, piling up two feet of new snow on the landscape outside his window. Alex looked forward to seeing his old girlfriend, Heather Maldutis, and some good sex, and maybe even a little skiing. The twitch in his eye was improving rapidly as he dreamed about what might be possible with her. He hoped it would be the same as where they'd left off a couple of months ago, and that he hadn't stayed away too long.

He'd known Heather Maldutis for almost twenty years, almost since she'd first started working for the government. After graduation, Heather had landed her first job as a GS-9 at the Pentagon. Good-looking, with a model's body lines, and interested in foreign travel, she'd quickly wormed her way into a GS-11 position in Stuttgart, Germany, where they'd met a year later. They'd dated for almost a year before she'd dropped him, explaining she wasn't ready to make a long-term commitment. At twenty-five, Europe beckoned, and she wanted to see it all. They'd seen each other less frequently after that and his thoughts of marriage faded. She saw other men, but hadn't married. Following other foreign assignments in Greece, Turkey, and the Philippines, she'd finally returned to Washington.

Disillusioned and no longer interested in foreign adventure, three years later she'd transferred to one of the Supply Squadrons on Hill Air Force Base, north of Salt Lake City. Since then he'd seen her about twice a year, and it always ended the same way. In bed, with her wishing he'd settle down to make her an honest woman, and him exploring every one of her orifices in detail and wishing she'd shut up so he could orgasm himself to death.

When he'd called her this time, she'd assured him she would take a couple of days off so they could go skiing. Her parents had a Condo north of Salt Lake at Snow Basin, but seldom used it, spending most winters in San Diego.

So much had happened in the past few weeks, Alex needed time to think. A couple of things were now obvious to him: his career in government was over, and it was time to look for another line of work. At heart, he felt betrayed, actually shafted. LePage had disappointed him. He tried to recall an expression his dad once used around the house when Alex was young; something about rendered fat and a goats ass.

As he emerged from the jet port he spotted her. She hadn't changed, and if anything had lost weight. She looked great.

* * *

As he was dressing the next morning he heard the phone ringing in the kitchen.

"Alex!" Heather called, "It's for you!"

It was Marvin Raoul in Washington, and from Marvin's tone Alex knew Marvin was upset. "Jesus!" Marvin blurted. "Have you heard, Ted LePage is dead! He was shot last night! The police think it was a drive-by shooting! I knew you were pissed Alex. But not that much."

Alex didn't respond at first. "What time?"

"Around six-thirty."

Alex realized what Raoul was driving at. "Don't be an asshole, Marvin! You know I left before it happened. You took me to the airport . . . remember? I got here before six yesterday. Tell me what happened?"

"I just saw it in the papers. He was killed in his car at a stop sign only two hundred yards from his home. Shot three times in the head and upper body at close range."

Alex recalled LePage's colonial at the end of a cul-de-sac, and the kitchen which was his wife's pride and joy. Alex had visited them twice for parties, and wondered how she'd take her husband's passing? "What do you think?"

"What do I think? I'll tell you what I think! After what you told me, I think he was executed. I don't think this was a random thing. No damned way! And if he was wasted because of what you know, Alex, then where does that leave you? Or me for that matter? Maybe it has something to do with those papers you have?"

"Let's wait and see."

"Wait and see what?" Raoul asked dumbly.

"I didn't do it. I am not involved with anyone who might have of done it. So what do you expect me to do? I would suggest you keep your eyes and ears to the ground and let's see what the newspapers and television have to say about it?"

"And if I can't reach you?"

"Then you will know that I've been wasted too!"

"Don't joke around Alex. It's not funny."

"I'll keep a weather eye on my six."

"How's the skiing?"

"I haven't been up yet."

"Don't break a leg!" Raoul hung up.

"Trouble?" Heather asked.

He hadn't told her anything. He looked at his watch. It was eight o'clock in the morning in Salt Lake which would make it eleven o'clock in Washington. He picked up the phone and dialed Scion Consultants. He had to call now. By the time he got back from the ski slopes this afternoon, they'd be closed. He recognized the familiar voice of Ted's secretary. He looked at his watch as Ted's secretary answered. "This is Alex. Just checking in. Any messages?"

She broke into tears as she told him what a wonderful man Ted was. The usual bullshit, Alex thought, as he waited for her to complete her rendition of the magnificent life and times of the late Theodore LePage. He hung up.

A minute later, he called her again. "The line went dead," she said.

"A bad connection here," Alex replied. "Any word on who's going to replace Ted?"

"The deputy I assume?"

"Chuck Bunn?" Incredulity was obvious in Alex's voice. She was just the secretary, she had no idea of the stupidity of what she'd just suggested.

"We haven't heard yet."

"Any messages?"

"None since yesterday. Ted told you about the two calls he took, didn't he?"

"No."

"He must have forgotten!" But Alex knew that Ted LePage didn't forget anything, and now Alex wondered what Ted hadn't told him. "Who were they from?" He hung up the receiver. Then called back again. "Bad connection," he said. "A detective in Florida called, hold on I'll check the phone log. His name is Arden Welsh. I don't know what the call was about, but I recall it concerned a murder down there. I thought Ted mentioned it?"

"It's okay. Anything else?"

"A Mr. Citwits also called from Cameron Station."

Alex made a note of the name and phone number. "Thanks, darling, I'll be in touch."

"Where are you?"

He hung up, again.

"You ready to go?" Heather asked.

"Just one more call!"

"Don't be too long. I want to get in a couple of runs before lunch."

He waited while the digits clicked through and finally a voice answered. "Welsh here!"

"This is Alex Balkan, returning your call."

"Yeah! What's his name—your boss? Did he tell you I called?"

"You referring to Ted LePage?'

"Yeah."

"No he didn't."

"When did you get back?"

"Day before yesterday."

"Strange he didn't say anything to you."

"A little difficult. He's dead, Detective! Gunned down last night in a drive-by shooting near his home in Washington!"

"Jesus. Any idea who killed him?"

"Not yet."

"I hope they get the bastard!"

"That would be nice," Alex replied assuringly.

"I mentioned two names to LePage the other day. One is a guy called Paul Carter and the other, some Peruvian creep named Eduardo Hernandez. The coroner also changed the old lady's cause of death from heart failure, to suffocation! So now her death is officially Murder-One!"

Paul Carter's name rang out like a cannon shot, and Alex wondered how Welsh had come across it. "This is all news to me. What did LePage say?"

"He'd never heard of either."

Alex thought of denying it too, but decided to listen first to what Welsh had to say before going into details. "What do you have so far?" Alex asked.

Welsh repeated the story about Carter's finger prints and the meetings with the Peruvian. "I know you are an intelligence type Balkan, but I've got to know why you saw her? Right now I've got two suspects, you, and this guy named Carter who appears to have died during the war. Then there's the Peruvian who is obviously heavy into drug smuggling. I've also got a witness who said he heard the Albion woman yelling at you, saw her throw you out of her house. Even saw her throw a flower pot at you. Is that right?"

"Yeah."

"Level with me, or I'll have to put out a warrant to have you picked up for murder-One."

What the hell, Alex thought, why not? He didn't need the police on his ass too. Especially not now that he'd been fired and his boss murdered. Alex had to admit that Raoul's observation about him wasting LePage did have a twisted sort of logic to it. "Okay. But you'll have to trust me. I saw her because of some calls made to her by a Russian defector who was living here in Washington. The defector was also murdered here in Washington this past Christmas!"

"Another murder?"

"Not so fast. I'm not saying they're related."

"What are you saying?"

"Only that I was asked by Scion Consultants, my employer, to investigate four long distance phone calls the defector made to Eve Albion last year. So I went to Key West to ask her about them."

"And she threw you out?"

"Yes. But not before confirming she knew the Russian defector."

"Of course she did," the detective replied, "you said the calls were made to her house in Key West."

"The circumstances surrounding the defector were always problematical, she'd been very valuable to us when she first defected, and so we had to follow all the leads to her murder."

"Understood. And all this other shit?" Welsh's voice dripped with sarcasm, "About you're being a writer."

"There are aspects of the case I can't discuss, detective. Issues of national security. I'm sure you understand?"

"What did the Albion woman tell you?"

"Nothing. We spoke for maybe five minutes before I asked her about the Russian defector who had repeatedly called her. She then became noticeably upset and clammed up."

"That when she threw you out of her house?" Welsh inquired.

"You got it," Alex replied.

"So they obviously knew each other?"

"Yes. Absolutely!"

"And Paul Carter's prints?"

"I can't help you with that."

"You know this guy?"

"Not yet. But if the FBI said he died so long ago why ask me?"

"Don't be a smart ass! You say shit like that and I might assume you put the prints around to cover your ass, and I'll have a warrant out for you so fast, it'll make your head spin. I know you were asking questions about submarines, Germans, and spies. Albion used to work here during the war, and if the FBI is right about his or her deaths, then this guy Carter may have died here way back then too?"

Welsh was clever to have made the connection. The hell with it, Alex thought. There was no advantage in his getting crosswise with this lawman. He'd tell him what he knew. "Detective Welsh . . . the truth is that Carter is an American who disappeared in China in early 1943. The Russian defector who called Albion, said she'd seen Carter alive in a Russian Gulag camp in the late eighties. I just got back from Russia but could find no trace of Carter in their system."

"So you knew the name all along?"

"Obviously."

"LePage said he didn't?"

"He lied."

"So maybe Carter's the one I want to put out a warrant out for."

"Maybe, but I don't think so. Not unless you want to look stupid. He's officially been dead forty years. What are you going to tell your boss? Are you going to spend a couple of months in Washington, trying to convince them otherwise? You think they're going to take a hick detective from Key West serious? No offense Welsh. But you got to realize that what I've just told you is not common knowledge. So you'd better be careful what you say about it. You are playing with a loaded shotgun."

"That a threat?"

"Just advice. If your suspicion about Carter is correct, then he's armed and dangerous, and will be out looking for whomever double-crossed him. And if you mention all this up here in Washington. Well?"

"That where you are now?" The detective interrupted.

"Yeah. I think you might run into others who might share Carter's agenda. They may not want you making waves."

"Meaning."

"Just trying to be helpful. I don't want something to happen to you."

"A conspiracy?"

"Something like that."

"And you are not part of it?"

"No."

"Was LePage?"

"I don't know yet. Maybe?"

"Then try to understand my position, Alex."

"It might be difficult, I've also been canned."

"Fired? When?"

"Two days ago."

"For what?"

"The Albion and Carter thing I suppose."

"I don't understand?"

"Neither do I. I can only assume I'm getting too close, so someone wants me out of the way."

"They got LePage out of the way?"

"Maybe."

"Are you in danger too?"

"I think so."

"So who's behind this?"

"LePage might have been involved, but I think it's someone higher up."

"Who's this character named Eduardo Hernandez?"

"Never heard of him."

"Your leveling with me?"

"Yes."

Welsh recounted the entire story about the Peruvian's background, associates, and that a notice would be issued to Interpol that the United States wanted him for questioning. Welsh mentioned the name of Eduardo's British lawyer and his London phone number, and asked if Alex knew of him. Alex didn't, but he made a note of it.

"I think I understand what's happening now," Welsh concluded. "I want you to cooperate with me."

"Okay, can you give me a week or two?"

"You got it! I'll be expecting your call Balkan!" The line went dead.

Alex transferred his scribblings about the Peruvian and the London lawyer to a note pad. Who was this Eduardo Hernandez who'd also tried to see the woman in Key West? If Hernandez was involved with the drug cartels; was Eve also? It was a side of Albion that Alex found hard to believe but stranger things happened every day and when he thought about it, she made the ideal link; low key, unknown and someone above reproach. He tucked the information into his wallet and headed for the door.

When he and Heather returned after dinner there was a message on the answering machine. Alex's mother wanted him to call. Heather chided him that he'd better do it before he got into trouble.

It was after midnight in Altoona when his mother answered. She told him that a man with a thick accent had called her from some unpronounceable place called novi-cyberspace or something like that. She'd asked for a phone number but the caller hung up.

A half hour later when Alex got through to Novosibirsk, it was mid-morning in Asiatic Russia, and Kaminsky's remarks were curt and cryptic! Three hundred and fifty Americans remained of those Alex had asked about, and Kaminski assured him he would find a way to let Alex know where they were. But Kaminski needed more time. The man Alex had asked about had been deliberately released by the Russian government, and provided with travel documents, and money, and allowed to leave the country. The release had to do with an unresolved problem dating back to Russia's Great Patriotic War.

Most disturbing to Alex was Kaminiski's summary that the man they'd released was being followed. Any additional information would be sent to the address Alex had in Moscow.

Two minutes later the operator called back with time and charges. Twenty-eight seconds. Alex smiled. Kaminski had deliberately kept the call to less than a minute, knowing it took that long for the Russian intelligence system to trace international satellite calls. He stared at the phone and reflected on what he'd just learned. Three hundred and fifty American POWs held by the Germans had been captured by the Russians at the end of World War II, and were still alive somewhere in Russia! Carter had deliberately been released, provided with papers, money, and was being trailed. So it was probably the Russians who were responsible for the murder of the two women and Ted LePage?

The question of the two KGB documents now became more pressing. He'd have to figure out the best way to use them. He decided he'd ask Heather to rent a safe deposit box at the bank where she banked. He'd also leave a copy of the two documents with a local newspaper in Salt Lake. He picked up the phone again and waited for his mother to answer. He informed her she was not to call him again under any circumstances, and tell no one where he was. She understood. What Kaminsky had told him now made sense. Carter was obviously in the States, and just behind him . . . his KGB tails. It explained Carter's prints at Key West. It explained the declassified document left with Slavchenko. It explained Ted LePage's murder. Then there was the Peruvian named Hernandez. Where did he fit in? Alex returned the phone to its cradle and headed for the living room.

The previous night when Heather picked him up at the airport, it was as if it had only a few days since they'd last seen each other. His lower back ached slightly from one of the more intricate positions she liked from her book on Kamasutra, which she'd alluded to last night during dinner. On the slopes today she'd stopped to peck his cheek a couple of times and made intimate remarks. She'd also told him how much she'd missed him, and hoped they might see each other much more frequently. Over an intimate dinner this evening she'd reminded him that he was getting older and she was too, and that she didn't care much about children, and now needed someone to share her life with. It was the most direct proposal of marriage he'd ever received.

Moving through the darkened living room he heard a noise, and glanced at the log fire and snowflakes sliding down the exterior glass. She'd cleared her throat again to let him know she was on the floor near the fire. Padding around the couch he stopped as she ran her hand up the inside of his thigh, then pulled on her terry-cloth towel until it fell away.

"You seem troubled," she observed later. What's the matter?"

"It's all coming to an end, Heather."

"Meaning?"

"I got a pink slip!"

"Fantastic, darling!" she exclaimed. Her voice was overjoyed. "Now you'll have time to do other things. There's a big world out there just waiting for us to enjoy."

He hadn't expected the response. "And what would I do?"

"Enjoy yourself, play golf, ski, sign up for college courses. Make clay pots, grow roses. Write a book!"

"Sounds boring."

"Move in with me until you get your feet on the ground."

"I'll give it some thought."

"Do it!" She laughed lustily, rolling over on top of him, sliding the wetness of her mons veneris over his withered manhood. "Make me an honest woman!"

He didn't tell her his other problems as she pulled his face to hers again and breathed heavily into his ear, her tongue lubricating its channel. The rest could wait, Alex thought. This time he was slower and more purposeful until she was exhausted.

After she'd left to shower, he decided there were two people he still needed to talk to. He looked at his watch, then, picking up the phone, dialed the long distance operator.

"A collect call to London. Name of the party is Nigel Smithers. Tell whoever answers that this in reference to Eve Albion in Key West." He waited while the operator did her thing and a man's voice with a pronounced stutter accepted the call. "Who is this?"

"I need your help. Its urgent. I must speak with Mr. Eduardo Hernandez. I was told you could put me in touch."

"May I ask how you got my number?"

"From the Key West Police. They said your Peruvian client provided your number to them. I assume you are his solicitor?"

"I see. And what does this have to do with you?"

"I was in Key West recently too and inquired about the same woman your client did, so the police have tentatively linked Mr. Hernandez and myself."

"What's the relevance? As I understand it, she passed away."

"Not passed away, she was murdered!"

"I believe I was aware of that too!"

"Why did Hernandez want to see her?" Alex asked in a demanding tone. "I must know what their relationship was?"

"Must? Sir! You have not even given me your name?"

"It's Alex Balkan. Your client has a real problem. Are you going to help me or not?"

"What kind of a problem does he have?"

"Interpol is about to issue a notice about him."

"A notice?"

"They will ask for him to be picked up, for questioning."

"On what charge?"

"I'll discuss that with your client. I may be able to stop it."

"May I ask what your work is Mr. Balkan?"

"I'm with the United States Department of Defense."

"My dear boy," Smithers voice stuttered on, now also a little incredulous. "that takes in millions of people!"

"Intelligence!" He shot back. "And that's about as specific as I want to get!"

"I'm afraid I can't give you his phone number."

"Fine! Write down my number in Salt Lake City. Ask your client to call me ASAP. Within a couple of hours if possible. Its critically important to him."

"I shall relay the message."

Alex took a hot shower and as he walked into Heather's room, he thought about waking her. She was asleep spread-eagled on the bed. She was beautiful with lanky legs, narrow hips and waist and petite bourgeois breasts. He stared at her for a few minutes, once again beginning to become aroused. When the sun comes up, he thought.

Snow Basin, Utah

Wednesday afternoon when he returned to Heather's apartment, there were two phone calls waiting for him. The first was from the historian at Cameron Station, and the second from the Peruvian, who'd left a number at Limassol—on the south coast of the Island of Cyprus.

Alex had spent the morning in Salt Lake City as Heather was unexpectedly called in to work, and not wanting to ski alone, he'd lunched downtown with the assistant editor of the Salt Lake Sentinel, a corpulent man named Waleston Thrower. He'd explained to Thrower who he was, and alluded to the possibility of live American POW's still being held in Russia. He also mentioned the recent deaths of Albion, Slavchenko and LePage—all of which Thrower could verify, insinuating that Alex knew about an elaborate government cover-up that was underway, and one for which Alex could provide significant insights. In the end Thrower seemed interested, and assured Alex that as long as Alex was not involved in the murders, Thrower would honor a confidentiality arrangement, and would sit on the story until Alex got back to him.

"You have the originals of these Russian documents?" the editor inquired after he'd examined their photocopies.

"And these are accurate translations of them?" Thrower demanded.

"Correct."

"But you have not had them authenticated?"

"No. But they are the real McCoy, don't worry. Besides, when you get the originals, I'm sure you have ways to validate them yourself."

"Such as?"

"Independent labs, maybe even the FBI or CIA if you like. But if you use CIA or the FBI, I'm certain you'll never see the originals again, they'd be deliberately lost in the mail somehow."

"Where did you obtain these, Mr. Balkan?"

"In Russia, from an old man whose conscience bothered him. Please write your home phone number and initials on the back of two of your business cards, Mr. Thrower."

"Why?"

"If anything comes to you in the mail from me, and it has your card with it, you'll know it's from me! If not, well, let's just say you might want to be suspicious."

* * *

As the reflection of the sun began to set across the Great Salt lake, Alex sat in one of Heather's captain chairs watching several F-16 fighter planes in the distance as they silently glided just above the lake's surface on their final approach to Hill Air Force Base. Alex had been debating if he should place the call now to Eduardo Hernandez in Cyprus.

LePage's death had raised too many questions, and Alex was beginning to get an uncomfortable feeling. It was becoming obvious to him that the sequence of events had inextricably embroiled him in an issue which he could no longer control. LePage's death had followed Alex's termination. Some might now wonder if the two were linked. One step at a time, he told himself. First he'd find out what Ted had told Stud Muffin in Washington. Then he'd find the retired Army Colonel who'd been at Bahia Honda during World War II, and see what he knew about Albion and the missing U-Boat? And finally he'd get back into Russia and check with Kaminsky's relative in Moscow, and see what he had? He looked at his watch. It was now five o'clock in the afternoon in Salt Lake City. It would be almost midnight in Cyprus. To hell with it he thought, he'd call Eduardo Hernandez and wake him up if he had to.

Metro Center

The well-dressed old man moved to the middle of Washington's Metro Center platform, stopping before a quadrangle of public phones. He'd just finished an early lunch at the Army-Navy Club at Farragut Square and walked the five blocks here. On the adjacent platform stood an identical quadrangle, one of which was occupied by the man he recognized. He moved into an empty stall and dropped in a quarter and dialed. He couldn't hear the single ring on the adjacent platform before it was picked up, and he heard the familiar voice.

"This is Jerry!"

Also known as Victor Indorenko and in the employ of Russia's national airline in Washington, Jerry was his handler: his case officer in the parlance of the CIA, and the old man's message would be relayed by his case officer to Moscow. The old man, and one of Jerry's predecessors had set up the arrangement a decade back when it became obvious the old order in Russia was about to collapse, and new security arrangements would be needed to protect the most critical of Russia's secret spy associations which Moscow desperately wanted to survive the end of the Cold War. Despite all this, some of the former KGB and GRU's best American spies had still been exposed in recent years—and the old man suspected that one day he too would receive the late night knock on his door, for a one way ticket to a padded isolation cell at some remote military prison. In recent years he'd been repeatedly amazed by the scope and depth of the Russian's Cold-War penetration of the American government and military. Aldrich Ames of the CIA had been blown. Robert Hanssen, the FBI's senior counter espionage connection had also been blown: along with three other agents. Those who remained were becoming hard to reach. The one that had amazed him most was Jonathan Pollard, the former U.S. Navy courier of the Jewish faith. He'd passed hundreds of thousands of sensitive American military documents to the Israelis and would spend the rest of his life in isolation at Leavenworth. What had never come out about the Pollard case was that his Israeli handler was a Russian mole in Israel who had immigrated to Israel and passed most of Pollard's stuff along to Moscow.

"You've got some serious problems Jerry," the old man said into the mouthpiece.

"As the Fiddler on the Roof said," Jerry's voice came back. "Life is problems, only death is not problems! What's the first?"

"A couple of people in Russia need to be silenced urgently. If not, they will cause a flap, which will be incredibly unfortunate for both you and me."

"Any details?"

"You'll get them through the usual channel. Let's just say they're very embarrassing. Two of your people in Novosibirsk have big mouths."

"And the second problem?"

"There is another loose tongue in your archives. Someone in Moscow offering us files for American military prisoners killed in

Russia following the Great Patriotic war. If the Rodina does not want to be severely embarrassed, you had better get on it right away. I've managed to contain it here for a while, but you must shut it down at your end as soon as possible."

"Anything else?"

"One last thing. Someone here has two of your documents. He obtained them from the people I mentioned in Novosibirsk. The person here must also be silenced forever."

"You have a name?"

"Alex Balkan."

"Have I heard this name before?"

"Probably. Back in December."

"Correct. Now I recall it. I also asked you if there were others who might be more suitable. You were insistent this was the right man for the job. It seems, my friend, that I was right?"

The American did not reply as the two men made eye contact between the platforms.

"How will I find him?"

"The particulars are also in the note. He has an apartment in Virginia and relatives in Pennsylvania. Be careful."

"I understand. Anything else?"

"That's it."

"Have a nice day."

Each left his respective booth a minute apart, blending into the platform traffic. Jerry boarded the next Blue Line train through the platform headed for Largo Town Center, while the old man caught the next Blue Line train for Arlington, where he had a luncheon appointment with the new man temporarily in charge of Scion Consultants.

FEBRUARY

ONE

Limassol, Cyprus

FROM THE BALCONY of his suite, Eduardo Hernandez surveyed the twinkling lights along the Limasol coastline. Out to sea an aircraft landing light moved through the blackness toward the British Sovereign Base Area on the south tip of Cyprus. Affectionately called SBA Akrotiri by the locals, Eduardo thought of the accusations made by the local taxi driver who'd brought him to the hotel this afternoon. Ever since the United States had placed restrictions on its citizens travelling to Lebanon, Akrotiri had assumed the role of a support base for the U.S. Embassy north of Beirut. Eduardo's taxi driver had railed about it all the way from the Larnaca airport: the Americans were spies, imperialists, hate mongers, and destroying the world's culture with their plastic society.

The cab driver said Americans were not friends of the Greeks and were indiscreet because they continuously launched secret planes from Akrotiri to irritate the Arabs. And in return, Arabs complained that the Cypriots were controlled by the CIA when in fact there was little the Cypriots could do about it, because the British had handed over twenty-two square miles of their Island to the British in perpetuity back in 1962.

In the 1950s Britain thought Akrotiri would protect access to their Empire in India and Hong Kong. But then the Egyptians seized control of the Suez Canal in 1955, and all of Britain's former imperial colonies became new independent states. Today Akrotiri was just another debit-item on the already bloated British defense budget. It was common knowledge around Nicosia that Britain defrayed its Akrotiri expenses by allowing the United States to use Akrotiri for a variety of overt and covert purposes in the region: paramount being Israel.

Eduardo glanced at the king-size Cypriot bed and knew his six-foot-two-inch frame would probably not rest well on it tonight. As he studied the twinkling lights along the shoreline he thought about his forthcoming meeting with the last name on his father's list.

For the last two months he'd been looking into his inheritance; and in the process, visited Hong Kong, Jakarta, the Netherland Antilles, Key West, and now—Cyprus. He'd resolved most of the questions regarding the first four names left amongst his father's papers. Tomorrow he'd meet the last of them.

Eduardo now knew he was a billionaire and controlled a vast empire of companies through a uniquely contrived arrangement of Bearer Share corporations which his father had set up. From the first two names he'd gleaned the scope and breadth of his wealth, but after that, things had clarified more slowly, leaving more questions than answers. The third name in the Netherlands Antilles was an insouciant policeman named Castries, who'd completely mystified Eduardo. He had absolutely no idea why Castries' name even appeared among the others. The name of the old woman in Key West was also a mystery. But she'd died late last year just before he'd been able to speak with her. Now this mysterious American from Salt Lake City had called Eduardo's solicitor in London, stating he urgently needed to speak with Eduardo about the dead woman in Key West.

Eduardo drained away his single-malt scotch and headed for a refill before turning in. He'd only arrived a few hours ago and already the city of Limassol bored him. It was obviously a summer vacation place, and in late January the city was dead. Everywhere entire apartment buildings owned by either well-heeled Arabs of the Persian Gulf Sheikhdoms, or even more wealthy nouveau riche Russians were unoccupied and totally blacked out. The few that were lit up bore names over their entrances like Narodni Palace, Perestroika House, and Nastrovia Condominium: places for Putinite friends and party hacks to escape Moscow's prying eyes. Street traffic was almost nonexistent and few tourists were in evidence. The Churchill Hotel where he'd taken a suite, had also seen better times, and he wondered if it were the best of the worst on the Island, or the worst of the best?

The jangle of the telephone in the darkness startled him. His luminous watch indicated it was just past three in the morning. The hotel operator informed him there was a Mr. Aral Bilkin calling from the United States. "Put him through."

"Heinkle?" the voice ten time zones away inquired.

"Yes."

"You know who I am?"

My solicitor said you'd called. You have any idea what time it is?"

"Late afternoon . . . why?" the American replied.

"What can I do for you?" Eduardo asked.

"We need to meet. It has to do with your recent visit to Key West. Are you planning to be in the United States any time soon?"

"I doubt it!"

"That's good."

The statement surprised Eduardo. "Why do you say that?"

"I think you would be interested in what I have to tell you."

"In reference to?"

"The old woman you asked about. You recall her?"

"What of it?"

"You also met a detective while you were in Key West."

"I did?"

"Welsh?"

"Correct," the American replied. "I've spoken with him. He doesn't like you. He believes you are linked with associates who own Blue Point Air, and, he plans to contact Interpol because he believes you are involved."

"Involved in what?"

"It's probably better if I don't mention it over the phone."

"Why?"

"I'll leave that until we meet. I may be able to save you some grief. But we must meet."

"I'm going to hang up, Mr . . . . ?

"It's Balkan."

"Why should I bother with you?" Eduardo demanded.

"If you want to be stupid . . . go ahead and hang up. But I would strongly suggest you either call your attorney in London or call Detective Welsh in Key West if you don't want to listen to me. But if you do call Welsh, I would make certain he cannot trace your call."

"And why is that?" Eduardo asked, his voice now becoming slightly annoyed.

The American told him that shortly there might be a warrant out for his arrest. “How can you help me?” Eduardo asked, his voice now level and trying not to show his annoyance.

“We are both interested in a very unusual woman, and I think we need to compare notes. The woman is what this is all about. Not Welsh or the folks in the Netherland Antilles. I could meet you anywhere in Europe.”

“I don’t understand. Why is she so important?”

“I can’t get into this over the phone. And believe me. You would not want me to.”

“Give me a hint of what it’s about?”

“World War II, and a lot of things which have happened since.”

“Fine. Let’s make it London then,” Eduardo said matter-of-factly. “But I cannot be indebted to you. So you shall be my guest. Tell me where you are and I’ll have a ticket delivered. I’ll also pick up your hotel bill for the London visit.”

“Very gracious of you. When and where?”

“Next Monday Mr. Balkan, at the Hyde Park Hilton, say . . . seven o’clock, in the bar?”

“I’ll be there, and bring receipts for my travel.”

“Good night, Mr. Balkan.”

A strange man Eduardo thought as he drifted back into sleep.

Kaliningrad, Russia

“You are in early today.”

“I received troubling word from Jerry, in Washington.”

“And that is?”

“Seems we have a leak.”

“What is it, Alexi?”

“Someone in Novosibirsk has a big mouth.

“According to whom?”

“Jerry’s friend in Washington.”

Alexi Poluostrov took a chair beside his boss’s desk.

Yevgeni Kosmutov swiveled his chair to confront his subordinate, trying to define whether what he was about to tell him was going to ruin his day, or just his first cup of coffee. “And who is this source who exploited the leak”

"An American called—Alex Balkan," Alexi replied.

Kosmutov's face contorted. He'd never personally met this American called Alex Balkan, but knew of him only because for the last decade Kosmutov had been responsible to approve all declared American intelligence personnel assigned to the joint U.S./Russian nuclear verification teams in Russia. Of the some-odd thousand Americans involved, Kosmutov recalled this man in particular, because of his unique native fluency in Russian. There were only a few with such a gift among the American verification teams, and the Russians had watched Alex Balkan closely over the years. Despite Balkan's retirement at the lowly rank of Major: to the Russians this only meant that Balkan was not able to kiss ass and maybe ignored shining his superiors apples.

Balkan called a spade a spade, believed in a creed which was rare among his American associates who deviated endlessly, and Balkan knew his business and especially what made people tick. Unlike most American intelligence agents who were unsuited for their work, Balkan was a consummate chameleon, a man never to be underestimated. Balkan knew Russia better than Russians themselves, and could disappear by passing himself off anywhere: as a native Russian, a Ukrainian, or a Belorussian. Balkan could be a Russian General, a cigarette smuggler, a priest, or even a street beggar. But Balkan's charter with the verification teams in Russia was strictly overt, so Yevgeni's report that they'd caught Balkan at his covert profession in Novisibirsk was of concern. More so was Balkan's apparent connection to the American who'd once been known as Paul Carter . . . and recently discharged from the Russian penal system last year—as Pavel Krasnov.

"When did this happen?"

"He was in Novosibirsk two weeks ago."

Now Kosmutov's became visibly annoyed. "Alexi . . . why were we not notified?" he demanded of his subordinate with a scowl.

"Obviously!" Alexi replied. "Because our system is in the parasha."

"He used his real name?"

"Yes. He arrived unannounced. A visa was issued at the airport, but they did not associate him with American intelligence until a week ago. We learned of it only yesterday, from our liaison office at Novosibirsk."

"Typical." Yevgeni observed acerbically. What was the reason Balkan gave for his visit?"

"His declaration said he was a tourist."

"No one was assigned to shadow him?"

"No."

"Have you checked with Novosibirsk?"

Alexi nodded.

"And why didn't they follow normal procedure?"

"Their staff had all been mobilized to trail some group of Iranians and Iraqis who were in Novisibirsk trying to buy heavy water and nuclear materials from some clerk in charge of a supply depot for the strategic rocket forces in the Fourteenth Teatr Voyennykh Deystviy."

"Crap!" Yevgeni muttered. "The military has lots of personnel, the Strategic Rocket Forces had no one to help with the Iranians? And they could not assign even one fucking agent to our American friend?"

"Seems not," Yevgeni replied. "It was the American's who'd tipped us off to the Iranians. The Americans do not trust our Rocket Forces. They say they are all selling equipment to augment their income. Seems the Iranians had recruited some retired supply man at the depot who had excellent placement. He used to be the Commander of the rocket forces. He was going to transfer thirty two tons of heavy water and a five kiloton suitcase warhead to the Persians."

"For how much?"

"Five thousand dollars."

"You must be joking?" Kosmutov remarked incredulously.

"I wish I was. Before we shot him he stated he needed the money to fix up his mother-in-law's apartment."

"And?" Kosmutov asked. Making it obvious he wanted Yevgeni to concentrate on the issue at hand.

"While they were attending to this it seems Balkan slipped by and has been making inquiries about Paul Carter."

"Shit!" Yevgeni replied. "Why now?" He wondered what had tipped off the Americans? Why the hell had they chosen this time to start asking about someone who'd been dead fifty years? "Do you think they used the Persians as a feint?"

"Doubtful," the younger man replied. "But passing through at the time when the American's knew we and they were about to make a sting and would have all our people committed . . . ? Well . . . their timing was good."

"And what did Balkan use as bait in Novosibirsk? Never mind." Kosmutov already knew the answer even before he'd asked the question. Kosmutov yearned one day to meet just one of his countrymen whom he could point to with pride—someone who hadn't committed treason for the goddamn almighty American dollar. "And what is this leak you spoke about, Alexi?"

"From what Jerry reports in Washington, it seems that they are two KGB documents which could complicate our future relationship with the Americans. The first is a 1948 document and the second, from 1960. They passed them to Balkan."

"If they are that old Kosmutov laughed. "Who gives a shit?"

"This is serious, sir!" Alexi replied. "Both documents pertain to information about American prisoners of war we held in our . . . ," Yevgeni left the sentence unfinished, pointing instead toward the blank eastern wall of the office. He could see his boss grasped the significance of his unfinished sentence. Russia's leaders, when informed about the reality of what could happen if the information became public, would not care to think about the political fallout. Ways would be found to arrange for the disappearance of all involved. Dead men kept their secrets and could not embarrass the living. "And who are these loose lips you speak of?"

"Two retired KGB officers in Novisibirsk. Their names are Kaminsky and Tukhachevsky. The latter provided the documents, but it is Kaminsky who is about to tell Balkan exactly where he might find the other Americans still out there."

"Put an end to this immediately, Alexi! You understand! See to it yourself! If you have to, make it look like the Chechins did it!"

"I'll leave right away."

"Alexi! Before you go, the Americans . . ." Kosmutov's voice was now threatening. He pointed toward the blank eastern wall of the office again. "Once you've attended to the two traitors, see to the Americans out there too! All of them! You understand, Alexi, they must all disappear forever, completely . . . without a trace! Understood?"

"I will see to it."

"Without a trace, Alexi! You understand?"

"It will be done."

"Oh, and, Alexi!" His subordinate stopped by the door. He knew the younger man could be relied on. "Make certain about all their guards and the camp administration involved too! Plus the records. And most important . . . get rid of their execution crew too! Leave nothing, no witnesses, no forensic evidence. Nothing!"

As Alexi closed the door, Kosmutov reflected on his problem with the old American in the United States. All of this could have been avoided if he'd left the old man in prison. His boss's plan had been flawed. Sending a fox to find the hen house had obviously failed. Instead Pavel Krasnov had found the hen house and was destroying its hens. It was time for Kosmutov to limit their losses.

He folded the most recent copy of the Washington Post. He was certain it was Pavel Krasnov who was responsible for the drive-by shooting of Theodore LePage two days ago in Washington. Now he realized it must also be Pavel Krasnov who'd murdered the old woman in Key West. The person the old American probably wanted the most was Tatiana Yevchenko, and it appeared that she'd still eluded him. What mystified Kosmutov was how the old man had found Theodore LePage? He smoked a cigarette and considered what must be done next. He picked up the phone and called a Chechen associate, suggesting an early lunch. The associate would have to find Krasnov, and kill him. One hundred thousand up front, and a half million dollars later should guarantee quick results.

The Chechen already controlled New York's Russian underworld, and a half million would make them jump through their ass holes. He picked up the phone and dialed. It was also time for an end-run as the Americans liked to say. For years the Spanish had wondered about their lost bullion. Now might also be an auspicious time to create a diversion, and inform Madrid where they might begin looking for their gold. If things didn't work with Washington, it would make a suitable quid-pro-quo, blood for money.

Troodos Mountains

The call from Alex Balkan bothered Eduardo and he'd slept fitfully. Twice he'd awoken, plagued by the same dream in which police chased him through his home town in Peru. It always ended the same way. They captured him, threw him into a dark room full of cockroaches who crawled over him in masses until he was about to suffocate. It was at this point he always woke up, just as they began to course down his throat, suffocating him.

He had no idea what the American's ultimate agenda was, only that it dealt with his connection to the Albion woman. He'd called

Smither's again this morning in London, and asked him to make inquiries about the enforcement of United States criminal warrants outside the United States? Smither's reply was not reassuring. Since September 11 and America's war on terrorism, governments around the world had been bullied, pilloried, and coerced into relinquishing significant portions of their own citizens sovereign rights, and were increasingly allowing American law enforcement to transport them to the United States where they were held incommunicado.

At ten o'clock Selvanian's chauffeur picked Eduardo up in front of the Hotel. Six kilometers north of the city they were into the foothills of the Troodos Mountains, climbing a steep road to the top of a hill where the car stopped before a sprawling villa. A servant appeared and showed Eduardo to a study. A half-hour later Eduardo was becoming annoyed because his host had still not appeared.

When Selvanian finally made his entrance just after eleven o'clock, the old man offered no apology as he strode past Eduardo and seated himself in a comfortable sofa across from his guest. The old man was the picture of health for an octogenarian, and from his brisk stride, obviously possessed the constitution of a man decades his junior. Selvanian's body was straight, his grip strong, and his eyes clear. His hands were steady as he reached forward and poured a coffee first for Eduardo and then one for himself.

For the next quarter hour he diverted Eduardo about his interests in horticulture, especially the cactus, which was able to survive despite long periods of hardship and drought—a trait Selvanian pointed out—the cacti genus shared with the Armenian people, of which he was one.

Selvanian glanced at his watch as a servant appeared and bowed slightly. "If you will excuse me, Mr. Hernandez," the old man said, "my barber awaits. It will only take a few minutes. Help yourself to more coffee."

Now more annoyed at this additional breach of etiquette, Eduardo wished he'd hired a car. Then he could have just got up and walked out and left instructions for the old man to meet Eduardo at his hotel. When Selvanian returned, he carried a black leather briefcase which he placed beside him on the settee.

"Now my young friend," he announced, "shall we get down to business?"

Selvanian waited for the manservant to top off their coffee, and asked him to leave them alone.

As soon as the door closed, the entire demeanor of the meeting changed, and accusations began rolling off the old man's tongue like thunder claps. Within minutes the old man had accused Eduardo's father of drawing up an illegal last will and testament, passing possessions to his son which were not his to give, and in effect being a common thief.

At first Eduardo tried to keep a straight face. But as the old man droned on, he realized Selvanian obviously had proof of what he spoke. When Eduardo had initially contacted the first of the five names on his father's list, a man called Hassan Khatoury in Hong Kong; Khatoury had been standoffish and noncommittal. Khatoury's Chinese lawyer also seemed befuddled as to the basis of Eduardo's claims. Now Eduardo realized that Khatoury's reaction had been prompted by confusion over what had obviously gone wrong in the relationship with Eduardo's father? And when Eduardo met a week later with the second person on his father's list, this time an old retired Chinese General called Chong Ki-Young, near Jakarta in Indonesia, Chong Ki-Young too had seemed out of sorts, and was not forthcoming with Eduardo. None of the first three had ever mentioned others on Eduardo's list, or that they had been contacted by others Eduardo had seen.

"So you see," Selvanian concluded, "your father illegally passed control of the CEBU Corporation to you when he had no right to do so. This was not our arrangement. Not our agreement! And we want CEBU back! As you know, the pyramid of interlocking corporations and holding companies below CEBU are substantial. Some assets of course are legally in your father's estate. Here I refer of course to those in the United Kingdom. But the others are held jointly and severally—not yours exclusively."

Smithers hadn't informed him about of any of this, or if he was even aware of what the old man alleged: and Eduardo was not certain about the best way to proceed. He already had more than enough from his father's British holdings, but was not about to let anyone move in on a portion of the rest unless it was legal. "And if I dispute your claim?"

The old Armenian shrugged. "Something untoward could happen."

"Is that a threat?"

"Take it how you wish, my young friend. None of it is of any importance to your lately departed dear father. And the same shall apply to me when the sum of my days have arrived. But for the moment I would suggest that you keep foremost in your mind that no one in the cemetery needs their wealth." The old man templed his fingers before him and stared at Eduardo.

Now the threat was palpable. Eduardo was almost in shock. He sat back and stared dumbly at his host. As an impoverished back-hills lawyer in Peru he'd been summoned to London a few months back, and informed he had a huge inheritance, plus an empire beyond Britain. Now it appeared Smithers had ignorantly, or otherwise, mislead him. He sensed that Smithers deft hand may have intrigued with his father against these men. Eduardo decided he'd wait and see what proof Selvanian offered to support his claim.

"I am a reasonable man," the Armenian concluded. "We must reach an accommodation my friend."

"What accommodation might this be?" Eduardo inquired.

"Two things. CEBU returned to our collective control, and I would like you to undertake a mission for me."

"For you personally?"

"For us," Selvanian countered.

"Us? And if I refuse?"

"It would be most unwise."

"Clarify unwise," Eduardo demanded, trying to appear nonchalant, knowing full well that if Selvanian didn't like what Eduardo was willing to agree to, then Selvanian could sue him. It would be difficult for anyone to prove CEBU's provenance, and could take the courts decades to decide which court could even hear Selvanian's complaint.

"I've tried to be forthright with you Eduardo. Since you seem resistant, let me be precise. You will die here in this house today," the old man said quietly over the top of his coffee cup which he'd raised to his lips but held it there as he spoke, his eyes glued to Eduardo's, obviously waiting for the first signs that stress was starting to overwhelm the younger man's composure—such as little beads of sweat for example, spurious eye movements, heavy breathing, or fidgeting. But the young Peruvian stared back at him as if he'd said nothing.

Selvanian liked what he saw. It confirmed to him that even though the young man before him was from the backwoods of South America, the rigorous regimen his father had put him through had obviously toughened the young man.

"I liked your father, Eduardo." Selvanian condescendingly observed after a long pause. "He was my friend. At least I thought he was? In any case. We all make mistakes. Mine it seems may have been an error in your character assessment. It did not occur to us that your dear father might deliberately undertake such a confrontation. But he is now no longer among the living, and is unable to defend himself, so it would not be fair to condemn him. And since you have come in his stead? So the question really is, shall we continue to cooperate as before, or—"

"Legally it is mine," Eduardo said. The moment he did so he knew it was a stupid thing to say and he regretted it. Eduardo clearly understood the old man's intent . . . whatever the legal playing field looked like, Selvanian intended to sweep it all aside and have Eduardo killed here at his home today, unless . . . they reached an accommodation?

The old man began to giggle, then laughed heartily until Eduardo realized he was mocking him. Selvanian rose and slapped Eduardo on the back. "Ohhh, to be young again and naive like you!" he exclaimed.

Eduardo was at a loss and hadn't the slightest idea how to proceed, and sat there almost in a trance. His entire life had been spent practicing legal matters within a recognized system of law and order, and in that system those practicing were not the victims, but those following the law. Law from the barrel of a gun was something he recalled from the Chinese communist takeover of China after the Second World War. Being from Peru, Eduardo was also familiar with the rule of the gun that had reduced Peru to the brink of chaos in the last three decades. First there had been the Guzman rebellion in which the native Americans had fought a bitter struggle for equal rights with the progeny of the Spanish conquistadors who'd taken control of the entire country two hundred years ago. When someone tells you to agree with them or be taken away and executed, it is usually only the moral and ethical questions for which humanity is willing to go willingly. When someone informs you that they are going to kill you unless you agree, threatening to sue them in the courts is the last thing anyone considers as a defense.

"It's quite simple, young man!" Selvanian continued. "Live and enjoy what was legally your fathers and ours together, or . . ." He didn't finish the sentence again and left the threat hanging. "It appears your father became greedy. A development that we hadn't anticipated! So your dilemma is simple really! Return the wealth that was never yours in the first place, and enjoy a long and fruitful association with us."

"Mr. Selvanian, what proof you have to support your allegations."

"In due course. First let me inquire what you know of your father's past?"

"Not much," he admitted.

"Maybe that is why you are a little confused at the moment. Would you like me to fill in the blanks for you?"

"If it has a bearing on your demand."

"I'll let you decide that."

Eduardo shrugged.

"Your father was born in eastern Germany. Did you know that? A small town called Bautzen."

"No," Eduardo replied. "I knew he was from Europe but not exactly where, and had always thought of Denmark."

The old man smiled. "Yes, and he moved to Peru after the war. He married your mother in Bella Vista in 1947, and you were born the next year. She died when you were six and your aunt, on your mother's side, was forced to raise you because your father secretly returned to Europe. You didn't see him again until you attended Oxford. Eight years later he arranged for you to enroll in the first class of the Institute of Strategic Studies in Peru, under the leadership of General San Lorenzo. Following that you returned to your law practice in Lima, and remained there until Nigel Smither's asked you to come to London on the fourteenth of December last year. Your accumulated income in Peru since Oxford, was a piddling one hundred and thirty thousand dollars. Not much for thirteen years work. Am I correct so far?"

The fact that Selvanian knew any of this didn't surprise Eduardo because anyone could learn such things by asking around.

"Now," Selvanian asked, leaning forward toward him "Who really was your father? Take a guess?"

It was a question Eduardo had frequently asked himself over the years. He knew his father had arrived in South America after the Second World War, but not much else. "You tell me?"

"His real name was Kaufmann. U-Boat Captain, Heinrich Kaufmann! I've known your father since 1943. After he arrived in South America he changed his name twice before settling in Peru, and taking the name you now bear. His first name belonged to a Chilean man who'd lived abroad for many years in Calcutta and suddenly disappeared while on vacation in central Africa. Then he assumed the identity of a second man, after all the records of this man's existence were erased in a court fire in Puerto Piramides, Argentina. A third identity belonged to a George Pehuajo, from Paraguay, who disappeared in a mysterious fire and was officially declared dead by the government. A few months later your father arrived in Peru, documented with your surname, and of a prominent Jewish family from Archangel who had all disappeared during the Second World war in one of Hitler's concentration camps."

"Stop me Eduardo if you knew any of this already?" Selvanian suspected the young man knew nothing about what he was going to say. "By now I suppose you are going to ask why he went to all this trouble? But first let me tell you a little about myself."

"Before the war I became involved in Swiss banking and frequently traveled to Russia, Asia and South America. In Germany I met influential people in the 1930s, some of whom would hold incredible power in the Third Reich while the others disappeared. By the time the war started, the leaders of the Third Reich had already acquired immense wealth which they'd sequestered from, well, let's say from those not in a position to object! At this point my association with both the haves and have-nots became a marriage of convenience. Both sides needed me to secure their investments outside Germany, and to make them legally disappear so that no one could trace them later. From this I earned handsome fees. You understand . . . ? Those in control would all die as the war drew to a close while those not in control could only hide away their valuables, hoping that someone among their kin might find it some day after the war. When the war ended, all of those I had helped were dead." The old Armenian held out his arms, a stupid grin on his face. "Only three survived who knew exactly where the three bullion shipments went. Myself, your father, and the old woman in the United States, who I believe you tried to see recently in Key West." He smiled insidiously at Eduardo again, waiting for the young man to ask him if he'd arranged to kill the old woman before she could confide to Eduardo what Selvanian just had just told him?

"What bullion shipments?" Eduardo asked, also wondering how Selvanian knew he'd tried to see the old woman in Key West.

"Patience, my young friend. In due course. There were three shipments that your father participated in. The first was in the

Mediterranean in early 1943. Then, a second to China just before war ended. And a third a few months later to South America. Extraordinary precautions were taken, because the Americans and British also knew about them. The last shipment contained almost half a billion dollars in Spanish gold coin."

Eduardo's amazement was obvious. "Spanish gold?" he asked stupidly.

"Yes," Selvanian replied. "You will understand that it was a lot of money even in those days. It had been secretly sent by the Spanish government to Russia during the Spanish Civil War. Germany captured it from the Russians two weeks after the German invasion of Russia in 1940. There were side agreements of course regarding the three shipments," Selvanian continued. "But these are incidental. What is important is that we got the first two gold shipments, but never recovered anything from the third. The third one was the one your father left off the Uruguay coast in August 1945."

"I don't understand any of this," Eduardo replied.

"My dear boy . . . all in due course. But by now you are probably getting the message loud and clear, that the genesis of your wealth is tainted, dirty, and even immoral. But that is a historical question, money has no master and is a whore looking to corrupt those who possess it. Your father scuttled his submarine twenty miles north east of La Coronilla, on the Uruguay coast. When we returned to retrieve her two years later." Selvanian held up his hands again. "Poof! The submarine was gone!"

"I see." Eduardo understood. "Maybe the crew came back for her?"

"They died when she was scuttled." The old man laughed.

"All of them?"

"Of course! Your father's instructions were to see to it and he did. There could be no witnesses."

"My god!" Eduardo muttered, his face an obvious mask now trying to conceal his disgust.

Selvanian laughed again. "Today, that shipment; including compound interest, inflation, rises in the price of gold, et cetera; would conservatively be worth a considerable amount. There were over six hundred tons of gold bullion aboard."

"And the first two shipments?" Eduardo asked.

"As you already know," Selvanian replied. "CEBU is worth about three hundred billion. Most of it was made in South America."

From what Eduardo had seen among the papers his father had left in England, the only portion of CEBU's portfolio which Eduardo truly abhorred was the six percent from the second shipment which had been invested in the narcotics trade in South America. The South American investment had been insignificant many years ago, but today it produced more profit than the rest of the portfolio combined. Eduardo recalled a ditty from his school years:

My name is cocaine, call me coke for short
I entered this country without a passport
Ever since I've made lots of scum rich
Some have been murdered and found in a ditch

As a youth he'd been educated by the Jesuits in Lima, before going to Oxford, and they'd infused him with a code which could accommodate most of the worst of human failings. He recalled the last four lines of the above ditty:

The day you agree to sit in my saddle
The decision is one that no one can straddle
Listen to me, and please listen well
When you ride with cocaine you are headed for hell!

"And the oil transactions through CEBU and the companies in Hong Kong?" Eduardo asked.

"Very good!" Selvanian observed with a smile. You are perceptive. I like that! Those are the final steps before narcotics proceeds are recycled into the legitimate world."

Eduardo knew that two-thirds of CEBU's wealth was physically in the United States, and the residual was split about equally between South America and Asia. The emphasis was changing however and increasingly there were concerns about America's long range financial viability as budget and trade deficits continued to erode the dollar.

Selvanian retrieved the brief case and opened it, handing over a sheaf of papers.

"As a lawyer. You should have no difficulty understanding what's in that file." Selvanian leaned back and thumbed through a copy of Time Magazine as Eduardo began to study the file.

It took him less than a minute to realize the old man was right. His father had betrayed his partners. He studied the notary markings to assure they were genuine. He handed the file back. "What do you want?"

"Keep what is yours in England, and take your father's place beside us."

"That's it?"

"That and the other point I mentioned earlier. We have a problem in Moscow. We want you to attend to it. I will be in London next Wednesday and we can discuss it then. There are other pro-forma issues of course, but all of these can wait.

That afternoon as Eduardo's Cyprus Airlines flight climbed out of Larnaca airport for London, he realized his life had once again changed forever.

Arlington

It was now Thursday and Alex's flight for London would not depart JFK until Sunday evening, he'd decided to head east immediately and clear up some issues before he met the Peruvian named Eduardo Hernandez in England. By sundown he'd arranged three east coast appointments, first with the historian Ted LePage had told him he'd seen at Cameron Station and who had been so helpful. Then he'd see the retired Army Colonel who'd fired on the German U-Boat at Bahia Honda in 1942, and finally . . . Alex's old friend Marvin Raoul. Heather was disappointed he was leaving so soon, and he confided some of the details of what he was involved in. The Russian documents fascinated her and she offered to help however she could.

Just before midnight she dropped him at the airport and he caught a Red-Eye for Baltimore. At nine the next morning he walked into Stouffers Hotel in Crystal City for his first meeting with Stan Citwits. Toward the rear of the coffee shop the waitress pointed to the historian who had his face buried in the morning papers.

"The name's pronounced Citwits," the historian advised, handing Alex a card. "Call me Stan if you like."

Despite the cold icy weather outside, Citwits was perspiring, and his breathing seemed labored, Alex wondered if the historian had recently kicked a tobacco habit. Stan Citwits recounted the highlights of his earlier meetings with Ted LePage at his office and again later at the State Department. It immediately became obvious to Alex that Citwits was unaware that Alex's employment with Scion Consultants had been terminated the previous week, and his security clearance also revoked at the TS/SCI/Code Word level. Before coffee refills arrived Alex also realized the historian was an unusual person with an encyclopedic memory; and a patriot with some very unconventional views for a government employee. Alex liked the combination and tucked the information away, almost certain too that he could call on the historian again if he needed some help outside normal channels.

Citwits seemed to know exactly what Alex wanted and offered that the Novosibirsk documents Ted LePage had mentioned were probably the real McCoy. The Russians, he assured Alex, had consistently lied about who they'd held in their prisons, and it was no secret that untold thousands of Americans had languished there in large numbers after WWII.

"The only problem in recent years," Citwits continued, "is that the central government's taxing ability has been almost completely co-opted by the Russian Mafia, and the government has had to cut back and close all nonessential services. The Russian government has been bankrupt for almost decade, and if it weren't for its energy exports the place would be a third-world country. The two documents you say you got in Novisibirsk obviously came out of someone's archive—probably in the Moscow area. But which one? All their archives have been closed for over five years. Even international work at the Hermitage in Saint Petersburg has been almost stopped. The real problem today is to prove that any of this is true."

"I hadn't thought about the archive aspect of it." Alex said. "Any ideas?"

"If it was one of Beria's prefifties documents, that would be the time Stalin was still around and most of those documents ended up in archives just northwest of Moscow. The camps of course spanned the entire length and breadth of the former Soviet Union."

"Exactly where?" Alex asked.

"Everywhere. Places with names like Ukhta, Kotlas, Syktyvkar, Kudyarsk, Kirov, Perm . . . do you want me to continue, there's probably several thousand altogether." Citwits studied Alex for a few moments as if collecting his thoughts. "So Mr. LePage never mentioned any of the details of his discussion with me?"

"Probably didn't have time," Alex replied. "I left before he and I had a chance to talk."

"Strange," Citwitz observed. "He told me he urgently needed the information to help you with your investigation. I'll have to ask him about it next time I see him."

"That will not be possible," Alex replied. "He was gunned down in a drive by shooting in McLean two days ago. That's why I called you. I thought you knew."

"My god, that was him? I saw the report, but didn't make the association. How unfortunate."

They spent several minutes reminiscing about others who'd been victimized around Washington, and finally the conversation drifted back to Paul Carter. Alex mentioned the possibility that there might be as many as 350 Americans still alive somewhere in the former USSR.

"I'm surprised Ted didn't mention it at the intra-agency meeting at the Foggy Bottom awhile back." Citwits recounted the Inter-Agency group's decision not to reopen the Carter case based on Alex's new information.

"I guess Ted was waiting for my written report before he went further," Alex said.

"Who will replace him, Alex?"

"No idea. I'd like you to keep all this to yourself until I know more about where they are."

"Sure, Alex. Can I give you a word of advice? You need hard evidence my friend. Without proof, folks on the Hill, and those over at the Pentagon and DIA will try their damnedest to discredit and marginalized you. They'll call you a rogue, someone whose crazy, irresponsible, out of control. They'll try to isolate you like the plague."

Alex knew it was true. He'd seen it happen to others. "Thanks for the advice."

"The information in these two documents," Citwits continued after scanning both, "is damning as hell. But if there are any survivors still out there, then you'd better sit on this until you can figure out some way to get them out. The documents complicate the naysayers' argument, and will make it impossible for anyone to ignore you: but it won't save anyone still out there. You say these are copies?"

"Correct. You can see the notary stamps on the bottom?"

"What do you intend to do with them?"

"For the moment, nothing. I'll follow your advice. They are only part of my problem. I'll need a couple of weeks for the rest." He thought about his meeting with the Editor of the Salt Lake newspaper and hoped he too wouldn't start talking before he got back to him. "When the time comes, I'll have to find a laboratory to do the document analysis and verification."

"I'd sure like to be involved when the time comes."

"I'll keep you in mind."

"Where's the originals?"

Alex smiled benignly. "In a safe place."

"Hopefully not here in Washington."

"Don't worry. Tell me Stan, you ever heard of Case Judy?"

"No. What is it?"

"Just curious."

"Look Alex. Mind if I make a suggestion?"

"Sure."

"What you're getting into could get hairy, know what I mean?" Stan breathed in heavily and rolled his eyes to emphasize the gravity. "My guess is that there are a lot of people around here who will not want your documents to see the light of day. They may not even want you around to talk about them. You understand what I'm suggesting? And if Moscow knows you have them, I would imagine they too might stop at nothing to see them out of circulation."

"What's your point, Stan?"

"Think about finding someone who's used to dealing with such problems. Somebody who might even find out where the three hundred are, and bring them out!"

"A macho type guy you mean?"

"Exactly!"

"Someone like Arnold Schwartzenegger?"

"You got it!" Stan replied with a big smile.

He suspected Citwits had seen too many movies. "You got somebody in mind, Stan? A real macho type guy."

"Matter of fact, I do! That's why I mentioned it."

"And who is this macho type guy?" Alex inquired.

"A retired Special Forces Colonel whose got a shit pot full of operational time on special missions, and just happens to have spent the last few years, up to his ass, in the POW/MIA mess. But he hates the creeps who run the program."

"Who in particular?" Alex inquired.

"Defense Intelligence Agency and the creeps over in Crystal City."

"Can I trust him?"

"Sure. DIA also shit-canned him. He's got a hard-on for them too, which is at least a foot long. He's good too!"

"What's his name?"

"Colonel Jose Santiago, United States Army, retired in lieu of courts martial." Alex remembered reading about it in the newspapers but had never met the man. "He's just north of the Beltway in Silver Springs, Maryland."

"What's his claim to fame?"

"First he's got the training and connections you'd need. He was involved in the Son Tay raid near Hanoi. He also worked on the Desert One scenario, but backed out when the hierarchy anointed the guy who eventually led it unsuccessfully. They fired my friend when he started to find out stuff he thought was wrong. He thinks the way the Vietnam POW issue turned out after the war ended was a national disgrace."

"How so?" Alex enquired.

"Our two senators, McCain and Kerry. The hearings they held in 1992 ignored the facts and wrote off all our POWs who were not released when McCain was released in 1973.

"How many?" Alex asked.

"A couple of hundred for sure. Santiago would love the stuff you've got."

"Vietnam's his specialty?"

"Yeah! But he has a good background in the others too."

"How could he help me?"

"Show you how to survive! What to avoid! Where the mine fields are. Where to plug in. Whose buttons to push! Stuff like that."

"You got his number?"

"I think so." Citwits withdrew an address book and scribbled the information down.

* * *

Santiago's residence in Silver Springs was sprinkled with paraphernalia of a military career. Modified automatics adorned his basement wall, and included the most lethal Russian, Chinese and Israeli types. At first Santiago seemed hesitant about the issue of Americans still being held captive in Russia and loosened up when Alex showed him a photocopy of the Novosibirsk documents. When he speculated about the circumstances surrounding his own firing and Ted LePages's death, Santiago's demeanor changed again, and he became deadly serious. "It may add up to something," he observed. "One should be suspicious when such things happen one block from home!"

"Why?" Alex said.

"Somebody is making a statement."

"So you agree with me then?"

"Not so fast. I'm only saying I thought it strange that they chose the execution site they did. The suburb is upper middle class and two blocks from LePage's house. Why were you fired, Alex?"

"I'm not really sure," Alex replied.

"Tell me about your career," the old man said.

Alex laid it out like it was. Leaving little out about what his intelligence work had really entailed. Santiago had been around, knew the community, knew what it did, and he had obviously done some of the same things Alex had.

"I appreciate your candor Balkan. I can read between the lines. How do you think I can help you?"

"Stan Citwits said you'd had a similar experience to mine and had operational experience. I would need someone like you if I actually find out where the three hundred are."

"Then you've come to the right man. I saw too much while on active duty which pissed me off. In the end it cost me my career. When they cashiered me, it was all very hush-hush, and took place behind closed doors. I'd be a General Officer today if I'd stayed out of the politics bullshit! But you know what, I sleep real good, and I walk around with my head high, and those who remember me mention my name with respect, and some of them cross the street when they see me coming because they are embarrassed. It's a good legacy. Know what I mean? I always followed my conscience. You seem to have the same problem."

"What happened to you?" Alex asked him.

"I got sideways with the Kerry Committee on the issue of what I call 'fishy milk'," Santiago replied. "I'm referring to our missing POW's in Vietnam of course."

Alex knew he was going to like this man. Santiago, by his own admission, had not thrived because of his inability to compromise when it came to matters of principle. Santiago had been cashiered for it.

"What got me started on all this," Santiago continued, "was a statement by Lieutenant General Tighe who was in charge of DIA in the early 1980s. Before Tighe retired, he said that too many of our missing in Vietnam had been declared dead on the flimsiest of evidence. I'd been expressing the same view for many years, but no one listened. So when Tighe said it in public, it rang like a clarion call to the colors. I asked the general what he meant by the statement a couple of days later and he said it was his opinion, and he preferred not to go into detail about it. I think Tighe was afraid to say more. I decided it was time for me to look into the matter, but I was in special forces at the time and I knew the only way I'd get anywhere near the truth was to get reassigned to where they keep the records at DIA."

"What I came to realize after I'd been with DIA for a while, was, that even as early as 1966, the Vietnamese held over eight hundred of our men; while we were saying the numbers in captivity were much less. Then the war escalated, and two years later the number of our POW's missing or in captivity doubled to one thousand five hundred, and then it doubled again by 1970. By 1973 when we pulled out of Vietnam, several of us within DIA were unanimous on the numbers. But then the decision was made to declare almost thirteen hundred of those we were carrying as missing in action . . . as killed in action. Then came Project Homecoming, and Hanoi released only 591. So logically there could have been another 722 who were alive out there in captivity who we had left behind.

"Throughout the Vietnam conflict," Santiago continued, "Hanoi never confirmed or denied a single prisoner they had. And even decades after the war, Hanoi is still as tight lipped as they ever were. All the statistics, which were assembled were drawn from our own estimates and guestimates—based on the best available data—and it was always ours, not theirs. The North Vietnamese just smiled and said nothing. The Russians did the same damned thing to us when the Second World War ended. The Koreans and Chinese too when the Korean conflict ended. To this day we still have no accurate accounting from any of these three countries. Did Stan tell you I was involved in the Son Tay raid?"

"Yes," Alex replied

"I realized after Son Tay that we didn't really know squat about their system, or how many of our prisoners they were holding, or where, or why? You ever worked with the Koreans or Chinks, Alex?"

Alex shook his head.

They all distrust round eyes. Can't say I blame them. We've screwed them over a couple of times pretty good in the last hundred and fifty years, exploited them, colonized them, fought over them, and left them in the dumps. China's problem is assimilation—there's just too many different types of Chinese thrown into the pot to ever get along; from Tibet to Yunnan and Manchuria, there must be close to sixty nationalities. Then there's the Koreans who along with the Japanese practice archaic forms of 'bushido,' whatever you want to define that as. And then there's Vietnamese, Laos and Thais. A swell low keyed gracious and polite bunch of people who I've loved to death over the years. Know what I mean, Alex? You ever been laid by one of them? From your expression I guess not. But make one of them mad and become their enemy and they become strange. And in war-time you don't want to be their enemy, especially if they capture you. Forget about everything you ever heard about decency. They will make your life hell on earth."

Santiago leaned back in his chair, wondering if Alex really understood what he'd just said. "And yet the armchair pencil pushers here in Washington meticulously expounded on who was still alive and who was dead when in reality they had no damned idea what they were doing, or what was being done with our prisoners! To make it worse, the intelligence assholes kept all the data so highly classified, and on a special need to know basis, that even our own government didn't know what was happening to our prisoners out there." Santiago stopped for a moment and looked inquiringly at Alex. "You really interested in all this detail?"

"Of course," Alex replied, I need to know whatever you think is important."

"Son Tay." There was a case in point." Santiago observed. "The camp had Americans in it before we arrived, but not when we got there. There was a DIA coordination failure in DC, or at least that's what some will tell you. After the fact DIA informed everyone that they knew our prisoners at Son Tay had been moved, but didn't tell us until after the raid. As a former air force colonel friend of mine who says he knew they were not there, informed me later that the Operations guys planning the raid did not coordinate with everyone they should have in advance because they were afraid of operations security. OPSEC failures that might tip off the enemy before we got there. We did check first, discreetly, and learned otherwise. But after the fact everyone was covering their ass and in denial."

"Some of us knew the estimates were wrong," Santiago continued, "and set out to prove it. Before the Son Tay raid we set the North Vietnamese up, so we could monitor their various prison locations; before, during, and after the raid. We thought we knew where all their camps where, and hoped to convince Hanoi we could raid any and all of their camps with impunity. You know what happened?"

Alex shrugged, recalling reading about it once, but unable to recall the details. "It was a long time ago, Colonel."

"First," Santiago continued, "someone tipped them off that we were coming. Secondly, their reaction at the other camps where we knew they were holding our prisoners, confirmed our suspicions. What we didn't expect though, was a similar reaction from seven other new camp locations at which we never suspected our people were being held. They were clever all right. It was then that we figured Hanoi was operating two parallel systems . . . and until then we knew nothing about the second system."

"How did they know you were coming?" Alex asked.

Santiago cut him off. "Let me finish. When our people came home during 'Project Homecoming,' debriefings of our prisoners produced absolutely nothing about the new POW locations. Then everyone forgot about the parallel system we'd just learned of as the war ended."

"Why?"

"Because the war was over and the seven other camps went quiet, and as the war drew down the existence and our men being held in them was also forgotten."

"Any ideas why Son Tay was empty when you arrived?"

"We were betrayed."

"By who?"

"Not the South Vietnamese. That is for certain. They were kept completely out of it. All the prestrike stuff was done right here in

Washington D.C. We were deliberately misled into believing that our prisoners were there."

"Where was the actual planning done Colonel Santiago?

"At the Pentagon. Why?"

"Just curious." Alex made a note to ask Marvin Raoul if he could find out where Eve Albion worked during the latter half of 1970. "Who exactly within DIA tracked the POW/MIA question then, Colonel?"

"DIA at Bolling."

"The aluminum palace?"

"Yeah."

"And now?"

"The folks at DMPO over at Arlington."

"Who are they?" Alex inquired.

"The acronym stands for Defense Missing Personnel Office."

"If DIA or DMPO," Alex asked, "wanted to check out a potential POW site today, how would it be done?"

"If you're talking about Vietnam, it's difficult. If you're thinking about Russia, forget it! It would be easier to check it out yourself!" Santiago wasn't smiling now. "As soon as we give the other folks notice that we suspect they're holding someone, our politicians start masturbating, and everyone waits for months, or years, until the whole thing can be coordinated by the respective bureaucracies in DC and Moscow. And by that time, you can guess the rest. And if it involves human remains at some crash site for instance, then it is several years before forensic teams may, and I repeat . . . may get to the area and start looking around."

"Who conducts the physical site survey?" Alex asked.

"An outfit called UMPC which stands for Unified Missing Prisoner Command." He noted Santiago's smirk. "Makes you want to throw up, don't it. Typical of our mamby-pamby leadership! They're all so damned proud because after twenty years, they're going to get us a final accounting of all our missing heroes out there! A final accounting . . . my ass. They only selectively look into politically acceptable stuff: never those still alive out there who for decades we have long ago said were dead."

"Where is this outfit located?" Alex asked.

"Hickam Air Force Base in Honolulu," Santiago replied. "They're subordinate to the Department of Defense and rely on it for all the political approvals prior to going into any country where we suspect the remains of one of our missing in action might be. Since they were formed in 1992, they've examined a few cites in Southeast Asia."

"Could a team be sent to Russia?"

"Don't know why not. DOD has arranged a couple of expeditions in the last few years to look for remains of some of our Cold War air crews lost along the northern Russian border in the late 1940s and early 1950s. But no recoveries. Once Moscow got what they needed from these air crews, they took what was left of them into a backroom and ended their misery."

"But," Alex asked, "if the Russians knew where the bodies of the aircrew were buried, why not eventually turn them over to us? Wouldn't it have helped relations between our two countries?"

"Alex, for a man of your experience, you sure ask some stupid questions. You ever seen a modern forensic team go to work on a set of human remains? They can tell your age, sex, condition of your body, and from skeletal remains—what kind of trauma you were subjected to before death. The way bones are broken, facial fractures inflicted, hands and feet mutilated—each reveals a detailed story. In the case of some of the bodies recovered from Vietnam, it was obvious many were severely tortured and then beaten to death."

"So if one of these forensic teams can be sent to Russia, that may be the way to go."

"Sure. But like I said, Alex, you'd need proof, lots of proof, the incontrovertible type, and the more political it is, you can multiply the coordination period by a factor of ten. And," Santiago exclaimed, raising his index finger for emphasis, "if you want to look for our prisoners who you believe may still be alive in Russia since World War II, it would be much easier to go yourself and bring them back."

"What about yourself, Colonel. You interested?"

"If you got hard data, I might consider it."

"Well, you've been very helpful, Colonel Santiago. I've got to be going."

"Mind if I ask what your plans are, Alex?"

"Europe to start. Then farther east. If I think it will pay off, I'll be back in touch with you."

"Want company?"

"Not right now. But I'll keep you in mind."

"Do that. You'll need help."

"One last question. You familiar with the term Case Judy?"
"No."

Timonium, Maryland

The following morning, Alex turned north off exit 26 on the Baltimore Beltway. Retired Army Colonel Svoboda's residence was in an upscale neighborhood just south of Timonium. But the expensive residence was run-down and had seen better days. Its paint was peeling. Two windows were taped with plastic, and the eaves were rotting in several places. He figured if Svoboda was in his early twenties when the war in Europe began, today he'd be approaching one hundred. The man who answered the door looked ancient. He looked decrepit. Svoboda's internal clock had obviously outpaced his peers, and he appeared shriveled and Methusalah-like, with one of the most extensive white beards in Alex's experience. His left leg dragged like a stump, probably the remnant of a stroke, which also affected movement in his right arm. From the interior of the house it was also obvious he'd shut himself off in the kitchen, and set up a mattress near the fridge while his meager assortment of old clothing hung dejectedly from a wall sconce. Everywhere the interior doors and windows were sealed with masking tape. In a command voice he ordered Alex to find himself a chair while he poured coffee.

Alex mentioned the story related by Mr. Solomon in Key West, who'd also shown Alex a copy of Svoboda's signed statement about the Bahia Honda incident.

"Damn right, I remember it," Svoboda exclaimed, his voice now becoming shrill. "There were two of them out there. One within range, and a second further out. The closest was at four thousand yards and barely moving. It was just past sunset; she was southeast of us on a bearing of 180 degrees. The second was at maybe seven thousand yards and 210 degrees from my position. We could clearly make out the silhouette of the first, and people on her deck. The navy was doing a lot of training around Key West back then, and it occurred to me she might be one of ours. Even though my orders were to shoot first and ask questions later, I didn't want a court martial for doing something stupid. So I called in."

"My commanding officer at Key West was really pissed that I'd called and ordered me to sink the bastards immediately. We were all kids then playing soldier. We had no combat experience. We'd only conducted firing simulations because ammunition was in short supply. My crew were so god damned excited that the first round overshot the Kraut by damned near a thousand yards." Svoboda began to laugh. "I damned near pulled out my revolver and shot my Sergeant. I was more worried that the bastard might shoot back and kill us before we could kill him." The old man smiled. "Now I know better. The Krauts must have been defecating in their britches and all he wanted to do was submerge. Our second round fell along her stern, and I'm certain we hit her. By now she was moving and starting to go down by the bow, so we threw another round into the breach, made a final correction, and fired. Nothing happened! The goddamn thing was a misfire—probably an old French round from WWI. I stood there having a hissy fit while they pried the thing out of the breech. By the time we'd loaded another round she was gone, and the other one further out had also disappeared. For good measure we laid another six rounds into the water where the first one had been but then darkness came and I called in my report."

"What about the people on deck?"

"Some were left in the water. We watched them through binoculars, but lost track of them when it got dark."

"How many?"

"Six is what we all agreed on."

"What about a hull number?"

"Never saw one."

"And those left in the water?"

"Don't know."

"You think she returned and retrieved them after dark?"

"Maybe. Who knows?"

"You seem uncertain?"

"That's true. Because the way it turned out."

"What do you mean?"

"The next morning my boss sent a staff car, and took us to a barracks on Trumbo where we were held incommunicado for four days. Then we were ordered on pain of death to sign top secret statements that we'd never discuss what we'd seen or done that evening. The whole thing never happened. Two days later I and my crew were shipped off to new assignments, and spent the rest of the war fighting the Japs in the Pacific."

"A cover up, Colonel Svoboda?"

"Didn't say that. Military security would be more appropriate. Stuff like this happens all the time in war. One learns to keep one's mouth shut."

"And you retired as a Colonel?"

"Goddamn correct! In 1974, with thirty-three years of service."

"And you never discussed this with anyone?"

"Not for fifty years. During a visit I made to Key West in 1992, I asked folks near Bahia Honda if they'd ever heard anything about that night? Met a real good-looker there too who also seemed to know about it. She asked me to give her what I knew about it. I used her type-writer and gave her a one pager with my name at the bottom, but I didn't sign it so I could deny it later if the CID tried to arrest me for disclosing an old secret." Alex did not mention that he'd got a copy of the document from the librarian at Key West. "Funny thing," Svoboda continued, "is I've read every damned book I could get my hands on since then, and have never seen a single reference to it."

"What about the rest of your crew?"

"There were four of us. I tried to look them up after the war. I was the only one who made it back."

Alex didn't want to get into all the details, he didn't have time, but he felt he owed it to Svoboda to give the old man some closure on an incident which had obviously been on his mind for most of his adult life. "Since you were involved and probably curious as hell about what it all meant," Alex confided, "I'm going to tell you what I can. But believe it or not, but all this is still highly classified stuff, and I'd hate to see you get your tits in a wringer with the Feds"

The old codger held up his hand. "I appreciate that, young man."

"German agents were in fact put ashore that night," Alex began. "Five. One was captured six months later on the mainland and was held incommunicado until the war ended and then offered American citizenship in return for his silence."

Svoboda's eyes twinkled. "Rumors I heard at Key West in 1992 was that three skeletons were also found nearby a year or two later, but no one had any records to substantiate it."

"Rumors are hard to kill," Alex continued, "I guess, and they die slowly. However that rumor was correct. The three were all killed by gunshot wounds to the head."

"Jesus," the old man muttered. I guess we executed them?"

"I don't think so," Alex replied. One person made it ashore that night who was never captured. That person has remained here secretly until she died recently." The old man's eyes twinkled. "She?" He chuckled, now thrashing around in an open counter drawer for cigarettes. "I know they're here someplace, the damned doctors tell me not to, but at a time like this. Who cares? You have put an old man's suspicions to rest." From another drawer, he withdrew a bottle of Dimple Scotch and poured two hefty glasses, passing one to Alex. "I always knew there was something strange about the way they treated us all after that incident. All the secrecy and stuff, then the dangerous assignments that followed to the Pacific. It's almost as if the army hoped the Japs would get us and eliminate any witnesses. Svoboda lit his cigarette breathed in deeply, enjoying the moment.

"There was also was a U-Boat stored clandestinely near Key West after, the war," Alex continued. "That too disappeared, but may now have been found. This is part of the reason I've come to see you about. Any idea whatever happened to the two U-Boats you saw that day?"

"No idea," he replied through a thick cloud of exhaled smoke.

"Well," Alex concluded. "Unfortunately everything I've just told you has to be forgotten, I hope you appreciate that?"

"Jesus! I'm glad you stopped by, young man. I can read between the lines! We never talked here today, Mr. Balkan. Where you headed from here?"

"Europe. But I suspect the real answer to what really happened, might lie further east."

"Russia?"

"Probably."

"Well, if you solve this, maybe you'll drop by again and we'll finish this bottle of Dimple."

"Thanks. You never know."

Half an hour later Alex was making his way north along Interstate 95 toward New York and JFK Airport.

TWO

Dry Tortugas

COMMANDER MERRIAM LOOKED at the wall clock at the rear of the bridge. "It's 1325 hours. I'm going below to my quarters. Maintain present speed and bearing."

"Aye-aye, sir."

At forty-four knots, she knew the hydrofoil would make Key West in time to snort a couple of beers at the Trumbo Officers Club. She was still three hours out, had plenty of fuel, and would make the run-in, through the reef to Key West, at high tide. The two knot Gulf current would cut a quarter hour from the transit time.

As she went below she hoped they wouldn't encounter any Cuban "balsamos" this far west. If they did it would screw up her plans for tonight. Cuban refugees anywhere in the Florida straits required her to stop and identify how many were aboard, and if there were any with critical problems, she was expected to render assistance. Merriman had a date and was looking forward to dinner and some fantastic sex with her boyfriend afterward.

She didn't anticipate any delays because the Cuban boat people were many things, but they weren't stupid, and knew it was suicide to launch their rafts west of Havana. Only east of Havana, and six degrees longitude, did the prevailing Gulf currents keep rafts in the Gulf stream, carrying them northward along the Florida coast past Miami. West of six degrees on the other hand, currents pushed them into the Keys reefs, and a slow death from exposure and dehydration.

PHM-4 had been out for four days on Operation SEEDY AJAX in the waters between Cuba and Mexico. PHM-4 was one of three hydrofoils based at Key West and used for the Caribbean drug war. Armed with a seventy-six millimeter gun and eight Harpoon missiles, she could engage even the largest surface combatant and outrun all her quarry with the sole exception of the ubiquitous Cigarette Boats. Merriam's hydrofoil was under the control of Atlantic Command's Fleet Headquarters in Norfolk, Virginia, but assigned operationally to Joint Task Force Four at Key West.

Merriam felt good about her performance the last few days. SEEDY AJAX had gone from concept to completion in five days, and she'd played a decisive part in it. ATF agents spotted several thousand kilos of refined Columbian cocaine being loaded aboard a ship a week ago at the port of Santa Ana on the La Guajira Peninsula of Venezuela. The cargo was transferred yesterday off the Yucatan, to a cigarette boat named La Conchita. La Conchita was well known to ATF because her four V-8 engines could propel her to 120 miles per hour in calm water.

The cocaine transfer had taken place just after sunset north of Cabo Catoche, on the eastern tip of the Yucatan, and Mexican authorities predicted Conchita would disappear during the night, and unload her contraband at any of thousands of inlets between Honduras and Texas. Nine countries were involved in the sting, but only the United States was in a position to intercept her at sea. So rather than let her get away, LANTCOM decided to wrap up the operation by forcing Conchita into the path of PHM-4.

In rough seas the Hydrofoil maintained forty-two knots and outran La Conchita who was forced to throttle back to less than thirty in the towering waves. The end came quickly, and the conclusion of SPEEDY AJAX had been an adrenaline high for Commander Merriam and her crew because Conchita was stupid enough to fire at the Hydrofoil. The contest was unequal and ended within a quarter minute, with five druggies dead and La Conchita badly damaged and sinking. Five hundred pounds of cocaine were recovered before she slipped beneath the waves. SPEEDY AJAX ranked among the biggest narcotics hauls for the first quarter of the year, and Merriam would get the credit.

"Captain, please report to the bridge!" The intercom squawked. Merriam closed her log and headed upstairs.

"What's the problem?"

"Radar contact, sir! Ten o'clock! Eleven thousand yards! She's in our declared no-sail zone."

Merriam raised her glasses, and through the haze could make out the silhouette of a ship wallowing in the swells. "What's our position?"

"Thirty two miles south by south east of Fort Jefferson."

"Druggies?" she inquired.

"Maybe," the pilot replied.

"Go to battle stations. Once we get within range, hail her, see who they are."

She waited as the target announced itself as the U.S. registry, Heron, out of Key West, with Captain Mike Gregoriou commanding!

Merriam grabbed the mike. "You are in a closed military training area Gregoriou. No parking! Were you aware of this?"

"Affirmative!" Heron replied, "We stopped to make repairs to the engine. We'll be on our way shortly!"

The unconventional Conchs, Merriam thought! They never paid attention to restricted areas, and were always the first to complain when their vessels were damaged. She supposed the Conchs inherited it from their pirate forefathers. The navy's announcement a month earlier had clearly identified the coordinates for an eight thousand square mile area south of Fort Jefferson, which was being used for low-level navy bombing operations.

"Do you want me to notify the coast guard?"

"Negative," Heron replied, "that will not be necessary! We are not in need of assistance!"

As she passed within six hundred yards, Merriam scanned Heron, and thought it strange she had divers over the side and a scuba buoy astern. Maybe her repairs were more serious than her skipper admitted. But since it wasn't her responsibility, she made a note in the log to advise the Coast Guard when she arrived at Key West.

Heathrow Airport

Eduardo Heinkle retrieved his case from the carousel and headed for the Foreigners Only line. It grated him to line up with the Asians and Middle Easterners, who always pushed and shoved and all seemed to have endless visa problems. When it came his turn he handed his declaration and passport to the officer.

"Nothing to declare," she inquired.

"No, ma'am."

"Purpose of your visit to the United Kingdom Mr. Hernandez?" she inquired as she tapped his data on a computer key board.

"Business."

"How long will you stay?"

"A week."

"Next destination?"

"Undecided."

"You have a hotel reservation?"

"Yes."

"And where might that be?"

"The Hyde Park Hilton."

"Very good." Eduardo failed to notice another officer who'd emerged from a doorway nearby, and now stood beside Eduardo. "Mind stepping out of the line and accompany my associate?" she said to Eduardo.

He was startled. "Is there a problem officer?"

"Next!" She motioned forward a Pakistani family behind him in the queue. She turned again to Eduardo, who was staring at her in disbelief. "There's a good chap! Just follow my associate. It is all right."

"But."

"Please, don't be difficult! This will only take a few minutes. Standard procedure." She nodded at Eduardo reassuringly as he move away.

What ensued was the most embarrassing half hour in his life. He was strip-searched—including a rectal orifice exam while observers stood by, assuring him it was normal procedure and for his protection so no one could abuse him. From their questions it was obvious they suspected he was carrying narcotics, which thank God he wasn't! Throughout the ordeal he'd thought of the phone call from the American, realizing this might be the first of many such encounters with Interpol.

On only a few occasions when he was young had he experimented with cocaine in Peru, but didn't like it. He recalled the ditties he'd thought of during his conversation with Selvanian in Cyprus. The customs officers also expressed surprise at the amount of cash he had in his possession, wondering aloud about its purpose? Few respectable businessmen moved around with twenty-six thousand dollars in cash. Eduardo cursed Smithers for handing him the envelope and not providing some credit cards instead. When it was over, the officer advised him that Scotland Yard would be contacting him at his hotel, and to have a nice stay in England.

At the Hilton he asked a porter to place his luggage in his suite, and headed to the bar for a couple of stiff drinks. When he called Smithers he got his answering machine. He left a message to immediately go and buy himself a cell phone so Eduardo could talk to him when he needed to, and to call him back ASAP. He had the Bellhop call him a cab and went out for dinner. Things were moving too quickly for Eduardo, and he wished he'd made the appointment with the American for the day after tomorrow instead of Monday. Now he had a weekend to kill.

His meeting with Selvanian was unsettling. He realized he was involved with people who dealt harshly with those with whom they had problems. He supposed he'd known all along that his father was not involved in completely legal activities. When he'd attended Oxford University many years ago, and saw his father for the first since he was a child, he'd realized then that something was amiss! His roots in Peru were middle class while his father's lifestyle and country estate just west of London at Maidenhead, were regal. The money obviously hadn't grown on a tree.

As he digested his dinner with a couple of brandies, he studied the view of the Thames River, trying to erase the old man's last warning which still rang in his ears: "henceforth only discuss legal issues relating to our business with a man named Maeki Zaki in Hong Kong." Shan Kew, Khatoury's Hong Kong lawyer had suffered an untimely heart attack. Selvanian told him, and Maeki Zaki had taken Shan Kew's place. Eduardo recalled Selvanian's advice . . . "If you are to enjoy your inheritance Eduardo, you must prove yourself. The matter I referred to in Russia, has to do with the Banque de Commerce e Credit International. You have heard of BCCI? Look into it as soon as you arrive in England. I shall also be in London next Wednesday to discuss all this with you further."

Eduardo knew it was no accident that Shan Kew had suffered a heart attack. The old Armenian obviously had him killed.

Eduardo drained away the last of the Brandy in his snifter. It was time for him to leave for the theater. When he returned to the Hilton after midnight, there was a note that Smithers would be by first thing in the morning.

London Hilton

"G-g-g-Good morning, Eduardo, have a p-p-pleasant trip?"

"Not really. The weather was foul, and I had some Englishman's finger up my arse at Heathrow yesterday!"

"Oh d-dear! They s-searched you?"

"An understatement!" Smithers was a competent international lawyer, seemed to have good breeding and an excellent education. One day Eduardo would ask him what he attributed his stutter to?

Smithers avoided his eyes and sipped his coffee. He seemed nervous, and Eduardo wondered what the solicitor was not telling him? "What is happening here in London?"

"Not, not not, nnn-ot good, I'm afraid. Not good at all! A Scotland Yard inspector named Haggerty popped around to see me the day before yesterday. Said he had some questions for you. I told him you'd just left England and would return. He's curious about your father. Enquired if anyone might have wanted him out of the way? Said the government would be making a request for his exhumation." He looked at Eduardo sheepishly, "I told him your father had no enemies, was respected and well thought of, at least as I knew anyway as his solicitor. They think foul play was involved."

"Did he say why?"

"I believe they know something, but he wouldn't say."

"And what did you tell him?"

"Nothing!"

"And what about suspects, do they have any?"

"He didn't say."

"Am I a suspect?"

"Good god. Shouldn't think so! After all, you were in Peru when he died."

"Smithers, I was told at the airport yesterday, someone from Scotland Yard would be around to see me, and based on what you've just told me, I assume it will be this man called Haggerty?"

"Most probably!" Smithers replied, "Inspector Haggerty is handling the case."

"What about their intent to have my father's body exhumed?"

"A British court will issue a request. It will be delivered to the Peruvian Embassy here in London."

"Why didn't you tell me about this when you called me in Cyprus, about the American?" He wondered what the Englishman did all day? Smithers only had two main clients; Eduardo, and some elderly woman in Scotland, whose estate was slowly being confiscated for back-taxes. Smithers had told him the Scottish account took less than three days a month.

"I thought it would keep until you returned."

"You thought! They gave me an asshole inspection for Christ's sake!" Shit, he thought. First the damned police in Key West and now Scotland Yard! What next?

The solicitor nervously searched among his notes until he found what he was looking for. "Here it is. I may not pronounce it correctly." Smithers stutter was becoming worse. "It's called Aipysurus Laevis!"

Eduardo waited.

"It's a type of venom. From a sea snake. Indigenous to the South Pacific. From what I gather, no antidote is available, and in small doses, the victim wastes away over a period of several days. In older people its symptoms are usually concealed behind other ailments normal in the aged. At first the victim experiences some discomfort and slight paralysis in the legs and arms. This worsens until respiratory failure causes convulsions and death. According to the medical profession, the venom is almost impossible to detect as only an infinitesimal amount is needed to induce death."

"Jesus, Smithers! You are up on all this?"

"Thought I'd better be able to inform you about it. I obtained this from a pathologist friend of mine."

"You should have met me at the airport yesterday." Eduardo was pissed off. The damned solicitor was starting to annoy him.

"Where would someone come up with poison like this?"

"They're checking around."

"Okay! What kind of man is this Inspector Haggerty?"

"Nice-enough bloke! Unassuming! Shouldn't think you'll have a problem with him!"

"What questions will he ask?"

"No idea!"

"What are my legal rights? As a Peruvian? Should I answer his questions without having legal counsel present?"

"You've nothing to hide, I mean, you weren't even in the country when he died. I should think the best course would be to be direct and above board with him. Be completely open. Tell him what you know."

"What about questions relating to inheritance and taxes?"

"Ahaaaa! Another matter!"

"So I should avoid those, then?"

"Yes!"

"And if he asks anyway?"

"Refer him to me. Inheritance matters are another question."

"My father was a Peruvian citizen when he died, wasn't he?"

"You are asking me! I thought you knew?"

"Oh come on Smithers! Did he have any other passports?"

"Yes. Aside from Peru, Portuguese, Brazilian, South African, and Armenian."

"Armenian?"

"Some friend acquired it for him."

"Christ almighty," Eduardo said. "Does Haggerty know this?"

"I don't know. He has not asked me the question, and it is not information I offer about clients."

"What about a German passport?" Eduardo continued.

"No."

"And he never applied for UK citizenship?"

"No."

Eduardo was beginning to care less and less for this Englishman. But suspected Smithers knew too much. Eduardo would keep him around until the problem with Scotland Yard was resolved. "A lot of things have happened, and I want to make sure you and I are on the same wavelength, Mr. Smithers. So if there are things you know, which I should know then you better tell me now. Tell me everything. Clear?"

"I . . . I . . . I underst . . . and!" he replied.

Eduardo could tell the Englishman was becoming more agitated. His stutter was worsening. "Good! Now, what else have you heard about my father's death?"

"Nothing Eduardo, God's truth!"

Eduardo suspected he knew more than he'd admitted. His father had used this man to draw up his Last Will and Testament. Smithers had included things in it he knew were at best questionable. How could two men associate for decades and not know something was amiss. He'd asked Selvanian if he knew Smithers. His reply was that he knew of him, but they'd never met. Selvanian had offered that he didn't trust Englishmen: especially solicitors who were usually men of meager means and with greed in their hearts.

"Okay, Mr. Smithers, I need your assistance with two things. Let me know if Scotland Yard contacts you, and contact Haggerty and tell him where I am. Secondly, I need a comprehensive data dump on everything you can get your hands on relating to the collapse of BCCI!"

"The bank?"

"Correct."

"What specifically are you looking for?"

"Everything you can find, right back to day one."

"I'll prepare a comprehensive dossier. Oh, by the way . . . ," he said leaning forward. "The cell phone you requested. This one is good for a month and you can call anywhere in the world with it. I've written its number on the paper with it."

* * *

Before lunch Eduardo was getting horny and arranged with the Concierge for a young woman to spend a few hours with him. He liked the young girls in London and always had. Their sleek bodies, long legs, and fine facial features were hard to find in Peru, and he'd come to enjoy their company during his University years in England. But when she left, he again felt empty, and thought about Mary Malagang. He called her in Geneva, and asked if she'd fly over and join him for the weekend. She agreed. She'd arrive Sunday evening . . . for two days.

Before his inheritance, as a poor man he'd relied on "donna di note" from time to time back home, when he needed sexual solace. Unlike most of his Spanish associates, whose cocks were embedded in their cerebral cortex; being of German background, his needs seemed more clinical, unemotional and detached. But Mary Malagang had awakened long forgotten chords in him.

Three days between her jasmine scented thighs, at her estate near Jakarta, had aroused long dormant feelings. He also recalled the four days they'd sailed the azure blue waters off Saint Martin, and realized she was not only beautiful and sensuous, but very intelligent. During their recent visit to Key West, and then Canada, he'd really come to like her. The only thing which nagged at him, was her ties to General Chong Ki—Young; the old Chinese general who was her father. Mixing business with pleasure was an area he was going to have to be very careful about . . . until he'd settled his relationships with Selvanian and the others who held the keys to his wealth.

That afternoon while Eduardo was out for a walk in Hyde Park, Smithers dropped off the dossier about BCCI, along with a note that Inspector Haggerty would be away from London until Monday. So there was no reason for Eduardo to remain in town over the weekend. He decided he'd take the afternoon train from Victoria Station and spend the weekend amidst his old haunts at Oxford. It would be good to look up old acquaintances and laugh about old times over some Guinness.

As he read through the BCCI material, he realized its demise was much more complex than he'd first thought. He recalled reading about it in Peru, but was only struck by the suddenness with which it appeared and then disappeared into history. A couple of points in the dossier stood out clearly. The bank was started in 1972 by a Pakistani named Abedi, was financed by money from the Arabian Gulf: and its principal owner was the ruler of the United Arab Emirates. In a decade it had expanded at an astounding pace, and when the end came nineteen years later, in July 1991, it died just as quickly—as regulators in sixty-two countries simultaneously froze what remained of its negligible assets. Incorporated in Luxembourg, it had maintained its principal offices in London, and, during its meteoric life, was surrounded by a host of the Who's Who of the era, many of whom had questionable links to the international crime world. Among its clients were Adnan Khashoggi of Saudi Arabia, General Manuel Noriega of Panama, Clark Clifford of the United states, Ferdinand Marcos of the Philippines, and even Saddam Hussein of Iraq.

It was the involvement of BCCI in three American banks which had brought about its downfall, and especially the involvement of America's intelligence agencies, whose close associations with the banks leaders had drawn attention to an unholy alliance. Not only was CIA involved, but also the security organs of England, France, Israel and Russia, until the world wondered who was running who? Was the tail wagging the dog? Throughout the dossier was a recurring theme that the United States Justice Department had consistently squelched investigations of people and institutions involved with BCCI. Those mentioned in the dossier included key leaders of CIA, DIA, and members of the president's national security staff!

International observers at the time thought it odd that the United States had called for BCCI's demise while at the same time continuing to shield those agencies and people who were alleged to have been deeply involved in scores of illegal transactions with BCCI. More knowledgeable observers opined that it was the same unholy troika which had led the Desert Storm coalition against Iraq. Selvanian's comments suggested he had serious concerns regarding this failed institution.

Truman Annex

"Rooooom, Tench-Hut!"

"As you were, gentlemen." Admiral Lange always attended the 0700 stand-up on Tuesday mornings. Staff summarized the previous week's activities and future events. It was also good for troop morale because the noncoms got to see him up close, and got "face time" with the "old man." Lange himself had come up through the ranks and he knew the value of "face time." It kept troop morale high when they got to see the old man, talk to him, joke, and mention issues which sometimes only he could solve. The average age of those in the operations center was thirty-one, which would have been twenty-two were it not for his two senior Watch Officers. But the kids at the monitors were mature beyond their years. Some had already done tours aboard various intercept platforms used in the never-ending war against the narco-traffickers and a few combat tours in Iraq and Afghanistan.

Congress's latest war against the narcos had pumped additional billions into the Colombian war and once again raised JTF-4's visibility within armed forces personnel systems. The war on terrorism was the latest newcomer to "operational status" which was important to the youngsters trying to get operational time on their resume's. With it they had a good chance of moving to the head of the promotion queue. Without it one had a slight disadvantage.

The admiral scanned the faces around him, momentarily acknowledging some and reassuring others. Those he didn't recognize he pointed to inquiringly, and waited as each identified themselves to him. "Okay, ladies and gentlemen, let's get started."

The 0700 briefing was a daily affair for the Key West staff who updated the leadership about the status of ongoing drug-related operations. Friday's and Mondays were the busiest days as it was the time the druggies made and received most of their shipments. Everyone liked to joke that the druggies were just normal business folks who worked a five day week like normal people, and spent the weekends at home barbecuing with their families. By Fridays, their work week was done and their product en route to market. Then it became the Key West Operations Center's responsibility, to track and intercept it before reaching United States soil.

By 1700 each Friday, everyone in the Watch Center was in high gear, as billions of dollars of military equipment deployed against the inbound shipments: from AWACS, to aircraft carriers, and the assets of several U.S. and international law enforcement agencies was focused on the mission. For the staff assembled here before the eerie back-lit green status boards, it was all about "end games." End games were the intercepts, at which the good guys actually confronted the bad guys; stared them down and took away his toys, his merchandise, and arrested him.

The admiral attended Tuesday morning briefings as by this time his staff had summarized the previous week's performance statistics. The format each week was the same. First came reporting on successful end games. Next up were planned end-games. And finally, status briefs for surface and air assets assigned to the Command. Last were staff updates on personnel. Admiral Lange's AOR or the Area of Responsibility, encompassed thirty-two countries from the Caribbean, to the tip of South America, and half the western African coast from Nigeria to Capetown.

Everything depended on kilos and tons of contraband captured. Tons captured annually were what the bean counters in Washington critically examined. Tons intercepted were the *sine-qua-non* and bane of Lange's existence, like body counts during the Vietnam War. Lange's promotion hinged on it.

"What's the first item?" he demanded.

"Operation Speedy Ajax is up first, Admiral!" the junior briefing officer replied. The lights dimmed and room quieted as the briefer presented a summary and video taken by a navy P-3 Orion which had circled the stricken ship as she slid beneath the waves, her name La Conchita prominently embossed across her stern as it pointed to the sky before going under. The last few slides were mug shots of the dead, contraband, and survivors.

"Isn't that Hermosa Sanchez?" the admiral pointed to the fourth photograph."

"We're still not certain, Admiral. We hope to have verification from Mexican dental records by noon. Hermosa Sanchez's identity could not be absolutely established as half of the drug runner's face was missing."

The briefer concluded that this event was the command's third "bust" of the quarter and had cost the Columbians six tons of Cocaine with a street value of three hundred million. Added to the two earlier busts, the command's capture rate for the second quarter was nine tons. Lange tried to be upbeat about the abysmal statistics and hoped they'd improve. The previous year's performance at this point was ninety-eight tons. His staff insisted the smaller captures proved that the good guys were finally winning the war. The admiral knew better! The Cartels had developed new delivery routes through Asia, Africa, and Europe, and in particular Mexico. LA's "La Familia" and "Los Zetas" were particularly effective in getting huge quantities across the southern US border at Mexicali, Ciudad Juarez, and Nuevo Laredo. JTF-4 had even intercepted two submersibles so far, one offshore at Puerto Rico and a second near Key Largo. Both captures were still classified, and the Cartels had remained silent about the losses. As the briefer covered the next eight items of interest, Lange wondered how much longer he could justify the lack of tonnage before higher headquarters began focusing elsewhere.

"Under highlights, Admiral, there are three items. First, a change in Bolivia's legal ruling on the death penalty for narcotics trafficking. We may not see any executions for a while! Secondly, the senior Columbian Naval Staff initiated an investigation into allegations of corruption in their Riverine Command. One riverine captain was caught last week trying to leave the country with a quarter million dollars in cash. This could affect our future cooperation. And last, Commander Merriam of PHM-4, filed a notice with the coast guard yesterday, that the salvage ship Heron, was stopped in a restricted area. Heron's captain stated she needed engine repairs. Merriam advises Heron had buoys deployed and suspects she may have been engaged in activity unrelated to engine repair or salvage. The coast guard will take this up with Heron when she returns to Key West."

"What's Heron's size?" the admiral inquired, recalling the name Gregoriou from around Christmastime, when he's asked one of his staff to look into the question of German submarines in the Keys during the war. He also recalled a retired navy captain he'd spoken with but couldn't remember the name.

"I don't know," the briefer replied.

"Well, you should!" Lange replied curtly. "Especially if you are going to brief it!"

Lange's XO interrupted. "If I may, Admiral?"

"Go ahead, Lynn!" Captain Lynn Davis had recently been made his assistant.

"I believe Heron is seventy-eight feet. Steel construction. And used by Dives Unlimited for deep wrecks!"

"Thanks." The admiral returned his gaze to the briefer who was obviously red faced.

"What will the coast guard do with this?"

"Inform her captain he was in violation of a warning notice, but not much else! It's up to ship owners to assume responsibility for their vessels, Admiral."

"What was Heron's location?"

"I don't happen to have it with me either, Admiral."

Lange's silence made it clear the briefer better have details next time. "Please send it to my office immediately after the briefing . . . continue."

London Hilton

Eduardo returned from Oxford at three o'clock Sunday afternoon and strolled through Hyde Park to clear away what was left of his weekend hangover from rounds at the pubs. By six he was back in his room and climbed into the jacuzzi in his suite.

Mary Malagang called twenty minutes later to tell him she'd checked into the adjoining suite. Eduardo ordered dinner in camera for two and suggested she join him as soon as she'd unpacked.

As he and Mary were working on yet another climax the next morning, the phone rang, and Smithers informed him that Scotland

Yard's Inspector Haggerty wanted to see him at the Yards Kensington offices at half past ten. To Eduardo's suggestion early afternoon would be better, the attorney strongly urged Eduardo to keep the morning appointment to avoid needless problems.

The meeting with Haggerty proved inconclusive, more form than substance, and Eduardo wondered if Inspector Haggerty already knew who Eduardo's father's murderer was and really wanted to find out more about Eduardo's non-UK inheritance. The inspector also repeatedly inquired about Eduardo's visits to Asia and Cyprus, visits which Eduardo assured him were for pleasure. Eduardo kept thinking of Selvanian's admission about how they'd planned to murder his father and wondered what Selvanian would think when he learned that someone else had apparently done it for him?

He returned to the Hilton just past noon for lunch with Mary. Another two hours between her thighs in her suite this time, had finally worn him out and he retired to get a few hours rest before his meeting with the Yank from Salt Lake City this evening.

* * *

"Mr. Balkan?"

"You're Hernandez?"

Alex pointed to a chair. He'd arrived earlier and deliberately selected a table along the rear wall where it would be difficult to overhear their conversation. He'd also checked for surveillance since his departure from JFK last night and found none, but he knew if anyone were on to him he'd probably never detect their surveillance anyway. Every once in a while it paid off: the sudden movement, the averted eye, or the odd and unexplainable, which led to that gut feeling.

A waiter took their orders. Eduardo leaned forward conspiratorially. "Is your name Bilkin or Balkan?

"The latter."

"Ohhhh. I checked with registration. I thought when we spoke on the phone, you pronounced it with two a's, and not two i's."

"You were correct," Alex replied.

"I thought as much!"

Hernandez was perceptive. Alex liked that. "I use variations at times like this when I'm in an unofficial status. You know how it is with us Intelligence types?" He withdrew his diplomatic passport and placed it before Eduardo so he could verify the photograph and name.

"And what do you really do for a living Mr. Alexander J. Balkan?"

"Right now nothing. I'm a retired air force intelligence officer who until just recently worked on a retainer with Scion Consultants in Washington. Their work too is intelligence related. As to what I actually did for my government, it's kind of mundane and boring. I verified the destruction of Russian intercontinental ballistic launchers used to launch nuclear weapons at the United States. Both sides agreed to get rid of a certain number under the SALT II accords. So I stand around a lot in the cold Russian weather and watch bulldozers squash their missiles. They have Russians in the United States doing the same thing."

"I see. So the Key West matter is unrelated to your normal work?"

"Correct!"

"So what's this all about?"

"You mind if we use first names?"

"Not at all."

"It's about the woman in Key West."

"You said as much on the phone."

"But how much do you really know about her?"

Eduardo had thought about how he would respond to this question when it came up and decided he'd force the American to reveal his cards first. "Not very much."

"Can you tell me what you do know?"

"Wait just a minute! Did I pay your way to London to answer your questions? It's supposed to be the other way around isn't it? Tell me what you know and then I'll see."

"I guess that's fair," Alex replied. He'd hoped detective Welsh's suspicions about this Peruvian were wrong. If Hernandez was a *Capo di tutti Capi*: a Columbian narco-king, then their conversation was probably going to be very brief and one way. If that were the case then Alex hoped it would end peacefully. He'd make the first move. He was running out of time anyway and had few options. "Just one more question before I begin. You involved with Peruvian intelligence?"

Eduardo started to laugh. "You must be joking! Sorry to disappoint you."

"What about narcotics?"

"Mr. Balkan, I'm just a dumb country lawyer from Peru. That's it! You called me. You wanted to tell me something important. You are here as my guest. What's this all about?"

Alex decided to believe him. "I stopped through Key West before Christmas to see this woman called Eve Albion because her phone number appeared on the telephone bill of a murdered Russian defector in Washington. Because the murdered victim was a defector, there was obviously concern that her death may have been intelligence related. So I was asked to determine why the Washington defector had called the woman in Key West? When I asked the old woman in Key West if she knew her, she got angry, and threw me out, and next thing I knew she died. That's about it!" Alex saw no reason to tell him just yet about the other information of her being a German agent and a spy.

"How was she killed?"

"According to forensics, by suffocation!"

"How does all this concern me?"

"I got a call recently from the Detective in Key West who interviewed you when you were in Key West. You remember him?"

"Yes."

"Well, he obviously suspects me," Alex continued, "because I was the last one to see the Albion woman alive, and people in her neighborhood remember her throwing me out of her house. But the Key West detective also suspects you because you're the only one who made enquiries about her since she died. But worse for you was what happened to you when you flew up from Saint Martin to the Bahamas."

"How did you know this?" Hernandez interrupted.

"Welsh told me."

"And what about it?" Eduardo asked.

"Let me finish. Welsh did a lot of digging. Most of what he's got sounds circumstantial. But in our courts, a foreigner from Peru or Colombia, does not get much sympathy on charges of narcotics trafficking. Even if you are innocent it could take years, and meanwhile you could rot in jail without bond while awaiting trial."

"Wait a minute," Eduardo interrupted. He was beginning to forget his legal training about getting all the facts first. "I have no idea what the hell you are talking about! I have been involved in no narcotics business!"

Alex studied him for a moment and wondered if the Peruvian was stiffing him. "Welsh says he's got proof you made a cocaine drop north of Cuba before you landed in Key West and went to see Albion. You going to deny it?"

"What?" Eduardo exclaimed loud enough for a couple nearby to take notice of him.

"Some outfit called Blue Point Air," Alex commented, "Dropped a center-line luggage container from low altitude on your flight."

"Il bastardo!" Eduardo exploded again. *"Il cunyo grande!"* Again a couple nearby stopped their conversation and looked at him. Eduardo's face turned bright red as he drained away his Scotch and signaled the waiter for a refill. "I should have known!" Suddenly it all became clear. Now it all fit. He recalled the pilot's excuse before takeoff that the center-line fuselage luggage compartment didn't work. They'd put his and Mary's suit cases in the main cabin. The rapid descent near Cuba for carburetor difficulties. Then the climb back to eight thousand feet, and the inexplicable loss of the underbelly luggage compartment in the rapid descent. The American was probably right. He'd been an unwitting player in a narcotics delivery. But why? He'd even paid Castries in cash for the aircraft lease. If Eduardo got a chance he'd teach the *cunyo* manners!

"Why was I so stupid!" He asked no one in particular.

Alex waited.

"Now I understand what you are talking about! Why didn't it occur to me sooner? You must believe me Mr. Balkan, I had no knowledge of what took place in that aircraft charter and have nothing to do with narcotics. You can check my credentials in Lima with the Bar Association."

But Eduardo had defended enough innocent men in Peru, and knew that circumstantial evidence was always enough to hang most. And in Peru most accused ended up being executed by firing squad. The Key West detective certainly had a *prima facia* case. "All right, I'll tell you what I know, but only in exchange for your help!"

"What kind of help?" Alex replied, wondering if his macho host was now about to blow smoke up his ass?

"In your business you obviously have connections. I had no idea Castries placed narcotics aboard the aircraft I chartered. Until a month ago . . . I was a back-country lawyer. Then my father died and left me with a substantial inheritance. I've been looking into it here in Europe.

Does the Castries thing sound like something a man in my position would do? I will tell you what I know but you must reciprocate."

"I'll do what I can!" Alex promised with his most engaging smile.

"Let me start at the beginning," Eduardo said with a congenial smile. "One of the things I found among my father's papers was a list with five names and addresses, but no explanation about their significance. I checked with my solicitor here in London. He'd heard of first three but never met them and knew nothing specific about their business, nor relationship to my father. He'd never heard of the last two names: a man named Castries in the Leeward Islands and Eve Albion at Key West. So I went to see them."

Alex was fascinated by all the stuff about holding Companies, bearer shares corporations, interlocking Boards and secret bank accounts. He also believed Eduardo was probably nothing more than what he appeared; a country lawyer trying to grasp the details of complex inheritance. Among the jewels Heinkle mentioned was a reference to a conversation he'd had with a Key West Realtor who'd spoken of the visit of a Slavic named woman to Eve Albion in the year before she died. Alex knew it had to be Tatiana Slavchenko. It was a point Alex completely overlooked during his visit to Key West, and he felt a little stupid on reflection. Eduardo concluded that once he realized Albion was dead, there was little he could accomplish in Florida so he and the Indonesian woman with him flew to New York, rented a car and drove to Canada where they remained a few days before returning to Europe.

By the time dinner was over it was almost half past ten when Hernandez looked at his watch. A good woman with a slender frame had just passed their table and his loins started to ache for the woman upstairs in his suite. "So do you think you can help me Alex?"

"I think so, I have friends."

Eduardo looked at his watch again.

"Something wrong?" Alex asked.

"I'm late for another appointment.

If you don't mind I'd like to continue our meeting tomorrow."

They agreed to meet for lunch.

When Alex got back to his room he placed a call to detective Welsh in Key West and said he needed a couple of weeks to put it all together. He also insisted that warrants for Eduardo Hernandez and his girlfriend be postponed. Finally he asked Welsh to check around Key

West and see if there was any record of Tatiana Slavchenko stopping there during the previous year: hotel reservations, car rentals or moped rentals and such.

Dry Tortugas

Mike Gregoriou knew visibility would be good at sixty fathoms. The half-knot current moving across the bottom only slowly dissipated the debris from their work. They'd arrived at the wreck just after dawn and spent the first hour refilming the exterior of the sub. Another hour was devoted to trying to force her deck hatches. Hatches atop her sail were also heavily encrusted with marine growth and resisted their efforts. To gain entry, their options at this point were two: C-4, or acetylene. Mike opted for the latter.

He knew something was unusual about this wreck. In the past two months he'd first been approached by retired navy captain named Millican, then the man called Balkan from Washington, and finally Admiral Lange's Executive Officer. In mid-February Mike had decided to reexamine the wreck.

He'd use acetylene initially to gain access to her inner pressure hull. The lack of any exterior hull damage suggested her pressure hull was intact. U.S. Navy records regarding her disposition reported she'd been sunk by gunfire, but there was no exterior hull damage anywhere from cannon fire. So either this wasn't U-2513 . . . or?

Mike's biggest concern was the sub's internal pressure hull. Were it still full of air, then the final incision through her plate could be dangerous, possibly opening her like a sardine can with a cherry bomb inside it. But the thought of what might lie inside intrigued him beyond words. Her exterior provided six known access points: a fore and aft deck hatch, two more aside the conning tower and one atop her bridge. All were hopelessly encrusted. Short of an explosive . . . cutting into her was the only option.

At sixteen hundred tons, U-2513 or whatever her designation was, she was among the largest wartime boats ever built and equivalent in size to American destroyers of that era. From blue prints he'd found, he'd decided the best way in was through her lower side between frames 37 and 38. They straddled her control room and at this point her exterior and interior hulls were only two feet apart and would simplify the work of cutting. He'd also cut close to her bottom, to minimize the escape of air if she were intact.

"Bottom-one to bridge! What's your status up there?" he demanded.

"All clear Mike. No problems so far. What's it look like?"

"We're going to cut her like we discussed. There's no other way in."

"How soon will you start?"

"A couple of minutes."

"How much time do you need?"

"Forty-five minutes for the first, maybe an hour for the second. I'll keep you posted."

"Okay. Please let us know before you start the second cut. Good luck!"

Bolotnoye, Russia

The black Ziv slid to a halt along the snow covered road amongst some heavy pines. When the thick snow melted next spring, if anyone ever found the two bodies it would be assumed it was the local Mafiosi or Chechen as Russian's referred to the local mafia, who'd done it. Everyone knew Pyotr Kaminsky maintained contacts with the Novosibirsk underworld, and was an unprincipled bastard. Kaminsky had many enemies and now that he was retired, everyone would assume old debts had been paid.

The frozen air almost took Kaminsky's breath away as he fell from the car into the snow. Alexi Poluostrov emerged next, and kicked Kaminsky a couple of feet off the road into the snow.

"Go ahead you shit!" Kaminsky swore as he rolled onto his back and stared at his executioner. "At least be a man and shoot me while you are looking me in the eye! "Go on, do it! Get it over with!"

They'd worked him over pretty good at an abandoned cabin down the road, but they were inexperienced puppies and he'd given them no satisfaction. He'd kept his mouth shut. He'd derived some pleasure from the realization that were their roles reversed even a few years ago, he'd have had himself shot for incompetence. Poluostrov had made feeble threats for the information, and seemed uncomfortable with physical violence, and the imbecile's efforts at torture were comical. If their situations were reversed, Kaminsky would have wrought unspeakable ruin, inflicting it in the most heinous and degrading manner and in the most intimate of places! There were ways to make any man talk. But no one seemed comfortable with the old ways anymore.

He was guilty of treason. Kaminski knew the rules. He'd played the game and come so damned close to winning, he didn't mind that he'd failed. At seventy-two he'd been retired two years, and his life now was no longer worth living anyway. He and his wife went hungry most of the time. An occasional bottle of vodka was the high point of his life. His pension of 250 rubles was a joke, today it didn't but a pack of cigarettes, and the ruble wasn't even good for toilet paper in the parasha.

The five hundred dollars the American gave him was enough to get them out of their shitty apartment, and into their own four room dacha. But now it wasn't to be. He'd have to enjoy his jackpot in the next life wherever that was.

Alexi Poluostrov raised his pistol and fired two rounds through Kaminski's knees. Kaminski wreathed and screamed like a stuck pig, and began crawling away in a vain attempt to avoid more pain, bellowing as his executioner fired again. But his third round was sloppy; a flesh wound through the upper arm.

"Shit, Alexi!" The driver in the car exclaim behind him, "Didn't they teach you how to shoot straight?"

Another round hit Kaminsky, this time through the elbow and he used his uninjured arm to push himself over onto his back. He stared at the sky, a smile peeking through the mucous smeared across his mustache. He watched as the man standing above him pointed the revolver. Pyotr smiled for what it was worth.

Poluostrov reloaded and watched as his associate pulled Tukhachevsky from the back seat next, and kicked him into the deep snow near Kaminsky. Six more reports in close succession echoed through the trees.

"Let's go!" Alexi had a flight to catch to Siberia.

THREE

London

ALEX STUDIED HIS watch for a moment as he thought about the number of time zones between London and Florida. It was seven in the morning in London and just after two in the morning on the east coast. To hell with it he thought. He'd call detective Welsh and wake him up.

Welsh's voice was groggy at first and then became angry when he realized what time it was. "You usually call people in the middle of the goddamn night, Balkan?"

Alex apologized, and explained he'd forgotten about the five hour time difference. "I'll call back later."

"Hold it!" Welsh replied. "You've already ruined my night, my wife is up and the baby's crying. Let me tell you what I found out. I never would have believed what I am about to tell you if you'd told me this last year Balkan. Everyone around Key West knew the Albion was a recluse who never went out, had no friends, and kept to herself. From an old man who runs a convenience store down the street from her house I learned that she'd confided to him that she had an elderly friend on the mainland who she visited occasionally. Her story about this friend was obviously crap! Each time she left Key West she'd gone gallivanting around the world like the damned queen of Sheba. Seven trips to be exact! And they cost her eighty-six thousand dollars! Included were cruises to the Caribbean, to Ireland, Alaska, Barbados, Hawaii, and a three week jaunt through China."

Welsh had also learned the Slavchenko broad had also travelled to Key West repeatedly, using the same travel agent as Albion. First last March and then August last year. Each time she'd flown-in first-class, rented fine cars, taken suites at Casa Marina, Key West's most luxurious digs, and spent lots of money. During her last visit, she'd also leased a private plane and flown down to Jamaica for four days.

"Where in Jamaica?" Alex demanded. Suddenly suspicious.

"Negril on the west end."

"Did you check with the pilot?" Alex asked.

"It was a wet lease," Welsh replied.

"Meaning?"

"She flew it herself."

"What!"

"You didn't know?" He laughed. "She had a private pilot's license . . . ? You CIA types are really something you know. You ain't so smart are you? I got a photocopy of it from the company she leased the aircraft from. It was renewed last year, at

Winchester airport near Washington."

Alex wondered what CIA would think? The terms of her resettlement didn't require her to inform them about the most intimate details of her private life, but someone at Langley should have known; they'd obviously dropped the ball. At least they should have known she'd left the country and went to Jamaica.

"I also found out she'd made several trips out of the country through the same travel agent in Miami. Were you aware of that?"

"No."

"Listen to this! Argentina last October for three weeks. Peru for a week in early November. Then England in December."

Alex couldn't believe it. "What were the dates for England?"

"Sixth through the thirteenth! Mean anything?"

It was around the time old man Hernandez died. The Vietnamese at her store in Washington hadn't mentioned her taking a lot of time off for her worldwide jaunts, and he wondered if CIA, or Ted LePage, had spoken to the Vietnamese man? For that matter, who the hell was her Vietnamese guy really?"

"One last question Balkan?" Welsh concluded. "Admiral Lange phoned me yesterday, and wanted to know if I knew where you were? What's that about?"

"No idea. I hope you told him you did not know."

"I did as a matter of fact."

Truman Annex

"I was looking for you earlier Lynn!"

"Sorry, Admiral! I stopped by, but you'd just left and I knew you wouldn't be back until three o'clock, so I got in eighteen holes of golf."

"How's your game?"

"Eighty."

"Good for a nineteen handicap! You've been at Key West too long. What did you find out about Heron?"

"A friend with Lloyds in New York has a program which monitors shipyard maintenance contracts in the States for all vessels exceeding ten tons. He ran a scan and found Heron went into the Chickasaw Shipyard in Mobile, Alabama, on the second of March for service. I called Chickasaw and their foreman confirmed Heron was fitted with an ROV—a remotely operated vehicle, which accommodates three people for dives to two hundred fathoms. She left a week ago."

"He say what her next destination was?"

"Didn't know."

"Thanks. I'll see you later."

After Lynn closed the door he checked his address book and dialed the number for Captain Millican. Maybe Millican knew something?

Michael Gregoriou of Dives Unlimited had departed Key West two weeks ago, and no one had seen or heard from him or Heron since. Lange suspected that the son of a bitch was up to something and it probably involved the lost U-Boat. Lange spread a navigation chart across his desk and checked the coordinates for yesterday's Hydrofoil report on Heron. It was one hundred and thirty miles west of Key West, twenty miles south of the Fort Jefferson National Monument on the Dry Tortugas. His charts showed water depths in that area of forty to seventy fathoms, and a current welling up from the nearby Cuba channel of one to three knots in some areas. The current could make bottom work a hairy proposition.

A few moments later Millican's phone rang, and Lange waited impatiently for someone to answer. Son of a bitch, he thought, probably has a call waiting service and knew it was Lange calling. The question of Alex Balkan and the god-damned submarine was one of the unresolved questions which had stuck in Lange's craw since Christmas. He knew Balkan was onto something down here, and it annoyed him he couldn't find out what? And now Gregoriou too was out there somewhere, and that pissed Lange off even more. As the senior military man in charge at Key West, the admiral wanted to know everything that was happening in his domain. A recorded voice came on and informed Lange that Millican was out fishing. Lange left an abrupt message.

A month earlier when he'd been in Washington for briefings at the Pentagon, Lange looked up an old associate who knew about such things. But Lange hadn't anticipated the response he got. His friend told him some things were better left alone, and it might be better if he just forgot about it completely. What the hell did that mean? His friend had refused to elaborate. Why forget about a fifty-year-old German U-Boat lying on the bottom; who cared? Why the mystery? His friend refused to speculate. Lange had decided to forget about it until last week's hydrofoil sighting of the Heron. Now he suspected it had to be that damned U-Boat!

Lange withdrew his wallet and pulled out a copy of Balkan's note the Shore Patrol had confiscated from Balkan the day they'd arrested him at Boca Chica. He studied it: 'Four bladed. Eisener Geselleschaft. Fabriken 22/X/1942, No: 399736. Plus Periscope.' What the hell did it mean?

The phone on his desk rang. His secretary told him a retired Captain Millican was on the line. She transferred it.

"Admiral Lange here. Who's this?"

"Millican. You called?

"Yes. How are you?"

"I'm fine Admiral. Yourself? Millican ragged him about his forthcoming assignment as CINC NAVSOUTH in Naples, Italy. Now that an article had appeared in the Key West papers, it was common knowledge around town that Lange would not get another star, and the Naples, Italy, assignment would be his last before he retired. "When do you leave?" Millican concluded.

"About a week."

"We shall miss you."

"Thanks," Lange replied, raising his middle finger in a rude gesture to the mouthpiece.

"And what can I do for you this fine day, admiral?"

"I was curious if you might join me for lunch?"

"I'm kind of busy. But don't worry, I'll follow your favorite issue and will try to keep you posted once you get to Italy—if that's what you want to see me about?"

"Please do that." The son of a bitch, Lange thought as he slammed the phone down, Millican didn't intend to tell him shit!

London Hilton

His bedside message light was flashing when Alex returned from breakfast downstairs. The Hotel operator informed him that his mother had called and said it was urgent. When he got through to her it was five in the morning in Pennsylvania, and she sounded groggy. A couple of things had come up. Another man with a strange accent had called, this time from Moscow, and wanted Alex to call him urgently regarding some papers.

He suspected it was Kaminsky's brother-in-law who'd probably now had the information that Kaminsky had promised. Next she told him there were a couple of goons making enquiries about him around town. She'd noted a late model car driving past the house repeatedly with two men in it. They'd parked down the street the previous night and she'd debated calling the police. The local gas station also asked her if Alex was in some kind of trouble after the strangers made enquiries about him there too. She'd contacted his office in Washington, but learned no one had seen Alex in a week, and they too were looking for him.

People asking about him in Altoona! Cars watching his mother's house? What was going on? Only his close friends even knew that his mother lived in Altoona. Alex called Marvin Raoul in Washington next and woke him up. Alex became even more concerned when Marvin mentioned a report in yesterday's newspapers about a break in at Alex's apartment in Ballston.

Just before eight Washington time he placed a call to Scion Consultants in Roslyn. Thank God Ted's secretary came in early and answered. She was working for Chuck Bunn now, and aghast at Alex's accusation that they might have put out the word that Alex was to be placed under surveillance. She assured him that as far as she knew, no one at Scion had anything to do with events in Altoona or Balston. He wanted to believe her.

"Hold on for a moment," she said, "someone wants a word with you?"

Chuck Bunn's voice came on the line. "Alex, you there?"

"Yeah!"

"What the hell's happening?"

"I'm looking for new employment."

"You heard about Ted?"

"Yes."

"Look, Alex, I won't mix words. Ted never confided much to me, and there doesn't seem to be any corporate history as to what you've been doing for him the last three months. But a lot of people are asking questions and I need answers pronto! One of them is the reason for your last trip to Russia and Europe."

"Is that the reason someone broke into my apartment and trashed it?"

"Don't know anything about that. Honest Alex."

"It's the Slavchenko syndrome!"

"The what?"

"Come on, Chuck, you know what I'm referring too."

"I've no idea."

"That's your problem then! Find out."

"And your trip to Europe? Who the hell is this Eve Albion woman anyway? Even the White House has been asking questions, seems they are pissed at you. I asked the FBI about her and all I got was that she retired from the Defense Department years ago."

"What does the White House have to do with this?" Alex demanded, now a little concerned that things might be reaching a point where his life might really be in danger.

"Damned if I know, Alex. But they asked about her?"

"Who in particular?"

"Langford Seeley, the president's national security advisor."

"Ask him then," Alex replied.

"I don't ask questions when the White House calls!"

"Well you ought to! Ollie North worked at the White House too. Remember?" Alex didn't care for Chuck Bunn. Bunn was a miscast in the intelligence business. He should have been a country preacher. He was Mr. Nice Guy; a patriot who believed gentlemen didn't read each other's mail and that spying was immoral. And in the lead-up to 9-11 it was guys like Chuck Bunn that had emasculated America's intelligence services. Now America wanted answers and the system was trying to cover its ass. There were thousands and thousands of incompetents like Bunn in the Beltway bureaucracy who couldn't be touched for negligence, stupidity or incompetence. The system had to go around them like a broken-down car blocking traffic on the expressway: eventually it would be pulled out of the way and everyone else drove by. Bunn had been broken down for years.

Alex laughed as he thought about the second Bush presidency. The people wanted a full-blown intelligence investigation to reveal all the negligence, but the White House wanted to go around the unions instead, and create the new Department of Homeland Defense. The White House also wanted to muzzle dissent and Bunn was too stupid to realize it.

For years everyone had tried to ignore Chuck Bunn, but because of his numerous advanced degrees, and eight ethnic minorities in his background, he'd been promoted into nebulous positions where they hoped he'd just eventually go away. But he hadn't, and now he'd had the good fortune to be at the right place at the right time, and would step into Ted LePage's shoes. Alex prayed Chuck was not heir apparent. Hopefully the wise men of the intelligence world would find someone with balls.

"What's your point, Alex? You comparing yourself to Ollie North?" Bunn demanded.

"I'll call you when I figure it out."

"Where are you now?"

"Can't say."

"What!"

"You heard me."

"Are you in the States?"

Alex ignored the question.

"Look Alex, you're still on my payroll until the end of the month and there are matters you must attend to."

"Chuck!"

"Yes?"

"Fuck off!" There was a pause and he considered hanging up before a trace was made on the call, but he needed answers. "Why do you have people looking for me, Chuck?"

"Look Alex, if you and Ted had misunderstandings let's work it out."

"We don't."

"The agency, then?"

"No. Why?"

"Then what's the problem, Alex?"

"Enquiries being made at my mother's place in Altoona. Cars surveying her house. My apartment in Ballston was ransacked. Why?"

"How the hell should I know! Stuff like that happens all the time."

"Not to me it doesn't."

I swear to God, Alex, I don't know anything about it. I'll check around."

"You do that, Chuck."

"Alex, there are documents you need to turn in."

"I don't think so."

"You gave them to Ted?"

"Did he tell you that I didn't?"

"Seeley mentioned you hadn't."

Alex caught himself. How did Seeley know Alex had documents? Alex had only mentioned the papers to Ted LePage, and Ted would not have mentioned them to anyone until they'd been published within the intelligence community as finished intelligence reports. Even though Seeley was legal counsel for Scion, Seeley was seldom briefed on operational matters.

"I'm afraid, Alex, I am going to have to insist that you turn in the documents immediately on national security grounds. If you do not wish to cooperate, then I shall have no choice but to notify the appropriate authorities under the Patriot Act. Under the Whistleblower Protection provisions I would strongly encourage you to turn in your government property immediately. I have proof of your misconduct. We'll put you away for fifty years without a trial."

Alex didn't need the threat and knew it could have serious consequences for him. But first they had to catch him. And if Bunn did it, it would blow back on Bunn in spades once the documents and the story hit the national papers. "Don't do that Chuck, you will regret it until the day you die if you do." He hung up the phone.

Checking the number in his phone book he dialed Kaminsky's brother-in-law in Moscow. The Russian asked him to stop by as soon as he could. Alex promised he would in a few days, and hung up. He looked at his watch and swore. He was late for his luncheon with Eduardo Hernandez.

* * *

At twelve-thirty, he found Eduardo waiting at the Hotel restaurant. "Sorry I'm late. Been trying to reach some people in Washington, to get the Key West problem off your back."

"I'm pleased to hear it. Any luck?

"Still working on it."

They ordered lunch and resumed their conversation of the previous evening about Eduardo's father.

"Oddly enough I didn't know much about my father until recently, when his associates provided some details." Eduardo covered the basics but avoided the sensitive information which Selvanian had confided to him in Cyprus. The American didn't need to know about that.

"My father was born in Germany, served in the war, and then emigrated to South America where he married my mother in 1947. I was born a year later in Peru where my parents worked a farm in the town of Bella Vista. I'm certain you probably have no idea where Bella Vista is. It's on the Huallaga River, about three hundred and fifty miles straight north of Lima, which is Peru's capital. When I was nine my mother died and a few months later my father left to seek employment in Europe, and I stayed behind with an aunt who raised me."

"What made you father choose Peru?"

"Don't know."

It didn't surprise Alex though. There was a German community in Peru, and over the years thousands had made their way there from Germany in search of a better life. Among them were many who obviously preferred to forget their past.

"Will you go to Germany someday to find your roots?"

"Doubtful."

"Why? Hernandez is not that common a name."

"It's not my original name!"

"Oh!"

"I learned only recently that my father's real name was Kaufmann and that he changed it when he moved to South America."

Alex's head cocked slightly to one side. Someone had mentioned that name to him recently. But where? "What branch of the German military was your father in?"

"Kriegesmarine. Submarines."

"Kaufmann?" Alex repeated. "That's it!" Uli Untermann on Usedom Island had mentioned the name Kaufmann to him. "What was your father's Christian name?"

"Heinrich."

"Jesus!"

Eduardo could tell from the American's facial expression that the name had hit him like a sledge hammer. "The name obviously seems to mean something to you?"

"Sure as hell does!" It had to be the same person. "A man called Heinrich Kaufmann skippered a U-Boat at Bahia Honda in 1942. Bahia Honda is in the Florida Keys, about forty miles north of Key West. And your father was also reported to have scuttled a U-Boat off the coast of Uruguay three years later . . . in August 1945." If it was the same man, then your father would have been at the three locations involved in the Case Judy deliveries. Ever heard of CASE JUDY, Mr. Hernandez?" He looked at Eduardo.

"It means nothing to me."

Leaning forward and pushing his sandwich aside, Alex's face became deadly serious. "Now I know why Eve Albion was among the five names on your father's list."

"Fantastic," the Peruvian replied. "Maybe you will be kind enough to inform me."

"Your father knew the Albion woman fifty years ago."

"Knew her?" Eduardo replied. "Should I take your statement as an insult? Knew her how?"

"Professionally is what I meant." As Alex's story unfolded, he could see its impact on the Peruvian's demeanor. At first his face blanched. Then he just sat there, morosely toying with his smoked salmon.

After a long pause, Eduardo repeated the phrase 'Madre Mia' several times. "You obviously know a lot more about my father than I do." Eduardo wasn't sure how to proceed. Much of what Selvanian had told him in deepest confidence, was also known by this American, and if Alex Balkan knew it, then others would too. "Who else knows about what you have just told me?"

"Just me for the moment," Alex replied.

Eduardo needed time to think this through and speak with the old Armenian again. "I will see someone the day after tomorrow who may be able to corroborate what you have told me."

"Mind if I ask who?"

"Someone who started out with him years ago."

"What's his name?"

"I don't know if I should divulge that."

"I need to know Eduardo!" Alex's voice was stern and insistent. "Don't you see! We're both involved in this up to our necks. You because your associates have implicated you with narcotics, and me, because authorities suspect you and I had a part in Albion's murder. If you are going to ask anyone about what I've told you, I must know who they are. Four people have died already, and you and I are also in trouble with Interpol. I need to know goddamn it!"

The American's logic convinced him. "His name's Garo Selvanian. His was the fifth name on my father's list. He's also the man I met recently in Cyprus. Selvanian was also aboard the submarine which my father sailed to South America."

"It makes sense," Alex interrupted. "And there is also the question of the thirty thousand kilos of gold bullion which was aboard."

Eduardo's face remained deadpan. "I know nothing of this Mr. Balkan. Who told you this?" Eduardo demanded with insistence in his tone.

Without revealing sources, Alex related the story which Uli Untermann had told him. Alex also threw in his own suspicions about the phantom U-Boat at Key West, and how the two appeared to be related.

"What do you really want?" Eduardo demanded.

"To solve a murder and if I can help you clear yourself, then so much the better."

Eduardo was dumbstruck. "The story you have told me must be true because the old man in Cyprus also told me of the submarine scuttled off Paraguay, but that it was not there when they went back to recover it later."

"That's right. And I believe that submarine is the one on the bottom southwest of Key West."

"So the United States has it?"

"So it would appear."

"Then they must also have the gold? You've seen this submarine?"

"Only a video of it. It appears to be undamaged, and is in about three hundred feet of water."

"And what is inside?"

"No idea," Alex replied. "But the secrecy shrouding its disappearance and its present resting place, makes it suspicious. It must be the same one."

Alex decided now was the time to introduce his 'piece de resistance.' "It's also my belief this man called Paul Carter is in the United States, and getting even with those who betrayed him. I'm sure he murdered the Russian woman in Washington and also killed Albion in Key West. I also suspect he murdered my boss last week in Washington. The first two victims obviously knew your father. So now the question is, who murdered your father in the UK? "Have you thought about that, Eduardo?"

"You think it was Carter who killed my father?"

"Most probably! When did your father die?"

"The twelfth of December."

"Six days," Alex muttered to himself.

"Excuse me?"

"Six days later on the eighteenth of December, the Russian woman was murdered in Washington."

"Coincidence?" the Peruvian asked.

"I don't think so! You still don't get it do you Eduardo? First your dad dies on the twelfth. Six days later on the eighteenth, the Russian woman dies. Then the Albion woman in Key West is suffocated a week later! Three people within two weeks."

"How can you be sure it's this man called Carter?" Eduardo asked.

"Because I now also happen to know that the Russians deliberately released him, hoping he'd lead them to the Russian defector whose name was Tatiana Slavchenko, and also the gold. But they didn't anticipate that this man named Carter would kill his victims instead."

"Okay, Mr. Balkan. How can I help you?"

"You have half the puzzle. I have the rest. Help me solve my half, and I'll help solve yours should you wish and get you off the hook on the drug problem."

"Agreed."

"Now tell me about the Armenian."

Heathrow Airport

Eduardo spotted Selvanian the following afternoon as he emerged from Heathrow Airport customs. The old Armenian expressed his pleasure that Eduardo would join their organization and assured him he would not regret it. Associates who'd been watching Eduardo for two months were anxiously awaiting his positive reply. Selvanian mentioned General Chong Ki Young in Indonesia and Hassan Khatoury in Hong Kong. As the cab pulled away from the terminal, Eduardo wondered if the old man knew he'd spent the last two days with Mary Malagang? He placed his index finger against his nose, still able to detect the last traces of her scent.

As the cab pulled into the traffic along the Heathrow access highway, Eduardo alluded to a new quid-pro-quo of his own.

"What is it?" The Armenian asked.

Eduardo hesitated, thinking this might not be the most appropriate time, but Selvanian insisted, and his smile was disarming; like a benevolent grandfather Eduardo thought. A kind looking impeccably dressed old man whom no one would ever suspect might be a serial killer, or a mass murderer.

"Money is incidental!" Eduardo observed.

Selvanian spread out his hands, palms open. His index fingers extended like a priest about to sanctify the host. "You have only to ask," he insisted magnanimously.

Eduardo knew it was a charade. But he'd decided to throw his fate in with these three men, and for good or bad, his life would now change forever. "There are three conditions."

"Name them."

"They are reasonable."

"I'm sure they are!"

"When I left Saint Martin, Michael Castries placed narcotics aboard the flight I chartered to take me to the Bahamas. The American authorities discovered what he was up to, and because of this, the police in the United States may issue a warrant for my arrest on drug trafficking charges. I think the son of a bitch did it deliberately. I want Castries taught a lesson!"

"There are many kinds of lessons," the old man observed casually. "Final . . . or just pain?"

"The son of a bitch has endangered my association with you. Must I go into details?" Eduardo asked.

"Done . . . !" Selvanian whispered. "What else?"

"I have an associate who can resolve my problem with the American authorities. I am going to offer him a position as my trusted confidant."

"What's his name?"

"It's not important at the moment, we can discuss that later."

"Fine. What about his occupation?"

"He's retired . . . a former military intelligence officer."

"What!" Selvanian said, obviously taken aback. "From . . . ?"

"The United States."

"You realize the implications, my young friend?"

"I trust him."

"I do not care for such people, Eduardo. Not in this business. They cannot be trusted. They are potential Quislings."

"It's my decision, not yours!" He waited silently, studying the passing traffic as they headed toward downtown London. Selvanian finally broke the silence. "I shall relent. But with a condition!"

"State it?"

"That you do nothing with the American until we conclude our arrangement."

"And when might that be?"

"Probably tonight."

"Agreed!

"And your third request?" Selvanian asked.

"It relates to my father's death. Scotland Yard suspects foul play. Even murder. They plan to have his body exhumed in Peru. Were you involved?"

"Absolutely not," Selvanian replied with such instant conviction that Eduardo believed him.

"Your word on that!"

"You have it! Do not ever ask me this question again . . . ever."

Eduardo turned to him. "I will need some time to attend to this issue regarding my father's exhumation."

"I agree. This is serious. When did you learn of it?"

"Two days ago. I was visited by an inspector from Scotland Yard. I met with them again this morning. One of their inspectors will leave for Peru shortly, to look into the exhumation of my father."

"Do they suspect you?"

"I suppose."

After a long silence while both studied the afternoon traffic struggling out of London, Selvanian turned to him, "Your father's death was not our doing! I want you to believe this."

"I do. Now, what is it you wished to talk to me about?"

"Tonight, my young friend. Tonight. We will discuss it over dinner."

Dry Tortugas

Mike moved back gingerly as the four foot section of heavy steel plate fell outward from the pressure hull, sliding silently down into the darkness, crashing into something below with a loud clang. Mike was the first through the opening and stopped almost transfixed as he studied the scene before him as his klieg light played across the interior of the submarines bridge. The feeling was eerie as he moved into the center of the control room and waited for the diver outside to join him. The water inside the hull was crystal clear, and everything was covered with a thin veneer of brown slime. The other diver signaled he was ready, and they made their way toward the compartment hatch at the rear of the control room. It was open and he flashed his light through and noted the hatch in the next compartment was also open.

They'd been lucky, the cut through the external hull had taken only an hour and a half while the interior pressure hull, considerably thicker, had taken the better part of a day and a half and numerous dives. Was she even partially filled, the initial cut through her pressure hull could have been catastrophic as inside and outside pressures equalized instantaneously. Five minutes later, they'd examined her from stem to stern. Both her diesel-electric turbines were in place which surprised him as her starboard propeller and drive shaft were missing. At six points along the inside of the pressure hull, her plumbing had been removed for cuts through her pressure hull before she'd been sunk here. Each of the cuts had been rewelded but not the interior plumbing, which made Mike believe she must have been towed on the surface to this place and then sunk. The most intriguing interior cuts were those through the deck beneath the bridge control room. These too had also not been replaced.

A half-hour later, they returned to the remotely operated vehicle which rested on the sandy bottom twenty feet from the submarines hull. He was disappointed. They'd found nothing of value. He was also a little confused. He couldn't explain the many incisions in her pressure hull which had all been resealed. If someone had wanted to inspect her ballast tanks during the course of her operational life, the easiest way would have been to cut through the outer hull which was not only thinner, but would not have affected hull integrity. But instead the cuts had been made from the inside, leaving few visible marks on her exterior hull. Strangest of all were the incisions below the control room.

German blueprints available for this type submersible showed three decks at her sail. The topmost for steering and radar, a middle deck for the captain's bridge, and the lowest for crew spaces. But the lowest deck contained two perfectly good water tight hatches which were still welded closed, and alongside each, a two by three foot slab of deck had been removed. Why had someone gone to all the trouble? Why had someone bothered to weld shut the two hatches? And why had someone then cut through the plate to reenter the compartment?

When Mike reached the ROV, he called the surface and told them they were done and would begin the four hours of decompression needed before they surfaced.

FOUR

London Hilton

SELVANIAN WAS FATIGUED from his flight from Cyprus and suggested Eduardo dine en suite with him. The bartender brought Eduardo's double scotch on ice to him by the fireplace.

"You might recall," Selvanian observed, "I mentioned BCCI last we met?"

"Yes."

"You had a chance to read up on it?"

"Some."

"You know their history? Who the principal owners were?"

"Yes."

"Good. Because BCCI is what brought on dear old Kew's untimely heart attack recently in Hong Kong."

"Untimely or induced?" Eduardo inquired indolently.

Eduardo knew it was a dumb remark! He wished he hadn't said it. He promised himself he'd take a more worldly view of his new circumstances . . . and associates. Now Eduardo had to be pragmatic. How many more years could Selvanian live? Or Mary Malagang's ancient father for that matter? Tonight he'd see what the old man wanted him to do in Moscow. Then he'd solve his problem with the Americans, and when the two old men were gone, Eduardo would bring in his own team.

Until now he'd been a stoic but not by choice, only necessity. It was easy to lust for a life of reason, restraint and self-mastery when one had nothing. Soon it would be time for him to challenge his epicurean tastes. Sin a little, he reasoned. Partake of the joys of the flesh. Lust fully after the beautiful things of life. Why not? He recalled his Jesuit mentor in Peru. Father Sebastian had hated the epicurean mentality which he considered the root of all evil. Its dogma, he'd insisted, was encapsulated in Omar Khayyam's saying; "Thou wilt not with predestined evil around, enmesh, and then impute your fall to sin!" Maybe Father Sebastian was wrong?

"Eduardo . . ." the old man almost whined. "Please! Don't be boorish! You disappoint me. Kew was one of my most trusted associates. We found him penniless in the stinking alleys of Canton and I raised him like my own son. I fawned over him, sent him to the best schools in Europe. Even arranged for him to work for a year with the London Institute of Strategic Studies. Paid him a fortune. Obtained his palatial home for him. But despite all this, the man was an ungrateful whore who betrayed us. Kew's behavior and that of BCCI was inexcusable."

Eduardo had no idea what the Armenian was ranting about. The Bank had been out of business for over a decade and Kew's body was barely cold.

"Let me explain," the old man continued. "I recently came in possession of information which indicates that Kew clearly accepted gratuities from BCCI before it collapsed. I have proof. Altogether he pocketed more than ten million dollars from them. They paid him to do nothing with CEBU's funds lodged with BCCI. Hundreds of millions of our funds were left with BCCI for almost two years, in low interest bearing accounts. BCCI made huge profits because of Kew's treason. Then BCCI collapsed, and . . . poof, our huge balances joined the ranks of other unsecured creditors. You saw Kew in Hong Kong. What did he say?"

Eduardo recalled the conversation. "He seemed resentful. He alluded to a lack of guidance from my father. He said my father should have visited Hong Kong more frequently."

Selvanian laughed, and for the first time, Eduardo realized the old bastard was really nothing more than a businessman in whom there was nothing inherently evil, just someone managing a portfolio and who didn't appreciate his bankers lifting his pocket change. "Typical Kew!" Selvanian observed, "Blame it on others . . . and a dead man."

"How was this accomplished, Mr. Selvanian?"

"Call me Garo," the old man commented insistently. "I have prepared a dossier for you and will leave it with you. It will explain why BCCI's former principals must reimburse us for the loss." Selvanian went on to explain that unlike Americans, who bankrupt their institutions and leave the Federal Deposit Insurance Corporation to bail out depositors; some international banks, such as BCCI for example, have no such safety-net. So international depositors relied heavily on men of integrity who owned the banks, supposedly men above reproach. "Consequently when one fails, and it becomes obvious the owner had his hand in the till then there is recourse, and depositors should visit this question with their banker."

"What's the point?" Eduardo inquired. "Your loss is an unsecured creditor account. And besides, the bank has been out of business for over a decade. Isn't it a little late to think about recouping your losses?"

"Good!" Selvanian exclaimed. "You have read about BCCI. But . . . those who created it are still wealthy men. They can tell me that I have no recourse against them because their money is theirs and not the bank's money. But not all men bear their protestations the same way. The key American officials of Enron, World Dot Com, and Arthur Anderson all enriched themselves by lying and falsifying their books. They screwed all their investors. In America people rely on lawyers to represent them before those whose money they steal. You have heard of Bernie Madoff?"

"No," Eduardo replied.

"You will one day. He's a whore who robbed his clients blind, but they were too stupid to realize it."

"In the international world," Selvanian continued, "it is a little different sometimes. There are ways to persuade those who steal your money to repay it. This is why I want you to go to Moscow. Some people will be there and I want you to convince them that it is in their best interest to return some funds to us. It will make a good introduction for you and the community will take note."

"You think I have the qualifications?"

Selvanian laughed. "Did you think, Eduardo, that it was by chance you attended the best British University when you did? You graduated eighteenth in a class of one hundred and forty. Clearly you were among the more intelligent of your peers. And did you think it was an accident that you were among the first to attend the newly opened Institute of Strategic Studies when it opened in Peru? I am aware that it is referred to these days affectionately as PMI for Peru Mafia Incorporated! You have influential friends, a good education, experience in the world, and a legal background. With these assets at your fingertips, you are ready to take you father's place."

Eduardo was flattered that the old man knew as much about him as he did. He wondered what remained unstated?

"Does it not surprise you," Selvanian continued, "that you were allowed to seek out the first four names on your father's list? And now that you have, ask yourself why we did not try to stop you?" Selvanian paused for effect, watching Eduardo digest what he'd said.

"We've known every move you've made since the first day you arrived in London, and flew on to Switzerland. Even the delightful young lady you arranged to spend the evening with in Zurich after you were told by your Swiss banker of your wealth! And the reports we received from Khatoury and Chong Ki-Young, were excellent. Both reported a circumspect mature young man in possession of the qualities needed for leadership. We didn't anticipate the problem with Castries, and I have already attended to that. As for the woman in Key West, I was not aware she'd passed away, but it makes no difference."

The statement about Castries surprised him. "What do you mean about Castries being taken care of?"

"It's of no consequence."

"I asked you a question . . . Garo?"

Selvanian hesitated a moment, his subtle smile one of new respect for his young associate, Eduardo had the right stuff and was exceeding Garo's highest hopes that they'd made the right decision to bring the young Hernandez into a leadership position. "All right. The poor man was found dead at his villa in Saint Martin, just this morning as a matter of fact. Expired from a heroin overdose as I understand it."

The old man had surprised Eduardo again. Eduardo realized it was time for him to begin playing the role they expected of him. "I'm pleased, Garo. It will hopefully send a message to others not to toy with me. Incidentally, while in Cyprus, I also asked you about an American partner of ours who was mentioned to me by Shan Kew?"

"In due course. In due course," the elder man assured Eduardo.

"Is there some reason you don't want to talk about it now?"

"When the time is right."

Eduardo decided not to push the question.

"Now," the old Armenian continued, "you asked for time to attend to your personal matters. I have no objection. But must insist you attend to the BCCI matter in Moscow first."

"What's the urgency?"

"We have a window of opportunity, and it cannot be missed. It should take a few days, then you can pursue your agenda and let us know when you are ready."

In the ensuing half hour Selvanian briefed Eduardo about an official State visit to Moscow by the ruler of the United Arab Emirates the following week. Selvanian had been trying to see the Arab ruler for five years. But . . . the old Arab had ignored his requests and forbid Garo's travel to the United Arab Emirates. Now that the old Arab would be visiting Moscow on a State visit, a Russian associate of Selvanian's, using false pretenses, would arrange a private meeting between Eduardo and the Ruler next week in Moscow. Eduardo was empowered to negotiate whatever settlement he felt acceptable for CEBU's damages. Both the Arab and Eduardo would be staying at the same hotel.

"I have prepared a file with the background and evidence. I think you will see we have the old goat by the pubic hairs. He is a wily bastard, and owes us every cent of the balance shown in Enclosure Eight. Review it carefully and we'll meet in the morning to finalize your strategy. The Sheikh will only be in Moscow for four days. So you will have to leave for Russia the day after tomorrow. With luck you will meet him this Sunday afternoon. May I have your passport?"

"Why?"

"To arrange your Russian visa."

Ust Charky, Siberia

Alexi Poluostrov was almost done. He gathered his overcoat around him to ward off the cold. "Jesus," he muttered, rubbing his nose to break off the tiny icicles which had formed from his breath around his nostrils. How could these American assholes have survived so long in such a godforsaken place? Pushing back his coat sleeve until the crystal of his four dollar watch peeped out, he again noted the time. It was just before three o'clock in the afternoon and already dusk was upon them. The barren empty wastes of Siberia chilled him to the bone.

It was his first time back in two years, and reinforced his conviction never to be assigned to the Fifteenth Military District. The Fifteenth was the most undesirable assignment in Russia. Second largest in area it contained four hundred thousand square kilometers of taiga and permafrost. Even its three largest cities, if they could be called that, were squalid affairs of narrow twisting dirt streets and dilapidated eighteenth century wooden Kulak houses with U-shaped shoe scrapers outside to remove the street filth before entering. Today the odd European tourist in the area offered local residents ridiculous amounts for the shoe-scrapers which no one in Europe had seen in a hundred years.

He'd flown in to the nearby airstrip at the city of Bilibino two days ago, and caught a creaky helicopter for the last hundred miles to the dirt airstrip across the Ugatkyn river ice from where he now stood. A decrepit air-dropped BMD tracked infantry vehicle, formerly of the proud Soviet Armed forces, its engine purring softly beside him, had brought him thc final forty kilometers here to Z-5. Last night his associates had also arrived with trucks and half-tracks which had been airlifted into the nearby airstrip before sunset yesterday.

During the past three hours he'd watched as prisoners; their guards, and the entire camp administration were loaded into large metal boxes aboard the trucks. Their rear doors then closed and padlocked from the outside.

A Spetznas noncom approached Poluostrov, saluting smartly. "Only a few left," he said, pointing to two old men being pushed forward toward the last truck.

"Quickly," Alexi yelled at the elderly prisoners, "Soon you will be in a warmer place."

"I want to be left alone. I'm too old for this," one of the old men replied in English.

"Where are you from?" Poluostrov demanded.

"Rochester New York to be exact," the old man responded weakly.

"And your friend?

"Fayetteville in Arkansas, also in the United States."

"What are your real names?"

"I am Private Allen Taylor," the old man responded. "And my buddy here is Corporal Bill Heffers."

"Army?" Poluostrov demanded.

"Yes, 101st Airborne. We were captured by the Germans near Cherbourg in 1944, during the Normandy landings, and shipped to a prisoner camp near Dresden."

"Ahhhh." Poluostrov smiled. "The Screaming Eagles."

"Once upon a time, yes," the first old man replied in a dejected tone. "But not anymore. You fucking Russkie bastards captured me and my friend at a German prisoner camp near Dresden in February 1945, and been treating us like shit ever since."

Poluostrov smiled, his demeanor suggesting feigned sympathy. "Well, who knows. Maybe things will get better now?"

"That will be the day." Taylor laughed.

"Poluostrov shrugged. His face scrunched, suggesting the possibility might now come to pass. Poluostrov helped push the two men into the last box and closed the door, watching as the guard secured a padlock to it.

"Everyone is accounted for and loaded, sir!"

"The final count?"

"Three hundred and fifteen. Just over thirty died in the last month."

"Of?" Alexi demanded.

"Old age, and the elements. We loaded their frozen corpses into the first of the trucks in the convoy leaving now."

"Very well, get them moving."

Alexi Poluostrov congratulated himself as the last of the tracked vehicles clanked past him. He'd anticipated some resistance, but no one had seemed disposed to question orders moving them to another camp in a warmer climate, and with better accommodations. The mid-winter move was ideal, and the low cloud base obscured space based platforms that might be observing such a remote area.

Hugging the Ugatkyn River's eastern shore, the convoy moved north through the gathering darkness for a couple of miles before turning west to cross the snow-covered river ice at its widest point. The Ugatkyn river at this time of year was covered with a foot of ice and easily supported the convoy of heavy vehicles. Topographic charts of the rivers course here showed the area was a small lake whose bottom lay over six hundred feet beneath the frozen ice. Alexi ordered the driver of his BMD to pull the half-track off to the side of the road as they approached the river ice. He wanted to enjoy the ambiance of the place for a while and withdrew a cigarette and leaned back and studied the barren scene as he lit up.

Five minutes later the convoy had reached the center of the frozen snow-covered lake and stopped. Poluotostrov watched dispassionately as the individual vehicle drivers emerged and gathered into a small cluster a hundred yards away. Moments later a series of explosions erupted around the stationary vehicles which slowly began disappearing as the shattered river ice around them gave way. Within minutes the scene before him was once again featureless, a barren snow-covered landscape.

He proceeded across the snow-covered lake and stopped midstream before the small group of drivers. A burst of gunfire cut them down; specks of their blood spattered here and there across the snow which already partially concealed the lifeless bodies.

Poluostrov's vehicle easily traversed the remaining thirty miles to the airstrip at Kolukoktov and found the IL-76 waiting, its engines idling as he drove up.

An argument was in progress between the aircraft's load master and the drivers of the four half-tracks which had preceded the convoy. The Illyushin's clamshell doors were open, but its vehicle ramp had refused to come down because of ice in its hydraulic lines. There was no way to load the vehicles. The loadmaster was also loudly demanding to know where the other eight vehicles were. Alexi told him there'd been a change of plan. Someone would return for them in a few days. Alexi ordered everyone aboard and instructed the aircraft commander to return to his base.

"And you, Comrade?" the aircraft commander asked Alexi.

"I shall remain here, I have transport coming from Bilibino shortly."

Nikolai watched impassively from the cab of his BMD as the clamshell doors of the IL-76 closed and the transports engines roared to full power. Within a minute the aircraft's hulk had disappeared into the gloom. He glanced at his watch; 2245 hours local time. Within a half hour the IL-76 would be ninety miles away to the southwest and over

the remote Anyuskiy Khrebet mountains. An onboard device with a barometric mechanism was set to activate at three thousand meters, and what was left of the IL-76 after that, would be scattered across hundreds of miles in one of the most inaccessible mountain areas in Siberia. It would be a week before anyone realized the aircraft was missing; and a hundred years before anyone found the wreckage because the Illyushin's flight plan filed at its home base was for Sevastopol in the Crimea.

London Hilton

The sound of the phone ringing seemed way off in the distance. His mind clicked and he realized it wasn't a dream. He'd had the damned dream again which had been haunting him since he'd left Limassol. Dark faceless men always chased Eduardo through the streets of his hometown in Peru. He never knew why. It always ended when he hid in a dark wet muddy cellar where cockroaches, lots of them, crawled over him as his antagonists searched for him. They always found him, tied him up and gagged him, then smoked cigarettes as hoards of the disgusting roaches crawled into Eduardo's nostrils until he suffocated. He always woke up in a cold sweat and yelling.

Groping on the nightstand he swore as the phone crashed to the floor. He untangled himself from Mary's arms and turned on the bed-side light.

"Hello." He had no idea what time it was, but could see light peeping beneath the thick curtains. He heard Smither's familiar stutter. Eduardo swore. He'd fire the bastard as soon as he returned from Moscow next week.

Eduardo had left Selvanian's suite after ten last night and gone out with Mary Malagang for a show, then dined along the Thames. They'd turned in after three.

"Yeah, what the hell do you want?"

"Sorry. I just had a call from Inspector Haggerty at Scotland Yard. He wants to pop around to your hotel in an hour."

"Not again, Smithers. His interviews are getting a bit tiresome."

"He's leaving this afternoon for Peru and wanted to see you before he left. I think you should see him. It's about your father."

"Tell him I'll be expecting him at eleven o'clock sharp!" He slammed the phone down and lay back and stared at the ceiling for a few minutes.

"Difficulties darling?" Mary whispered. She laid her length against him and licked his ear.

He'd agreed last night with Selvanian, to see the ruler of the United Arab Emirates in Moscow. Most of the Arabs he'd met over the years hadn't impressed him with their business acumen, and what he'd read about BCCI, impressed him even less. The thought of presenting Selvanian's claim excited him. He couldn't recall hearing of anyone ever making such a preposterous demand. But if that is how much Shan

Kew's connivance had cost CEBU, then Eduardo supposed there was no harm in sticking it to the old Arab who'd absconded with it. The worst the Arab could do would be to throw Eduardo out. Now Mary's tongue was probing his ear with penile-like thrusts and the sound of her breath in his ear erotic beyond imagination.

A half hour later he called room service and ordered breakfast. Afterward they agreed to spend the afternoon at the London Museum and Mary returned to her suite.

Twenty minutes later Alex Balkan called and explained that something had come up and he too had to leave for Moscow. It was a small world Eduardo told him. Eduardo was headed the same way. They agreed to meet briefly at noon to coordinate a Moscow rendezvous.

Haggerty was obviously annoyed when he arrived. He'd been escorted to the penthouse suite by a Pakistani employee of the hotel, and the Paki had stood in front of Haggerty, apologizing profusely to Eduardo, inquired in a sing-song voice if he were expecting a Mr. Higgirty. As Haggerty pushed by, Eduardo assured the Paki would be all right to allow the inspector in.

"Coffee?" Eduardo asked as he closed the door.

"Please. Two sugars and milk."

Eduardo deliberately dallied over the preparation, slowly buttering two pieces of toast, applied marmalade, quartered each meticulously before placing them before the Inspector. Eduardo sat opposite him and held up his own cup. "Cheers."

The Englishman ignored it. "Smithers told you I am off to Peru?"

"He did."

"I wish to convince the authorities to move quickly. Time is of the essence."

"Oh! Why is that?"

"Ever heard of Aipysurus Laevis?" the inspector inquired.

"A prehistoric monster of some type?"

"No. Only a sea snake."

"Get to the point, inspector."

"No need to be uppity, dear boy."

The comment pissed Eduardo off. The Englishman was being condescending. "My apology Haggerty. Being an Oxford don, one tends to be abrupt with commoners."

The Inspector blushed, his annoyance now barely controlled. The age of royalty had died long ago in England but still the trappings were everywhere, and the common people resented the former aristocracy's belief that they were better than others. Haggerty decided to forget the innuendo, having himself shown bad form when he pushed into Hernandez's suite a few minutes earlier. He supposed this nouveaux-riche South American gaucho had a right to be annoyed this morning.

Eduardo had no idea what the Inspector wanted and didn't care. He sipped his coffee and helped himself to more toast as he waited for the inspector to calm down.

"This poison is what killed your father. Sure you've never heard of it?"

"Inspector, I already said no. If you persist, I suggest you get a subpoena. Or find someone who understands what the word no means."

"No need for histrionics my dear boy."

The Englishman was beginning to really annoy him. "I'm not your dear boy either, Haggerty! Get to the point!"

"We now know that your father was murdered, we know how it was done. And . . . now we have a suspect."

Now it was Eduardo's turn to be surprised, but he didn't show it and waited for Haggerty to continue. In a way Eduardo supposed he already knew the answer since he'd met with the American.

"Aren't you even a little curious?" Haggerty demanded. Eduardo returned to the breakfast cart for more coffee.

"Of course I am. But it occurs to me you are here to tell me, so please proceed."

"Yes . . . We've traced the poison to a chemist near Trafalgar Square. He sold it on the eighth of December. The chemist's record shows it was sold to a Bulgarian named Pavela Krasnov, whose address was given as 23c Chetwith Street in North London. The address is bogus. A computer search turned up another person with almost the same name. A man who debarked from a Russian cargo ship last November. "This chap, documented as a Bulgarian, and with a Bulgarian passport was given a six week visa and left from Gatwick Airport on the twelfth of December, for Toronto, Canada."

"The day this Bulgarian left, was the same day your father was killed! The Bulgarian Embassy tells me the passport was stolen.

The Canadian Embassy passed my information to Quebec, but unfortunately they kept no photograph of the subject, and Krasnov's present whereabouts in Canada is unknown."

"Well, Inspector. It seems you've solved the case, but lost the murderer."

"There's a fly in the ointment! The person who bought the poison was a woman. The Chemist is emphatic. She spelled her name Pavela Krasnov. The man who debarked at Portsmouth was Pavlo Krasnov. Two names are almost identical. Very odd."

"Mr. Hernandez, I also had another talk with your father's butler and inquired if a woman had visited him before he died. The butler described the same woman who'd visited the Chemist. Late thirties or early forties, attractive, blond hair. She saw your father three days before he died."

"You ever heard either of these names, Mr. Hernandez?"

"Never." Eduardo made a note to mention it to Alex when they met at noon.

FIVE

Northern Moscow

ALEX'S KNOCK ON the discolored dirt encrusted chipping varnish bearing the inscription # 214/V.Z. reverberated down the bleak stairwell. A woman somewhere on the other side demanded to know who it was. He replied in Russian that he was expected. The door swung open partially to reveal an elder woman with puffy eyes holding a black hanky to her mouth. She'd obviously been crying.

"Is Vitali Zitalko here?" Alex asked in Russian. He'd just spoken with Vitali two days ago from London and spoken with him again briefly this morning. "Da! He is inside."

"Please tell him I'm here."

"*Da*!" She motioned for him to enter and pointed to a chair near the window. "He's dressing, he will be out in a moment. Would you like tea?"

"Kharasho," Alex responded, "that would be very nice."

"You speak our language very well!" She observed sarcastically, her statement more accusatory than a compliment. He assumed she was anxious about his visit because Russians suspected all non-Russian's who spoke their language fluently. Most who did were almost always somehow involved with intelligence.

When Vitaly joined him, it was obvious there'd been a death in the family. Vitaly's coat sleeve bore the traditional black arm band, and from the strained expression, it was obvious, that Vitaly too was upset.

"You know about my brother-in-law?" Vitaly inquired, pointing to the arm band.

"No, I did not."

"We were just advised of his death a few hours ago."

"My regrets."

"He was a good man . . . a little gruff maybe . . . but a patriot . . . someone who deserved better."

"My condolences." Then it struck Alex that Vitaly Zitalko was speaking of Kaminsky. "My god . . . how did it happen?"

"The Chechen as I understand."

Alex tried not to show his disbelief. The Chechen syndicate had in fact sprung up everywhere in the vacuum following the collapse of communism. But in recent years Putin had conveniently fostered a shibboleth of them: that they were like an octopus with activities throughout the entire economic fabric of the former Soviet Union. Every sort of evil was now blamed on them, and Alex had to admit that they deserved some of the fame.

The Chechen came in all shapes and sizes, from the corner thug, to the big city syndicate boss who controlled everything from prostitution, to black marketing, illegal arms transactions, banking and international trade. The Chechen nomenclature, labeled one of Russia's smallest states, the Checheno-Ingush Autonomous Soviet Socialist Republic, was a mere seven and a half thousand square miles of rugged mountains on the north slope of the Caucuses. Chechniya was hemmed to the east and west by the Caspian and Black Seas, Armenia to the south, and Georgia on top. A contentious mountain people, they'd been relentlessly pilloried by all the empires of history, and most recently by Joseph Stalin, who'd sent most of them to their deaths in the camps during WWII for collaborating against Russia with Hitler's Germany. Then came the postcommunist era and Moscow's effort to constrain their bad habits. Like their Armenian and Georgian brethren the Chechen were notorious for their exceptional business acumen, and their ability to create something from nothing—including terror. In recent years Chechen traders had spread across Russia like dandelions on the wind, and no Russian street corner could successfully survive without them.

"They found him with another man along a country road near Novosibirsk," Vitaly Zitalko explained. "Both were shot many times. It is the Chechen's way of letting us know they were unhappy with Pyotr. His wife will see to my brother's burial and then she will move here to Moscow to be closer to my wife and me."

"You mentioned another victim Vitaly."

"An associate of Pyotr as I understand it—a man called Tukhachevsky. You knew him?" Vitaly demanded.

"Yes. I met him through your brother-in-law."

Alex wanted to kick himself. He'd obviously been careless in Novosibirsk, and used poor tradecraft with his two clandestine sources, and now both had paid for his stupidity with their lives. It wasn't too difficult to figure out what had happened. The secret police were obviously on to Alex sooner than he'd anticipated. They'd followed him. Now he regretted taking the rental taxi driver to the camp near Novosibirsk. He should have considered a car from the American consulate. He'd also met Kaminsky in a public place and then gone with him to meet the other man. He'd even given Kaminsky his true address and phone number in the States. He wondered if the old woman, Anna Yarakino who'd met him at the hotel had also been caught up in the net? Now he wondered if it was KGB who'd burglarized his apartment in Ballston?

"It's a shame about Tukhachevski, do you know who he was?" The old Russian asked.

"Not offhand," Alex replied.

"He was from a noble Russian family. His father, Mikhail Nikolayevich Tukhachevsky was from Slednevo, and was executed in 1937 in the Stalinist purges. The father was actually reinstated by the Russian government in 1988, because they realized he was not only a patriot but had made tremendous contributions to the advancement of the Russian military system He led the defense of Moscow in 1918 and fought the Bolsheviks on the Eastern Front. From 1925 to 1928 he was the Chief of Staff, then deputy commissar of defense after 1931 and received the Order of Lenin for his contributions. Regrettably he was purged in 1938—a tragedy for Russia when Hitler attacked us."

"And the son?" Alex asked.

"He had a distinguished career too in the intelligence field."

"You do not believe it was Chechen then?" Alex asked.

"Absolutely not."

"I didn't think so either."

"Why?"

"I know Pyotr. I does not make sense."

Vitali reached for the tea pot. "I do not know much about you, Mr. Balkan, and that may be better for me. Pyotr spoke highly of you in his letter and that was the only reason I agreed to help him, and called you. Pyotr referred to you as a good man, a patriot, and a man whose word he respected. From him that was something! But I must ask you what this was about, and what was so important that they had to kill him?"

"It's a complicated story," Alex replied.

"Clandestine things usually are," the older man observed casually.

"True." Alex wondered when the tick in his left eye would start-up again. He was upset. He could feel the blood throbbing in his neck. If they'd killed Tukhachevsky and Kaminsky because of Alex, and now knew what they'd passed to Alex, then they'd be after him too . . . and anyone else who Alex might have involved with the documents. He also wondered if they now knew he was back in Moscow? Had they followed him here this afternoon? Were they waiting outside right now? "Vitaly," Alex continued," a Russian woman was murdered a few months ago in Washington, and I was asked to investigate her murder because the victim had reported many years ago that she had met an American in one of the Gulag camps near Novosibirsk." Alex skimmed the highlights down to the present.

"So. Pyotr agreed to help you find this man?" Vitaly observed.

"Unfortunately," Alex said.

"And then you learned about others too."

"From Tukhachevsky, yes."

"And this is why you asked for this meeting with me?"

"No. That was Pyotr's idea."

"Pyotr must have been crazy! But I suppose the system makes us this way! Our history is replete with so many such disgraces that it is time for some of us to stand up and be counted as you Americans say. I am glad you told me." Vitaly reached into his pocket and withdrew an envelope. "It's from my brother-in-law, and he asked me to give it to you."

In it were two papers. The first was a handwritten note from Pyotr, the second an old document.

The man you seek no longer exists with his original name. Today he is Pavlo Krasnov. On the 18th of September last, he was issued a Bulgarian passport, number 8776-A-726. When released he was told he was free to go where he wished. It was arranged for him to acquire rubles and dollars in a manner which did not arouse suspicion that his release might be deliberate. He sailed from Yalta on 20 October aboard the Captain Bastrov, for Portsmouth, England.

Regarding the others you inquired about? There are three hundred and fifty-six of them still alive at a place called Z-5. The person who gives you this can locate it for you.'

Your enquiry about the man in Krasnoyarsk led nowhere. But it is rumored that the old woman you spoke with died the day after you left. A mysterious fire killed both her and her grandson. Was her name Anna Yarakino?

He looked at Vitaly. "Jesus Christ!" Alex exhaled slowly. The Scotland Yard inspector had mentioned the name Krasnov to him two days ago in London. Krasnov was obviously on the move, in the United States, and today was probably documented as Paul Carter or God knew who. Now a lot of things made sense to Alex.

"Do you know where this place is that he mentioned in this letter?

"I inquired discreetly about Z-5," Vitaly observed. "It's in the Chukotskoye mountains, about eighty miles south of the Arctic coast, along the Ugatkyn River in Siberia."

Alex briefly thought about an area in which he had difficulty placing major cities. "How can I get there?" he asked.

"I'm afraid that is impossible. It is in a remote place. Pevek and Bilibino are the nearest towns. It's another two hundred miles east to the river and there are no roads! I wish I could be more encouraging."

I must try!"

"Forget it! The entire region is also a restricted military area. Without a military pass, you would be arrested as soon as you got off the plane!"

"I would reimburse you well for your help."

"Please!" Vitali raised his hands. "I have helped you because I know Pyotr would have wanted me to do this. I must think of myself and my wife. More I cannot do."

Alex unfolded the second document which was brittle onion paper and yellowing with age. Its top and bottom were torn away, leaving parts of several discernable letters showing its classification:

21 February 1942
Comrade Stalin,

Discussions with the American representative in Moscow yesterday, indicate Roosevelt agreed to give us until the Fall of 1944, to capture Berlin. In the interim the United States will devote its principle effort to the war in the Pacific.

While the American representative refused to speculate on the rationale, you will recall from earlier meetings with the British and Americans regarding CASE JUDY, that both have made their 'quid pro quo' arrangements. That aside, we will inherit enough of Europe to prevent future upstarts from ever threatening our homeland again from the west. To realize this, we must reach Berlin by late 1944.

President Roosevelt's letter which was given to me yesterday is also attached to this memorandum. A translation follows: (Quote). "Dear Josef. Now that we have embarked on a course which is acceptable, we shall strive to create a post war United Nations, which will have superimposed on it, an American/Soviet alliance so that we dominate world affairs in the post war era. You and I have agreed on the division of Europe, that Russia will not negotiate a unilateral peace. Our post war struggle is with colonial imperialist empires, who for too long have embroiled our world in catastrophes. I am confidant, that unlike the First War, which strengthened colonial powers, our new world will be made safe for our peace loving peoples. Regards, Franklin.

Signed, Lavrenti Beria

Alex looked up.

"It's something, eh?" The old Russian smirked.

"How do you mean?"

The old Russian smiled. "It is your president Roosevelt who wrote that. But Stalin was obviously the grand master of the double-cross." Vitaly laughed. "Even I remember Stalin's observation that 'sincere diplomacy between countries is no more possible than dry water or wooden iron.'"

"But it worked," Alex countered. "For sixty years a difficult peace prevailed between our two countries, and now America alone is the only remaining superpower on our planet. I appreciate your taking such a chance to get this to me. Your wife has already lost her brother and I do not want to see any more difficulties come to her or you."

"We have done it for Pyotr. I too have had enough. When Glasnost and Perestroika came we Russians thought the great democracies of the world would come and help us get our house in order. But after almost a century of Communist idiocy, things have only gotten worse for the average Russian. But we are free I suppose." He smiled insidiously. "Many of us have difficulty eating our freedom when hungry. I want to help you in any way I can. My wife also agrees."

"But this is dangerous," Alex replied.

"The old order is gone," Vitaly continued. "Nothing is the same anymore." He removed a communist party card from his wallet. "This too is worthless! This was my life's work. My monthly pension today cannot buy a carton of Russian cigarettes. And now they have killed my wife's brother. For what?"

"Where do you work?"

"I'm retired for five years now."

"And before that?"

"I was a clerk."

"With the government?"

"Yes. Military security."

"GRU?" Alex inquired.

"The Second Chief Directorate."

"We have a lot in common."

"Ahhh!" Vitali observed, "you know something about the old order?"

"Some." Alex pointed toward Vitaly's lapel pin. "I'm also retired military. We were opponents back then."

"Mortal enemies is more like it." Vitaly laughed. "Yesterday enemies and today friends?"

Alex smiled in agreement. "Was it you who told Pyotr about the Z-5 camp?"

"No."

"And this man Pavlo Krasnov?"

"I do not know of him either."

"Could you inquire?"

"It wouldn't be wise," Vitaly observed.

"Where exactly did you work in the Second Chief Directorate, Vitaly?"

"The fourth of Department, under General Dimitrievich Volkgonov."

Alex laughed. "What luck. The same Volkogonov who was a confidant of Yeltsin, and in charge of the Russian POW Agency?"

"Yes, why?"

"I saw him briefly in early 1992 when he visited Washington for discussions on establishing a Russian American working group to look into the prisoner issue. Our two countries established the working group in March of that same year. If anyone could find out what really happened it would have been Volkogonov."

"I know," Vitaly replied. "Life is strange that way. His death was untimely."

"Especially since the initiative has gone nowhere until today. Most regrettable. I sure could use your help."

"In this particular area?"

"One of the men who assumed his responsibilities is Valeriy Yeniseysk. You have heard of him?"

"Of course."

"Kaminski wanted to help me more, but of course . . ." Alex left the statement unfinished.

"I'm sorry, Mr. Balkan, I can't."

"I understand." Alex retrieved his wallet and removed ten one hundred dollar bills and placed them on the table between them. "I owed this to Pyotr. He asked me to give it to you for him. It is yours now. I would like to make it ten times more—if you would help me?"

"Thank you. If you are serious, I would first have to discuss this with my wife. Could I see you at your hotel later?"

* * *

Alex checked with hotel reception when he returned and was told that Mr. Eduardo Hernandez was expected to arrive tomorrow. From a lobby phone he called the American Embassy on Ulitsa Chaykovskogod and asked for Jose Ramani in the Defense Attache Office. Alex had spent time with Ramani inspecting Russian missile sites, and the two had become close friends. Jose was the Embassy's liaison assigned to the Russian military. Under various SALT and associated inspection agreements, Russia was deactivating hundreds of its older SS-11 and SS-18 ICBM's, and Alex and Jose's job had been to document their physical destruction.

"Jose, I need a favor!"

"This who I think it is?"

"Yeah!"

"Jesus. You here in town?"

"Yep!"

"I heard you were retiring in a few days."

"You can't always believe what you hear.

"Guess not."

"Got time for a drink?"

"Sure! Where?"

"Your place?"

"When?"

"Half an hour?"

"See you there."

Rimani occupied the embassy quarters: a rat's warren of ancient prerevolutionary Russian royal apartments which had been repeatedly subdivided and redivided over the decades, to accommodate an ever expanding Embassy population. Being senior enlisted Jose got more space than most.

A quarter hour later, Alex flashed his identification to the Marine guard and passed through the various security screening devices. If anyone had taken note of him he didn't' notice it.

"So what's this all about?" Rimani demanded as Alex removed his overcoat.

"Did you tell anyone I called?"

"Didn't have a chance. Why?"

"I'd like to keep it that way."

"Spookville?"

"I'm here for something else this time." His expression hinting it might be a special operation which not even the Embassy knew about.

"I understand!" Jose replied. He knew better that to inquire about compartmented operations. They were going on all the time out of the Moscow embassy and one became bored with them after a while. "How can I help?"

"I need to make some calls."

"Is that all?" He dug into his pocket and handed Alex his cell phone.

"Not with a cell phone, it's not secure."

"Got it," Jose replied, pointing to another phone on the sideboard beside him.

"Do you mind?"

"No problemo."

Jose was on call, so the Army installed an STU-3 in his apartment, which allowed him to make round-the-clock top secret calls anywhere in the world from his apartment.

Alex dialed Marvin Raoul's number first, depressing the "Go Secure" button. As he watched, the LED display reflected the number dialed, then the Department of the Navy-Historic Records, USN-AHJ-4D, ext. 3562 Anacostia, and finally, Top Secret—Secure. Marvin's familiar voice came through with a slight accent.

"Hi, Marv. It's Alex."

"What the hell you doing in Moscow?"

"I'll explain later! Two issues! You remember the guy I was checking on? The one who's been gone a long time? Well he's been travelling recently with a Bulgarian passport, under the name of Pavel Krasnov." Alex spelled out the details to make sure Marvin got it right. "Krasnov sailed from Yalta on 20 October aboard the Captain Bastrov for Portsmouth, England. Then to Canada around the eighteenth of last December. See what you can find out from the British and check with immigration, see if he entered the States from Canada. Secondly, I need you to run a code-word system search for anything with Judy in it. Specifically 'Case Judy.' Got it? But be careful, I mean it! How long do you think it will take?"

Rimani watched with feigned interest as Alex balled his fist, and moved it up and down above his zipper to symbolize an orgasm coming "Marv, I need answers. This has to do with the issue I mentioned! One last thing. I'm sending you a letter. Take a look at it and hold it for me till I get back." Alex hung up and made two more calls, first to his mother who didn't answer, and then his girlfriend in Salt Lake City.

Before Alex left they had a couple of shots of vodka for old times and he handed Rimani a sealed envelope and asked him to drop it in the embassy's pouch to Washington.

* * *

At six that evening Alex stepped into the shower and let the tepid water loosen up his muscles for ten minutes. The last couple of days had tired him out and he still suffered from jet lag. He decided he'd have a couple more vodka's before dinner, and crash early. An hour later he emerged from the elevator and made his way toward the dining room off the main lobby. He didn't spot Vitaly Zitalco who was reading a newspaper near the wall. The old Russian folded his paper and rose, following Alex until he noticed another man approaching Alex.

Vitaly watched as the two spoke briefly, and tried to memorize the other man's face as Alex turned and followed him out the front door. What Vitaly saw next as he stood at the hotel entrance, convinced him that Balkan had probably just been kidnapped, and he made a note of the vehicle and its license plate as it sped away. Vitaly also thought he recognized the man who'd just spoken with Alex.

By five the following afternoon Vitaly had asked around and suspected he knew where they'd taken Alex. He decided to wait for Balkan's Peruvian friend to arrive, and see if he were interested in ransoming his friend? It was the only way.

Downtown Moscow

The half-hour of useless discussion was obviously getting Eduardo nowhere. "Gentlemen," he interrupted the arguments and shouting of the supposed bankers seated around the table. "If you will excuse me, I have to use the toilet."

A Russian seated by the door pointed down the hall.

The negotiations with Selvanian's Russian friends were obviously stalled. According to Selvanian they owed him money, and arranging the meeting with the old Sheikh would constitute partial payback. But the Russians viewed the deal differently. They smelled money and wanted to know what would be discussed with the old Arab, and what was in it for them. The senior Russian at the table had hinted a one percent cut of whatever it was that Eduardo would get from the Arab might be appropriate. Eduardo was not about to agree. If the old Sheikh met Eduardo's demand, the one percent for the Russians would represent thirty six million. For what? To make an appointment? Eduardo could do that himself if he had too.

Thirty feet down the passage he could smell yet another of Russia's famous Parashas. He'd only been in Moscow a day, but already he'd encountered the odor several times. It reminded him of the back alley behind Cantina Esmeralda in his hometown of Bellavista. Entering the Parasha, the toilet resembled his negotiations with the folks down the hall—unclean, odoriferous, and shitty.

The Russian chief executive was an ignorant goon named Valery Zeinoviev—an engorged cretin with ham-hock hands, dirty nails, bear like arms that strained the seams of his wrinkled coat while the man's mind knew as much about banking as a thief—banks had rooms full of money and he was entitled to it. Zeinoviev also smoked like a chimney, hacking and coughing when he laughed. Eduardo's comment as he'd left the negotiations was that Zeinoviev arrange the meeting with the Sheikh, or else. The ultimatum had brought on another coughing fit which turned the bastard's face redder than the now obsolete Communist flag on the wall behind him.

Eduardo had to be careful. He couldn't push the fat bastard too far. Now that Putin's goons controlled the political and oil apparatus of the new Russia, they no longer needed to kiss bankers assholes to get state loans, and in the last few years forty-two bankers had been murdered in Moscow, along with almost three hundred *Enterpreneurskis*. Men like Zienoviev were the latest industrial giants of modern Russia, and from what Selvanian had told Eduardo, two years ago Zeinoviev, was a nobody who'd eked out an existence under a rock somewhere near Kharkov. Today he was a senior bank executive with a *coterie* of well-paid thugs.

Zippering his fly he stepped back and pulled the toilet chain. Nothing happened. He looked at his watch as he returned to the negotiations. Now he'd give them his best and final offer, and if they refused, he'd walk out and let them stew. They could call him later at his hotel.

There were other things too that Eduardo needed to do today, one of which was to see how he could find out what had happened to Balkan? He'd repeatedly asked about Alex at the hotel reception, but been told he wasn't in. Then he'd been approached by a Russian named Vitaly Zitalko, who alleged Alex was kidnapped, and might be released for a fee. Not believing him, Eduardo agreed anyway to pay three times the Russian's demand, but only to be paid after Alex confirmed to Eduardo personally that he'd been kidnapped, and that the kidnappers would release him. Zitalko agreed. The Russian would arrange the American's release.

Back at the conference table, Eduardo held up his hand for silence. He told Zeinoviev he'd reached a decision which they could take or leave. He'd pay them twenty thousand dollars to arrange the meeting with the Sheikh for tomorrow afternoon. If the meeting actually took place there would be another forty thousand for Zeinoviev and twenty thousand for his friends. The fat Russian agreed but only, he said, because of his long friendship and love for his good friend Garo Selvanian.

The Dubna Dacha

"This is airport security at Sheremetyevo calling. May I speak with Colonel Yevgeni?"

"Speaking. Who is this?"

"Maximov Shetlin. I was told to report the arrival of an American to you."

"What do you have?" Yevgeni was tired. He'd been up most of the night, and the only positive development so far was a call from his assistant in the town of Bilibino, advising him that the Z-5 problem had been resolved.

"The subject arrived two days ago, aboard the British Airways flight from London."

"*Sutkin yar*!" Yevgeni exploded, "It took you this fucking long to find that out?" Cupping the phone he looked across the darkened room at the bound figure slumped in the chair. "This is a call from the Moscow airport, Balkan, no one realizes you are missing yet."

"Tell me, Shetlin . . . how long did his application say he would stay?"

"Twenty-four hours. I can confirm he still had not left Moscow as of this morning."

Yevgeni started to laugh. The airport guy couldn't confirm shit. "Report anything else you hear to me immediately." He dropped the phone into its cradle. Of course the American hadn't left Russia he mused. He never would. After they'd grabbed Balkan the night before last in front of his hotel, they'd held him in a Moscow garage before moving him here to this Dacha last night. Twenty miles east of Moscow the dilapidated affair at Morino had once been a whorehouse for long dead Party bosses during the Khruschev and Brehznev era. Old fashioned and outdated, it had gradually fallen into disrepair, until today when no one frequented it anymore during the winter months. Morino's upkeep had been entrusted to a disfigured veteran from the Afghan war who looked after it. Napalm had burned away most of the caretakers face and mottled his arms and legs. The caretaker would also have to be disposed of with Balkan.

"Make me coffee!" Yevgeni shouted at the caretaker who cowered on a filthy cot by the wall.

The caretakers tongue flicked repeatedly across the exposed membrane of his lower jaw; burned away in a momentary inferno somewhere near Kabul when a Russian airplane had dropped its ordinance too early. The cretin's tongue resembled an albino rats head poking out of its hole, slurping continuously around in a vain effort to moisten the raw tissue of an exposed saliva gland. The hairless eyelids were pulled back to expose half his corneas while the corners of each eye were packed with congealed mucous.

Yevgeni turned away and entered the darkened bedroom. It was just past five in the morning, supposedly a victim's worst time psychologically.

"You know who I am?" He spat at Alex again as he stood before him.

Alex shrugged his shoulders dejectedly,

"Yevgeni Kosmutov?" The Russian slapped him. "Talk to me! Then I will let you go."

"Why should I tell you anything?" Alex replied.

"Because you want to live, don't you? Now my friend, tell me about Carter?" He waited but the American said nothing. "What about Slavchenko?"

Alex continued to ignore him.

The Russian kicked him in the kidney and watched the American's face contort with pain.

"What about Case Judy?"

Still no response.

"I want the two documents you obtained from Kaminsky in Novosibirsk! Where are they?"

Alex was surprised at how much the Russian knew. But he still hadn't killed Alex, so he obviously still needed something.

"If you don't cooperate, you may never see your mother again Mr. Balkan," Kosmutov commented finally.

"Doesn't matter to me," Alex replied. "She's dead already."

"Is that so." Yevgeni observed. "This is new information that I didn't know." He scribbled something on a notepad. "She seemed alive and kicking the other day when we made enquiries about you in Altoona?"

The twinge in Alex's eye gave him away.

Maybe the old woman was the key Kosmutov thought. "Such a small house she has." Kosmutov's tone was insulting. "A real shack from what I'm told. You lived there as a youth didn't you?"

Alex said nothing.

"Will you inherit it when she dies? I shall arrange it. It is obviously not the bourgeois palace I would have expected for someone as famous as you. It's even smaller than my parents humble home, so you must be from a peasant background."

Again Balkan didn't respond.

"Your mother must be one of the whores from Bosnia who fled to America rather than be stoned to death by the Moslems for adultery, eh? An unclean wench whose thighs relieved the juices of all the passing Ottoman armies? She obviously escaped Karadzic's ethnic cleansing?"

"Up your ass," Alex replied.

Kosmutov slapped him.

"Your coffee is ready excellency," the housekeeper interrupted from the doorway.

Yevgeni whipped around. "Get out scum!" Turning to Alex he continued. "We made enquiries Alex, and even spoke with your mother. It would be a shame if something happened to her. She's such a nice old woman. I hope you do not want us to make her suffer needlessly?"

"Fuck you Kosmutov!"

"Ahhhhh, he cares!" The Russian laughed, moving his face only inches from Alex's. Maybe she has the two documents I want? We will need to talk to her about them again. But this time with some persuasion to make mama cooperate, eh! We know you didn't give them to Ted LePage before he died!" Alex's reaction to this piece of information confirmed to Kosmutov that he was getting through to this American. But were their roles reversed; Kosmutov had to admit, the reference in the same breath not only to the American's mother, but his boss by name, and the Novosibirsk documents, would have devastated Kosmutov too.

"Maybe your mama stuffed them in her bra? Or in some other body orifice? I know that women from the Balkan's are famous for concealing valuables between their thighs. I will call my friends and tell them to strip her and do a cavity search? Any guidance? Does your mama like big or little cocks? Maybe some cigarette burns on her arms, pins in her eyes, or some wires on delicate places?"

"What rock were you born under you fatherless piece of shit!" Alex responded.

"And if she doesn't cooperate," Kosmutov continued sarcastically, "maybe a fire; a traditional American barbecue? Aawww," Kosmutov cooed noting the hatred now obvious in the American's face. "But then you would not inherit her puny house. And you could pour what's left of mama into a vodka glass."

"Up your ass." Alex realized he was handling this poorly as Kosmutov slapped him again, this time harder.

"Be careful Amerikanski! Perhaps a broomstick, or the housekeepers prick up your ass for a couple of hours would prove you are nothing special. My housekeeper hasn't had a woman in years, and he's not fussy anymore about how he satisfies himself," he shouted to the caretaker, asking him if he'd like a night alone to fuck this American? "Daaaa! Daaa!" the cretin exclaimed, appearing in the doorway, his hands already unbuckling his belt.

"Maybe I should leave you with him for a couple hours. Eh, tell me where the documents are, Alex, and you'll be on the next plane from Sheremetyevo. Think about it. I'll be back after I have my coffee."

Three days ago Yevgeni had spoken with General Valeriy Yeniseysk, and ordered him to pick up Balkan if he was ever stupid enough to return to Russia. Yeniseysk had also reminded Yevgeni that the FSB might have to arrange not only for his own liquidation, but if Yevgeni failed, maybe even for his entire family as well. Too much was at stake. The POW/MIA issue with the United States was explosive; if the documents about what happened to so many Americans in Russia now became public, they would eliminate any likelihood of *rapprochement* between the two countries for a decade or more.

Yevgeni knew that Yeniseysk meant what he said. For several years now the General had been the president's military confidant, and the man in charge of Russian POW/MIA affairs. And just in case Yevgeni had missed the point, the General reminded him of the Case Judy confession he'd signed years earlier, admitting that Yevgeni had fathered the entire conspiracy; right down to the defection of Tatiana; in hopes that she'd lead them to the missing Spanish gold. Last Fall Tatiana had been ordered to pursue new leads in Argentina, then Peru, and finally England. But when she was ordered to return to Moscow for debriefings she'd balked. And before they could silence her, she'd obviously been murdered in Washington. Carter's release too had been a mistake. Again Yevgeni had miscalculated. The American had led them nowhere, and was obviously only interested in getting even with those who'd betrayed him sixty years ago. Now Yevgeni would have to find Carter and silence him too.

Case Judy had first come to Yevgeni's attention on a warm spring day in the late nineteen seventies; the type of day one clearly remembers: when the Moscow air was pungent with the scent of spring, and one appreciates the beauty of life. His second daughter Katerina had just been born the previous day, and he'd visited his wife at the hospital before walking to work. Two hours later his boss had called him in and told him to sign for the Nasdreli Kachou file. Nasdreli Kachou related to Case Judy, and in retrospect, he now wished he'd been somewhere else that day.

As Soviet armies rolled through Germany in the closing days of the Great Patriotic war, thousands of tons of Hitler's records were being vacuumed up by advancing Soviet Divisions and shipped to Moscow where most of them had been left to rot away in dark rooms. Only recently had Russian analysts begun pouring through them, piecing together a story which hinted at the existence of a hitherto unknown secret German submarine, one which went deeper and moved faster than anything available at that time.

The first reference to it had appeared in 1949 from German files captured at Rostock. The files bore the imprimatur Case Judy Construction. But the four sheets of paper provided no details, and were eventually forgotten. Then in late 1989, forty years later, newly acquired KGB computers had made a match between a file in the Volodarsk archives outside Moscow, with another file maintained inside the Kremlin. Both files had contained references to Case Judy.

Subsequent investigation tied the Kremlin file to an Anglo American agreement delaying an American invasion of Europe until late 1944, so as to give Russia time to capture most of eastern Germany in accordance with a secret understanding between Stalin and Roosevelt. The second file hinted at a wider conspiracy regarding Anglo American cooperation to remove wartime gold bullion from Germany. Suddenly Moscow analysts realized there was obviously more to the obscure agreements than they'd originally thought. Both files were immediately placed within the KGB's Nasdreli system and assigned the designator, Kachou. Kachou became the Kremlin's most closely guarded secret, known only to three men—the new Russian president, the Director of the KGB, and . . . Yevgeni Kosmutov.

Implicated in the file was the United States and Great Britain, who had obviously each agreed to delay the defeat of Germany until 1945 . . . in return for the transfers of bullion. This delay also provided Hitler with sufficient time to reduce his minorities problem to a level manageable for resettlement in Palestine after the war, and gave Russia half of Europe—in return for a commitment not to negotiate a separate peace with Hitler. The UK's *quid pro quo* was the realization of the Balfour declaration and the creation of a pro-western State astride Britain's carotid artery, its lifeline to its empire east of the Suez. Most insidious as far as Yevgeni was concerned was Roosevelt's side-deal to help German leaders smuggle their treasure out for the postwar era, treasure which Washington had then misdirected and stolen for herself. The Volodarsk papers also proved that Hitler had gone to incredible lengths to build a unique submarine whose sole purpose was to smuggle his treasure abroad, and to do so in such great secrecy that no one would ever find a trace of its existence . . . or the cargo: during or after the war. Altogether several thousand tons of gold had disappeared from wartime Germany. And for starters . . . Spain's gold which had been captured from Russia near Minsk on the nineteenth day of Operation Barbarossa. Where had it gone? That was the question Yevgeni had devoted decades of his life to uncovering.

But the mystery did not end there. Russia, for fifty years, had a highly placed sleeper in Washington. And it was this man he hoped would lead them to their gold.

During the summer of 2005, Yevgeni thought he'd made a breakthrough. It was a false start! Police in the Mongolian Republic of Ulan Bator had caught an itinerant Mongol trying to sell gold coins in the bazaar. When the FSB realized they might be Spanish Pesetas from the Caballero shipment, Yevgeni was dispatched to investigate. But Mongol security goons had tortured the old man to death before he arrived and the genesis of the Mongol's coins remained a mystery.

Promotions for Yevgeni since the collapse of the Soviet Union had come regularly in recent years, along with bigger apartments and better cars. The old system might be dead for most, but not those loyal to the security services. Somehow the government was always able to pay them.

The caretaker asked him if he wanted more coffee.

"No," he replied. Handing him the mug, he arose and returned to his interrogation of Balkan.

"So, Alex, tell me about the Novosibirsk documents."

"I don't know what you are talking about."

A fist slammed into Alex's mouth. Blood trickled down his jaw and his tongue told him there was a loose tooth.

"Don't treat me like an ass! If you do, I'll remove each of your teeth until you are babbling like an old babushka. We have an agent inside the White House so we know what is true and what is not." He moved a chair closer and sat down facing Alex, his face only inches away.

"I gave them to my boss," Alex replied.

"And his name?"

"You know who he is."

"Entertain me."

"Ted LePage!"

"How convenient! We know you didn't give them to him. Plus, LePage is dead!"

Alex tried to look surprised. "I didn't know that." Again his eyes saw stars as the Russian's fist slammed into the side of his head.

"What did you do with them?"

"I told you. I gave them to LePage."

"What did he say?"

"That it would be interesting to see if they were the real McCoy. He thought they were not."

Maybe Balkan was telling him the truth. Maybe his own information from Washington was wrong? "You mean he thought they might not be real?"

"LePage thought it strange they appeared now, and felt it might be a provocation to embarrass your leaders."

"Where would LePage have stored them?"

"How should I know? Maybe his personal safe. Or he might have registered them, in which case they're in the official system somewhere."

"But you don't know?"

"I didn't ask."

"What about Paul Carter?"

"I know he's in the States and wasted Slavchenko."

"You are certain?"

Alex glanced at him for a moment before responding. It was a strange question from the Russian. "Yes."

"You are certain she's dead?"

He continued to stare at Kosmutov. "Why?"

"You saw the body?"

"What does that have to do with anything?"

Kosmutov smiled and changed the subject. "They will never find Carter." He observed with a sarcastic grin.

Alex almost made a catastrophic error when he started to acknowledge that he knew Carter was using an alias, but caught himself.

"How did you meet the two Russians in Novisibirsk?"

"Kaminsky found me at the hotel and introduced me to the other guy."

"And Case Judy? What do you know about that?"

"Nothing," he lied, and hoped the Russian wouldn't pick up on it. "What is it?"

Yevgeni studied him for a few moments before deciding not to believe him. He grabbed Balkan's lower jaw and pulled it toward him, then smashed his fist into Alex's nose. "I would suggest you tell me the truth."

Alex's eyes were tearing badly. He'd already been caught in one lie and if caught again, knew Kosmutov would administer even more violence. "Honestly I don't know what you are talking about!"

"You'd find Case Judy fascinating." Kosmutov observed finally as he sat back and lit up another cigarette inhaling deeply before blowing the smoke in Alex's face. It is maintained in Washington. I have part of it."

Alex hoped he'd continue.

And the Russian did. "America was afraid Moscow would sign a separate peace with Hitler like we did in the first war. So Roosevelt agreed to give us Eastern Europe, and half of Germany, in return for our commitment to stay in the war. "You Americans," the Russian spat, "you think you know all about war and suffering but you don't know shit. When Roosevelt agreed to give Russia all of Eastern Europe it was because he knew it was the only way to avoid American casualties, so he let us do his dirty work for him. You lost a hundred and fifty thousand and we lost twenty million, we lost a hundred and thirty people for each of yours."

Your people call your firemen who died in the World Trade Center heroes. They were thieves who probably deserved to die. Why didn't your government say anything about all the stolen merchandise which was found in their fire trucks? Boxes and boxes of jewelry, clothing, and electronic stuff all looted from the nearby shops by the firemen before the World Trade Center buildings collapsed and buried their equipment.

"So is this what Case Judy is about," Alex asked, "a complaint about how many people you lost compared to ours?"

Kosmutov shook his head slowly. "I am disappointed. It is okay, play stupid if you want, there is a lot of time left for you to come around."

"So what's your point?" Alex inquired in his most disarming manner.

"I'll tell you," Kosmutov replied. "Roosevelt knew it would take us two or more years to reach Berlin anyway, which was more than enough time for that bastard Hitler to solve his minorities problem. But this is only half of it. The Case Judy file also proves that Roosevelt cooperated with Germany to hide treasures stolen by Hitler."

Alex tried to look surprised as he licked the blood running from his mouth.

"I have spent the last two decades of my life working on this. You and I Balkan, we both want the same thing. We both want to find Paul Carter. You also want to find out where the Americans are that we are still holding, and I want to know where the gold is that America is hiding. Interested in a deal?"

"For what?"

"What I want and for what you want."

"An interesting story," Alex replied.

"Then let's make a deal."

"And the exchange?"

"The two documents and the gold for our prisoners."

Alex didn't believe he'd keep such a bargain, Kosmutov couldn't. "I wish I could help!" Alex muttered.

Kosmutov stood up and kicked him in the chest so hard that Alex careened over backward onto the floor. "You will tell me everything Balkan, you bastard! But first I shall have some more coffee and a cigarette, then we will get started in earnest.

Eastern Moscow

Seinoviev, from Simcha Bank, called before lunch to confirm Eduardo's appointment with the Arab for two-thirty that afternoon. After lunch Eduardo returned to his suite, showered and selected one of his dark blue suits and a power tie. He wanted to project authority and poise during this meeting, knowing the Sheikh's aversion to all men with blue eyes. He'd also contacted reception and asked to be notified if anyone called. It was over twenty-four hours since he'd agreed to pay for Alex's release and he was becoming anxious.

At quarter past two he answered the knock on his door and joined Zeinoviev as they moved down the hall toward a slight man attired in white desert garb. Zeinoviev would make the introductions and then make his excuses and depart; leaving Eduardo to present his case to the Sheikh.

The evidence against the old Arab was compelling. In a Peruvian court, both the Sheikh and the Chinese man he'd conspired with would both have been quickly found guilty: the former for conspiracy to defraud, and the latter for bribery and grand larceny. Selvanian had thoughtfully provided a quotation from the Koran which Eduardo intended to use. *God will call you to account for the evil intention in your heart.* The bedouin guard opened the door and ushered them into an anteroom.

Another man appeared from a side door, introducing himself as Jassim Ali bin Thani al Khabar ibn Salwa. Eduardo asked him which name he preferred?

"Call me Jassim." Jassim was to be his translator for the meeting with the ruler. The old man spoke no English. They filed into an adjacent room and he recognized the Ruler from photographs Selvanian had showed him in London. The old man seemed disinterested in the proceeding and was speaking animatedly with two younger men seated beside him. Finally he turned and looked at Jassim.

"Eh ya huwaagaa, shoo fee hessa?"

Jassim turned to Zeinoviev and asked if they were ready.

The obsequious Russian expressed his pleasure at once again having the opportunity to meet with the great ruler of the Arabian Arabs. He hoped that Simcha bank might continue to be of valuable service to the Arab's cause against Israel. The old ruler's face feigned a smile of satisfaction. It was obvious he had no recollection of who the Russian was. Eduardo glanced repeatedly at Zeinoviev as his remarks droned on interminably and he suspected Zeinoviev had forgotten why they were here and who was paying his fee? Finally Zeinoviev concluded, assuring everyone that Eduardo was an influential man, a friend of Russia's, and a man who could be trusted.

Eduardo waited an appropriate interval while the Russian excused himself and departed . . . maintaining eye contact with the old Sheikh whose hooded eyes remained deadpan above a copious white beard.

"It is my understanding," Eduardo began, "there are amongst this assembly, those who know of a company in Hong Kong called CEBU. Also a Chinese man named Shan Kew who was once a client of yours!" He waited while a translation was made and sat in stunned silence for what seemed minutes while no one acknowledged anything he'd said. "Ask the Sheikh if he is familiar with the persons I have mentioned?"

"Laa. Il Sheikh mabarif huwwa," a young man to the left replied.

The translator looked at Eduardo and informed him no one was familiar with these names.

"Well, he should be!" Eduardo replied. "And I expect he will make it his business to find out more. Shan Kew was paid ten million dollars from the Sheikh's personal account in Dubai, for parking billions of dollars of our deposits with BCCI, for which BCCI paid a low interest rate. Despite repeated guidance not to, CEBU continued to maintain huge balances with the bank until it folded. Conservatively we estimate our loss at two and a half billion dollars. Which, with accumulated interest since that time, comes to an additional two hundred and twenty-eight million. This comes to a grand total of—"

Jassim interrupted Eduardo, raising his hands and requested a moment while he translated

Moments later as the translation was finished the Sheikh began to laugh and slowly stroked his beard as he mumbled a series of staccato statements which seemed to confuse the interpreter.

Jassim finally turned to Eduardo. "The Sheikh states he has many accounts, and many foreigners come with their hands outstretched, but leave with nothing. He does not know what you are talking about. He suggests you seek a handout elsewhere."

Eduardo stared first at Jassim, then at the ruler. Maybe Jassim hadn't comprehended and translated what he'd said correctly?

Jassim assured him that he had.

"He will not pay?" Eduard demanded.

"He says he has no idea what you are talking about." Jassim shook his head slowly. "I am sorry."

"Thank the Sheikh for his time. Tell him we wish him well and shall not bring this inconsequential matter before him again. Before I leave however, please inform him that my associates allow American Banks to screw us from time to time, like ignorant virgins—because when American banks fail—even if due to theft or malfeasance of the officers involved, the Federal Deposit Insurance Corporation usually reimburses us. Because of this we seldom bother to hunt down criminal American Bankers when they have fucked us, and bury their bodies in cement."

Jassim's eyes widened.

"Tell him, Jassim."

Two young men beside the Sheikh became noticeably upset as the translator continued, but no one said anything as they looked at the old man.

Eduardo continued, "So please inform His Majesty." Eduardo had now decided to use the term deliberately to let the old man know that Eduardo was being polite, but also obviously mocking him diplomatically, "that since BCCI has no Federal Deposit Insurance Corporation, that BCCI's owners have stolen something which is not theirs, and the Islamic sanction for such theft, at a minimum, is to have one's right hand and left foot chopped off. And for large thefts . . . even one's head."

Jassim threw up his hands. "A moment! You use offensive language, Mr. Eduardo! I cannot tell him this."

"Tell him!" Eduardo shouted.

"I cannot," Jassim insisted.

"Of course you can my friend. After all, I am only reminding everyone about what your Holy Book says. If he chooses to take it as a personal affront, then that is his problem. Tell him Jassim!" Eduardo ordered. His tone now so strong and abrupt that it surprised even him. He waited as the old man's demeanor remained deadpan. But the younger men around the Sheikh had begun fidgeting nervously with their worry beads.

"Is that all?" Jassim asked, looking at Eduardo.

"No. Tell him that because the Sheikh personally was the major owner in BCCI that my associates have decided to be magnanimous, and assume it was not His Majesty who was personally involved, but his trusted associates who stole our money. We thought His Majesty, as an honorable man, would see to his just obligations. If not we can only assume your Sharia law applies, and justice will be administered accordingly in accordance with your Koran."

Now the old man was frowning as he conducted an exchange with the man to his left. Finally Jassim informed Eduardo he still had no case.

"Then I am still not finished," Eduardo interjected. "As I said earlier, my associates don't care about the eight to ten billion dollars of other people's money stolen from the now defunct BCCI. This was the Sheikh's business."

Jassim was obviously becoming agitated again and asked Eduardo to wait while the man to the Sheikh's left leaned forward, his hand on his dagger and making gutteral sounds for which Eduardo did not ask a translation.

"What exactly is it that you want to tell his excellency?" Jassim asked Eduardo as the man to the sheikh's left demanded in impeccable English. "What's the bottom line, Peruvian?" The young Arab, probably in his late twenties sported a huge black beard and the eyes of an Egret, set aside both sides of a prominent beak-like nose.

"The bottom line," Eduardo told him, "is that unless we get back what is ours, we assume the man who took it is no better than a common bazaar thief and must be treated accordingly!"

It was a hell of a gamble Eduardo was taking, but it was Selvanian who'd given him the wording. The old Armenian had insisted that the old man had to clearly be informed that he could pay or be assassinated. According to Selvanian the Sheikh knew he owed the money and had been playing with them for over a decade. Also that the old Sheikh had billions and enjoyed stiffing other former Christian associates by making them wait forever for their money. Selvanian had told him that an associate had personally heard the Sheikh refer to the seventeenth Sura, verse twenty-seven of the Koran, when asked about the money he owed to CEBU ten years ago. The old man had said, "Verily spendthrifts are brothers of the evil ones and the evil one is ungrateful to his Lord."

The man with the stubble glared at Eduardo. "Is this a threat, Peruvian? Are you with Peru's Shining Path? Or maybe Tupac Amaru? Are you a terrorist? How dare you make such a statement! How dare you call this man a bazaar thief! If I tell him what you have said, he will let you watch while your tongue is cut out and stuck up your ass, then remove your eyes and have them placed on tooth picks."

"Then so be it!" Eduardo replied, "but you better tell him. I have not come here without authorization. I am but a messenger" He wondered if Selvanian would really arrange for Eduardo's funeral details and have him buried beside his father if one of these goons decided to cut him up? "Tell him that if the CEBU account is still unsettled next week, I have been asked to tell you, that my associates suggest the Sheikh sleep with both eyes open from now on."

The man with the stubble shouted to his security people to remove this dhimmi from their presence. They jostled Eduardo into an adjacent room and pushed him into an arm chair and stood before him with drawn revolvers. Eduardo could hear Jassim and the man to the Sheikh's left yelling at each other in Arabic.

Finally Jassim reappeared and signalled for Eduardo to follow him.

"Bi-kaam floos huwwa aiyse?" the old Sheikh demanded as Eduardo was brought in.

"What is the exact balance due?" Jassim asked.

"Two point seven."

"With a 'b' before it and eight zeroes I assume?" Jassim asked.

"Yes."

The Sheikh shook his head slowly with a condescending expression as he stroked his beard. Foreigners with the nerve to confront him like this obviously knew what they were doing. He barely recalled the CEBU deal in Hong Kong. So many had stood in line over the years, trying to get back money they'd entrusted to him one way or another over the years. He wished he'd never met those who'd first suggested an Islamic Bank, one that could avoid the filthy Christian habit of charging interest.

The banking world had always been run by the Christians and Jews, and the blessed Prophet Mohammed—praise and blessings be upon his name, had discouraged banking and forbid the payment of interest just as had the Christian religion in its early years before men got greedy. Now this nonbeliever threatened to have him exterminated unless he made good on their loss plus the cursed interest. "Gulli, wayne il pakistani akroot hesse?" the old Arab asked Jassim.

"Musharrafak?" Jassim knew it was the Pakistani who'd arranged the deal with CEBU, but the Pakistani had not accompanied them to Russia and Jassim suspected the Pakistani's life might be considerably shortened if the Sheikh settled this account with this Peruvian.

"Tayyib! Galti Mustapha, shoof awal, ow baadayn untini haitha kharregia il floos."

The Sheikh nodded toward Eduardo, then to Jassim. "Fee tanny?"

"La!" Jassim replied.

"Quayyis. Allah Ma'ak!" the old man stated as he arose and left.

The older of the two men seated to the Sheikh's left approached Eduardo. In precise California accent, he informed Eduardo that the Ruler wished for God to be with him, and that a deposit would be made to Dai Itchi Bank in Hong Kong within seventy-two hours.

"There is another man called Hernandez?" the Arab demanded in English, staring at Eduardo.

"How do you mean?" Eduardo asked.

"There was another of the same name. But much older than you! Maybe your father?"

"Maybe," Eduardo replied.

The Arab laughed. "We hope to never see him or you again."

Eduardo didn't think it would be a problem as they escorted him to the hotel hallway and closed the door. He asked where Zeinoviev was and was told he'd already been shown downstairs to the lobby.

SIX

Outside Dubna

THE TWO VEHICLES halted in the thick woods. The low cloud cover in the night sky to the southeast glowed from the lights of Moscow while before them the road jogged to the right along a frozen creek into the darkness.

Vitaly Zitalko emerged first from the lead sedan, and studied the woods. The place didn't appear to have changed much as he recalled years past at this place. As a younger man he'd visited Morino on numerous occasions for weekends of debauchery amongst perfumed thighs. In the last decade this hideout had obviously been replaced by others more modern and comfortable which the rich and famous now demanded. It was also obvious from the road surface that only one other vehicle had passed this way recently, a sedan he guessed from the shallow imprints in the snow. He was certain that Yevgeni Kozmutov and Alex Balkan were just down the road in the run down Morino Dacha.

He turned to a bulky man with a peasant face who'd moved forward from the truck behind him. The bulky man used the *nom de guerre* of Boris and was reliable. Boris, now slightly paunchy and gray around the temples, was still in excellent condition and as big as a bear. He'd spent eighteen years with SPETSNAZ, Russia's equivalent of America's Special Forces, and had seen combat in Yemen, Afghanistan and the Caucuses before his retirement four years ago. This morning's enterprise almost bored Boris, but he feigned attention when Yevgeni was round as Yevgeni was the brains behind this effort, but Boris was the man who would lead the motley assault group which he'd assembled for this evening's work.

Vitaly pointed at the road. "Only one vehicle has passed."

"No problem," Boris replied. If they behave friendly, it will take a minute. If they are unfriendly—maybe two. Everything is possible for big bucks."

"I do not want the American harmed." Vitaly reminded Boris yet again. "Remind your men again."

Boris motioned those in the truck to dismount. One group of four and another of eight fanned out into the woods. The Dacha faced the river a hundred yards away and the main assault would parallel the river and go through the front door to disarm those who surrendered and shoot those who didn't. The second would catch those who fled into the woods from the rear of the Dacha.

He wondered where Boris had found the ragtag assembly. But from the way they checked weapons, all obviously had military training and none seemed nervous. Maybe the promise of two hundred dollars each had hardened their stools, Vitaly thought.

Five minutes later the silhouette of the dacha was discernable through the trees. No matter how many times Vitaly was out before dawn on such days, he always found it ominous and foreboding, maybe it was because it was the low point of most living things circadian rhythm, and this morning was no different. Crouched against a tree in the darkness he recalled hunting trips earlier in his life when he'd waited for game to move in the predawn darkness like this. Then he'd hunted wild boar and deer, this morning it would be other humans.

Boris nudged Vitaly, handing him a Tokarev pistol. "Know how to use one of these?" he whispered. He didn't wait for an answer, pushing it into Vitaly's hand. "If you need it, don't hesitate! Nine-rounds. Just pull the trigger but don't forget the safety!"

"I do not need this!"

"I know. But I want to get paid when this is over!" Boris smirked.

"Don't worry," Vitaly whispered as the bear-like Russian moved passed him cautiously.

Moments later they could discern movement amongst the trees along the river bank and hear the crunching sounds of boots through the crusty snow. Then staccato gun-fire erupted amidst sounds of a door being kicked in. Men yelled and screamed as muffled shots followed. Vitaly was into the house a half minute later and saw Alex's surprised expression as he sat tied to a chair in the back bedroom, his muffled voice obviously screaming through a gag.

"Untie him!" Vitaly ordered.

"Only three here," Boris replied. Your friend over there, another in the bedroom who is now terminal, and this cretin here." Boris pointed at the housekeeper who sat dumbly by the wall obviously terrified, his eyes like swollen peeled eggs in his face as his tongue flickered even more feverishly now. The specter began whining for his life; and swore he would never say anything. A round from Boris's pistol froze the flickering tongue. A second sprawled the ogre onto the stove like a ragdoll where he now lay motionless, his flesh sizzling on the hot metal.

Alex's initial surprise at seeing Vitaly passed as he realized the badly wounded man Boris referred to in the other room was his interrogator. He struggled against his bonds as they were cut away. He pushed his way into the bedroom where Yevgeni lay sprawled by the wall. "Out!" Alex ordered the Russians standing around with bored expressions on their faces, "I need to be alone with this man." He slammed the door after them and knelt beside Yevgeni. "Where are they?" he demanded, hoping the dying man would offer the information before he departed for the next world. "Tell me where the three hundred Americans are? You are finished. It's too late for you, so what difference does it make? At least let me end their misery and return them to their families and loved ones." The Russian smiled briefly as his eyes tried to focus.

"Shit." Yevgeni muttered. "You knew all along . . . !" He gurgled. "You knew about them? How?"

"You don't have time for the explanation," Alex said gently, studying the Russian who had been stitched across the chest by an AK-47 burst and his life was ebbing quickly. Blood was bubbling from three holes in his shirt. "Tell me where they are?"

Yevgeni's lips formed words but nothing came out.

Alex placed his ear next to Vevgeny's mouth. "Try again!"

"Uga . . . , Ug . . . , Uggg . . . aaaaaat . . . sssshn . . ."

"Ugatkyn? The camp called Z-5?" Alex demanded. "Blink your eyes if that is the place."

The Russians eyes opened wide and stared back in surprise as Alex grabbed him by the shirt and lifted him to a sitting position.

"Blink damn you! You bastard! Tell me!"

Yevgeni blinked.

"And this mole of yours in America. What is his name?"

As he waited, the whites of the Russians eyes appeared, as a death rattle escaped his lungs. Too bad Alex thought. At least the bastard had confirmed the existence of the prisoners at Z-5. He rifled through Yevgeni's pockets but found nothing of value, some Rubles, a laminated ID card identifying the corpse as a member of the FSB's intelligence service, two rubbers and a spent 9mm cartridge.

The door opened and Boris peered in. "We must go, Alex. Now! It is dangerous to stay and I must collect my big bucks."

"Tell Vitaly Zitalko to come here!" Alex ordered, waving him off and stared at the Russian until he closed the door. Moments later the door opened and the old Russian walked in and studied the dead man on the floor for a moment. "I thought it would be him," he muttered. "I've seen him before."

"I owe you my life Vitaly," Alex said, squeezing the Russian's shoulder. "How can I thank you?"

"In good time," Vitaly replied. "Boris said you wanted to see me. About what?"

"I need another favor."

A few minutes later they called Boris in and he quickly agreed he might be able to arrange a visit to eastern Russia. Boris had a friend near Bilibino with a decrepit YAK aircraft. The YAK could take them anywhere. "But it will cost many dollars." Boris observed, greed now exuding from every pore of his being. "And you already owe me big bucks which I have still not seen?"

"My friend will pay you well," Alex assured him.

"First let me see if your rich friend will pay me for tonight's work, then we can discuss even bigger bucks!"

Vitaly explained the arrangement to Alex regarding his release, and that Eduardo had agreed to pay everything.

"A deal's a deal!" Boris quipped. "We are capitalists now, Da? As soon as your friend pays, I pay my friends outside and we discuss new business! Da?"

The Oymayakonskoye Mountains

Alex watched the silhouette of their YAK aircraft flitting across the snow-covered forests and peaks which at times threatened to rip out the plane's belly as it cleared ridge after ridge of sheer rock by mere inches. His knuckles were white and his stomach was in his throat so often that he thought he'd lose his breakfast of boiled potatoes and cabbage. On more than one occasion he'd involuntarily lifted off his seat cushion as they'd barely cleared ridge lines. The pilot was good, desperately hugging the terrain so as to avoid detection by the Krasnoyarsk radar a thousand miles away. It was still a potent threat to their survival even in these days of reduced budgets. Alex suspected the massive air defense radar was probably inoperable anyway and prayed that the god damned thing was offline or broken down. They needed a lot of luck if they were to survive the next few days.

Krasnoyarsk's Cold War function had been to detect inbound low flying American bombers inside Russian airspace. Its four massive three hundred foot radar faces were designed to look over the horizon and detect even the smallest aircraft skimming above the earth's surface.

Alex wasn't about to complain about the inherent danger of today's flight because Russian air defense squadrons in the area had standing instructions to shoot first and ask questions later. The entire militarized area still contained some of Russia's best kept secrets and the Kremlin wanted it kept that way. Nonmilitary traffic in the area was coordinated weeks in advance and if not and detected: blown out of the sky and a search mounted for survivors later. The whine of the turboprop pulled to full power again as they accelerated up a mountain face and dropped across another ridge-line into a pristine untouched valley. The beefy Russian next to Alex smiled. "The pilot's good, Eh?" Boris's feigned bravado was obvious. Boris pointed to the cockpit door. "But big bucks not worth parasha droppings if he makes a mistake. Da?"

Alex laughed and pulled a vodka bottle from his pocket and offered it to him. Boris upped the bottle and drained a quarter of its contents without swallowing. "To big bucks!" Alex shouted as Boris handed it back.

"Daaaaa!" Boris replied, punching his chest with his fist.

They'd been airborne two and a half hours, and were somewhere deep in the Chukotskoye Nagoroye Mountains of northeastern Siberia. Anytime now they would be crossing the southern reaches of the Ugatkyn River valley. They'd skim the river's course northward for a couple hundred miles to the camp known as Z-5. In the three days he'd known Boris, he'd come to appreciate the Russian's sense of humor. At heart Boris was a teddy bear who liked to laugh, play jokes and drink, but he killed with equanimity. Although raised in a communist society, Boris's capitalistic instincts were superb and he hadn't missed a trick during the negotiations for this expedition. When Alex mentioned Siberia, and inquired if Boris knew the area the son of a bitch had broken into a huge smile and laughed heartily until everyone around him had joined in. The Russian could smell more than big bucks; especially after Alex outlined the location.

Boris accurately described the area as a restricted military region where unauthorized foreigners and Russians usually disappeared—and without a trace. Eduardo had sarcastically suggested that Alex forget about the endeavor as no one wanted Boris to violate Russian law, endanger his life, or the lives of any of his men. The Russian went for the bait. There was no need for concern Boris had insisted. Boris excelled at such things. He'd fought the Mujaheddin in Afghanistan and personally killed hundreds of them in hand to hand fighting. Near Kandahar he'd taken many prisoners, disemboweled one and eaten his liver while three other Muhajeddin had begun crying for their mothers and begged for mercy. Mercy! Boris had laughed as he'd cut off their cocks and stuffed them into their mouths then taped them shut and left them tied to a fig tree as a warning to others in the area not to screw with him.

Avoiding the authorities in such a vast area where Alex wanted to go was no problem Boris insisted, because now there were few security forces, and with Boris's assistance, they would easily pass in and out of the area unnoticed. However, to do all this Alex needed lots of money, and enough to help Boris obtain their own aircraft. Eduardo had suggested Boris get started, and to get a flying machine big enough for four people. Boris, Eduardo, Alex and he had looked at Vitaly Zitalko, who reluctantly agreed to join them. Boris had asked for one hundred thousand. A quarter up front. The demand didn't even faze Eduardo. He'd deftly unbuttoned his shirt and counted out fifty one thousand dollar bills while Boris's eyes greedily followed the rest of the trove as Eduardo returned it to its envelope in his waistband. They'd given him twice what he'd asked for, Boris gushingly told Eduardo, with a puzzled look. Eduardo assured him an equal amount would also be forthcoming once they returned from the trip and were safely across a western border. Boris's frame had shaken with laughter at his unbelievable luck, and he reached into a battered suitcase, withdrawing yet another small bottle of vodka which he upended and splashed over several glasses. "Nasdrovia Kamaradsky!" he'd announced. "I love capitalists. Long live American money."

Two days later they'd driven east to Electrostal and the following morning boarded a domestic flight for an insignificant place called Ust Nera. One of Boris's associates met them at Ust Nera, and put them up for the night at a farm near the airstrip.

Unfortunately, Boris's associate explained, the Yak aircraft he'd arranged for was no longer available. A Chinese oil survey crew had arrived unannounced and taken it for two weeks into the hinterlands. An alternative had already been arranged, and two hours before sunup they awoke to the sound of engines overhead and watched as a twin-engine plane fitted with snow skis as it slid to a halt outside.

"Much better than the Yak," Boris exclaimed, "two engines better than one! Faster too! More people. More vodka."

Alex recognized the modified Tupolev-2 light bomber. Designed too late for wartime service in the Great Patriotic War, thousands of them had entered service in the post war era, but today only a few survived. The TU-2 could sprint to four hundred miles an hour, and had a range of two thousand miles—more than enough to get them out and back if it didn't fall apart first.

They departed before first light, and when the sun rose, the unspoiled landscape reminded Alex of what the United States must have looked like before the arrival of the white man: virgin forest for as far as the eye could see with no clearings, no roads, and no sign of civilization. Three hours later, they were into the barren mountains of the Arctic, and the forests gave way to desolate Taiga. He hoped the pilot knew about compass bearings and wind drift. Siberia was a place where the lost were seldom seen again.

"Ugatkyn!" the pilot yelled back as the aircraft slid across another ridge and went into a hard left turn along a river valley off their right side.

"Keep your eyes peeled!" the pilot shouted. Alex's plan was to land at Z-5, inform the residents that their compass was out and would need a few hours to make repairs. It would give them time to look around. A half-hour later the first sign of habitation appeared at a bend in the river, but what they saw surprised them. Fire had consumed several long earth covered huts, whose roofs had obviously collapsed into their foundations and only a few of the outlying structures appeared undamaged. "It is deserted the pilot shouted.

"Look for a place to land," Alex replied, and five minutes later they taxied to a stop. It was the utter stillness and quiet they all immediately noticed once the props stopped.

"You sure this is the right place?" the pilot asked. "Looks like everyone moved away. Maybe we should check further north?"

"This has to be the place," Alex said heading toward the rear door of the aircraft.

The concertina wire enclosure consisted of fourteen long earth covered structures half buried in the ground. A gate on the north side was down as were two sections of the wire to the west. Their buildings insides were lined with center poles supporting roofs of rough hewn logs above which was piled earth and snow. Those not burned were littered with an aberration of broken furniture, wrecked multi-tiered bunk beds, and trashed cooking areas. Dank, damp, and filthy, it was difficult to believe humans had occupied them. It was also obvious that the inhabitants had recently left in a hurry. Strewn everywhere were old clothing, newspapers, worn out boots, and other extraneous detritus of human habitation.

They spread out and searched the camp. On a partially burned table in one of the sheds Alex made out the inscription "God Bless America" and on another "Live Free or Die." Everywhere old carvings of hearts and arrows with initials and names were in evidence. He wanted to kick himself because he'd forgotten to bring a camera. On the charred remnants of a roof beam were inscribed Harry Smith. And below it, Papillion, Nebraska—March 14, 1925.

A shrill whistle outside distracted him and he stepped through the door. In the distance the pilot motioned him toward him. Everywhere around them were partially snow covered prints of tracked vehicles which had headed away northward along the river. Whoever was here, had gone in that direction.

"Let's go!" Alex shouted as they headed back to the Tupolev. "Once we're in the air," he told the pilot, "follow the tracks."

The pilot looked at him. "No. We must go back. There are only a couple of hours left, and the instruments are unreliable this far north, especially at night." He bulged his eyes for emphasis.

"Fifteen minutes only!" Alex insisted. "Then we'll head for Ust-Nera."

"Not possible," the pilot insisted. "Money no good to me if dead. We return home now." They headed west through the foot hills and suddenly Alex noticed more vehicle tracks in the snow which were heading southwest.

"Follow them," Alex ordered the pilot, who brought the aircraft around to follow the tracks. Moments later they crossed what appeared to be an abandoned airstrip where they saw the burned-out hulks of four halftracks and snow-ski imprints of a large aircraft which had obviously departed recently.

"Land!" Alex ordered. "I want to check it out."

The pilot shook his head, repeatedly yelling nyet, nyet above the engine noise. There was no time the pilot insisted. "We'll get lost in the mountains at night if we stop."

"Land!" Alex screamed as he pounded his fist on the instrument panel.

Boris turned to the Peruvian and rubbed his forefinger and thumb together. Eduardo held up five fingers.

"Hundreds?" the Russian asked.

"Thousands," Eduardo replied as Boris leaned toward the pilot and offered him half the amount. The Tupolev immediately slewed into a sharp turn and landed.

Ten minutes later Alex's confusion was apparent. A heavy lift transport had obviously been here and left with whoever had been in the half-tracks. But where had they gone?

Toronto, Canada

The phone rang. It had to be his friend from Washington because no one else knew he was here. The familiar voice of Marvin Raoul inquired if this were the famous world traveler Mr. Alexius Balkanovitch?

"When did you get here, Marvin?"

"A few minutes ago. I'm downstairs at reception and will be moving into 2345."

"Great! I'm just above you. They told you I'll pick up your tab?"

"Yeah!"

"Any problems on the drive up?"

"None."

"Look, Marvin. It's almost five o'clock. Grab a couple of hours' rest and let's meet in my suite around eight. We'll have some drinks and then go out for dinner."

"Sounds good. See you then."

Things were looking up. Alex padded to the picture window and sank into the soft cushions as the orange orb of the sun slid toward the western end of Lake Eire. The weather tomorrow promised to be clear, a good day for their drive south. They'd follow Route 219 through Western New York and then east to his mother's place in Altoona.

Marvin had warned him before he'd returned from Russia that the FBI were looking for him, so Alex had flown to Toronto instead. Border procedures at Niagara Falls were more problematical since 9-11, and hopefully no one would notice the return of two American tourists in a Virginia rental car. After Z-5 Alex had flown east and dropped Vitaly Zitalko near Moscow, and while there called General Valeriy Yenisysk, informing him where his subordinate could be found. The General told him they would meet in hell one day. From Rybinsk he and Eduardo flew west across the tree tops into an Estonian airstrip twenty miles from Tallinn on the Gulf of Finland. Visa formalities at the Estonian airstrip were nonexistent and hundreds every month passed through the same way. For fifty bucks everything was arranged and they kissed Boris good-bye and took a ferry across to Finland.

In Helsinki they checked into the best hotel in town and went shopping. Alex needed to return to the States while Eduardo was headed for Peru to follow up on Scotland Yard's efforts to have his father's body disinterred. Over dinner their second night in Helsinki, Eduardo made a business proposal to Alex. He already knew the American's future with his former employer was over and Alex was out of work. Eduardo's business interests on the other hand were substantial and he needed someone with Alex's expertise at his side. He suggested Alex take a month or two vacation to wrap up his affairs, and then join Eduardo as a pseudo business/security assistant or majordomo. Alex liked the arrangement, knew it would give him something constructive to do until he made more permanent long range plans. To seal the deal Eduardo handed him fifty thousand dollars in cash: three months advance pay.

* * *

"You've been travelling I guess?" Marvin asked as Alex admitted him to his room.

"That's an understatement."

"What happened to your face?"

"Some asshole roughed me up one night near Moscow," Alex said. He made Raoul a drink as he recounted the highlights of his experience in Russia.

Jesus." Marvin observed, "Incredible. Especially being kidnapped and then being busted out."

"Did you get the envelope I mailed from Moscow?"

"Yeah!"

"You bring it?"

"I thought it better to leave it at homc."

"Any thoughts about it?"

"Who is this guy called Pavlo Krasnov?"

"He is Paul Carter."

"No shit? I loved the document from Beria to Stalin. A typical James Bond conspiracy. Ian Fleming couldn't have done better. What do you plan to do with it? Use if for a Hollywood movie script?"

Alex didn't appreciate the cynicism. He'd considered telling Marvin about his new job, but suspected Marvin might not understand. "Maybe. By itself the document is incriminating as hell. But I don't think anyone will believe it unless you can get your hands on Roosevelt's original letter."

"Unlikely," Alex replied. "But it mentions the Case Judy conspiracy."

"Sure does! But again, without Roosevelt's signed letter, the question may be dead in the water."

"You hungry?"

"Yes. Let's eat."

Niagara Falls

At noon the next day they crossed at Niagara Falls amidst heavy lunch hour traffic, and were waved through U.S. customs and immigration with only their drivers licenses. By the time they reached Altoona it was half past ten and no one was home. At a nearby gas station Alex called his sister nearby in Tyrone. She told him she'd meant to drive over and check on Mom, but hadn't, and that there was a front door key below the fourth flagstone along the side of the house.

The first thing Alex noticed inside when they entered was the mess, and then the odor. He tried the lights but the power had been disconnected, and so was the phone which lay amidst a jumble of overturned furniture in the living room. The house had obviously been ransacked, and he could feel his pulse quicken as he found a flashlight in the kitchen and checked upstairs.

All Alex could recall later was the sound of Raoul gagging somewhere, and when he found him in the basement he was throwing up. His mother's body had been stripped to the waist, beaten, and strangled with her nylons.

"What are you going to do?" Marvin asked.

"Kill the son of a bitch when I catch him."

"I know, but in the meantime?"

"We'll head for Washington."

"What about the police?"

"Forget the police Marvin! It's too late for my mother! If I'm here when the FBI hears about this, then I'm off to the pokey." He headed for the stairwell. "Be right back."

Upstairs in his old bedroom he pried up the window sill. His secret childhood hiding place was undisturbed and he reached down and removed a 9mm Ruger in a ziplock bag. Further down where he'd left it five years earlier were six boxes of ammunition. He replaced the sill and wiped the area before returning downstairs.

"Jesus Christ!" Marvin exclaimed when he saw Alex fitting the silencer to the Ruger. "You going to start a war?"

"It may come in handy. Come on, we'll stop at some Motel down the road and crash for the night."

The next morning after calling his sister, he and Marvin were having breakfast at a diner nearby when he noticed a red Firebird pull up outside. The passenger got out and after pausing momentarily next to Marvin's rental car, headed for the diner. Alex could make out the driver's black wavy hair and swarthy complexion. The guy at the door paused by the cashier and looked around before asking for change and then left. The Firebird screeched its tires as it pulled out and left.

Ten minutes later as they drove south through the hilly Pennsylvania countryside toward Centerville, Marvin noticed the

Firebird in the rearview mirror. Alex glanced back, his shit detector telling him they were in trouble. "Speed up Marvin, see if he does too."

The Pontiac stayed behind them.

"I got a bad feeling Marvin! Something about my mother's place."

Marvin studied the rearview mirror again. "What do you want me to do?"

"Don't let them pass, and if they try, run them off the road. Take the next left on that country road up ahead."

"What the hell you talking about?" Marvin whined as he noticed the Ruger laying in Alex's lap.

"Just do as I say."

"I'm worried Alex."

"Not now goddamn-it! Just do what I told you."

The Pontiac crossed the double line and pulled alongside.

"Goddamn it, Marvin, push the son of a bitch off the road!" Alex hollered as his window shattered. He jammed the barrel through the opening and squeezed off three rounds. The Pontiac careened off to the left, through a barbed wire fence and came to a halt amidst a swale of young poplars.

"Jeeeesus, Alex!" Marvin exclaimed as they sped away. "This is more than I bargained for."

"Turn the car around. I want to go back."

"What! Are you crazy?"

"Turn around! They're probably unconscious anyway. I've got to find out who they are."

Marvin looked at him in disbelief. "No damned way! We're heading for the nearest police station."

"Sorry Marvin. Can't let you do that. If it turns out they're the ones who killed my mother, then I'll take them into the woods and you can wait until I'm through. And for Christ's sake, slow down before you kill us."

"We are not going back." Marvin's hands were shaking. Gun fights were obviously not part of his stock-in-trade and Alex was afraid his friend might completely lose his nerve. "All right, all right. Head south. And obey the speed limit! They can't run that fast."

"How did they know who we were, Alex?"

"Must have picked us up last night."

Two minutes later, he swore as he looked in the rearview mirror. "The bastard is back! Hang a left at the next road up there."

The Pontiac overshot the turn. "Keep your speed below fifty, and, for Christ's sake, don't lose it! I don't want to be out in some damned cow pasture and up to my knees in cow shit with them picking us off from the road. If you find a straight away, let him get right behind us and jam on the brakes real hard. Make him rear end us. Let's see if we can bust-up his radiator."

As they continued to weave down the narrow road, Alex waited until the Pontiac was within fifty yards and emptied an entire clip at it. Two of them hit the windshield and the Pontiac weaved, lost speed and dropped from sight.

Marvin's voice now was high pitched. "You'd better count me out from here on. Sometimes it's better to ignore big fish unless you got a big hook or lots of dynamite. We got neither."

Fifteen minutes later Alex was sure they'd lost them.

Key Cudjoe, Florida Keys

"My god! What a surprise. I didn't recognize you in civvies, Admiral!"

Lange obviously hadn't driven up from Key West to wish Mike Gregoriou a good day. The admiral's Hawaiian shirt, Bermudas, and sandals clearly indicated his visit was unofficial.

"Nice place you got here, Mike. Mind if I come in?"

He stood aside with a sweeping gesture, watching Lange suspiciously as he passed. "Want some coffee?" Mike asked.

"Please."

"If you'll follow me through to the pool deck." Mike's residence was a hollowed-out Roman design, with a colonnaded atrium in the center which was surrounded by living areas off three sides while a portion of the atrium was a two story screened aviary with hundreds of birds. Behind the house, adjacent to the pool, was Mike's pride and joy—a four-engine Cigarette boat with the unlikely name: Unruled.

"So what brings Key West's admiral to my humble abode?" Mike sat easily across from him as the butler poured coffee for them.

Lange appreciated the younger man referring to him as Admiral, and hoped it was indicative that his host was in a mood to share confidences. "Your recent out of town trip below the Dry Tortugas."

Gregoriou stopped sipping his coffee and put the cup down. "Come again?"

"You've been away for a few weeks."

"Yeah. So what?"

"I wanted to ask you about it. You've been out diving." Lange withdrew a slip of paper and read off the coordinates from the hydrofoil sighting.

Gregoriou's face hardened. "Should this mean something to me?"

"A naval unit reported Heron there. She's registered to your company?"

"Get to the point!"

"Why was she stopped?"

"Engine trouble."

"There were divers in the water."

"So what?"

"It wasn't engine related, was it?"

"Matter of fact, it was Admiral. But I don't reckon that it is any of your business. What's this all about? Washington pissed because we stopped in an area used by the navy?"

"No."

"This an official call?"

"No."

"So?"

"I'm here in my personal capacity."

"Get to the point then."

"As I said, you had divers in the water."

"Checking the screws." Mike smiled.

"There was a man here a few months back asking about U-Boats."

"This man have a name, Admiral?"

"Alex Balkan. You've met him."

"Briefly. So what?"

"Just curious? Balkan is asking questions and Heron is out there with divers out." Lange knew he was not handling the meeting well, and Gregoriou was obviously becoming annoyed.

"Look, Lange! Diving is my business. I've been doing it twenty years. I have an immaculate record. No drugs. No arrests. And no illegal operations. I resent your inferences that I was doing anything other than what I have already told you I was doing twice now. So unless you have something else you want to tell me, I suggest you forget about the coffee and show yourself out."

"Tell me about the submarine, Mike."

Gregoriou began to laugh. "Am I going to have a problem with you, Mister Admiral?"

"I don't think so," Lange replied.

"Am I going to have a problem with your employer?"

"I'm not certain."

"Meaning?"

"I really do not know."

"Then why are you really here?"

"I told you, its unofficial."

"In your personal capacity, as just plain old citizen Lange?"

"Correct!"

"My god!" It hit Mike. This son of a bitch was probably interested in salvage, and maybe planning to double-dip on his employer. "So what are you really looking for, Admiral? You want employment with my company? We don't usually hire senior navy officers, they are too uppity and don't work well with us stupid civilians."

Lange's embarrassment showed. "You've misread me, Mr. Gregoriou. My interest is purely academic. I have no monetary interests whatsoever. However, I believe you might be getting into something you know nothing about, and may be in way over your head."

"Is that a warning, Admiral?"

"Friendly advice if you wish."

"Look, Admiral, I'll tell you what I tell everyone. It all comes down to the law of the sea around here. In my business you abandon your ship on the high seas and I find her. I salvage her. She's mine! Finders keepers, losers weepers! You are sticking your nose into my business and it is not welcome. So—"

"Is she the 2513?" Lange came back at him.

Mike didn't respond.

"You've seen her? Haven't you?"

Again Mike ignored the question. He'd never physically thrown an admiral out of his home. The thought didn't please him. He stood up and pointed toward the front door.

"You are aware of her history?" His guest continued, "When I inquired about her in Washington, a senior associate privately suggested, "I forget about it." Hinting it would be healthier if I did so."

Lange's statement surprised him. Now Mike was intrigued. "So you are warning me?"

"As I said. Friendly advice."

"And why were you advised to forget about it?"

"I don't know."

"Well, Thanks! I think we are wasting each other's time and you know how to find your way out. Have a nice day, Admiral."

Washington D.C.

The phone rang six times before someone picked up the receiver. "Colonel Svoboda?" Alex asked.

"Speaking."

"This is Alex Balkan. We talked awhile back."

"Sure. I wondered what happened to you?"

"I just got back."

"Where you been?"

"Russia."

"What you got?"

Alex's world was imploding. His hand shook as he stood in the darkened phone booth in the gas station parking lot. First they'd killed his mother. Then the road incident yesterday in Pennsylvania. And tonight they'd somehow found Marvin Raoul's apartment while Alex was out getting groceries, and now Marvin was dead too.

"I need a favor Colonel

"Sure."

"A room for a couple of nights?"

"You in trouble?"

"Some. But it will give me a chance to tell you the rest of the story."

"Come on over."

"I'll need a couple of hours to get there."

"There's a magnetic key box under the left front bumper of my car in the driveway. If I'm asleep when you get here, take the first room at the end of the hall, I'll see you in the morning.

Alex and Marvin had returned to Washington yesterday and somehow the red Pontiac must have picked up their trail again, or maybe through the rental cars license plates. Marvin had turned it in this morning, and since there was nothing to eat in the apartment, he'd borrowed Marvin's car to get groceries and run some errands. When he got back the apartment was trashed and Marv had been badly mangled before they'd executed him with a round through the back of his head.

Alex rubbed at the twitch in his eye and could feel his heart pounding in his chest. He had to get a grip on himself. He'd just narrowly escaped death for the third time in a week. If he'd returned a half hour earlier, his brains too would be splattered all over the apartment.

He'd just got off another call with Heather in Salt Lake City, begging her to fly east. She'd agreed to be here Friday night and hire a rental car which they'd drive back to Utah. He couldn't afford to risk flying, and now there was no way he could rent a car without giving himself away. She'd agreed to meet him at Svoboda's place north of Baltimore.

He climbed into Marvin's car and headed south into Maryland's Prince George's County. He had to see General Putnam first, and would chance a late evening cold call to Putnam's home.

At a quarter to three he pulled into Svoboda's driveway and parked as the porch light came on. Alex crunched through the ice and snow up to the old man's door. The stop at General Putnam had gone better than he had hoped. Putnam recognized him but at first seemed reticent to talk. Being polite he'd asked Alex in for a cup of coffee which gave Alex the opening he needed. Alex's discussion with the director of America's second most powerful intelligence organization went better than he'd hoped. Putnam listened attentively and made notes as Alex explained the highlights of his story. The only pained expression was elicited by Alex's mention of the three hundred American prisoners at Z-5. Alex suspected Putnam already knew about them, and if so, realized Defense Intelligence Agency would have much to answer for if all this became public. Alex hadn't confided the part about his plan to have the Russian documents published in the Utah newspapers. That would be Putnam's enema—if the general were double timing him and had devious intentions.

"You look like hell, Alex," Svoboda commented as Alex slumped in a kitchen chair.

"It's been a long trip, Colonel."

"Productive?"

"Very! And if it is okay with you, I'd like to stay here a couple days until my girlfriend picks me up. That is if your offer still stands?"

"No problem. We can use my car to do some shopping in the morning. I have an empty stall in the garage out back. Take a minute and park your car in it so it's out of sight." He handed Alex a key. "Lock the door once your car is inside."

Over brandy and cigars, Alex swore the old man to secrecy and regaled him with events of the last few days and the new information about the submarine and the gold. During their second brandy the old man's head settled against his chest and he began snoring.

SEVEN

The White House

"GENERAL PUTNAM! WHAT is the meaning of this?" The president had deliberately left most of his schedule open for the day so he could do long range planning for the various forthcoming congressional and state election races which needed his help. The GOP still controlled both houses of government and he hoped to change that in the next election cycle. And now this General stood before him, insisting he had something so urgent it couldn't wait!

Putnam was only the director of the Defense Intelligence Agency; not one of the president's senior staff or important legislative peers. Putnam had repeatedly insisted his national security issue was so critical that he had to see the president immediately on a personal basis, and without the normal Pentagon or military service brass coordination. The president would have the general's resignation on his desk by sunset if Putnam's issue was less than that demanded for such an audition.

"My apologies, Mr. President, it's very sensitive!"

"I hope so, general. So sensitive you couldn't prebrief my staff?" the president demanded, his face reflecting his annoyance. The president had already been through the wringer several times over security leaks within his administration and hoped this wasn't the start of yet another. He himself had served in the military and understood the chain of command. Chain-jumpers always started out the same way, and even now he thought of dismissing Putnam and telling him to coordinate his matter with his staff along with his resignation.

"Yes, Mr. President. It is that important."

"A DIA matter?"

"No, sir!"

"The military?"

"No, sir!"

"National Security?"

"No, Mr. President."

"Okay. You have three minutes, General. What's on your mind?"

"An old issue which if not handled correctly, Mr. President, might get into the public domain, and well, sir, I don't think you would want that to happen on your watch?."

"Let me be the judge of what should be in the public domain, General."

"Yes, Mr. President." Putnam's biggest concern was the POW/ MIA aspects of the Case Judy file. These would probably not be the president's concern. In the last few decades DIA had repeatedly been tarred and feathered over the status of prisoners and missing from the Vietnam era. Congressional hearings in the early nineties had created a new organization to attend to America's huge backlog of unaccounted for POWs and MIAs. It too had failed and been repeatedly criticized for incompetence: and most recently two GAO reports which recommended the entire bureaucracy involved be fired and a new program built from scratch. And Alex Balkan's information about hundreds still alive in Asiatic Russia.

Deep down Putnam knew the real issue was caused by Congressional appropriations. The Department of Defense had escaped recent appropriations cutbacks because everyone agreed that good intelligence about one's enemies became more important during times of national emergencies. For a half decade since 9-11 the U.S. military was chasing the Taliban across central Asia and the Mideast while others hid out in Africa and right here in the American heartland.

"Mr. President, an ex-air force civilian case officer named Alex Balkan is about to go public with proof that Russia still has over three hundred of our soldiers who were captured in World War II by the Germans sixty years ago, and maybe others from Korea and Vietnam. According to Balkan they are all that is left of tens of thousands of our POWs who we knew were shipped alive into their Gulag between 1945 to the 1970s. The Gulag, as you know, Mr. President, was the Russian's camp system equivalent of Hitler's extermination camps for the Jews.

"Please, General, give me some credit for intelligence, I know what the Gulag is."

"This man, Balkan, Mr. President, he has proof that the executive branch of your government already knows about this, and has done nothing. He asked me to let you know, Mr. President, that your administration is going to have its—excuse me, sir—its ass in a wringer if you don't take action on it."

"Continue General." Putnam was sweating around the forehead. And well he should, the president thought, this son of a bitch was so far out of line that he'd seriously think about turning him over the Attorney General's office and getting him relieved and put away under section 135 A. 1(d), of a Secret annex to the recent Patriot Act legislation: for spreading unlawful chaos and dissention in the populace. "I am listening."

"Two nights ago this man stopped at my home. In my career I've heard some incredible stories, Mr. President, but nothing this bizarre. So yesterday I checked with various archives around Washington. There was no reference to Case Judy anywhere. But in an old wooden file cabinet on the third floor of building C-3362 at Fort Belvoir I found reference number K39974/4/LD.311 to Celtic Judy. It took a half hour and two more cross references before I retrieved a manila envelope from an archivist, it contained an envelope which had been sealed for over fifty years . . . since April 1944, by order of Pres. Franklin Delano Roosevelt. The file jacket bore the caveat that even after fifty years, only three men in America could inspect the contents: the president of the United States, the director of the Office of Strategic Studies, or the director of Military Intelligence."

"You opened it?" the president demanded.

"Yes, Mr. President. In my capacity as director of military intelligence."

"And?" the president replied, a look of disdain now obvious. Something so sensitive, the president thought it would have occurred to General Putnam that he should have forwarded it to the Oval Office for action. But he deferred to the general who may not have used the best judgment.

"What I saw," Putnam continued, "convinced me that the incredible hair-brained story has merit. There was an agreement between the allied leaders and Hitler. Conceived by Roosevelt—he'd offered tidbits to each of his wartime allies—and enemies too but kept the grand prize for himself. Even six decades later the information is explosive. Fearing others might somehow get access to it, I illegally put the original documents into my overcoat, resealed the empty file with some newspaper, and left.

"So, General, what you are about to show me . . . and speak of . . . has not been coordinated with anyone?"

"Correct, Mr. President." Putnam didn't care much for this man, he'd never served in the military. But Putnam wasn't about to let idiosyncrasies cloud his judgment. How the president handled Celtic Judy was his call.

"You speak French, General?" The president had also learned early in his administration never to screw around with the military's secrets—unless the issue was a no-brainier and something the congress and the American public obviously supported. Gays in the military for instance wasn't a no-brainer. "You speak French, General?"

"A little."

"Maintenant je pense que, Il ya un naf naf sur l'air!" The president laughed coyly.

Putnam smiled too. Deducting the president too realized something was afoot.

"Well, General. I suppose we should get started." He picked up the phone and asked his secretary to ask the National Security advisor to join them. "It'll only take a minute," he said reassuringly to Putnam.

"Please, Mr. President," Putnam insisted, "this is for your eyes only, no one else!"

The president eyed him with obvious annoyance and cupped the phone. "No one? You telling me how to run my office, Mister? You telling me I can't have who I want in the room?"

The General decided he would make one last plea and then fold. It wasn't his call. He was only trying to be helpful. Only four intelligence agencies could report directly to the Oval Office, and DIA was not one of them. DIA reported to the CIA and he feared CIA already had an agenda with regard to Case Judy.

"Mr. President, I have brought my resignation with me." Putnam pushed the paper across the desk to the most powerful man in the world. "Withdrawing an envelope from his inside jacket pocket he placed it on the desk. "I suggest you at least give me the courtesy of looking at this first in private, then show it to whomever you wish."

"Cancel the request!" The president ordered his secretary and slammed the phone into its cradle. "Okay Mister! Go on!"

"Have you heard of Celtic Judy, Mr. President?"

"No, what about Celtic Judy?" The president said as he opened Putnam's envelope on his desk.

Putnam then related the entire story. When he finished, the president turned and looked out the window. "Three hundred and fifty eh? I heard something about this man a couple of days ago. Isn't he the one Moscow's complaining about?"

"Yes, Mr. President."

"I was advised Russia has also requested his extradition for two murders in Moscow."

"As I understand it, the two died during an assault to free him from kidnappers."

"We'll straighten that out later. Give me the file."

A few minutes later he threw the papers on his desk. "I see, and Balkan gave you these copies when he met you the night before last?"

"That is correct," Putnam replied.

"And where did you say this Z-5 place is?"

"Siberia."

"General Putnam. I want to see this Mr. Balkan this afternoon."

"That may be difficult, Mr. President."

"Oh?"

"He's disappeared."

"Dead?"

"Hiding most probably."

"Then find him! You have resources to do that." The president checked his calendar. "I'll be on the west coast over the weekend and return here Monday evening. Have a briefing ready for me at 0800 next Tuesday morning. Just you alone, I'll clear it with the staff. I want to know everything we've got on the Russian question; this place called Z-5, the POW/MIA question. And, General, do it yourself. Here's a number you can reach me at if you have to, I'll accept your calls for the time being.

Thanks was all the president said as he watched Putnam leave. Then he picked up the phone. "I want to see you, pronto!"

He reread the last two documents. The first was a copy of a handwritten letter to the Russian dictator, dated 21 February 1943, and reflected not only Roosevelt's initials but his naiveté. The president smiled at the simplicity of Roosevelt's last line, "This time the world will be made safe for democracy." The president supposed it was true. A half-century had passed and there had been no more world wars. He placed the second memo before him. It was written only a few weeks before Roosevelt died and must have been one of his last.

> Warm Springs: 2 April 1945
> Subject: Case Judy.
>
> Latest coded transmission indicates a second shipment will depart Kiel this week for Asia. Assurances are a third will occur soon, to the destination off SA. Seems Berlin keeps promises. Camps are worse than anticipated. We must distance ourselves quickly from this issue.
>
> Franklin

Christ, the president thought. General Putnam was correct. He needed to be assiduously circumspect with this. Nixon was undone by Watergate. Reagan almost forced out because of Iran Contra, and Clinton for his pecker in the wrong orifice. What would have become of FDR had he survived the war? The document was malevolent. Its subject matter corrosive. And when exposed, the media would have a field day . . . but at whose expense?

The phone rang. "Mr. Seeley is here, Mr. President."

"Tell him to come in."

"I've got a problem, Langford. What do you think of General Putnam?"

"In what regard?"

"Any hidden agenda?"

"He's a straight shooter, Mr. President. One of our best."

"What about his political aspirations?"

"Good god, no! Why?"

"He was just here. Told me a story, which if true, I need to get on it pronto! Three things. You familiar with Case Judy or Celtic Judy?"

"No, sir."

His NSC advisor was among the most astute men in Washington, and the president valued Langford's judgment above most. Seeley had been in the Washington political woodwork since Christ was a corporal; knew everyone, and kept his hand on the national pulse. Langford would know how to proceed with this.

The only son of wealthy nineteenth century Connecticut ship owners, young Langford had attended Harvard Law, and at thirty-two appointed Under Secretary for International Security Affairs. Next followed appointments to the Council on Foreign Relations, Assistant Secretary of Defense, and a tour at the United Nations before the State of Connecticut sent him to Congress for eighteen years. He'd also served on Committees for military appropriations, intelligence and preparedness. Then he left government for a decade or two in industry until the president appointed him as his National Security Advisor.

To say Langford was affluent was an understatement. And a right wing hawk too. His parents left him twenty million in the early fifties. He'd invested wisely in Wall Street, South America and Asia. Then he'd speculated in gold in the early seventies and made another fortune when gold soared to almost five hundred dollars an ounce. He'd taken another quick ride when the Hunt brothers cornered the silver market and rode it up from five to thirty-two dollars an ounce. The president knew Langford's background; he'd seen the FBI work-up before he'd offered Langford his National Security Council position.

"Take a look." The president pushed the folder toward Langford.

"Is this a joke?" was all Langford said a few moments later.

"I don't think so."

"It is very untimely."

"How so?"

"Where did this come from?"

"General Putnam found it." The president provided the highlights of what Putnam said about Balkan.

"These are Roosevelt's original memo's Mr. President. If this were to become public, Mr. President, it . . . Well, just the fact that this guy Balkan and General Putnam brought it to your attention is untimely."

"You've used the word untimely twice now."

"First of all, Putnam had no right to dig into this document. That was your purview—or mine to bring to your attention."

"He was trying to be helpful."

"My ass. Mr. President. This is political. His conduct in this instance is unprofessional. You should ask for his resignation."

"He offered it to me this morning. In writing."

"And?" Langford inquired.

"I told him I would think about it."

"And your other comment about 'untimely,' Langford?"

"State received a request last week from Madrid. The Spanish Ministry of Finance wants to know what we know about the Caballero Bullion." Langford could see from the president's face that he'd better explain.

The president pointed to the file on Seeley's lap. "You telling me there's a connection?"

"Most likely! You've seen FDR's memo regarding the shipments from Kiel. Where did this man Balkan say he got this document?"

"Not Balkan. It was General Putnam who found it, in Fort Belvoir's archives."

"If it were up to me, I'd make discreet enquiries to ascertain the scope of the problem. Then I'd throw that file into the shredder, Mr. President. If the financial markets get wind of it, well, it could be very serious for your administration."

"How serious?"

"Mr. President, as you know this recession is the most serious in our history and may be about to get worse. I don't want to use the D word, but we may be looking over the precipice now."

"I'll take it under advisement. But first I want to know what could happen economically from this. Find someone you trust who can track the Spanish enquiry, and how we should respond to it. I'll also need a legal opinion about the impact of the Spanish request too. What's the worst we could expect from that sort of thing? Finally, there's this matter of the three hundred Americans at Z-5. What do you think?"

"I'd urge extreme caution Mr. President. If we tell the press, they'll go crazy. If we confide in the Russians, they'll deny it. And then there's the man in the street. There's no telling what the public would demand were we to find out this story is true. Pressure to break relations with Moscow could become intense! The Tea Party could even holler for war with Russia over it. Where is this man Balkan?"

"I don't know."

"Pity."

"I asked General Putnam to try to find him."

"Also a pity."

"Langford?" the president inquired. A look of confusion on his face.

"I meant that we do not know where he is at a time like this."

* * *

The son of a bitch! Seeley thought as he walked back through the tunnel toward his office in the old executive building adjacent to the White House. The no-good, goddamn bastard! Balkan had somehow escaped again. He had to be found and wasted. Without Balkan the entire problem would go away like last night's wet dream. The file too was bad news and could bring down America's financial house of cards. The huge Clinton-era surpluses left to the new two-term Bush administration had fostered one of America's most irresponsible spending sprees on foreign adventures, domestic government expansion and an insane unsustainable housing boom. The earlier dot-coms and accounting scandals had initially challenged the American public's economic faith. And now this, and at a time when America's financial house was so vulnerable. But the president had the only copy of the document and must be persuaded to shred it. Langford could feel perspiration soaking his armpits. First Carter's escape, and now this! He wondered what the Russian leader and his cronies were really up to.

By noon Langford was livid and took a couple of tranquilizers to calm himself. State had sent the Spanish request to the Federal Deposit Insurance Corporation in Virginia! Was that logical? Hell no! Even a damned first grader knew FDIC was the wrong place to be informed of it. But could State Department figure out something that simple? Obviously not. But maybe the screw-up was a blessing because it would provide more time. Langford knew Henry Zeugma over at FDIC, and Henry had agreed to meet Langford after lunch.

Just after one, Langford stopped at a phone booth on the corner of Eighteenth and H Street and dialed a number. It was almost a month since he'd last spoken with Victor Indorenko. When the answering machine came on, he said, "This can't wait! See you in three days' time, at ten." Indorenko would know it was a distress signal and know he must be at a predesignated phone booth this afternoon at five o'clock.

FDIC-Ballston

Henry Zeugma was in a quandary. As director of 'F-Dick' as insiders referred to it, as the director of the Federal Deposit Insurance

Corporation, he'd held his post for a year, and it was on days like this he wished he'd never left commercial banking. His latest problem was unlike any he'd experienced heretofore. There was a serious cover-up underway somewhere in the financial markets, and he'd unwittingly become involved.

Only supposed to bail-out one or two failed banks from time to time which had worthless portfolios and were in default, FDIC's reserves of six billion were never intended to bail-out the entire system's two hundred trillion of insured bank accounts—all at once. Most failures in recent years had been averted by forcing the banks with valuable portfolios to assume responsibility for the few that were weak and dying. That way FDIC paidout nothing. But FDIC's widened responsibility in recent years was one referred to as the 'essentiality doctrine.'

Conceived in 1971, and reaffirmed in 2007, the doctrine would save the entire system from collapse. Initially FDIC bailed out an insignificant bank, then they bailed out another four that Congress ordered be saved. Why? Because of inter-linkage. Then came the dot-coms, insurance and the automotive business fiasco with GM. The concept was that when one failed it impacted others which were all interlinked in the markets. The original four Banks were the 11.4 billion bailout of Unity Bank and Trust Company of Boston, the 1.5 billion Bank of the Commonwealth of Detroit, the 9.1 billion First Pennsylvania Bank of Philadelphia, and the 41 billion Continental Illinois National Bank and Trust Company of Chicago. Continental had already been brought down once before by bad loans for utilities, and more recently by bad oil and gas loans. The four had failed because of their single-minded pursuit of growth at any cost. Go for the fast buck because the bigger the banks the bigger management's compensation. The experience made an indelible imprint on Henry Zeugma's mind, especially about how to avoid such failures in the future. But now, as FDIC Director the buck stopped at Henry's desk.

FDIC was once again under stress because of the monstrous housing market mortgages which were worthless. And now there was this gold thing in the background, and Henry did not want to be remembered as the man at the helm when FDIC went tits up.

Ten days ago he'd been called by Parker Quink at state, and told a document was coming over. It was a terse note from the Spanish foreign office in Madrid, enquiring about the whereabouts of the

Caballero Bullion. Henry vaguely remembered the subject from a Freshman college course he'd taken forty years ago as a cadet at the military academy at West Point. But why now? And why had Spain sent it to the State Department? And why was State passing it to Henry? So he'd rerouted the inquiry to the Financial Center with a cover note.

Langford Seeley, the president's National Security advisor had just left Henry's office, and now Henry really wished he'd taken the afternoon off to play golf. Langford Seeley had patronizingly confided that he knew Henry was a loyal American who'd served honorably in the Army: had an impeccable record in banking, and was discreet. There were two things he wanted Henry to do. Fly to Luzerne and find out what the Swiss Bank's future plans were if a financial crisis was afoot. Langford then advised Henry that he was going to be 'read-in' to a SPECAT program about which he could say nothing to anyone—not even to his wife. SPECAT was a special category for government secrets of incredible sensitivity.

Langford handed him a file stamped Top Secret SPECAT, and just below that in large bold handwritten letters: CELTIC JUDY. He asked Henry to read and sign it. Curious as hell what it was all about, his reticence was instantly overcome by his curiosity. He threw caution to the wind and signed it.

That was Henry's first mistake.

The United States stood athwart a financial precipice which could exhaust the nation's gold reserves overnight and undo the existing world financial system a day later, leaving the United States in another Depression. The scenario, improbable as it was, had finally come full circle and now stared him in the face. During World War II the office of Special Services had clandestinely recovered gold from a German U-Boat in South America. There was no genealogy for the gold. So Washington allowed it to be secretly used, first by the OSS and then by the Central Intelligence Agency. By the eighteenth year of the CIA's existence the last of the gold had been expended for its covert operations. The CIA had also disposed of the source of its funds off the Florida Keys. If exposed today, the submarine's cargo and genesis would cause incredibly grave damage to United States national interests. Therefore it could never be disclosed. The file's contents reminded him of the story about the "Boys from Brazil."

Henry had inquired why the problem was being brought to FDIC?

Seeley's response was candid and blunt. The president needed someone he trusted implicitly. After Seeley left, he realized all the SPECAT bullshit was only to protect the guilty. Gold reserves at Fort Knox would be exhausted seven times over if foreigners' debts were repaid with American gold this afternoon. He also recalled his visit last week to New York's Federal Reserve Bank in Manhattan. Five stories below street level, behind a ninety ton door, was a vault with forty percent of the world's gold, thirteen thousand tons worth over $150 billion. Unfortunately three quarters of it too was already owned by central banks of other countries.

And then there were America's treasury obligations. International creditors held nine and a half trillion dollars of it while American institutions owned the rest. Gold covered a pittance of the total, and if creditors all demanded payment, the only way out was to print paper money. FDIC's reserve covered barely a penny on the dollar for American bank obligations. If forced to print money, within a week the price of a loaf of bread in New York would exceed $200 while a gallon of gas would surpass $500. The thought prompted Henry to reach for his Maalox.

Rosslyn

From the FDIC headquarters it took Seeley ten minutes on the Metro to reach Arlington station and Scion Consultant's fifteenth floor offices. The guard behind the desk with the gold emblazoned logo, recognized him instantly and deferentially waved him through.

"How's everything?" Langford asked once Chuck Bunn had closed the door behind them. A few minutes passed in idle chatter while Chuck fawned over his distinguished visitor, hoping he might mention his name to the president and get him the Scion appointment.

"So what brings the president's National Security advisor to Scion on a Friday afternoon?"

"I need your help, Chuck. It is about your man Balkan."

"My man? He's not my man. As a matter of fact he's not our man any longer. His employment has been terminated."

"That's unfortunate." Seeley observed caustically. "When?"

"End of last month."

"For cause?"

"Retired might be more appropriate."

"Too bad. This Russian thing is getting out of hand, Chuck." Langford Seeley emphasized the last five words. "Now it has even come to the president's attention." He let the words slowly roll off his tongue, hoping Chuck would see the advantage of cooperating if he wanted to be promoted into Ted LePage's vacant position at Scion Consultants. "Who did your man see in Europe and Russia?"

Discussing Alex made Chuck uncomfortable. As acting Scion chief, he was supposed to be on top of things and to know what his people were doing, but his predecessor had confided nothing, treating him like a mushroom most of the time. And in Balkan's case, everything between LePage and Balkan had been arranged verbally so there were no written records anywhere. Alex Balkan had also refused to talk to Chuck before he left.

"We don't know Mr. Seeley. We don't hear from Alex anymore." Chuck deliberately used "we," hoping it would draw off any blame prior to his assuming command.

Langford leaned forward. "He's still on your payroll isn't he?"

"Technically, yes! But he has a lot of accumulated leave and sick time to burn off. He's using it up now."

In the ensuing few minutes Langford felt reassured until Chuck's reference to the call from a detective in Key West, in which Alex's name was mentioned in connection to a Peruvian with cartel connections and the missing American called Paul Carter. Turning pale Seeley tried to conceal his discomfort as he chewed on two Tums. It was the first time he'd heard Carter's name spoken in many years. And the finger prints found at the Albion residence in Key West. That sent shivers through him. The son of a bitch was obviously here in the United States and it must have been the Russians who had released him! They'd lied to Langford. But why? Langford thought of asking his Russian case officer, but he knew Moscow would lie about that too. He needed to know what they were really up to.

"Well, Chuck, thanks for the update. Good to see you again. If you hear from Balkan, call me immediately. The president thinks highly of you and I shall put in a good word with him for your promotion. In these times of national peril and the War on Terrorism we need good people in charge."

Adirondaks, New York

"When do you want to go out and get something to eat, Paul?"

"About seven." He was tired and she was the reason. He'd gone for a walk in the woods, and they'd made love when he returned.

Cimeon Kannapolis was twenty years his junior; a cute divorcee with petite breasts, a narrow waist and plump thighs. Somewhere in her background were children, grandchildren and even great grandchildren—two of them. He'd met her by chance last fall at a Bacchanalian Washington festival called Rally in the Alley downtown in the District. He'd recently arrived from Canada, needed a place to stay and after a few dates, had moved in with her.

For him Cimeon was a godsend, because not only did she provide a comfortable place for him to live, but had a car, and with no driver's license it provided Paul with a way to get around during the days when she rode the Metro to her work at an office supply store just beyond the Beltway. When she'd announced she would take two weeks off and spend them at her camp in the Adirondaks, Paul readily agreed to go along.

"What do you feel like for dinner?"

He missed the bland Russian diet. All the red meat and junk food in the States constipated him and chocolate flavored laxatives made him laugh as he thought about the idiocy of it all. Too much food and then chocolate to loosen one's stool. "Whatever pleases you."

"Mexican?"

"Sure!"

The last two weeks at her remote cabin in the woods by a mountain stream had rekindled memories of his interminable years at the Silent Camps along the Ob River where he'd whiled most of his adult life.

"I'll wake you at six." She draped a leg over his waist and pressed her body against him, waiting for his tap-root to probe her copsed thighs yet again. She smiled and gently kissed his throat as his snoring began. It was good to have a man in her life again after a long solitude, even if he was old and slow. Her children had chided her about it but things hadn't seemed to work out until she met Paul. She needed him, loved him in a way, and enjoyed his company and intrusion into her life, but suspected they would never marry. Marriage wasn't in her lexicon anyway, his neither, and she hoped they would remain intimate friends for as long as they enjoyed each other's company.

Later as he watched her primp herself, he luxuriated between the warm sheets. A well-fed woman, sex with a woman, and good food! What else could a man ask for in paradise? And he was still in good shape for an old man, he thought, as he ran his hands down his flat stomach and skinny-sinewed thighs.

Was it almost three-quarters of a century since his eighteenth birthday and the day he'd signed up at the Marine Corps Recruiting Station on Linden Street in Brooklyn? His last day at boot camp seemed like only yesterday, and then he'd been commissioned an Army second lieutenant and sent on his way to his first assignment in the nation's capital.

As a newly commissioned officer he could tell there were serious concerns about Japan's war in China. After a decade slugging it out with Hirohito's army, no one in Washington knew how much longer China would hold out. And if she collapsed there was nothing left in Asia to stop Hirohito's bandy-legged legions. The big question in Washington was where would Hirohito's boys attack next: in Hong Kong, in the Philippines, in Vietnam, or further south at Singapore or even Australia? In those days no one across America cared about anything beyond the United States. Bread and soup lines snaked down streets from New York to San Francisco. Millions were out of work, and for the rest, "peace at any price" and nonintervention was the battle cry—of even the great Americans of that time, like Charles Lindberg and Charles Chaplin. Senior American officers knew it was a question of time before America got involved. And when it came there would be quick promotions for men like Paul Carter. Asia fascinated him so he read up on China and studied the language; memorizing several hundred words and expressions in a few months.

In late 1937, as Chiang Kai-shek's best troops were decimated before Shanghai and Nanking, Chiang's government retreated inland to Chungking. Then the Japanese rolled westward after him. Hong Kong fell next, then Vietnam, Burma, and many of the Pacific atolls and island groups. Paul's superiors sought ways to convince China's warlords to join Chiang Kai-Check's Nationalists. But they would only fight for money and Chiang's treasury was bankrupt. In early 1940 all this was coming to pass as Paul held his first unscheduled meeting with the president in Washington.

Coordinating an assignment at the State Department, the president had asked the Army for a certain Officer's dossier and Paul was asked to deliver it. The president studied Paul closely, interrogating him about his background, interests and capability. The president was intrigued with Paul's experience in China and in particular, his capability with the Chinese language. Days later Paul was reassigned again to China, and during the months it took him to reach Chungking, Paul came to understand Japan's vulnerability. With no infrastructure in China to facilitate fast moving war machines, the lack of roads, bridges, and fuel, quickly bogged down Japan's army and guaranteed China's eventual survival, because she would eventually exhaust the Japanese interlopers.

In the months that followed Paul became familiar with the various Chinese factions and by the end of the year was placed in charge of liaison with coalition warlords. Liaison had only to do with money, and money to the Chinese warlords was gold bullion, not paper. It didn't take long for him to become known as the golden American. But there were others who came to hate him, and in the end he suspected it was one of these who'd eventually done him in. He recalled one meeting in particular which involved a bullion delivery to Chong Ki-Young, the young son of a powerful warlord. The warlord had withdrawn his army from the field, and refused to fight until paid. Paul had finally negotiated a settlement with the warlord's son that angered the father who was then forced to return to a fight which he lost.

Chong Ki-Young had an evil laugh and a cruel streak longer than the Great Wall of China, and when Chong's subordinates failed to bow low enough in his presence, a sudden sword stroke would lop off their legs where they stood. At the conclusion of Paul's last meeting with Chong, the young kid ordered one of his lieutenants to bring the American round-eye more tea. Chong's tone made it obvious that he was angry with Paul and wanted to insult him. The lieutenant correctly assumed his liege's intent and failed to bow respectfully to Paul. That cost the lieutenant his legs. Chong concluded his negotiations with Paul as the legless lieutenant bled to death before them.

Another of Chong's subalterns was an unpleasant bastard named Shu Chan, who'd also taken a strong dislike to Paul and threatened him repeatedly. He ignored the subaltern, but three years later, in January 1943, realized he should not have. It was Shu Chan's troops who had waylaid Paul's mission to south Burma and then beheaded everyone except Paul, leaving him to contemplate his end. But then they had somehow forgotten to execute him.

In August 1940, Paul left China to join General Douglas MacArthur's staff in the Philippines, and a year later, in November 1941, luck again smiled, and he was ordered to carry urgent dispatches to Washington two weeks before the Japs attacked Pearl Harbor. He recalled with fondness the huge Pan American World Airways China Clipper that carried him to San Francisco, and even more fondly, the young stewardess who repeatedly introduced him to the Mile-High Club while in transit.

Mid-December 1941 he was summoned to his second meeting with the president. This time he was asked to undertake a special mission for the president. Two weeks later he boarded a train for Grand Central Station in New York, and spent the next six months working across the street from Rockefeller Plaza at the British Passport Office in Manhattan. In June 1942 he boarded another train at Grand Central, this time for a farm near Oshawa, on the north shore of Lake Ontario. Three months of intensive training in the clandestine arts of demolition, parachuting, murder, assassination, and agent operations at Oshawa made him a lethal weapon of a secret organization called the Office of Special Operations. He then returned to Manhattan, this time to take up work in one of the war's most secret diversions of wealth.

At the end of 1942 he went to Cuba for some final training prior to making his first foreign mission. Two weeks later in mid-January 1943, he was picked up by the president's flying boat at Key West, and before the end of the following month commenced six decades of imprisonment in Soviet Asia.

Falls Church, Virginia,

"It is a call for you, Chuck," his wife called from the kitchen.

It never failed. When he was cleaning up the yard, someone called, and his mobile phone was always buried somewhere beneath a mountain of junk in one of his daughters' bedrooms.

"Who is it?" he hollered.

"A collect call from a man named Alex Balkan."

"I'll be right there!"

Yard work was his Sunday afternoon chore. First Church, then brunch near Tyson's Corners, then the yard. He kicked off his shoes as he entered the kitchen.

"Chuck speaking." He grabbed a pencil off the refrigerator and frantically scribbled down the area code and number where Alex was calling from. Where the hell was area code 402? "You caught me in the middle of cleaning up my property, Alex," Chuck said. "Where are you?"

"Can't say, Chuck, but I have a question though, and I need an answer to it now!"

"So do I, Alex. Lots of them."

"No time for yours, Chuck! Listen or I hang up!"

"Okay, I'm listening."

"When I called a couple of weeks back, you mentioned there were documents that I hadn't turned in. How did you know about them?"

"Which documents?"

"Don't screw around, Chuck! The ones from Novosibirsk!"

"Let me think for a second."

"Don't think, Chuck. Did Ted LePage mention them to you?"

Chuck's mind was racing. What was Balkan really after? Where was area code 402 in the States? He grabbed the phone book and started looking. "No he didn't tell me! Why?"

"Who then?"

"What's this all about?"

"Goddamn it, Bunn! Who mentioned the goddamn documents to you?"

"We need to talk, Alex. When can I see you?" There it was as his finger stopped on Omaha. What was Alex doing in Nebraska?

"You are in over your head, Chuck. Be careful who you speak to about what I was doing."

"You took off in a huff, Balkan, and ever since I've been backstopping you because until you use up your accumulated leave and sick pay, you're still on my payroll. What's this all about?"

"I tripped over a conspiracy."

"Such as?"

"There's 350 American prisoners from WW II who are still alive in Russia. They are all that is left of tens of thousands of them who were shipped there right after World War II, and others during Korea and a few from Vietnam. They were all kidnapped by the Russians and then shipped illegally to Siberia, and we never called the Russians on it. Since then we and the fucking Russians have been suppressing the information about their existence in captivity."

No wonder everyone was pissed, Chuck thought. Balkan's wild-goose chase had taken him off on a tangent into some crazy dead-end. "Who's trying to suppress it, Alex?" Bunn demanded. "Who is trying to kill you? Where are these Americans? Who are they?"

"Answer my question first, Chuck."

"The president's national security advisor told me," LePage replied with an exasperated tone. "Langford Seeley stopped by last Friday. The president is concerned. Moscow has accused you of trying to bribe their ministers." Chuck's expression changed as he spoke. "Hello! Alex! Shit!" The bastard had hung up. Chuck redialed the number in Nebraska.

"This is the Regency Court Marriott. May I help you?"

"Put me through to Mr. Alex Balkan's room, please?"

"Just a moment please. Sorry! There's no one here by that name."

"Operator. I just took a collect call from this person at your number. Please check again."

A few moments later she advised him that the call had come from a room registered to another party. "Just a moment and I'll put you through."

No one answered.

Chuck called Langford's pager and left Alex's current location information in Omaha. Then he returned to his yard work.

Tacoma Park, Maryland

"Hey, baby, hurry up! I need you!"

"Got to shave first," he replied. He'd just finished another of his incredible twenty minute hot showers. God! How he loved American showers and their inexhaustible supply of hot water. You've come a long way he thought as he studied his reflection in the mirror and rubbed shaving cream across the stubble of his prominent chin. It was a strong chin he thought, obviously indicative of a man who'd survived life's worst trials: betrayals, prisons, depravities, and sicknesses. Like most caged animals, it was those who adapted quickest that survived the longest.

When he first arrived in Siberia in 1945, only one in five of the Americans he knew survived the first year, one in twenty survived the second year, and maybe one in a hundred to year five. They'd perished like flies—of dysentery, of starvation, of exposure, or systematic execution. Remembering so many he'd befriended briefly here and there before they perished along the way made him morose. It had all been so unreal, unbelievable, and inexplicable—virtually all believing their country would come to rescue them before it was their turn to die. And now many of their memories screamed out to him from the corners of his mind when in sleep, begging for revenge, accountability, or at least the mention of their name to those who had waited for so long some word of their fate.

As he shaved away the stubble, Paul was pleased with his reflection. At ninety-two, his body was scrawny but muscled. He attributed much of it to his Marine training and a monastic life of self-denial. He flexed his wasted pectoral muscles and studied the sinew beneath the pale white skin. Not bad for an old fart. Most Americans his age around Washington had well-padded bodies inflated by the excesses of soft living and gourmet diets: fat old men with distended paunches and puffed out throats with multiple jowls. The most noticeable change over the years in Paul's appearance was his height, which had shrunk considerably, he supposed because of a lack of calcium. He'd lost six inches and now stood just over five and a half feet.

"Paul baby," Cimeon's voice called. "Hurry up and come play with me, lover boy!"

"A couple more minutes," he called out.

When they'd told Paul last year in Russia that his camp was to be closed and everyone was free to go home, he'd been skeptical. He'd spent the last two decades known to everyone around him as Malin Patel, which for years had become his nom de guerre in the camp; everyone had one. He believed they had somehow lost or misplaced his records about his real identity. The day he was set free, a faceless camp bureaucrat handed him his identity papers, a thousand rubles, a new shirt, trousers, a coat, and an open train ticket valid for thirty days. He'd slowly made his way to Odessa, contacted an old camp associate who'd fixed him up with a passport and boat tickets for passage for Southampton. From England, he'd stowed away on an oil tanker bound for Canada, and then illegally crossed into the States through the woods along the New Hampshire border.

As he turned his attention to his other cheek, he could feel his arousal returning as she called again. Then he saw her reflection in the mirror. She pressed herself against his back, then moved around and sat on the sink before him and hiked her legs around his hips. My god! he thought. She was going to kill him if he weren't careful, and he decided he needed to start pacing himself if he wanted to avoid blowing a head gasket. An old poem came to mind: *The peacock's pride was the glory of God. The goats lust—God's bounty. The lions wrath—God's wisdom. But the naked woman—that was God's work.* What the hell, he would labor once again in God's vineyard and then rest awhile.

There were no women in his Gulag. He'd always wondered where the Russians kept them. Paul had been horny as a youth and wanted every girl he saw on the streets in Brooklyn, even the ugly ones. But girls in those days were proper, and unavailable until one married. Things changed for him when he arrived in China in 1940. His first year on the mainland and then in Manila were an orgiastic odyssey of exploration of the three-haired Asian love-machine. Chang Ming still haunted his dreams. Eighteen and from a well to do Xingtai family, her father had been educated in Italy and had Chang tutored in English, Greek, and Roman history, the arts, western music, and hoped to send her to the Sorbonne in Paris. Paul met her at an official function and danced waltzes with her for several hours. Two nights later she'd opened the petals of heaven for him. There had been others, but Chang stood out in his memory because he'd really loved her and always wondered what became of her once the Japanese moved farther inland in China.

Sated for a while when he returned to the States just before Pearl Harbor, he sought out his childhood sweetheart and married her, only to realize once they were married, regrettably, she viewed sex as, according to her Parish priest, a necessary evil of procreation and to be endured only temporarily to accomplish God's divine plan. The Asian women on the other hand had lived for sex, were unabashed about it, and spent hours and hours in foreplay. Paul's American experience with his childhood bride were brief joyless interludes in a dark room. His normal heterosexual sex life had then ended completely with his betrayal and capture in Burma in 1943.

In retrospect, the first two years of his imprisonment were the worst because nothing in his training had prepared him for the never-ending rounds of interrogation, torture, starvation, and rape which delighted his captors. Reflecting back on his capture, he still couldn't understand why they hadn't killed him along with the others. Why had he alone been spared?

He'd landed with the gold shipment at a remote airstrip near Myitkina on the China-Burma border in February 1943. His flight had been diverted at the last minute to Myitkina, the pilot having been informed by radio that their primary airfield had just been overrun by Communist forces during the night. On arrival at the remote secondary airstrip, he realized the diversion was a trap.

Everyone aboard the two C-47 transports with him were manacled and marched twenty miles to a mountain village where they were held incommunicado for weeks. Then one morning at sunup they were all assembled in a courtyard, and one by one, placed head down on a wooden table, and beheaded. It was the most horrendous experience of Paul's life, watching associates stretched out while sloppy sword strokes hacked at them until heads came away. They saved Paul for last, and just before him went the Englishman named Jack Horner, who'd accompanied Paul on the last leg of his secret mission from Egypt. Horner was a gutsy bastard who'd told his executioner in fluent Chinese to shove their sword points up their mothers' cunts and tickle her tits as they held his arms out and dropped his head into the pile.

Then it was Paul's turn. They forced him face down on to the table while he contemplated the macabre jumble of horrified heads before him. But the stroke was delayed while they toyed with him.

"*Hoondan yaosa teusa!*" he screamed, begging them to get it over with. His executioner then climbed up on the table, his feet straddling Paul's chest, and he urinated on Paul, to the screams of delight from the assembled spectators. Then they untied his hands, pulled him off the table, and manacled him as they led him away. "*Shim hoy pong guo wah,*" Paul screamed. Demanding to know why they had not killed him.

A guard told him a warlord had decided to spare his worthless life.

"*Weh tiang yee pa tsi, dee yee tien*!" Paul replied, spitting at his captor.

The man cautioned him never to tell a great warlord he would see him in hell! "*Junong bouqu whea hantio eho*!" the guard replied. Assuring him his fate was to be worse than the flames of hell.

"*Waite jum mor . . .* ?" By whose order had his life been spared, Paul demanded.

"*Femg xi . . . Shu Chan*!"

The answer stunned Paul. He recognized the name but hadn't seen Shu Chan among his captors. He also hadn't seen Chong Ki Young's former subaltern either for the last two years, not since his days in China. He asked his captor to pass the word to Chong Ki Young that Paul Carter was a prisoner and to come to his rescue. He assured his captor that much gold would come to him if he did as he asked.

The next morning, Paul's grueling decades-long odyssey into oblivion began. Its first chapter only ended months later in the mountains of northwest China, where a three-year ordeal began in a three by five foot offal pit. A second cross-country trek followed in the winter of 1945, which ended at a railroad siding somewhere near the Russian border with China. Two days later a train arrived at the siding and Paul was stuffed into a boxcar already packed with captured Japanese troops who had surrendered in Manchuria. Most of them were sick and dying, and from one of them Paul learned that they'd worked on secret Japanese chemical and biological weapons. It explained why so many of them were now sick and dying.

Seven days later, Paul thought they were all going to die when the train stopped in a snow-covered valley where thousands along the track waited to board. When the doors were opened, chaos ensued. Then the doors closed and the train began to pull away. A riot erupted outside and machine gun fire echoed through the valley. The next morning Paul noted the guards along the tracks were no longer squinty-eyed Chinese, but round-eyed Russians and Mongols. They'd obviously crossed into Asiatic Russia during the night and were now heading west along a spur of the Baykal-Amur Rail-line.

Three days later, the train stopped again and those still able to walk were marched through waist-high snow drifts to a massive fenced enclosure with rows of long windowless earth covered huts. He estimated that fewer than one in eight who'd been aboard the train when he'd boarded still remained when they entered that camp, and the huts only accommodated one in ten of the new arrivals. The rest remained in the open that night and froze to death.

Each hut was crowded cheek to jowl with Europeans and American servicemen liberated of those captured by the Soviets in Eastern Europe, Poland, and Czechoslovakia. By Paul's estimate, there were at least eight to ten thousand men at the camp the day he arrived. The few of the new arrivals who gained access to the huts were shoved and pushed toward the rear to the place of honor for new arrivals—the notorious Parasha. Most didn't care because for the first time in weeks they were warm in the stinking indoor toilet. But during the nights that followed, those who needed to relieve themselves stood in and around the door and urinated and defecated over the prone bodies of the new arrivals, rather than risk stumbling over them in the dark. Each morning those who had succumbed during the night were unceremoniously stacked in the snow outside.

Paul watched and waited, and days later quietly bludgeoned one of the unwary men in a lower bunk halfway thorugh the shed and quietly dumped his body outside with the rest. He'd developed open sores which he knew would kill him if he didn't get away from the urine and feces of the Parasha. Now he would learn the difference between two unfamiliar Russian terms: Kontriki and Blatnyaki—it was a distinction he'd never forget.

Blatnyaki prisoners ran the camp while the Kontriki did all the work. The former were the hardened criminals who used violence to get what they wanted. Kontriki were the political types, school teachers, musicians, bus drivers, monks, shopkeepers; people who basically abhorred violence. Paul's move without Blatnyaki approval was disrespectful for no other reason than he lacked their permission. Several in the bunks around him had whispered warnings which he had ignored. The last thing he remembered were several Kontriki avoiding his stares as he was dragged from his cot and beaten unconscious.

When he awoke he was once again face down in the Parasha.

Two weeks later his salvation came from Pacho. Pacho was a senior Mongol Blatnyaki who'd decided to take Paul for his lover, a role Paul was initially unaware of. So once again Paul was beaten senseless and this time when he came too, he'd been spread-eagled to a plank in a private room where he remained for two weeks while Pacho had his way when he felt amorous. Pacho eventually switched his attentions to a young Chinese boy who'd just arrived. Pacho told Paul he would be returned to the hut and allowed to live if he kept his mouth shut and behaved.

In the months that followed, Paul was befriended by a Ukrainian called Semyon, who taught Paul the skills he needed to survive. Semyon's work was gathering wood for the camp's stoves. The improved food and outdoor work gradually restored Paul's health and his strength returned. But Semyon's friendship, like most Paul would make in the camps over the years, didn't last.

While out cutting wood two months later, Paul heard a gunshot in the woods and ran toward it. He and others were warned away by a guard who'd just executed Semyon for trying to escape. Trying to escape? Semyon lay where he'd been working. The guard gave Paul a sick smile as he passed. They'd obviously killed Semyon because Pacho was jealous.

One of the wood gatherers' responsibilities also included the disposal of the dead each spring. Thousands died each winter, and by spring the heaps of thawing snow-covered cadavers presented a serious health threat to the camp administration. As Paul stood watching the huge funeral pyre consuming the dead one day, he took a moment to sing a new Russian ballad he'd learned:

As I crossed the great lake of Baikal
When whom should I meet but my mother.
Good day to you mother, my dear,
What news do you bring, dear Mother?

Your father's long since in a common grave, my dear.
The grave lightly covered with earth now.
Siberia also knows where your brothers have gone
The cold where their leg irons are clanking.

And when I die, that's it,
They'll stack and bury me too!
And where I die, I'll lie,
No one to see, no one to care!
Yet, in the early spring
A nightingale will sing.

July 17, 1947, stood out in Paul's long prison memory. It was the day he was given his first opportunity to tell a Russian officer visiting the camp who he really was, and that America was Russia's ally during the Great Patriotic War, and so why was Paul in a Russian prison? It had to be a mistake Paul had insisted. That interview had not gone well for him right from the start.

"Sit down!" the Russian officer had bellowed. "And shut your imperialist capitalist mouth!"

Paul sat and waited, realizing from the Russian's collar tabs that they represented the MVD, Russia's State Security police.

"I am not used to being given orders by prisoners, is that understood?" the officer shouted when Paul again politely tried to explain.

"I believe from your dossier that you are number K-8873664. Is that correct?"

"Yes."

"You are certain?"

"Yes, it's the number I've had since I got here. But my real name is—"

The officer withdrew his side arm and forced its barrel into Paul's mouth, pushing it so hard that Paul's chair leaned back against the wall. "I didn't ask you that! You have no name asshole, only a number" was all the officer said. "How long have you been here?"

"A long time," Paul mumbled around the gun barrel. The pain was excruciating as the steel pushed against his tonsils.

"Minutes, hours, days, weeks, months, years? Are you stupid, Kontriki?"

"About two years," Paul replied, "But I was also held in China before that. My name is Paul Carter, I am an American officer, and . . ." his explanation was cut off as the officer withdrew the gun barrel and kicked him in the groin, knocking him on to the floor. The guard by the door smiled, anticipating some fun might be about to come his way.

"We already know that," the Russian replied. "Why are you telling me these lies?" the officer demanded.

"It is the truth!" Paul grunted as he raised himself and sat again in the chair.

"You are lying! Prove it."

"How?"

"Show me your passport!"

"I do not have it."

"Identification papers?"

"They were all confiscated."

"Witnesses?"

"I have none here, but there are many in America who can . . ."

Again Paul's face turned beet red with pain and anger as the Russian ground his boot heel into the arch of his left foot.

"I am an American officer," Paul muttered as tears streaked his cheeks, "and entitled to privileges afforded prisoners under the Geneva Con—" Again he couldn't finish the statement as the guard slammed his stick into his stomach. Moving around behind him he kicked Paul repeatedly in the kidneys.

"And did the authorities not tell you to always keep your documents with you?" the Russian officer asked

Paul looked up at him incredulously.

"Then where are they?"

"Somewhere in north Burma."

"North Burma, how convenient!"

"It is the truth."

"What were you doing there?"

"I was with an official mission."

"What kind of official mission?"

"To see the Chinese."

"Who, about what?"

"To discuss operations against the Japanese."

"What proof do you have?"

"None."

In the next few minutes, hoping to entice the officer with greed, Paul told him the real nature of his mission to Burma, alluding to the fact that some of the gold might still be in the area.

"But you can prove none of this?" the lieutenant demanded. He began to shout that Paul was a liar and that the punishment for liars was six months in solitary. And those prisoners who persisted with their lies were shot.

"We have checked." The Russian spat. "Do you think I come here like some asshole? Someone who you can tell to eat your shit! You lied to me! Do you know who I am?" the Russian screamed. His face inches from Paul's. "How dare you play games with me! I am in charge of sentencing enemies of the State, all those revolutionaries scheming and plotting against the People's Proletariat. You are a revolutionary pig! We know about you, you will be taught a lesson!"

Paul didn't know what to say and frantically tried to remember all the techniques he'd been taught about how to deal with interrogation. "What is it you wish me to do?" Paul asked in a contrite tone.

"Think for a while." The lieutenant rose and left as the guard pushed Paul into a side room. His feet were bound together with rope. Another was forced between his teeth like a bridle bit, and the ends placed over his shoulders and run between his feet and then drawn tight. Paul began to scream as his body was bent backward into the shape of a wheel; his heels almost touching the back of his skull. He remembered screaming so hard he thought his lungs would explode in the seconds before he passed out.

When he regained consciousness it was dark and he'd lost feeling in his extremities. He'd heard of the notorious Swan Dive, but never appreciated its effect. He would have told them anything they wanted to know and then made up stories to meet their every fancy if it would ameliorate the pain.

The next morning, the lieutenant returned and ordered the guard to untie him. Paul couldn't move so they threw him on the floor as his agony began anew.

"Now, I shall read your sentence." The lieutenant picked up a document on the table.

"The Special Council of the MGB in session on July 18, 1947, heard the case of the defendant Pavlovich Krasnov, born 1916 in Sofia, Bulgaria!"

"But I am not this man!" Paul interrupted."

The lieutenant raised his hand. "If you interrupt again . . . more Swan Dive? I have much to do, and if you persist, you will be shot!" He resumed reading where he'd left off. "The accused is guilty of crimes cited in Article 58, paragraphs 4 and 11 of the criminal code of the republic. The defendant has given aid to the international bourgeoisie in its attempts to overthrow the government of the USSR, and by participating in war on the side of the Hitlerite forces. Therefore in the name of the Union of Soviet Socialist Republics, the defendant, a political prisoner, is sentenced to life in the Correctional Labor Camps."

He placed the document on the floor next to Paul. "You will notice it already bears the signatures of the Special Council. Sign it at the bottom!"

"I cannot!" Paul replied.

"As you wish! The sentence stands. For insolence and refusing to sign, a month in the potato shed." The Russian placed an x in the prisoners name block and left the room.

Paul never understood the purpose of that meeting, and still didn't understand it today. They knew who he was because he'd told them everything. Thirty-four years later when he was at the camp near Novosibirsk, he'd been interrogated again by the Russians about the wartime gold delivery. But why had they waited so long?

As they hauled him out of that first interrogation, he swore he would survive, and he had. The potato shed was the closest he'd come to death during his initial years in the Gulag. Designed to break a man's health first, the potato shed eliminated most within weeks. And for those who survived, next came a broken spirit, and finally a useless mind. Those who survived one visit usually did anything to avoid another. He'd seen thousands dragged to them and their cadavers pulled out weeks and months later with ice picks. Log-lined pits twelve feet deep, their only opening was a four-inch hole at the top. In summer their rancid feces-covered bodies consumed half of their victims while a mere five percent survived winter sentences. Paul was among the lucky ones.

In the years that followed, he never discussed his real identity again with anyone, and by the end of his fifth year there were only three left in the camp who recalled that he was ever an American, and they too were all that had survived of thousands of Americans there years earlier. To help survive, he'd learned fluent Russian and almost every one now knew him by the pseudonym of Malin Patel. By the end of his eighth year, his camp had moved four times as the railroad wended its way eastward.

Conditions suddenly improved in the spring of 1953; the administration provided additional rations: an effort was made to improve conditions. The sick were given time off, and everyone wondered if the administration had lost its mind. Rumors circulated that the Presidium of the Supreme Soviet had issued a new law making the murder of Gulag prisoners punishable by death, and for a while Paul thought there was hope he might even be released. The reality was the Russian camp system was in serious trouble because too many had been disposed of too quickly and after the horrendous losses of the Great Patriotic War, new replacements were becoming increasingly hard to find in the post war years. The camps were also no longer able to meet production quotas for raw materials and precious metals. Like a tarantula, they had too efficiently devoured their offspring and the carnage was ordered stopped.

On the fifth of March, Paul's detail was inexplicably recalled from the forest in mid-morning. As they approached the camp he noticed the flag at half-mast. Rumors circulated that the "Great One" back in Moscow had died, and everyone in the camps were confined to barracks until further notice. It was the only time in Paul's memory that prisoners got two weeks off with full rations. Everyone contemplated a better life without Comrade Stalin, and for a while hopes soared. But the old ways soon returned.

Paul's first decade in captivity taught him everything he needed about survival. His first two years in China exposed the futility of confrontation; five years along the railroad, the futility of escape, and the last three, the art of conflict avoidance. He also recalled his significant birthdays when he paused to note events around him. His thirtieth passed along the railroad in Siberia. His fourtieth near Tulun. His fiftieth near Vikhorcvka, the big six-zero north of Kolpashevo, seventy at Buytenlag-23V near Novosibirsk. At seventy, he realized he'd probably never see freedom and became resigned to an ignoble end in an unmarked grave somewhere. In the late nineties, rumors circulated of new and foreign concepts sweeping Russia. He and the other survivors with him were given small plots of land to farm. Gorbachev and Yeltsin came and went with their radical ideas of Perestroika and Glasnost. Paul was resigned to the finality of life, his only wish being retribution against those he knew had betrayed his mission to China a half-century ago. If he made it home in this life, he would find them and make them accountable.

Then it happened. The survivors of his camp were lined up and informed that the Russian government had ordered the camps in Paul's area closed. In three months, inmates would be released. Each would be provided clothing, identification, and money. Paul became fearful that someone would recall who he really was and would not release him. For the first time, he prayed that if there was a God somewhere, that his release would come, and this was not another of the long line of cruel jokes he'd endured in his life.

"Darling! What's the matter?" Cimeon's voice cut into his consciousness. "Your peckers gone limp, lover boy!"

Paul looked down and realized his erection had withered. "Can't concentrate, babe." He kissed her on the cheek. "I need a couple hours' rest. After dinner?"

"I'll be waiting." She placed his hand on her mons venerus. "Think about it until you awake."

Key Cudjoe

Mike Gregoriou was in a quandary. He clicked the remote and froze the video image again of the submarine's sail and walked out onto the lanai: he needed to come up with a strategy. Retired Captain Millican had first aroused Mike's suspicion last year when he'd come into his shop before Christmas, enquiring about U-2513. Then a day later Balkan too had inquired. The only official U.S. Navy record concerning U-2513's disposition reported her sunk by gunfire south west of Key West. Mike had rerun the tape several times and this couldn't be the same U-Boat! On his desk lay the Illustrated Military History of German U-Boats. Page 138 contained a worldwide map of coordinates and hull numbers for all known wartime U-Boat sinkings. Several appeared around Florida. But none existed near the Tortugas. The submarine itself had enough variations which made it certain it was not the 2513. And then there were the mysterious interior pressure hull sections that someone had cut out and replaced. Somebody was looking for something. But what? The welded hatches and missing deck sections beneath the conning tower intrigued him the most. Mike suspected they were the key.

Mike had flown to Miami and poured through the public libraries to learn more. The official navy history about U-2513 stunk the worst and had obviously been fabricated. The official record stated: *She was moved to Key West on 2 September 1951 when the Chief of Naval Operations ordered U-2513 sunk by gunfire. Presumably, that decision was carried out soon thereafter—although the exact date and location of the action is not recorded.*

The navy had fabricated it. But why?

Either the frozen video image of the submarine's sail was U-2513, or another U-Boat, maybe an unrecorded one. He suspected it was the latter. What the hell, he thought! He'd take a chance and see if the admiral was in this morning. He picked up the phone and called the operator. "Give me the number for Admiral Lange's Office at Truman Annex please?" He dialed the number. After the way he'd treated the admiral when he'd visited his home awhile back, he wouldn't blame Lang for refusing the talk to him.

"Admiral Lang's office," a voice announced.

"This is Mike Gregoriou. Would you tell the admiral I would like a word with him?" The secretary told him the admiral was at his residence, packing out of quarters. She transferred the call.

"Admiral Lange speaking."

"Mike Gregoriou, Admiral. Remember me?"

"Sure, Mike. How could I forget. What's on your mind?"

"I've got a question. Last time we met you told me that when you were up in Washington that someone warned you to forget about the subject we spoke of the other day."

"Yeah."

"Any details?"

Lange's response amazed him.

Salt Lake City

Terekli knew that Balkan and the Maldutis woman would show up eventually. Maybe they'd been delayed by the lousy weather between Omaha and Salt Lake City?

He didn't want to miss them when they arrived, so just in case, he'd parked in a handicapped parking slot thirty feet from the apartment building's main entrance where he had an unobstructed view of everyone coming and going. He had no idea what the woman looked like and hoped she'd walk in with Balkan. But even if she came in alone it didn't make any difference, because Vedeno, his associate, was waiting upstairs in her apartment.

Terekli's mission was almost over. He'd accepted the contract to kill Alex Balkan three weeks ago in New York. A half million dollars; split two ways would guarantee his future for many years. His only problem was he'd missed his target several times already, and his victim obviously knew he was being stalked; first at his mother's place, and then along the road in Pennsylvania. Terekli had thought they'd nail Balkan for sure when they'd busted into his friends place in Washington DC. But the son of a bitch had just left, so they'd worked Balkan's buddy over for a couple hours, but the asshole had refused to talk so they'd wasted him. For a while they'd had no idea where Balkan had gone, until the night before last when Terekli got another call from New York. Balkan was now in Nebraska. So they jumped the first flight to Omaha. But again he'd just given them the slip, and from hotel reception they'd got his girlfriend's name and address in Salt Lake and hopped another flight here.

This time Balkan wouldn't get away. Terekli didn't intend to make the same mistake twice.

Adirondaks, New York

Paul had spent the last two hours in the local library pouring through POW reference material when the name Igor K. Severinlik leapt off the page at him. This had to be the same Severinlik he'd known for several years at a Baikal-Amur rail camp. Known then as Iggy. Iggy had moved to another camp in the spring of 1953 and Paul never saw him again.

The article before him repeated the identical story Iggy had told Paul decades back. Iggy had returned to Russia in 1937 to see his relatives, and got trapped when the war started. Iggy survived the war years in the Soviet Union, only to be arrested by the Russians for having no identification when it was all over, and then shipped off to the camps. The article alleged that Iggy was still alive as late as 1970. When the United States demanded an accounting, Moscow denied it.

Paul had befriended Iggy because Iggy was an American who'd lost his passport in a German bombing raid, and when the Russians liberated him in 1944, the poor bastard then had no proof of who he was. The article concluded that according to a high-ranking American bureaucrat in the POW/MIA accounting program, that Valeriy Yeniseysk's information had to be correct. After all, Yeniseysk was one of the prime movers in the American/Russian POW/MIA Agency. The bureaucrat concluded that at most, there might have been ten Americans still unaccounted for throughout Russia since World War II, and that while allegations that tens of thousands were there, without forensic proof of this, such as dog tags, DNA, identification cards, and such, there was no proof to support the charges.

"Christ!" Paul exclaimed aloud. "On that basis, the Holocaust also never took place!"

He noticed the librarian sitting next to him was giving him a stern look.

"The son of a bitch is a lying whore." Paul muttered. He recalled seeing piles of American ID cards and passports and other documents being burned by camp officials.

The librarian cleared her throat. "Excuse my English!" Paul quipped.

"I'm sorry, sir," she told him, "Patrons are not allowed to use vulgarity like that. And library patrons are only allowed fifteen minutes on the microfiche readers. There are others waiting."

"I'll be done in a moment!"

"I'm sorry," she insisted officiously, "but your time is up."

Up yours, he thought! He checked his watch. He still had a quarter hour before Cimeon would meet him in front of the library. They'd driven into Johnstown this morning for provisions and she would return for him at noon. A cold front had moved through the area and there wasn't much else to do on a cold rainy day. Paul was going to finish the article and the librarian could go play with herself. She finally moved away.

The article concluded that all liberated World War II American prisoners were repatriated after the war, and the few still missing were those unable to substantiate their identity. Paul didn't buy Yenisekysk's assurances. Paul recalled the three thousand odd Americans with him in the Siberian camp in the late 1940s. They'd all perished in the years and decades after the war. He also recalled a guard at one of the Siberian camps who'd himself been imprisoned. That man had told Paul about another camp in the Arctic two years earlier, where thousands more Americans from the Korean war were disposed of.

All those in the camps had seen such atrocities many times. Camp inmates were nonpersons. Their identification documents and personal possessions were stripped away and destroyed before they were entrained. And when they arrived at remote locations deep in Asiatic Russia and Siberia, additional searches rid them of last vestiges of identification. The camp guards were deities who did what they wanted, when they wanted, and to whom they chose. And when there were not enough rations to go around, the weak were field stripped and marched off to some remote place and disposed of. Interrogators made prisoners eat their own documents: one another, and even their own excrement.

Guards and prisoners were all condemned to the same fate, but the prisoners died first. Paul had seen six-foot-high piles of identity documents doused with gasoline and burned at one camp. At another camp he'd seen rooms full of confiscated letters, books and other contraband taken out and also put to the torch.

Paul glanced around him in the silence of the library and grimaced. Americans! He thought. What did they know? They didn't want to know about such things. Americans were naive and almost childlike regarding conditions beyond their own borders. To an American, it was inconceivable that their local police department might indiscriminately arrest thousands of their neighbors each morning; dispossess them of their identification, money and other valuables before lunch, and then cram them into empty freight cars destined for unknown destinations where they would be murdered in mass graves. And those who resisted, they and their women and children were summarily executed by gunfire where they stood. Who would believe such a thing possible? And if someone did such things in America, American's reasoned the legal system would provide attorneys to represent and protect the victims who could sue the police involved and have them sent away to prison instead. The first Russian officer who'd interrogated Paul in 1953, stood out most starkly in Paul's memory. Paul had told him that as an American Paul had legal rights. The statement had obviously stunned the Russian who struggled with the incredulity of the concept for a couple of moments.

Later that evening Paul and Cimeon sat before the fire sipping brandy. She was a good woman. She'd accepted him for what he was without too many questions. Didn't want to know about his past, or what problems he many have . . . even if he were previously married. He'd told her nothing about his background, only that he would get around to it eventually because it was too painful. They'd been here two weeks already, and the day after tomorrow she'd start back to Washington. She had to be at work Monday morning. Paul had enjoyed his time in upstate New York. In many ways the area reminded him of his last camp along the Ob River in Asia. But here there was no barbed wire or guards.

Lucerne, Switzerland

At two meters five centimeters, Henri Dagobert easily outpaced his shorter assistants as they walked along Kapelgasse into the Korn Market in Lucerne's old town section of the walled city. The weather was already unusually warm for early May. The snowcapped Titlis mountain behind Lucerne reassured Henri that some things in his life had not changed. He pushed back his dishevelled main of white hair from his craggy face, and stopped before a store front, checking his reflection in the glass to see if his tie was straight. He wondered why he even bothered. It was only an American he was about to meet for lunch and most of them were poorly dressed.

From one of Lucerne's oldest families, the Dagobert name dated to one of the most senior trusted Knights Templar's who fled France in the thirteenth century. And Henri, as the eldest son in the direct line, was entrusted with his genealogy and the knowledge of the origins of accumulated Templar wealth in Switzerland. Regrettably the rest of the senior Templar leadership had stupidly remained behind in Paris in 1312, were arrested, and then executed by the bankrupt French monarchy. Few in today's world bothered to reflect on how Switzerland had become a world banking center so many hundreds of years ago. In earlier centuries, rumors had circulated about it and still did today. But without confirmation from those with the secrets, few had a basis upon which to explore or challenge the disposition of the Templar's treasure which had so suddenly disappeared in the thirteenth century.

"Herr Dagobert," his assistant continued as they traversed the Korn Market, "our estimates of our exposure in the U.S. subprime catastrophe is conservatively two to three times what U.S. authorities suspect. So our issue with the recent arrest of our representative in Washington is more serious, especially if the Americans push the question of tax evasion. A way should be found to quickly end it with the Americans. They too have their problems and will probably react positively to our assurances to help them quiet their troubled financial markets."

"Do not preach to me," Henri scolded him. "I have been in this business before you were conceived."

They turned the corner, the river now in sight as he moved the last one hundred meters to the tree lined river bank. Henri's favorite place for lunch on such nice days was in the shade of the Japanese Walnut trees that lined Lucerne's riverfront. Today he knew the nearby Kapellbrueke covered bridge and Jesuit Cathedral across the river would comfort him, reminding him of the two things he would have to play at with his guest over lunch; defeating his enemies without a fight and the politics involved therein. The former because of its simplicity had stopped Lucerne's enemies in the last four hundred years from harming the city. And the latter: because when its worst enemies, like the Jesuits, became difficult, the city had ostracized them. The Jesuits secretly suspected the origin of the Swiss banking systems' wealth, and who its earliest depositors were. It was no secret that the Knights Templar's loss of Acre in 1291 and the disappearance of Acre's immense treasury took place the same year that the three areas of modern Switzerland, Schwyz, Unterwalden, and Uri, first agreed to form a political union, with a new mint in the Alpine town of Sion. In the intervening centuries, the residents of Lucerne had gradually become uncomfortable with their relationship with the Jesuits and ordered them out of Switzerland. Two years ago, the city fathers asked the 160,000 residents of the Canton of Lucerne to vote yes or no in a referendum: "Should the Jesuits be allowed to return to Lucerne and reopen their church and missionary endeavors beyond Switzerland's borders?" It had passed by a two-thirds majority.

The damn Americans on the other hand were now also trying to pierce Switzerland's legendary bank secrecy laws, much as had the Jesuits and then France's King Louis the XVI eight hundred years earlier when he sought to confiscate France's Knights Templar's wealth in 1307. Henri wondered what Washington's real issue was this time. Henri was the bank's main commodities trader and followed the investment strategies created by his superiors. For thirty years, he had made the bank wealthy, but then came their entry to the American market and things in other areas of the bank's portfolio had become cash-cows. It was these cash-cows that were now a serious problem. The Yankees were such sanctimonious bastards! Henri found these people from the colonies immature and alarmingly curious. They were unrestrained, childish, and aggressive. They spoke loudly, called aloud to each other across crowded rooms, wore sloppy clothes, pushed their opinions on others as if they were in charge of everything, and bragged incessantly about how much they had and how much money they made.

A Washington court had recently ordered the arrest of Stefan Altman, Union Banque Swiss's U.S. representative for North America. The Americans said he was helping his American depositors to avoid income tax by placing their funds abroad. Henri knew it was all so much horse dung, but still had to be taken seriously. Even Mitt Romney, a past governor of Massachusetts had Swiss accounts. American shenanigans had already hurt Swiss banking interests when Zurich agreed to reimburse WW-II Holocaust victims for one and a half billion dollars in damages for long-dead gold deposit accounts. Now it seemed new exposures regarding failed U.S. subprime market operations might be more serious than first advertised. Henri's young assistant had just clarified for Henri that the original UBS exposure estimate of one hundred and thirty eight billion dollars was ultra-conservative. Henri knew the real truth lay far beyond this and hoped it would take his assistants and the bank's auditors many months to realize it.

UBS alone had a conservative sub-prime exposure of just over seventy billion, two and a quarter times UBS's equity reserves. If the American economy continued to decline, Henri knew it could kill UBS and take most of Europe's large nongovernment banks with it. Unlike American banks, all of Switzerland's banks were private institutions with no government backing. Had there been no FDIC in America the current crisis would have brought on another Great Depression. It was always easy to take risks at the poker table when someone else had to pick up the loss. The specter of UBS's failure terrified Henri. Not in his memory had such a possibility existed in Switzerland's history. Across the Atlantic he knew U.S. real estate mortgage defaults were serious and that only two U.S. mortgage giants remained: Fannie Mae and Freddie Mac. If loans were called on the others they would collapse. And even in the case of Fannie Mae and Freddi Mac, their combined reserves of about eighty billion dollars was all that underpinned a troubled obligation of six trillion—less than a dollar per seventy exposed. As a young man he'd spent a couple of years with one of the major U.S. investment houses in Manhattan and learned a lot about risk management—American style.

Henri stopped at the river front and dismissed his associates before turning down-river along the cobble-stoned roadway to Hotel de Balances where his American visitor waited. Moments later the hotel's maitre-d' showed Henri to a river side table.

"Henri, I'm Allistaire Bancroft," the American said. "My boss, Henry Zeugma at FDIC, sends his warmest regards."

"I appreciate that," Henri replied, noting dourly that the American did not even have the courtesy to use his family name. Henri nodded to the headwaiter that he would have his usual midday schnapps. "And what brings you here this fine day?"

"You," Bancroft replied.

"Me," Henri said with feigned surprise.

"We know how serious the subprime issue is. We know your exposure. We know how serious it is for UBS and other major European banks like Deutche Bank, Royal Bank of Scotland, Banco National de Lavoro in Italy, and scores of others."

"And?" Henri inquired testily. Hating emissaries like this who loved to overplay their roles.

Bancroft smiled. "The tide has obviously gone out, Henri, and UBS has been swimming without a bathing suit."

"So what," Henri replied. "Everyone has been skinny-dipping it seems, otherwise why would you be here pointing this out to me? As you Yank's like to say, what's the bottom line?"

"No more UBS write-downs until the fourth quarter of this year," Bancroft almost whispered it as he leaned forward over the table to make his point. "We know you are in the market for new financing. We know it will be forthcoming from "certain interests" in the Middle East."

"You do?" Henri smiled mirthfully. "And may I ask who?"

"It's a small world Henri. Sheikh Seyyed of Abu Dhabi. A first cash infusion of twenty-two this week and a second and third within a month."

"You are well briefed," Henri complimented the American.

"We have to be. This is one of those times when we sink or swim together. But the infusion will only stabilize your asset base for the time being. You guys fucked up!"

"Please avoid such language," Henri interrupted, "it is offensive to me."

Bancroft continued. "As you wish. We made mistakes too, but we are not the one in critical condition here. In the last two years your balance sheet equity ballooned twenty percent to 2.6 trillion Swiss francs, and as of last December your assets were sixty times greater than your equity, making you the highest leveraged bank in the world."

Now Henri knew where Bancroft was going. The Americans needed his cooperation to save themselves. All Bank assets had value, but if that value suddenly declined, as was the case with the U.S. sub-prime mortgage disaster, it left the liability side of balance sheets covered with red ink—red ink that could only be offset by new cash or equity infusions. UBS's bank's shareholders had already made their opinion known a month earlier when seven thousand shareholders gathered at a stockholders meeting in Zurich and cashiered most of the Bank's leadership.

"If you do not acknowledge the reality until the end of this year" Bancroft concluded, "the international market will have time to recover."

Henri laughed. "You know what really happened at our recent stockholders meeting? It's true that all the senior leadership got their notices and now we have the Swiss Federal Banking Commission all over us."

"Henry Zeugma knows this. He and the president do not want to see Switzerland's biggest bank fail. The UBS's shares have already lost half their value. Your new management team will know how to avoid more write-downs. Just pass the message quietly to them, and FDIC will reduce your exposure in the United States."

"What?" Henri asked. "What does that mean?"

"Things will be arranged for Stephan Altmann, your UBS guy under arrest. It is all a mistake, a misunderstanding of our complicated tax laws. The charges against him and UBS of tax evasion and such will be resolved, but it will take a while. UBS's name will be cleared. Henry told me to make sure you understood this. We need your cooperation on the write-down question. If you cooperate everyone will be better off and we can get back to business as usual.

"And the Arabs?" Henri asked.

"Don't worry about them."

"What do you mean?" Henri demanded.

"Jesus . . . Henri. We are the Arabs! And . . . they are in this with us, up to their necks, and they know it. More expensive oil will replace most of their medium term investment losses, but it will take a few years. In the meantime they can either lose it all, or cooperate and graduate with us. The FDIC's exposure right now exceeds almost a quarter trillion, a potential bad debt of almost a thousand dollars for every man, woman and child in the U.S. If not controlled it will create a creditmeltdown. If we and you fail, then the Arabs fail big-time too."

The White House

"Have a seat, General Putnam." The president pointed to one of the chairs before his desk. "Langford will join us in a few minutes. You have a good weekend?"

Putnam suspected the president knew he hadn't. "Yes, Mr. President."

"Good. What have you got?"

"Three items, sir."

The president leaned back, hoping what he was about to hear would put his mind at rest.

"If there were three hundred and fifty Americans there, it is important we get an accounting for them this time. Mr. President, we abandoned approximately thirteen thousand of our captured prisoners to the Russians when World War II ended, maybe more."

"What?" the president replied. "What is the exact number?"

"Uncertain. Some say thirteen thousand. Others as high as twenty or more thousand."

"I was not aware of that."

"Most Americans at the time weren't and still are not, Mr. President."

"What happened?"

"Following Yalta, we agreed to exchange all prisoners liberated from German cages by our respective armed forces as the war drew to a close. Some ninety thousand American servicemen were liberated by the Red Army from German POW camps in the eastern areas of the Reich during Russia's five month final push in early 1945. Many of these men walked west and eventually reached our lines. Many died during the march. At least sixteen to twenty thousand however were physically shipped east into Russian holding camps to await the cessation of hostilities, and of those, 2,900 Americans were eventually turned over to our liaison personnel in April 1945 in the port area of Odessa."

"The problem, Mr. President," General Putnam continued, "was a Russian law passed about six weeks after the Germans invaded the Soviet Union on June 22, 1941. Stalin enacted Law No. 270. It stipulated that any Soviet soldier becoming a German prisoner was automatically guilty of treason against the Soviet motherland and prescribed two penalties: death for Officers and imprisonment at hard labor for 25 years for the enlisted.

My research indicates that while all Russian POW's knew of the law, few in the spring of 1945 really believed Stalin would apply it when the war ended. But Stalin did, and reports from our American escorts with the first groups of Russian POW's returned by us to Soviet control, confirmed the validity of Law 270. NKVD troops and political-commissars shot most of the returnees in plain sight of their American escorts at the turnover points. These executions went on day after day for almost two solid weeks before this news reached our Russian POW cages in France. Then chaos erupted. Russian POWs under American control refused repatriation. They staged mass camp breakouts and mass suicides. In one incident over six hundred Russians died. The British were the first to agree to involuntary repatriation, and shortly thereafter we followed suit. In the end almost one point seven million Russians were forced across the embarkation lines to Soviet control."

"Can't you speed this up a little, General?" the president asked. He had never served in the military and didn't care about all the minutia. All he wanted was the bottom line.

"All right. When Stalin learned of our breach of contract regarding repatriation, he—"

"But you said the Russian POWs refused."

"I'm stating the facts of history, Mr. President."

"All right. Get to the bottom line."

"Throughout the war, the Red Cross visited all of Germany's prison camps holding Americans. In December 1944, we knew they were holding just over 93,000. We had their names, ranks, service numbers, and American address from the Red Cross lists."

"And?" the president interrupted.

"Five months later the war ended and when our final accounting was made, comparing the names on the German lists with those we recovered alive, 17,870 of those who were alive in December 1944 had suddenly become unaccounted for four months later in April 1945. The total was probably five to eight thousand more as none of those captured in the Battle of Bulge had yet shown up in their camp records system.

"And the bottom line?" the President inquired.

"We informed the Russians we were concerned about these men's whereabouts, but Moscow denied any knowledge of them and continued to do so through the end of 1945 and into 1946. They never did admit they had anyone. So eventually the State Department and Provost Marshall realized we were not going to get them back from Stalin, and we had to tell the families something. So toward the end of 1946, we declared them all killed in action and their bodies not recovered. The technical term was KIA/BNR, and the men's families were then so advised. But behind the secret stamp, in the late 1940s we knew they were still alive somewhere in the USSR."

"Jesus, and you think the men reported in Russia at this place called Z-5 are some of them?"

"Yes, Mr. President."

"Why did Stalin do it?"

"We told him we had returned all of his Russians held by Germany and us. Stalin obviously did not believe us, so he held some of our troops as hostage, I suppose. The reality is that we secretly held back almost half a million of them who we quietly resettled around the world and we never admitted this to Stalin either."

"Jesus Christ, this is outrageous."

"I know," the general replied.

"The question is what do you want to do with it . . . Mr. President?"

"What else?" the president demanded with frustration.

"The latest information from AFDIL, the Armed Forces DNA Identification Laboratory in Maryland, in addition to the seventy-two thousand missing GI's from the Second World War, they list another 8,100 from Korea, 1,950 from Vietnam and about 130 from the Cold War."

"Enough . . . enough, General! Let's move on."

Putnam continued, "The question of the camp called Z-5 is next. Mr. President. Sir . . . it's located in the Nagorye mountains facing the Chukch Sea in northern Siberia." Putnam pointed to the location on a map he'd placed before the president. "The Ugatkyn is the largest of five tributary rivers converging east of the town of Ust Chaun on the Bay of Chaunskaya Guba." Putnam pointed to the town. "The largest town in the area is Bilibino over here. It's two hundred miles away.

"What do we know about Bilibino, General?"

"Not much. Its claim to fame is a secret nuclear power plant located in the rolling hills about thirty five miles behind the coast. It's a huge four unit complex contains twenty nine reactors which produce forty percent of Russia's weapons grade fissile material. If we ever go to war its on our strategic target list for a two megaton surface weapon."

"General, just tell me what I need to know about the problem at hand."

"Sorry Mr. President. Population density across the region is sparse, less than one per ten square miles."

"No wonder the Russians put the camps there," the president quipped.

"Yes, sir. As for the camp known as Z-5, it was, or still may be part of the Sev Vostochini Administration. In the 1960s, there were fourteen complexes in the area which contained a total of two hundred and eighteen camps and a grand total of about twenty five thousand prisoners. In the early 1980s, fourteen camps were still operational. Today I believe that one or two remain. And one of these may be where our Americans are rumored to be."

"How do you know for sure?"

"Satellite imagery indicates hotspots where human habitation can still be detected; such as heat from buildings, road traffic, etcetera. Current imagery indicates only two probable sites, and I assume one of them is the camp Alex Balkan visited. It's here." The General pointed to a mark he'd made. "It's one of the hotspots I mentioned."

"Who controls the area?"

"It is a military area, Mr. President."

"Which military?"

"Russia's, sir. It's still part of the Sixteenth Military District."

"Don't we have a source out there, General, someone who can confirm this for us?"

"Ground assets you mean?"

"Of course."

"Unfortunately not."

"CIA?"

"Maybe. But I don't think so. The military controls the region, but they have nothing to do with the camps."

"Who does?" the president asked.

"The FSB, Russia's former KGB."

"Okay. What else have you got?"

"My last item. What became of the people who were there?" Putnam placed a large aerial photograph before the president. "Imagery taken last Monday confirms what Balkan told me. No activity can be detected at the Z-5 cite now. I asked a National Military Intelligence Collection Center analyst to take a more exhaustive look, and he also reconfirmed Balkan's data. It seems the camp was evacuated sometime within the last few weeks. The analyst detected four vehicles parked at a remote airstrip thirty miles away. But aside from that, nothing." Putnam placed another photo on the table in which he'd circled the image of the vehicles. "The airstrip is seldom used, but from this next photo you can detect the traces from the landing and takeoff of heavy aircraft."

"What type?" the president demanded.

"From their depth and footprint, probably an Il-76."

"Any idea where it might have gone?"

"We don't have the air tracks for it yet. But I've got someone digging into old satellite imagery. Something should come up."

"It is important, General. I want to know where the goddamn thing went! Also if there were prisoners aboard. Were they ours? I need to be absolutely certain, damn it! No more intelligence failures!"

"I understand, Mr. President." And he really did. The events of 9-11, Iran's nuclear weapons, Iraq's weapons of mass destruction, and endless unresolved conflict in Iraq and Afghanistan highlighted America's inability to orchestrate successful end-games. In the halls of international power America's current leaders were perceived as rogue cowboys bitten by some mad varmint from the plains of Texas or craters of Hawaii. They behaved more like the leaders of third world countries like Nigeria, Ethiopia, and Somaliland. "From the graffiti Balkan alleges he saw at Z-5, it is reasonable to assume Americans may have been there."

The president rolled his eyes in disbelief as his phone buzzed and Putnam waited while he answered.

"Good, ask him to come in," the president said.

The National Security advisor looked fatigued and the president assumed Langford had also been working the same problem over the weekend.

As Seeley took a seat across from the president, Putnam reviewed the highlights for him again. The old man's interest perked regarding the transport at the adjacent airstrip. "Could be something to the story." Seeley observed. "How soon will you know where the aircraft went?"

"Day after tomorrow."

"Anything else, General?" Seeley asked in a suspicious tone.

"That's it."

"We appreciate the input," Seeley replied. "Thanks for stopping by," he said without looking at the president. "Will you excuse us, General?"

"Yes, thanks, General Putnam," the president added. "See me as soon as you have more information."

"What have you got, Langford?" the president asked as Putnam showed himself out.

"Not all good I'm afraid." He hoped that by now his Russian contact had already arranged for Balkan's extermination in Nebraska. Chuck Bunn had left a message on his answering machine last night about the call made from the room registered to the Maldutis woman in Omaha. Whomever she was didn't matter. If she was travelling with Balkan it would be one more corpse that wouldn't make any difference at this point.

"Conditions at Kiev continue to deteriorate. Moscow is getting concerned."

"Why?"

"Moscow saw our hand among the rebels in Georgia fighting Russian troops. They see our hand in Kiev. Moscow is concerned about continued access to its warm water ports in Crimea."

"I do not have time for this, Langford. Some other time. What else?"

"There's a couple of loose ends which will have to be tidied up concerning what the General just told you. This assumes, Mr. President, that you have decided not to go public with this issue."

"You referring to the coverup of the POW thing, Langford?"

"No, sir! I'm referring to the ahhhh, the economic impact of the Spanish claim."

"Oh! Okay."

"In the instance of the first two gold deliveries, Mr. President, the United States would be considered to be an accessory to conspiracy. Even though we did not benefit from it materially or otherwise."

"We'd still be liable for damages?"

"Correct. It will take years to get through the courts, and the outcome would probably fall to the next president."

"And the last?" the president inquired.

"It is the most damaging. The OSS was supposed to have unloaded the cargo off South America right after the war. That is what they were supposed to do. But because of technical difficulties at the time, ahhhh, involving the 'Schechter thing,' they brought the damned submarine here to the States."

Seeley went on to explain that midway through the war, Germany developed a new cypher which defied our code breaker's efforts to decrypt. Developed by a German called Schechter, the code was unique and only used in reference to a single submarine's operations. When the war ended, America captured part of the Schechter's research in the Baltic port of Keil and were eventually able to decipher some of his war-time traffic pertaining to the final disposition of the unique submarine. What queered the problem however were the Russians. Thinking they'd captured Schechter's entire research, the Russians went on to developed their own postwar code around it. The Russian's used these codes throughout the Cold War, enabling the United States to read most of their diplomatic traffic. Realizing this, the United States needed to compartmentalize the Schechter's association with the submarine in question.

"So we were both able to figure out where the submarine was sunk in South America?" The president inquired.

"Yes, sir. But we got there first. Moved it, and the Russian's never figured it out."

"They never suspected?" the president asked.

"Don't know. They probably assumed her skipper sank it in the wrong place. And for the next twelve years Moscow used Schechter's code without realizing his basic research had also been compromised and we could read their mail. So we said nothing."

"Jesus," the president muttered. "Where is it now?"

"The submarine?"

"Yes."

"Even that is not certain, Mr. President. The navy attended to it and reportedly sunk her near Key West."

"Jesus Christ! In our own territorial waters?"

Seeley nodded. "Unfortunately."

"Christ! Who else knows about this?"

"Right now, no one."

"For how long?"

"We may have a break. The navy doctored its records and recorded her as the U-2513—one of Germany's last production types, which was brought here for exploitation. It's on the bottom somewhere near Key West."

"Who knows exactly where she is?"

"No one at the moment."

"Even the navy?"

"No, sir. There may still be some alive who participated in her sinking back then, they'd be the only ones. We're trying to locate some of them right now."

"Incredible! Why didn't the navy just take her out and deep-six her in mid-Atlantic?"

"We'll never know, Mr. President."

"Anything else?"

"I spoke with Henry Zeugma at FDIC about the economic impact. It is bad! Damage claims could run into the trillions. Even more once it gets into the courts. The numbers are enough to cause a financial panic. This must be avoided at all costs."

"I want it in detailed estimates, Langford."

"Yes, sir."

"Is that it?"

"One last niggly detail, Mr. President. It seems Balkan also started asking about this submarine in Key West last December. Some people down there now believe something fishy happened."

The president leaned back. "So we do have a problem then?"

"Maybe. But I believe its manageable. There's an Admiral down there who took a keen interest in the subject after Balkan left, but he's been reassigned to U.S. Sixth Fleet Headquarters in Naples, Italy, so that takes care of him. But there's also a commercial diver there who supposedly knows where she is. It may be difficult to get him reassigned like we did to the admiral."

The president's face blanched. He hated conspiracies.

In the next few minutes Langford revisited the subject of the applicable laws of the sea as they related to such matters. Wrecks in international waters had traditionally been open game, but more recently the laws had begun to change. Individuals and governments increasingly were able to lay financial and humanitarian claims on cargoes, hulls and even the human remains aboard. He also covered the navy's record regarding the U-Boat's disposition. The president thought the record screamed of conspiracy and couldn't understand why someone hadn't already blown this wide-open years ago. "So if someone could raise her, and prove she wasn't 2513, when the navy said she was, then we'd have our ass in a sling?"

"Yes, Mr. President."

"Is the gold still aboard?"

"All of it was removed. But we can't be sure. They might have missed some."

"Jesus." The president observed. "Jewish gold stolen by the Nazis, Spanish gold heisted by the Russians, then illegally misappropriated by our navy and spent by the CIA for clandestine operations around the world . . . while tens of thousands of our boys were worked to death in Russian camps after the war? If ever there were a smoking gun and a recipe for disaster! This has got to be it." "Of utmost concern, Mr. President, is the lash-up with Case Judy."

"What do you think?" the president inquired.

"One links the United States to the other, sir. Each can be disproved separately. But together? Without the wreck and gold however, there's no incriminating evidence. Then everything becomes circumstantial and Madrid's suspicions would be impossible to prove. We must distance ourselves from the Caballero matter quickly."

The president swiveled and studied the photographs of his family on the sideboard. Off in the distance, hundreds of people stood amongst the necklace of flagpoles around the Washington obelisk. Christ! What could he tell them? What Seeley hinted at could bring down the American financial house if it became public knowledge. The media would orgasm over it endlessly—until everyone was bankrupted and millions were standing in bread lines. And long before that came to pass Americans would be storming the White House gates demanding to know why the president had allowed it to happen in the first place. He'd be damned if he'd be remembered in history as another

Harding. He was not going to be the president to introduce the first Great Depression of the twenty-first century. No fucking way!

"All right," the president quipped, "you've convinced me. What are the options?"

Langford Seeley appeared relieved. "We'll get a special operations group to use the wreck for a demolition exercise. It is done all the time, Mr. President. The navy will decide that the wreck is a hazard to navigation. They'll send out a team and blow her up. And without the wreck, presto! No incriminating evidence."

"How difficult is it to do?"

"This would be easy because it is in a remote area where there is little shipping."

"Make it so, Langford," the president ordered. "Make it look like a training exercise. Talk to those you trust in the navy and ask them to see to it. Now, how will you track the Spanish request?"

"As I mentioned a couple of minutes ago. Last Friday I briefed Henry Zeugma at FDIC. Henry will keep his mouth shut. He's unwitting about the Schechter issue, but he knows about the gold."

As Seeley left, the president withdrew an old Rolodex and began thumbing through it until he found the number he wanted. It belonged to one of the original founders of the CIA who'd retired years ago out in Arizona and had told him to get in touch if ever he needed a favor.

EIGHT

Snow Basin, Utah

ALEX WAS BEGINNING to feel better. He leaned back in the stuffed captain's chair and studied the panoramic view below him of the huge salt lake to the southwest. Too much had been happening in his life and he knew that eventually he was going to have to standdown for a week or two and really relax. His two weeks in Russia had challenged his body and mind. The drive from Canada to Washington had been too exciting for a man no longer wired for deadly confrontations. The cross-country drive from Washington to Snow Basin on the north side of Salt Lake City had been mentally unchallenging, but physically it had taken a toll. He thought the trip west from Omaha would take him under two days, but too many halts for meals, for restroom facilities and fuel, had stretched a day and a half to three days. By the time they reached Omaha last week he'd almost driven off the highway into a bridge abutment and Heather convinced him it was time to stop. They'd pulled into a Regency Court Marriott for a couple hours sleep.

Another six hundred miles lay beyond Omaha and they'd arrived here yesterday. This afternoon he and Heather went downtown after lunch and retrieved his stuff from her Bank safety deposit box. He needed to make exact translations of the two Russian documents into English.

Alex's biggest regret as he studied the Russian documents was that Kaminski had been unable to provide the original of Roosevelt's handwritten letter to Stalin. He believed that the four documents when reviewed together would be a clear indictment.

Tomorrow morning he would provide the originals and translations to Waleston Thrower and let him get them authenticated through a laboratory in San Francisco. Then he and Heather would head to Florida. Alex picked up the phone and dialed Gregoriou's number in Key West.

"Still working?" Heather asked as she emerged from the bedroom wearing a terry cloth robe.

"Almost finished. Just this last call. Got any snacks, I'm hungry."

She opened her bathrobe and pressed her breasts against his face. Since she'd picked him up in Washington four days ago, both of them had been on edge and tired by the long drive. He could smell her perfume as he waited for Grigoriou to answer. To hell with it he thought. There were things in life that could wait. Prioritize objectives, define principles he mumbled as he hung up the phone.

Salt Lake City

"It's been a couple of weeks. I wondered if you'd forgotten," the newspaperman posed.

Alex paused while a waitress refilled Waleston Thrower's coffee, then he recounted events since they'd last met. Thrower was agog; suddenly more somber too as he realized the scope of what Balkan was up against; and by extrapolation—probably himself too.

"How much did you say was lost by Spain?"

"About eight hundred tons of gold bullion in 1940."

"And then the Russians lost it to the Germans?"

Alex nodded. "That's affirmative."

"How fitting," Waleston continued. "The thief is himself robbed. What lengths do you think they will go to keep this under wraps?"

"The Russians? Whatever it takes."

"Meaning?"

"Just what I said."

"Murder?" Waleston asked with concern now obvious in his voice.

"Seven have already died."

The newspaperman now had a healthy respect for this man who sat before him. It was just over three weeks since they had last met, and Waleston had used the time to extensively research Russia's abysmal human rights record. Also the Caballero Bullion story. Nothing Alex had told him so far seemed too outrageous. The world of international intrigue was a whorehouse of confidence men and murderers, and the deaths of this man's mother, his best friend, and five others, all made Waleston uncomfortable. Waleston had also spent enough time in the international arena to appreciate just how different other systems viewed the issue of respect for human life. Russia was still a police state—run today by a thin veneer of capitalist politicos who relied on Mafia organizations to support them and to raise taxes. Somewhere in the mix were the security organs.

Waleston glanced around furtively; as if to assure himself no one was watching them.

"I would suggest you be very circumspect Waleston, until this is out in the public domain. Then the danger will go away."

Waleston had covered some controversial stories in his life, and even exposed some blockbusters, but they'd always been at someone else's expense, and none had ever directly threatened his life. This time it was different. He could sense the danger. He too stood in harm's way. Balkan was right. He had to be careful, especially if the story he planned to write were exposed before it hit the tabloids.

As a graduate of New York's Moorehouse School of Journalism at Syracuse University, Waleston had an interesting career since he'd first started out as a stringer in Washington D.C., then pounding the pavements of Eastern Europe for a while before moving on to cover the Moscow coup of August 1991. After a few years in Asia he'd returned to Washington to work the capitol scene again before tiring of it all and taking his last job here in Salt Lake City. His credentials seemed ideal for what he now had in mind. He'd covered the Ollie North expose; the BCCI and Ames Spy scandals, and remembered the various telephone threats against his life. He understood the Potomac Potentates penchant for concealing their perfidious double dealings which Washington insiders always insisted was in the national interest. Most of those he'd exposed were good God-fearing people who'd been raised in rural America, and started out with strong Christian values. But when they reached Washington something changed and the artificial aspects of power and fame changed many who forgot where they came from, and the values they'd been taught at their mother's knees. Waleston's opinion was that given enough time, even the purest Americans became jaded and tarnished in the nation's capital.

"If seven have already died," he asked Alex, "am I also in personal danger?"

Hoping to reduce his concerns, Alex played dumb. "How do you mean?" The statement sounded inane and he decided to allay the other man's fears. "No, you are not," Alex lied. "No one goes after the press. No one knows you have the documents, and once all this hits the tabloids, no one can hurt you or me."

"Alex, let me summarize what I believe you have here. There are in fact four stories which are all related. First there is the three hundred and fifty Americans who until recently, were still alive at this place called Z-5 in Siberia."

Alex nodded in agreement.

"But they are not there anymore?" Waleston continued.

"Correct," Alex said.

"Secondly there's the Novosibirsk documents." Waleston leafed through Alex's translations. "Which support your contention that thousands and thousands of American servicemen never came back after the war, and that the three hundred and fifty are all that remain today."

"Right again," Alex replied again.

"Then there is this string of murders." He examined the sheet of paper on which Alex had printed out the names and dates of each of the seven were murdered and who they were. "Which, according to you, represents but the tip of a conspiracy called Case Judy. Which brings me to the fourth point, that Case Judy involves these last two documents and the Caballero bullion which was never accounted for after World War II, and someone out there who knows where the gold is, would prefer the information remain out of the public domain and is willing to silence those who might? Is that a good synopsis?"

"I guess," Alex replied, amazed at how his information had been so neatly divided into its critical components so that anyone could grasp. He watched the newspaperman's finger as it kept drumming on the name at the bottom of the list he'd given Waleston. It was the most critical link in the entire patchwork, and yet also the weakest link in Alex's case. To expose Russia for holding American prisoners was one thing; to accuse a member of the president's cabinet of committing treason was something else! He suspected Waleston still needed to be convinced about the latter.

"And the president's National Security advisor's name here at the bottom," Waleston asked. "According to you, he is guilty of treason. Pretty heady stuff."

"The evidence condemns him."

"I'll get back to him later," Waleston replied. "Let's discuss this mysterious submarine which you intend to look into further in Florida."

"I'll get the proof you need next week. Documentary evidence and some eyewitnesses."

Leaning back Waleston stroked his chin as he mulled over the multi-tiered plot this stranger from the secret Washington world of espionage and skullduggery had brought to him. There were two problems confronting him. What could be proved and substantiated and that which couldn't be? If the Z-5 camp were deserted, it would be almost impossible to prove who'd been there unless someone could get into it immediately and look for forensic information. The two Novosibirsk documents were a smoking gun that Waleston would stick with for the present. The submarine information he hoped would come next week, and if compelling, could link the others. And finally would come Beria's letter regarding Case Judy and its link to the Spanish gold.

First things first, he thought. He'd get the two Novosibirsk documents and the one from Beria authenticated.

* * *

Maybe relieved was the way Alex would describe his feelings as he headed west toward Heather's condo near the University Medical Center. His meeting with the newspaper editor had assuaged Waleston Thrower's reservations. Thrower now had the documents and would get them authenticated. That would take a couple days, and by the end of the week the first story would appear in the Salt Lake papers. As soon as Alex picked up some of Heather's things at her apartment downtown, he'd return to her condo at Snow Basin where they planned to have dinner with some of her friends from work. Then they'd hit the ski slopes early tomorrow morning.

He parked a half mile up from Temple street, beneath a row of oaks and crossed the center divider into the parking lot of Heather's complex, threading his way between the rows of parked cars. Turning left at the last row he proceeded a couple paces before he froze. A hundred feet away at the building entrance was a face in a car window.

Hewas absolutely certain he had seen once before . . . at his mother's place in Pennsylvania.

He circled around and approached the car from the driver's side. Stopping suddenly by the open window he pressed the nose of his revolver into the base of the man's neck. The man froze. "Feel that shithead! Please. Give me an excuse to blow your brains out through your ear." Alex ordered him to lift the weapon gingerly from his belt and toss it into the rear seat. Alex opened the rear door and forced his gun into the back of the driver's neck as he climbed in.

"You got two choices asshole: do what I tell you, or—"

"Hey, you're in control," the driver exclaimed in broken English.

"Right, asshole. Start the car and back up."

Alex couldn't discern the man's accent. "Where you from, dick brains?"

"New York."

"And your folks?"

"None of your business."

"Let it pass, Alex. He'd find out soon enough."

Once out of the northern suburbs, they threaded their way north into the mountains past a public camp ground appropriately named Memory Grove. *Memory Grove*, Alex thought. Memory Grove for his mother. Memory Grove for Marvin Raoul. The park was closed and Alex ordered dick brains to drive around the barrier and they pulled into a thicket away from the main road.

"Get out slowly dipshit," Alex ordered.

"What you going to do?"

He slid out of the rear seat and sat on the hood, facing the driver who now stood against a tree.

"Who hired you."

"Don't know what you're talking about. I was waiting for a friend when you kidnapped me."

"Kidnapped you?" Alex started to laugh. "We met before shit for brains! Remember?" He leveled the gun at the man's groin, "Last week in Pennsylvania. Remember? You had a friend with you. So did I. Mine's dead. By the way . . . how's your friend?"

"Hey man, you must be crazy!" his victim exclaimed.

"You got it." Alex laughed. "I'm screwed up in the head. People killing my mother like they did, it messes up my brains. Makes me act crazy, and I think about doing strange things to people. Know what I mean, asshole?"

"What you going to do, man?" The tone of his victim's voice had risen slightly.

"That depends on you. What's your name?"

"Ned Yadkin."

"You got documents, Ned Yadkin? Throw your wallet over here and empty your pockets, and don't play games with me shit head." A New York State driver's license, a Costco card, laminated Social Security Card, and some credit cards were the sum total of this man's American existence.

"What kind of a name is Yadkin?"

"East European."

"Come on, Yadkin! Eastern Europe is a big place. You are pissing me off."

"It is Polish, I think."

"Where in Poland?"

"Don't know. My parents never told me."

"Where were you born?"

Yadkin's driver's license stated Queens, New York. And his date of birth made him just over thirty-five.

"Queens," Yadkin replied.

"How long you lived there?"

"What is this?" Yadkin laughed. "Twenty questions?"

"Which hospital?" Alex said.

"How should I know?"

Alex had been searching his memory for a Polish word and finally found it, and said in fluent Polish. "There are only two hospitals, the south or north hospital. Tell me, or I am going to shoot your worthless ass now." Alex pointed the silencer at Yadkin's forehead.

"Crakow," Yadkin replied in Polish. "I'm an immigrant. I escaped from a prison work detail three years ago near the Baltic."

"What's your real name?"

"Charles Semorovsky."

"And what do you do for a living, Mr. Semorovsky? What is a law abiding American citizen of Polish ancestry doing in a Salt Lake City parking lot, with a loaded gun and a silencer fitted to it?"

Yadkin didn't reply.

"Why did you kill my friend?" Alex demanded.

"I don't know what you're talking about, man!"

Alex moved back a couple of steps and pointed the silencer at Yadkin's feet.

"Say good-bye to your foot, Ned."

"Wait!" he screamed. "I'll tell you what I know, man. But you'll let me go, right?"

"Right." Alex promised crossing his heart with his index finger.

"You promise?"

"Sure man. Know what I mean? I'm a man of my word. If I get the truth and you promise you'll blow town and I'll never see your ugly face again. Sure, you got my word of honor on it. Why not?"

"My buddy did it. I swear. I swear it on my mother's milk! The idiot is crazy, know what I mean? He's from one of those crazy Arab countries and has scores to settle. I never meant you no harm. I needed the money, that's all."

"Where's your buddy now?"

"I didn't like him so I dumped him."

"You're here alone in Salt Lake City?"

"Yeah."

"And why are you here?"

"Hey man, like I said, I was waiting for a friend."

"You are pissing me off Yadkin, Semorovski, or whatever your real name is. Now tell me who hired you, and where is the other guy who was with you in Pennsylvania. Tell me and you'll be tied up and left here until someone finds you. Otherwise?" Alex pointed the silencer at his feet again.

"In Manhattan!" Yadkin blurted. "Some creep in lower Manhattan hired us."

"Details Ned. I need details. Know what I mean, my friend?"

"Names Orthon Royster," the pole continued. "Don't know if it is his real name though. He hangs out on Twenty-third Street, between eighth and ninth avenue on the south side. Number 1737. Can't miss it. It's a crummy-looking gray apartment building in the middle of the block with a creaky elevator at the back. He's upstairs, fourth floor rear. Number 408."

"Office or apartment?"

"It's a three-room dump. He's there by himself. The guy is a snake."

Extending his arm Alex rubbed his thumb and forefinger together. "How much?"

"A lot man! He must really want you."

Alex continued the gesture with his fingers. "Whose paying Royster to get me?"

"Don't know. Honestly" the pole whined as the gun barrel rose further, now pointing at his lower abdomen. "He gave me your address in Washington and your mother's place in . . ." Yadkin halted in midsentence. His face paled. He knew he'd just made a very serious mistake and admitted something really stupid.

Hoping the Pole might think Alex didn't know what they'd done to his mother, he ignored the comment and kept rubbing his index finger and thumb together as he waited. Alex had to find out who wanted him dead. It obviously wasn't this guy Royster in New York. Royster was only an intermediary. "Royster get his requests from Washington?" Alex quipped, hoping the Pole would blab.

"He just told us where we could find you. We almost had you in Omaha, but you left before we arrived."

"We? I thought you said you were alone?"

"I, ahhhh," the Pole stuttered.

"Royster told you I was in Omaha?"

"Yes."

The connection suddenly flashed through Alex's mind like a thunderbolt. The only person Alex had called from Omaha was Chuck Bunn, the temporary CEO of Scion Consultants. Chuck Bunn was the link. But Chuck Bunn on his own was too stupid, so it had to be someone higher up that Bunn had unwittingly told? "And how did you get the address of the lady with me here in Salt Lake City?"

"From the Marriott registration desk in Omaha."

Alex made a note that he'd have to tell Heather to be more careful. "You haven't told me how much they paid you?"

"A half million."

"Each?" he said with incredulity in his voice.

"No. Split two ways."

"Your associate, the Arab with you in the car in Pennsylvania and in Omaha. Where is he?"

"You promised you'd let me go."

"Yes. But I think you lied to me."

"I didn't mean to."

"I'm waiting?"

"Yeah, he's here. He left just before you arrived, to get some cigarettes and candy. He calls himself Abdul, and his last name is Beerziet or something like that. Royster introduced me to him and that's all I know about him."

"Where is he from?" Alex inquired.

"Said New York City, but all his relatives are in Israel."

"Jewish or Moslem?" Alex demanded.

"Says he's Moslem. But I noticed he had a Star of David on his key ring. Said it was from some Hebrew he'd killed, but I think it's his religion. He's got several sets of documents too, in different names, so I am not really sure who he is."

The Pole screamed as a soft nosed bullet tore out most of the back of his left knee, exposing shards of broken bone as he collapsed to the ground.

"You shouldn't lie to me Yadkin or Semorovski, or whoever you are?" Alex's face hardened. He'd trained for decades in the arts of wet interrogation and murder but only killed twice. This would make his third, and each time it got easier, especially when personal issues were involved. "What you did to my mother must have been one of your finer moments. You good at killing old women?" Alex seethed through clenched teeth.

"It wasn't me, honestly," Yadkin pleaded, "that's my associates specialty." He whined. Blood was seeping between his fingers as he tried to staunch the flow around the wound. "I wanted to tie her up while we waited for you."

Alex didn't think he could do it. He pictured his mother's nude body and this bastard burning her with cigarettes. He hesitated for a moment and turned away, thinking he might be sick.

Yadkin lunged, hoping to knock Alex down, but with one knee gone, his momentum fell short as Alex stepped back, and Yadkin sprawled beside him on the pavement.

"Oh please, oh please!" Yadkin begged, tears filling his eyes as Alex pointed his gun at him again. "You promised. I never hurt anyone. You promised."

"So I lied," Alex assured him soothingly.

Six indentations erupted across Yadkin's shirt as the soft lead tore out most of his respiratory, circulation, and other life support equipment. Yadkin's chest spasmed as he tried to form words, his eyes riveting Alex with an accusatory look. Alex pointed the gun at Yadkin's face and squeezed the trigger again but he'd already expended the entire clip.

He felt like a zombie as he drove out of the park. But his mind was clear now. He was caught up in something he had to finish. There was still Yadkin's partner. He had to go back for him. Alex knew that for a half a million Yadkin's associate would pursue Alex until he died of old age.

Washington D.C.

"Leben Julius."

"Yeah, Leben, what you got?"

Julius periodically briefed the White House Staff, and Langford Seeley had called him earlier and requested he keep in touch should anyone ask for information about coordinates in north-eastern Siberia. Julius had inquired why but been assured it was only an administrative matter and to please keep him informed. The Office of Strategic Reconnaissance controlled the release of all satellite imagery, and all such requests crossed Leben Julius's desk first.

"Two calls came in during the last twenty four hours, Mr. Seeley. One from DIA, the other from a retired army colonel I know. I told both I would have to get back to them."

"You did the right thing. What's the two people's names?"

"It doesn't matter."

"Yeah it does!" Langford insisted. "Higher ups want to know."

Julius sat back and studied the rolling countryside beyond his window. Suddenly he felt nervous and uncomfortable.

"Come on, Julius, I don't have all day. The president wants to know."

Putnam's name didn't surprise Langford when he heard it. But who was this other guy. Langford made a note of retired Colonel Jose Santiago's name, address, and phone number. This Santiago guy was probably another of Balkan's friends he would have to look into immediately.

Snow Basin, Utah

"What's the matter, Alex?" Heather inquired her voice concerned. She'd noticed the change in Alex when she'd picked him up at the home of Mr. Svoboda on the north side of Baltimore a week ago. Something serious had obviously happened while Alex was in Russia, and several times since he'd been with her, he'd screamed in his sleep.

"Something is seriously wrong, isn't it?"

"Problems to attend to, that's all."

He'd confided some of what had happened to him in Russia, but nothing about events since his return. He didn't think Heather would understand what they'd done to his mother or Marvin, and he couldn't tell her about the two men he'd just killed here in Salt Lake City. Not just yet anyway and probably never.

Heather's expression was sincere. She knew he was uptight and could sense it in their lovemaking. She recalled reading once that when the male animal was under increased stress, its thoughts of reproduction declined. But when under intense danger on the other hand, the urge to copulate sometimes become insatiable. It was as if one cancelled the other she supposed. Tonight his interest in sex seemed inexhaustible.

"It will pass," he whispered as they lay nude before the fireplace.

"When will you return?" she asked.

"About a week. I've got a couple of things left to do back east."

He'd shot the second assassin in Heather's downtown apartment. He wrapped the body, whose identification identified the corpse as Abdul Beerzeit, in garbage bags and stuffed it into the trunk of Yadkin's car which he was able to find nearby from the Alamo electronic key in his pocket. Beneath the spare tire in the trunk, he also found additional identification documents for Beerzeit and two passports which initially intrigued Alex. and then began to worry him. The first was an Israeli passport for Moshe Solomon, and a second for Abram Herzel from Brazil. What was this guy really doing in the United States when he wasn't looking for Alex? Whomever his assassins really were, Alex was certain this Royster guy in New York City would know where their contract money was coming from. Alex would catch a flight to New York first thing in the morning and find out.

On the way back to Heather's place, he'd stopped at a Mobil station and called Waleston Thrower at the Salt Lake City newspaper to tell him he had to leave town for a couple of days. Then he called Mike Gregoriou in Key West. Gregoriou sounded pleased when Alex told him he was ready to pay Gregoriou the ten thousand to film the interior of the submarine.

Heather whispered in his ear. "You ever considered making me an honest woman?"

"Yes. I love you. We should do it."

"In the morning?" She teased, running his hand over her still wet mound.

"Soon. I swear it. Once this is all over."

"A couple of days?"

"A month, not more."

Boca Chica NAS

Admiral Lange was furious. He'd been asked by the Chief of Naval Operations to go to the flight terminal at Boca Chica Naval Air Station this morning for an unofficial and "off-the-record" meeting with the president's National Security advisor. And the first thing the president's advisor did was to open an old wound; by raising the question of the damned submarine off the Tortugas.

Lange initially pleaded ignorance of the subject, only to be challenged by his visitor, who asked him not to be petulant. Lange demanded to know the reason for the enquiry. The president's security advisor told him it was none of his business, repeating the question. Who the hell did Langford Seeley think he was? Outside on the ramp stood an air force twin-engine Gulfstream II jet which had flown the son of a bitch down from Washington for this off-the-record meeting? The CNO could have ordered Lange to fly to Washington instead, saving the taxpayer fifty thousand dollars. What got under Lange's skin even more was Seeley's condescending tone and haughty manner. The issue, as Seeley described it cryptically, involved the national security, and he couldn't divulge more. He knew that Lange had asked questions and therefore knew about Balkan and strongly suggested that Lange cooperate fully and not conceal evidence. Who else, Seeley demanded, knew about the submarine?

Lange mentioned his executive, retired Captain Millican, and Alex Balkan. Seeley noted the names.

"That's it?" Seeley inquired officiously.

"As far as I know," Lange replied. "How long will you stay in Key West?" he asked.

"I have other business to attend to," Seeley replied dismissively, "and shall depart 0600 in the morning."

Business to attend too! Lange thought as he watched the man climb into the Official government stretched limousine outside the passenger terminal doors. What crap! Seeley had come to see him, and had just dismissed him like some errant school boy! Lange watched as the car pulled away. Then he went to a public phone and flipped through the book until he found the number he wanted. He dropped two quarters and waited.

"I want to speak with Gregoriou."

"Mike, this is Admiral Lange," he said in a deadpan voice. "I'll be departing Key West tomorrow and thought you'd like to know, someone is around asking unofficially about anyone knowledgeable of the subject we discussed. I did not give him your name. I don't know what this is all about, but thought I owed it to you before I leave."

"Thanks! Who asked?"

"The president's National Security Advisor. He just arrived fifteen minutes ago at Boca Chica. He'll be here until tomorrow morning."

"Why is he here now?" Mike asked.

"No idea. But suspect the issue we discussed must be very important to him."

"Is he going to try to see me?"

"For some reason I doubt it."

"Thanks. I hope you enjoy Italy."

Hotel Pierre, Manhattan

Alex walked through the empty hotel lobby and took the side door onto Sixty-first Street. The late February weather was still unseasonably cold and he zipped up the inner lining of his overcoat. He picked up a newspaper at the corner and descended to the subway platform where he stood awkwardly staring around at the dirt and filth interlaced with the pungent odor of urine. 9-11 he guessed had not done much to improve New Yorker's pride in their public transportation system. He rubbed at the corner of his eye nervously as he waited, glancing at his watch repeatedly. He chastised himself for not having inquired at the reception desk about how often the subway trains ran at this hour of the morning. He felt the rush of air begin on his face and heard the approaching train as it rolled into the station. Thank God! He'd taken a noon flight yesterday out of Utah, with a plane change in Chicago, arriving at Newark Airport just after eight. He'd dined at one his favorite restaurants in the East 70s and slept fitfully all night. He climbed aboard the subway car and pulled the mornings paper from his overcoat and turned to the article in the first section and scanned it once again.

He suspected the FBI had made him when he bought his round-trip ticket for cash at Salt Lake City Airport and decided he'd use another of his old alias documents for his trip to Florida.

Twenty minutes later he reemerged at street level on Fifth Avenue and thirty-second street. The four floor walk-up a couple blocks away on west twenty-third was right where Yadkin had said it would be. Alex quickened the pace. He had to get to this guy called Orthon Royster before Royster saw the morning papers. Page twenty-two carried a report about a body found in the trunk of a rental car in Salt Lake City. From Interpol fingerprint the office of Homeland Defense identified the victim as one Ned Yadkin who was really Vassily Nizhniye and wanted in Poland for escaping from prison three years ago. The other victim was Butros Vaniak, a Russian Jew who had emigrated to Israel and a Mossad operative wanted by Russian intelligence for murder, extortion and rape.

Alex checked his watch again as he approached the building's entrance, noting that mailbox number 407 bore no name. If Orthon Royster handed out half million dollar contracts, the building definitely didn't exude his affluence. Alex rapped three times on a dirty door at the rear of the fourth floor and waited.

"Who is it?" a man's voice demanded gruffly.

"Yadkin sent me."

"What about him?" the voice demanded.

"Ned needs money. He's in Salt Lake City with Vaniak. He told me to see you. Said it is urgent!"

Thank God there were no peepholes in the door, Alex thought. If pinhole cameras observed him from above, none were evident. The sounds of locks and chains being removed echoed through the door, the last almost at floor level. Alex threw his shoulder into the door as it opened, knocking Roykin back into the room. Before Roykin could get up, Alex kicked the door shut behind him and pointed his automatic in the old man's face. He'd picked up the 9mm Brazilian special from a friend in lower Manhattan last night and hoped the damned thing worked.

Roykin's three small rooms and a bathroom were filthy. Roykin's front business was obviously a shoestring operation.

"Who are you, what the hell do you want?" Roykin demanded. His voice bordering on outrage. "You an idiot? You know who I am? Get out of here you two-bit punk before I have you dissolved in nitric acid."

Alex kicked him in the groin to shut him up, and stood back and waited while the old man tried to assuage his bruised testicles. Removing duct tape from his pocket Alex bound Roykin's hands and feet and slapped strips across his mouth. Hauling him into the bathroom he taped Roykin's neck to the steel drain pipe coming down from the water tank above the commode. If the son of a bitch struggled too much he'd strangle himself.

Rummaging through desk drawers revealed two handguns, a loaded revolver and a Smith and Wesson, along with some old pornography magazines and hundreds of pages of 900 number phone billings. On shelves near the door were eight recorders which clicked on and off as incoming calls were automatically being redialed to some international number.

Alex pushed one of the monitor buttons and listened as a sexy woman's voice assured the caller that business in Russia was not only profitable, but tax free. Callers were advised to carefully note the following information; and a long list of names addresses and phone numbers ensued for Russian companies involved in various types of business, and what they needed to export from the United States. He whistled softly. Roykin's operation was a telephone scam. He laughed. Callers were billed five dollars a minute by the phone company, and reimbursed Royster four. The machines probably produced six to eight hundred bucks an hour. Maybe a quarter million a month. The old man was probably a millionaire, but he lived like a penniless cockroach in a shithouse.

"My name is Alex Balkan," he said in Russian as he returned to the bathroom. Royster's eyes were impassive. Alex tore the tape from his mouth. "Now, who called you from Washington and told you I was in Omaha?"

"Up your ass," Royster spat in Russian.

"I see. You speak Russian too. And who told you to put a half million price on my head?"

"Fuck you," Royster replied.

Alex pulled the New York Times from his overcoat and held up the front page so Royster could see the date. Then he turned to the article on page twenty two. "See this," he demanded in Russian. "The two you offered a half million to, the worms are eating them. You should read the papers earlier each day."

"What does this have to do with me?"

"They told me about you. Now. Who was it in Washington and who in Moscow?"

"I don't know what you are talking about!"

Alex tapped on the wall behind Royster with the butt of his gun. "They're awful thin. Maybe someone will hear you." Alex ripped more duct tape from the roll and slapped it across Roykin's mouth. Then he wound the rest around Royster's calves and thighs. Royster had at least ten to twenty years on Alex and appeared weak and emaciated, but Alex didn't want any surprises, so from a closet he got three leather belts and used them to further secure Royster to the pipe and commode.

"I already know the names of your goons," Alex told him, "the Salt Lake police found their bodies yesterday. You should always read the local papers at the beginning of the day, then you might not be in this situation you are in right now. You, my friend, are going to tell me about the others. That I promise. Or the coroner is going to need five years to figure out who you were and exactly what it was that killed you? Understand? All you have to do is nod your head."

He glared at Alex.

"Mr. Tough guy, huh? That's okay. I suspected as much. I know you won't talk, but should you change your mind, nod your head up and down." From his windbreaker, he removed an ice pick and pliers. Dispassionately he buried the ice pick in Royster's knee. He set the pliers on the desk and went into the adjacent room. Yanking the lamp cord from the wall, he stripped away the insulation from several inches of wire. Straightening two coat hangers, he secured the wire to it with duct tape. Over that he wrapped hand towels and more tape, and placing the two bare wire ends apart on the carpet, he pushed the plug into the wall. "You understand what this is?"

A tough bastard, Alex thought. He could feel his bile rising. He swallowed hard and pictured Royster's goons working his mother over. He pictured Marvin Raoul's contorted face as they'd slowly killed him. Alex poured a glass of water into Royster's lap and another over his bloody knee. Touching the coat hangers together produced a cascade of sparks.

"Last chance asshole," Alex confided with disinterest.

Placing one of the coat hangers into the wet material in Royster's crotch, he touched the other one to the haft of the ice pick. The body jerked and contorted violently, the neck bulged like a blowfish. Royster's head jerked back against the pipe as his nostrils flared and his breath hissed as he repeatedly sucked in air. Again the probe hit him, this time on the side of his neck. The bastard had a lot to hide, Alex thought, as Royster's body wreathed before slumping forward unconscious.

Too much too quickly, Alex thought. He hoped he hadn't killed the bastard. He continued his search of the apartment, this time in minute detail. Awhile later Royster began to mumble. Alex ripped away the tape and waited until he was no longer gasping.

"Who is Ned Yakin?"

"Russian intelligence," came the reply in Russian.

"Not bad," Alex replied. He thought he'd had it all figured out already, obviously he hadn't. Gutsy bastard, Alex thought. Even on his way to the next world Royster had still stuck to his cover story. "And the other guy?"

"Israeli intelligence, but really working for Moscow. He's a recent immigrant sent to Israel and lives in an Israeli West Bank settlement near Ramallah."

"Why him?" Alex asked.

"He was available I guess."

"Who in Moscow?" Alex asked, picking up the two coat-hangers for emphasis that the question was one Royster should answer.

"Yevgeni Kosmutov."

"And in Washington?"

"Victor Indorenko."

"And where do I find Indorenko?"

"The Russian airline office in Washington."

"Indorenko told you I was in Omaha?"

"He gave me the name of the hotel."

"Who told him?"

"No idea."

"Nooo," Roykin pleaded as Alex replaced the tape and more muffled screams turned his throat gray and his face crimson.

Alex waited a minute and then removed the tape again. "Who told him?"

"I don't know. Kill me if you want, but it is the truth."

"Who paid you?"

"Indorenko, but only one hundred thousand up front. The rest was to come afterward."

Fifteen minutes later Alex took the subway uptown. The only thing which gave him satisfaction was that he'd eliminated the jackals around the sheep pen, and now the rest of his prey would be grazing peacefully, unsuspecting of their own stalkers presence.

MARCH

ONE

The Oval Office

"OKAY, GENERAL, WHAT have you found out?" The president demanded as Putnam was shown into his office by one of his staff. The president intensely disliked conspiracies, and every time one had cropped up in the past, he'd relentlessly discouraged it or avoided it like the plague, but this time he felt he'd been unwittingly coerced into one and was annoyed with himself. The DIA general was starting to take up a lot of his time. He'd intended for his National Security Advisor to handle this afternoon's meeting with General Putnam, but Langford Seeley was still down in Key West looking into the submarine matter, and had calledin to say he couldn't make it back to Washington until this evening.

Now the president wouldn't see Seeley until early next week because he himself had to leave in a few hours to speak at the National Governor's convention in Denver tonight, and after Denver, there were whistle stops in Seattle and San Francisco over the weekend and he would be back in Washington next Monday afternoon. The president looked at his watch as Putnam approached his desk and indicated a chair along the wall.

"I located the aircraft wreckage in Russia, Mr. President. From SATCOM tapes in storage we were able to develop a track for the aircraft. It started out from Chita near Lake Baikal. The transport departed Chita on March 12 at 1530 local, stopped at a Russian vehicle overhaul depot called Aldan, five hundred miles away. An hour after arrival at Aldan, it left again, this time headed for Z-5 where it landed at 0200 local."

"Eight hours, General?"

"It crossed two time zones, Mr. President. Normal flight time for the distance is four hours, about two and a half thousand miles."

"Who does the Chita base belong too?"

"How do you mean?"

"Who in the Russian military?"

"Voenno Transportnaya Aviatsiya, which is their equivalent of our Air Mobility Command. VTA's commander is three star lieutenant general named Vassiley Gorbatyuk. Chita's normal compliment is twelve Il-76's. From KEYHOLE and TALENT satellite imagery of Chita after the twelfth of March, there have been only eleven IL-76's on the flight line. One is obviously someplace else."

"And the stop at Aldan?"

"To pick up vehicles, Mr. President, Aldan is a vehicle depot." Putnam passed a photograph of the Z-5 strip. "This was taken on 19 March. A week after the flight. If you look carefully you'll see four abandoned APC's."

He passed another photograph. "This was taken the day in question." The president could clearly make out the image of an aircraft.

"This proves it was there Mr. President. Balkan's story checks out."

Now they were getting somewhere, the president thought. If he were going to confront Moscow and accuse the Kremlin of duplicity, he needed proof. And the Keyhole imagery was substantial. "Where did it go?" he asked.

"It was lost, Mr. President."

"Lost!"

"It crashed."

"When?"

"Within minutes after takeoff as near as we can tell."

"Jesus!" the president exclaimed. Where's the proof?"

"NSA's communications intercepts during the twenty four hours following the IL's arrival at Z-5 on the thirteenth of March produced this for 2242 local time at Z-5." He withdrew a small recorder from his briefcase. The sound of Russian voices floating through the Oval Office were in distress. One man was screaming while another, his voice obviously more authoritative, kept interrupting the cacophony of sound. Then nothing. Putnam pushed a transcript across. "This is what those voices said, Mr. President. Coordinates for the communications intercept indicate the aircraft was about eighty miles south-east of Z-5 when this transmission took place."

The president scanned the transcript, muttering portions of the English language transcript aloud as he went. "Explosive decompression; the right wing has come off."

He looked at the general. "A mid air explosion?"

"Yes, sir. If what Balkan told me is true, there would have been hundreds aboard. It is worth having a look!"

"Photography of the wreckage?"

"It'll be shot this weekend. A Keyhole satellite is being redirected right now. Its next pass over that location is scheduled for early Sunday morning. I'll have pictures for you noon Sunday."

"And Russian Air Force Headquarters in Moscow, what have they said?"

"Neither have announced the loss. Nor is there any indication of any search or recovery effort underway. It has been a month. I called our Air Attache in Moscow. He has also heard nothing."

"Suspicious as hell!" the president said. "I want a team in there. If you are correct, then there will be bodies strewn all over the landscape for a hundred miles."

"It is their airspace and territory Mr. president. And the location is nowhere near any missile or nuclear sites that we could use to justify a preemptive challenge."

"Hell, General. Find a way then."

Putnam knew the United States had three preempts each year and had already used one. But Washington's worsening relationship with the Kremlin over its Crimean demands would make Moscow's cooperation difficult. Unconditional challenges were serious business. Very serious, and usually signalled one sides belief that the other was cheating on its international nuclear nonproliferation programs. Preagreed treaty rules for such a challenge required that the challenger be afforded "access to the designated facility, building, location, area, or site, within six hours of notification." It was the only fail-safe way that either country could be certain the other wasn't building a doomsday machine somewhere.

"If we do, the press will get a hold of it and the spin doctors will have a field day. What justification would we provide?"

The president picked up the red phone. “Get me the Russian president.” His demeanor changed moments later as he glanced at his watch. “Never mind. I’ll call him later.”

“Too late in Moscow,” he quipped as he replaced the phone. “Keep snooping around, General. You’ve done a fine job. I want to see you first thing next Tuesday morning.” He looked at his calendar. “Eight o’clock sharp! Bring me what I need to challenge the goddamned Russians.”

The president reached his National Security advisor in Key West moments after Putnam left and was pleased to learn that events there too were moving in the right direction. Seeley assured him that in about an hour, the submarine would be history.

“I’m leaving for Denver this afternoon Langford. We must talk. Can you meet me in Seattle?”

“I’ll be there, Mr. President.”

“Think up an excuse for the Seattle trip so people don’t speculate.”

Key West Officers Club

“What’s the matter, Colonel?” the bartender asked.

“Life sucks!” the colonel replied. Signaling her for another double vodka.

Ruth had worked the Trumbo Officers Club for several years and knew everyone. Key West was a small place and most of the hundred and fifty officers frequented the Club several times a month. Except Lt. Col. Vincent Astove. Astove was a loner. A quiet and secretive man. She’d heard rumors a month back that his career might be over.

Astov was commander of Seal Team Twenty-Eight, or ST-28 as the locals called it. Forty-two officers and men, they were housed a mile away on the north end of Fleming Key. ST-28 was the elite called upon to do the most dangerous missions, and no one knew what the Seals really did when they were not in residence at Key West. And when in Key West they were always dropping out of airplanes or running around in gray and black rubber boats at all hours of day wearing wet suits.

As she placed Astov’s drink on the bar she considered asking him what last December’s incident had really been about? Astov and some senior Air Force intelligence officer who was involved in clandestine counter-narcotics operations against the Cartel's had been admitted to the local hospital with serious injuries. The rumor mill immediately went into high gear about inter-service rivalry and even speculation about their involvement in the failed 1982 Desert One disaster in southern Iran. But Astov's concern this afternoon lay elsewhere. Officer assignments had called him an hour ago to notify him he had twenty-four hours to present himself to a new assignment at Fort Sill, Oklahoma. He downed half the vodka and sat back smiling at the barkeep. He'd miss Key West and the lifestyle because Fort Sill sucked! Oklahoma sucked too! It was a dead end assignment.

He'd apparently been shit canned. But why now was the question he couldn't ascertain? Before coming to the Club this afternoon his XO informed him that he too had just received orders, to a Chemical-Biological Incident Response Force with the third battalion of the eighth marines who were forward deployed to Bagram Air Base in Afghanistan. His senior enlisted group leader had also been reassigned to the first platoon of the 1st FAST Company at Rodman Naval Station in Panama. Astov suspected the sudden assignments of all three had something to do with a classified operation they'd completed yesterday.

And only last night, at a special closed ceremony, he and eight of his men were commended by none other than the president's National Security advisor for a special Top Secret demolition job they'd completed southwest of Key West. They'd also been briefed two days earlier by the president's National Security Advisor who'd flown in personally from Washington. Astov's team was ordered to sign Top Secret statements never to talk about the mission. The Navy brass had obviously decided a wreck nearby was a hazard to navigation. Astov knew better. Three things made the mission suspect. A wreck in three hundred feet of water? Why after so many decades. And why use so much explosive?

Before sunset yesterday he'd watched the underwater detonation from the fantail of a cutter, after which he and his team were retrieved by Helo for the flight back to Key West. He'd felt good about the mission until a couple hours ago. Now he had to pack his gear and ship out. His family would have to follow later.

Washington DC

Paul watched as the beige chauffeur driven Cadillac emerged from the side entrance onto Seventeenth Street and turned south toward Constitution Avenue. The unstretched model was unassuming amidst the rush hour traffic; it's owner's concession to the plebeian need of his countrymen to know the governed were no worse off than those who led them. Paul knew it rankled the Cadillac's occupant, who in any other milieu would have departed with his personal helicopter from the roof of the building. As the Caddy passed by, Paul could see the old man seated in the rear, and wondered if he were nervous?

Yep, Paul thought to himself, citizen Seeley was obviously homeward bound after another grueling day at the office. It was only half past two and if he were homeward bound, Seeley's trip up the Potomac would take thirty minutes to his estate thirteen miles away at Cropley. Paul knew the route, and watched as the chauffeur turned left at the corner toward the Memorial Parkway.

For the last four days Paul had waited for the beige Caddy, and spotted it Monday and Tuesday, but not the last two days. Then it reappeared this morning. Seeley either didn't report for work, or had left town. Paul smiled as he ambled down the pavement toward the corner; reflecting on the possibility that citizen Langford might be so terrified that he was varying his travel routines and had avoided the trip downtown altogether for the past two days.

Just before noon this Monday, Paul placed a call to Langford's White House office from a pay phone at Union Station. At first his old friend was incredulous. Until Paul recalled an anecdote about Langford's inability to compute ballistic trajectories while attending OSS training in Canada in 1942. He reminded Langford of the instructor's observation, that if Langford didn't master ballistics he was bound to succumb to return fire. "And for you, my oldest friend," Paul concluded, "it's time for return fire. I've waited a long time for this." Paul hung up as Langford insisted they meet because Langford could make him a wealthy man and they could work something out.

Paul turned right at the corner and headed to the Metro stop at Foggy Bottom. He'd parked Cimeon's car on a side street near the Hyattsville metro.

* * *

Alex arrived the same afternoon aboard National's Shuttle from New York and rented a nondescript black car. Before departure from New York, he'd called information and learned there were only two listings for Indorenko; and only one for a Victor Indorenko. Alex noted the address and phone number and called it. A woman's voice answered. He asked casually in Russian if Victor were home. He wasn't. He observed to her that business in the airline industry must be good. "Very good," she replied. He hung up before she inquired who was calling.

A half an hour later, he parked in a garage and walked to the Russian airline office. From a corner phone, he called and asked if he could speak with Indorenko. The airline receptionist said he was on another line and put him on hold. Alex hung up, crossed the street, walked into the office, and casually browsed through some travel brochures until one of the sales agents became available. Again he inquired if Indorenko might be available? The agent pointed to a man behind a glass enclosure. Alex studied the face for a moment, thanked her, noting he was obviously busy and would return later.

At five, Indorenko emerged onto the street and walked around the corner to a parking garage. Moments later he emerged in a late model BMW convertible with Virginia tags. Alex noted the distinctive face again and license plate number as he followed him to his apartment in Silver Springs. When the doors of the Russian's elevator opened on the eighteenth floor his body was found by a resident.

* * *

Jose Santiago picked Alex up that evening at National Airports curbside passenger waiting area.

"Christ!" the retired Special Forces Officer exclaimed as Alex recounted the highlights of his recent trip to Russia, and the last couple of days. He left out the part about killing the two men in Utah, the one yesterday in New York City, and Indorenko an hour ago.

"What a story!" The old man observed. "Wish I'd gone with you."

"The most fascinating thing though," Alex continued, "Was my interrogator at Monino. He worked for Valeriy Yeniseysk. They knew about the Novosbirsk documents. They'd been tipped off by someone here in Washington." Santiago glanced at him, aware of the implication. "He also knew where my mother lived, what her house looked like. He knew I'd stopped in London before going to Moscow. And he told me they have a mole in the administration here; someone who keeps them informed about everything going on. Even down to what's going on inside Scion Consultants—the outfit I used to work for until they fired me."

"Jesus," Santiago replied."

"But even more interesting," Alex continued, "was his statement that he and I were really after the same thing; which is what this whole mess is all about? It seems we stole a lot of their gold during the war." Alex paused for effect. "And now they want it back. How naive I was. At the beginning I thought it was all about their trying to find and kill the Slavchenko bitch. She was just a bit player."

As they negotiated the evening traffic northwards around the beltway to Silversprings, Alex related everything. What he knew about Case Judy and the three wartime bullion shipments; how he'd met Eduardo Hernandez: whose father commanded the mysterious submarine. Alex concluded with his suspicions about the U-Boat wreck in south Florida.

"Young man . . . ," the old colonel exclaimed, "you have made this old man happy. I appreciate your sharing all this with me. You're secrets are safe with me."

"Thanks," Alex replied.

"You really think it is down there?"

"Colonel. That's the sixty-four thousand dollar question?"

"And the Americans at Z-5?"

"I was hoping you might agree to check it out."

"Me? Why?"

Alex described the Z-5 graffiti he'd seen. "I didn't have a camera. I know it was put there by Americans. The huts just at this one place were large enough to accommodate at least 500. And the authorities in DC have never admitted more than 200 across the entire former Soviet Union. You'd need an hour or two on the ground at Z-5. The whole thing out and back would take four to five days. I'd take care of all your expenses and make it worth your while." He glanced at the colonel, who was now obviously more interested.

"Give me some examples of this graffiti you speak of."

"One said, I volunteered to fight in Korea, and am abandoned in this shithole 52 years now—I think? And another . . . tell Cindy in

Omaha I loved her dearly . . . DK. JB. 101st Airborne . . . Cherbourg, France 1944. And another . . . Damn those who abandoned us!"

"I don't work cheap," Santiago said.

"Ten thousand! Plus all expenses."

"Shit, Alex, I'd do it for free. When do you want to start?"

"You got a passport?"

"Two!"

"One's black?"

"Sure enough. It has another two years validity left on it too. But I'd use the Tourist one for travel out of the States, and the Dip one only if challenged by some asshole in Russia."

"How soon could you leave?" Alex asked, hoping it would be immediately.

"Long as it takes to get a round trip ticket to Moscow."

Two hours later it was arranged. When he contacted Boris in Russia, Boris demanded an additional ten percent, insisting that Alex's friend arrive in Moscow within four days. Otherwise transportation to the location they wanted would have to wait awhile.

Seven Corners, Falls Church

The next morning Alex borrowed Santiago's decrepit station wagon and headed into Virginia. Saturday morning traffic on the Beltway was light and a low overcast threatened rain. At nine o'clock he passed Chuck Bunn's residence in Fairfax and noted Chuck's late model Volvo still in the driveway. He turned at the corner and after another pass, pulled over and parked.

Chuck emerged a quarter hour later, and after refueling at the neighborhood gas station, stopped briefly at a hardware store, then pulled into the Safeway at Seven Corners. Alex parked two rows away and waited. Chuck finally emerged from the Safeway and left his groceries behind a store barrier and went to retrieve his car.

Alex knelt next to the car adjacent to Bunn's, tying his shoe laces until Bunn had the door open and was getting in. Alex walked over and kept the door open. "Move over," Alex ordered pushing Bunn into the passenger seat.

Chuck's expression bordered on speechless incredulity. "You been following me?" His voice expressed outrage. "How dare you."

"We need to talk, Chuck."

Bunn's demeanor was petulant. "How dare you follow me?"

"Shut up for Christ's sake. Don't act like some born again Christian! You of all people should know better. Who called out the FBI on me?"

"I Don't know, Alex." He stared at Alex's left hand which was inside his windbreaker. "What are you holding there?"

"A peace-maker. Just in case." Alex smiled. "Now, tell me about Case Judy."

"I have no idea what you are talking about."

Alex studied him for a moment and decided he was probably telling the truth. "How did you know I was in Omaha when I called?"

"Easy. I have Caller-ID service on my phone."

Alex hadn't thought of it. "And who did you tell after we spoke?"

"Why?"

"Because people showed up and tried to kill me."

"Who?"

"That's why I am here, asshole! Three are dead since I spoke with you from Omaha."

"Watch your language, Balkan. I am your superior, you know."

"Are you kidding?" Alex insolently demanded. "Don't you read the papers, Chuck? They also killed my mother and an old friend named Marvin Raoul . . . right here in Washington . . . that's five."

Bunn looked aggrieved for a moment. "I'm sorry about your mother. I didn't know. Also about Raoul. I read about him in the 'Earlybird' but had no idea it had anything to do with you. My condolences."

"I don't need your condolences, Mr. Bunn. What I need is the name of the person or persons you called last week and told them I was in Omaha."

"You are assuming I told someone. Why?"

Alex was starting to lose his temper. "Think about this, Chuky baby!" he said. "I called you Sunday afternoon. No one else knew where I was. Seventeen hours later, a Russian hit team arrives at my hotel in Omaha, but I'd already left. So they followed me, and staked out the next location where they knew I'd show up."

"Where was that?" Bunn asked.

"I'm not going to tell you shit! You've already betrayed me once and you'll stupidly do it again. Luckily for me I spotted the assassin's first and now they're dead."

Bunn's expression transcended disbelief. "Jesus Christ! You murdered two people?"

"They both tried to kill me. One of them admitted killing my mother. The other admitted wasting Marvin Raoul here in Washington."

"This is outrageous Balkan! You can't go around this country murdering people for Christ's sake! That's law enforcement's job!"

"Shut up!" Alex yelled, his face now inches from Bunn's, and a mask of anger and frustration. "Don't be such a goddamn asshole and try to engage your mouth only after your brain has had a chance to process data! For two weeks these guys tracked me. Someone paid them a half-million dollars to kill me! They almost succeeded . . . twice! And you sit there acting like some stupid outraged cunt whose been dildoed in a whorehouse and you are going to call the police! Forget about your haughty moralistic bullshit and tell me what I want to know, or so help me you dickhead, I'll shoot you too, right here."

Bunn's face was ashen and aghast. "You've got to turn yourself in, Alex," Bunn told him. "The FBI will protect you. I'll guarantee it."

Alex started to laugh.

"You are out in left field, Alex. You have got to let the law handle this."

"I'll be dead within hours if I do," Alex replied. "These guys are good and they are connected. They're getting their instructions from someone much higher on the totem pole than you, Chuck. They want me out of the way because of what I know. Without me there's no witness. And whomever that person is, it is someone you have been talking to, and you unwittingly informed them where I was so they could get to me. Tell me who you called, that's all I ask, and I'll be on my way."

Chuck was nervous and sweating despite the cold early morning temperature. Alex considered Bunn an unwitting part of the problem, but kept his left hand on the automatic pistol inside his jacket just in case. If Chuck made a false move, he'd blow him away too.

"I'm waiting, Chuck?"

"I can't, Alex. You have to follow the laws of our country just like the rest of us."

Alex withdrew the automatic and pushed it against Chuck's ribs. "What they did to my mother is indescribable. Marvin Raoul too. Would you be upset if some criminal visited your house while you were out, did unspeakable things to your wife before killing her, then played with your daughter, despoiling her until she too died in incredible agony, and they did this for money. Would you tell anyone who listened that the law should take its course, and you would have no problem if the courts let the criminal off on a technicality. Well, all of us don't have your view of justice Chuck, so tell me whom you spoke too, or I have no choice but to assume you are part of the problem and also want me dead."

"You are not the type Balkan."

"I'm out of time, Chuck. You betrayed me. Because of you they killed my mother and my friend. And now they are trying to kill me. Well, if it works for you Chuky baby, it works for me to." The distinct sound of the hammer being clicked filled the car.

"It was Seeley," Chuck blurted.

Alex uncocked the gun and returned it to his jacket.

"I thought so. But I had to be sure. If I were you Chuck, I'd strongly suggest you forget you saw me here. I'm serious. Give me your cell phone." Alex smashed it on the center console. "You tell Seeley what you just told me, and I guarantee you and your wife will die mysteriously before nightfall."

Alex pulled the keys from the ignition and dropped them into his pocket as he closed the car door. "Sorry to inconvenience you. AAA can make you a new set within an hour."

Twenty minutes later, Alex pulled off Wisconsin and parked near a public phone. He called the Defense Intelligence Agency office at Bolling Air Force Base and asked for General Putnam's office.

Alex recounted the New Yorker's story about Indorenko's half million dollar contract to have him murdered, and his belief that Indorenko was Langford Seeley's Case Officer. There was a long silence and Alex could feel Putnam's hesitancy.

"Did you tell the president about Seeley?" Alex demanded.

There was no response.

"A hit team tried to kill me in Omaha last week. The only man who knew I was there was Seeley."

Putnam suggested he come in and get debriefed. "I just have," Alex replied and hung up.

That evening Jose Santiago told Alex he would leave for Moscow via Lucerne, Switzerland, the next evening."

"Lucerne?" Alex asked.

"An old girlfriend is there." Santiago smiled. "Just an overnight."

"Don't be late, Jose."

"You got it."

Boris had arranged Jose Santiago's flight to Z-5 for three days hence. Alex would also leave in the morning for Key West and stay with Mike Gregoriou until they finished next week's dive. By next Friday he'd have the video footage of the submarine and Santiago would be back from Russia with the pictures from Z-5. Alex smiled. In two weeks Larry King Live and Good Morning America, would offer Alex millions for an interview.

Silver Springs, Maryland

"Glad you returned my call, Alex," Waleston Thrower replied on the phone in Salt Lake City. "I left a note on the answering machine. Did your girlfriend tell you? The inks and paper checked out against other documents used in the Soviet Union during and just after World War II. There was no doubt either about the paper. The signature too is authentic!"

"Glad to hear the documents checked out. What happens next?"

"The story will appear in the morning edition, front page, section D. If it is not spiked."

"Spiked?"

"It means my editor decides not to go with it for some reason."

"This late in the game?"

"He's still nervous about referring to you as a confidential source in the article."

"Waleston. I don't want my name mentioned. Got it!"

"That's where it stands right now. Anything more on the submarine?"

"I should have it in a couple of days."

"Okay. Watch the news tomorrow. Your story should go nationwide by evening."

Alex hung up. He'd wanted to tell Thrower what Royster had told him in New York, regarding Indorenko, and that Indorenko was the Russian Case Officer handling Langford Seeley. Also that the Russians had paid Royster a half million to arrange Alex's execution. But it probably didn't matter anymore. With Indorenko dead, Seeley probably knew his world was unraveling, and it was just a question of time before the scales of justice would decide Seeley's destiny.

Seattle, Washington

"Good news, Mr. President." Langford strolled vigorously into the top-floor hotel suite and shook his boss's hand. "The submarine is history! The day before yesterday."

"No traces?"

"Shouldn't think so. Four hundred pounds of C-4. I'm assured even one hundred along its keel would have been enough!"

"Everything all right, Langford?" Seeley seemed preoccupied.

"Just tired from the trip, Mr. President. It has been a long week."

"Okay. Let's get started. This will only take a couple of minutes. I want to talk to the Russian president about the Z-5 issue as soon I get back to Washington. I'd like you to set it up personally."

"What's new?" Langford asked as he helped himself to a cup of coffee from a decanter.

The president wondered how the old man's heart stood all the caffeine. "General Putnam found an NSA intercept for the thirteenth of last month. Seems Russia lost a heavy military transport, an IL-76, south of Z-5. It has to be the one that took the prisoners out. It arrived before first light and departed that evening, then crashed within a quarter hour after takeoff."

Seeley's demeanor was indolent and he almost seemed disinterested in the conversation. "You sure you are all right, Langford?" the president inquired a second time.

"Yes, sir. It is just jet lag. Being in my late eighties doesn't help either." The president guffawed and related the rest of the highlights of his meeting with Putnam.

"Langford, I intend to tell the Russian it is vital we be allowed to inspect the crash site. I've got to be certain none of our POW's were aboard that transport. So what I need by Tuesday morning are some ironclad arguments to support our demand."

"You sure you want to dig so deep into this? It will upset the world equilibrium, Mr. President."

"Goddamn it, Langford, look into it. When Yeltsin was here a few years ago he informed us there were still some live Americans here and there around the Soviet Union, but was not definitive, and he, and you too by the way were among those who promised to look into it. But then he had a run in with Putin and some of the party hardliners, and the issue seemed to come to an end. There was that Russian general too, Volvogonav, Volkoganev or something like that. He too informed us he was aware of lots of former American military imprisoned in the USSR, but then his information also seemed to go cold when he got home. You could start with that outfit in Alexandria who follow the POW/MIA issue for this country. I was informed they have produced a couple of reports on the Gulag which report Americans by the thousands here and there across the USSR in the 1950s to the 1970s.

"Sure you want to go there, Mr. President?" Seeley opined quietly.

"Excuse me?" The president asked, annoyance again creeping into his voice. "Do it, Langford . . . If there are Americans there, then we'll open Pandora's box all the way. The American public and Press will probably go banana's and we will have to take our licks as the saga unfolds. If I'm wrong about all this; then we forget about everything—including Case Judy! This man Balkan will have been discredited, and Russian American relations can return to normal."

"And the Caballero question now appears to have evaporated as of two days ago." Seeley smiled.

"Thank God," the president muttered. It was not one of his prouder moments. But Langford had eliminated a problem neither of them had wanted to deal with.

"Now, Langford. How to handle the Russian next Tuesday? My inclination is to come right out and tell him that we know. Put our relationship on the line! If he has nothing to hide, he'll agree. If he refuses, then we're in for some rough sailing."

"Who else has been brought it on Case Judy, Mr. President?"

"No change from last Monday."

"You and General Putnam, and Zeugman at FDIC?"

"Yes, plus Balkan, and whomever he's confided it to."

Seeley shook his head. Mention of Balkan's name had quickened his pulse again. "He will be discredited, Mr. President if the crash site is clean. Without the Case Judy documents, and without the submarine, there is no case. And if the crash site opens Pandora's Box as you just alluded to, it won't make any difference anyway because the POW thing will probably lead to a break in diplomatic relations anyway."

For the last week Langford had debated submitting his resignation. He hadn't slept in three days; not since he'd received the call from Paul Carter. It was his worst nightmare unfolding; being stalked by a man from his youth, one he wouldn't recognize, couldn't find, and dared not expose.

But even if he did resign and disappeared, he'd only avoid Carter for a while. Carter was resourceful, obviously a survivor, and a man who would find him no matter where he went. Langford was better protected while he remained NSC advisor. He'd wait a couple of weeks and reconsider. Maybe the old bastard would drop dead first from a heart attack?

"Jesus, Langford," the president quipped, "you really don't look well. You want my doctor to take a look at you?"

"It is all right, Mr. President."

The president studied his itinerary. "I return to Washington late Monday. First thing Tuesday morning; make it 0800, I want you and Putnam there. Bring a list of talking positions I can use with the Russians."

"I'll get right on it."

"See you Tuesday."

San Francisco

It was a typical beautiful Sunday morning in San Francisco. Clear skies overhead and just to the west along the city's ridgeline hung a wall of morning clouds drifting in from the Pacific Ocean that would burn off by mid-afternoon. The president had just concluded his remarks at the Desert Storm memorial in San Francisco when a squat reporter jumped up with a clipping grasped in his pudgy hand.

"Mr. President!" He screamed, "What do you intend to do about this POW report which appeared in this morning's Salt Lake Sentinel? Are you going to demand a full accounting for the thousands of Americans reportedly held, and then abandoned, in Soviet camps after World War II? Or was it more, as high as 25,000 from a report allegedly made by General Eisenhower when he was in charge in Europe just as WWII ended? Will your administration sever relations with Moscow if they refuse to cooperate? If it is true why didn't Defense Intelligence Agency or the CIA expose this abhorrent state of affairs long ago?"

The president glanced around nervously as he raised his hands. "Hold it, hold it! I haven't seen the report." Where's my Press Secretary he thought, frantically wondering what the hell had gone wrong, and how the leak had started?

"According to the article, Mr. President," the pudgy heckler persisted, "there are as many as three hundred and fifty American servicemen still being held prisoner in secret Russian camps somewhere in the Siberian Arctic. Any comment?"

"As I said. I have not seen the report," the president replied. He pointed next to the NBC reporter.

"Mr. President," the NBC man shouted. "The Salt Lake City report hints at a wider conspiracy between the United States and Russia regarding the POW issue. There are rumors of a conspiracy between our two governments. Is your administration aware of this?"

Once again he disavowed any knowledge and sought other questions, but it kept coming up. He noticed that the chief of his secret service detail was trying to get his attention.

People at the back of the crowd were now holding up a huge banner: "SHAME! Bring them home NOW or RESIGN."

He thanked everyone and headed for the exit.

The Alexandria Yacht Club

Professor Schenke was not so familiar with the Washington area as it had been many years since he'd been here and on previous visits had never rented a car. Now the sudden upward swing in the EURO's value made it too cheap not to. He'd landed at Dulles International Airport yesterday from Zurich and was staying with a nephew whose home was in Westmoreland Hills, seven miles northwest of the White House. Tomorrow he would drive north into Pennsylvania and visit another relative before returning to Washington and then back to Switzerland. He'd had no problem finding the turnoff a mile south of Reagan

Airport and could clearly see the Potomac River and the yacht basin and sailboats from the parkway. He was temporarily distracted by the noise of a Continental Airlines passing overhead on its final approach to Reagan Airport. He slowed to watch it before proceeding to the Yacht Club parking area just south of the airport. A waitress showed him to a table by the window where a lone man waited in the sunlight.

Professor Schenke recognized him, but the American gave no sign of recognition as he approached.

"You are Mr. Reinhardt Staples. Isn't it so?" The professor asked in a thick Swiss accent.

"Yes, and you are Schenke?"

"Yes, I am," the professor replied as he took a seat across the table from Staples. "It's good to see you again."

"Again?" The American asked.

"You are being humorous?"

A strange statement. But anyway, what brings you to Washington, Mr. Schenke?"

"You, and my relatives."

"Yes, you stated on the phone that we had met before?" The American observed.

"Yes in fact, several times," Schenke replied.

"Please refresh my memory if you would be so kind."

"Our profession has few people like us," Schenke replied, realizing that this man was going to annoy him again. He'd already done so during several occasions in the past when they'd met in Europe. When he'd called Staples yesterday, Staples had trouble recalling who he was and insisted they had never met. Staples was also noncommittal on the phone, refusing to meet with him until Schenke threatened to take his concerns higher in Washington.

As a world military power, Schenke could appreciate the arrogance of American power, but not ignoring the fate of so many of their captured soldiers after twentieth century wars which America had won. On both sides of Schenke's family were relatives who were involved with the downfall of world powers of their time. On his mother's side was Count Franz Conrad von Hotzendorf, the chief of the Austro-Hungarian general staff in 1914. On his father's side was Lord Balfour and at a time when Pax Britannia reigned globally. A Swiss national himself, Schenke's citizenship was through his mother, jus sanguins.

"My reason for wanting to see you, Mr. Staples," Schenke said as he ordered ice tea, "is, as I mentioned yesterday, I saw Yakov Ghranov again in Moscow ten days ago, and once again, he asked if I had reminded you of his earlier offer to you. I assured him I had, but he seemed puzzled that you had never contacted him and he asked me to see you personally while I was here. He is upset that neither you nor anyone in Washington has contacted him."

"Ghranov?" Staples observed somewhat distracted. "Have you mentioned that name to me in the earlier phone call you allege you made, or yesterday's call?"

The professor's expression became pained. "Allege! What do you mean *allege*, Mr. Staples? You do not remember?" Exasperation now clearly evident in Schenke's tone. "We spoke about it at considerable length last year when you were in Lucerne, Switzerland. September 20 was the date to be exact."

"I'm sorry, Mr. Schenke. I checked my logs and must have forgotten it. What did we speak about?"

"What did we speak of?" Now Schenke's tone became incredulous. He now understood the annoyance of his research associate in Paris, who'd already informed him of his suspicions about this man called Staples; and others too in Washington who were entrusted with the resolution of America's huge case backlog of eighty-three thousand POW/MIAs, a significant number of whom had ended up dying secretly in the USSR after WWII. The Americans seemed uninterested in the Russian offer, apparently seeing no future in digging up or accounting for old American skeletons in Russia, even if there were fifteen or twenty thousand of them. Schenke had personally called Staples earlier and informed him Moscow was ready to make available thousands and thousands of its secret dossiers compiled for over twenty thousand American servicemen they'd captured from the Germans as WWII ended, and then secretly shipped into the Gulag and never admitted they had them.

Schenke knew the American files existed. He'd already seen hundreds of them and their name cards in the FSB's Moscow archives. The archive director had also shown him scores of the American dossiers—many of who had perished in the Gulag: five, ten, and even twenty years after WWII had ended. It was the FSB's archive director, Yakov Ghranov, who had made the offer to Washington and wanted to make the files available.

Staples continued to stare at him expectantly.

"Mr. Staples, you know Yakov Ghranov?"

"The name is not familiar to me."

"For god's sake!" Schenke's voice exasperated. "What are you saying! I know that you have met him. Ghranov also told me he had met you several times in Moscow with Special Group-Moscow and also at symposia in Luzern, Switzerland, three years ago in August. I attended that symposium and so did you. I recall you speaking with him on several occasions."

"Well, of course, I recall being there, but there were so many people. How do you expect me to remember all of them?. What did he look like?"

"Two meters in height, eighty-five kilos, a little fat in the stomach, a clean-shaven hawklike face and graying hair with a bald spot on his crown. He spoke no English, and you spoke to him in Russian. You and he exchanged three vodka toasts to American Imperialism's success in China, Russian capitalism, and Korean reunification. Remember?"

"I still am having trouble placing him, Professor Schenke."

"What is all this about, Mr. Staples?"

"Sir?"

"Why do you refuse to acknowledge that we spoke about Ghanov earlier? Why do you refuse to acknowledge you have met Ghranov?"

"I am refusing nothing. I see many people. I just do not recall him, nor this offer you allege he has made to us."

Schenke was not a stupid man. He and Staples were part of a handful of experts investigating the worldwide unresolved POW/MIA community. He, like Staples, knew the countries that had seriously abused prisoners legally and otherwise in the latter half of the twentieth century. Both men had written papers on the subject. Schenke was a senior research assistant who for the past two decades conducted research in Moscow's most sensitive intelligence archives. His mission: find still missing WWII Europeans captured and imprisoned in the former Soviet Union and never admitted by Moscow. Staples offices in Washington had the same mission—did exactly the same thing. In last twenty years Schenke had documented the fates of a quarter million of his fellow countrymen who'd died in Gulag camps in the decades after 1945. Some had even been found alive and repatriated to their families in Europe. Staples organization on the other hand had accounted for less than four hundred out of over eighty thousand.

Three years ago Ghranov had offered to account for thousands of Americans for which he said he had dossiers in his archive. These dossiers described in excruciating detail who each of these men were and where and when each had eventually perished in the Gulag. He indicated there were over twenty-five thousand of these dossiers. Schenke had also passed this offer to Staples three years ago in Washington. But then nothing happened and the Russians were curious. Why not? And now, the man across the table from him could not recall the offer?

"To remind you, Mr. Staples. Ghranov informed you that there were 25,237 American servicemen in three separate holding camps around the Odessa area in late April 1945. All of these men had been liberated months earlier by Soviet forces from German prison cages in eastern Europe as WW-II ended. Those in a fourth camp in the Odessa area were 2,983 to be exact. These were turned over to American liaison officers in the Odessa port area that month and documented by the United States before they were shipped home. The rest, some 22,250, whose whereabouts in the Odessa area were obviously unknown to U.S. authorities at the time, were secretly entrained east to Gulag camps in Soviet central Asia and Siberia were they were eventually disposed of."

"How do you know this man Ghranov can be trusted?" Staples asked.

"Acchhh!" The professor rudely waived away the waiter who'd arrived with his ice tea and asked about their lunch order. "Leave us!" he abruptly ordered the waiter.

Leaning forward he said. "Get the dossiers, Mr. Staples! What have you got to lose?"

"Ask Granov to put his subject to me in writing and send it to me and we will get back to him."

"Are you joking? They have done it several times already and got no reply."

"As I said. Put it in writing."

"But I am asking you now, why has no one replied?"

"Put it in writing."

"Why bother if you know no one will reply?"

"Put it in writing. Ghranov wants money for the dossiers?" Staples observed quietly.

"Yes. Two dollars per dossier to cover photocopying and retrieval of the dossiers.

"America does not pay ransom demands from anyone." Staples informed him officiously. "And it is our national policy not to pay ransom. If you do not know this then you should. We cannot pay ransom."

Schenke's expression was incredulous. "Surely you are joking with me?"

"No, sir. We do not pay ransom."

"I feel sorry for you, Mr. Staples. May God forgive you for your indolence and stupidity."

"No need to be obtuse, Professor. For your information. We also do not believe there are any of our people who were not accounted for. Therefore the Russians are probably lying."

"But I too have personally seen hundreds of these American dossiers in the Russian archives. Are you suggesting I am a liar, sir?"

"A man of your pedigree, I would not presume to pass judgment," Staples observed. "I do not believe the dossiers exist."

"Ya . . . ya . . . I know," the professor replied with incredulity. "And that is why you still have over seventy-five thousand still listed as POW/MIA from WWII. Am I correct?"

"There are various reasons for this," Staples replied. "Mostly accounting errors and some confusion on names."

Schenke threw up his hands in frustration. "My American colleague. Is it not possible," he observed, "in your mind, that even a couple may have been lost and could now be accounted for?"

"Our policy, my dear Swiss associate, is that any who remained were obviously traitors and turncoats, and deliberately volunteered to remain in Russia, as have others in Korea and Vietnam, so why should we look for them?

"Unbelievable!" Schenke muttered with disgust. "You have been there. You have seen the USSR. And you make such a ridiculous statement to me?"

"We have been through this before. There are none. I appreciate your coming to inform me of your concern, Professor Schenke." Staples looked at his wristwatch.

"What should I tell Ghranov when I see him?" Schenke demanded.

"Whatever you like. It is not my concern."

"And your government?"

"As I have repeatedly told you . . . Mr. Schenke. My government does not pay ransom, and since none are there, why should we listen to you or others?"

"Now I understand why your program is under investigation by your congress."

"It has nothing to do with Russia." Staples tone now defensive.

"Not yet." Schenke observed. "But one day."

"We do what we are told."

"Mr. Staples, I will be back in Washington next week, may I follow up on this with you?"

"Regrettably I will be on vacation for a month. You can leave a message."

Cropley Manor, Maryland.

Langford Seeley was tired. He knew his condition bordered on exhaustion. Like most animals being hunted: fear and self-preservation frequently enabled them to function far beyond their normal condition. A long week had turned into a longer weekend, and thank God he was home. Maybe tonight he'd get some sleep for the first time in a few days. The phone calls had been incessant, and he'd finally had the damned thing disconnected and also turned off his cell phone and hot line to Washington. Screw them all he thought. They could charge him with dereliction of duty for making himself inaccessible to the administration for a day or two. But he suspected worse things awaited him.

He studied the sporadic ribbon of headlights making their way to and fro between the homes across the valley in the Virginia hills. Below, in the foreground, he could discern the Potomac islands from the back-lighted sky of Washington. He loved this scene. So much history lay before him in the Virginia countryside—historic battles of the Revolutionary War and Civil War eras, as well as the constant turmoil of the Washington scene ever since.

After Key West he'd flown to California for his meeting with the president and then northward to Seattle where he spent the night with his grandson before returning cross-country to Washington this afternoon. He and his wife of many years had just finished a light dinner before watching the evening news. Only one item referred briefly to the president's media encounter in San Francisco.

"I'm going to bed dear." His wife's voice cut through his thoughts.

"I'll be up in a while, Esteve."

They'd lived as man and wife twenty-four years. His third, her fourth; and neither had reservations any longer about the reality of love's passage. For him she represented legitimacy, and a thing to grace his arm in public forums. America's puritanical electorate demanded it of those in public office. They bore each other a grudging respect. He didn't need her, just her physical presence. She didn't need him, but enjoyed the perks and interminable round of socials and dinners that his position garnered. The glitterati of their lives was something both used for adrenaline. Her last divorce had made her wealthy; although inconsequential compared to his, but still, neither knew what to do with it all anyway. So they'd reached comfortable compromise. Lust was for the young and inconvenience for the old. There was a familiar comfort to their arrangement, like the furniture and other accoutrements of a familiar staid existence.

Men were bastards, he smiled as he reflected on the bonfire of the vanities; and women were bitches. But each needed the other for the perpetuation of the interminable game. When he'd first met his German lover in Berlin just before World War II, Marta was seventeen, he eighteen; she five foot four and ninety pounds—with an incredible eighteen-inch waist, prominent breasts, and a face like the icons of Aryan perfection. She had long slender legs, blue eyes, and blond hair, and Langford was instantly smitten by the rose-scented cleft of her mons veneris. They'd made love on their third outing. He thought he'd seduced Marta with his suave New England breeding and good looks. How naive he'd been then. How naive he still was.

Well born and used to the finer things, he's stupidly thought she loved him because she'd given him her body. In those days he loved Marta because she willingly slept with him and he couldn't live without her body. She was something fine, beautiful, desirable, and forbiddingly irresponsible. As a student temporarily having a summer holiday abroad, he thought nothing of it. So he'd taken up residence in her bed and drowned himself between the mountains of her breasts and valley between her thighs.

Germany, before the war, was a halcyon place of quaint towns with cuckoo clocks and streets lined with gingerbread houses. But behind the straight-laced facade lay the urge to participate in aberrant fantasies of a social system which had been totally corrupted. Within a week after he'd met Marta, she'd introduced him to the finer arts of love in Berlin's prurient clubs and bars where the most outrageous fantasies could, and were, played out. Scion of a good family who'd sheltered him, Langford never imagined that such sodomitic pleasures existed nor was he smart enough to suspect the obvious.

In the postwar years, he'd continued to worship her from time to time, like a narcotic dependence but differently. And as the decades passed, it was his earliest memories of her that sustained him. It was the unstructured life or irresponsible adolescence, the incredible fun, the sensuous eroticism of the time, and the totality with which she'd overwhelmed his defenses that his mind reveled in whenever he thought of her. He knew too that he'd do it again if he could. He wanted to, but without the aberrant sodomic experiences in Berlin.

On a few occasions in Berlin he'd consumed too much Schnapps and passed out. He recalled awakening at Marta's apartment near the railroad station, and being told that he'd made an ass of himself in his drunken stupors. He suspected what had happened, but couldn't clearly recall the details. But his body knew. After washing up he'd returned to her bed.

Two years later, after he'd graduated from Harvard and obtained his first job in Manhattan, he was approached one Sunday afternoon at Coney Island by a nondescript man with bad teeth, worse breath, and a thick accent. The man informed him of certain indiscretions, hinting all would be well if Langford were cooperative. But if not? The man handed him an envelope. Its contents mortified him. The man assured Langford that there was no need for concern. All the stranger needed was a favor and would contact him again. Before Langford could reply the man turned and left.

Ever since that day his recollections of his alcoholic stupors in Berlin had haunted his subconscious. Photographs of him posed indiscreetly with dogs, sheep, and even a pig were repulsive. How would he explain it to his parents, his employer, or his friends? He'd be a laughing stock and lose everything: power, position, respect, authority, and social stranding. He was certain Marta knew, but she never let on. Had she been a part of it? Again, she denied any knowledge and he believed her.

Three months after the first Coney Island incident he received a New York Times newspaper article in a plain envelope which contained a picture of the nondescript man from Coney Island. He'd been deported to Germany for espionage. Also enclosed was a glossy photograph of the spy handing an envelope to Langford months earlier at Coney Island. Soon Langford's Walter Mitty career began in earnest, and in the years that followed he betrayed his family, his friends, and his country . . . in spades.

He'd held his breath, wondering when the FBI knock would come, but it never did, nothing happened, and Langford's Berlin indiscretions were apparently forgotten. Then, years after World War II was a distant memory in the United States, a chance encounter on a Manhattan street corner convinced Langford otherwise. It was suggested he travel to Brazil for the forthcoming Carnival and wait for a man with the initials GS to contact him.

He encountered Garo Selvanian at a cocktail party at the American Ambassador's residence in Rio de Janeiro. A gregarious well-connected and apparently wellhealed Armenian expatriate, Selvanian, like Langford; lived well and partied with the paparazzi of Rio. Langford had just arrived in Rio, and in the weeks that followed, the two men became inseparable on the Rio social circuit. Selvanian introduced him to a Peruvian whose investments later became incredibly profitable for Langford too. And as the Peruvian's wealth multiplied so did Langford's. A year later the web thickened when the Armenian introduced him to another of his friends, this time a wealthy Hong Kong real estate mogul named Hassan Khatoury. Hong Kong born, with unorthodox ideas, Khatoury further expanded Langford's investment horizons in Asia. Langford at first suspected the genealogy and genesis of these men's wealth but then chose to ignore it when they confirmed his suspicions. Most problematic for Langford initially was their involvement with the Caballero bullion.

Over the ensuing decades Langford's fortunes continued to multiply while his association with the two men faded into the background. He hadn't seen Hassan Khatoury in decades, nor the Armenian for that matter for four years. Over the years Selvanian had appeared unannounced from time to time, always amidst a crowd, and always when Langford was abroad on private vacations. And now the

Armenian had appeared again. This time to assure Langford that the wars in Iraq and Afghanistan had been good for sagging economies, and proposed yet another insidious approach to protect their assets and generate even more wealth.

Langford yawned as he arose from his favorite chair and stretched. He knew he would not sleep well this night. His body was exhausted but his mind raced as he moved to the sideboard for another of his favorite Cypriot brandies. Funny he thought how his life had come full circle. The Seal Team at Key West had trashed the submarine. That nightmare was gone. Sipping the Five Kings Brandy, he studied the ribbon of headlights across the river as he reflected on Eve Albion who was also now dead. He'd known her so many years ago in Berlin as Marta and cursed Paul Carter for killing her. A part of him had died with her. Strange how two men's lives could be interwoven with the same woman he thought! They'd both shared her, like two knots in a rope; and once one was undone, so was the other.

God! Could it have been sixty-plus years since he'd first met Paul Carter in one of the hundreds of temporary wooden State department buildings that had once littered the Washington Mall's landscape where the Vietnam Memorial now stood. The Marine Corps had agreed to "loan" Major Paul Carter, USMC, to the British Passport Office in Manhattan for the duration of the war. Langford Seeley's employer had also agreed to transfer Langford to the same office in New York. Langford, already a closet idealist then, knew Paul Carter's life until then had made him a hard bitten pragmatist—steeped in the seamier side of life in the Far East. Carter had seen death and murder up close in Asia. The British Passport Office served as a cover for the newly organized Office of Special Services, Donovan's OSS. Donovan, at the time, was assembling a team of young men to handle the nation's forthcoming wartime need for clandestine operations, and among the scores he had assembled from various backgrounds were Langford Seeley, Paul Carter, and Ted LePage.

On arrival in Manhattan, Langford and Paul became involved in planning for the first of three wartime gold transfers. With the outline of a plan in place by mid-1942, the two men attended special agent training on the Canadian side of Lake Erie, where they ended up as room-mates.

Too bad Langford thought as he sipped at the Five Kings. If the Chinese had gotten rid of Carter when they were supposed to,

Langford wouldn't be sitting here watching the darkened Virginia landscape tonight, and contemplating his destiny? Now, as he cogitated surviving the next few days, he desperately wished he'd get an opportunity to speak with Paul Carter before it was all over.

TWO

Key Cudjoe

ALEX TOOK A deep breath of the pungent air as Mike Gregoriou's vintage 1967 Boat-tail Alfa Romeo hummed northward along the Overseas Highway northwards from Key West. Alex was glad to be back. He liked the sharp contrasts between the cobalt blue sky, white cotton ball clouds; thousands of tiny atolls, and luxuriant green shades of flora. His senses were repeatedly assailed by the earthy contrasts of rotting vegetation mixed with pungent Frangipani. By Alex's calculation barely one hundred days had elapsed since his last visit to Key West, and the approaching summer sun was perceptibly warmer now.

"Yeah," Mike observed as their speed dropped off for yet another of the long columns of motor homes slowly moving northward. "Snowbirds heading home," he observed acerbically.

They hadn't spoken much at the airport. Alex's concern about how soon they could visit the wreck was ameliorated by Mike's up-front assurance that everything was ready and Heron was already at sea. Gregoriou's body was still as lean as Alex remembered, only the tan was more pronounced, and the crow's feet etched a little deeper around his eyes.

"Still doing a lot of exercise, Mike?"

"Five miles each morning, fifty laps in the pool most days. Not so much time for the bicycle though."

"Why the heavy routine?" Alex ran his hand around his girth a little self-consciously. He'd been taking too much solace lately in food and the abuse showed. He swore to himself that as soon as all this was over that he was going to join a gym and lose fifty pounds and get in shape.

"Marathons," Mike replied. "You familiar with them?"

"Something about running?"

"It commemorates the Greek defeat of the Persians in 490 BC. Some unknown Greek named Pheidipides ran the twenty-six miles plus 385 yards to Athens after the battle of Marathon to let Athens know she'd been saved. I do several a year." He looked across at Alex. "Got another one coming up in Athens, Greece in August. It's a bear I'm told. I've got a couple of route maps and the first five miles are over flat land away from the coast at Marathon, then its increasingly more and more uphill for nine miles until you cross a ridge. From there on it is through the congested and polluted streets of the city. Friends tell me that Athens air is the equivalent of smoking five packs of cigarettes a day from the pollution." He glanced at Alex and shrugged.

"So why do it?" Alex inquired.

"Because another Greek did it. My grandparents were Greek, if you hadn't guessed?"

"Okay," Alex laughed. "That's good enough for me."

"Incidentally, Alex. Someone mentioned your name here last Wednesday. Seems you are still a popular guy around here."

"Didn't know anyone cared."

"Lange does. Recall that name?"

"Sure. The Admiral."

"He was transferred to Italy you know, and left two days ago."

"Sorry I missed him."

"Yeah, I'll bet." Gregoriou glanced over at him again. "Didn't know you'd met him."

"Yeah! We had lunch together. How'd my name come up? I'm still mystified why he called me." Alex waited for Gregoriou to continue.

"Out of the blue last Wednesday Lange calls and tells me he's up at Boca Chica NAS, and had mentioned your name in regards to some official enquiries in Washington about U-2513. He said he'd also mentioned the names of two other people here who knew about our project. Lange's Exec, a Captain Millican who is a retired navy goomba down here. I asked him who wanted to know. Lange said it was the president's National Security advisor."

"Langford Seeley?" Alex asked, his voice obviously troubled.

"Yeah. Jeezus . . . You know him too, Alex?"

"Of him, Mike. Who exactly is Millican?"

"Some retired navy guy down here who also asked me about the sub the day before you did last December. I mentioned him to you last time."

"Yeah, now I recall it."

"I got the impression Lange was warning me." He turned and looked at Alex. "Anything you want to tell me?"

"No, why?"

"Trouble maybe?"

"Don't think so." But Alex made a note to contact Lange's office at Truman Annex.

"I haven't told you this Alex, but I returned to the wreck about a month ago."

"Thought you might!" His voice obviously annoyed that Mike hadn't already mentioned it earlier.

"Don't get hostile on me now. It's my business."

"And?" Alex asked politely.

"Everything is fine. I'll give you the details as soon as we get you settled in."

Alex leaned back and relaxed as Mike turned onto a secondary road toward a sumptuous gate and long circular drive. From the size of the house it was obvious Gregoriou lived well. An elder man appeared with white jacket and black slacks as the car halted beneath a portico.

"Manuel, please show Mr. Balkan to his quarters. I'll be out at the pool Alex."

Alex dropped his bag on the bed, combed his hair and headed through the lanai to the pool.

"Swim?"

"No thanks, Mike. I didn't bring a suit."

"Don't need one!"

The orange orb of the sun was just above the horizon and already the temperature was cooler. Mike shed his shirt and trunks and climbed into the jacuzzi beside the pool. "Don't need one here either."

What the hell, Alex thought, as he got comfortable in the hot water. Manuel appeared with drinks.

"Manuel has prepared dinner, what time you want to eat?"

"No hurry," Alex replied. "Tell me about the sub."

"I've got a dive ship called Heron. A month ago I parked her above the wreck and we looked her over more closely. Also cut through her side and checked out her interior. Whoa!" Mike exclaimed, noting

Alex's immediate accusatory expression. "Relax man! She's not yours you know. And I already knew about her. Take it easy! She's in excellent condition, no hull damage. She was definitely not sunk by gunfire like the official navy records report."

"You got it on video?"

"Only her exterior. That's why you are going to pay me the ten grand, so I'll go back and get the interior stuff. We didn't take cameras inside earlier because we were concerned about safety. Then we ran out of time and had to surface. No matter, we'll get it this time." He studied Alex. "You obviously know more than you've let on from the start. Mind telling me what this is all about? Someone has obviously done a lot of exploratory work inside."

Alex gave him one of his innocent expressions.

"Come on, Alex! Lange calls to tell me he's been warned by Navy Brass in Washington to forget about the sub. The president's NSC Advisor comes down here and makes enquiries about it. It is obvious the navy falsified her record. And her insides are intriguing."

"Such as?" Alex demanded, his ears perking up.

"Ahhhaaaa!" Mike exclaimed. "Finally! An expression of interest?"

Alex smiled.

"Parts of her interior pressure hull were cut away a long time ago," Mike continued, "and then replaced. There's strange modifications to her lower deck, some hatches are welded shut, and holes later cut into her interior pressure hull. Comparing her to German records available, I can't figure out what Type she is."

"Can you be more specific?" Alex asked with obvious interest. He was almost certain now she must be the one reported lost off South America. The navy had obviously raised her, brought her here, and then disposed of her secretly. Two more days and he'd have the internal video footage. Then it wouldn't matter.

"This is what I think, Alex."

Oval Office

The president's expression became pained as he waited for a Moscow translator to explain a linguistic idiom used by his counterpart in the Kremlin.

Instead of a calm weekend on the west coast, he'd encountered a media piranha-feed frenzy following the Sunday morning expose by Salt Lake City's largest daily newspaper. The press had confronted him initially at a fund raiser breakfast in San Francisco, and then everywhere later in the day. There was still no hint anyone knew yet of the Z-5 site, or the IL-76 crash, and for that he was grateful. If he had to, he hoped to get out in front on both issues before those too were raised.

He'd asked Langford Seeley to be in his office at eight this morning for the Moscow call, but Langford had obviously overslept, and hadn't responded to his pager, so the president started without him. General Putnam seemed troubled. The president wondered if the pace of events had given the general second thoughts about having come to the president?

Unbeknown to the president, the general had debated calling him several times over the weekend, to tell him what Balkan had confided to him last Friday about Langford being a Russian mole who reported to a man by the name of Victor Indorenko here in Washington.

Putnam had checked every U.S. intelligence data bank he could find about Indorenko, but had found nothing to indicate an intelligence affiliation anywhere in the Russian's background. That didn't surprise him though, because he knew the Russians were getting better at hiding spies in the U.S. in the postcommunist era. Until the late 1990s Americans knew Russia was their enemy, but since then the Russians had become good guys trying to make a living like good capitalists. The 450,000 Russian immigrant community that had overwhelmed Brooklyn, Miami Beach, and San Francisco, since the end of the Cold War, were an attestation to their new status. Putnam wondered how many former KGB, GRU and Stasi agents had been dropped into the stream and were now burrowing into America's deepest military secrets. Putnam already knew of sixteen. They were being watched in various positions in the Department of Defense, America's nuclear weapons program, and large defense related corporations. Putnam suspected that within three years the FBI would be tracking even more, and might exceed those already known to be on Israel's payroll.

Even without the corroborating back-up evidence, he wanted to tell the president what his real concerns were about the POW issue. But Putnam had already stuck his neck out once by coming to the president and not going through his normal chain of command, and didn't want to risk his career again. He still had no proof. And senior generals did not go around informing American presidents that their most trusted advisors were spies.

Balkan hadn't provided a single shred of hard evidence to support his claims about Seeley, aside from some dead man's word in New York, and even then, an underworld type whose dying words had been tortured from him. No one would take such evidence at face value. Balkan's history was also one full of controversy, and the general wasn't about to bet his career on another roll of the dice. While waiting for Seeley to arrive, Putnam briefed the president with satellite photography of the aircraft crash site south-east of Z-5. There was little doubt that the ugly blackened slash down a ridge, and blackened pock marks in the snow, were the wreckage of the IL-76. The largest piece was a recognizable wing section a mile from the main cite. Its location away from the main site seemed to support the cockpit voice tapes that one of the aircraft wings had come off in flight. The wreckage lay fifty miles from the settlement of Llirney in the mountains of the Gora Dvukh Tsirkov. It would be an incredibly difficult location to reach, and even more difficult to exploit.

The translators voice interrupted the general's thoughts as the Russian leader's response came through.

"I just learned from our Ambassador in Washington, Mr. President, that an Aeroflot employee of ours was murdered in Virginia over the weekend."

The president's face crinkled. What the hell did this have to do with what they were discussing. "A Russian Aeroflot official?" the president inquired dumbly. "So what?"

"So what?" the translator's voice repeated accusingly.

"Make a note of the name. Find out what happened," the president said to General Putnam.

"Also, Mr. President," the Russian translator continued as a crescendo of mumbling emerged in the background at the Kremlin end of the phone line. "One of our advisors, Valeriyesk Yeniseysk, who is in charge of our POW/MIA affairs here in Russia, is here with me now. As you may know he also serves on the defunct American/Russian POW/MIA Agency. Mr. Yeniseysk informs me it was your Mr. Alex Balkan, who arranged for the release of the Novosibirsk documents with provocateurs here."

"Meaning?" the president demanded from the Oval Office.

"Meaning, that the documents you refer to are obviously forgeries and meant to provoke a confrontation between our two great democracies."

"The president's voice became testy; he desperately wanted to believe the Russian, but he had to be sure. He himself, had never served in uniform, and he didn't want to sweep the missing Americans under the carpet unless he was certain it was a nonissue. "You have proof that they are forgeries?"

Again there was background mumbling, intermittently spiked with shouts and exclamations. "Absolutely!" Came the Russian reply.

"I must know for certain," the president insisted.

"Mr. President," the Russian translator continued. "You will hear from your ambassador in Moscow within the hour. Valeriy Yeniseysk and the Foreign Minister are leaving for your Embassy here in Moscow now. We have another issue to discuss at this time."

"What is it?"

"The United States new policy of being free to take preemptive action against terrorists in states with weapons of mass destruction."

"The president looked at Putnam with a blank look. He cupped the phone. "What the hell is he talking about?" he asked Putnam."

The general shrugged his shoulders.

"What about it?" the president inquired.

"Russia has decided to adopt your second convention, that no country or combination of countries will ever be allowed to challenge Russian military superiority or our security if they have a common border within a thousand miles of our border. We have also decided that international treaties and organizations cannot provide protection for our people against international terrorists and have therefore agreed with your unilateral intervention measures as a preferable approach. Consequently, Mr. President, I am informing you that two days hence, three Russian Divisions will occupy the Crimea. Russia must rid herself of the threat of terrorists in this place."

"Mr. President," the American president replied with some surprise evident in his voice, "you realize that after the events of 9-11, only America is justified in such responses and that only we, as a world superpower, can be allowed to resort to such measures. America cannot support such unacceptable behavior by any state which is a member of the United Nations."

The president waited while laughter subsided at the Moscow end of the phone line.

"Never the less," came the Russian leader's reply, "Conditional sovereignty is not a concept which applies only to America. Under current American doctrine, any nation which has weapons of mass destruction forfeits its sovereignty. We are informed that some rebels in Kiev may be about to acquire a small nuclear weapon from Iran's Ayatollah's, so we must protect ourselves."

"You must be joking," the American president replied. "No we are not." The translator's voice in Moscow replied.

"You cannot put yourself above international treaties," the president's voice was now beginning to show some signs of annoyance. The Russians were playing his own game with his ground rules, but the basics were not the same. America' s terrorist threat was different.

"International treaties?" the translator Russian replied, followed by a long silence as voices arguing in the background became audible. Then the voice picked up again. "The Russian president asked me to inform you that America cannot have it both ways. America ignores international treaties and sends a message to the world that it does not give a damn about anyone else. You walked out of the Kyoto Accords on Global warming, You unilaterally abrogated the international Anti-Ballistic missile treaty. The international criminal court's rules apply to everyone but America, and the only country in the world with 122 United Nations Resolutions against it for human rights violations and every other form of violation, is Israel. And you say nothing to the Israeli's. America also walked out of the South Africa world conference on Human Rights. It is regrettable that America does not wish to work to make existing organizations better, and prefers to abuse its leadership mantle and behave boorishly. We are going to send Russian troops into the Crimea soon and when we do I would suggest you downplay its importance."

There was a click and the line went dead.

"Son of a bitch," the president exclaimed, "the Russian hadn't even had the courtesy to say good-by before hanging up." He swiveled toward Putnam, "Would you be kind enough general, to tell my secretary that I want her to find Langford now!" He tented his fingers and studied the distant crowds of tourists around the Washington Monument.

"Where the hell is Seeley?" he demanded as Putnam returned.

"He left his residence forty minutes ago, Mr. President. They're trying to reach him by phone now."

"The damned Russians allege that Balkan's documents are forgeries, general. He states they have proof. The proof is being delivered to our Ambassador in Moscow right now. We should be hearing from our Embassy any moment. Any idea what this is all about?"

"No, Mr. President."

He looked at Putnam. "If the Russian is right, the fall-out in the press will be disastrous. Will anyone here believe the Russians after it got this far? And the Salt Lake paper alleges this expose is only the first of three installments. What else do the Salt Lake people know that we don't? What have they got up their sleeve? Can you find out for me?" Concern streaked the president's face.

"It's a First Amendment issue, Mr. President." Putnam shrugged. "Not an area I should become involved in."

The president paused. Maybe it was a question he should pursue through another venue. Freedom of the Press was something the White House had to dance around in this instance. No one in the United States wanted to help Russia. After all the Russians too were Capitalists now, and Capitalists were supposed to take care of themselves. But the president knew capitalism in Russia was a veneer beneath which lay its disgruntled military, corrupt politicians, a huge criminal class, and worst of all, thousands of Russian ICBM's still deployed across central Russia, which in the wrong hands contained enough warheads to end civilization.

"General . . . I really would appreciate your looking into what the Salt Lake City newspaper's documents are all about." the president's voice now an order and not a request.

Putnam wasn't about to get involved with the Press. The president was already getting a bad name with them. The president, his secretary of defense, attorney general, and vice president were increasingly being described as Pit Bulls who brought down their prey by piling on in a vicious free for all. Yesterday's New York Times had described them as the Gang That Couldn't Shoot Straight, men who manipulated civil rights and freedom of the press to their own purpose, ignored and ridiculed allies, violated international agreements, confused nations with terrorists, and loved preemptive drone strikes.

The world had moved on since Perestroika and left the former Soviet Union in a worse mess than under Communism. With the reunification of Germany, Europe was also a different place. Asia too had indelibly changed, and the two superpowers no longer ruled anything. And then there was the damned Spanish claim which Seeley had assured Putnam, had been put to rest . . . or had he? The best outcome would be to discredit the Spanish report completely, and get the Salt Lake City's Lake Chronicle newspaper to recant its report.

"I am sorry, Mr. President. I cannot," Putnam replied. The president yanked the phone from its cradle. "Get me the CIA director!"

Turning to Putnam while he waited for the CIA Director to call in, he asked, "You ever heard of Victor Indorenko with Aeroflot here in Washington?"

The general hesitated. Should he mention Balkan's suspicions about Seeley now?

"Yes sir, Mr. President. I have seen his name among Russians here in Washington."

"The Russian president told me this guy Indorenko was killed here in Washington over the weekend. So what? Why would the Russian president point this out?" He noted the general's obvious discomfort. "You all right, General?"

"Yes, Mr. President. Just something I ate I guess."

The president laughed as the CIA director came on the line.

"Jenkins," the president said, "I want to know everything you've got on a man named Victor Indorenko. He's Russian; with their national airline here. Yeah! That's right, Aeroflot. I am informed he was supposedly murdered in Virginia over the weekend. Check your files. Have someone check with the local police. Call me back ASAP." He slammed the phone down.

There was a knock on the door, and the president's chief of staff came in. Putnam could tell from his expression that something real bad had happened. The man was visibly shook up. "Bad news Mr. President, the chief of staff said. Langford Seeley's dead! Apparently murdered . . . maybe assassinated for all we know? It just happened moments ago along the George Washington Memorial Parkway."

"Jeeeesus!" the president exclaimed, now also visibly shaken.

"His car was stopped in traffic, and someone shot him through the window. An off duty policeman pursued the assailant on foot into the woods and caught him. He's an old man. The officer thinks the assailant had a seizure or heart attack. The assailant had no identification on him. He's under heavy guard at Walter Reed and the doctors report he is in a coma. The police have no idea who he is."

The president walked into the adjacent room and flipped on the television and hit the remote for CNN. "They're good," the president muttered aloud as it became obvious that CNN was already all over the story. "Sometimes too damned good." He observed as his Chief of Staff joined him. A helicopter view showed miles of backed-up south-bound traffic along George Washington Parkway.

"Mr. President," his chief of staff interrupted, "Under the circumstances I think we should notify the press that this might be international terrorism, and that we are notifying the Armed Forces and Homeland Security to be extra vigilant in case this is part of an Arab or Al-Qaeda plot to assassinate our senior leadership. Put all our local airports on alert . . . that kind of thing."

"I agree," he said. "Make the call."

"Is this the right time to make such a statement?" General Putnam inquired aloud of the chief of staff as he passed him.

"Who asked you?" the president's assistant demanded. "This is a matter for Homeland Security, not military intelligence."

Putnam shook his head. "It's just one man for Christ's sake." No wonder the American people were becoming indifferent to the external threat he thought? Osama bin Laden's repeated warnings to the American people were clear. It was time for America to address two critical issues which only America could resolve. Provide the Palestinian people a homeland somewhere, and avoid overt support for corrupt Arab regimes around the world. Putnam knew there would be more terrorism because Israel was the tail wagging not only this administration, but the entire American dog.

"Shit!" the president exclaimed. "What else can go wrong this morning?"

"Do you want to call Mrs. Seeley?"

"Right away," the president replied. Twenty minutes later the American ambassador to Russia came on the phone from Moscow.

"Mr. President, Valeriy Veniseysk is here with me. He has some documents which I've reviewed. They are handwritten confessions and appear genuine. They state that the Novosibirsk documents were forgeries meant to embarrass Russia and agitate the American public. Yeniseysk assures me the motives of those involved was to ruin relations between our two countries, and inflame firebrands hoping to bring down the Russian government."

Ask who they are? Putnam scribbled on a note handed to the president.

"Who are the these men involved in the forgeries?" the president asked.

"There are three, sir. A Yevgeni Kosmutov," the ambassador replied, "a second is Pyotr Kaminsky and the third a man called Tukhachevsky. All are former KGB officers. While the latter two are bit players, low level types, the general informs me that all three were secretly disposed of recently for treason."

"Recently disposed of?" the president asked incredulously.

"That is what they have informed me, Mr. President," the ambassador replied.

"When?" General Putnam cut in.

Some indistinguishable conversation could be heard in the background before the Ambassador's voice came back on the line. "Sometime within the last few weeks as near as we can tell, sir."

"Sound too convenient?" Mr. Ambassador?"

"I have no way of knowing, Mr. President."

"Do you believe them?"

"The general has always been forthright and cooperative with us heretofore."

"Do . . . you . . . believe him?" the president's voice was slow and measured.

"As you know, Mr. President, his boss too has done his utmost to cooperate with us on a broad spectrum of issues from nuclear force reductions to—"

"Damn it! I'm aware of all this!" the president interrupted. "Do . . . you . . . believe them?"

"The confessions appear genuine, Mr. President. They are dated several weeks ago, and the foreign minister assures me that had they known the documents were actually not passed to us, they would have brought it to our attention earlier. As you know, Mr. President, our government-to-government agreement reached with Russia back in 1993, specifically states that any POW/MIA related classified documents passed between the parties will automatically be protected at the same classification level, and not made available to the American public."

"Then," the president asked, "the secret Russian documents passed to Balkan, by agreement, must be considered secret by the United States?"

"Per our agreement," the voice in Moscow replied, "Yes."

"Any comment about this, Mr. Ambassador?"

"I must confess it is a strange arrangement, especially concerning the American POW/MIA families who might be interested to know what became of their loved ones in the Soviet Union after WWII, and other twentieth-century conflicts."

"Okay, thanks. Anything else?"

"No."

"Thanks," the president concluded. "Stay at your office for a couple of hours, I may need to get back to you in a while." The president hung up. "Get me the Russian leader!" He turned to Putnam. "What do you think?"

"If the documents were forgeries, Mr. President, then the POW question is a chimera, and all that remains is the report about the three hundred and fifty at the crash site. If they are out there, then DNA and forensics, dental records and such, should leave little doubt. If they aren't, then the prisoner question is also moot."

"And if the Russian documents are real?"

"Well . . . I suppose Balkan would be guilty of a security violation. But under the circumstances I am not sure it would be wise to charge him publicly. The American public might not understand."

"Who would charge him then?" the president inquired.

"Maybe the FISA court in a secret enclave. The public would not have to be informed."

"And this place called Z-5?"

"Mr. President." Putnam struggled with his answer. "If there is no one at Z-5 then they must have been aboard the downed aircraft. You've got one challenge." He left the obvious conclusion unstated.

The president agreed. This only left the problem of the Spanish enquiry. The phone buzzed and he picked it up. The Russian president was on the line. "Mr. President, I just spoke with our Ambassador in Moscow. We want to close this matter between us as soon as possible. There is only one issue left."

"And what is that?" his Russian counterpart replied.

"You lost an IL-76 a month ago in Siberia. My advisors inform me we can close the entire issue here, if you would allow us to examine its wreckage."

There was a long pause, after which the translator replied that the Russian leader was unaware of such an accident.

"On the thirteenth of last month," the president replied. "Near a town called Lliney in northern Siberia."

"And what does this have to do with the documents?" The translator eventually demanded. The Russian leader's voice in the background now obviously testy.

"We understand there were prisoners aboard!"

"Whose?"

"Ours."

"Yours" The Translator shot back. There was a long silence. Then the translator's voice returned—his voice now strained and curt. "My president believes this is a matter which will have to be coordinated. Our president is not aware of what you are speaking of and wants time to consider the request. Do he have your word this will end the entire problem, if we concur?"

The president cupped the phone. "What do you think, General?"

"If they are not in the wreckage, then it is a closed case."

"If you agree," the president replied to the Russian, "we will consider the issue completely closed."

There was the sound of arguing for several moments. The voice came back. "My president insists that if you wish to review this location, and we agree, then it must be under your last preemptive authorization in the nuclear verification program."

"Just a moment," the president asked, noting General Putnam's hand gesture for a time-out. He cupped the phone. "Yes, General?"

"Give him your word instead, Mr. President."

"We would prefer that you accept my word as gentleman," he said, waiting for the Russian to translate to his Russian counterpart.

"Not possible." Was the response.

"Sir?" the president asked.

"Use your nuclear challenge or forget about it."

"Then tell Vladimir I accept," the president replied.

"We will call back," the Russian translator replied.

"How soon?"

"Very soon."

"A moment, please," the president continued. "I may have one more question."

The line had gone dead. The president smiled. "We are making progress." He noted the yellow blinking light. It was Jenkins at CIA calling back.

"What have you got, Jenkins?"

"Mr. President, the man named Indorenko, worked for the Russian airline. He's been here two years, and was murdered while driving home Saturday night near his home; shot repeatedly at close range."

"I just got off the phone with the Russian president, he mentioned it to me. Why would he mention the death of some airline employee?"

"No idea, Mr. President.

"Christ almighty!" The president observed. "With Seeley, that's two inside the beltway within forty-eight hours." He wondered if moving the nation's capital to the heartland might not be such a bad idea after all?

Key Cudjoe

Alex awoke at half past eight and after a shower, learned from Gregoriou's manservant that Mike was out running, and would return in a while. Alex accepted a cup of black coffee and sat in the aviary watching Mike's raucous collection of parrots. He felt better this morning. A couple of aspirins had already assuaged his hangover from the bottle they'd wiped out last night. By noon tomorrow he'd have the film footage he needed and it would be up to others to prove it was not the same submarine that had been used to deliver the Case Judy bullion. He suspected there was little the government could do but admit there had been a cover-up about the bullion years ago. From what Gregoriou had told him of the alterations below the U-Boat's control room; she sounded like the real McCoy.

Yesterday he'd borrowed one of Mike's cars and driven to Key West and visited Truman Annex, but Lange's ex-secretary was abrupt, providing only a forwarding address for her ex-boss in Naples. He'd thought of stopping in to see Detective Welsh but hadn't. Instead he drove north and lunched with Kate Rheiner on Ramrod Key. She remembered Svoboda and enjoyed hearing Svoboda's confirmation about the landings which took place many, many decades ago at Bahia

Honda. Then she'd asked the obvious. If the navy knew about the landings right from the start, why hadn't they arrested those involved, and who was this mysterious person Alex was talking about?

Kate's question had nagged Alex all night. It was one of the obvious questions he'd overlooked. If the navy knew about the landings in Hawk Channel and had deliberately falsified the reports for the two ships involved; then they'd also deliberately shipped Colonel Svoboda and his crew to the Pacific Theater to eliminate all the witnesses. Then five or six years later they'd again gone to excruciating lengths to conceal events surrounding the disposition of U-2513. And finally there was Eve Albion who'd replaced her twin sister and queered Paul Carter's mission to China? How come she'd never been arrested? Why had she been allowed to spend the next fifty years here in the United States, and be employed in sensitive government work? More loose ends?

Alex returned to the kitchen for more coffee and flipped the TV to CNN's nine o'clock news—and then froze! He watched in horror as a helicopter scanned a traffic jam along the George Washington Memorial Parkway. Ex-Senator Langford Seeley, the commentator announced, had just been assassinated by a lone gunman. Someone at the scene stated ex-Senator Seeley appeared to have been on his way to his office at the Old Executive Building adjacent to the White House, when an old man walked up to his car while it was stalled in traffic and executed him gangland-style with several shots at close range through the side window of his car. The assailant was pursued from the scene by an off-duty policeman who captured him a short distance away. As of this time, police were unable to identify the assailant who carried no documentation and appeared to have suffered a heart attack or stroke before police could question him.

The camera panned toward two men who the commentator explained had witnessed the incident. "Tell us what you saw?" the commentator asked. A portly man in a three piece business suit explained the traffic had stopped because several cars ahead appeared to have had their tires shot out, causing an accident which backed up traffic. Then a lone man crossed the center divider, stood alongside the Seeley's Cadillac, removed a gun from his coat, and repeatedly fired it into the rear window at point blank range. The off-duty policeman explained next that the assassin collapsed a short time later while being pursued through the woods away from the scene. The camera focused on the reporter who added that word had just been received that the Bureau of Homeland Security was asking all Americans to be extra vigilant because the shooting was suspected to be the work of international terrorism and Al-Qaeda was apparently involved.

"Jesus Christ!" Alex exclaimed.

He walked outside toward Mike's cabin cruiser tied up in the wide canal. What the hell would Alex do now? Half his satisfaction was gone, and yet another of those involved had obviously been blown away! Even after he got the underwater photography on the submarine; so what? He picked up the pool phone and punched in the numbers for the Waleston Thrower's residence in Salt Lake. Waleston's voice sounded annoyed.

"Balkan, its six o'clock in the morning for Christ's sake!"

Alex had forgotten the three-hour time difference. "Have you heard the news from Washington?"

"Yeah! My office called a couple minutes ago. I'm on my way in now. Where are you?"

"On the east coast."

"Call me back, Alex! Make it two hours. You have the number at my office. My editor and senior staff will be there. We want to talk to you about future releases."

Alex could tell there was something Thrower had left unsaid. "What's the matter? What's this about?"

"I'll be expecting your call. Alex, I've got to go." The line went dead.

Just after eleven o'clock the operator connected Alex to Waleston again.

"Alex, I've got my senior editor and several other staff members here with me. We've got a serious problem. It is with your story!"

"What is that?"

"The president's National Security advisor called and spoke with us yesterday."

"Jesus Christ!" Alex interrupted him. "The son of a bitch is dead. He was just assassinated in Washington an hour or two ago. Doesn't that tell you something?"

"We know. We've seen the reports."

Alex sat down and tried to steady himself as he felt his bile rising. The bastard would undo him even from the grave. Thrower explained that Seeley had informed him that the president was pissed-off over last Sunday's expose and could emphatically dispute the story's validity. The president demanded the newspaper give him a one week hiatus on additional reporting. The White House would provide proof. After a week the newspaper could proceed as it liked.

"And you believed Seeley? His death this morning shouldn't have been a surprise to you," Alex commented sarcastically. "Haven't you wondered why? Haven't you wondered who his assailant is? So what if the president is pissed? He should be! He's probably got his tit in the wringer too! Besides I'm not even certain the president knows any of what I've told you."

"Look, Alex," Thrower replied more curtly. We need to talk this through. When can we meet?"

"Follow through, Waleston, as we agreed. You will regret it if you do not. I'll contact you again tomorrow evening, your time."

"No sooner?" Waleston asked.

"You better wait that long," Alex replied and hung up.

THREE

Z-5, Siberia

BORIS STOPPED IN midstride and sniffed at the air for a moment. He thought he'd heard something. Checking his watch, he continued toward the last building where he knew the American colonel named Svoboda was still looking around.

They'd arrived just after noon and were waiting for the American colonel to finish his reconnaissance of the site. Boris knew one thing for sure, people had obviously lived here, and not too long ago because the fleas and lice were still alive and starving. Boris scratched through his heavy clothing at a particularly mean bite just below his nipple. Fleas and ticks had danced around on them when they first arrived, like Cossacks dancing to a fast balalaika. Boris would be relieved to leave this vermin-infested shit hole. The American colonel had videoed the interiors of the buildings. Boris thought him a little strange because the bastard also got close-ups of the outdoor parasha doors and their interiors as well. Boris assumed he was recording the graffiti carved into them, most of which was in English.

The Tupolev pilot was also getting increasingly nervous, and had just reminded Boris it was way past the time they should have left. Their agreement was not more than four daylight hours on the ground. Boris stopped in midstride, now only fifty feet from the American who'd poked his head into yet another doorway in one of the partially collapsed buildings.

As the American reemerged, Boris noticed him lower the camera, a question now obvious on his face too. They'd both heard something. The day was heavily overcast and still, and one could hear boots breaking through the white crust a hundred meters away. He looked south. Whatever it was they'd heard was from that direction. He began moving again, this time to the right, away from the building next to the American; he wanted to get an unobstructed view to the south to see what the sound was. As he did so the sound became familiar. It was a helicopter engine, by its sound, a Soloviev D-25V single shaft-free turbine to be specific. And from its tone probably fitted to a Mi-6 heavy transport helicopter. As Boris cleared the building he spotted it, then a second, both skimming the terrain toward them. He stood mesmerized as the two huge transports bore down on them. He glanced sideways at the American Colonel who now had his camera aimed at them.

"They're Mikoyan-6 heavy lift heli's," the American colonel shouted, "NATO's code name for them is Harke . . ."

"Who cares!" Boris screamed at him. Boris didn't give a shit what NATO called them. What the hell were they doing here? Boris knew they were in deep shit and they had to get airborne immediately. He broke into a run toward the Tupolev. "Run, asshole!" he shouted over his shoulder at the American as he ran.

Boris knew what would happen if they were caught. To hell with the American colonel, Boris thought as his legs carried him as quickly as they could through the deep snow. If they could get the Tupolev into the air they could easily outrun the helicopters. The alternative was enough to loosen Boris's bowels; he wanted to see his wife and kids again. The thought quickened his pace. The pilot also emerged from the building near the aircraft and also broke into a run for the Tupolev.

One of the giant shadows passed overhead and slowed to a hover a couple of hundred meters to Boris's right. Beneath it was a sling slowly lowering an olive drab bulldozer which clanked as it impacted the ground and its harness fell away. The second bird hovered a couple hundred meters away, also lowering a palletized cargo of trucks. The first Mi-6 began to turn toward him as the Tupolev's right engine sputtered to life.

Boris hit the aircraft's rear door opening and sprained his leg jamming himself through it. The left engine kicked over next and started. Thank God for well-maintained equipment he thought as he screamed, "Go, go go!" as the pilot squeezed past him heading for the cockpit. "Get this piece of shit the hell out of here!" He could feel the aircraft start to move, and through the blowing snow could see the rotating blades of the MI-6 overhead.

"Go, go go," he screamed again, watching mesmerized as white clad men began debouching from the rear of the second helicopter which had settled into the snow a quarter kilometer away. The white clad troops were deploying in a skirmish line as the Tupolev gradually began to pick up speed. Boris hit the deck as the staccato sound of spent bullets rattled through the fuselage. A half minute later they were airborne and out over the featureless frozen river. The giant helicopters were now tiny dots as the two purring Ivchenko Al-20D turboprops continued to put distance behind them.

"What the hell was that all about?" the pilot screamed.

"Hopefully just some army maneuver group that accidentally strayed by."

"I don't think so!" the pilot replied, his voice several octaves to high. It had been a close call. Too close! "And the American?"

"Screw him," Boris replied as he squeezed into the copilot's seat. "We can't go back. We'd best get the hell out of here and hope the authorities don't get anything from the American until we're halfway to Moscow." Boris already had half the down payment in his parka pocket. The pilot didn't know it though.

South of Dry Tortugas

"What's the problem?" Alex demanded as the skipper turned the eight hundred ton ship into yet another three hundred and sixty degree circle. The weather was idyllic, balmy and clear, and Alex had enjoyed watching some porpoise frolicking below the ship's bow wave as it carved through the calm surface. They'd been at it now for over an hour and Gregoriou's initial conversation over the intercom from the submersible below had now become sparse.

"I'm not certain. Mr. Gregoriou is still trying to locate her," the captain replied.

"Where's the marker you mentioned that was left?"

"The buoy must have broken loose. She was tethered twenty feet below the surface. Very strange that it is not where we left it. It is here somewhere, we've just got to find it."

A quarter hour later Alex felt Heron's engines slow and then stop. The captain opened the bridge door. "Mike's coming up." Alex headed toward the fantail and could hear the winch start up as it rolled the inch thick cable slowly onto the spool. When Mike finally emerged from the diving bell, he was upset and motioned for Alex to follow him.

In the main cabin Mike broke open the video camera's water tight shell and extracted the cartridge which he jammed into the VCR and punched the play button.

"What the hell's the problem?" Alex demanded petulantly, annoyed at the way Grigoriou had rebuffed his questions and ordered him to follow him like an errant schoolboy.

"Watch the screen!" Gregoriou muttered.

Alex focused on the images as the camera panned along the now familiar anchor chain which he recalled from the earlier tape Gregoriou had made. Then his pulse quickened when he realized it no longer rose up to a knifelike bow; but seemed to drop away into a trough in the sandy bottom. As the camera panned further he could see pieces of torn and mangled hull plate, debris strewn everywhere.

"Someone blew it up!" Gregoriou's voice cut through the silence like thunder. "There's nothing left but pieces of mangled plate. Incredible . . . sixteen hundred tons of metal completely shredded." Alex watched mesmerized as the camera froze on a mangled diesel engine piston. "The biggest piece of her engine I could find. What the hell's going on Balkan? Who did this?"

Alex didn't reply for a couple moments and continued to watch the unfolding chaos of scattered debris across the sandy bottom as the diving bell reversed course and moved across the wreckage from another angle. Toward the back of the trench he could make out what appeared to be pieces of her shredded diesel engine casings.

"What does this mean?" Mike demanded again.

"I'm not sure," Alex replied dumbly.

"You are not sure? You damn well ought to be! Lange tried to warn me about this last week." Gregoriou scowled. "Why? Who would want to do this?" The camera panned across a piece of shredded confetti connected to a length of bent tube; "that is her left propeller shaft!"

* * *

Just before sunset the helicopter dropped the two men behind Gregoriou's house. Neither had spoken much after Alex told Mike about his suspicions regarding the submarines true pedigree, and the nature of its last mission to South America. Both men now appreciated more fully that they were up against something more insidious than either had realized at first. Alex's disappointment was tempered by a new sense of foreboding. Whoever was behind this would stop at nothing to thwart him, and he recalled Uli Untermann's warning over lunch in northern Germany to "be very careful because what you seek is a dark and ugly secret, one best left alone."

Without the submarine his case wouldn't hold water. They'd already second-guessed him on the two Novosibirsk documents and queered the Salt Lake City's newspaper expose. At least for the time being. But Alex still had one ace card left. Colonel Santiago's pictures from Z-5.

Santiago wasn't expected back until the end of the week, and without the submarine video footage, there was no sense in Alex returning to Salt Lake City just yet. So he decided to get in touch with Eduardo Hernandez. Through a phone number in Peru he learned that Eduardo had left two days earlier for Switzerland, and could be reached near Geneva. When he got through, Eduardo insisted he fly over immediately with Heather and spend some time skiing at Zermatt. The spring skiing was fabulous this year and they would be his guests. Eduardo also insisted that they needed to discuss business.

Alex agreed, and a phone call to Heather convinced her to meet him at Miami's International airport this Friday afternoon. They'd fly to Europe together. Alex would also arrange for Colonel Santiago to meet him in Switzerland. Convincing the folks at the Salt Lake City newspaper to conduct their discussions with Alex telephonically was more problematical.

Yeniseysk's Apartment

"Yeniseysk, your Excellency?

"Yes."

"This is Colonel Kamov. A moment, sir."

Yeniseysk noted the blinking light to the left of the keypad and realized the caller was activating the encryption package. He glanced at his watch. Christ, it was six thirty and already time to get up! The last couple of days had tried his patience. Especially the endless rounds of debates with his gutless leaders in the Kremlin.

The American's demand to inspect the Siberian crash site had not set well with any of the senior Russian Air Force leaders. They demanded to know why Russia's president had even agreed to discuss such an issue with the Americans. Then to Yeniseysk's surprise it also took the Russian Air Force two hours to even admit that they'd lost an Il-76 a month ago. It wasn't a conspiracy, just a total breakdown in the chain of command. With all the former Soviet Republics to their south now independent States, what was left of the former Union of Soviet Socialist Republics and their myriad of air forces and air defenses had become totally disconnected and uncoordinated. No longer was there any centralized command and control which they'd all taken for granted a decade ago. And today, the situation was so bad that no one even was certain where all their inventory was. The air force chief of staff seemed only slightly concerned when he learned one of his transport aircraft was missing.

Kosmutov had done a superb job! While Yeniseysk listened yesterday to the two presidents arguing, he realized the Americans were now convinced that the Z-5 survivors were aboard the downed transport; and not at the bottom of the river nearby. Let them explore the crash site to their hearts content. All they'd find were the aircrew, and the carcasses of some Spetsnaz special forces troops he'd arranged to be aboard for training! Now it would be Russia who had been the one falsely accused.

Smiling, he rubbed the stubble on his chin. The situation had definitely developed to his advantage. He'd won all the moves in the chess game so far. Even his trusted aide Yevgeni Kosmutov had been found gunned down in the Dacha at Morino, the victim of a CIA plot in league with some Peruvian drug runner. And soon Alex Balkan too would have a fatal encounter with a bullet, and the fruits of Yeniseysk's plan would be realized.

Several hours had been wasted last night arguing with senior air force and army general officers over the obscene American demand to inspect the Siberian crash-site. Most vociferous was Chief Marshal of Aviation, Yefimov, who was pissed off beyond belief over a host of perceived Kremlin insults which had brought them where they were now: inventory cuts, declining budgets, and manpower reductions, all of which Yefimov screamed were also directly responsible for the recent IL-76 crash. Yefimov smelled a plot behind the American demand. He'd heard that America's Aviation Week and Space Technology magazine intended to publish an expose later this month about the unreliability of Russia's military transport fleet. America's bottom line, Yefimov raged, was to stop a four billion dollar Russian air-transport sale to Syria, India, and three commercial aircraft sale to Asian and African markets.

Luckily for Yeniseysk, logic prevailed, and the Kremlin agreed to let the Americans take a look at the Il-76 crash site. Last night before leaving his office, Yeniseysk ordered a special team into the Z-5 site, which was fifty miles away from the crash site, to raze whatever was left of the flea-infested Z-5 site. The team would then deploy to Bilibino, and await the arrival of the American inspection group who would fly into Bilibino from their base at Hickam Air Force Base in Hawaii. Yefimov agreed to allow the American Air Force to land at Bilibino and provide ferry service onward to the Il-76 crash site. Yefimov estimated the operation should take no more than a day or two. To be magnanimous, the Kremlin agreed to give the Americans seven days on site.

The yellow flashing light turned green and Yeniseysk said hello. His expression darkened as he listened. The lead element into Z-5 had encountered a lone aircraft which fled as they approached. It had left behind a retired American Colonel. The lone aircraft was intercepted and shot down a couple hundred miles away by fighters from a Russian airbase nearby. Colonel Kamov had used superior management skills and immediately isolated the American at Z-5 and wanted to know what should be done with him?

"The man was a spy," Yeniseysk replied. "Make it appear he too had died when the bandit Tupolev crashed. Make sure he is dead, but not with a bullet, and then drop him into the Tupolev wreckage." Hanging up, he laughed. The Americans would now truly have their ass hanging out for the entire world to see. With the body of this Colonel amidst the Tupolev wreckage, Yeniseysk would have one more needle to stick up the American's ass when the time came.

The Kremlin

"It's taken us a while, Mr. President, but we did it!" General Valeriy Yeniseysk's expression became sinister. "We must speak privately."

The Russian leader ordered his English translator to leave.

Valeriy removed another Rothman and tapped it repeatedly on his silver cigarette case, a gift to him from General Dimitri Volkogonov who bought it for him during a trip to Washington in 1992, when Dimitri was in charge of the Russian side of the newly formed Joint U.S. Russian Agency to account for thousands of WWII American POW/MIAs secretly held in the USSR. That accounting, as preplanned between the parties, had produced nothing, and now it seemed, some crazy low-level American agent might expose the secret everyone had agreed was forgotten. Valeriy's cigarette case was an outrageous bourgeois statement for a man high up in the communist party, but in these capitalist times it gave Valeriy satisfaction as it reminded him of how naive the Americans were. He leaned back and lit up, enjoying the English tobacco. Cigarettes were something the British still did well.

Volkogonov had led a group of eight senior Russian officers to Washington for initial POW/MIA liaison conferences in the early 1990s, one of which was held at Defense Intelligence Agency's most sensitive facilities in Virginia. On the day of Volkogonov's visit, DIA's public conference room was already in use by some visiting boy scout troop, so the American security officer escorted the Russians to another conference room deep within the building. Incredibly awed by their good luck, two of Yuri's associates had left pin-head low-frequency burst transmitters behind, and for eight months the Kremlin monitored discussions about America's best spies.

"From your expression, Valeriy," the Russian president said, "you seem pleased with yourself."

"Several developments, Mr. President. I Just learned we intercepted a hostile aircraft near Z-5."

The president stiffened. "Hostile?"

"Not authorized to be there."

"Whose?" The president's face now deadly serious.

"Not to worry!" Valeriy continued, "It's been attended to." He explained how the advance team to Bilibino had stopped en route at Z-5 and surprised an old Tupolev which fled, but was intercepted to the south west and forced down into the mountains. "The Tupolev pulled out of Z-5 so fast when our team arrived," Valeriy laughed, "that they left one man behind. A retired American army Colonel!" Valeriy drew another long drag on his cigarette, and as he exhaled, muttered, "There must truly be a God of justice."

"Be serious, Yuri!"

"I am! The American was so stupid, he didn't think to destroy his documents or a video camera he had with him with which he was documenting what he saw at Z-5. As our SVB officers frisked him, the ignorant bastard began shouting something about his rights under the Geneva Convention. I am making enquiries through our Embassy in Washington as to who he is?"

The Russian president's composure hardened. "First this man called Balkan, and now this? Do the American's know we have him?"

"Probably not. They may not even be involved at all. The guy appears to be a loner. We'll know more in a few hours." Yeniseysk waited while the president ranted on about the two-faced Washington president who he repeatedly called an imbecile. Following Gorbachev and Yeltsin's trysts with Perestroika and Glasnost the American's had promised much but delivered nothing. And now that he'd agreed to allow them to inspect the crash site, they had the temerity to send in a cloak and dagger type to snoop around elsewhere nearby. The president wished he'd told his American counterpart to go to hell. He shouted for his assistant to get the American president on the phone, now!

"Mr. President," the Russian leader hollered into the phone, not even waiting for his translator to catch up, "How can I trust you when you behave like a buffoon all the time? You promise your people to build a bridge with us into the twenty-first century, but you try so hard to burn all these bridges with us. You gave me your word yesterday, and today I realize your word is Parasha droppings."

The American's surprise was problematical. His denials of knowledge about it contrived. But he agreed to immediately look into it.

Typical the general thought as the phone connection was terminated and the Russian president turned to look at him. Russia's new capitalists got nothing from the Americans, only eight dollar MacDonald Hamburgers, and five dollar Dairy Queen ice creams in Moscow. With Russian unemployment near thirty percent, and under-employment close behind, he more clearly understood the American term: rip-off. At least the long years of Communism had left them their national pride.

"What about the others, Valeriy ?" The Russian leader demanded.

"It has been taken care of Mr. President. One of my men, realizing he was American, immediately concealed him from those preparing the site. The colonel's body will be found amidst the Tupolev wreckage.

Once the Americans start examining the IL-76 site, we'll inform them we've also found the Tupolev crash nearby, and let the Americans find their dead colonel. Then we can watch Washington play out its usual bag of tricks before we rub their nose in shit. It will give you a good card to play with the world press about your Crimean concerns.

The Russian president leaned back into the soft leather of the sofa. He liked the idea. "You mentioned other developments."

"Nasdreli Kachou has been resolved."

"How?" The Russian president's expression turned to curiosity as he leaned forward in anticipation. Nasdreli Kachou was Yuri's personal baby, and only three in Russia knew of it. Himself, Yuri and one of Yuri's underlings—a man named Kosmutov who'd recently been killed.

"We have found the pinnacle and those atop it."

In the next few minutes he confirmed to the Russian leader that the Bearer Share company registered in Hong Kong, named CEBU, was in fact the entity that now controlled almost a third of the bullion captured by the Wehrmacht near Minsk at the beginning of Russia's Great Patriotic War against the Hitlerite Socialists.

They'd known for years the Americans were also somehow involved, but were never able to trace the gold's whereabouts. Now he had found it.

"You have done very well, General! Very well indeed!"

Yuri went on to describe the complex architecture behind the construction of CEBU, and how the legal ownership of a Bearer Share Corporation was established and how its control was insured. Whoever controlled the Shares, had voting rights, and these voting rights represented control.

"Only three people control all this Valeriy?"

"Correct! A few minutes ago I passed instructions for the three principals to be discreetly picked up and secretly brought here. Once we have them under our control, it will be a short time before we've restructured CEBU's ownership so that it will do our bidding." He went in to considerable detail about the old Armenian's background, the one who lived most of the year in Majorca. Then there was the elder Chinaman named Chong Ki-Young who resided in Indonesia. It was the latter he said who had been the organization's kingpin in Asia. And finally he addressed the Peruvian: whose father was the notorious Heinrich Kaufmann, the German they'd been looking for all these many years. Unfortunately, the Hitlerite Nazi criminal had recently died, but his half-breed progeny had replaced him, and the son too would soon be picked up.

The president smiled. Things were beginning to look more positive. "And how do you steal it back?"

"Knowledge is power, Vladimirovitch!"

"Always," the Russian president replied. At this point he didn't mind Yuri taking such familiarities in private. After all they now shared incredible wealth and secrets together. "What is the key?"

"The security of such ownership is anonymity. And as long as others do not know who possess it, then control is arranged and maintained through intermediaries."

"The seven veils?" The Russian leader laughed.

"Exactly!" Valeriy exclaimed.

"How did you acquire this information?"

"Oddly enough, from a pissed-off Arab." He stubbed out his cigarette and withdrew another Rothman's. "You remember your meeting with the old Arab Sheikh a couple of weeks back?"

"The one from the Gulf?"

He nodded. "Seems while the old Arab was here in Moscow, Heinrich Kaufmann the recently deceased father, sent his son here to Moscow and threatened to have the old Arab killed unless he repaid a debt owed them. The old Arab was so annoyed he sent one of his siblings to see us. We were told we might be interested in the Peruvian's background, and given a dossier which exposed the Gordion Knot. The dossiers contents showed us how to cut it."

"I'll be damned!" The president laughed. "How much did the Arab owe him?"

"Three billion dollars."

"Jesus!" he replied. "That much?"

Yuri lit up his Rothman's and smiled.

"And the Arab paid?"

"In full! Within days."

The president opened a side drawer and withdrew a Vodka decanter, pouring two hefty shots. Pushing one across, he downed his in a single gulp.

"And how long will all this take?"

"A week. Once we have them here, we shall convince them to share their dirty little secret with us. Then we will liquidate them, and their assets."

"Is it going to be so easy?"

"I think so." Valeriyi didn't need to explain all the details to the president just yet. The sledge hammer he intended to use with Eduardo was the part the Peruvian had played in the recent execution of Yevgeni Kosmutov and the housekeeper at Morino. The penalty for espionage and counter state activities in Russia was death by firing squad. The punishment for anyone convicted of first degree murder in Russia was death. Conspiracy to commit murder was life in prison without parole. The penalty for illegally leaving the country was twenty years, and finally, smuggling currency on the other hand was another twenty years. The Peruvian would be shot and never see the light of day again.

"How much is involved?"

"At least five hundred billion dollars! Maybe a hundred more." Valeriyi smiled as the president whistled. It was more than enough to build themselves a small dacha outside Moscow, outfit it with some liquor and women. For sure it was enough for the Russian president to get himself reelected several times. "There would have been more," the general laughed, "but unfortunately the Americans beat us to the rest of it after the war." He explained how the U-Boat scuttled off Paraguay in 1945 had been removed by the CIA.

"So that's why it was never found?" The president observed.

"You got it! As the Americans like to say."

"And Washington spent it?"

"Who cares. They stole it. What happened to it at this point is irrelevant. They're guilty like a thief. An American court would sentence them to jail for twenty years and order indemnity. The international courts will do no less. I've arranged for hints to be passed to Spain, that the United States has their missing gold."

"And where exactly is this wealth which the three men control?" the president asked, wanting to terminate the conversation because he had to urinate.

"Sixty percent of it is in the United States, and the rest divided between South America, Europe and Asia. And most interesting is South America, where 7 percent of CEBU's wealth produces profits exceeding the rest of their assets combined."

"Narcotics?"

"Yes. Cocaine."

Now the Russian leader knew how to deal with the American president.

Oval Office

"Mr. President," his chief of staff signaled, "the Russian leader is on the Moscow commo-link."

"Thanks," he replied as he headed across the room to the phone on his desk.

In five days the POW question had leapt to national prominence since the Salt Lake City expose and the press were having a field day. No one knew what to believe? And now the area around the Vietnam War Memorial had become a hotbed of Veteran organization protests. It seemed to the president as if all the damned crazies and fringe groups had come out to have a party. Veterans marches were held in several cities across the country while national POW/MIA organizations in Washington were planning a million man march to the White House next week. Congress was also making noise about sanctions against Russia.

Congressional party leaders demanded that the administration come clean with whatever dark secrets the intelligence community was still hiding about prisoners in Russia. The president knew he'd have to make an announcement soon if he hoped to defuse the gathering storm. But first he had to get a team into the Siberian crash site. If body parts were found and forensic matches made to relatives of the dead here at home, then all bets would be off, and the president could take credit for exposing the problem and be the hero of the hour. General Putnam had assured him that the initial results from the crash could be available within a day or two of their arrival on site. Putnam also assured him that a POW/MIA recovery team from Honolulu was ready to deploy anywhere in the world and would be moving within hours of the Russians agreement and in place in Siberia within twelve hours after that.

"Good afternoon, Vladimir," the American president said.

"Mr. President." the Russians voice boomed back. "If we agree to your terms mentioned yesterday, do I have your promise this ugly chapter, and the incredible accusations being made against Russia will cease?"

"You do." The president had already kicked it around with bipartisan groups on the Hill, and all had concurred that a way must quickly be found to defuse the issue before Russian firebrands like Zhirinovsky and others could denounce the U.S. and call for a break in diplomatic relations, a reality which was already being advocated by others because of Moscow's chess moves along the Black Sea.

"And do I also have your word," the Russian continued, "that you will refute the newspaper reports from Utah?"

The president shrugged. Refute was a lot to ask. But if the documents were forgeries, why not! "If they are forgeries . . . or course!"

"My people are upset, and my government is not in a good position to challenge America as we once did."

Screw you and your vodka drinking people, the president thought. Is it America's fault that you fell in love with Communism and allowed such shitty leaders to lead you down the garden path?

"And, Mr. President," the Russian continued, "there are other matters which we must discuss as a part of this accommodation we are about to make."

"Vladimir, this must be a stand-alone agreement between us," the president insisted. "America cannot be coerced into agreements that are not blessed by our Congress. You know that."

"Please do not use that familiar term with me again," the Russian's repy clarified. "You insult the dignity of Russia's highest office."

The president's face reddened as he heard laughter from others who were with the Russian leader.

"Everything is moral hypocrisy. Don't you agree?" the Russian asked. "You demand democracy in Iraq and Afghanistan, but overlook Saudi Arabia, Pakistan, Syria, Egypt, and Libya. And I will not deign to even address your country's record with the Pahlevi's of Iran, Marcos of the Phillippines, Mobarak of Egypt, or Idi Amin of Uganda. As you probably know, Mr. President, I was a part of president of the USSR Podgorny's security detail when he attended Pahlevi's 2,500 anniversary celebrations at Persepolis in October 1971. The Vodka was not as good as ours, nor the Caviar for that matter, but your CIA station chief in Tehran; he personally approved all visas for each of the thousands of international visitors to the Shah's party. I remember this because my associate at the time was turned down, and I only learned the reason why a decade later when the Iranians captured your Embassy in Tehran. There is no need now to discuss this further."

"And your point?" The president decided not to push his luck with his Russian counterpart and avoided the trivializing nickname his predecessors had used earlier for Russia's leader.

"Georgia."

"What about it?"

"Russia is also going to reoccupy it again and install a responsible new government there, and then dispose of all its terrorists who have been causing us so much trouble."

"America could not support such overt aggression and you know it," the American president replied. "You have no right to occupy a sovereign state. I hope you are not serious."

"Very."

"Washington will oppose you with all means at our disposal. I can promise nothing. You know that. Can we send in our team to the Il-76 crash site in Siberia or not?"

General Putnam's hand covered the microphone for the Moscow hotline and the Oval Office became silent. "They are going to say yes," Putnam said. "They have to settle the crash site issue with us before it inflames world opinion against them."

"We agree," the Russian voice boomed back over the line. "But with three provisos. Regretfully Moscow is unable to compromise on the three. It is a take it or leave it. Everyone around me insist on them. I am sure you appreciate there are many among my military and government, who are exceptionally difficult these days. You will appreciate also that our experience with democracy is only a few years old, and many around me do not yet share my strong belief that Russia should remain a democratic state. So I must insist on the three. They are reasonable however, and I do not think you should have any trouble with them."

"I'm listening, Mr. President."

"First! Your teams will only have access the crash-cite through a camp we will set up for you nearby, and your people must use our internal transportation which we will provide for this purpose. Second, your search area will be restricted to twenty miles around the crash site. And last. Your team will only have access to the site for seven calendar days; starting on the 21st, that's the day after tomorrow. I think you will agree the three conditions are reasonable?"

The president glanced at his chief of staff, then at Putnum, whose face remained deadpan. "A question, Mr. President," Putnam said. "As you know, our personnel assigned to the forensic group in Hawaii, according to the latest congressional restriction placed on them, are only allowed to use American flag aircraft anywhere in the world. We must demand that the Russians allow us to bring in our own helicopters and use them in their airspace."

"You must be joking, Putnam. You expect me to start arguing over some god damned congressional legislation at a time like this? To hell with it, get a waiver."

"I understand." Putnam nodded in assent.

"I agree," the President said. "Moscow has been more than accommodating on this matter. Is that it?"

"Yes," the Russian replied.

"There's one final matter, Mr. President, which I too would like to mention," the American leader commented. "Our information is that your IL-76 flight originated at Z-5 on the Ugatkyn River. You are familiar with it?"

"I have heard of that River." There was muffled laughter in the background. "Siberia is a big place you understand? It is three times the area of the great United States, and our rivers number in the thousands."

Again there were muffled sounds of laughter in the background.

"We would like to inspect that location too."

Sounds of Russians curses and expletives were audible. The translator shook his head signifying he hadn't been able to pick all the various background comments, but mentioned a synopsis of six of Russia's most descriptive adjectives for indiscriminate sexual intercourse. "I think we have already reached an agreement, Mr. President, and this is not part of it." The Russian's voice came back overriding the background conversation around him. "I am sorry."

"One of my staff just mentioned it to me. I apologize. It was an oversight."

"And why is that?" the Russian president demanded.

"I just told you. Washington believes the IL-76 originated there."

"That is not true, Mr. President and you know it," the Russian's annoyed voice replied. "The flight originated where the plane was home-based. That was elsewhere."

"I misspoke," the American corrected himself. "The plane stopped at Z-5."

There was a long silence. Then the Russian translator hesitated as sounds of shouting again slipped past the cupped mouthpiece. "Just a moment please!" The translator asked, and then continued. "I am sorry but that too is a lie." Then another long silence. The White House communications room assured the president the link was still intact.

The president twiddled a pencil as he waited, wondering if the Russians would agree? He had to admit it was a long shot, and if the tables were reversed, he would have told the Russians to go to hell on both counts. No foreign power would ever be allowed to unilaterally conduct such an investigation into the loss of an American military aircraft on United States soil. No way!

The Russian translator's voice wavered slightly after a long silence as he related his boss's response. Russia would graciously agree to either of the requests. But not to both! America must choose, and choose now. If not the issue was closed and no inspection at all. His chief of staff leaned forward. "I agree with general Putnum," he said, "Mr. President. There's no one at the camp anymore! We know that. Whoever was there left aboard that aircraft. Go for the Il-76 crash site, Mr. President."

"Okay, the United States agrees to your conditions. I will also ask General Putnam who is here with me right now, to contact whomever you designate, and to coordinate arrangements. We would like to have a team in place within twelve hours."

"Twelve hours? So soon?" the Russian inquired. "Flying time from Hawaii to Bilibino is that much time."

"Well, they will be underway then within twelve hours or so." No problem was the last thing the Russian translator said before the Moscow line went dead.

Five minutes later his chief of staff returned and switched on the CNN news and indicated the president should watch.

"In a late breaking development," the CNN announcer began, we have just learned that a woman has advised the Washington police that she recognized the gunman who killed ex-Senator Langford Seeley yesterday. Reports are that she met the assailant during the Christmas holidays last year and spent the last two weeks with him in upstate New York. She states the assailant was known to her as Pavel Krasnov who she thought was a Canadian citizen. FBI sources however believe that Krasnov is not Canadian. The porous Canadian/U.S. border has been a favorite entry point for terrorists in recent times and an anonymous U.S. intelligence spokesmen who spoke to CNN off the record, indicate that Seeley's assassin is believed to be connected with the Al-Qaeda terrorist group. Stay tuned as we provide more on this fast breaking story."

"Who is she?" the president demanded.

"Some elder divorcee named Cimeon Kannapolis, Mr. President."

Turning to Putnam he said. "Have her picked up and held incommunicado under the Patriot Act. I don't want her talking to anyone until we know the extent of this new terrorism against our country. And get with the FBI. I want to know what they've got on her and this guy before they release anything to the public."

Once again the president had that feeling events were slipping beyond his grasp.

FOUR

Bilibino, Siberia

THE AIRCRAFT COMMANDER of the lumbering USAF C-5 of the 416th Nevada Air National Guard Reserve Squadron thought he would wet his flight suit for the first time in his eight year air force career, as the sixteen main landing gear wheels of the aircraft softly settled into six inches of new fallen snow and did not collapse beneath the aircraft's 278,500 pound weight. A local Russian air traffic controller had assured him from his mobile trailer beside the almost invisible snow-covered runway, that if the C-5 touched down within a thousand feet of the outer marker that a twelve-thousand foot concrete runway lay between the two rows of flare pots. The C-5 stopped with a half-mile to spare. The pilot got on the intercom to his load master.

"Sergeant Smith, I'm going to leave the engines at idle. Open the rear cargo door and await the arrival of the locals who are supposed to tell me to taxi into this godforsaken darkness around us." He checked his watch. It was 0513 local, and there were another four hours until sunup.

Two minutes later Smith was back on the intercom. "Two Russkies are here, sir. They followed us down the runway in a tracked vehicle. Some lieutenant says to shut down our engines and he will help us unload at sunup, and clear the snow around us. They want everyone assembled in the cargo bay, sir."

"I'll be right down, Sergeant."

Down in the cargo-bay Russian Second Lieutenant Yuri Vassily and his political sidekick, Sverdlov Karpov were already being difficult hosts.

"This is our rule at Bilibino." Yuri informed the C-5's pilot and mission Commander Colonel Gellman who was standing beside him. "My orders from Moscow are clear. You comply immediately. If not then you can restart your engines and use the rest of the runway outside and get-out of Dodge." Yuri's expression looked foolish. "You understand?"

The Russian lieutenant beside Yuri demanded all thirty-two Americans aboard to hand over the military ID cards and their passports to him. He'd also handed the aircraft commander a sheaf of papers for a full accounting of all official and nonofficial cargo aboard.

After a nose-to-nose hostile stand-off of ten minutes the two Russians agreed they would accept photocopies of the American's military ID cards, but still had to have their passports. And for American/Russian friendship, the Americans could hand in their cargo manifests when completed—but warned that nothing would be unloaded until—in Lieutenant Yuri's words . . . "Peeper wark is complet . . . Hokay!"

"God damn it!" Colonel Gellman exploded. "Give the mother fucker what he wants and lets get this show on the road."

"Dis is good. Dis is good!" Yuri's political sidekick informed everyone. "American's obey our regulations—just like in America . . . Da? You big mutha fucka . . . me big mutha fucka, all responsible, same same."

Karpov then opened a rucksack and produced four pint bottles of vodka. Yanking the cork from each with his teeth, he spat them onto the deck and handed the bottles around. He held the fourth bottle up. "We drink to Russian/American friendship and a successful mission . . . Da," Karpov exclaimed.

Colonel Gellman looked around at his men and politely refused: informing the Russian that it was against regulations for any of them to drink while on duty.

"You do not drink to American/Russian friendship?" The two Russian's exclaimed in pained voices.

"I am sorry," Gellman replied.

With a disgusted expression Yuri, with considerable aplomb, retrieved the corks from the deck and replaced them in the four bottles, then replaced them in Karpov's ruck sack, and was getting back into his vehicle a few yards from the rear loading ramp when Gellman caught up with him.

The C-5 crew watched with fascination while their Colonel withdrew one of the vodka bottles from the Russian's ruck sack, yanked its cork with his teeth and spat it into the snow. Holding up the bottle for all to see Gellman shouted. "To American/Russian friendship. Nasdrovia!" He drained away a quarter of the contents before handing it to the sergeant beside him who did likewise.

"Welcome to mother Russia Amerikanski's," Yuri exclaimed. He grabbed the bottle from the sergeant, finished it off, and tossed it into the darkness beyond the runway.

* * *

Twelve hours later Colonel Gellman surveyed the activity at the barren helicopter landing zone around him. Some eighty-five miles from the Bilibino air-strip, his reception here too was definitely among the more unusual he'd encountered in his career. Assigned to UMPC's Central Identification Laboratory in Hawaii, he'd been with the organization three years, and made deployments to Thailand, Cambodia, Korea, Vietnam, and Iraq. Thrown together on a moment's notice, Operation Brilliant Oyster was his first flight into the former Soviet Union.

A half mile away stood the foreboding jagged peaks of the Strachny mountain range. Somewhere about twenty miles beyond the closest ridge lay the wreckage they had come to inspect. The basic logistics of food, fuel and accommodations were always the same for these missions no matter where you were in the world, but environmentally this area was starting out to be among the most remote and challenging he'd seen. Despite it being late April, the weather was still brutally cold and a thirty mile an hour wind reduced the chill factor to eighteen below zero. He hoped it would be less windy up in the nearby mountains where they would go in the morning.

"Sergeant," he said to the man alongside. "Make a note, stress to our men the need to keep all exposed skin covered. Especially their faces and hands. I don't want any cases of frostbite."

He and his team had been ferried the last eighty-five miles here to Camp One aboard a creaky Russian helicopter whose turbo-shaft engine vibrated so bad that Gellman feared it might come apart in mid-air. He'd been assured by the Russian liaison officer at Bilibino that the rest of the their cargo and food aboard the C-5 Galaxy would be delivered before nightfall. As Gellman watched the heavy-lift helicopter lumbering back from Bilibino with yet another load, he knew they wouldn't get it all here today, and maybe not tomorrow either. The Russian's organizational skills appeared rudimentary to Gellman and he shook his head as he noticed the helicopter pilot pouring vodka shots for his crew as they unloaded the cargo.

Camp One wasn't much to write home about and not what he'd expected. A barren snow covered waste in which four tents now stood. The biggest was for the American team and fifty feet away a smaller one for the Russians. Two other smaller ones accommodated their survival gear and supplies if they ever arrived. A bevy of Russian guards had already strung a single coil of razor wire around the camp to keep out wild animals and wolves which the Russians assured him were nearby, and hungry.

As another helicopter came down through the overcast, Gellman thought about the special intelligence briefing he'd received in Hawaii just before they departed yesterday. A colonel named Hendrickson from DIA had flown to Hawaii specially to inform Gellman that about a hundred and thirty miles to the northwest of where Gellman now stood, lay a special Russian prison camp which for fifty years had been known to the Russians as Z-5. Hendrickson told him "on a Top Secret 'Specat' basis," that DIA's intelligence was that Z-5 had until recently, held up to as many as 350 captured American military prisoners, all of whom were believed to have been held in the USSR since World War II. Be very discreet Hendrickson had warned Gellman. But if Gellman was given a chance to visit Z-5 while he was at Camp One, he was ordered to take the opportunity at all costs.

Gellman understood the implication as he looked around. But he didn't think he'd be able to do much from this far away. All around him the landscape was flat and snow-covered. Anyone wandering beyond the wire stood out like a sore thumb against the snowscape. And besides, to Gellman . . . it seemed impossible that anyone could survive in such a desolate area for so long.

Walter Reed Hospital

"We need him resuscitated!"

"It might be awhile."

"Come on, Dr. Micklem! There must be something medical science can do to make this son of a bitch wake up!"

"Excuse me, Special Agent Collins, or whatever your real name is?" Micklem, shot back. His face expressing his concern over the agent's reference to his patient as a son of a bitch. "You want me to kill him?"

"If you have to." Collins leaned over the unconscious man and grabbed his arms and shook him as screamed. "Hey, shit-head . . . wake up you murdering old bastard and talk to me!"

Micklem shoved the young man back against the wall. "Call security," he ordered the nurse. "Get this secret agent the hell out of here."

"I am security!" Collins yelled at the doctor. And get your god damned hands off me, or I'll have you detained too for assault on a federal officer."

Micklem asked the nurse to wait in the hall and closed the door. "What's the problem here, Collins?"

"He's our prisoner, not your patient," the younger man threatened, "Got that? That old son of a bitch, for all I know is an al-Quaeda terrorist with orders to assassinate others of our leaders. Under the Patriot Act he has no rights. So we'll have people here in an hour to move him to one of our secure facilities."

"Where?" Micklem asked. "Your dog cages at Guantanamo?"

"You got a problem with that . . . Doctor?"

"Look at this man, Collins. He's got to be in his eighties. You think he is a terrorist?"

"Not my call, doctor."

"When I was a young man . . . Agent Collins, we used to demand due process. To you it is obviously not important."

"I got a job to do."

"So did Hitler's Gestapo. And last time I looked," Micklem observed, caustically, "this was still a U.S. Government facility and not Abu Ghraib, so you better be careful, Collins, because this is still my clinic and that man is my patient."

Collins gave him one of those condescending smiles. "Stay out of this, Doc . . . if you know what is good for your career."

"That a threat?"

"Goddamn right it is."

"Collins," he replied with obvious annoyance, and getting up a head of steam over the younger man's crass behavior. "You can address me as Colonel Micklem. I have a Top Secret clearance, and I clearly out-rank you, and I am in charge here, so get your skinny little ass out of here . . . or I shall have you restrained by force and sedated."

"Okay, okay, calm down," Collins replied. "I'll back off. Can you explain what his problems are?"

"He's suffered an embolism. A clot has cut off the flow of blood to parts of his brain. His coma indicates its more than a mini-stroke which normally starts with speech, confusion and paralysis. His heart seems to be okay for the moment. We've administered blood thinners and anticoagulants which should ameliorate further damage. It may even dissolve the thrombosis and allow blood to reach areas now being impacted. If that happens he will regain consciousness. We've scheduled him for a battery of tests which should explain problem areas. As regards his recovery, once out of the coma, early rehabilitation efforts are critical. So you understand exactly what has happened to this man, Agent Collins, it's like expecting your computer at home to work when you've pulled out its electric supply. Or worse, run a power surge through its hard drive. Yelling at it and shaking it accomplishes nothing."

"If he regains consciousness, Doctor, can he get up and walk around?"

"Maybe in three or four weeks, but only with therapy."

"Thanks, Doctor."

The comatose patient in room 9B-312 in the psychiatric section of Walter Reed was Micklem's responsibility. If the old man had shot a street bum in Washington no one would have given two hoots about him. But the president's National Security advisor was obviously another matter.

The majority of stroke patients normally regained consciousness within days. Others, however, never did, and when they didn't it was usually a blessing because in such cases it involved massive brain damage—their owners were essentially brain-dead.

Glancing at Special Agent Collins as the younger man's anger subsided, Micklem realized that the new generation, just like those that came before, thought they were shit-hot G-Men: with their Kevlar vests, earpiece communications, and concealed weapons under their armpits and elsewhere. But in the final analysis nothing had changed, they too were loyal Americans just trying to do a job in a world they didn't fully understand. For Micklem, the old man lying before him, aside from his cerebral problems, was a unique anomaly, and he wished he could bring him around and privately determine his genesis. This patient had a story to tell. The old man had obviously survived a lot of severe physical abuse in life. The type of abuse seldom seen in Micklem's profession. An X-Ray of his chest, head, arms and legs, looked like a child abuse victim's paradise. There were bone fractures everywhere, and the more serious ones were healed broken bones. This man had obviously been so severely beaten and so many times over an extended period of his life that it was a miracle he was still alive, and at the age he was. The nails of his right and left foot had all been removed, and two had painfully regrown at odd angles, suggesting his toe nails had all been removed by someone deliberately trying to inflict pain. Portions of his right foot and heel were missing. Micklem had only seen one similar case in forty years of practice: a Jewish survivor of one of Hitler's medical experiments who had survived the war and emigrated to the United States. Micklem debated contacting a local Rabbi to come and pray over this patient just in case he too might be Jewish.

Above the East Coast

The orb of the sun along the horizon seemed more spectacular from thirty five thousand feet as Alex squinted out the window. Heather's eyes flitted in his direction every few minutes from across the narrow isle of the twin-engine Citation II. As if to reassure her that all this was really happening and that he was still there and everything would be okay, he'd nodded his head and winked at her. She seemed more composed now, but was obviously frightened out of her mind. Now she understood more about what he was involved in because he'd confided most of what had transpired before the men at the airport in Miami had surrounded them and escorted them away.

From the long squiggly ribbon of lights along Interstate 95 below and the familiar city plan of Richmond, Alex knew they were approaching Washington. He pointed to the tape over his mouth. The FBI agent seated facing him leaned forward and removed it.

"Which airport you going to land at in Washington?" Alex demanded. The agent ignored the question and replaced the tape. Alex shrugged. If things had gone the way Alex had planned, right now he and Heather would have been somewhere over the Atlantic heading for two weeks of fun with Eduardo and his Indonesian lady friend in Switzerland. But two hours ago his skiing plans at Zermatt had suddenly changed.

He was such a fool. How could he have been so stupid? His biggest concern now was for Heather's safety. She'd had nothing to do with any of this, and was now caught up in something she didn't understand. He didn't think these people would go to all this trouble if they intended to waste him, but he had no idea who they were nor who they worked for. What worried him most was that they might lock him and Heather up somewhere and throw away the key forever. He knew it happened frequently in cases of dire national security, especially in these days of the War on Terrorism and the Patriot Act.

Heathers reaction from the start had been superb, she had more spunk than he'd given her credit for. She'd laced her escort with a string of obscenities and struggled like a wildcat as they'd manacled her, and in the process had kneed two of her assailants in the groin and brought one to his knees. Heather Maldutis was no pushover. Studying her across the aisle he promised himself he would ask her to marry him when this was all over.

In the last two hours he'd had a chance to reflect on what had happened. Mike Gregoriou had dropped him at Miami airport after lunch. Two hours later Heather's flight arrived from Salt Lake City and he'd suggested Heather pay for their First Class tickets to Switzerland with her credit card and they'd travel as Mr. and Mrs. Maldutis. It had been a mistake. He should have bought his own economy class ticket in a variation of his own name as he'd done so many times already, hoping the airline didn't notice the typo on his ticket. He knew law enforcement agencies monitored passenger lists, but seldom had time to study the infinite variations which might occur. His name was easy to vary, Balkan became Bulkun, Bilkin, or Belken. The economy class counters were swamped when they'd checked in, and the operators would never have noticed. The First Class counter on the other hand was damn near empty. So the clerk asked to see their travel documents, and studied Alex's diplomatic passport and Heather's tourist passport. It was their first mistake. Then she'd inquired casually if he worked at the American Embassy in Zurich? Alex replied he didn't. Right then and there he should have walked out of the terminal. But he thought he could pull it off, and ten minutes later as they drank coffee near the boarding gate, he noticed two men watching them and knew he'd blown it. When two more appeared Alex knew it would be difficult for them to escape. He could have made a run for it but knew Heather wouldn't make it and would be held until he turned himself in. Minutes later, handcuffed, they emerged from a sedan on the far side of the airport and were airborne within minutes.

Alex pointed to the tape on his mouth again and mumbled louder this time.

The Agent removed it again.

"Where are you taking us?"

The tape was replaced.

Twenty minutes later on their final approach to Andrews Air Force Base through the pelting rain, he could make out evening traffic along the Washington Beltway, and beyond it, the red and white checkered water tower with Andrews Air Force Base emblazoned across it. As they glided over the motel on Allentown Road below, his mind flashed back to the three day binge he'd gone on after his separation from the Air Force so many years ago. The jet taxied to a hard stand near the end of the Operations Apron and shut down engines as it rolled to a stop. The sound of a helicopter turbine became discernable as the forward door was opened and the agent across from Alex leaned forward and removed the tape from his mouth.

"No need to make this any more unpleasant than need be, Balkan. We'll leave the tape off if I have your word you'll keep your mouth shut outside. Deal?"

Alex nodded.

The agent looked at Heather. "And you miss Maldutis?"

She too nodded her assent.

They moved quickly across the hundred yards to a waiting chopper. Once into the Sikorski, Alex began to protest as the tape was reapplied. A new agent beside Alex yelled at him in a threatening voice to cut the crap or they'd knock him out with chemicals. The two men who'd accompanied Alex from Miami stood on the tarmac and watched as the chopper lifted off. The helo headed west across the Potomac into the inky black Virginia countryside. Alex knew they were going west because he'd seen the heavy ribbon of Friday evening headlights backed up across the Wilson Bridge over the Potomac.

Salt Lake City

"Thanks," he told the building custodian. "I don't think we'll be needing you any further. We'll lock the door when we leave."

"I'll hang around," the elder custodian replied. "It's Friday night, and I've got nothing to do." He sat in an easy chair by the door and watched them. They'd tried to order him to leave, but realized he was not about to go quietly and had threatened to call the police if they forced him to leave the apartment.

These guys with the FBI might be official and all that crap, the custodian thought to himself. The document they'd presented appeared to be a bona fide search warrant. But what did he know about what real and artificial warrants looked like these days? He'd seen enough shit on TV to know about the abuses of power by the Feds, and there was no way he was going to leave these young puppies alone to rifle through Miss Maldutis's things. He also didn't trust these guys who'd officiously flashed their FBI badges at him but refused to let him study their documents, so he could note their names or verify who they said they were. He might be a no-count apartment building security guard, but he'd fought under the Marine Corps colors for three tours in Iraq and knew what it was to love his country. He also thought highly of Heather Maldutis, and considered her a God-fearing Mormon woman.

As the two FBI agents continued their search it became obvious the Maldutis woman was a typical middle aged lady; without a life, no photographs of boyfriends, no secret love letters, no address books with old phone numbers or pornography. Not even a dildo under the mattress.

"You check the answering machine Barry?" The agent in the bedroom called out as his buddy finished pouring through the contents of the various paraphernalia in Heather's medicine cabinet.

"I'll get it."

Special Agent Barry was bored and obviously ready to retire. Eighteen years with the Bureau were exciting until he got assigned here to the Salt Lake City office. Utah was a dead sort of place far from the madding crowds of the east and west coast. The Salt Lake office was no-wheres-ville! Their biggest cases were those of the far-right militant groups spread across northern Montana and Wyoming, who were convinced Washington had sold out to the United Nations and that an international conspiracy was afoot to take over the United States and disenfranchise freedom loving Americans of their heritage.

Barry had been the first to receive the incoming Maldutis message from Washington two hours ago and had placed the pertinent points in a warrant which he'd taken up two floors to get Jamie Duzeman's approval on. Barry suspected that Jamie Duzeman, a bona fide federal judge for Summit County, was on a retainer with the Bureau under the Patriot Act. The rumor was that Duzeman was a FISA court member, a secret member of the intelligence community's Foreign Intelligence Surveillance Court. If true then this Maldutis woman might be something special. Barry knew that in the last decade, the FISA court had only disapproved eleven out of some 34,000 such requests. After a cursory inspection Jamie had approved an open-ended search warrant for Heather Maldutis apartment and other properties which the Bureau might find in the next sixty days. Barry's summary pointed out that Maldutis had just been placed under arrest in Miami as a terrorist suspect trying to flee the country while an associate arrested with her was wanted for the illegal sale of classified government secrets.

The building custodian watched as FBI Agent Barry pressed Heather's answering machine rewind button. The first call was from Heather's father, wishing her bon voyage and good skiing in Switzerland: expressing the hope she'd return in two weeks a married woman. The second call was from her sister, telling her she should marry her man; that he was a good person and would make a great husband.

"Hello," the third caller's voice filtered through the room. "This is Mary Malagang calling from Switzerland. Its early Saturday morning here, and I just returned from the police station in the town of Thonon, near where I live on the south side of Lake Geneva. I've got terrible news. I hope this reaches you before you leave for Switzerland. Eduardo was kidnapped last night. The local police are waiting for a ransom demand. I also heard from Jakarta that my father is missing. Please ask Alex what he thinks all this means? Please call me as soon as you can. If you decide to come skiing anyway, call me when you arrive and I'll have the driver meet you."

Agent Barry popped open the recorder and removed the tape, dropping it into an evidence bag as the custodian told him he wanted a receipt for it.

"I don't think so," Barry replied. "Espionage, kidnapping, a terrorist trying to leave the country."

Crash Site, Siberia.

Nothing could have prepared Colonel Gellman for the macabre scene around him. He was used to examining forty to fifty year-old crash-sites in Southeast Asia and Europe from time to time: where human remains were little more than bone fragments and the odd pieces of clothing and equipment. The Russians said the mountain range around him, which bore no official name on Russian maps, was referred to as Strachny by the locals. Gellman had not inquired what Strachny meant, but thought it would be appropriate if it meant abattoir. The Strachny crash site resembled a slaughterhouse of the Mad Hatter. From the angle of the slash down the mountain side, the doomed aircraft's forward motion had spewed wreckage down the slope for five hundred yards into a ravine.

The deep snow and intense cold had instantly frozen everything into surreal art which Dante might have envisioned in his 'Inferno.' Yesterday several of Gellman's crew, and again this morning, were forced to stop because of the gore. The whole place was a meat locker of gory body parts and not the environment usually experienced by those of UMPCs usual forensic work was crash sites were victims had died decades back. Excavating this site involved the horror of instant death more familiar to those of massive bomb explosions in the public markets of Baghdad. It was a new experience for Gellman.

The Russian's assisting him seemed to have less trouble with the work, pulling flesh and viscera from the wreckage with almost a mechanical disconnect. They paused only occasionally to wipe their gloves with snow before lighting up more cigarettes. Gellman glanced at his watch. Another two hours of daylight remained, but he was now ready to call off the mission. They'd found about all they needed.

This evening when he returned to their base camp, he would confer with his Russian counterparts and then his headquarters in Hawaii. He intended to tell his superiors, that for all practical purposes, that their work here was finished. In the last two days they'd physically accounted for eight whole bodies; almost complete assemblies for another three while the rest were miscellaneous bits and pieces which might constitute another ten to twelve. All they'd found so far were young Russian males. The aircraft on impact contained less than twenty people. Gellman also knew the difference between old and young victims. First there were the pieces of uniforms and insignia. Facial parts were clearly those of young Caucasian males. It was the teeth and jaw bones which made a conclusion inevitable. All belonged to men in their twenties.

Forensics could pour through the remains for a couple of weeks if they wanted to dot the i's and cross the t's. But it wouldn't change Gellman's conclusion. If his pre-mission briefing in Honolulu was to be believed, several hundred elder males should have been aboard, and the teeth of old men were easily identified—even by a high school kid with five minutes instruction. It was the boots which further simplified the final body count.

Eighteen pair of Russian military issue boots stood in three ranks off to his left. He knew there would be a few more somewhere beyond the impact point, but to remain a few more days so as to find them at this point seemed futile. The boots sickened some of Gellman's subordinates because most still contained the feet of their owners.

Gellman paused to listen. Another helicopter was approaching from the north east. A voice crackled on his radio. It was one of Gellman's subordinates who asked him to stand by; the Russians were coming in to pick him up. There was something nearby which they wanted him and his senior enlisted man to see.

A couple of hours later as he sat around in the mess tent back at the base camp, Gellman knew something really weird was afoot. He recalled his conversation with his Russian counterpart that afternoon as they stood shoulder to shoulder at the crash cite. A Russian somewhere else had called in to report they had just found another crash cite nearby. It was the wreck of a small twin-engine Russian light bomber which lay twelve miles away from the Il-76 site, and amidst its wreckage was a dead American. Gellman suspected this new victim might somehow be connected to DIA's suspicions about Z-5?

There were three bodies at the site. Two Russians and the American who appeared to be retired Army Colonel Jose Santiago. His body contained not only a wallet with the usual paraphernalia of photographs and credit cards, a retired military ID card, but also his last month's pay stub from the Army Accounting and Finance Office. Included also was a list of cryptic phone numbers, one of which was the name of a Russian named Vitali Zitalko who lived in Moscow. His Russian counterpart showed the phone number to Gellman with a smirk of satisfaction, and an insolent tone. "Look," Gellman's Russian counterpart said. "Phone number 338-861 is in Moscow, and in parenthesis, on the paper . . . KGB and an associate of Alex Balkan." Other names and numbers were under the headings, CIA and DIA. The notes seemed to conclusively suggest that the dead American colonel was obviously up to no good. Very unfortunate too for the United States, in Gellman's opinion, was the dead Colonel's diplomatic passport which was obviously the real McCoy!

From the way the Tupolev crash was laid out, Gellman assumed the aircraft had experienced engine trouble and tried to land in a narrow clearing in the mountains and disintegrated amongst a stand of heavy trees. No fire ensued and the cockpit area had remained intact. There were what appeared to be bullet holes in one of the tail empennages, but he could not be certain when they'd been made.

When Gellman reached his boss in Honolulu by radio, it was just after dinner in Hawaii and midnight in Washington. It would be eight to ten hours his boss told him, before he could get back to Gellman with definitive instructions to pull out.

Camp David

The president was taller than Alex expected as he extended his hand. Nattily attired in black slacks with a pale blue cardigan over a white golf shirt, he appeared well rested. Putnam who entered behind the president, approached the two Secret Service agents and signaled them to wait outside.

"I believe you two know each other," the president quipped. "The general informs me you have briefed him on occasion over the years."

Alex was almost speechless. For the last two days they'd kept him blind-folded in a locked windowless room. No one had told him where they'd brought him two nights ago. They'd been airborne for over half an hour out of Andrews Air Force Base and he figured they'd landed somewhere around Gainesville in western Virginia, or maybe somewhere on the grounds of Fort Meade south of Baltimore.

An hour ago they'd provided him with clean clothes and told him to shower and shave. Then they'd traversed a short hallway to the room where he now stood. "Everything okay?" The president inquired.

"I guess that depends? Where am I"

"Camp David," the president replied, glancing at Putnam.

"There was a lady with me when I arrived, Mr. President. Where is she?"

"Two rooms away," the general replied as the president expression changed to a knowing smile. "Don't worry. She's just fine."

"I want to see her."

"You will. After we talk."

"Why am I being held, Mr. President? What are the charges against me and Miss Maldutis?"

The general leaned forward. "After your talk with me at my home the other night, the president also wanted to see you."

"A strange way to issue an invitation?"

"Alex," the president began, "I apologize for the way you were brought here. There were allegations by you that assassins were trying to kill you, and others too, so we needed to speak with you."

"And I'm held incommunicado for two days?"

"As I said," the president continued, "my apology. There are things you know about which we must speak." From Balkan's expression it was obvious he was not mollified. "The General has told me all about your meeting two weeks ago in which you expressed certain concerns. You have had an interesting time the last few months and I congratulate you for a superb job well done. My condolences for the loss of your mother and your associate." He studied a piece of paper, "Marvin Raoul, I believe was his name. It's also very unfortunate that things worked out for you as they did at Scion. It was regrettable and we intend to rectify that."

"Mr. President!" Alex looked at the general, then back to the president. "Can I assume you know the truth about Langford Seeley?"

"The General has told me all about your concerns and your beliefs. I have taken certain measures to check-out your allegations. I have also taken cognizance of the contents of the articles which appeared in the Salt Lake City newspapers, and your concerns about our people in Russia who may have been overlooked. I have concluded that these issues must be forgotten in the national interest."

"Forgotten?" Alex's body language stiffened. He crossed his legs and folded his arms across his chest. "Mr. President. Are you serious?"

"Yes," the president replied, sitting back into his chair and obviously waiting for Alex to digest what he'd said.

"I assume you know the entire story, Mr. President?"

"Mr. Balkan," the president replied abruptly. "That is why I am the president and you are a cog in the wheel of government. Suffice it to say I have initiated certain enquiries and clarifications. At the moment I am satisfied you did the right thing."

"And?" Alex asked dumbly.

"It is all behind us." The president nodded reassuringly. "Our men you thought were in Russia and Mr. Seeley."

Alex looked at Putnam who gave him a blank stare, and then back to the president who also nodded in affirmation.

"Why our people in Siberia?"

"It is the national interest," the president said with a deadpan expression.

"But, Mr. President," Alex shot back. "They are there. And that son-of-a-bitch Seeley is a god damned spy! God knows he's probably betrayed every secret you ever discussed with him, and that's just his latest duplicity. I realize you do not wish to embarrass yourself with such a high level expose like this, but the rest of it?"

"As I said," the president repeated himself again. "I am convinced you did the right thing and I am not questioning your patriotism. It may come as a surprise to you, Mr. Balkan, but Seeley was murdered two days ago. Shot in his car while in traffic. And I can assure you, I, nor anyone in my Administration had anything to do with it."

Alex still wasn't certain he understood president-speak. But he knew that he did not want to forget the issue about the missing prisoners. "I agree that some dirty laundry may best be washed in the back room, but our men?"

With his National Security advisor dead, there was obviously no longer any need for the president to further embarrass his Administration nor the intelligence agencies at a time when they'd already taken a drubbing. The presidency had concentrated too much national power among too few, and without strong checks and balances a couple of former Potomac Potentates, mostly former administration retreads, had assumed virtual police state powers. "And what do you intend to do about our American prisoners in Russia?"

"Do? As I said," the president replied, "you did the right thing, and now it is time for you to move on,"

"You are going to forget about them?" Alex said in disbelief.

"Mr. Balkan, I told you once already, that both of these issues are best forgotten and never spoken of again. Do you understand? Expediency dictates it, Mr. Balkan. One of the advantages of being the president is that I have access to a wide range of information, and options usually unavailable to the average citizen. I want all this forgotten, Mr. Balkan. I would also like you to consider returning to your earlier employment for Scion. I would also be disposed to make it worth your while should you consider to pursue alternatives. We can explore these too if you like."

"A bribe . . . ? Something to insure my silence. Mr. President?" It was a dumb statement, and Alex wished he hadn't said it the moment it came out. But he was getting mad. Too much had happened. There was no way he was going to look the other way, especially regarding the men at Z-5. If America's leader wanted to push this secret under the carpet, then he'd have to do it without Alex Balkan. "They were Americans there Mr. President, I saw the graffiti, the names and dates and places where they came from."

"I know," the president replied. The president's demeanor indicated he was upset over Alex's inference to bribery. "Mr. Balkan!" The president countered. "I'm going to overlook what you just said. Let me be brutally frank. I've already told you we are grateful that you uncovered some serious problems dating back a long time. But these are behind us now. It is my intention that they be forgotten. We cannot afford to endanger our precarious understandings with our former Soviet enemies. Do you understand? With regard to the other two issues, I think it only fair that you know why I've made this request of you." He produced a broad engaging smile, trying to reassure Alex no malice was intended.

"I know a considerable amount more than you think! Most of it so sensitive that it must remain cloistered. So that which I am about to say must be kept in confidence forever. Between you and I. You understand?" The president paused. "I realize you may think you are no longer bound by secrecy agreements, Alex. But you are. Your employment at Scion involves a clearance. Your recent trip to Russia was within Scion's purview. What you learned there, comes under the purview of our secrecy act. I know you are a patriot. Do we have a deal?"

"I would like to hear what you have to say first."

"I must insist!" The president smiled engagingly.

"I will agree to say nothing if I agree with your logic," Alex replied.

This angered the president. Balkan was an arrogant asshole who was way out of his depth and needed to be taught a lesson in humility. But on the other, hand he could tell too that Balkan was a patriot and believed fiercely in what he was doing. From what Putnam had informed him about Balkan's earlier career, he also knew that Balkan had always called a spade a spade, and was a no bullshit type of person who because of his strong belief in the moral aspects of life, had always had problems working in organizations which required accommodations. The president opened his palms upward in a gesture of conciliation and waited.

"Okay," Alex replied, "if it is reasonable."

The president seemed placated. General Putnam too. Putnam adjusted the front of his uniform; brushing away specs of lint. A Rubicon had obviously been passed.

"There are several things you need to know up front. Our laws regarding missing POW/MIAs dictate that they be declared dead a year after we last heard anything about them. When WWII ended, we knew from earlier German military reports to the International Red Cross, that tens of thousands of our POWs were still alive and being held in German Stalag prison camps in the eastern areas of Germany and Poland. Soviet Red Army troops overran all of these camps and deliberately kept our men behind barbed wire and refused to admit any knowledge of them. They also denied us entry to their occupied areas area. We knew they then transshipped them through Odessa into Asiatic Siberia. Mr. Stalin had in effect illegally kidnapped them. We knew in mid-July 1945, that some twenty-five thousand of our men were in cages in the Odessa area."

"So," the president continued, "at the time we had two options, demand their return by a date certain or declare war on Russia. We pursued the former but not the latter through late 1945. The Pacific War against Japan was still underway, and we desperately needed Stalin to attack Japan as soon as possible. He had agreed to this. So we ignored the POW problem for a while. With Japan's surrender the Cold War began immediately and left us with only a nuclear option.

Regrettably by that time the families involved had already been informed that all their loved ones were dead . . . killed in action and their bodies not recovered. General Eisenhower knew about it as did most of our senior leadership in the post war era. Re-surfacing this saga today will only frustrate and bring pain to tens of thousands of our families who have moved on, remarried, and raised new families. There are also serious legal issues to be taken into account. These legal matters are also to be left unaddressed." The president looked at Alex, then Putnam, then back at Alex. "I hope this provides some sense of reason for my insistence that you keep your silence, Mr. Balkan. You obviously tripped over something you shouldn't have and I respect you for pursuing it as you did. But now it is time to rebury it."

Alex shrugged. "All right."

"Now, you also need to know about Case Judy. There is only one copy in existence and I have it, and I can assure you that its contents are irrelevant to our discussion here this morning. It's moot."

"Moot?" Alex replied.

"Correct!"

"Nothing to do with our POW's in Russia?"

"Nothing!"

Alex's expression once again showed his incredulity.

The president's demeanor showed his annoyance at being questioned again by this public servant.

"Nothing! I swear it," the president repeated in a low insistent voice. "You have to take my word for it, Mr. Balkan. Let me continue. "You are familiar with the name Pavlo Krasnov?"

"Yes, Mr. President."

"May I ask in what context?"

"A source in Moscow informed me he'd left Russia last October, for England, and from there he went to Canada."

"You know who he really is?"

"Yes. I do."

"And?" the president asked, waiting for Alex to reveal the name.

"Paul Carter."

"Good! You are aware of Carter's background?"

"As much as I need to know, Mr. President."

"Also good. Then let us move on to the next point."

Alex kept a straight face. He supposed the president would eventually get around to telling him how he'd made the connection. He didn't have long to wait.

"I wonder if you also know that the seven millimeter automatic pistol used to murder Theodore LePage, was the same one used four days ago to kill Langford Seeley?"

"Paul Carter?"

"Correct."

"I hadn't heard it on the news."

"And you won't, because this is one of those issues I must insist, not leave the Oval Office. The information has not been released to the Press and will not be. It would serve no purpose. Nothing useful would ever come of it."

"But they will find out Mr. President."

"I don't think so! Not if you don't tell them. And you won't! Will you?"

"Why not?" Alex inquired.

"Because, for a start, it will have a devastating impact on our military intelligence."

Putnam looked relieved and withdrew a handkerchief and wiped his brow, then the lenses of his glasses.

Alex understood. The information would implicate America's intelligence services in a scandal more serious than Gulf War Syndrome and the cover-up of the United States extensive chemical and biological weapons program supplied to Saddam's regime during the 1980s, so Saddam could use them against the Ayatollah's in his eight-year war with Iran. Alex understood that if this came out now it would do grave damage to America's military intelligence systems in the international arena.

"Now, Alex," the president continued condescendingly, "so you will completely understand why I must insist on your silence. The third point I wanted to make is that there is no trace of any Americans which you believe were at Z-5. And if there ever were, it is now impossible to prove."

"But," Alex interrupted.

"Let me finish!" the president cut him off. "Following your report to the general, we looked at the area and the adjacent airstrip you mentioned."

"I saw the aircraft marks in the snow, Mr. President, and . . ."

"Please!" the president insisted, holding up his hands. "I believe you. It is not the point here! We know the aircraft in question was a heavy transport. We know when it took off. Where it came from, and, where it was probably going."

Alex relaxed. "So?" Alex demanded petulantly.

"Unfortunately it crashed shortly after takeoff."

"Then," Alex interrupted him, "It is—"

"Shut up, Balkan!" the president exploded. "For Christ's sake! God damn it! Will you at least give me the courtesy to finish what I have to say."

"I apologize," Alex replied red faced.

"Accepted," the president replied. "Imagery and communications intercepts indicate there was a mid-air explosion about a hundred and fifty miles south west of Z-5. From an analysis of the data it's obvious the large transport's left wing suddenly came off in flight and it went down. So I contacted the Russians. I told them what we suspected and based on what you passed along to General Putnam, I demanded that we be allowed access to the Z-5 site and the wreckage location! They agreed, but only to one location which we had to choose. Since you indicated they were at Z-5, but left, we demanded access to the crash site. Our team chief at the crash site is a Colonel Gellman, and he just submitted his report." He held out his hand to General Putnam who opened his briefcase and passed him a folder.

"Have a look."

"What!" Alex said a half minute later. What he'd read shocked him. NSA intercepts of cockpit conversations made it obvious the aircraft was destroyed by an on-board explosion. The Colonel's report on the other hand indicated not more than twenty aboard the aircraft when it crashed, which on site forensics indicated all were young men in their twenties and thirties, and all attired in Russian military gear, and all documented as Russian air force personnel.

"Mr. President, the document I got from the source in Moscow indicated there were at least three hundred and fifty elderly American WWII prisoners at Z-5. I saw the graffiti myself, it was everywhere; people's names inscribed in beams, dates of birth, hometown names." He looked imploringly at both of them. "It could only have been made by Americans."

"I'm sorry," the general replied. "At this point there's no way we can go in hot pursuit of tarnished cenotaphs. Aside from your word about the graffiti, there's no shred of proof that they were ever there. And they, like us, now are only silent sentinels who can't speak."

"What about an original copy of a late 1948 KGB document, signed by Beria himself, admitting there were still at least thirteen thousand Americans still alive in their system at that time?" Alex asked.

"What are you referring to?" the president demanded.

"The Salt Lake City, Lake Sentinel newspaper announcement," Alex replied. "I gave the original Russian documents to the newspaper."

"You had original documents?" the president's voice was now incredulous.

"Of course," Alex replied. "You think the newspapers would have raised such an issue based on my word and promise? They had the documents checked out by some lab in San Francisco, who . . . confirmed their authenticity."

"Interesting," Putnam observed. "I'll get in touch with them and get back to you right away, Mr. President." He turned again to Alex. "Even if your story checks out, Balkan, which it hasn't. You realize we still have no concrete proof that any Americans were ever held at Z-5."

Alex dejectedly handed back Colonel Gellman' report and inquired about its reference to enclosures and a second accident site?

"That too is interesting," the president replied. "Give that report to me, General." Putnam handed over the additional photography and report for Gellman's second aircraft accident site.

"How did you get to Z-5, Alex?" the president asked.

"By private plane."

"Take a look at this," the president demanded, handing over a grainy aerial photograph of the wreckage of a small airplane in a forested area. The president handed over another photograph. "And this one?"

Alex still couldn't discern what the wreckage might have once been.

"It is a Tupolev." The president observed unemotionally. Probably the same one you used."

"Probably?" Alex said with disbelief. "Where was this taken?"

"Less than twenty miles from the other wreckage."

"What's the significance, Mr. President?"

"Of the wreckage? Nothing! It's who was in it, and what he was carrying that's become a serious problem."

"I don't understand."

The president searched through the file and pulled out a glossy photograph of an officer in full formal military uniform, the type usually placed in Officers promotion files. He held up the picture. "You know this man?"

Now Alex understood. "My god, is he still alive?"

"He's very dead, unfortunately! We just learned about this from our team chief leading the accident investigation for the Il-76 crash. The Russian's informed Colonel Gellman there was another crash-site close by, and Colonel Santiago's body was found in the wreckage. Moscow has conveniently provided a list of his documents to us, all of which check out. I have the names of two Russians aboard also. The pilot and an ex-Speztnaz guy. The Russians are really outraged, so unless I can defuse this somehow, they intend to make it into an international incident. Santiago's wallet contained compromising phone numbers, names and addresses. Moscow allege he was on a clandestine spying mission for the CIA, and was responsible for the sabotage of the Il-76! This is obviously not the case." He studied Alex for a long moment, waiting for Alex to say something.

"Goddamn it. Balkan! You asked him to go didn't you? The Russians also found your name and phone numbers of your contacts in Moscow among Santiago's papers. You asked him to go, didn't you?"

"Yes."

"To check out Z-5?"

"Yes."

"May I ask why?"

Alex mentioned the graffiti he'd seen at Z-5, but without a camera, was unable to document it. Without photographs it was Alex's word against impossible odds. So he'd arranged for Santiago to go and get the pictures.

"I'm truly sorry he didn't make it Alex," the president replied. "If he had, we probably could have supported your case. From what you told General Putnam earlier, we thought the latter was the best option. We obviously may have made a mistake. And once we chose the crash site, they sent in a team to trash the Z-5 location." He held up his hands to ward off Alex's obvious question. "I know what you are going to say. Don't say it! We sent someone to Honolulu specifically to brief our on-site team chief, to snoop around if he got a chance. He did and flew over the location on his departure. His report is that there's nothing left of what you described. The entire place was burned to the ground, and all the facilities bulldozed into the permafrost."

"Bastards," Alex muttered. "If there was one, there will be others. We'll just have to find them."

"I don't think so, Mr. Balkan. Forget about all this. You must." The president also suspected he might be hearing shortly from others in Russia. But not the way Alex thought. Russia's government was no longer the secretive monolith it once was under the communists. If any of the radical Russian firebrands got a hold of the information that the United States had demanded to inspect a Russian crash site, and Kremlin leaders had caved in and agreed, all hell would break loose. A Russian firebrand like Zhirinovsky could cause havoc with it. And on the other hand, if there were still other camps, or survivors, he would have the resources of CIA and DIA begin secretly delving into it again. Maybe they would get lucky next time.

"Well, Alex, I guess we'll never know the truth now about Z-5? Without Santiago's photography, and without bodies, there isn't much to go on. Can we agree the issue is closed?"

"I suppose."

"Your word on this?"

"Yes," Alex replied reluctantly.

"What are your plans?" the president inquired.

Alex shrugged. How the hell should he know. Last time he'd thought about it he and Heather were bound for some good skiing and sex in Europe. Now he only wanted to get away somewhere for a while and think. Once things calmed down he'd call Eduardo and join up with him.

The president looked at General Putnam. "Mind if I have a word privately with Mr. Balkan? Be kind enough to check on Miss Maldutis and bring her here. I would like to meet her. Oh! And General Putnam. Please follow up immediately with the Salt Lake City newspaper on the Russian documents, Alex referred to."

He turned to Alex as the door closed.

"Who is Mary Malagang?"

Alex's face showed his surprise, "A friend of a friend, why?"

"And Eduardo Hernandez?"

He studied the president for a moment. Now he understood the president's earlier comment about having access to information not normally available to most. "Why do you ask?"

"Something I thought you ought to know, that's all. The FBI may have got a little too excited when they picked you up in Miami, and they obtained a search warrant for Miss Maldutis's apartment in Salt Lake. I'm sorry. Had I known, I would not have allowed it."

Alex gave him a condescending look.

"On Miss Maldutis answering machine was a call from a woman named Mary Malagang in Geneva. Her message to you was that a man named Hernandez had been kidnapped. Also something about her own father disappearing. My regrets that I was unable to inform you of this until now. What was their relationship to you?"

Alex ignored the question and shook his head in disgust. Maybe the common man in America was right. Maybe big government had outgrown its usefulness. Without any formal charges or legal grounds for a search warrant the FBI had searched her apartment.

The president's eyes riveted him and Alex became uncomfortable. "Why are you staring, sir?"

"Sorry. I was waiting for an answer."

"It is not important."

"I hope not. I heard about another name once applicable to this man Hernandez. It was Heinkle, I believe? Strange how that name keeps popping up all of a sudden. The other Heinkle however was much older. A German as I recall. He commanded a submarine during WWII. Heinrich was his first name. It has all been forgotten now however." He squinted; his crow feet extending out from the corners of his eyes. He slowly templed his hands before him, his index fingers tapping each other. "Alex . . . I hoped you might forget this also?"

Alex understood. The president knew! He'd obviously made the connection. He had the CASE JUDY file and knew its secrets. Alex suspected he knew most of what was in the file, but there were gaps. Did the president also know about Alex's arrangement with Eduardo? He would let the president confirm it if he did. "Tell me something, Mr. President?" Alex inquired deferentially. "Since we are trading confidences and making accommodations. Why was the submarine off Key West destroyed?"

"I'm sorry Alex. I do not know anything about that."

"Langford Seeley was there just before it happened."

Again the president's response was immediate and open and appeared forthright. "If you say he was, I'm sure it is true. But I did not know that and do not know the answer to your question."

Incredible. Alex could detect no trace of deception in the president's response. "Maybe as much as four hundred million in Spanish gold was aboard that submarine at one time, Mr. President. What happened to it?"

"No idea."

The two men continued to eye one another. The pause pregnant with innuendo.

Alex broke eye contact first.

"Where is Paul Carter, sir?"

"In confidence, he's still at Walter Reed. But his coma is not likely to abate. His physician advises he may never recover."

"What a shame," Alex concluded.

"Yes. That is true."

"Sure you do not know about the submarine . . . Mr. President?"

The president arose, giving Alex a frown. "Wish I could help you, but I have no idea what you are referring too. Well, Alex, I guess that wraps things up. Take a few minutes with Miss Maldutis, then I'd like to meet her. I'd suggest you and she take that vacation you planned. And when you get back, let the general know. We'll take good care of you."

Alex had thought of telling the president that he'd already made other arrangements with Eduardo Hernandez, but decided against needlessly prolonging the meeting further. If Eduardo had been kidnapped as the president indicated, maybe his arrangement with Eduardo was now history too.

The president got up and headed for the door, then stopped, and looked back. "One other thing. "If you are going to travel, I'd suggest you avoid Moscow. There's a warrant out for your arrest, for the murder of two Russians at a place called Morino."

Alex smiled.

So did the president.

FINCEN, Washington D.C.

"What the hell is going on?"

"Beats me, Henry," the voice in Manhattan replied. "It is obviously developing on two levels. What's real and what's rumor."

"What's real?" Zeugma demanded, pulling his eyes away from the computer screen just long enough to study the expansive lawns outside Washington's FDIC's headquarters in the Virginia suburb. Spring was in the air outside and everywhere people were out strolling along the streets and through the parks. Things like this shouldn't be happening when the weather was so nice, he thought.

"We're still trying to find out, Henry," the voice in Manhattan answered. "So far all we know is that its institutional, it started in Europe, and everyone over there is nervous as a wet hen in a fox's lair."

"Where in Europe?"

"According to sources, it started in Frankfurt and Paris. They tell me there are several international groups there whose computers automatically kicked in last week when the DAX and the Paris Bourse reached certain trading points."

"What trading points, for Christ's sake!" Henry demanded. He'd seen the last weeks activity just like the asshole in New York had, and there was nothing unusual about the levels or numbers of trades.

"Damned if I know. That's all it is though. Trades kicking-in automatically when certain conditions exist. Then, if it moves too quickly, other institutional programs are tripped too, and all of a sudden you've got what we have right now. That's all it is!" There were a few moments of quiet on the line as each was deep in his own thoughts. "Hopefully that's all it is, Henry. If it is? Then everything should recover nicely by the end of the week. I'm assured its nothing serious."

"Is it the Crimean issue?"

"Not yet."

"The levels are awful high," Henry chided.

"True. And our economy is in terrible shape. Inflation is down." All the major indicators supported a weak and stagnating economy. "My guess is this will blow over by the end of the week."

Henry hoped the New York expert knew what he was talking about. Deep in the recesses of his mind he suspected it was the opening gambit of the Spanish question. But what could he do? Officially he did not know about it, and if he admitted anything, how would he explain it further? In fact, he really didn't know that much anyway, and most of it was hearsay. Only yesterday morning, government computer programs monitoring CHIPS transfers had also started sounding alarms. Then, other alarms also chimed as the unusually high level of CHIPS activity slewed into adjacent investment areas. CHIPS stood for Clearing House Interbank Payment System. It was an automatic electronic transfer network used by the world's financial system to facilitate worldwide funds transfers between banks. It functioned along an electronic highway that could move vast amounts of funds and assets around the world at lightening speeds.

After thousands of years of snail-like movements of money between customer's accounts in different countries, the new CHIPS system amazed everyone with its speed, agility and simplicity. Where it once took several days to move a dollar between New York and Tokyo, now it happened in a second, and billions coursed through the system in every direction like a huge interstate highway interchange. But on the flip side of simplicity, lay the unknown: things could happen so quickly today that no one could always anticipate them in advance: and worse, if no one understood the underlying issues . . . especially government's, then what little useful interventions there might be, ceased to be of value. You went to bed at night and everything was fine, and when you awoke in the morning, the world had emptied your vaults because of some rumor.

CHIPS had become fully operational in 1990, and handled thirty-seven million transactions worth two hundred and twenty trillion dollars in its first year. Projections for the end of the millennium were ninety million transactions worth eight hundred trillion. And last year, the activity surpassed one thousand two hundred and eighteen trillion. The volume dwarfed the United States GNP, and in terms of a single days operation, last week's 760,000 transactions exceeded 29.2 trillion dollars. The staggering speed at which all this happened and the volumes involved made Henry's job of monitoring CHIPS almost impossible.

One of the first oversight functions to fail when CHIPS was first introduced were the United States law enforcement programs against illegal drug launderers. Little in the last five years had been available to satisfactorily monitor or stem the tidal waves of dollars swishing through the system. Next came the counterfeiters. In the last four years Iranian and Russian owned printing presses in southern Lebanon and Moscow had produced forty-three billion in bogus one hundred dollar bills. The counterfeits were so good European and Asian banks couldn't detect them. Planeloads of the bogus currency to various points across the Mideast and the former Soviet Union, had made it the new unit exchange. Since 90 percent of all the one hundred dollar bills ever printed in the United States were now held overseas, new one hundred dollar bills would be introduced next month in an effort to slow down international counterfeiting.

What concerned Henry most as he watched some kids throwing a Frisbee on the lawn below, was the Executive branch's incessant screaming about terrorist transfers being conducted within the CHIPS flow, and the need to stop it. Henry's information was that the total movement in the last four years totaled two hundred and eighteen million dollars: only .000000000002 percent of the system total, and the U.S. Treasury oversight of CHIPS was now threatening to stifle the international movement of trillions of dollars in trade! But the flip side now was that many were already moving to the European EURO.

What would happen if the current financial outflow continued to gather momentum during the next few days. Henry suspected a worldwide panic would result. And at its core would be the international faith in the United States currency. Backed by gold and silver decades back, nothing backed it today, only Washington's promise to pay, a triple *A* bond rating and the strength of the United States economy. Henry feared that "In God We Trust" was all that really stood behind the FDIC and bankruptcy. Trillions out there sloshed around in a system whose owners believed the paper dollars were worth something because the United States would somehow make good on its debt. But the United States was the world's largest debtor, owing over thirty trillion dollars.

By the close of business yesterday, transaction volume against the dollar was only up four percent; nothing to worry about the experts assured Henry. They said the unusual level of transfers was just a momentary spike in the market. But by the end of the day, the four percent had surged to eighteen percent. Dollars flowing abroad had grown from a trickle to a river.

Then it started again this morning. And by noon today, dollar outflows had redoubled. Almost sixty billion above normal had moved, and there seemed no end. Henry knew it was no fluke. At mid-morning he'd received a call from the Federal Reserve Bank in New York, informing him that Chase Manhattan and the Bank of America had received instructions from foreign affiliates not to roll over four trillion 90 to 180 day Treasury Bills due next Tuesday. And there were rumors of more to follow. Within the next thirty days almost a quarter of the United States short and medium term debt was due to roll over. If others followed suit, trillions would go bidding in search of higher interest rates. If the Bond markets also moved above one and a half percent, there was no upper limit to which it could surge, possibly even eight to ten percent like back in the early 1980s. Was a financial meltdown about to take place?

"Whose really behind this?" he asked the voice in New York.

"I'll have details this afternoon, Henry," the voice in New York replied.

The federal government was constantly in the markets, borrowing funds needed to finance the government's massive fifteen trillion dollar national debt. Most of it was made up of long term interest bearing bonds. But in there amongst it too, were the short and medium term stuff more critical when things like this got underway. If the debt weren't so massive the problem wouldn't have been so serious. But in recent decades the Congress had been remiss in its spending policies, and allowed the Treasury to print trillions to give to foreign governments and institutions in payment for the nation's largess.

"Could it be junk bonds?" Henry inquired.

"Ancillary to the main issue at this moment I should think," the voice in New York replied. "There had been an unprecedented flood of bad debts cascading through the markets from distressed and bad corporate bonds, especially after the ENRON, dot coms, housing bubble, and other assorted scandals. Small investors by the millions saw themselves as the victims of a massive con game sanctioned by the government which had cost them multiple trillions. Part of the problem too was the incestuous relationship between the major commercial and investment banks. With FDIC to back up their incompetence, thousands of small banks had allowed their basic functions to become blurred following the repeal of the Depression-era Glass-Steagall Act. The fox was into the hen house again and no one was asking about the actual value of institutional assets, portfolios, or savings. It was clear to Henry that just over the horizon was another 1929 disaster all over again.

The retrenchment of American industry after the Cold War eliminated five million high paying jobs. The president bragged he'd grown the economy by creating six million new jobs—all minimum wage. Eight years and two foreign wars . . . on credit, along with massive tax reductions, had eliminated a three trillion surplus left behind by Clinton and now approached a twenty trillion deficit. How had it happened? Where had it all gone in seven years?

What really scared the crap out him was the suspicion that somewhere in the background was Celtic Judy.

Washington's reply last week to Madrid had in effect suggested that Spain reconsider a formal demand to Moscow instead. The reply didn't answer Madrid's question. The Spanish already knew the gold went to Russia in the late 1930s. Why rub their nose in it? All Washington needed to say was that the response to their request was negative.

Per Langford Seeley's request, Henry had passed the information on. But now, Langford was dead and Henry's last two attempts to contact the president had been rebuffed.

Before calling New York a few moments ago Zeugma also checked on the latest projections of U.S. currency holdings abroad. Of the thirty-two trillion sloshing around outside the country; thirty percent was believed to have been reinvested in U.S. Treasury instruments while the rest represented illegally printed currency circulating in the former Soviet Union, Southeast Asia and Middle East. Of that, approximately a third was held by foreign governments and quasi-government organizations who Washington could pressure to leave it in place. Henry suspected this would have to be done soon if a panic were to be avoided. The total numbers were terrifyingly mind-numbing.

"Where will the funds be parked?" Henry asked the New York person.

"No idea," his associate in New York countered. "I wish I knew."

Parking was the term used when money moved between investments. If it were in bonds today and stocks tomorrow, there had to be a brief moment at which they momentarily became liquid as they moved from one instrument to another. Whatever that brief moment was during which they were parked, they drew bank interest. In most instances the park lasted minutes or less. But there were times, especially during periods of uncertainty such as now, when funds might be parked for considerable lengths of time while undecided investors watched and waited.

"What about currency cross?"

"Too risky," the voice in Manhattan replied. "The Yen is a quarter point off, Sterling a sixteenth, and the Euro an eighth right now. But it might last a couple of hours. There's systemic imbalance within the Euro however, France and Germany is off almost a point, but the French couldn't take this much on short notice?"

"Over the weekend?" Henry demanded.

"Possible, Henry, but they'd probably go long, or short, according to their experience with the exchanges in Asia."

Currency crosses were short term placements that gambled against minor spreads between various currencies. They were very risky and seldom used by regulatory agencies. If the dollar bought 1.04 Euro's, but the same 1.04 Euro bought 120.00 Japanese Yen, and the Yen/ Dollar rate was 119.00, the three way cross represented a gain of 1.00 Yen, a tidy overnight speculator windfall of 1.8 million on a billion dollar deposit. Risk avoidance however was the cardinal rule of institutional liquidity. If the anticipated profit went into a loss at opening of business the next day, then huge losses would be incurred.

"What about precious metals?" Henry had the metals indexes displayed on his screen as he inquired and knew this market too was volatile. Silver was already above its three year ceiling of $45.70 an ounce and gold above two thousand.

"Buy orders have outstripped sells all day in Europe so far," the man in New York replied. "The market in Asia opens in seven hours. No telling how high it could climb there if this continues. We could see a five to six percent adjustment."

Only a few times since the CHIPS system was introduced had levels moved so unpredictably and so fast. When they did, it presaged economic and political instability somewhere in the world. This too was an issue that concerned Henry. At the moment there was absolutely nothing going on anywhere.

"Okay thanks. I'll get back to you before the market closes."

Moscow

"Yes, my darling."

"Of course, my love."

"How can you ask such a thing, my sweet?"

He glanced at his girlfriend beside him on the bed; more than slightly embarrassed that he had to indulge his wife on the phone while his manhood shriveled inside his mistress.

"Things are happening, my love," he continued. "I am required to attend to important matters of State at the Kremlin. Of course you and the children are important! Anna, how can you ask such a question?" He smiled at the beautiful blonde naked beside him. She smiled indulgently as she slipped out of the bed and headed for the bathroom to freshen up. He ran his hand down her back as she passed, coping the flesh between her legs, cupping the mouthpiece with his other hand as he did so. "What a wet dream? You are still the most beautiful woman I know."

"Yuri, you really are a bastard!" she murmured.

"Hurry, my love," he whispered, "be quick in the bath."

Returning his attention to the phone, he feigned a loud yawn. "Anna, my love," he assured his wife again, "I shall be home over the weekend."

Tatiana closed the bathroom door quietly while Yuri told his wife the interminable lies she knew were required to assuage his Kulak bitch! In reality Tatiana and Anna both hated Yuri, but for different reasons. She too had once loved him, but that was over twenty years ago when they were stationed in Central Asia together. In those days too, Yuri's wife was gorgeous and sought after by many, but had refused to leave the comforts of Moscow to join Yuri for his three-year assignment in eastern Russia. Now Yuri had power and position and lots of young cunts in his bed whenever he wanted them. Yuri was a real shit who liked a bitch in every port, and when he called, still came, just as she had two decades ago.

Yuri Valeriy Yeniseysk today was far beyond middle age; had a paunch, and body odor from too much liquor. He never shaved his coarse beard close enough, which was annoying because it chaffed her crotch. And more frequently these days he consumed too much vodka. It was the latter which troubled her most because the Vodka frequently made him nasty. Almost sixty years old and overweight, Yuri's once formidable sexual appetite had declined to two basic courses, meals at the Y and the missionary position. Even the latter quickly exhausted him, and now the American expression, "wham bam thank you, ma'am," came to her mind as his flab was slapping her thighs.

Tatiana could leave him any time she wanted, but she knew she wouldn't get far. Certainly not here in Russia. And beyond Russia . . . there was no place left for her to hide. She knew too much, and now she'd come home to Russia after decades in the United States and would have to make the best of what time she had left. Tatiana heard the phone slam down as she stepped into the shower, humming the theme song from Golden Girls.

"Damned bitch!" Yuri exclaimed as he pulled aside the shower curtain and kissed her shoulder. "Take your time darling! I've got to leave for the office right away. I'll call you later."

Zagorsk, Near Moscow

Through a deep sleep, somewhere in his subconscious, Eduardo heard a key clanking in a lock and several bolts fell back. Opening his eyes, the door to his cell opened. Two uniformed men with black boots stood stiffly at attention beyond the threshold, a third motioned him forward. Eduardo was depressed. With less than twenty-four hours before his scheduled execution, he had few illusions left. No longer did he bother to hold his shoulders back or keep his head erect. His captors were unimpressed with their victims appearance.

"Is it time?" he inquired.

"Da," the guard replied.

Eduardo's pulse quickened. He thought he was going to faint. He put his index finger to his chest, his thumb simulating a pistol hammer.

"Nyet." The guard in the doorway laughed, raising his head as he said it. His index finger transcribing a half moon in the air signifying later.

Passing a central courtyard he noticed four chairs along the wall, two askew amidst dark brown stains on the wet concrete. Nearby he could see the glint of spent brass shell casings strewn everywhere. On three occasions last night he'd heard prisoners passing his cell toward this place. Then, after some silence, sometimes came a plea; shouting, or a wail which were followed by automatic weapons fire. And then the lone report which he knew must be the 'coup de grace.'

The way things stood, Eduardo too would be seated on one of those chairs tomorrow and executed like a common criminal.

Emerging into a small courtyard they proceeded beneath an architrave to an oak door bearing Cyrillic script and the Roman numeral four.

The guard opened it, pushing Eduardo forward toward a high back chair. He shivered as they removed his chains and ordered him to sit.

Before him, behind a spindly desk sat a woman with flaxen hair and blue eyes. Attractive and in her late forties, her blue eyes and blond hair were striking. "Una donna magnifico" was how he'd have described her back home in Peru. And were his circumstance different he'd have subconsciously thought about what it might be like to be screw her brains out. Was she the type who would arch her back and moan loudly in orgasm, or moan obscenities in his ear? That he would never know ordinarily would have saddened him, but now he no longer cared.

On the desk before her lay a file.

He waited as she opened it, studied the contents briefly and then closed it.

"Who I am is irrelevant." She began, as the guards left, leaving them alone. "Just so you know however. My name is Tatiana Slavchenko. I am a Colonel in Russian intelligence."

Recognizing the name he replied. "Might I have heard this name before"

"Probably, from your American friend, Alex Balkan?"

"Alex told me you were dead?'

"Oh!" she commented.

"That's what he told me."

"When?"

"He said you were killed last December."

"Where?"

"In Washington."

"And he believed it?"

"Of course. You are the same person?"

"Yes."

"So you are not dead after all?"

Tatiana studied her hands and finger nails with a distracted air. "So it would appear."

"Alex seemed very upset about it, he spent a lot of time trying to find out who killed you."

"Poor man," she replied. "He thought many things."

"How did this happen?"

"It is no longer important."

"What have I done?"

"That too is no longer important."

"Why am I here?" Eduardo asked.

"Because you have been condemned."

"I know that. I mean right now, here . . . with you?"

"Because of your father," she replied.

Eduardo waited for her to complete the sentence.

"And who your father was?"

Eduardo still had no idea what she meant. "He's dead."

"I know that. Last December in England. From Aipysurus Laevis."

Eduardo recalled Haggerty's reference to this snake poison in London, and then again last week in Lima. "How did you learn this?" he asked. "Nothing appeared in the newspapers about it?"

She laughed.

He waited.

"You know what it is, Mr. Hernandez?"

"Yes."

"And you are surprised I know?"

"Yes," Eduardo replied. "How?" He recalled that while in Peru recently, the Scotland Yard Inspector had tried to get a Peruvian court to honor London's request for his father's exhumation. Eduardo didn't want it to happen, and mentioned this to his old friend, the Director of the Institute of Strategic Studies in Lima, and received his assurances that since his father and Eduardo were both men of means, that no Peruvian court would honor the English request.

"I was there," she informed him.

"You murdered him.?"

Her smile became insidious. "The poison did. After I left."

"Why?"

"Why?" She countered with a smile. "Because he was stupid and refused to cooperate. Finding him was the biggest problem. Over sixty years had elapsed since our gold was stolen at Minsk. The trail was cold. When I found him I was afraid he might spread an alarm."

Smiling at her reference to *our gold* and *stolen*, Eduardo thought of laughing at the idiocy of her observation, but decided he'd better not. Before his trip to England he'd been an ignorant country bumpkin, only to become one of the richest men on earth. Spain's Conquistadors stole the gold from the Aztec and Inca; then Russia stole it from Spain: the Germans from the Russians: and finally his father from the Nazi's. And in an ultimate twist of fate, Eduardo's father had stolen some of it from his coconspirators while the Americans got the rest. All Eduardo wanted now was to escape death and walk out of this room a free man. They could keep it all.

"We knew the gold went to Berlin," his interrogator continued. "We know Hitler ran handful of it through his fingers like King Midas had done. After the war we traced the transfer from Berlin to the port of Bremerhaven. From there the trail became cold. But we did acquire a lot of Germany's secret records and new computers in the late seventies enabled us to cross-check millions of old German files at various places in Russia. This uncovered new leads. Then the trail went cold again after a Mongol sold some of the Spanish gold coins in the central bazaar in Almaata." She could see he had no idea where that was. "It's the capital of Mongolia. We hoped the Mongolian would lead us to the rest. He was killed before we could ask him."

"So you see, Eduardo, we had bits and pieces of the puzzle, but no idea how they all fit together. We cooperated with America to defeat Germany and had side agreements with Roosevelt. We knew the British were involved. We suspected the Germans were too. But again we had no details. What we didn't know until recently was the United States had double crossed us right from the beginning. Washington knew where the gold was the whole time because she'd misdirected it herself. So Moscow arranged my defection to the United States to find out what became of it. By 1980 I had completed all my briefings and training and left for the United States."

"So you know all the answers then?" Eduardo observed. "Then why am I here?"

"Most. But still not all . . . unfortunately," she replied.

"I don't follow."

"There were three shipments. We have the first two. Now we want the last."

Suddenly it dawned on him, she was referring to the South American shipment which had disappeared off the South American coast of Brazil . . . or was it Key West?

"The last cargo was huge compared with the first two," she told him.

Maybe Eduardo had something he could bargain with after all? What was it Alex had said about seeing a video of the wreck. That it was undamaged and lay in three hundred feet of water? And that the American Navy had conspired in covering up its final resting place?

"Last year," she continued, "we got close."

"And?" Eduardo pressed, suddenly realizing he really might be able to save himself.

"We found the woman who you also were looking for in Key West."

"Eve Albion?"

"Yes." Tatiana smiled, revealing perfectly aligned white teeth. A whiff of her perfume reached him. He wished their circumstances were different because this woman was formidable and obviously concealed deep pools of erotic and uncontrolled passion. Latin men could sense such traits. He envied Alex Balkan because he'd obviously experienced this woman's passion.

"But she was already dead when I got there," Eduardo told her.

"I know that too."

"So what's the point?" Eduardo asked.

"When I saw Albion, she hinted there might be someone in England. But she was a cagey old bitch and wouldn't say more. Eventually I was able to befriend her and reduce the English field to only four people. Knowing an American prisoner in Novosibirsk who'd once met your father during the war, we hinted to him that your father was still alive and involved in his betrayal. We provided him with just enough evidence to prove it. Then we let him go and he led us to your father."

"Paul Carter?"

"Very good! I see my old associate Alex Balkan confided even this to you."

"Where did Carter meet my father?" Eduardo inquired.

"In the Mediterranean. The gold was transferred from his submarine to a flying boat off the coast of Cyprus. Carter then escorted the airplane to Asia. That was where he came to be captured."

"And so, I assume Carter didn't tell you everything you needed to know?"

"Yes and no. We had to devise another way." Tatiana wasn't about to tell Eduardo that Carter was more interested in killing those who'd betrayed him than helping Russia recover its gold.

Eduardo waited as she leaned back, obviously enjoying his discomfort.

"So we got to your lawyer instead," she said.

"Smithers?"

"Yes."

"I see." "He was willing to cooperate in your inheritance."

"How?"

"He changed some of your father's documents. Leaving to you more than was his to give." She smiled insidiously.

"To what end?" Eduardo demanded. But he recalled the old Armenian's anger in Cyprus over his father's efforts to screw his business partners.

"So we could follow you."

"To the others?"

"Bravo," Tatiana replied. "There . . . now you have it!" she exclaimed. "And all we had to do was watch as you led us like a fox to its lair."

"You seem to know everything already. Why waste time with me now?"

"As I said I need your assistance."

"How can I help?"

"Interested in a deal?"

"For my life?"

"What else?"

"Maybe," Eduardo said.

"Maybe?"

"Depends what you want."

"Just bits and pieces."

"Such as?" Eduardo decided he had nothing to lose.

"The old Armenian in the next room," she jerked her thumb toward the far wall, "has been very difficult. And being old, he's too stupid to realize the game is over for him. He's given us everything we need already. The Chinaman too. The old Chinese General is more pragmatic however. Chinese people seem to be more fatalistic. It is a frustrating trait sometimes, but we already have control of CEBU and the entire pyramid below."

"Who are you referring to?" Eduardo asked.

"Your associates of course."

"They are in the next room?"

"Come," she said, rising and moving to the door behind her. She opened it and stood aside to let Eduardo look.

What he saw shocked him. Selvanian's eyes met his accusingly, but the eyes in his face were about all that Eduardo could recognize in the physically beaten bloody face. Chong Ki Young, a heap beside Selvanian, appeared to have been less brutalized. Before he could say anything the guard in the room slammed the door shut.

"So why do you need me?" Eduardo inquired.

"Because," she replied, "do you mind if I use your first name Eduardo? As I said a moment ago, the United States, and not CEBU, got the last shipment which your father and the Armenian stole. What can you tell me of it?"

"In exchange for?"

"No execution."

"Why should I believe that you would release me?"

"I'll be honest. In fact we can't. Not for a few more weeks anyway. It will take us that long to liquidate most of CEBU's assets. After that there is nothing you can do about this. So if you agree to cooperate, when this is all over you'll walk out a free man. Do you want to cooperate?"

"And my two friends in there?" Eduardo asked.

"Don't be stupid. They are not your friends, only associates, and believe me they mean nothing to you. Partners maybe, but not even that any longer. Forget about them, if you want to go free and enjoy the rest of your life?"

He wanted to believe her. A month was more than enough to transfer ownership. And with the three principle bearer share holders here in Russia and issuing orders for the divestiture of their assets, the system would dumbly comply as long as the documentation was authentic.

Tatiana's smile became sensuous as she tried to reassure him that her offer was one he couldn't refuse. He'd suddenly won the lottery and just as quickly lost it. Eduardo's interrogation two days ago with an elder Russian named Yeniseysk, had laid out the Russian government's case against him. Eduardo had conspired with, and paid a Russian to assassinate two Russians who were also members of the intelligence community. The government had witnesses to Eduardo's involvement, including photographs and sound tapes. Moscow's case was airtight. They had him by the balls and because of the intelligence connection, a Russian court had already reviewed his case and found him guilty of murder, and his execution scheduled for dawn tomorrow.

"Well, to answer your question. I guess I have no choice but to cooperate with you."

"An understatement, Eduardo. But the right decision."

She withdrew a paper from the folder and placed it before him. "It is a pardon. You leave Russia in three weeks for Lima, Peru. In the meantime you will be released from prison, but kept at a comfortable villa nearby."

Eduardo could not read what it said, but could make out the signature of the Russian president at the bottom.

She removed a second sheet of paper. It was a quit claim, written both in Spanish and Russian, that he had no further legal rights to any assets of CEBU, nor the pyramid companies below.

Eduardo picked up the pen. "Where do I sign?"

As he did so, she picked up the phone and ordered the operator to place a call to CEBU's new lawyer in Hong Kong. "You will confirm to him Eduardo, that you, the Armenian, and General Ki-Young, are all here together, and have decided to liquidate everything. That he will be contacted by me personally there in Hong Kong within forty-eight hours, with all the required documentation, and that he is to comply with the instructions I carry. If he has any questions, I shall provide him with a number at which you can be contacted. Questions?"

"And if he asks why?"

"Tell him it is none of his business. You are divesting your interests for other considerations."

Eduardo signed the various documents.

APRIL

ONE

FDIC Balston

THE PROBLEM HAD obviously started with CHIPS.

Across the manicured expanse of green grass, resembling a sea of greenbacks, stood the rose granite and green gables of the headquarters of Federal Deposit Insurance Corporation, looking more like a beached Albatross, than the last resort for the guarantee of America's national currency. Behind the opaque mirrored facade above the entrance, Henry Zeugma smiled as he considered the anachronism of his dilemma; his undoing and maybe even his demise.

FDIC was a paper tiger. "He that hath pity on the poor lendeth unto the Lord," Henry thought. But who would lend money to FDIC? No one seriously believed anymore in the government's ability to pay its debts and knew they would just have to print more paper money. FDIC was supposed to reassure the nation that it's banking institutions and currency were solid. Neither were. Neither could pay and only the twenty-two carat gold inlaid letters over the main FDIC portal outside was worth something. The rest was all bullshit!

As Henry Zeugma watched several of his aides depart, he knew his mission was doomed. Through the mirrored glass of his eighth floor office, he viewed the featureless monoliths lining Wilson Boulevard. Each bespoke investments based on the people's belief that each tomorrow would be better than the day before. If some bank failed, its depositors had nothing to fear, not as long as an insured by FDIC plaque was displayed prominently on the counter. But FDIC was never intended to bail out the entire system at once. Henry smiled at the gallows humor of it all. Within a year, America's financial house could resemble that of third world places like Nigeria and Uganda, where government's squandered the peoples patrimony and runaway inflation and worthless currencies reduced humanity's expectations to poverty, chaos, and a peripatetic scramble for the next meal. Everything in the United States could soon be indexed. And if not, then men making fifty thousand dollars today would be earning two hundred thousand a year hence. And a million the year after . . . when a gallon of gas would exceed fifty dollars and a loaf of bread, twenty-five.

Henry had testified before Congress that it had neglected the domestic problem for too long. It had ignored the international banks too. Now the International Monetary Fund was being highlighted as a problem area. Out there were hundreds of mortally sick American banks that should have been allowed to die years ago. All had been preserved from the axe-man, absorbed by healthier ones, those too big to fail. Too big to fail in the name of socialized government. And if it were only the banks that were the problem, it wouldn't have been so bad. But the Congress's endless hand-wringing ad-nauseam and irresponsible approval of huge bail-outs for America's automotive, insurance, housing sectors, and out of control social programs had pumped multiple-trillions of newly printed paper money into a system that should have been left to adjust itself.

His wife confided to him that Washington's accounts now resembled those of the Roman Empire in the fourth century of its existence. America's social fabric too had unraveled. No one had responsibilities anymore, only rights and privilege. Marriage and family life, child rearing, commitments to others, taking care of parents, all were things of the past. One in three whites were born out of wedlock, one in two blacks, over twelve million illegal Hispanic immigrants drew social program benefits who had never paid a dime into them. White men called women bitches, blacks . . . their whores.

Henry jumped involuntarily as the phone beside him rang. It was Kenneth Dilanian, the treasury secretary on the line.

"Henry, I got problems. Got a minute?"

"What is it Kenneth?"

"We've known each other a long time, Henry."

"Twenty-five years at least."

"This is not a social call, Henry. The IMF has serious problems."

"Things are tough everywhere right now, I think it will all work out."

"Always the optimist, Henry. I don't know if I can agree."

"How's your wife and boys?"

"They're leaving town. I have a place up in Vermont. I think that's where they should be right now."

Henry paused a moment, trying to figure out what Ken Dilanian was telling him. "Your children are in high school, aren't they? You are pulling them out of classes?"

"I think it is best, Henry."

"Jesus, Ken. What are you telling me?"

"I'm afraid. No! Its more than that! Remember . . . a couple of years ago, we damned near had a meltdown of the International Monetary Fund because of its bailouts of deadbeat nations. You know me, Henry, I've spent an honest career in industry before being asked to serve publicly. This is not what I expected. No one in the Oval Office seems to give a shit about details while the congress and senate only care about getting reelected and blaming everyone else for our country's problems."

"You think it is that bad?"

"Yes, I do."

"So what's the bottom line, Ken?"

"IMF and the World Bank may have to close their doors within the week, for a while anyway. Our economy is also on the brink of collapse . . . in my opinion."

"You can't just walk away like this, Ken."

"I don't need the job. My resignation is on my desk."

The line went dead.

Henry closed the door to his office, picked up the phone, and dialed his residence. "Don't ask any questions?" he told his wife. "Just do what I ask. We've already been over this. I want you to gas up the pickup. Then hit a couple of supermarkets in the area and buy a couple of thousand dollars' worth of staples for the house and leave them in the garage. Remember, only food staples, stuff that will last a long time without refrigeration. Oh . . . and don't forget to charge it."

When the panic started, there would be anger in the streets. The stores would be emptied and hoarding would become rampant.

Once it started, Democrats would blame the Republicans and vice versa. The Senate would blame congress. All would say it was the White House's fault. Tempers would flare. The public would seek revenge.

The president had agreed and Henry had just ordered his subordinates to carry out the FDIC's disaster plan. Now it would depended on the hundreds of millions of individual depositors out there. What would they do next Monday? Next Tuesday? The banks would be allowed to remain open for a while if a rush of depositors began to withdraw their funds, but would eventually have to close if the rush became a torrent.

If everyone lined up to withdraw deposits next week, the system would collapse. If not the system might survive.

The latest edition of the London Economist lay open on Henry's desk, aptly describing the perfect storm that was brewing. A Fed spokesman in this morning's *Wall Street Journal* was quoted: "If this crisis serves as a catalyst for constructive action, it will have served a useful purpose. And if not . . . God, help us." And typical of the Italians, they opined, "Americans, as individuals, can, by borrowing, live beyond their means but only for a limited period of time. Why, then, should America think that collectively it is not bound by the same limitations as the rest of humanity? It is time for America to learn a bitter lesson everyone else has known for decades."

In utmost secrecy over the weekend, eight commercial aircraft would depart military airfields around Washington at random for cities across the country. Each would carry hundreds of billions in newly printed currency to be distributed to any bank who's depositors sought to withdraw their money next week. If everyone did, and the banks did not close, then by this time next week, the country would be awash with trillions of dollars, and Henry's worst fears would be realized.

The Kremlin

Communism was dead after decades of hard times in Russia. Massive new oil and gas discoveries across Siberia had enabled Moscow to once again reassert Russia's place on the international stage. Capitalism, as envisioned by the signers of the American Declaration of Independence, had gradually morphed into an all-inclusive socialist system controlled by a wealthy elite who comprised only one percent of the American people but controlled over half of America's wealth. Europe, always a kaleidoscope of conflicting interests, also had the cancer of widespread social subsidies that were inexorably hollowing out its cradle-to-grave social mandate.

Yuri Veleriy Yeniseysk smiled. Despite Russia's problems in the Ukraine and Crimea, the tide of world opinion was turning against America and Europe like a morning mist after sunrise on a clear day. For fifty years of the Cold War, the main question in the Kremlin had been what would bring America down first, financial collapse, nuclear war, or American's naïve belief that its democratic experiment would forever be invincible. In the decades since the collapse of Marx and Engle's communist dream in the USSR, Washington had arrogantly run rough-shod over the world with her military might. The world today viewed her as a society uninformed, indolent, overweight, self-indulgent, and most important, afraid. Her incredibly expensive all-volunteer military forces were virtually useless against the scores of lone terrorists that now came at her with hatred in their hearts from the four corners of the world.

"Soon it will be our time!" Yuri stated to no in particular as he listened to the end of the intelligence briefing on domestic issues in Russia and three of her former republics.

"Excuse me, Colonel General," Yuri interrupted him, rising from the comfortable leather chair at the long conference table. "Let us take a five minute break. I must use the men's room." Yuri arose and walked briskly from the room.

Examining his face in the bathroom mirror, Yuri grinned as he studied his smile lines for a moment. He was still handsome. Almost sixty, he looked forward to another decade of vigor. As he proceeded to the first stall, he stopped at a window for a moment to watch the sparse traffic crossing Kremlin square beyond the walls. Recovering 40 percent of Spain's Caballero bullion lost to the Germans in 1942 at Minsk wasn't so bad, he thought. Especially after more than a half-century. It would support his plans for quite a while.

CEBU and its various sub-entities had nurtured its patrimony into a three-trillion-dollar prize. He realized that the rest of the gold was probably now lost forever. But no matter. Garo Selvanian and Chong Ki-Young, after considerable discomfort induced by Yuri's experts, truly didn't seem able to account for what had become of the last gold shipment to South America. Both suspected the United States of concupiscence, but neither could offer specific evidence to support it. It no longer mattered anyway. Eduardo Hernandez's information about the mystery U-Boat near the Dry Tortugas had provided a new starting point. Since it lay within United States territorial waters, he doubted Russia would ever be able to recover it without the United States finding out. The next best thing therefore was to use it as a weapon against Washington. Now he knew how the Americans had recovered the gold. In a way it was better this way, he would find a way to introduce the information to the world court and let it undo Washington.

Through the Russian Embassy in Spain earlier this week, Yuri learned of the U.S. State Department's reply to Spain's Caballero inquiry. Washington said it knew nothing. It suggested Madrid recontact Moscow. Spain had . . . and Moscow suggested Madrid look into a wreck off the Florida Keys and thoughtfully provided coordinates. Yesterday the Spanish ambassador sought out the Russian president and asked for clarification.

Yuri smiled as he considered the vagaries of human travail. The Americans thought they knew everything. But they would now be undone by their own indolence. Aristotle had first inquired about what constituted the good life. Aristotle examined how people were ruled, should be ruled, wanted to be ruled. He examined how people related to each other in their various forms of governance and those governments to one another. He concluded that his Greek compatriots adopted democracy because it worked for them. And that in reality it only involved five thousand Athenians while for the rest of the Greeks, there were no privileges, only responsibilities. The Egyptians had their Pharaoh, the Babylonians a bicameral house with vetoes by the king. Persia's Shah's represented his people to Persia's trinity, Ahuramazda while the Americans? Well . . . they insisted the world adopt the American democratic model of one man one vote which was ludicrous in mankind's experience.

Tatiana too had done well. It had taken her too long, but eventually she'd found the woman at Key West. Unfortunately Tatiana was now unhappy since her return to Russia and Yuri supposed it was probably because she had secretly become a capitalist during her American sojourn. She was still a beautiful woman, haughty, demanding, and luscious. Still . . . she was now a problem he'd discussed with the president: who concurred their world would now be better without those knowledgeable of their part in the Caballero transfers.

Yuri would see that her remains received a fitting funeral. Yuri was particularly pleased with her performance with the Peruvian lawyer.

The son of Heinrich Kaufmann had betrayed his associates in spades, and now the son, Eduardo, had followed suit. Once CEBU's rape was complete, the son and his associates would also be disposed of.

The information the Peruvian had provided about the submarine in the Florida Keys was fascinating. But Yuri knew the gold would not be there. The fact the submarine was where it was and secretly moved there by the American navy, and its record falsified was proof enough. He'd prepared a confession to which they'd forged Heinkle's signature. It confirmed Heinkle's guilt, provided names, places, dates, and the part each of the conspirators had played. The information would infuriate Washington when it hit the media. Moscow had also suggested Spain preposition her navy at the Florida site until an international team could be brought in to inspect the wreck.

Washington had its pants down. Exposed too was its participation in the Nazi's conspiracy to steal property belonging to Europe's now extinct wartime Jewish community. Now America's powerful Jewish lobby would go crazy with cries of anti-Semitism in America's highest office. They would demand reparations. Powerful law firms would initiate class-action suits that would tie up the courts for decades.

Then there was Spain's bullion. The potential settlements for that treasure were staggering. A run on the American financial house might undo it as happened in 1929. Yuri smiled as he reflected on the huge financial transfers out of the United States which had already started. The world's media was abuzz, and soon the unwashed masses would join the stampede to cover their risk.

"Now we will show the bastards." Yuri's voice echoed through the empty parasha stalls. And it was all possible because of the three men Yuri had kidnapped last weekend.

First, was the young Peruvian lawyer who'd been careless. It took three men a couple of seconds to spirit him away. The Armenian had also been easy. His villa on a remote promontory near Santa Eulalia del Rio, on the east coast of Ibiza, was an ideal place for a kidnapping. The minute they had the old Armenian, word was sent to the Russian Embassy in Jakarta, and the old Chinese General named Chong Ki-Young was also picked up and spirited out of Indonesia.

CEBU's rape in the last five days had already progressed beyond Yuri's wildest expectations. The transfer of all the group's liquid assets would be completed by early next week. Semi-liquid assets within 180 days. The liquidation of her fixed assets would take longer.

Just over a fifth of CEBU's assets had already been converted to bullion in Switzerland, and another eighteen percent would follow by mid-summer. To date, 4,500 tons of new bullion resided in their Zurich gold accounts. It was enough to finance Russia's economy for a couple years and secure Yuri's continuance in high-elected office in Russia for several more terms. He wiped his hands on the soft warm hand towel and returned to the briefing and resumed his place in his comfortable chair. Looking around the conference table, he noted that everyone was present.

"We may now resume the briefing," Yuri ordered. "Are you almost done?"

"Yes excellency."

"Good then get on with it."

The colonel general of the second intelligence bureau, Andrei Goryainov, dimmed the lights and the small red dot of his laser pen traced the next topic heading: Anti-American events.

"It is the unanimous assessment," Goryainov said with conviction in a deep resounding voice, "of our senior diplomatic, military and national security intelligence analysts that the United States has irretrievably lost the third world's goodwill at the United Nations. It is also the consensus now that ten of the leading industrial states are also in this category and are suffering from their inability to justify continued traditional pro-American policies. Among these are India, Pakistan, Egypt, Indonesia, China, the Stan states of central Asia, and Brazil. We have just changed our national objectives with regard to these entities and will be bringing new policy proposals within the next two weeks for your review."

"What do you have in mind?" Yuri inquired.

"Some challenges."

"Continue." Yeniseysk replied through a yawn.

"Four," Goryainov began. "Encourage a new nonaligned group of states like those formerly of Nasser and Tito that existed during the Cold War. These will create a new anti-American block. Next is more enhanced radicalization of Islamic groups inside the European Union: to undermine the Union's cohesion. Despoil Washington's endeavors in Afghanistan, Iraq, and Iran, and finally to make NATO irrelevant.

"Interesting," Yuri observed.

Goryainov continued, "Following is a summary of current American crisis issues, which will be summarized for you by Major Ligachev."

The luminous green screen changed to a blue background with eighteen lines of highlighted white items in five areas: Asia, Africa, Mideast, Europe, and America.

"You'll notice that the internal threat level ratings for all the country's shown has been raised, signifying their rising concerns over Washington's growing inability to do anything about the Ukraine and Crimea." Washington is clearly on the ropes and weak." Yuri slammed his fist noisily on the table. "I don't want to hear such talk. If the American's want to go down to penury, let's not send them any signals that we are laughing about where they are going or what will happen to them when they get there."

Red-faced, Ligachev apologized for his poor choice of words.

"Has anyone seen the CNN report an hour ago," General Goryianov interrupted, "with Rev. Jesse Jackson, America's pseudo-black? Jackson announced the white man has no business being in Africa and have already done enough damage there."

"Our Chechens and Georgians need someone like Jackson," Yuri interrupted. "Maybe we should the offer Jackson a Chechen passport. How many more briefing items, Ligachev?"

"None."

"Thanks, everyone have a nice day."

TWO

The White House

"THE VICE PRESIDENT is here, Mr. President."

"Tell him to come in."

The president smiled as his alter ego entered. "Good to see you, Chain." Chain's hair had become almost completely white around his bald pate since he'd become vice president.

"The family is well, Chain?"

"Yes. Thank you, Mr. President."

The president hoped to keep Chain's visit brief. Chain had asked for a few minutes with him alone. "What's on your mind?"

"What's happening, Mr. President?"

"Chain?"

"I am hearing things."

"What does that mean?"

Chain looked pallid and needed to lose weight. But the blue eyes riveting the president from behind wire-rimmed glasses were lucid.

"I am concerned, Mr. President. There are things happening of which I should be informed. Events in Bahrain, Qatar, the Crimea for instance."

"The attempted coups? They failed. What about it?

"Our troops were involved in Bahrain, Mr. President. We manned roadblocks, we rounded up local nationals. I was not informed."

"Christ, Chain! You get the daily intelligence reports, what's the problem?"

"Did you authorize our troops personally to get involved in putting down the coup?"

"And if I did? The leadership there are our friends."

"The Khalifa's and Al-Thani's you mean?

"Whatever!" the president replied dismissively.

"What about the Spanish issue?" the vice president asked next.

"You know as much about it as I do."

"I do?"

"Yes."

"I don't believe you."

"Look, Chain. I'll tell you what I know so far. The Spanish allege they shipped 520 metric tons of gold to Odessa in 1937 for safekeeping. The Germans captured it from the Russians in the opening days of World War II. At the time, Spain had already received armaments deliveries to General Francisco Franco's opponents in the Spanish civil war worth 95 million: for aircraft, tanks, artillery, machine guns, and rifles. So the Russians still owed Spain the balance of some 435 million."

The buzzer on the president's desk sounded.

"Hold on a second, Chain." He moved around the desk and sat down. His secretary informed him the chairman of the joint chiefs of staff at the Pentagon was on the line and urgently requested to be put through on an issue regarding an Admiral Lange who had been assigned until recently at Key West in Florida. Lange had reported something about which the president should be aware.

"Put him through."

"I'm in a meeting, Admiral," the president told his caller. "You got fifteen seconds."

A half-minute later, he gently replaced the phone and turned to Chain. "Where were we?" The president was furious. What he'd just been told scared the bejeezus out of him. He should have foreseen it. Until now it had all been too good to be true.

The president had hoped the comatose old man in Walter Reed was the final chapter to Langford Seeley's treachery. Only five men knew of the effort to control the conspiracy. The president, General Putnam, Langford Seeley (who was now dead), Alex Balkan who would say nothing and Paul Carter who was comatose and would probably never regain consciousness. What he'd just been told was that the conspiracy had once again jumped the boundary fence.

At the request of a member of the joint chiefs of staff at the Pentagon, Admiral Lange had informed them about Seeley's visit to Key West a couple of weeks ago. The admiral was upset, believed he'd been involved in a conspiracy without his knowledge, and then been passed over for promotion and now sluffed off by not only senior naval personnel but also the White House. It was all a matter of public record. Seeley's visit to Key West had been to meet with the commander of the local Seal Team who'd then also been transferred a few days later, following the destruction of the submarine.

Now the navy was upset as were some senior Seal personnel. All someone had to do now was ask the right question and put Seeley's visit together with the submarine's destruction. Even a moron would make that connection.

Even though there was a cover story for the submarine's demolition, the president knew it wasn't worth a damn under close scrutiny. Like most cover stories, they got past the casual observer but seldom when under a microscope. How could Seeley have been so stupid? The president should have asked CIA to do it. Outside already, just beyond the White House fence, a beefed-up press presence besieged the gates waiting for him. It wouldn't be long before they'd also demand to know why the president's National Security Advisor went to California to confer with the president after Key West? Why had Seeley then been shot by this unknown old man? Were Al-Quaeda terrorists really involved? Was there a conspiracy?

Yesterday he'd asked the Secret Service to find Alex Balkan. Now he wished he hadn't suggested that Balkan and his girlfriend get lost for a while and take a long vacation. The son of a bitch had and disappeared into thin air. And to make matters worse, last night the president learned that two Spanish warships were anchored southwest of the Dry Tortuga's. A U.S. Navy hydrofoil on routine patrol had spotted them and inquired if they needed assistance. They didn't. The U.S. Navy ship informed them they were inside U.S. territorial waters. The Spanish response was that a Madrid *Pronunciamento* was forthcoming and would be delivered to the White House. The Spanish secretary of state informed the president that his government's statement signified a formal *demarche:* an official government-to-government complaint and something had to be done. The U.S. Navy was confused and had already requested the Spanish warship's to move beyond our waters, but they refused. Having no idea what the pronunciamento was all about, the incident was dutifully reported through coast guard and then Naval channels to the Pentagon. The chairman of the joint chiefs of staff had passed along an unclassified report about it to the State Department with a courtesy copy to the White House.

Before the president, on his desk, now lay a copy of the Madrid pronunciamento. It was a veritable stick of dynamite with a lit fuse. It accused Washington of piracy on the high seas, misappropriation of stolen property, and conspiracy to defraud the Spanish people. Spain demanded compensation of 1.3 trillion dollars. The Spanish ambassador when he called on the president this morning, explained sheepishly, that the amount included accrued interest—a multiple for price increases in value of gold since 1938 . . . and finally, unspecified damages.

He went on to inform the president that Madrid would maintain a naval vigil at the coordinates contained in Annex-1 of their complaint, for a period of two months. Madrid alleged the proof to support their allegation lay within the coordinates provided in the Florida Keys. The president's part in recent events left him highly vulnerable to criticism. Seeley's ineptness would now almost certainly be revealed and the White House's involvement with it. Even if General Putnam held ranks with him, which the president hoped he would, Putnam too would be pilloried without mercy. And if Putnam caved in regarding what he knew about the CASE JUDY file, he'd illegally removed from Fort Bellvoir, then all was lost.

"Where were we, Chain?" he asked the vice president again.

"I need to be kept in the loop, Mr. President. What's behind this POW/MIA thing?"

"Like I said, Chain, you know as much as I do."

"And Iraq?"

"What about it?"

"You are going to let others get involved in exploiting Iraq's petroleum?"

"The Kurds are our friends."

"Not the Kurds. The Iranians."

"Meaning?"

"We have a formal embargo against Iran. We are supplying weapons and munitions to Baghdad and its leaders, who are violating our embargo, are allowing their friends in Basrah to ship oil into Iran."

"You cannot speak about this, Chain. It's the Kurds we must worry about. Theirs will be the next independent state in the area. Their democracy is vibrant . . . Chain. Have faith. The Kurds will work for the good of all their people."

"What the hell does that mean, Mr. President? Whose people?"

"Calm down, Chain."

"Calm down, hell, Mr. President."

"Chain," the president replied calmly. "I think our meeting is over. Please give your missus my regards. You know the way out."

"Not yet . . . Mr. President . . . not yet." Chain withdrew a document from his jacket pocket and placed it on the president's desk.

"What is this?" the president demanded.

"A photocopy of a satellite photo of a recently abandoned camp in Siberia."

"And?" the president inquired. "Where the hell did you get this?"

"It's time for you to resign," Chain replied. "I'll give you a week to consider it."

"How dare you, Chain."

"For the health of our country, Mr. President, please think about it."

"Or?" the president demanded as Chain turned toward the door.

"Or!" the president demanded again as his vice president closed the oval office door behind him.

The president pushed the Spanish government notice and Chain's paper aside. He picked up another which his press secretary had dropped off earlier. It contained two statements. The first was an outright denial of the Spanish claim. The second, an admission, it might have merit and would be studied further. Spinning his chair around, he watched a couple walking hand in hand across the expanse of grass beyond the rose garden fence. Should he resign the presidency? He thought first of Dick Nixon, then Bill Clinton. They'd also confronted their ghosts; the first lost while the second survived. He didn't see himself placing among the latter. Picking up the phone he called general Putnam.

"I guess you've heard the reports about the Spanish claim?"

"Yes, Mr. President."

The president waited for Putnam to offer some additional explanation or sympathy. He offered neither.

"What are your intentions, General?"

"Mr. President?"

"There are only two of us who know about the file. What do you intend to do?"

"What file, Mr. President?"

"You know exactly which one I am referring too!"

"Sir. As I said, what file?"

"I see," the president said.

"And as regards the rest, Mr. President, that I leave in your capable hands. Good luck! May God be with you. And whatever you thought I knew about Seeley, I can't remember a thing about that either."

"Thanks, General."

"As I said the other day, Mr. President. Some tarnished cenotaph's are best left undisturbed."

The president hung up. Even if Putnam tried to keep his silence, the president suspected the inevitable pack of hounds who'd pursue them might tear the general into small pieces while he still lived. He suspected the general was a man of his word and would somehow endure what was to come. As for himself, it would be the same. He'd committed no crime. Done nothing wrong. Reaped no personal benefit. His only sin was that he'd been in the wrong place at the wrong time, and now he or others might now have to humble the United States in the forums that awaited her. Maybe it was all inevitable anyway? He hoped not. He was many things, but above all, he considered himself a patriot and a honorable man.

He returned his attention to the second of the two documents which he intended to read on national television at some point. Picking up a pencil he wordsmithed it as he read it:

> The president of the United States and the American people offer their sincerest condolences to the people and government of Spain, for this grave miscarriage of justice. Whenever government's conduct unacceptable policies, there are consequences. In this instance a grave miscarriage has occurred a half-century ago, for which an apology is due.
>
> At the conclusion of World War II, the United States came into possession of a certain German submarine in the waters off South America. It was unique for two reasons: aboard was some six hundred tons of bullion smuggled out of Hitler's Germany in the closing days of the war. A portion of that bullion we later came to learn belonged to the government of Spain, and the rest, to unknown victims of the Holocaust.

> More importantly, however, was the recovery of a_German cypher. Within months of the war's end the United States realized this new cypher had been put into use by the Soviet Union. This enabled the United States for the next half-century to read the Soviet Union's most sensitive communications and avoid nuclear war.
>
> For national security reasons previous presidents decided not to reveal either the information about the submarine, the cipher, or the gold aboard. Information about the gold has now come to light and it is time for the United States to discuss a financial resolution. I have, therefore, directed my administration to meet with Spanish counterparts and negotiate a satisfactory conclusion to this matter.

At the end of this announcement, he also intended to make a statement that within twenty-four to forty-eight hours there would be another important announcement from the Oval Office.

Spetses Island, Greece

Inishkeen lay back into the soft leather and surveyed the plush layout of his stateroom, his eyes focusing on the curve of his favorite knife hanging on the wall; it was an Omani Khanjar, with its four silver rings and finely chased silver thread and bone handle. It had once belonged to the Wali of Sur in the sixteenth century. The dagger had been made at the end of another era as the Portuguese arrived and overthrew the local Omani Dynasty. Today, for Inishkeen, was the end of yet another era, but this time for that of Sean Inishkeen. Now it was time for him too to leave the stage.

His yacht had been tied up in the Spetses anchorage for a week, and the late April cold and rain had been despicable until today. Now the sun cascaded in and brightened his stateroom. He'd always known his life would end one day and suspected it might end like this. Now it was no longer a case of whether he might die naturally of old age or if his life might be caught short. Events had now overrun him and ninety years of good living were his reward—not bad for a poor bloke from the hills of western Ireland. He arose and walked to the window and studied the steep house-covered hillside which he'd come to know so intimately over the years. Along the quays the last of the town's morning shoppers struggled up the narrow alleyways to their homes above the harbor. God, how he would miss all this!

He drew the blinds. The call from his solicitor in Dublin this morning informed him that a senior Inspector from Scotland Yard had been around, accompanied by an officer from MI-5 and were making inquiries. They wanted to know where Sean was. It was urgent they said.

His solicitor feigned ignorance, replying only that Mr. Inishkeen was frequently abroad as the damp Irish weather bothered his rheumatism. They'd insisted it was urgent, a matter of national security and instructed the solicitor to advise them immediately if he became aware of Inishkeen's whereabouts! As he moved through the darkened cabin, he assumed it was the American called Alex Balkan who'd put it all together and exposed him. He should have arranged to have Balkan killed that day months ago, when the American appeared at his home in Shannon. Now the headlines of the international papers on his coffee table screamed about the Caballero Bullion scandal. Washington seemed unable to control the disaster as the Wall Street's Bears wrought havoc on the Dow Jones, Amex, and elsewhere: Germany's DAX, Japan's Nike, the Paris Bourse, and London's Fleet Street.

Postwar divisions of Europe would never have arisen had the damn Yanks listened to Churchill! Sometimes he thought the Americans had agreed deliberately so they could occupy only half of Europe at the end of the war. What the Yanks had really accomplished was the dismemberment of the world's twentieth century colonial empires, especially Britain's. Churchill had argued without success at Casablanca that the Allies invade Europe from the east via the Dardanelles and not through France. That way, the Americans could mass their army through the Red Sea, move up the eastern Mediterranean, into the Black Sea, and fight alongside the Russians in the final march into Berlin. Had the Yanks agreed, Eastern Europe would have remained in the democratic camp after the war.

But instead, the Americans took the long way around and fought every Jerry in Morocco, Algeria, Tunisia, Sicily, Italy, France. And finally Germany itself, giving Moscow the time it needed to occupy eastern Europe and Hitler time for his final solution.

Predestined is the way Sean Inishkeen would describe the outcome, recalling a top secret document he'd seen in the MI-5 Library in late

1949. At the time he was en route to a new posting with the British Embassy in Cairo. That document had tied the conspiracy together for him and also his own part in it. With the unlikely name CASE JUDY, the document reflected a nefarious secret: a Churchill/Roosevelt side agreement at Casablanca. American airpower based in Britain, with the help of the Royal Air Force, would pound the German heartland to rubble through 1944, allowing Soviet armies time to wear down Hitler's eastern front and push the Whermacht into the rubble of Berlin. This would allow the Soviets to incur the huge casualties they did. And in the process save England and America the human cost. This much of the document had seemed perfectly reasonable to Inishkeen. So logical in fact that even the simplest moron could understand it. But then came the really bizarre justification behind it.

The two men had secretly concluded that a continental invasion as late as mid-1944 would provide Hitler with more than enough time to resolve his minorities problem to insignificant numbers. And these remnants then accommodated in the Palestine area of the eastern Mediterranean after the war. With the Island of Cyprus a short distance away, the Judaeo-Christian enclaves straddling Suez would secure access to her majesty's postwar colonial empire east of Suez for decades. Sean understood Hitler's quid-pro-quo for the deal. Nazi's postwar wealth would be available at several locations around the world where his goons could live well while they planned their comeback in the postwar era.

Both must have been out of their minds and borne bitter grudges to have undertaken such an insidious conspiracy. On the other hand one could only speculate about what might have happened had the 1944 Normandy invasion failed. The Red Army would have pushed to the Atlantic seaboard from Norway to Spain by mid 1945, and all that would have remained in Europe would have been old men and women. But it succeeded, and the new Jewish state in the eastern Mediterranean became a post war garrote around America's neck as the Moslem world endlessly reminded the United States of their annoyance with the new post-Crusader cancer reality in their midst. For the last half-century everywhere Washington turned, her diplomats were killed, her citizens taken hostage, her airplanes hijacked, and her Embassies attacked.

Leaving the salon, Inishkeen moved down the stairs toward his cabin. Picking up the phone he dialed the bridge. "I'll be taking a nap for a few hours, Luigi. I do not want to be disturbed."

Opening the drawer by his bed, he removed his favorite engraved Beretta and placed it on the table as he took another sip from his single malt Whiskey as he removed six bullets from a case and pressed them into the magazine, studying the last round particularly carefully. Pulling the slide a round chambered smoothly.

For Sean's part in the 1943 betrayal, he'd received a hundred thousand gold sovereigns. He'd deposited them in a secret Swiss gold account and—at the suggestion of certain superiors—lived frugally for the next two decades: withdrawing only enough to acquire a small apartment in Marbella and a ten-meter sailboat which he kept at Koropion, to the east of Athens. Then the price of gold escalated in the nineteen-seventies, and within years his Geneva account was astronomical. Only in recent years had be acquired visible assets. A penthouse in the Voula district of Athens, a pied-a-terre in Malta, and a splendid rooftop place above Rio de Janeiro's Ipanema Beach.

"Inca Gold," his forty-two-foot cabin cruiser here at Spetses had been a gift to himself for his eightieth birthday. Fingering the gold chain around his neck, he examined its .22 carrot Inca peseta for the last time. "Old friend," he cooed. "Now you will need another neck to grace." He emptied the glass of whiskey.

EPILOGUE

A Week Later, Central Mexico

MAYBE IT WAS all because too much power had been concentrated in the American presidency. Or maybe it was as simple as one of Alex's local neighbors had told him—that all empires had a normal lifespan from birth to death. His neighbor quoted Toynbee's Rise and Fall of World Empires. Toynbee's belief was that the birth to death span was normally between two to three hundred years. By his neighbor's rationale America had another half-century. Alex thought he had a point.

He wondered if it were Yeniseysk who'd finally started the ball rolling through the international financial markets this time? The last few weeks were among Wall Street's worst. Certainly amongst the most depressing in most anyone's recent memory. First came the slide in the stock market's and then attacks against the dollar, followed by the Spanish government's demands. The president's resignation: instead of creating further instability, actually strengthened the markets for a while. The world's loss of faith in America's lack of leadership over the Ukraine problem had not helped. Then rumors resurfaced about more home mortgage concerns, banking and insurance problems, subprime's, and unemployment.

The American president had left America's problems to his vice president. As the economy continued its tail spin, the Caballero expose drifted further from the front pages, replaced by the financial catastrophe consuming the international monetary system. Americans were now saving their nickels and dimes as the economy ground to a halt in a sea of fear. Alex wondered where Eduardo was right now. His repeated calls to Mary Malagang indicated Eduardo and the two other principles of CEBU had vanished without a trace. Alex suspected he knew where they were but he hadn't mentioned it to her.

A page-three article in one of the old Washington news papers he'd bought this morning caught his attention. "Can Spooks save POW's?" It carried a Washington dateline:

> Following a complaint of bad odors from a neighbor in Baileys Crossroads, police found the body of Mr. Rhinehard Staples at his apartment two days ago. Staples lived alone and was employed by the Defense Department in Arlington, Virginia, and had taken a month vacation and not been seen for some time according to neighbors. Mr. Staples had complained of unsavory phone calls.
>
> A Pentagon spokesperson who requested anonymity, confirmed Staples had spent a career in the search for POW/MIAs, and had been working on a case concerning a WWII American servicemen who recently escaped from Russia. This ex-serviceman is now believed to be somewhere in the United States, and, according to the spokesman, using the alias of Paul Carter. Carter is thought to be a WWII turncoat and traitor who requested sanctuary in the former USSR. He is considered dangerous and is believed to be involved with the recent deaths of not only Rinehard Staples, but also Langford Seeley the recently murdered Secretary of State, and Theodore LePage the former director of Scion Consultants in Arlington, Virginia.
>
> The Pentagon spokesman observed that Carter is considered dangerous and if apprehended should be held incommunicado until turned over to representatives of the Department of Defense or Central Intelligence Agency. Local police admit they have little to go on and at this time suicide does not appear to have been the cause of death.

Alex smiled. Washington and the White House had obviously spun yet another fabrication to avoid responsibility. Maybe there was justice after all? May, in central Mexico, was beautiful. He and Heather had decided to make a go of retirement here and bought a place. Heather would return to Salt Lake at the end of her month's vacation and put in her papers for an early retirement from her job at Hill Air Force Base. She'd already been notified anyway of manpower cuts coming and been offered an incentive to leave early. She'd rent out her apartment in Salt Lake and then rejoin him here. With thirty-two hundred a month from his air force retirement, eighteen hundred from his years at DIA, eight hundred from Scion, plus eleven hundred from Social Security and Heather's three thousand a month government retirement, they could live comfortably in Mexico on a third of it.

They were in a predominantly foreign retirement community in the Ental Mountains north of Mexico City. With the money left over from Eduardo's advance, he'd purchased a three-bedroom villa from an elder couple who'd decided to sell out and return to the States. The white-washed house with a red-tiled roof and open interior courtyard with a fountain was cozy. Surrounded with terrazzo balconies dotted with huge clay pots sprouting riots of red, magenta, and war-bonnet yellow bougainvillea, the home was a place where Alex hoped he could comfortably spend the rest of his life. What convinced him to buy the place was the lattice enclosed Jacuzzi atop a rocky outcrop at the rear of the villa. It commanded a breathtaking view of the surrounding valleys and distant peaks, and already he and Heather had joked about the need to constantly change its water because of miscellaneous body fluids.

"Alex," Heather called from the kitchen. "Don't forget, we have to leave in half an hour! You will be ready?"

"Yeah!" He swizzled the ice around in his tequila, studying the view as he fished out the lime.

"Not like that you won't." She laughed. Smiling at him from the doorway to the terrace.

"Soon as I finish this article in Life Magazine." It was the March 16, 1953 copy which he'd bought at a neighbors garage sale a few days ago. The pictures of Malenkov and Stalin on the cover had caught his attention.

What was it about Stalin, Alex wondered, that had caused him to send so many to Siberia. And among them so many Americans. *Life* magazine's eleven-page article offered no answers. But it concluded that Stalin was the epitome of a sadistic control freak, the grand master of the double-cross, a man who callously purged dissenters, liquidated legions of suspects, and dishonored all his agreements by violating them. Alex noted one point, however, where Stalin's foresight was almost biblical. In a red-bordered Editorial on page 34, it reported that in Stalin's last speech before he died, he said the major capitalist countries, America, Britain, and France, would eventually atrophy, and it would be China and Germany who would once again assume U.S. hegemony.

Already the latter two had distanced themselves from the mounting U.S. financial disaster and seemed to be on the road to recovery. Alex recalled Citwits, the Washington historian, and for a moment wondered if he too would be caught up in the new round of manpower cuts. It was Citwits who opined that the American's POW issue with the Russians had really been sealed at the seventeen-day Potsdam Conference of late July and early August 1945. The participants had haggled endlessly over spoils and reparations and only at the very end gotten around to the issue of war crimes. It was Stalin who'd thrown up all the roadblocks, and then when everyone was exasperated at Yalta, suggested they just draw a line through Europe: everything eastward for Russia, westward for his American and British friends, and get home so they could finish off the Nazi tyrant. The Cold War had already begun, and the new border ended meaningful discussions on what had become of America's missing sons in the east.

"Ten minutes, Alex!" Heather called again from somewhere within the house.

He emerged from the Jacuzzi, toweled himself off and slipped into his white cotton slacks and shirt. He headed into the house to comb his hair and brush his teeth. They'd been taking bridge lessons for a week, and tonight was their first game with neighbors up the road.

"Ready," he said as he came out and stood beside her in the driveway.

"Jesus, Alex," she exclaimed laughing. "Put some shoes on."

51417610R10352

Made in the USA
Lexington, KY
23 April 2016